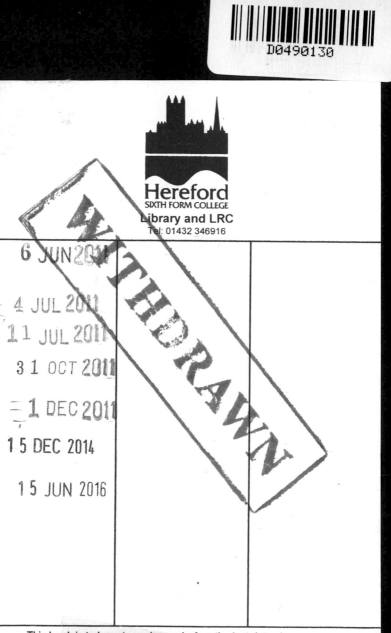

# THE RELUCTANT MAGE

# THE RELUCTANT MAGE

## FISHERMAN'S CHILDREN

### BOOK TWO

# KAREN MILLER

orbit

www.orbitbooks.net

ORBIT

First published in Australia in 2010 by HarperCollins*Publishers* Australia Pty Limited
First published in Great Britain in 2010 by Orbit

A CIP catalogue record for this book
is available from the British Library.

ISBN 978-1-84149-785-3

Typeset in Times by Palimpsest Book Production Limited, Falkirk, Stirlingshire
Printed and bound in Great Britain by CPI Mackays, Chatham ME5 8TD

Papers used by Orbit are natural, renewable and recyclable
products sourced from well-managed forests and certified
in accordance with the rules of the Forest Stewardship Council.

**Mixed Sources**
Product group from well-managed
forests and other controlled sources
www.fsc.org  Cert no. SGS-COC-004081
© 1996 Forest Stewardship Council
FSC

Orbit
An imprint of
Little, Brown Book Group
100 Victoria Embankment
London EC4Y 0DY

An Hachette UK Company
www.hachette.co.uk

www.orbitbooks.net

*Dedicated to*
*Robert B. Parker*
*Who lifted crime fiction into the heady realm of*
*sweet, spare elegance,*
*Kage Baker*
*One of the most gifted and consistently under-rated*
*writers in the field of speculative fiction*
*and*
*Dick Francis.*
*I read* Hot Money *so many times the book came*
*apart in my hands.*
*If that doesn't denote genius, I don't know*
*what does.*
*I can't believe we lost three of my favourite writers in*
*the space of a few weeks. Thank you, thank you, and*
*may you all rest in peace.*

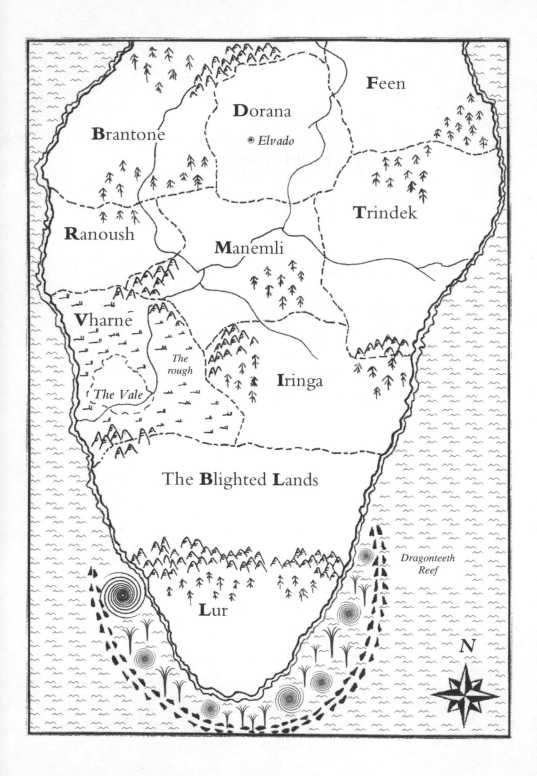

# ACKNOWLEDGEMENTS

Stephanie Smith, the ever-vigilant. Glenda Larke, Mary G. T. Webber, Elaine and Peter Shipp, for the nitpicking. Abigail Nathan, who often saves my bacon. Greg Bridges, for his sublime cover art. Ethan Ellenberg, my agent. The Voyager Team. The Booksellers. And, as always, The Readers

# PART ONE

# CHAPTER ONE

**B**ecause he was Doranen, and a Garrick, Arlin refused to avert his gaze.

*Of all the ways a man can die, I have to think this is the worst.*

Worse even than drowning in the chaos of a whirlpool.

Kneeling on cold, glimlit flagstones, Morg's latest victim trembled and keened as his little life was slowly extinguished.

Arlin shivered. The first time he'd seen Morg kill like this, with magic, the victim was Father's dear friend Sarle Baden, who'd wept so hard at Rodyn Garrick's empty-coffined funeral he'd made himself vomit.

Since Sarle there'd been three other killings — well, four, counting this one — all of them as gruesome, and he had to believe there would be many more. As many as it took for Morg to absorb the scattered pieces of himself until he was whole again, and entirely unstoppable.

*But Asher sundered him years ago. I wonder why it's taken him so long to attempt this rejoining? I wonder how long it will take him to succeed?*

He didn't have any answers. He wasn't sure he wanted them.

The morning after Sarle Baden's murder Morg had ordered him to kneel. Then, glancing at Fernel Pintte and the idiot Goose Martin and the other captives, bound and gagged, he'd smiled.

3

"You are Doranen, Arlin. I would not treat you like these cattle. You are free to ride behind me, unbound — provided, of course, that you behave yourself. Will you?"

He wasn't a fool. Swearing obedience, staring into Rafel's haughty face, he'd seen no hint of the man whose body Morg had stolen. But then, as Morg gestured for him to stand, he'd thought he caught a glimpse of something familiar and desperate in the sorcerer's dark Olken eyes.

Angry with himself, he'd smothered the surge of pity and did not look for Rafel again.

For the next five months Morg led them through the wilderness beyond Barl's Mountains, often willy-nilly it seemed, but always edging north, league after league, over fallow fields, through woodland and across sluggish rivers. If there were villages or townships in the lands they travelled, the sorcerer kept well clear of them — and the few unbidden souls they encountered on their journey he captured and yoked to Pintte and the rest.

But the bidden souls? The men Morg summoned with mysterious arcane ritual because they carried a small, sundered part of himself?

Those men he killed.

Twice, the possessed had come to them out of the night, haggard and half-mindless, and once the sorcerer had hunted his quarry to ground as though he was a harrier hound and could scent the man's terror. Or perhaps he was simply scenting himself. Like calling to like, evil to evil. Each time Morg sucked his victims dry and moved on, but where he'd abandoned Sarle Baden, leaving the aged Doranen's broken body behind to rot, he did not abandon Rafel. And with each death, each swallowed morsel of himself, Morg grew stronger and more confident.

At long last, ragged and dirty and exhausted, they'd reached Lost Dorana — that almost mythical land for which his dead father had spent a lifetime pining. And twenty-four days after crossing his ancestral land's almost extinct magical border they reached Elvado, the city of mages, Dorana's cradle of knowledge.

It was a wasteland, smashed to ruins in the great mage war and never rebuilt. There'd been no-one left to rebuild it. Morg said, carelessly, "I killed everyone who opposed me, you see. In the end there was no-one left." He'd shrugged. "It was better that way. I do my best work alone."

Arlin rode through the haunted silence with his eyes closed.

Unmoved by Elvado's profligate destruction, Morg took his captives to an ancient, magically preserved mansion some three leagues distant from the city. "My once and future home," he called it. There he set them to airing and cleaning the chambers and corridors, grooming the estate's grounds and taming its fields and orchards. Forbidden to use magic, Arlin toiled alongside the other prisoners and made sure to keep his offended feelings hidden.

Nine days later, just after sunrise, another witless soul arrived, answering Morg's summons like a dog obeying its master's shrill whistle.

And now the man was dying.

This one was young, barely escaped from boyhood, with light brown hair and not much chin, peach fuzz on his cheeks and a voice that remained lodged in his throat . . . though by the time Morg was done with him, like all the others he'd have screamed it right out.

Arlin felt unwelcome fingers pluck at his sleeve, stirring him from memory and sour contemplations.

"Arlin."

The whisperer was Fernel Pintte, who insisted on treating him with a loathsome familiarity—and was so afraid of Morg he had no fear to spare for anyone else, which meant there was no way to stop him from being familiar, short of murder.

But murdering Fernel Pintte was out of the question. Morg had a use for him, so Pintte must stay alive.

"*Arlin.*"

He snatched his arm free. "What?"

Fernel Pintte wasn't faring well. After so many months of strenuous captivity he was a loose collection of bones draped in folds of sallow skin. Being Olken, and inferior, even though he was useful he was not treated kindly.

"Arlin," Pintte whispered, "how much stronger will this new death make the sorcerer?"

"How should I know?" he said, making sure to keep his voice soft. "Why don't you ask him?"

Fernel Pintte flinched as though he'd been struck with a whip. "You're a bastard."

"Pintte, be quiet," he said, impatient. "You think because he's killing someone he won't hear your rattling tongue?"

Flinching again, Pintte shut his mouth.

They stood in the underground chamber below the mansion that Morg had chosen for his arcane slaughters. For some reason the sorcerer liked them to witness these monstrous deaths, him and Fernel Pintte and the other three Olken, whose names he'd not bothered to learn, and Rafel's idiot friend Goose. Why Morg kept that halfwit alive he couldn't begin to understand.

*Unless it's to torment Rafel.*

And torment him it would, if he truly was still alive and aware within the cage of his body.

*But I'll not lose sleep over that. If anyone deserves some torment, it's Rafel. And why would Morg be merciful? Rafel's father murdered him. He must want his sweet revenge.*

Peach-fuzz's skin was peeling off his naked body now, rotting strips of human hide sliding from blood-and-pus slicked muscle as though he were already a week-old corpse. Pintte was retching. He always did at this point. Rafel's idiot friend was grunting like a pig. The others controlled their bellies, but they were snuffling. Weeping.

*Good thing I'm made of sterner stuff. As the last surviving Doranen in this forsaken place I do have a position to maintain.*

Morg's stolen face was a mask of physical pleasure as he consumed another lost and found sliver of his sundered soul. If he had a soul. If he was even human. Did he know how many more pieces of himself were out there in the wider world, waiting to be found and harvested?

If he did, he never said so. On the whole Morg said very little—or very little to the point, at least—and Arlin knew better than to ask impertinent questions. Not of this mage.

*For I'm anything but a fool. And Father had thrashed the impertinence out of me by the time I was six.*

Fernel Pintte began moaning under his ragged breath. "Finish it, finish it, for the love of Barl just *finish* it."

Pintte was a maggot, but even maggots could be right. Morg's lascivious lingering over what was, at its heart, a simple, straightforward task? Revolting. Obscene.

*I know why we're here. He's reminding us that we're his chattels. His slaves. We're to remember, waking and sleeping, that we breathe because our breathing amuses. And the moment we cease to be amusing . . .*

Dead at last—*what a blessing*—the young man slid from Morg's embrace and struck the chamber's stone floor with a wet slapping sound. Pintte gagged and turned away.

Ignoring him, Arlin watched Morg instead. Spine and shoulders pressed to the wall, the sorcerer shuddered and quivered, the chamber's cool air rasping in his throat as he absorbed his reclaimed powers. Just like every other time, something peculiar happened to his face, a shifting of feature upon feature, Morg's and Rafel's strangely combined. Blue eyes masking brown, a nose at once both straight and crooked. As though the mind inside the body wasn't sure whose face to wear.

And then the mind settled, and there was Rafel again. More or less. Morg indulged in a luxurious stretch, blithely oblivious to the bloody smears staining his forest-green silk tunic with its gold-and-obsidian buttons. He'd let Rafel's hair grow so it brushed his shoulders in a thick, black mane. Very dashing. Rafel surely must hate it.

"Pintte," he said, with a sleepy, half-lidded smile at peach-fuzz's corpse. "You and your friends clean this up. And once you've done that you can butcher the latest kill and prepare it for roasting. Arlin, walk with me."

At the crooking of Morg's finger Arlin abandoned Pintte and the other Olken to their filthy tasks and fell into step beside the sorcerer, permitted that indulgence because he was Doranen, a novelty, and something like kin.

*And because he knows I have no hope of hurting him.*

They wandered out of the stinking chamber, along a wide corridor and up a flight of stairs to the mansion's ground floor. From there they made their way through its echoing stillness and outside to the newly tended gardens, shy with autumn blooms and lavish with as-yet-uncut grass. The sky was a pale milkish blue, the early morning sun thinly veiled by cloud.

Waiting for the sorcerer to speak, Arlin took refuge from recent horrors in the surrounding countryside.

Morg's mansion stood on a gentle rise overlooking wild woodland thick with birds and game, a larder on their doorstep. Beyond the woodland, Elvado's surviving magic-twisted spires winked and glittered in the rising light. Seeing them, Arlin felt a pang of grief for the ruined city. Once it had been thriving and beautiful, with Doranen magic soaked into its bones. Riding its empty streets behind Morg he'd heard the faded power whisper, felt it sigh against his skin. Elvado had been colourful, as Lur's Dorana City was colourful. Now only hints and echoes of its brightness remained, bleached by the long years to a mournful memory of joy.

*I'm glad Father never saw it. Ruined Elvado would have crushed him.*

It was odd to feel such a detached compassion. If the wearisome, wandering journey from the blighted lands to Lost Dorana had done nothing else, it had given him ample time to reflect on his life. On his father and their brutal, unloving relationship. On Rafel and *his* father, and why seeing them together had made him sick with rage.

*Not that it matters any more. My father is dead. Doubtless Asher is dead now too. And Rafel, well, he can't survive in there forever. Sooner or later Morg will crowd him out.*

Drifting on a light breeze was the sound of Fernel Pintte's grating voice barking orders at the other Olken as they disposed of peach-fuzz's emptied body. It seemed he'd chosen a patch of field beyond the stables for a graveyard, and now wanted the idiot Goose to scrounge stray rocks for a headstone—an impulse of decency that must be foreign to this place.

*I wonder how many stray rocks there'll be in that field before Morg is done here, one way or another?*

As though the sorcerer could read his thoughts, Morg rested a heavy hand on his shoulder. "I must confess, Arlin, you intrigue me," he said, fingers briefly dabbling. "I thought you'd be more curious. About me. About my plans. Months and months of travelling—and there were no questions. We've been here for days and still you ask no questions. Was I mistaken? Are you a dullard? Is there *nothing* you wish to know?"

When Morg wore Sarle Baden he'd been half-mad, unable to decide if he was a *me* or a *we*. But since clothing himself in Rafel the sorcerer had adopted a light, bantering tone and there was never so much as a hint of madness in him. Remarkable, given there was more of Morg in Rafel now than there'd been in poor old Sarle.

*So why is he not raving? Because he needed more of himself to be sane? Or because Rafel is truly a mage like no other, able to contain the spiteful power of this . . . man?*

"Arlin," said Morg, with a bite in his fingers, "do you really think it wise to ignore me?"

He stopped breathing, just for a moment. The sound of his racing heart boomed in his ears.

*Show no fear. Show no fear.*

"Master," he said—on pain of death they were required to call Morg "master"—"forgive me. I wasn't ignoring you. I was merely contemplating my reply."

"Which is what?" said Morg, letting his hand drop.

"I've asked no questions because I didn't want to anger you. If I need to know something, I trust you'll tell me."

Morg stared at him with Rafel's wide and honest eyes. "Sink me bloody sideways, Arlin! I never took you for a prosy fool."

Arlin's surprise was so great he took a step back. "*Rafel?*"

"No," said Morg, amused. "But his speech is so quaint, don't you think? I wanted to try it. And *I* was curious, to see what you'd do if you thought he'd returned."

*What would I do? I don't know. Beg him to save us, probably.*

A lowering thought. "Can he return?" he said, careful to sound disinterested. "I wasn't sure. In truth, I thought he must be dead."

"Not yet," said Morg. Gloating malice fattened his voice. "There's too much pleasure to be gained from his pain."

So Rafel was aware. "I see."

Morg considered him closely. "Does it please you, that he's suffering? And he is suffering, Arlin. I'm making certain of that."

*Does it please me? Yes. But . . .*

He shrugged. "Rafel's no friend of mine."

That made Morg laugh. "I know. And so does Rafel. Would it astonish you to learn he bears no grudge against you? Your father's death haunts him, Arlin. Asher's son is soaked in grief and drowning in regret for the loss of Rodyn Garrick." Another laugh. "When he's not screaming, that is."

It was easier to do this if he didn't look at Morg, so he kept his gaze pinned firmly on Elvado's few, distant spires. "Master, I tell you honestly, what Rafel feels means nothing to me. *He* means nothing. How could he? Rafel's an Olken. He comes from common stock. He's inferior—and a liar."

"Really?" Now Morg was mocking. "And yet I chose him and not you to sustain me. Tell me you're disappointed, Arlin. Tell me how devastated you were when I passed you by and chose *him* for my vessel."

*How can I? I was never so relieved in my life.*

"Master—"

Morg cuffed the back of his head. Rafel's loutish strength meant the blow hurt. "*Look at me*, Arlin Garrick, and tell me that's so."

Slowly, his heart thudding again, he turned and looked at the sorcerer. Was this it? The moment of his death?

*If it is, I will not die craven. I am a Garrick, and a Garrick does not beg.*

**10**

"I can't. And you know I can't."

"Arlin, Arlin." Morg's soft laughter was frightening. "You are such a Doranen. So proud. So arrogant. I've *missed* that. It's been far too long since I kept company with my own kind."

Uncertain, Arlin stared at him. This was a Morg he'd not seen before. As they journeyed through the miserable, blighted lands that stood between themselves and Lost Dorana, collecting a man here, a woman there, as he'd been forced to witness the deaths of those few poor knaves who'd hosted Morg's shredded essence, the sorcerer had kept himself aloof. And though Morg had spent the days since their arrival at this estate supervising his prisoners, still he'd not spoken a word save for giving orders or uttering spells.

This Morg was . . . unexpected.

And though he was frightened, he was also curious. Filled to the brim with questions he never thought he'd ask. Perhaps then, with Morg in a talkative mood, he might take a small risk.

"Does that mean I am allowed a question, Master?"

Morg tipped his face to the pallid sun. "Yes, Arlin. You're allowed. And since I'm feeling expansive I might even answer it."

He found it unsettling to see the small changes in Rafel's face, now that a different intelligence ruled the Olken's body. A quirked eyebrow here, a thin sneer of lips there, a head tilt . . . Even his voice was changed. It was less brusque. More mellifluous. No hint of pain showed in him anywhere.

*Forget Rafel, you fool. Forget him and his screaming. Think of him as dead.*

"Master, are there truly none of us left, save for the descendants of those mages who fled Dorana with Barl?"

Morg slid his fingers through his hair, a languid gesture so at odds with Rafel's blunt muscularity. "You're wrong, you know," he said, musing. "Rafel never lied. He had no idea of the power that's in him. His father kept it a secret. If you could feel his resentment—his *rage*—about that?" Another laugh. "One might almost feel sorry for him."

Arlin had no desire to talk of Rafel or his misbegotten father. "Well, if you say he was truthful then of course I must believe it. Master—the Doranen?"

Morg's expression tightened, and he tutted impatiently. "Why does it matter?"

"Because Dorana's mages are a part of me, Master. They were my distant family, some of them. I used to think that if ever I found my way to this place I might meet someone whose face looked like mine."

"Family?" Morg shook his head. "It's unimportant, Arlin. You've missed nothing. And no. None survived."

He did his best to hide his grief. "I see. Master—another question?"

Morg sighed. "If you must."

"Are we—were we—the only mages in the world?"

"Counting the Olken?"

The *Olken?* "Do *you* count them, Master?" he said, shocked.

"The only counting of Olken I intend," said Morg, this time with a smile of greedy anticipation, "is the counting of skulls as they pile higher than Barl's Mountains."

Arlin looked at the grass. Once that might have been something he would say. Even now, after everything, a part of him responded to the raw and ugly threat. But a greater part of him recoiled from it. The Olken were a peasant race, good for nothing but grubbing in the dirt. But even so . . .

Morg was watching him closely again. "We could count skulls together."

"We could, Master," he said, his throat dry. "So, there are no other mages?"

"None."

Which meant no hope of an alliance against him. "Master, there is another question I'd ask you."

"One more," said Morg, dangerous. "My patience wears thin."

Such casual menace. He felt his belly churn. "Master, where *is* everyone? You rid Dorana of its mages, but did no one else live here? Is our homeland empty of people? Is the *world* empty?"

"It's true, the world is emptier than once it was," said Morg, drifting to the nearest half-weeded flowerbed. He plucked a bronze blossom from its stem and brushed stubby petals over his cheek. "When I was myself, before, so long ago, even after I destroyed the Doranen, I ruled people. I ruled nations. Every land we travelled through, Arlin, and lands you've not seen, I ruled them all. And though eventually I left crude flesh behind, still I ruled. There were people and there were creatures. Fantastic beasts of my devising." His face clenched in a scowl. "They perished when Asher murdered me."

"And the people? What happened to them when you . . . fell?"

"I assume those in Dorana fled," said Morg, shrugging. "Back to the lands whence their ancestors came." Then he smiled, caressing his lips with the flower. "Where now they hide with their countrymen, thinking I'll not notice them—the fools."

Arlin swallowed. "So you remember what happened? You remember your life? Even though you were—"

"Dead?" Morg let the plucked blossom slip from his fingers. "I was never dead, Lord Garrick. I can't be killed. At least—not for long."

*Lord Garrick.* The tone of Morg's voice made the formal address an insult. "Master, all mortal things die."

"Yes, Arlin, but I am *im*mortal," Morg said gently. "I transmuted myself. And when I am whole again, then will I transmute again. I will leave this sorry prison of flesh and blood and bone—ruined, of course, for it's the least Asher deserves—and once more I will spread myself upon the wind. The nations and kingdoms and principalities that once served me, they will be punished and then serve me again."

"And what of Lur? What of the Doranen there?"

"Lur . . ." Morg said the name caressingly. "Barl's unlikely refuge. The bitch whore was always lucky." He shrugged. "Lur is dying. You know it. Rafel knows it. Rafel is sick with grief for that. Are you?"

Was he? He'd grown up despising Lur as an unwanted place of exile, but was his contempt for the kingdom anything more than a habit? Had he only longed for Lost Dorana out of self-preservation, so he'd not be thrashed for disobedience and disloyalty?

*I don't know.*

But this wasn't the time or place to admit his doubt out loud.

"Lur was a pretty place, once," he said, with care. "Abundant. Peaceful. Over-run with Olken, but you can't have everything. Even so, it was never our home. Dorana is our true home. Many Doranen harbour secret hopes of finding their way back."

"Tell me . . ." Morg plucked another flower, a yellow one this time, and petal by petal began to shred it. "If I spared their lives, Arlin — the Doranen of Lur. Would they agree to serve me? Bow down and do my bidding?"

"Many would, Master," he said, thinking of his father's friends. Their greed for magic, their yearning for more. Given the chance to become true mages he had no doubt the Doranen like them would serve. "But some wouldn't. You know they turned Barl into an object of worship? There are clerics and churches. They think she intercedes."

Morg sneered. "Interferes, more like it. Or she did. Yes, I remember. That creaking old woman — what was his name? Barlsman Holze. Loved the bitch like a moonsick calf, that one. But she's dead, Arlin. And unlike me, she's never coming back." A sharp glance. "Rafel says you're not a believer."

What an odd conversation this was proving to be. Arlin Garrick and the sorcerer Morg, chatting like old friends. Discussing *theology*. It had to be a dream.

"No, Master," he said, and meant it. "I'm not. Barl was a mage. There was nothing divine about her."

Never in his life had he seen Rafel smile the way Morg was using him to smile now. "Nothing whatever. Arlin, I think I *like* you."

*Really? In that case, I think I'm going to be sick.*

"Master," he said, after a moment. When he could trust himself. "The Doranen of Lur. Will you spare them?"

Morg smiled, swift and sly. "I might." Bits and pieces of yellow petals littered the grass at his feet. "If you behave yourself."

"And the Olken, Master?" His empty belly was churning again. "You'll really slaughter them all?"

This time Morg's laughter was soft, and sinister. "Arlin, you're too gullible. I promise you, the peasants are perfectly safe. I have plans for them."

Staring at the sorcerer, Arlin thought he saw Rafel trapped behind his own eyes and screaming. "Plans?"

"I can feel them, you know," Morg murmured, and tossed aside the petal-stripped flower. His chilly gaze turned soft and warm, lingering on distant Elvado. "Those scattered, tattered pieces of my self. If you were me, Arlin, you'd surely go mad. I was a mirror, and I shattered, and each shard contains me."

"Then am I truly speaking to Morg?" he said, after another long hesitation. "If I ventured back into the world beyond Dorana, would I meet you in the wilderness? Would we then have this same conversation? If you're sundered how many Morgs are out there?"

"Arlin . . ." Morg patted his cheek. "You know, Rafel thinks you're quite the mage but I'm not so sure. *Think*, my doughty little Doranen. Put you in a room full of mirrors and how many Lord Garricks exist?"

"One," he said. "Just one."

"Exactly," said Morg. This time the pat on his cheek was more like a slap. "Now don't ask me any more stupid questions or I'll change my mind about talking to you. And I enjoy talking to you, Arlin. After centuries of silence and these past years of incompletion I find this return to humanity surprisingly refreshing." He grimaced. "Well, now I do. Now that I've a body worth wearing. Although Conroyd was a good fit. For a while. 'Til he betrayed me. He was better than Durm, at least. That fat old fool was gross."

"Master, why didn't you choose me?"

The question was slipped off his tongue before he could swallow it. Not that he *regretted* Morg's choice, but there was no use in denying his pricked pride. That Morg had chosen Rafel, an Olken, over one of his own kind . . .

*If Father had a grave he'd be spinning in it.*

"I had my reasons," said Morg, his voice flat and cold.

"Master," he said quickly, and made sure to bow his head. Morg might have kept himself mostly separate on the journey here, but that wasn't the same as keeping his nature secret. The sorcerer was capricious and nasty and thought nothing of using magic to punish in ways that made sight and hearing a curse.

Silence, as Morg closed his eyes and tasted the world. "There's another one coming," he murmured. "Only a small piece of me in her. She's a whisper, this vessel. Weak and faltering, like all women." His eyes opened. "I have work to do here. You can fetch her to me, Arlin."

He felt his jaw sag. "*Me?*"

"Yes, Arlin. You," said Morg, mildly enough. "This is a world of flesh we live in. Until I transmute I must live in it as flesh, which means I cannot be in many places at once. So you will fetch myself to me, Lord Garrick, and you will safely bring me home."

"Master, you'd trust me to—"

"*Trust?*" Morg struck him, hard. "No. Not yet. You'll be warded and escorted. I am not a fool."

Face burning, Arlin bowed his head again. "Master."

"Come," said Morg, and turned for the mansion. "It won't hurt for you to see this."

Mutely compliant, all his fears rewoken, he followed the sorcerer back into the mansion and downstairs to the extensive honeycomb of cellars which were given over to housing both the Olken and the dribs and drabs of humanity they'd collected during the journey to Dorana. Twenty-two souls in all, eight women and the rest men, from three different lands with only an odd, cobbled-together muddle of the Doranen tongue between them. Morg had yoked each prisoner with severe compulsions, which made it safe to send the strongest, nimblest men into the woodland to hunt game. Those five men he left untouched, but six of the other men and four of the women he singled out.

"Come," he said, and snapped his fingers. "Arlin, you can herd them from behind."

Weeping, obedient to the magic branded in them, the chosen captives followed Morg upstairs to the mansion's empty entrance hall where they huddled like sheep.

"Stand out of the way now, Arlin," the sorcerer commanded. "I don't want you caught in the nimbus. You're far too pretty a man for this."

Arlin backed against the nearest wall, feeling his palms slick and his breathing quicken. Something dark and dangerous curdled the air. Power was building, like a storm sweeping in. His exposed skin tingled. The hair stirred on his head. Morg was laughing as the snivelling captives cowered. One by one he touched them, and whispered, and moments later they changed.

Remembering the stories he'd heard of the day Asher killed Morg, Arlin felt his eyes stretch wide. Here was pure Doranen magic, savage and primal and unapologetic. Fascinated, revolted, he watched the chosen men and women sprout hides and scales and tails and horns. Watched their skin deepen to animal colours of grey, brown, chestnut, brindle. Heard them scream and grunt and snuffle, lose their speech and every vestige of humanity.

When he was finished, Morg turned. "Your escort," he said. His eyes were shining, his face flushed. "And because I do like you, Arlin, here's a word to the wise. Even if you knew the words to undo this working, you never could. Accustom yourself to the truth, my little lord. You're mine, as they are mine. As the world was mine and will be again. You'll ride to fetch the summoned vessel and your escort will run with you. Beware. My *dravas* never sleep. They do not tire. They obey me, and only me. Take the best horse and find the road we came in on. Follow it without turning. You'll meet the woman within a day."

He bowed. "Yes, Master. I'll just fetch water and some food to—"

"No, Arlin," said Morg, approaching. The men and women—the *dravas*—followed him slavishly with their inhumanly human eyes. "You won't need them. And you'll not flirt with the notion of running, either."

The heat that seared through him as Morg sank a spell into his flesh was part pain and part pleasure. Stirred, humiliated, he stared at the floor.

"That will keep you," said Morg, indifferent. "Go now. Don't stop. And remember this, Arlin: I will see you through my *dravas*' eyes.

Should you displease me, on your return I will thrash you so hard you'll think your father's beatings were a kiss."

*He knows about that? How can he know about that? Rafel never knew.*

Shamefully, his legs trembled. "Master," he whispered, "there'll be no need."

He escaped from the entrance hall and the look in Morg's eyes, retreating to the field behind the mansion where their motley horses were kept. There might be stables, but there was no straw for bedding and no corn for their feed. The *dravas* followed him, claws and hooves clicking on the mansion's stone floor and then thudding and scratching on the grass. A kind of feral intelligence glowed in their sunken, bestial eyes. They had fangs and talons. They could kill him with a blow. Would Morg command them to kill him?

*He might, if I lifted a hand against them. If I lifted a hand to him I'm certain he would. Watching them tear me to pieces would be more amusing than killing me himself. They are my keepers as he is my keeper. He's diminished and I can't touch him. He's diminished . . . and I'm terrified.*

And yet Asher had defeated him. Remembering that, for the first time in his life he felt admiration for Rafel's father. Then, on the heels of admiration came a dreadful, crushing grief.

*The world is lost again. The Innocent Mage has come and gone and now there's no one. Morg is reborn and not a soul can defeat him.*

Despairing, watched by the *dravas*, Arlin clung to the field's crooked gatepost and wept.

# CHAPTER TWO

D orana City's Olken graveyard was woefully crowded, these days.
Hanging back so Charis could at least pretend she was alone
with her father, Deenie let her blurry gaze wander over the new headstones shoved higgledy-piggledy into every spare space between the
older, ordered rows of graves. Though the sky was patchily clouded,
for once it wasn't raining—but so much rain had fallen of late that
some of the headstones were starting to sag. Soon they'd be falling
flat, squelching into the soggy ground. And if the weather didn't soon
clear for good then the soggy ground would turn to muddy soup, surely,
and coffins would rise out of their holes and wash away down the
graveyard hill into the living city below.

She pinched herself.

*Stop it. You're being morbid. Think of Charis and her grief.*

Not quite two months had trudged by since poor Uncle Pellen
breathed his last. He'd held on for much longer than anyone expected.
Just on a month after Rafe left home she'd overheard Pother Kerril
talking to Mama, saying as how she daily thought to get word that the
old gentleman had gone, or was going, but days and days passed, turned
into weeks, and more weeks followed, became months—and Dorana
City's former mayor clung to life, refusing to die.

But then, because even Uncle Pellen had to let go in the end, he did die, and things in Lur were so awful by then that his funeral had been swift and plain and hardly noticed. Not like Darran's, say, or the funeral for the royal family he used to tell her and Rafe about, when they were small.

Deenie felt her throat clutch tight. *Rafe*. Blinking hard to keep the tears at bay, she pinched herself again. She mustn't think of her lost brother. At least not here, in this cold, miserable place crowded with sagging headstones, and weeping mourners who placed sad sprigs of flowers on the wet ground then went home alone and bewildered by the world's capricious cruelty. And not when Charis stood half a stone's throw away, either.

*Two months? That's nothing. That's no time at all. She doesn't need me here, weeping. Charis needs a strong friend, not Deenie the mouse.*

A shiver ran through her. But it wasn't from the chilly damp. This time it was a warning. She stared at the sky. Fresh clouds were streaming into the kingdom from over the mountains, dark and ominous and blotting out the scattered patches of pale blue. A bad storm was coming.

Her unwanted mage-sense leapt again, pricking her. Not a day went by now, sometimes not even an hour, when it didn't niggle at her, complaining. Her only consolation was that out of desperation she'd cobbled together a few tricks, little ways to throttle her power, muffle the worst of it when it shouted for attention.

But her control was far from perfect. And while her mage-sense no longer wrecked her the way she'd been wrecked down in Westwailing that terrible day Rodyn Garrick and his son and his ignorant friends had tried to break Dragonteeth Reef, still it caused her enough misery that some nights she sobbed into her pillow for the pain in her bones.

Charis, though possessed of her own mage instincts, hadn't noticed the shift in the air. She was mired in grief, blind to everything but her father's grave.

*I do wish she'd stop coming here. It doesn't do any good.*

But poor Charis, she wasn't ready to leave her father behind. So many years had gone by since her mother died, and in the years that came after, it was just her and Uncle Pellen. Closer than peas in a pod, they'd been. Of course Charis missed him. Of course she felt bereft.

*Just like Mama's bereft, even though Da's not dead.*

But that was another thing she couldn't think about, her mother so lost and withdrawn these days, and Da in his silent bed, breathing, swallowing gruel, and doing nothing else. Pother Kerril said she was baffled by his illness and couldn't find a cure. For herself, she'd given up talking about the blight she could feel in her father. There wasn't any point. Nobody believed her. At least it wasn't growing any stronger. She could feel that much. It was all the good news she was likely to get.

Overhead the dark grey and black clouds jostled, bullying each other as the temperature plunged.

"Charis," she said, calling softly. "Charis, it's going to storm."

Charis pressed her hands to her face, smudging tears, then turned. These days there was never enough colour in her cheeks. "I know."

"We should go. There's ague about the city and we don't want to catch it." Not when half the new headstones in this graveyard could be laid at its door.

"A few more moments," said Charis, her eyes tragic. "Just a few."

Deenie swallowed a sigh. "Only a few. And then, truly, we do have to go."

"You start walking," said Charis. "I'll catch up. *Please*, Deenie. You hover, and you know how I mislike it."

*If I didn't hover, Charis Orrick, you'd sit yourself down and never walk out of this place.*

"All right," she said, reluctant. "But you have to come, Charis. Don't make me turn back and drag you out of here."

Charis's eyes flooded with fresh tears. "Don't be mean to me, Deenie."

She loved Charis like a sister, but even so . . . 'I'm not being mean. If you get agueish I'll have to pother you. Neither of us wants that."

"I said I'll come, and I'll come," Charis snapped, turning her back. "In a few moments."

*Sink it.* Deenie tugged her shawl tight and headed for the grave-yard's iron gates. The other mourners were leaving too, huddled into their coats and coverings and casting resentful glances at the lowering, leaden sky. Two of them, a mother and son it looked like, noticed her. The son, close to her own age, tugged his mother's arm then veered between the headstones. The mother followed, her face protesting.

"Meistress Deenie," the son called out, a young man with eyes as tragic as Charis's. "You are Meistress Deenie? The Innocent Mage's daughter?"

He and his mother reached her and stopped, so she had to stop too. She'd never laid eyes on either of them before. Could be they were country Olken fled into the city to escape the hardships further south. Since Da's illness and Rafe's leaving she didn't often come down from the palace grounds. She didn't like being stared at and whispered about because of what had happened to them. She didn't like it when strangers wanted a word. But she couldn't rebuff this polite young man or his mother, because Lur was in sore strife . . . and Asher and his family were the closest thing to royalty the kingdom had left.

"One of the other visitors," said the young man, vaguely gesturing. "He told us who you are. He was right, wasn't he?"

"Yes," she said, and let the small word tell him what she wasn't supposed to say.

*You're a nuisance. Leave me alone.*

The young man heard what she'd left unspoken, and didn't care. "Your father, Meistress Deenie. How is he?"

It seemed to her that every Olken in the kingdom thought they owned a piece of Da. Thought that because he was Olken too, and had saved them twice, it meant they could ask impertinent questions and act as though they knew him. If she thought for one heartbeat this young man's question was about Da and not about how frightened he was, most likely she wouldn't want to slap him.

But it wasn't, and she did. She clasped her hands behind her back. "He's the same. He doesn't change."

"We're sorry to hear that," said the young man's mother. Her dark hair was streaked grey. She looked old and tired and very sad. "It's a trial for your poor mam."

A cold wind whipped up, sudden and sniping. The gnarly mab trees in the graveyard rattled their bare branches and the last trickle of watery sunlight vanished.

"Mama will be touched to know you think of her," Deenie said, and tugged her shawl tight again. "Meistress, it's closing in nasty. You might want to get safe indoors afore the clouds break."

The sad-eyed woman nodded. "I do."

But as she turned to go, her son held her back.

"Meistress Deenie," he said, fervent, something more dangerous than sorrow in his gaze. "What do the pothers say? Will your father wake in time to save us?"

Months of misery sharpened her retort. "What gives you the right to ask me that? And why would you think I'd bandy words about my da with a rude young meister I never met in my life?"

"There now, Phin, see what you've done?" the woman scolded. "She's Asher's daughter and you've riled her. Silly boy. You take me back to the hostelry."

The young man Phin flushed dark red. "No offence meant, Meistress Deenie. But we're in a sorry way and I thought—I hoped—"

"I know what you thought," she snapped. "And what you hoped. But it's not for you to think or hope anything when it comes to my da. Our wrack and ruin's got naught to do with him."

"Come *away*, Phin," the woman said, tugging him. "You want us outside when the clouds break?"

Mother and son hurried to the graveyard gates. Deenie watched them go, her heart thumping. Tears prickled her eyes but she wasn't going to let them fall. She *wasn't*.

"Your papa wouldn't know you, Deenie, if he could see you now," said Charis, behind her. "Not such a mouse these days, are you? You've grown cat claws and you're not frighted to use them."

She scowled as Charis came to stand at her shoulder. "That young meister was rude. He asked about Da."

Charis's delicately arched eyebrows lifted. "And that's rude, is it?"

"The way he asked? Aye, it is."

Grumbling high above them, the first ominous rumble of thunder. Charis looked at the threatening sky and grimaced.

"We'll never make it back to the Tower," she said. "But if we run we'll likely reach my house before we're soaked."

Deenie could feel her friend's trepidation. Charis hadn't set foot under her own roof since the day Uncle Pellen died. "You're sure?"

"I'm sure I don't want an ague," said Charis. "And that's all I'm sure of."

So they ran, slipping and sliding in the graveyard's mud and on the city's cobbled streets, their long skirts wrapping round their legs as they dodged carts and carriages and other Olken on foot.

*Almost*, they out-ran the vicious storm.

Not quite soaked through, they fell across the Orrick house's threshold. Charis slammed the front door on the wind and the water. Deenie, her teeth chattering, conjured glimfire then collapsed onto the staircase and hugged her knees to her chest. She wasn't cold, even though she was wet. It was the storm raging through her, in the sky and in the earth beneath the streets and houses of battered Dorana City.

Charis sat on the staircase beside her and held her hand.

To take her mind off her own troubles, Deenie tightened her fingers. "You all right, Charis?"

"I should come back here for good," Charis whispered. "I shouldn't leave the house empty."

Deenie bumped her, shoulder to shoulder. "You can't live in this big old place alone. How can you live here alone?"

Hard rain slashed at the windows and drummed the tiled roof so far above their heads. More thunder rumbled and the glass panes rattled a warning. Charis whimpered a little.

"I should be used to these storms by now," she said. "But I'm not. I don't think I ever will be. Deenie, are there tremors coming?"

She couldn't feel them. As a rule she could feel the earth's ructions, shuddering her bones before ever they shuddered the streets and the city's buildings and everywhere else in poor ruined Lur.

"No. All's quiet this time."

Sighing, Charis pressed her other hand to her eyes. "Good. Oh, that's good."

"Yes, it is," she agreed. "They spasm me something awful, and I'm sick of Pother Kerril's nasty potions. Especially since they don't work so well any more."

The last tremors had rattled them six days ago, bad ones that ripped up half of Cherry Street and all of Princess Way and put most of the Livestock Quarter in a hole. Not that much trading went on there now, but even so. And there was bad damage in the Home Districts too, many of the few remaining, unblighted apple orchards twisted to rotting fruit, and farmhouses flattened to damp dust and rubble. Even with Kerril's possets she'd felt all of it, the earth's pain and the city's fear too, escaping its wall and running wild in the country.

"Deenie . . ." Charis's voice was wobbly. "Maybe I could come back here if you came with me."

She stared. "Leave Mama in the Tower alone with Da, you mean? Oh, Charis. I couldn't."

"Then what will I do?" Charis wailed. "I can't live there with you forever, can I?"

Deenie slid her arm around Charis's slender shoulders. "It won't be forever. Not the rest of your life. Just a while longer. Charis, you can't stay here on your lonesome. It's not safe."

"It's not safe to leave the house empty," Charis retorted. "Every time I come past here I think I'll see the windows broken or the door off its hinges or —"

"Don't be a goose," she said, and gave Charis a little shake. "You know that won't happen. The City Guards come by regular to make sure there's no mischief."

Charis took hold of the banister and pulled to gain her feet. "And they'll come by more often if they know I'm living here again. For Papa's sake they'll make sure I'm unharmed." She trod the three steps down to the floor then turned. "Deenie, I *miss* him. And I—I feel close to him here."

Well. It was better than feeling close to him in the graveyard, but she still didn't like the notion . . . 'I know you do. Only Charis—he's gone. You can't be a rabbit and bury yourself here."

"Why can't I?" said Charis, mutinous. "You bury yourself in the Tower, missing Rafe."

She heard her breath catch. "That's not fair."

"Isn't it? Why isn't it?" said Charis, her damp cheeks pink. "It's what you do. It's been months and months since Rafel crossed the mountains, Deenie, and I only need my fingers to count how many times you've set foot out of the Tower. So don't tell *me* you've not been hiding."

*Rafe*. "Mama needs me, Charis," she protested. "You know she needs me. Da can't be left, someone has to sit with him, and it can't always be her. You should understand that better than anyone."

Charis nearly stamped her foot. "And *you* should understand that I want to be alone a bit! I want to be alone in my house and remember Papa and me laughing here and—and—" Face crumpling, she dropped to the staircase's bottom step. "Deenie, why don't you ever talk of Rafel? You never so much as mention his name."

"Oh, *Charis*." Deenie pressed her forehead to her knees. "I can't. It hurts to talk of him. Even saying his name is like stabbing myself with a knife."

"I don't care!" said Charis. "Deenie, you don't even say if he's still alive. Is he? Please, at least tell me that much!"

"Yes, he's alive," she said, lifting her head sharply. "If I thought he wasn't, if—if I *felt* he wasn't, don't you think I'd have said so? Do you think I'd keep a truth like *that* secret?"

"I don't know!" said Charis, wildly. "You're so far away these days, Deenie. Almost a stranger. You've gone somewhere I can't reach you."

Stung close to tears by Charis's resentful misery, she had to look away. "I'm sorry."

"I know what's happening to Lur hurts you," Charis said, still upset.

"I know you have to drink Kerril's horrible possets to dull what you feel, and they make you sick and drowsy, but—Deenie, I miss *you*, too. All my life, after Mama died, there was Papa and there was you and there was Rafel. And now—"

Beyond the windows, the storm battered the city. They could hear the rainwater rushing off the roof, and down the sloping street past the front path and gate. In the gloom and the glimlight, just the two of them, it felt like being alone in the world.

Deenie shook out her damp skirt. "He's alive, Charis. I promise. Rafel's alive."

"How do you know?" Charis whispered.

"I just do," she said, shrugging. "I can't tell you where he is and I don't know what he's doing, but I know he's alive." She rapped her knuckles to her chest. "I can feel him. In here."

"Oh," said Charis, her voice wobbly again. "Oh, praise Barl."

So at least Charis felt better.

*But I don't. It's not enough to know he's alive. I want to know what's happening. I want to know when he's coming home. If he could magic those stupid Councillors back to Dorana, why can't he find a way to tell us what's going on? If he's such a powerful mage why does he let us torment ourselves with worry?*

She loved Rafel. She did. But at times she thought she hated him, too.

"I'm sorry, Deenie," Charis said, her voice still small. "I don't mean to go on at you."

Her head was pounding, hammers of pain beating at her temples. Despite months of constant storms and tremors, still Barl's Weather Magic wasn't shaken loose from Lur. It clung to the earth like a tattered autumn leaf to a tree, stubbornly refusing to abandon its home.

"It's all right."

"Sometimes—" Charis took in a deep, shivering breath. "Sometimes I can't believe what's happening to Lur. Why would Barl let this go on? Why doesn't she intercede? In chapel Barlsman Jaffee says we're being tested and to prevail we must stay strong in our faith and

27

observe Barl's Laws but—" She bit her bottom lip. "Deenie, the chapels have never been so full, yet nothing changes. What is Barl waiting for, do you think?"

Though she was two years older, sometimes Charis seemed very *young*. "You still believe in Barl?"

"Well, yes," said Charis, uncertain. "Don't you?"

Deenie pulled a face. "I stopped thinking of her as anything but a dead Doranen mage long ago. I think Arlin Garrick's horrible father was right. Jaffee's talk of Barl saving us is nonsense."

"*Deenie!*" Shocked, Charis shoved to her feet again. "It's wicked to say things like that."

"Truly? Well, I don't care," she said, feeling her face scrunch into a scowl, the way Da's did when he was fratched. The way it used to. *Da*. "I don't see how sitting around waiting for Barl to save us has done Lur much good, do you?"

"What choice do we have?" said Charis. "No matter how bad things get here, we've nowhere to run. Olken and Doranen, we're all of us stuck between the mountains and the reef. The only hope we've got is Barl."

"And Rafel," Deenie reminded her. "He's out there trying to save us, Charis. Him and Arlin Garrick. If Arlin's still alive. I can't tell about him."

"Rafel," said Charis. Her voice broke on his name. "Oh, Deenie. All this time without word. What if he's in trouble? What if he needs help?"

*Then he's on his own, Charis. There's nothing we can do.*

But she couldn't say that aloud. "He'll be fine. He's Rafel."

"And Lur?" said Charis, still fearful. "Deenie, how long do we have before the kingdom's utterly ruined? Do you know? Can you tell?"

Not for certain, but she had a nasty suspicion. Only she couldn't share those fears either, even though if she did she'd maybe not feel so alone. Da would want her to be strong, even though she was his tiddy timid mouse. So she had to be, didn't she? For him, for Mama, for Charis—and for Rafe.

*I wish there was someone to be strong for me.*

"Deenie?"

Stirred out of bleak thought, she looked at her friend. "I can't say how long we've got, Charis. And I can't say what'll happen when time runs out."

Charis crossed to the entrance hall's window and rested her hand against it, palm-first and spread-fingered. "The whole world's weeping," she said sorrowfully. "That's what it looks like. I heard someone say yesterday almost a third of the kingdom's gone under water, with the Gant and the riverlets breaking their banks in so many places. I wonder . . ." Now she rested her forehead against the glass. "Will we drown first, or die of hunger? Or will the ground open up and swallow us instead?"

The storm aching in every one of her bones, Deenie tightened her arms around her pulled-up knees. "Don't talk like that. How is it helpful, you talking like that?"

Charis shrugged. "How else should I talk? You might not come down to the city, Deenie, but I do. I talk to people and I listen. Food's growing scarce everywhere. We've got the kitchen gardens up at the Tower, and chickens, and we muddle along—but that's not the same for the rest of Lur. Folk are hungry and frighted. The Council doesn't know what to do, and the few Doranen who've not run back to hide on their country estates, their magic can't fix any of it either. They're as lost as we are, even if they won't admit it."

She knew that. Didn't she talk now and then with the Olken who came to work in the palace? They told her things. Of course, mostly they told her because they hoped she'd confide things to them in return, tell them about Asher and how he'd be up and about soon and saving them again. But she didn't need their selfish secrets. They only told her what her mage-sense had already made clear.

*It's all falling apart now, faster and faster, and if there's someone in Lur who can stop it, well, I don't know who that is.*

Another shiver ran through her. "Storm's passing," she said, relieved, and stood. "We should head home. Mama will be fretting."

Charis turned away from the window. "You go. I want to stay here tonight."

"Here?" Deenie frowned. "No, Charis. You can't. I know you're missing Uncle Pellen, but you don't want to—"

"Don't you tell me what I want!" Charis retorted. "I think I know what I want better than you do, Deenie."

Hurt, she looked past Charis to the easing rain beyond the window. Was that a glimpse of blue sky or her tricky imagination?

"You don't have to have my room, Charis. I did offer you Rafe's. We can swap. I don't mind."

"I don't *want* Rafe's room!" said Charis, tears spilling. "Or yours. I want *my* room, Deenie, in *my* house. I want my papa back. I want Lur the way it was, with sunshine, not storms. I want to trust the ground beneath my feet. I'm so tired of being afraid. I wake up afraid and I go to sleep afraid. I used to be *happy*. I used to laugh and dance and sing. I want to be that Charis again but I know—*I know*—I never can be. She's dead and Papa's dead and Lur is dying and Rafel's lost and I can't bear it . . . I can't bear it . . ."

"Oh, Charis," said Deenie, and went to her, and held her friend as she sobbed. Not even at Uncle Pellen's little funeral had Charis wept like this. She must've been saving up these tears ever since. "Please, Charis, don't fratch yourself," she murmured. "Things will get better. You'll see. They will."

"You really are a terrible liar," Charis said, hiccupping. "You shouldn't even bother trying."

Deenie let go of her and stepped back. "You truly want to stay here?"

"I do."

Sighing, she smoothed Charis's damp hair. "All right. But only tonight, mind. Mama won't have you staying here longer, Charis, and neither will I. What if there's a tremor and the house falls on you, or it falls down a hole and takes you with it? It's happened before. I'm not about to let it happen to you."

Charis's teary eyes widened. "You can feel a tremor coming? *Deenie*—"

What a shame she was such a bad liar. If she was more like Rafel she could say "yes" and make Charis come home with her, and then maybe by the morning she'd have forgotten this nonsense.

She sighed. "No, not now. But there will be more tremors some-time and I don't want you caught."

"I won't be, I promise," said Charis. Turning, she looked again out of the window. "The storm's passed. You should go. I'll see you tomorrow."

Since there was no talking Charis out of staying, Deenie left her friend behind in her memory-crowded house and toiled up the long, puddled High Street to the palace grounds. The sky hadn't cleared completely — a few clouds still remained, spitting sulky rain onto the city. By the time she passed through the open palace gates her feet were soaked to the ankles, her shoes horribly squishy. The day's light was waning, the autumn night closing in. Now when she shivered it was from proper cold, not dread anticipation of wild, magic-born weather to come.

"Mama," she called, climbing the spiral staircase up to her parents' apartment. "Mama, I'm home."

Mama didn't reply. She never did. Any strength that was left in her these days, she saved for Da.

"Mama," she said again, standing in Da's open bedchamber doorway, "you should rest before supper. I'll sit with him a while."

Still Mama didn't answer. Small in the armchair beside Da's bed, she held his hand gently, her gaze resting on his sleeping face. She always said she'd never been a beautiful woman, not even when she was young, but Da never saw that. To him she was the most beautiful woman in the world, especially when she was scolding him with fire in her eyes.

Looking at her mother now, Deenie felt a sharp pain.

*These days her eyes are like burned-out coals. I can't remember the last time I heard her laugh.*

Hiding her dismay, like always, she crossed the rug-covered floor to the bed. "Please, Mama. Go and rest."

Mama glanced up. "Deenie," she said, her sorrow softening almost to a smile. "There you are. Is Charis with you?"

"No, I'm on my lonesome. Charis is sleeping in her own bed tonight."

"Oh," Mama said vaguely. "Well, I suppose that's all right."

It struck her then, like a slap across the face: Mama looked worse than weary. She looked *old*. Old and frail and on the brink of surrender. Had she stopped believing that Da would recover? Was she like everyone else, thinking Rafel was long lost?

*I don't know. I'm afraid to ask.*

But Mama *couldn't* be giving up on them. She was Jervale's Heir. Against the most terrible odds she'd seen prophecy fulfilled and Lur saved from a nightmare. Morg's destruction was as much her doing as Da's.

*What will I do, if Mama gives up?*

"Deenie? Is something amiss?"

Swallowing hard, she shook her head. "No. Of course not. Mama, please, go and rest a while."

Mama's brows pinched. "I'm fine."

"Mama—" But there was no point arguing. Her mother could be so stubborn, a real slumskumbledy wench. "Then go for a walk in the grounds. There's still a little light left, and some fresh air will do you good. And I'd like to sit with Da for a while."

Now Mama did smile, properly. "Ah."

Deenie watched her lift Da's hand to her lips and kiss it, then settle it carefully on the quilt. Not helping her out of the chair was hard, but Mama snapped whenever anyone tried to coddle her. Even though she needed coddling. Even though she'd become a shadow of herself.

"Is there supper?"

"I put an egg pie in the oven to slow-bake before I went out."

Mama squeezed her arm. "You're a good girl, Deenie. If you need me, I'll be taking that little walk."

"And afterwards, you'll have a lie down before we eat?"

"Deenie—"

"Don't fratch at me, Mama," she whispered, her throat tight. "It's just . . . you look tired."

"Do I?" Mama said at last, her gaze once more on Da. "Well, perhaps I am, a little. And if I am . . ." Her voice was suddenly pale, like winter sunlight. "I've got cause. Call me when the pie's baked."

Alone with her father, Deenie sat in the chair by his bed. His hand when she picked it up felt cool and dry and disinterested. She had a dream that one day when she wrapped her warm, desperate fingers around his she'd feel them move and see his eyes fly open and hear his loving voice say, *Hello, mouse.*

But he'd been lying here silent and still for so long. When was it foolish to keep on dreaming a dream?

Overwhelmed, she stroked his silvering hair. He liked to keep it cropped close, but Mama had let it grow so he'd not be bothered with scissors while he was poorly. He didn't react to that touch either.

"Hey, Da," she said softly. "It's me. Deenie."

Not even a tiny twitch of his eyelids. Mama didn't speak to him, not any more. But she did. She had to. Though her voice hadn't woken him yet, she wasn't about to give up.

Djelba logs burned in the chamber's fireplace, a cheery crackling. The last tremor had tipped four of the palace's oldest trees out of the earth. The nightbirds who'd roosted there had been so loudly offended, especially since the birds in the trees on either side refused to share their homes. The dispossessed nightbirds had flown away and not returned. Mayhap they'd found new lodgings. Mayhap they'd perished. Not even birds were safe in these troublesome times.

"Da, I need your advice," she said, watching the slow, steady rise and fall of his chest. "I don't know what to do about Charis. She misses Uncle Pellen so much and I don't know how to help her."

Da didn't either. He never said a word.

She tightened her fingers around his. "So how are you feeling, Da?"

When he didn't answer, she woke her mage-sense and sent it questing inside him for the deep blight only she could feel. Hoped—prayed— that this time she'd not find it.

But no. There it was, a dark, rippling curtain dropped between him and the world. Oh, how she hated that blight. Her hatred was so fierce it made her feel sick. And guilt twisted through her, for not knowing how to save him from it.

"Keep fighting, Da," she whispered. "Please. You mustn't let it win. I'll find a way to free you. I will. You just have to hold on."

His sunken eyes shifted behind their closed, translucent lids. She held her breath.

*Open them, Da. Look at me. I'm here.*

But he didn't.

She kissed his forehead, feeling him cool and so far away. Then she told him of her day, glossing over the part where yet again she'd mucked about with Doranen magic. She had to keep that from him. All her life he'd done his best to protect her from mage doings. He'd be cross and disappointed if he knew what she'd been up to.

*But I have to try, Da. Could be one of these days I'll finally get a Doranen spell to work three times out of three, not just one. And if I do, I might be able to help Lur.*

After that she read to him for a while, one of Mama's sloppy old Doranen love stories she used to pretend she despised. Then her empty belly started rumbling. Supper time. And after supper Kerril's novice assistant Pother Ulys would come and sit with him partway through the night, so there could be a little sleep for her and Mama.

"Da," she said, leaning close. "Our Rafel's still out there somewhere. He is. I can feel him. Don't you lose hope, Da. I haven't. I won't."

It was safe to leave him alone for a short stretch here and there, so she smoothed his undisturbed blankets, kissed him again, then went down to the Tower kitchen to slice the egg pie for supper. After making sure Mama ate hers and drank her mulled wine with some sleeping herbs dropped in it, she greeted Pother Ulys and after that at last fell into Rafe's bed for a snatch of rest. Worn out from the storm, and other people's turbulent emotions, she tumbled swiftly into sleep.

And, for the first time since he rode away, dreamed of her missing brother.

# CHAPTER THREE

"**Y**ou *dreamed* him?" Charis squealed. "*Deenie!* Could you see where he was? Is he unharmed? Did he speak to you? What did he say? Is he coming home? Deenie—"

Grabbing Charis's arm, Deenie hustled her out of the Tower foyer and down the wide sandstone steps to the untidy gravel forecourt, and kept on hustling until they reached the tree-lined carriageway leading to the stables. There she dragged Charis behind a djelba's sheltering trunk. Leaves fallen from the nearby piplins were drifted against its exposed, knobbled roots, and rustled as she and Charis scuffed amongst them.

With a look round to be sure it was safe to speak, she gave Charis's arm a little shake. "*Hush.* You *know* how voices carry in there, and Tibby's come to help me clean today."

Momentarily chastened, Charis smoothed her plain green linen sleeve. "Sorry. But Deenie—"

"I can't have Mama knowing I dreamed him," she said, hearing herself fierce and unfriendly. She didn't care. "I can't have her stirred about, Charis. If she knows that much she'll want to know everything and I can't—I can't tell her—"

"Tell her what, Deenie? Please—" Now it was Charis's turn to take hold and shake. "You're frighting me."

Sink it. "Not here," she muttered, as she spied Pother Kerril approaching along the main carriageway up to the Tower. "We'll take a wander to somewhere private and I'll tell you. Just let me speak with Kerril first. Wait."

Feeling Charis's alarmed stare on her back, she hurried to meet the pother.

Kerril greeted her with a frown. "Deenie. You're looking peaked this morning."

Trust the eagle-eyed Doranen pother to notice. "Really? Because I feel fine. There's no need to fratch over me."

Kerril's fingers drummed the bulky leather satchel slung against her hip. "No need? Deenie, you're a young girl cooped up in a Tower with one parent ailing and the other pushed far past her limit, you've a brother lost in the wilderness and on your shoulders is the weight of a kingdom you can't help. So don't stand there and tell me you're fine."

*Yes, well, when you put it like that.* "It's the way things are," she said, shrugging. "I can't change them, so I have to live with them. We all do."

"And that's true enough," Kerril murmured. She glanced at the cloud-scattered sky, and then at the scars the latest tremors had left behind: uneven folds and ripples in the earth, gaping holes where trees used to be, aimlessly tumbled sections of the wall around the mostly empty stables. "But I mislike it, Deenie, you trapped alone in this sad place."

"I'm not alone," she protested. "With Da and Mama and Charis, and the folk who come in and out to help me keep the Tower to rights —how can you call me alone?"

Kerril wore her silver-gilt hair pulled back from her narrow face. It made her frowns seem all the more severe. "You know what I mean, Deenie. This is no life for a young lass. I think it's time you—"

"No," she said, and stepped back. *Leave me be, you bothersome woman.* "I'll not do that. Pother Kerril, I did ask you not to ask me again."

Kerril sighed. "Deenie, I'd be derelict in my duty if I didn't try to change your mind. I know the notion distresses you, but—"

"This isn't about me," she said. "It's about Da. You think I don't know how much easier my life would be if I convinced Mama to let you put him in a Barlshouse hospice? I can't do that. I won't give him to strangers, even if they're Barl's strangers. He's my *da*."

"And if your da weren't so broken," said Pother Kerril, gently cruel, "would he let you break yourself over him?"

She met Kerril's compassionate gaze with the stony strength she'd never known was in her. The strength she hadn't needed until Rafel went away.

"Pother Kerril, please," she said. "I don't want to fratch with you. Your care for Da means a great deal to me. If it turns out I can't do right by him, I'll tell you. But until that day comes . . ."

*Which it won't. I swear. I'll never abandon him.*

Grudging, Kerril nodded. "Until that day, then. Deenie, you're Asher's daughter and no mistake." It wasn't entirely a compliment, the way she said it. Then her gaze shifted. "How is Charis faring?"

There was so much she could say to that, but to speak would be a kind of betrayal. "She misses Uncle Pellen."

"Grief has as many faces as there are folk who grieve," said Kerril. "And for some it takes a goodly while before they can let themselves believe the loss. Be patient with her, Deenie. Charis will find her way."

She wanted to believe the pother so badly. "You think so?"

"I know so," said Kerril firmly. "And now I'll see to your father. I've brought fresh herbs for his gruel, and some strengthening possets."

"Thank you," she said. "Pother Kerril—"

Kerril paused. "Yes, Deenie?"

"It means something, doesn't it, that Da hasn't—that he's not—" She swallowed. She never could bring herself to say those words out loud. "He's still with us, after all this time. He takes his gruel and tea. He's not wasted away entirely. I'm not coddling myself, am I? It does mean something?"

"It means your father is the most stubborn man breathing," said Kerril. Then she sighed again. "But if there's more meaning to it than that, Deenie, I'm sorry. I can't say."

Discouraged, she left Kerril to make her way into the Tower and returned to Charis, who was hopping with impatience.

"Come along," she said, as Charis opened her mouth. "We'll take a wander through the palace grounds."

But really there was only one place where she knew for certain they'd not be disturbed or overheard. She couldn't risk them walking the grounds' public pathways, because with Lur in so much strife folk came up every day from the city to loiter in the Garden of Remembrance and whisper prayers. And then there were the comings and goings from the palace where the secretaries and messengers and coin counters worked, busier than ever these days with so much trouble to contain.

"Deenie, where are we *going?*" Charis asked for the third time as they left the palace's cultivated grounds behind and struck out into its woodland. "And if you say 'you'll see when we get there' again I declare I will *smack* you!"

One of the earth's great upheavals had struck all along this section of tangled, brambled path. "Mind yourself here," Deenie warned as she stumbled and staggered through the ruts. "If you turn your ankle I'll never carry you back to the Tower."

Cursing under her breath, Charis stopped. "That's it. I'll not take another step until you—"

"Sink it, Charis, what does it *matter* where we're going?" she demanded, spinning round. "Somewhere peaceful, somewhere private. Why do you have to be such a ninny about it?"

Charis slitted her eyes. "I think I liked you better when you were a mouse."

Abruptly contrite, Deenie bit her lip. "Sorry. I don't mean to fratch at you, truly, it's just—" She grabbed her thick brown braid and tugged it, hard. "I have to boss so many folk these days, it's turned into a habit. There's Mama and Pother Kerril and the stable lad and Tibby and the Councillors who come to bother us and—" She let go of her hair and sighed. "I almost forget what it was like to be a mouse."

Charis's lips twitched. "You left me off your list. You boss me more than anyone."

And that was true. "Only because you need it," she said, fighting a small, silly smile of her own. "You were all right last night? In the house on your lonesome?"

The woodland straggled around them. Instead of answering the question, Charis watched a biddy-bye flutter from branch to branch on a half-uprooted nirrin tree. The bird's red and white plumage was the only splash of colour in the surrounding damp drabness.

"It was very . . . quiet," she said at last. "I thought being there would bring Papa closer."

She'd thought the same thing, sleeping in Rafe's bed, living in his Tower apartment while Charis lived in hers. "But it didn't?"

"No," said Charis, thoughtful. "He seemed further away than ever. I sat on the staircase after you left, and I stared at the front door waiting for him to walk through it. I knew he wouldn't, but I sat there anyway. I expect that makes me soft in the wits."

*Grief has as many faces as there are folk who grieve.*

"No softer than anyone who's lost someone they love."

Charis looked at the rumpled earth and the soggy woodland. "Tell me about your dream, Deenie. Please."

"Soon," she said. "We're almost there. Come on."

"Almost *where?*" wailed Charis, following. "Slumguzzle it, Gardenia . . ."

"Sorry," she said airily. "I don't know anyone by that silly name."

And she would have grinned over her shoulder at her dearest friend, her almost sister, only they'd come to the end of the muddy, overgrown track which meant they'd reached it at last, the place nobody but her family knew she knew about.

"Oh," said Charis, crowding beside her. Her voice was small and hushed. "Deenie. Is that—*was* that—the *Weather Chamber?*"

Stunned, Deenie stared at the pile of brick and glass and timber before them. Stared at the violently uneven ground of the clearing, where tremors had lifted and torn and crumpled the earth like a handkerchief.

"How do you know about the Weather Chamber?" she whispered. "Nobody's meant to know. It's s'posed to be a secret."

"Yes, but Papa was mayor forever, remember?" said Charis. "And he was your da's best friend. I heard lots of things when I was a tiddler, 'cause either they didn't think I was listening or they reckoned me too young to understand. How did *you* know?"

"Mama brought me here, once," she said, and blinked away the memory of Da thrashing stricken on the Chamber's floor, and Rafel stricken beside him. "I swore I'd never tell of it, but everything's different now."

Fretting, Charis hugged her ribs. "How long has it been tumbled, d'you think? You don't suppose *this* is why—"

"No," she said. "I think it must've come down in the last big tremor. Look—there's no moss grown on the rubble, and the broken timber's not rotted. And things have been going wrong for ages." She pointed to an uprooted djelba. "Let's sit."

Perched side by side on the smooth-barked, sloping tree trunk, they gloomed at the ruined Weather Chamber. "Weren't there important mage things in there?" Charis said at last.

"I think there must've been," she said. "It's where all the Weather Magic got done."

"D'you think we should—"

"No." Deenie shivered, feeling the dregs and drizzle of leftover power in what remained of Lur's most powerful place. "We stay well clear. If a brick fell on your head and cracked it, however would I explain that to Pother Kerril?"

"There was so much magic here," said Charis, awestruck. "After all this time abandoned, it still skritches."

*Skritches*. That was one of her brother's words. She felt a breath catch in her throat. "Yes, but never mind that now. Charis, Rafe's in trouble. Terrible trouble."

Charis took her hand and held on tight. "Tell me."

Even sleeping, she'd known it wasn't an ordinary dream. She'd known it was a sending, a warning, a desperate cry for help. The oddest thing about it was she couldn't see Rafe's face. Not properly. Though he'd been standing in sunlight an odd darkness had cloaked him, and in the dream she'd heard him screaming.

Charis's clutching hand tightened. "Screaming? Oh, *Deenie*."

"I know," she said, her voice catching. "It was awful. I woke up and for a moment I didn't know where I was."

"Did you see where Rafe was?"

"No. At least, not exactly," she said slowly. "He was outside. In a garden. I didn't recognise the flowers. There was blue sky and sunshine. There was a grand house behind him. He was wearing— I don't know—" She screwed her eyes shut for a moment, trying to recapture the sight of him. "Something *fine*. There were jewels. I remember jewels."

"*Jewels?*" Charis stared at her. "That doesn't sound right. If he's wearing jewels, in a garden, how can he be in trouble? Are you sure this wasn't an everyday dream?"

"I want to think so," she said, and tugged her hand free of Charis's tight clasp. "It's true I've dreamed about him before, but—"

"You have?" Charis slapped her, a cross little sting on her arm. "You wretch. You never told me!"

No, because those dreams had made her weep. She and Rafe had brangled like puppies, growing up. Her mousiness fratched him. Brash and bold, he never could understand why she was so timid—and she'd never worked out how to explain. But beneath his crossness he loved her. She knew that. With Rafe gone, in her sleep she'd revisited every laugh, every smile, every precious moment when the two of them weren't at odds.

"Those dreams were different, Charis. They were just memories. But this time—he's in trouble, I tell you. *That's* not a dream."

Charis leapt off the tree trunk. Now there was a damp patch on her dark green skirt, and clinging bits of bark, but she didn't notice. "Then we have to help him."

"How?"

"I don't know. Another expedition, maybe."

"Another expedition?" she said, staring. "Charis, you're daft. The Council would never agree. Not after all the fuss and flap over what was found beyond the mountains. Those Councillors Rafe sent back from the blighted lands, they put the wind up everyone so bad there's no one as'll listen to me. Besides, the Council's declared Rafe and Arlin Garrick dead, remember? And now most everyone believes it. The only person who believes me when I say Rafe's not dead is you."

Uncertain, Charis frowned at her. "And your mother."

"I don't think so," she said, after a difficult moment. "I think Mama —it's been so long, with no word, and I think—"

"Oh," said Charis, and sat on the tree trunk again. "Deenie, I'm so sorry. Why didn't you tell me?"

*Because it's something else that hurts too much.*

"It doesn't matter," she muttered. "Mama's not herself these days. And it's not the point, anyway. Even if the Council did give permission for another expedition, all I can say for certain is Rafe's in a garden. And what use is that?"

Charis leapt up a second time. "Nonsense. If you dreamed him once you'll dream him again, and could be next time you'll dream his exact whereabouts. As for the Council, who cares about that gaggle of old blowfish? We don't need their permission to go after Rafe."

"Charis, Charis," she sighed, "you've taken leave of your senses. We *can't* go after him. Even if we could survive the blighted lands, Barl's Mountains are warded against crossing and the reef's impassable."

"Must you be such a noddyhead, Deenie?" Charis demanded. "Perhaps an *ordinary* mage couldn't find us a way out of Lur, but you're not an ordinary mage, are you?"

"Oh, Charis. I'm not *any* kind of mage," she said, despairing. "I feel things, that's all. And every so often I can get a Doranen spell to come out right. That's it. Honestly, I'm practically useless."

Charis planted her fists on her hips, everything about her offended and determined. "Deenie, I swear, this is no time for you to turn back into a mouse. Rafe's your brother and he needs you. How can you give up without even *trying* to save him?"

Deenie shoved off the tree trunk and put some breathing distance between herself and Charis. "And what d'you expect me to do, Meistress Orrick? Snap my fingers and magic myself to where he is? When I don't *know* where he is? When I don't know how to *do* that?"

"Rafe did it," Charis retorted. "He sent those Council ninnies Dimble and Clyne and Hambly home from the blighted lands. And if he did a spell like that then so can you, Deenie, because you're his sister. You're *Asher's daughter*. It doesn't matter if your magic's unreliable and it frights you—somehow you have to find a way to use it. Because right now you're Rafe's only chance."

"Well, I don't *want* to be his only chance!"

Charis grabbed her by the shoulders and shook. "*I don't care*. This isn't about you, Deenie." She let go, shoving a little. "In case you hadn't noticed, Lur's falling apart, faster and faster every day. Stupid people keep hoping your da's going to wake up and fix things but we both know that's not going to happen. There's only one mage who can keep this kingdom alive and that's Rafel. So if Lur's going to live, *he* has to live, and that means you have to save him, Deenie. *We* have to save him. Rafe's the only hope Lur's got!"

All her life she'd known Charis, and she'd never once seen her like this. Stunned, Deenie found her way back to the tree trunk and thumped herself onto it.

"Charis . . ."

"And if that's not a good enough reason," said Charis, panting, "then think about *this*. I'm mad in love with your brother, Deenie, and I know your brother's got feelings for me. I kept waiting for him to speak but he never did, 'cause he's a noddyhead, and then he left and —and—" With an effort, she steadied her voice. "So if we don't at least *try* to save him I swear I'll *never* speak to you again!"

"*Charis*—" Deenie clenched her fingers. "Of course I want to save him. I'd give *anything* to save him. But wanting it isn't enough. *It ain't possible.*"

For a long time Charis stood there, her wet cheeks flushed, breathing quickly. She was a pretty, flirty young woman and she never lost her temper. Not like this.

*She really does love him. And he left her behind and now most likely she'll never see him again—and neither will I. Did I know that when he rode away? Did I know in my bones Rafe was riding to his death?*

Some days she thought she had known it. Some days she hated Rafe so much for leaving, for breaking Mama's heart, for not being at home to share the burden of Da. For not being in Lur to use his magic when his magic was so sorely needed.

*And I think I hate him for asking me to help him when he must know there's not a thing I can do.*

"Charis," she said, fighting her own tears, "please say you believe me."

"Yes," Charis said at last in a small voice. "I believe you. I don't want to, but—" She dried her face on her sleeve, then let her hands fall by her sides. "So that's the end of it. Rafe's in trouble and he's going to die. We're all going to die. And nobody can save us."

She sounded so *defeated*.

"We're not dead yet, you know," Deenie said, sliding off the tree trunk. "Maybe Barlsman Jaffee's right. Maybe Barl will send us a miracle before it's too late."

Charis's expression darkened. "Don't say things like that just to make me feel better, Deenie. I don't need coddling. *I'm* not a mouse."

And that stung, but she wasn't about to let the hurt show. "I'm not coddling. I'm trying to make the best of a poor situation."

"I know," Charis muttered. "I'm sorry."

Deenie shook her head. "No, *I'm* sorry. Charis—"

"Don't," said Charis. "It's not your fault."

Lost and bewildered, they hugged each other. Then Deenie stepped back and looked past Charis to the tumbled wreck of the Weather Chamber, keenly aware of a deep, aching regret. After everything their parents had fought through and survived, it was hard to accept it had all been for nothing.

"Lur used to be so lovely," she said softly. "Before Barl's magic ran out."

Charis scuffed her mud-sticky shoes against the grass. "When Papa realised his time was short, instead of sleeping, like he was s'posed to, he stayed awake and told me stories about King Borne's day, and how peaceful and prosperous and safe the kingdom was then."

Linking arms with her, Deenie sighed. "Darran used to tell me and Rafe the same stories. He said Lur under King Borne was a golden age. He said he'd thought things would only get better, with King Gar on the throne and Da his good right hand."

"And then everything went wrong," Charis whispered. "It made Papa so sad, remembering what we've lost. He said it broke his heart to leave me alone in a world grown so uncertain. He told me to fight for Lur however I could. And I want to. I *would* fight. I just don't know how."

Guilt seared her. "I don't, either. I wish I did, I wish I wasn't so *useless*."

"You're not," Charis said sharply. "And I'll smack you if you say that again. If it wasn't for you, Deenie, we wouldn't know for sure Rafe's alive."

"But I can't *help* him."

Charis sighed, resigned. "You aren't to blame for that. Besides, anything could happen. Maybe there *is* a way for you to save him, and we just don't know what it is yet."

Startled, Deenie stared at her. "You really think so?"

"I have to," Charis said, after a long silence. "If I give up hope I'll disappoint Papa." Then she heaved another sigh. "I should go. I promised Meistress Dindle I'd lend a hand in the bakehouse. Her nephew found wheat good enough for flour so she's doing a brisk trade again, and with her husband gone . . ."

Meister Dindle, killed three — no, four — storms ago. Twelve city folk had died that day, two of them spratlings. So much loss and pain in the city. Was it never going to end?

"I mustn't linger, either," she said, stifling sorrow. "I've chores to do, and cooking, and I need to sit with Da so Mama can get more rest."

Dispirited, and trying to hide it from each other, they left the Weather Chamber to the elements and made their muddy way back to the palace's public grounds. There they parted company, Charis promising to bring home some fresh bread. Deenie returned to the Tower—where she found Pother Kerril, ominously waiting.

"What's wrong?" she said, feeling her heart pound. "Is it Da?"

Kerril's lips were pinched tight. "No, Deenie, it's your mother."

Weak-kneed, she sat on the settle in the Tower's marble-floored foyer. "She's tired, I know."

"Tired? She's *exhausted*," snapped Kerril. "I've never seen anyone fail so fast in a week. Deenie—"

"I do what I can to ease her, Pother Kerril," she said, flinching. "But I can't drag her from Da's bedside like a criminal, can I?"

"The way she's driving herself *is* criminal," said Kerril. "And so I've told her. *And* I've told her it's time to do the right thing, for herself and for you and most importantly for Asher."

"The *hospice?*" Furious, Deenie leapt up. "Pother Kerril, we've already talked on—"

"No, Deenie, *I've* talked and *you've* refused to listen," Pother Kerril retorted. "Now it's high time you stopped this nonsense and—"

Cold and close to shivering, Deenie glared at her. "It's not nonsense. Pother Kerril, Mama and I are grateful for everything you've done, but that doesn't give you leave to march in here and bark orders. If you can't treat Da without upsetting the way we live, then perhaps you shouldn't come again."

"And perhaps *you* should stop fuddling yourself with the notion that one day your father will wake!" said Pother Kerril, glaring back. "For he won't, Deenie. I promise you that. He'll linger a while yet for it's the nature of this malady, but he's never coming back to you and—"

"You don't know that!" she said. "You don't even know what this malady *is*. I tell you it's unnatural and you won't listen. You say there's no blight in him because you can't feel it. Well, *I* feel it, Kerril. And to best it Da must stay strong, but he'll only stay strong here at home, in the Tower, being cared for by me and Mama. You put him in a hospice with strangers and I tell you straight, you might as well be putting him in the ground!"

Kerril's mouth pinched tighter than ever. "I can see there's no persuading you."

"None."

"Well, if you won't see the truth now, you'll see it soon enough," said the pother. "And when you do, you'll call for me. In the meantime I've left possets for your mother too. I've already given her one, but make sure she takes the rest, two a day, *and* eats nourishing food."

"She does!"

"But only a few snatched mouthfuls, I'll wager," said Kerril. "Or will you stand there and tell me Dathne guzzles three courses at a sitting?"

No. Mama didn't. It was a task to make her finish a single slice of egg pie. "She's my mother," she muttered. "She won't let me feed her like a child."

"I know you're trying, Deenie," said Kerril, softening. "But this sad state of affairs has grown bigger than your heart."

"We're managing," she said, and stepped back. "But I thank you for your concern, Pother Kerril. And for the possets."

Kerril sighed. "Deenie, I've known your father since first he came to the city. Whatever harsh words I say, I say them out of love." She sighed again. "I've sent for Ulys. As soon as she comes, cajole Dathne to bed. You could sleep more too. And if you've any concerns, send for me at once."

After Kerril was gone, Deenie trudged up the spiral staircase to find her mother. The day wasn't even half over and already it was full of pain.

*Prob'ly I shouldn't have told Charis about Rafel. But I had to tell someone. I couldn't sit on that, like an egg.*

And as for Pother Kerril . . .

"Mama," she said, entering Da's sweetly scented, silent chamber. "We need to talk."

Seated by Da's bedside, his hand in hers, Mama looked round. Her eyes were heavy with the herbs in Kerril's posset. "I'm not sending him away, Deenie. I'm not giving him to strangers. So if you've come up here to rail at me on that, you can—"

"No, Mama, of *course* I haven't." Distressed, she hurried to her mother's chair and dropped to a crouch. "How could you think it? I don't want Da in a hospice any more than you do."

Sighing, Mama stroked her hair. "Good."

She had to blink back a swift sting of tears. "But, Mama, Pother Kerril's right about one thing. You need to rest more. If Da could see how fratched you are he'd start throwing plates."

"Deenie." Mama looked at Da, so quiet beside them. "How can I waste my time in sleep when every hour I sit with him might be the last?"

"*Mama*—"

"Poor Deenie," Mama said softly, still stroking her hair. "These past months have been hard on you, haven't they?"

"And on you." *Rafel.* "But Mama—"

Breathing deeply, her mother smothered a yawn. Kerril's posset was fast taking effect. "Have I disappointed you, Deenie? Do you wish I was out there, fighting for Lur, instead of staying cooped up here in the Tower?"

*Yes. No. Maybe.* "Mama, it's all right. I understand."

"No, you don't," said her mother. "How could you? In many ways you're still a child. Deenie, I was younger than you are now when I learned I was Jervale's Heir—and almost every day since, I've fought for this kingdom. But I can't face another battle, not on my own. Not without your father." Her voice broke. "I just can't. I'm worn down, Deenie. I'm done."

"Mama . . ." Hearing her own voice crack, Deenie pressed her lips tight until she could trust herself to speak. "What about the Circle? Couldn't it help?"

Mama raised Da's hand to her cheek. "The Circle's long broken, Deenie. Aside from me only Jinny is left—and neither of us have the magic in us that Lur needs."

"Rafe does," she said, troubled. *Should I tell her? I should tell her.* "Mama—about Rafe—"

And then, between heartbeats, she changed her mind. The last thing her mother needed now was something else to fratch her. Especially when there was nothing either of them could do.

"What?" said Mama. Her head was nodding, her eyes drooped almost closed. "Deenie, is something wrong?"

Deenie kissed her cheek. "No, Mama. Everything's fine."

The sound of footsteps on the spiral staircase reached them, and a moment later the novice pother Ulys was tapping on the open chamber door. So she left Ulys to keep Da company and helped Mama to her chamber and into her bed. And then, even though she had chores, and cooking, she pulled up a chair and settled herself to make sure her mother slept.

Before the posset claimed her completely, Mama opened her eyes. "I love your father, Deenie," she whispered. "I love him more than my life. But I tell you, I'm so cross with him for doing this to me I could *spit*."

Deenie rubbed her mother's thin arm. "I know, Mama. I know."

Her mother slid into sleep then, and she drowsed a little herself, only to startle awake when Mama began to toss restlessly beneath the bedcovers.

"—*should've* burned that diary, Asher. You had no business keeping it. You had no right to lie!"

Shocked, Deenie stared. Her mother might be muttering now, but once she'd shouted those words. Shouting and anger were loud in her sleeping face.

*Da lied to Mama? I can't believe it. And I've never heard of a diary, either. Not one that should've been burned.*

So what story had she never been told, not even by that ole rattle-tongue Darran?

"No secrets, we promised," Mama muttered, resentful. "He broke his word to me. To *me*. How could he? That sinking diary. More trouble than it's worth. *Asher*—" On a gasp, Mama's eyes fluttered open. Mizzled with sleep and Pother Kerril's posset, she blinked in the chamber's gentle glimlight. "Deenie? Is something wrong?"

She leaned close. "Everything's fine, Mama. You were dreaming. Mama—" *Go on. Go on. You might never get another chance.* "Why d'you think Da should've burned the diary?"

"Why?" said Mama, her half-lidded gaze blurry. "Because it was Barl's, of course. He had no business keeping it. Horrible thing. Full of old Doranen magic. He told me he'd burned it." Her face twisted, tears threatening. "But he lied."

Deenie felt her heart thud. "Barl's diary? That sounds important, Mama. If Da didn't burn it, where is it now?"

"Mustn't tell," Mama said, her eyes drifting closed again. "It's a secret."

Heart still thudding, Deenie watched her mother slide back into sleep. *Barl's diary.* No wonder it was hidden. No wonder Da had lied. He was right to lie, if lying meant Doranen like Arlin Garrick and his father never knew it existed.

But even so . . .

*Oh, Rafe. If only you'd known of it. If you'd had that diary with you perhaps you'd not be in trouble now.*

# CHAPTER FOUR

ꚛ

**H**earing soft, shuffling footsteps on the brickwork behind him, Arlin stopped cleaning his saddle and turned. It was Fernel Pintte and his faithful shadow, Goose—drooling idiot and Rafel's best friend.

*We should have left him behind in that rotted village. He serves no useful purpose . . . and he makes my skin crawl.*

"You're riding out again?" said Pintte, standing with the idiot in the aisle between the still-empty stables. "So soon?"

He'd returned to the mansion only two days ago, after six days spent finding and dragging back with him another three pathetic victims of Morg's sundered self. Two men and a woman, this time. The sorcerer had consumed and discarded them in swift succession, too greedy for leisurely, luxurious murder, then locked himself away to seek out other vessels. The more pieces of his power he collected the more he needed, it seemed . . . and the less willing he became to simply wait for their vessels to answer his call.

*Which is just what we need, of course. An impatient, unpredictable, all-powerful sorcerer.*

"I ride when Morg commands," he said, and scrubbed a brush over the dried mud on his saddle's girth. "Why? Does my absence inconvenience you, Meister Mayor?"

"You think there's cause to mock me?" said Pintte, his face flushed

51

a sickly pink. "Why would you mock me, Arlin? What harm ever did I do to you?"

The stables were smothered in cobwebs. Idiot Goose had shambled across the brickwork to the nearest dirty window and now stared open-mouthed and vacant-eyed at a fly caught up in sticky strands.

Arlin stopped scrubbing the dirty girth. "What harm? Let's see . . ." He pretended to think. "Oh, yes! You got my father killed. I think that's harm enough to be going on with, don't you?"

"I never did," said Pintte, chin lifting. "That was Asher and his son."

"Perhaps. But you helped."

"And you're blameless?" Pintte retorted. "You were there, Arlin. You're a mage. And I don't recall you lifting a finger to help him." The Olken's face twisted. "But then there was no love lost between you and Rodyn Garrick, was there?"

Unthinking, reacting with blind fury, he lashed out with fist and power, hurtling Pintte across the stable block's aisle and crashing him into a closed stable door. Dust belched. Echoes boomed. The shambling idiot Goose dropped to the brickwork floor moaning, arms clutched to his head.

A thread of blood trickled from Pintte's right nostril. Sprawled on the bricks, splayed awkwardly against the old, bleached timber, his thin chest heaved and heaved for air.

And then, shockingly, he laughed.

"You think you scare me, Lord Garrick? After *Morg?*" With a grunt he rolled over, found his unsteady feet and crabbed to the half-wit. "There now, Goose," he crooned, one dirty hand gently patting a broad shoulder. "No harm done. No harm. Pay no mind to our Doranen friend, there. He's a noisy, blustering shit but he can't do us any mischief."

Vaguely ashamed of himself, and furious for that, Arlin watched Pintte help the idiot scrabble to standing. Almost rags, their clothes were now. Morg refused to give them any of the fine garments that were stored in the mansion. Hollow-eyed, hollow-cheeked, Pintte was a harried servant now, hounded to keep the estate and its captives in some kind of order. The idiot Goose had just enough wits left to fetch and carry, to chop wood and pull the guts out of dead deer and boar. Since neither man was fodder for beasting, they lived by capricious Morg's lightest whim.

*As do I. And Pintte knows it.*

"So he commands you to ride out again," said the once peacock-proud Olken. "How many more of his pieces will you bring back this time?"

Arlin stepped sideways, clear of his saddle on its wooden stand, and slumped a shoulder against the brick wall. The mud-brush dangled negligent in his fingers. "I don't know."

With his arm still sheltering round the idiot's shoulders, Pintte ran a hand down his drawn, stubbled face. "How many more are out there? Has he said?"

"He says little."

"He says enough," said Pintte, his voice raw with bitter pain. "Arlin, can't you stop him?"

He felt his lips peel back in a savage smile. "Why, yes, Fernel, of course I can. The reason I haven't is because the sight of him slaughtering innocents and turning men and women into beasts amuses me so much I can't bear the thought of being deprived of the entertainment."

Fernel Pintte looked at him, his eyes bleak. "There's not a day gone by when I was wrong about your kind. The Doranen are a blight and a curse upon the world."

For once he wasn't in the mood to argue that point. How could he, when Morg's existence made it true? But even so, no mere Olken could be permitted such disrespect.

"Idleness offends, Pintte," he said curtly. "So you and your addled pet can make yourselves useful. My horse needs fetching from the field and saddling. See to it."

Dull rebellion seethed beneath Pintte's silence, but the Olken didn't dare disobey Morg's favoured assistant. To do so would be to invite an unspeakable retribution. Instead he caught idiot Goose's ragged sleeve in a tight grip and tugged the doltish creature out of the shadowed stables and into the bright, unforgiving light of day.

Arlin shook his head.

*And so the ignorant leads the idiot. What a world this is.*

He returned to the mansion. Each of its doors was guarded by Morg's mindless, faithfully obedient bestial slaves. Familiarity with the *dravas* had not bred contempt. It didn't matter how many times he was confronted by a snout, a tusk, a horny hide or a barbed tail, every time was like the first. Every time he felt his breath catch and his heart thump and a prickle of sweat break out on his brow and down his spine. The magic made the creatures slept unquiet beneath their skins. They tainted the air. They darkened the sun. They were unnatural in such deep ways there was no easy abiding them.

As he entered the mansion through its side scullery door, forced to pass between two viciously tusked beasts, Arlin dropped his gaze to the flagstones. *Dravas* could—they would—disembowel in a heart-beat if they detected a threat. He'd seen it as he travelled to collect Morg's summoned pieces. The stink of spilled blood and shit and guts never left him. The sound of claws and teeth tearing. The animal shrieks of the dying. Whenever he closed his eyes he found the memories behind his eyelids, waiting to pounce.

He wasn't sleeping so well, these days.

Heavy with resignation, he made his way to the mansion's top floor, one vast space beneath its old, gabled roof. Morg spent most of his time there, sending arcane summons, reuniting himself, sitting in silent meditation as he gathered his strength. Plotting his second subjugation of the known world.

*And here I am, helping him. Wouldn't Father be proud?*

Plodding step by step up the staircase, he wondered yet again why he didn't just kill himself. He might be denied self-harm by an unbreak-able compulsion spell, but doubtless if he provoked a *dravas* he could get the job done. The trouble was . . .

*I don't want to. I have no desire to die.*

Doubtless Rafel would call that craven. But he wasn't about to let that bother him, since it was unlikely Rafel would ever know.

At last he reached Morg's eyrie. Standing on the other side of its closed, brass-bound door, he waited to be summoned within. He never had to knock. Morg always knew when he was there. But this time he waited, and he waited, and no summons came. So at last he did knock. Not hard, just a light, respectful tap.

Still no summons.

On a deep breath, with a pounding heart, he unlatched the heavy door and pushed it open.

Morg sat, as he always sat, in a plain high-backed wooden chair facing the chamber's large circular window. The morning's sunlight fell on him like a benediction, bathing him in a suffused, golden glow. Aside from the chair, the room was empty. Unimpressive, even. Its floor was unadorned polished timber, its plain walls painted an unremarkable cream. Nothing about the chamber suggested power or cruelty. It was a vacant space, filled entirely with the presence of one man.

Arlin closed the door behind him and stood, silently waiting. Morg shared the same silence, his ring-laden fingers clasping the wooden chair's arms. Malleable in the sunlight, time stretched on and on without purpose.

At last, sick with fear and hating himself for fearing, Arlin softly cleared his throat. "Master?"

The man in the chair did not reply or even stir. But he wasn't dead. The power in him was vibrant, swirling the warm, dry air.

"Master," he said again, "I am come, so you might command me."

Still, Morg said nothing.

"*Master*," he said yet again, his heart pounding harder. Dangerous, treacherous hope flickered, a tiny flame in the dark.

*Let this be over. Let him be sitting there poisoned by his own sick soul.*

When Morg continued silent, he risked his life by approaching the chair without permission. By circling it until he could look into Morg's face.

Eyes wide and unblinking, Asher's son stared back at him. Beneath the sorcerer's jewelled silk tunic his chest lightly rose and fell. Shocked almost speechless, Arlin dropped to one knee and reached out his hand.

"No, don't touch me," Rafel whispered, with a tiny, desperate shake of his head. "You'll wake him."

Rafel. It was *Rafel*. But how was that possible? And how was it possible he should feel such relief? Such joy? Yet he did. Ridiculous.

*This man murdered my father. Helped murder my father. What does it matter that I never loved Rodyn Garrick? He was my father. He was Doranen. The Olken should pay for his death.*

And yet . . . and yet . . .

"I know," said Rafel, still hushed. "I can't believe I'm glad to see you, either."

He ignored that. "You say Morg's *sleeping?*"

"Not exactly. It's more like a trance."

Incredulous, Arlin rested his fists on his bent knee. Oh, for a sword. For a dagger—or even a rock.

*I could beat his brains out. I could kill him where he sits.*

"No, you couldn't," whispered Rafel. "You're compelled to obedience, remember? That includes no act of murder. You'd turn a dagger on yourself first."

"You know that?"

A single tear fell on Rafel's pallid cheek. "I know all of it, Arlin. I know everything he's done and everything he plans to do. He makes sure of it. He likes to feel my agony when he kills. When he savours the coming enslavement of every land that escaped his tyranny after Da UnMade him. Or tried to."

There was truth in that. Another man's agony, to Morg, was better than fine wine. "And why does he permit you to speak to me now?"

Rafel smiled, as a ghost would smile. If there were ghosts. "He doesn't. I've outwitted him, but I can't stay surfaced for long."

"*Outwitted* him?" Disbelieving, Arlin shook his head. "That's not possible. He isn't a mage, Rafel, he's a *sorcerer*. His powers—what he knows, what he can do—not even *you* can—"

"Yes, I can," said Rafel. Beneath his anguish there was pride. "And this isn't the first time. But it's getting harder and harder to break free. Arlin—"

"How are you doing it?" he demanded. "Tell me. Show me. There might be a way—"

"For us to link in a working and expel him?" Another ghostly smile. "You think I've not thought of that? We daren't even try. One touch and he'd taste you. He's still *in* here, Arlin. It's just that for these precious moments he's oblivious. He's seeking. Summoning. There are still many parts of himself he's yet to consume."

"How many? How *complete* is he? How soon will he be ready to transmute?"

"I don't know," said Rafel, slowly blinking. "Some things he glories in showing me. Others he keeps hidden. That's one of them. All I can tell you is that he's like an artist, creating a self-portrait. And every gathered piece adds another layer to the picture."

He struck a fist to his knee. "Rafel, you *must* know more than that!"

"I know he's widely scattered, across hundreds of leagues and several sovereign lands. And I know many of the vessels carrying his scattered powers sicken and die, so those pieces are lost to him until they find a new vessel to sustain them. Some are even lost for good."

Arlin felt himself lean closer. "Then there's still time. While he's flesh and blood he's vulnerable. So how do we kill him? Can you do it, Rafel? Trapped in there, can you kill the bastard?"

Another tear, and then another. Rafel shook his head. "No."

After months of seeing Morg behind those dark brown eyes it was so *odd* to see Asher's son. Odder still to feel himself moved to an overwhelming pity.

"You say there are some parts of him he'll never retrieve," he said roughly, because he had no desire to feel pain for Rafel's pain. "Does that help us?"

"Not enough," said Rafel. "Arlin—he has so much power to summon. For him to lose a piece here, a piece there, it's like us nicking a finger and losing a drop or two of blood. We're not vanquished by that—and neither is he."

He could have smashed the chamber's round window in his

57

frustration. Or ploughed a fist into Rafel's face, hoping the blow might hurt Morg. "I refuse to believe there is *nothing* we can do!"

"I didn't say there was nothing, Arlin," Rafel whispered. "But it won't be easy. There's a price to be paid in blood and tears and terror. And I find it odd that you'd be willing to pay it."

"You think I'm *lying?*"

"I think you could be."

"You think I *care* what you think!" he spat. "You stupid, ignorant *Olken.*"

Rafel's lips twisted into a smile. "And there's the Arlin Garrick I know and don't trust."

"You don't have a choice, Rafel. You have to trust me."

"I know," said Rafel, after a long silence. "Because I see who Morg really is. Worse. I *feel* it. And I'm doing my best to thwart him. But every time he feasts on his own essence he fastens another lock on my cage."

Arlin felt a stabbing fright. "You talk of thwarting him but it sounds like you're giving up. Rafel, you can't. *Look* at you. You're talking to me and he doesn't know. If you fight harder, if you *try* harder, surely—"

Rafel's eyes blazed. "*I am fighting Morg as hard as I can!* You don't know, Arlin, you can't *imagine* what—"

And then his blazing eyes rolled back and he started to shudder. Frothy, blood-tinged spittle oozed over his lips as his fingers spasmed on the arms of the wooden chair.

Arlin grabbed his wrists. "Rafel! *Rafel!* Can you hear me?"

*Don't go. Don't leave me here to face him on my own.*

"*Rafel?*" said Morg, and struck him hard across the face. "You dare to call for that Olken upstart? What a fool you are, Lord Garrick. What a puling, puking *fool.*"

Head ringing from the blow, pain bursting and burning, Arlin dropped to the floor in a posture of absolute submission. "Forgive me, Master, I was only—"

Morg surged to his feet. "You were only *what*, my little puppet?

Seeking to free my greatest enemy's son? Seeking to harm me? To *betray* me?"

How close was he to death? Not so close, surely. Morg still needed him. *Let me not be close to death.*

"Master, I came to you as you commanded but you were strangely silent," he said, staring at Morg's boots. "I waited and waited but you did not speak. I grew concerned. I called your name and still you did not answer. I thought you might be ill, I—"

"You *hoped* I might be ill!" Morg shouted. "Am I a fool, Garrick? Do you imagine I think you serve me *willingly?*"

Now he looked up—and that wasn't Rafel's face. Those weren't Rafel's eyes. Rafel was gone as though he'd never existed. Grief and fear and panic churned through him.

*I am alone, most likely for good. And now I stand at a crossroads. I can fight Morg by myself . . . or I can surrender and serve him.*

He tried to swallow, but his mouth was sucked dry. "Master, I don't know what you think. You are the most powerful sorcerer born and I am a young, inexperienced mage, whose true birthright was stolen centuries ago."

Morg laughed. "Am I to believe you *revere* me?"

"No, Master. I was raised to fear the sound of your name. You are the monster hiding beneath my childhood bed."

Silence. Then Morg bent low. "Little mage, little mage . . . what is it you want?"

"Master—" Sickened, sweating, Arlin made himself meet Morg's pitiless eyes. "I want to live."

A tiny tug of smile, then Morg straightened. "What else?"

*The trick is to distract him with a truth. To lead him onto different pathways so I won't be forced to tell a lie.*

"Master," he said, feeling the sweat soak through his shirt. "I grew up with the words 'you cannot' ringing in my ears. Every day the inferior Olken told me what I could and could not do with my power. But I believe I could be a great mage."

"And why would I desire a great mage around me?" said Morg,

idly. "We Doranen are an ambitious breed. One taste of greatness feeds a ravenous appetite for more. Do I not know it? Was *I* not once *you?*"

Was Rafel listening to this? And if he was, what was he thinking? "You flatter me, Master. I admit ambition, but I confess my limitations. I am Arlin Garrick. I am not Morgan Danfey."

Morg's eyes narrowed. "You do not answer my question."

"I fear to answer it, Master," he said, lowering his gaze. "I have seen what happens when you're displeased."

Again, Morg bent low. Arlin flinched as the sorcerer took his face between Rafel's strong, peasant fingers, tightening his grip to the point of sharp pain.

"Little mage, you have *never* seen me displeased."

Morg's dark power beat through him, waking pain and rousing fear. "Master, you need me."

The sorcerer flung him away so hard he struck the floor with his face.

"*Need you?* Do not flatter yourself, Lord Garrick."

Dazed, blood from a split eyebrow smearing his vision scarlet, Arlin made no attempt to protect himself. "I'm not. *You need me*. You are Morg . . . but not completely. You're still sundered. Still searching. Master, until you are whole you need a mage you can trust."

"And that mage is *you?*" Morg laughed. "Arlin—"

"Ask Rafel," he said, and cautiously sat up. "If he's still in there. If he's still alive. Ask him what kind of mage I am. What kind of man. He hates me, and with good reason. I am no friend of his. I never was. I never will be."

Truth piled upon truth. No lie for Morg to smell.

Morg turned away and began to pace the chamber. "You think with these touching declarations I'll free you from compulsion? You think I'll share my power with you?"

"Of course not, Master," he said quickly. "You would never be so reckless."

"Then what *do* you think?"

"I think—I hope—that you will ungeld me. I have some small

**60**

power, Master. Let me use it to serve you. Let me *use* it. I never have. Not properly. I have never been a true Doranen."

Morg turned back. "And you ache for it. You *burn* for it. You yearn to be set free, to break the chains others have laid upon you. Is that it?"

"Yes," he whispered. Because it was true. He wanted his birthright as he wanted air to breathe. All his life he'd been trammelled by Olken like Asher, and by treacherous, cowardly Doranen who believed the lie that their own people were to be controlled and feared. "Yes, Master. I ache. I burn."

Morg smiled. It was terrible. "You will if you betray me, Lord Garrick. You will ache and burn unto the end of time."

The threat—the promise—nearly loosened his bowels. "Master, I have told you the truth. Your need of me is already proven. Who else have you trusted to gather your sundered pieces and guide them home? No-one. There is no-one else you *can* trust. But I can be so much more than—than a *shepherd*. Let me show you. Let me help you rebuild everything that was lost when Asher of Restharven sought to end your life. Let me help you rebuild our homeland, Dorana. She was a shining jewel once. Let her shine again. I *beg* you."

A warm silence. Then Morg smiled again. "Rafel's weeping," he whispered. "Oh . . . his tears. His *tears*."

Arlin shrugged. "Let him weep. What does the pain of an Olken matter?"

"Interesting," said Morg. His smile faded. "I could almost believe you hate Asher's son as I hate the son's father."

"Believe it," he said, brutal. "Master, believe I hate them both. Am I not orphaned because of them? Am I not *small?*"

"What you are, Arlin, remains to be seen," said Morg. "What you might be? Come. You can show that to me now."

Morg swept from the chamber and Arlin, scrambling, followed him. Down the creaking staircases, along the corridors, through the mansion's rear scullery door and out to the back of the grand old house where Fernel Pintte and the idiot stood guard over a saddled horse.

One look at Morg and the shambling half-wit bolted. Morg laughed and made no attempt to stop him. That left Pintte, whose knees buckled with fear.

"Master," he croaked. An acrid whiff of urine. He'd pissed himself.

Incurious, their thick, horny hides shining brindled in the sun, the *dravas* guarding the scullery door and every ground floor window watched as Morg snapped his fingers and summoned a dagger from somewhere. Its blade was long and thin, a shining promise of death.

"Take it, Arlin," said the sorcerer, holding out the knife. "And kill Fernel Pintte."

The horse's reins dropped from Pintte's clumsy fingers. Unnerved by the *dravas*, by the roil of power in the air, the danger, the animal tried to bolt. Morg halted it with a word.

"Lord Garrick?"

Arlin closed his own fingers about the dagger's hilt. There was nothing arcane in the weapon. Iron and bone and a dragon's-tear gem. Fernel Pintte's death was to be a commonplace butchery.

*If I close my eyes, will I hear Rafel weeping?*

"Arlin . . ."

And that was Pintte, small and dismayed. Ignoring the Olken, he turned to Morg. "Why?"

Morg's eyebrow lifted. "Does it matter?"

"It does."

"For what reason?" said the sorcerer, considering him closely. "He's Olken. You hate him."

"Master—" He breathed out a slow sigh. "It matters because it matters to you."

"Ah." Smiling so sweetly, Morg reached out his hand. "Arlin, I believe you begin to understand."

He let himself flinch at the sorcerer's touch, because not to flinch would rouse instant suspicion. But then, as Morg's palm pressed to his cheek, Arlin waited—and waited—then let himself lean into the caress.

*Believe me. Believe me. I understand too well.*

"Arlin," said Fernel Pintte. "You can't—you're not—" He was

heaving for air, great shuddering gasps. "You're an arrogant little shit, Arlin, but you're not a *murderer*!"

Morg withdrew his caressing palm. "You want to know why? Because jewels must be paid for, Lord Garrick. Trust must be earned. To be great one must do great things. Make great sacrifices. Purge every impulse towards humanity. With your eyes fixed upon the mud, how ever can you hope to see the stars?"

Arlin looked at the dagger loosely clasped in his hand.

*Fernel Pintte was never going to survive this. Since he crossed the mountains he has been living on borrowed time. And if he was always going to die, does it really matter how?*

He knew the answer, of course. But if one death could prevent thousands . . . and besides, it was *Pintte*.

"Arlin?" said Morg, so gentle. "Show me how truthful you are. Show me how faithful. Show me the face you show no-one else and then, perhaps, I will believe you."

The Mayor of Dorana tried to run, but like the saddled horse he was halted with a word. Halted—but not silenced. He could beg. He could weep.

*Show me the face you show no-one else.*

He could kill Pintte swiftly. Push the dagger through his throat or his heart and quickly end the miserable little man's existence. But Morg was watching, and what he wanted wasn't mercy.

*If I fail this test the known world loses.*

"No," Pintte whispered. "No, please, *no*."

Arlin clenched his jaw. All his life he'd been tested. And if he were found wanting, punishment came swift and sure. Because he was a Garrick, and no Garrick could fail.

*How well did you teach me, Father? I think we're about to find out.*

The dagger's sharp blade slid without resistance through the flesh of Pintte's ageing belly and sank to its hilt against the Olken's ragged shirt. When he pulled it out, bright blood eagerly followed.

Pintte stared at the blood in silent shock.

He stabbed the Olken again, this time through the fragile cage of his ribs. Pintte released a bubbling cry. Flecks of red appeared on his lips. Without Morg's holding spell he would have fallen.

"You pig," the Olken whispered. A pulse was beating frantically in his throat. "You stinking Doranen. You magespawn offal. You—"

He plunged the dagger back into Pintte's belly. Twisted it this time, to spill the contents of his gut.

Pintte squealed.

Arlin watched as the Olken spat blood and bled shit, aware of a distant and cool curiosity. Where was the grief? Where was the revulsion? Where was the shocking pain, that he could *do* this to a man?

*Show me the face you show no-one else.*

From the cradle he'd been taught to revile the Olken. That was a lesson he'd learned eagerly, with little prompting. This puny race, these pretend mages, these keepers of secrets who presumed to judge their betters and passed laws to limit greatness because greatness was beyond them.

*I hate them. I hate them all.*

A hand on his shoulder. A soft breath in his ear. "I see you now, Arlin. That's enough. You can end him."

He pushed the blade into Pintte's heart, and stepped back, and watched him die.

Morg snapped his fingers. Pintte dropped to the ground.

"I have found two more of my lost pieces, Lord Garrick. They travel here from Brantone. You'll find them some six hours hence, upon The Chilling Way. And when you return we will talk. Keep the dagger. It might come in useful."

"Master," he said. He had no way to safely wear it.

Morg laughed and snapped his fingers a second time. Held out the dagger's leather sheath and a belt to hold it. Bending, Arlin wiped the dagger's blade clean on the dead Olken's sleeve, then sheathed it and belted it round his hips. As he reached his horse, the sorcerer released it. The animal tossed its head, eyes rolling at the stink of fresh blood. Snatching at the reins, he shoved his foot into the stirrup and swung himself up and into the saddle. How he missed his own stallion, a beast of superior bloodlines and beauty. This thing was nothing more than a nag.

Silently summoned, his *dravas* escort appeared in the open space between the mansion and the empty stables. Always the same beasts, created by Morg to be swift and cunning, light on their feet. Tireless. Able to keep up with a cantering horse and run down a fleeing miscreant.

Morg's gaze lingered on them, proud and loving. And then he frowned. "Lord Garrick? You tarry. Is there a problem?"

"No, Master," he said quickly. A kick in the flanks and a tug on the reins had his slug horse shifting. The *dravas* stepped aside to let him pass. But as he rode between them he heard a garbled cry. Turning in his saddle he saw the shambling idiot Goose creep out of the stables' shadows towards the punctured body on the ground. Gobbling noises in his throat. Mangled words. The pathetic creature was trying to talk.

*Not all his wits lost then. Just most of them. A pity Morg didn't test me on him. It would've been a mercy and the result would be the same.*

Wailing with grief, Rafel's ruined friend collapsed to the ground beside dead Fernel Pintte. Gathering the cooling corpse into his arms he rocked the Olken, blubbering like a child. A spitting sound of impatience and Morg raised his arm. Spread his fingers. Opened his mouth to curse and rid the world of the half-wit.

Watching, Arlin saw something flicker over the sorcerer's face. Saw a ripple of muscle beneath his temper-flushed skin and felt a swift, uneasy churning of power. Morg's eyes widened. His breath quickened. His spread fingers spasmed, then clenched into a fist. Still as stone he stood there . . . he stood there . . . and Goose Martin lived.

*Rafel.*

Slowly, Morg lowered his outstretched hand. A shifting behind his shadowed eyes. Another flicker across his emptied face.

Rafel's brief ascendency was over.

Arlin kicked his horse into a bounding leap and shot off towards the mansion's carriageway. The *dravas* pounded after him, compelled to follow in his wake.

\* \* \*

Ruined Elvado was laid out in a circle, with four main thoroughfares leading from its heart to Dorana's four neighbouring borders. The Winding Way pointed towards Trindek. The Swift Way led to Feen. To reach Manemli a man rode The Narrow Way, and took The Chilling Way to Brantone. The old roads and the old lands were laid out on a map in the mansion. Arlin had studied it carefully but learned nothing of Dorana beyond how not to get lost.

The Chilling Way was tree-lined, its broad grey bricks weathered with age. Keeping his inferior horse to a steady, jarring jog, the *dravas* clopping and padding and clicking behind him, he closed his eyes and tried not to think of Fernel Pintte. Better to think of Goose Martin and how Rafel had saved him.

*I'm not alone. I'm not alone.*

Up ahead, approaching, was an entire troop of *dravas*. They were coming back from a raid—most likely into Brantone, but maybe further, into Ranoush. They brought with them more captives, fodder for Morg to turn into more beasts. An army of them, he was creating. He needed *dravas* to retake the lands around Dorana, that he'd ruled once before and was determined to rule again.

*Lands he thinks I want to rule with him. Because I let him think it. Because I made him believe it.*

The soft surrender of Pintte's belly as the dagger's blade thudded home . . .

*Show me the face you show no-one else.*

And so he did. He'd had to. There'd been no other way. But in showing Morg that hidden face he'd also shown it to himself.

*Did I know? Is that truly me? Or is it someone else?*

He waited until the approaching *dravas* and their filthy, exhausted, terrified captives were past, and then he heaved up his guts in the road.

*Don't believe what I showed you, Rafel. Don't leave me alone.*

# CHAPTER FIVE

The clashing, clanging ring of heavy swords kissing echoed through the frosty air. Autumn was come early and stern to the Vale, with the blue sky wide and cold, the ground crisped white and all the red-leaved trees stripping themselves naked, shameless.

Ewen the Younger spun himself clear of Tavin's long reach, gloved fingers wrapped tight round the hilt of his training blade. The sword-master was blowing hard, plumes of white breath smokily curling. The old seamed scar across his nose had pinked up and his broad, flat face was pink to match it.

"Think you're clever d'you, boy?" Tavin wheezed, taking a step back so he could assess the situation.

Grinning, Ewen shook his head. "Don't think it. I know it. Come on, old man. Have at me again."

"Hah!" Crooked teeth bared, Tavin held his broadsword one-handed and dragged his vambraced forearm across his sweat-stippled forehead. "Arrogant pup."

"Not arrogant. Confident."

"Is that so? Well, let's see how confident you are when you're sprawled on your arse! Huzzah!"

Ewen laughed and met him blade for blade. The shock of impact ran through his fingers and his tempered wrists, through the sibling bones of his forearms and up to his shoulders. Beneath his booted feet the cold-nipped grass of the tiltyard flattened and tore, clods of dirt coming loose as he clashed in mock combat with a man taller and heavier than he would ever be. But that was all right. He'd been crossing swords with Tavin since he was fourteen, and after ten years he'd learned a trick or two. Besides, in fighting above his weight and reach he trained himself to survive against uneven odds: a strategy not to be sneezed at in these dark and difficult times.

Stroke, parry, stroke, deflect. Stroke, parry, stroke, deflect. Blood burning, breath rasping, muscles lithely obedient, he fixed his gaze to Tavin's deep-set brown eyes and surrendered conscious thought to the strangely dreamy otherworld of swordplay, where instinct was king.

The sun was not long risen. It meant they were alone in their training, which was how he liked it. The days of a pompous and ceremonial court were long dead and buried and not even Vharne's release from mage bondage had brought them back. He felt no sorrow for it. Empty talk was a waste of air. Deeds mattered. Only deeds. Perhaps if his mother had lived, his father's court might at least have found its bright clothes and smiles and put them on again. But she'd died, so much for gaiety. And freedom hadn't freed them from anything, it turned out, so the court's colours remained sombre and every morning, very soon after daybreak, he met with Tavin in the tiltyard and they bashed at each other with long, heavy swords.

Round and across the tiltyard they fought each other, seeking that one moment of opportunity, looking to force the happy misstep that would see an opponent disarmed, or fallen onto his back and asking to be split wide chin to balls. His muscles were complaining loudly now. Teeth gritted, eyes stinging with sweat, Ewen ignored the pain and blocked Tavin's bone-shuddering blows. He wore a padded jerkin and their training blades were blunted but even so, if he made a mistake he'd pay a steep price for it. Tavin said a man who trained safe died unprepared and he had his reputation to think of, so he never went easy just because he sparred with the king's elder son. The sword-master took even mock-fighting seriously, never letting himself think it was *only* a game. And he didn't let his pupils think of training that way, either. No respecter of rank, respecting naught but the sword, Tavin wasn't afraid to use the flat of his blade like a cane and mark the hide of a king's son who offended in this way or that.

"Come on, come on, luffkin, keep your mind on the business!" the swordmaster shouted. "Woolly-noggined, you are, boy, and that'll be the death of you!"

To make his point he feinted then brought his sword up, around and over in a brute-force swinging arc. Ewen parried, caught back-footed, misstepped and lost his balance.

"Hah!" shouted Tavin, as he hooked him round his booted left ankle and jerked him off his feet to smack the tiltyard ground with his spine and skull. "Turtle!"

Winded and groaning, seeing stars but still with his sword gripped tight, Ewen squinted up at him. Tavin was grinning, all the empty spaces in his gums on show, short badger-streaked hair plastered to his skull with sweat.

"Think I've got a noggin to spare, do you, Swordmaster?" he said, the words coming in fits and starts as his emptied lungs spasmed.

"Didn't see the harm," said Tavin, still grinning. "Seeing you weren't hardly using it." Bending, he held out his hand. "Boy wants help standing, does he?"

"Boy's not a boy," he retorted, and whipped his sword up so its point rested at Tavin's crotch. "Steady, now."

Tavin froze. "Oh, now that's dirty, that is. There's still some life in the old pecker yet, son. We'll call it quits and even. How's that?"

*Boy. Son.* Only Tavin could get away with such familiarity. He'd earned the liberty, and more besides. Vharne would be a sadder and sorrier place this day without the swordmaster's staunch presence these past bleak years. The sorcerer's grip on the kingdom might well have loosened, but other troubles crowded in his wake.

Ewen lowered his blade. "Quits and even."

"Hah!" Tavin flexed his fingers. "That's a lad."

Pleased with himself, he grasped Tavin's hand and helped haul himself upright. But that wasn't the end of his training session, oh no. Sword-master Tavin was a stickler and a tyrant. At the start and finish of every session there were drills, drills and more drills. Not a man in a fight for his life there ever was but didn't lose a little or a lot of his mind, said Tavin, what with the screaming and the bleeding and the rest of it, so he needed something to fall back on when his mind let him down.

And in Tavin's world, that meant drills.

Lifting his blade, Ewen gave Tavin a respectful student's nod and waited for the first command. He knew men who resented drills, but he wasn't one of them. There was a comfort in the sound of the sword-master's steady voice as it barked the set patterns of swordplay passed down from master to pupil for years and years beyond remembering. Pacing steadily from one side of the tiltyard to the other and back, over and over, strongly and smoothly flowing from position to position, he felt the separate sweepings of his sword as much a part of him as his shoulders or his knees or the long bones in his thighs.

That was another reason why he welcomed sword drills with Tavin. With every thought and all his energy poured into the physical, into the sword in his hands and the perfection of his form, with his will bent on earning Tavin's praise and not his sharp displeasure, there was no time to dwell on uncertainty and the gnawing fear in his gut.

*Something dark is waking beyond the Vale. I can feel it.*

"*Ewen!*" snapped the swordmaster. "Elbows up. *Up*. And keep your chin tucked in. You're woolly again, boy. Eager for a taste of my blade on your backside, are you?"

He shot Tavin a dirty look then wrenched his mind to its proper place. Blanked it to everything save the sweep of his blade from guard left to guard right to overhead extend to underhand retract back to over-head round to cross-body left hip into cross-body right hip back to overhead extend and start again from the beginning without a pause. Faster and faster Tavin called the drills until he was at a killing battle pace, his phantom opponent a madman. Time blurred and thought blurred with it. He was running sweat, he was breathing fire, he was a sword and he hungered for blood.

But the enemy was whispers, and rumours, and shadow.

*Can't kill a whisper. Can't run a rumour through or decapitate a shadow.*

"All right!" Tavin said at last. "That's enough for today."

Fetched up against the tiltyard's solid wood enclosing wall, Ewen thudded his shoulders to the weathered boards and let his swordpoint drop to rest on his right boot. His heart pounded so hard his ribs ached, and his throat was raw with his gasping.

"Curse you, Tavin, I'm nigh on half-dead."

Tavin's reply was to pluck the training sword from his lax right hand, then sink probing fingers into the muscles of his upper arm. The bite of it made him shout and try to pull away but Tavin's grip was like iron.

"Hold still," the swordmaster grunted. "It's a little griping. Women in childbirth hold their tongues in more pain."

"If we could but swap places, Tavin, you'd not call it 'a little griping'," he retorted, then sank his teeth into his lower lip as the swordmaster's fingers probed down to the bone. "Spirit curse you!"

Tavin prodded a moment longer, then let go and clapped his shoulder instead. "You're over-using that arm again, Ewen."

"Tav, it's right-handed I am," he protested. "What do you—"

"Is it blind I am, not to see it?" Tavin snapped, and cuffed him. "If I *was* blind, I'd see it. Right-favoured you're fighting, and how's that to the good? You've got two hands, boy, and it's time you used both of them. Come tomorrow you'll be a left-handed swordsman 'til I say elsewise."

He groaned. "Tavin—"

Up went Tavin's clenched fist. "It's your swordmaster I am, and I've spoken."

Barracks discipline killed the impulse to argue. "Swordmaster," he said, and that was that.

Come tomorrow, Ewen the Younger would hold his sword left-handed.

"Good," said Tavin, and held out the training sword. "So it's hot water and a liniment you need on that arm, you do."

"Liniment," he scoffed, taking back his weapon. "That's for horses. Stick to swordplay, you should."

"Stick to sticking a sword in you," Tavin snapped. "It's stinking like a horse, you are. Come on. Not too fancy for a barracks bath, are you, boy?"

Tavin could be such a cross-grained man. "When did I turn up my nose at a barracks bath?"

Taking a fistful of shirtsleeve, Tavin tugged him along. "I misremember. I'm sure you did once."

"Well, yes, maybe when I was six and the water was cold!" he said. "Save your long memory for sword drills and old skirmishes."

"Snippety snip," said Tavin, and flung an arm about his shoulders. "You keep talking, boy, and the water'll be cold again, you'll see."

Companionably irritable with each other, they abandoned the tiltyard and retreated to the barracks. Awake now, the soldier-heart of the old court buzzed with vigorous voices and dogs snarling over bones and horses stamping in stables. Men tumbled out of cots into wool and leather and boots, and from there to barracks duties while they waited for breakfast to cook. Their swordplay came late in the day, once other soldierly tasks were completed. Seeing their prince and their swordmaster side by side and amiably bickering, they grinned and nodded and saluted with clenched fists. Ewen saluted in reply, at home here in these barracks. At home with the rough men and the rough life of a man and his sword. For him it was a kinder place than the cold stone castle where memory slept and woke and slept again, never satisfied unless it was causing pain.

He left his and Tavin's training blades in the armoury for later cleaning, then joined the swordmaster in the stout-walled, lamplit bath house. The air beneath its low roof was warm and damp, its flagstoned floor crowded with wooden tubs and huge iron pots of water over burning coals, heating. Presiding over the sparse luxury was wizened old Shyvie, who kept order in the place, with younger men and brats to help when he yelled for them.

Tavin was already nose-deep in a tub, his scarred, bent knees poking out of the water. He had soap in his cropped hair and was vigorously scrubbing his scalp, just like an old woman. Ewen smothered a grin, pulled off his boots and socks, then stripped out of his padded jerkin and his long-sleeved wool shirt and his cotton undershirt and his leather trews. Leaving them haphazard in a pile on the bath house's wooden bench, he climbed into the other tub Shyvie had seen filled with steaming water, wincing and hissing as the heat bit his cooled-down skin.

Tavin rang the bath-house bell. "You might want to nip up yonder and fetch the Younger some clothes as aren't wringing with sweat," he suggested to the barracks brat who'd come running. "Take his mucky ones to the castle laundress while you're about it—but leave his boots behind."

"Yes, Swordmaster," piped the brat.

Ewen watched the lad stagger away under his burden of dirty, sweat-soaked clothes. "You spoil me, Tavin."

A bucket of rinsing water was sat beside Tavin's tub. "Spoil the Vale, more like it," he said, reaching for it. "You've got the morning in Hall with the king, yes? Coop you in a room 'til midday in those clothes and there'll be folk passing out from the stink every which way you look, there will."

Laughing, Ewen tugged off the thin leather thong tying back his hair, dropped it to the floor, then let himself slide beneath the surface of his bath. Eyes closed, he revelled in the heat and darkness, holding his breath until he could no longer ignore his body's demands for air.

"Soap?" he said to Tavin, who'd sloshed his head free of suds and was now scrubbing his back with a knot of rags tied to a long wooden handle.

The swordmaster stopped scrubbing and lobbed him the soap pot. His hair was long enough now it needed a large scooped handful. To keep the king his father pleased he should cut it—and he would. Most like. One of these days.

Done with lathering, he emptied his own rinsing bucket over his soapy hair, spat out suds then looked across to Tavin. The sword-master's brooding face killed his careless training question stone dead.

"What's wrong?"

Elbows braced on his tub's sides, chin sunk to his chest, Tavin frowned at his wriggling toes. "There's a whisper of strife. Tickled my ear late last night, it did. You need to hear it, boy. And the king too."

He sat up. "If the king needs to hear it, Tavin, then tell the king."

"It's all morning you're spending with him, isn't it? You can tell him," said Tavin, still frowning.

Ewen stifled a sigh. Not so much the length of the tiltyard had his father the king and Swordmaster Tavin ever walked in step, side by side. The king's father, Ewen the Elder, had made Tavin barracks swordmaster. By the time he died, seven months later, every barracks man was ready to sword himself following Tavin. Ewen the Elder's son Murdo knew better than to fiddle with the barracks, so Tavin stayed swordmaster—and they tossed words at each other only when it was needful. Beyond barracks business they did their best not to cross paths.

Why that was, he'd never found out.

"Tav, you rile me," he said. "When Padrig and I tread toes you knock our heads together until we're put straight. It's knocking your head to the king's that's needed now, I'm thinking."

"Try it, boy," Tavin growled.

No, he didn't think he would. "You should tell me why you and the king clash swords."

"If it was business of yours I'd mention it here or there," said Tavin, fiercely scowling. "Do you want to know what I know or do you want to poke at me 'til I bite off your finger? Choose you should, and quickly. I've a day waiting with work in it."

The swordmaster's barrel body was hooped and criss-crossed with scars. In his time he'd hunted boar and stag, skirmished the kingdom's borders and ridden down desperate men charged as outlaws. He'd killed a beast, the only man in Vharne to do it. Never did the swordmaster startle at shadows.

*So if Tav's uneasy . . .*

"Tell me," he said. "I want to know."

Instead of answering, Tavin ducked deep into his own bath water, splashing it onto the flagstoned floor. Exasperated, Ewen waited for him to come back up.

"Tavin," he said, once the swordmaster was breathing air again, and gave his voice a little weight. "I'm the king's son. I can't pretend I never heard you."

"Boyde came in from riding the rough country," said Tavin, after a silence. "It's a good man, he is. Not fanciful. Sees what he sees and doesn't see more than that, or pretend to."

Ewen felt his belly tighten. "I know Boyde. What did he see? Share the news, Tav. Don't be a selfish man, you."

"Riding the rough, like I say, he came across three brain-rotted wanderers," Tavin said, keeping his voice low in case Shyvie or one of his brats were anywhere close enough to hear him. "Out of their wits, babbling and drooling, like they do. He put them down, kindly. They crossed the border from Manemli, he says."

A shiver prickled across his wet shoulders. "Is he sure? We've had wanderers over to us from Iringa—seven in less than a month. That's a worry on its own, that is. But Manemli?"

"Boyde's a canny man," said Tavin. "He's sure. Seen a stripe-haired Iringan ever, have you?"

There was no such thing as a stripe-haired Iringan.

Ewen reached over his tub's side for the soap. It was slippery, like his thoughts. Scowling at his scooped handful, he dropped the jar back to the wooden bath stool, soaped his chest and under his arms then grabbed a bath cloth and scrubbed them free of grime and sweat. Scrubbed the rest of his body after, not looking at Tavin. Not voicing those thoughts.

*I knew something was twisting. I felt it in my dreams.*

He ducked himself into the water, then came up streaming. "So it's wanderers from Manemli and Iringa now. When there's been no Manemlin set foot in Vharne since the end of sorcery. What do you say it means, Swordmaster?"

Tavin stared at the bath house's timbered ceiling. Lamplight gleamed on his wet hair and skin, and plunged his eyes into masking shadow. "The north's stirring, son. Ghosts are on their feet and walking, I say."

"What kind of ghosts?" he said, his belly tight again. "Not sorcery, Tav. That's behind us, that is. Dorana's dead."

"Is it?" The swordmaster pinched the end of his nose. "Sure of that, are we?"

Clearly Tavin wasn't. *And Spirit save me, neither am I.* "You should tell the king your misgivings, you should. Come to Hall with me. *Tell* him."

"You tell him."

"*Tavin*—" Ewen kicked his bath water to waves. "This is king's business, this is. I'm not the king."

Tavin looked at him from under lowered brows. "You'll be sitting your arse in the king's seat one day."

"One day. Not today."

"I'd not waste his time," said Tavin, after a moment. "King Murdo values a proven truth, he does. I say the north's stirring and I think it is. That's what my gut tells me and I listen to my gut. But what my gut thinks, that's not enough to sweeten your—the king."

He sighed. It was true. His father the king was a plain man who liked plain facts. There was no patience in him for guesswork and half-truths and airy-fairy feelings.

"Could be we should think twice about putting down them we find with brain-rot," he said. "Was there a word of sense Boyde could get out of those wanderers? Did he even try, or did he whip out his dagger at the first sign of madness?"

"He says they had the wits of beasts," said Tavin, shrugging. "Raving crazy like all the rest, he says. Covered in sores and pustules and black blood. Not much point trying to chat with that, is there? Boyde says it was a mercy to slit their throats quick."

"That may be, Tav, but how will we know what ghosts are stirring beyond Vharne's borders if we never wait long enough to ask a man who's maybe seen one?"

"Ewen . . ." Tavin shook his head, disappointed, and held out his hand for the soap pot. "Shame you don't have my memory, boy. If you did you'd know not to ask that foolish question."

He tossed the pot, hard. "It's not foolish. And I remember full well what happened before. I was there, wasn't I?"

"Then remember it was only by the spirit's grace your mother was there too," said Tavin, glaring. "With a dagger and no squeamish womanly misgivings, so the king wasn't bitten and sent mad himself. Bless her, she could see with one look that *talking* wasn't a thing to be done with that beast."

Tavin wasn't only cross-grained. Sometimes he was flint. "That man was no beast, Swordmaster. He was a misbegotten soul touched by the blight, like all the others. Not his fault. Do you say the king's pity is a bad thing?"

"Pity's fine when no lives are at risk, boy," said Tavin, snorting. "But pity misplaced can kill as fast as a sword."

They could argue about this until their bath water froze solid and nothing would change. "That madman was years ago," he said flatly. "Leave him behind, I say."

Tavin slathered soap across his broad, hairy chest. "Glad to."

"But that still leaves Boyde. If we've got wanderers from Manemli, the king has to know. And he has to know it could bode trouble from the north."

"I'll send Boyde to him to make a report," said Tavin. "Best the king hears that tale first-hand. But Boyde won't spin it further than what he saw with his own eyes and did with his own hands. You could mention trouble in the north, if you like. Then it's your ears the king'll chew, boy, and not mine."

He snatched up a handful of cooling bath water and threw it. "It's a scrag-beard, you are!"

"Ha," said Tavin, briefly grinning. "You want to cork me for holding my tongue?"

"I do."

"Then tip me over turtle in training tomorrow and we'll call it quits and even," said Tavin. Then he sighed. "Ewen, when it comes to the king it's not a rich man, I am. I can't squander my coins on a maybe. On my gut."

"You're Vharne's swordmaster, Tavin. The king praises you."

Tavin pulled a face. "He's no fool. He knows I serve him honest.

But there's reason for his doubt. Don't cobble me hard done by, boy."

More than ever, he wanted to know what had happened between the king his father and Tavin. And there'd come a time when he'd find out, even if he had to get Tav drunk to prise the tale loose. But until then—

"Do I misremember, or are there three more scouts still out beyond the Vale?"

Tavin nodded. "Three, that's right."

"Then it's fools we'd be, to panic," he said. "Once they ride home and tell what they've found, that'll mean a different picture, I say."

"You hope," Tavin said. He stood in his tub, the bath house lamplight playing over his stitchings of old wounds. "But one thing's sure, boy, and the king needs to be reminded. Stern to save ourselves we've got to be. No brain-rotted wanderers inside our borders."

Ewen stared. "You'd kill them all?"

"It's them or us." With a grunt, Tavin clambered onto the flagstones. "You know how fast the rot can spread from man to man, unchecked. This is no time to go soft. The south might be as dead as it ever was, but the north's stirring, I tell you. And no good ever came to Vharne from the north."

Shyvie kept towels on pegs by the long fireplace, so they'd be warm for using after a bath. As Tavin dried his hair and his skin, Ewen sloshed himself wet all over one last time then came up again, spitting water.

"Could be you're glooming for nothing, Tav."

The swordmaster looked up from pulling on his clothes. Seemed he was heedless of his own sweat and stink. "Could be, son, but I'm not. And you know I'm not, so save your boyish quibbling and look harsh truth square in the eye, as fits a king's son."

He slapped the side of his wooden tub, his wet hand waking hollow echoes. "If I'm quibbling, Tavin, that's only because you're playing the slippery fish."

"It's not any kind of fish, I am," said Tav, stamping into his boots. "It's fishy you are, I say. Time to dress your thoughts in words, boy."

Hostile again, they glared at each other. Then he slapped the tub again, vexed. "I have thoughts, yes. Troubling thoughts. But I don't *know*, Tavin. And well-schooled I am not to talk when I don't know."

"Well, this is what I know," Tavin murmured, bulky in front of the fire. "I know my years are twice yours and a few more for luck. I know when I had no more than your years the world was dark and I lived in it and fearful it was. I know when you were a small boy the dark lifted and I thanked the spirit. And I know . . ." The swordmaster's lamplit face fell into sorrow. "I know the dark's back, Ewen." His pointing finger jabbed. "And that's what you know. Shame on your head for not saying it like a man. Now I'm off to see about my barracks business. Tell your brother I want him in the tiltyard with a training sword two hours past noon."

As the swordmaster thumped his way out of the bath house, riled into a temper, he passed Shyvie's brat coming back in, laden with clean clothes fit for a prince.

Ewen smiled, because the brat was a small boy who didn't deserve a snarl. "My thanks."

Grinning, the brat dropped the clothes in a pile and fled to Shyvie for another task. Ewen clambered out of his tub, snatched a warm towel from its peg and pressed the water from his hair, Tavin's grim words echoing.

*I know the dark's back, Ewen—and that's what you know.*

Yes. He knew it. It was the creeping cold in the marrow of his bones, the rattle in the back of his throat, the fleeting shadow in the corner of his eye. Premonitions of disaster. Dread for what was yet to come.

*The king scoffs at such feelings. For once the king is wrong.*

With liniment rubbed into his over-used right arm, dressed snug in the embroidered wools and linens the brat had brought him and with his damp hair combed and tied back in a thick tail, he left the barracks a prince again to take his customary breakfast with the king. Five minutes inside the castle, he found his brother in a window-nook near the dining hall with his hand shoved down a maid's unlaced blouse.

"Ow!" said Padrig, aggrieved, rubbing his head where he'd been cuffed. "Ewen!"

Ignoring him, Ewen grabbed the maid's wrist and hauled her out of the nook. "Encourage my brother again, Maise, and I'll see you beaten out of the Vale. Grasp that, do you?"

"Yes, sir," whispered Maise, a plump young armful.

"Then lace yourself decent and get about your proper tasks."

"What call have you to spoil my fun?" Padrig complained, staring after the maid. "Spoil yours, do I?"

"What call?" Ewen stared at him. "So you want to plant a bastard in her, do you?"

Nineteen, nearly twenty, and Padrig could still sulk. "Vharne needs more people in it. That's what the king keeps saying."

"True, that might be," he retorted. "So let Maise find a groom or a barracks man to fondle her tits and give her a baby for the Vale. Little brother, you can do better than a maid, you can."

Padrig had their dead mother's hair, a bright red-gold. He had her pale blue eyes and her short, straight nose. But his lusty swaggering was all his own. So was his smile and the laugh that made any who kept company with him laugh too. Like the weather he could shift from sunshine to rain and back again, in a finger snap.

"I can," he agreed. "But Ewen, must a man marry to scratch an itch?"

Ewen thumped his brother's shoulder. "No. But when he's the king's son he needs to be careful how he scratches it, he does. Said that before, I have. Remember it this time. Have you broken bread this morning or do you eat with me and the king?"

"Waiting for you, I was," said Padrig, flashing his charming, mischievous smile.

He grinned back. "And it's touched, I am. Next time think of a more useful way to wait."

Bumping shoulders, they wandered along the corridor to the dining hall. The king was already seated at the high board, his neatly clipped dark red hair silver-glinted in the morning light. Hearing them enter, he looked up from the parchment unrolled across his empty plate.

"Food's on its way. Eat fast, you'll have to," he greeted them. "And forgo Hall you will, Ewen. There's a man blighted in the Eastern Vale. It's both of you I'm sending to deal with the strife."

Surprised by that, Ewen slid into the chair by the king's right hand. Padrig took the chair on the left, his sulk over the buxom maid forgotten.

"Blight in the Eastern Vale, Father?" he said, concerned. "That's not happened before."

Vharne's long years of struggle were written deep across the king's thin face. "No," he said heavily. "It's news I much mistrust."

"And there's more to mistrust, I'm sorry to say," Ewen told him. "One of Tavin's scouts is back from the rough country. He put down three brain-rotted Manemlims, close to the border."

The king's sparse eyebrows lifted, his gaze cold and critical. "You learned this crossing swords?"

Careful, careful. "Tavin's sending the scout to you during Hall."

"And I'll send Tavin—" the king started, then held his tongue as servants entered bearing platters of food and a large jug of ale. He rolled the parchment, tucked it inside his leather vest then sat back as his plate was filled with coddled eggs and hot flatbread and pottaged meat.

Served after him, belly rumbling, Ewen breathed in the warm, welcome aromas. Once Padrig's plate was filled, and the remaining food and ale jug was left on the side board, the king picked up his knife and spoon. His first swallowed mouthful was the signal to eat.

Ravenous after training, Ewen ate as fast as manners allowed. Easily he could shovel it in, but the king frowned on a rowdy table.

"Father," said Padrig, around a mouthful of pottage, "this blighted man in the Eastern Vale. Is he of Vharne, or is he a wanderer stumbled over the border?"

With his plate only half-emptied, the king shoved it away as though food was a disgust to him. "The message says he's a Vale man."

Leaning back in his chair, Ewen exchanged a look with Padrig behind the king. His own mouthful of flavoursome flatbread tasted abruptly like ashes. He washed it down with some ale.

"Father, we've not had any in the Vale infected for months."

"Nigh on a year, I know," said the king. The lines engraved in his face seemed to sink further into his flesh. "This bodes nothing good, it does."

He dropped his gaze to his plate. *Do I tell him? I should tell him. I'll leave Tavin's fears out of it and speak only for myself.* "Father . . ."

The king stared. "You mouth the word as though I've put a sword to your throat, you do. Would you say something? Say it, you should."

He could feel Padrig staring, too. "Father, it's not a man for fancies, you are. But I can't be a good son and hold my tongue on this. There's a fear I have, that trouble's stirring in the north."

The king's short fingernails drummed on the board. "A fear with proof, or without it?"

"Wanderers from Manemli proves something is wrong," said Padrig. "Blight in a Vale man? That's wrong too, it is. And Ewen's a canny one, Father."

"He is," the king admitted, his stern expression easing. "Another canny one is the swordmaster. You talked of this in the bath house, Ewen?"

*Sorry, Tav.* "Father, I did."

Again, the king drummed the high board. "I'll talk with him on it, I will, before Hall. You two should ride now. Get to the Eastern Vale, see to the wanderer, and we'll talk when you return. Padrig—"

"Father?" said Padrig, wisely leaving aside his displeasure that he'd not had time to clear his plate.

The king gestured at the dining hall doors. "Go ahead to the barracks. See to your horses—and hold your tongue. It's a private word I want with your brother."

Padrig knew better than to question the king. "Father," he said, snatched up his half-eaten flatbread, and withdrew.

The king held out his emptied goblet. "Pour me more ale, Ewen. Then hear what I have to say.'

# CHAPTER SIX

Refilling the goblet, Ewen glanced at the king. "Was I wrong to talk of Boyde and the north with Tavin? No slight to you was meant, by him or me."

"No slight is taken," said the king. "After my death the kingdom's caretaking falls to you. It's offended I'd be if you took no interest in Vharne and the Vale."

So Tavin and the king could agree on that much, at least. Ewen handed the refilled goblet to his father, but didn't retake his seat. "I thought you'd scoff at my misgivings, I did."

"Scoff I would, if there weren't more wanderers crossing into Vharne," said the king, and drank deep.

Ewen folded his arms. "But they are. It bodes ill, I say."

"Most ill," the king agreed. "Since the sorcerer's fall, Vharne has muddled along. We've kept ourselves peaceful. We've avoided tangling with anyone beyond our borders. But it's determined they are to tangle with us, it seems."

"Must it be seen as a tangle?" he said, after a moment. "If trouble does stir, is facing it alone the best choice?"

"Ewen . . ." The king frowned at him. "Years of silence beyond our borders, there's been. Now the silence breaks, but not with words of friendship. No. All we see of our neighbours are brain-rotted wanderers. An alliance with madmen? You'd advise that, you would?"

"Of course not, Father. But are all men beyond Vharne's borders mad?"

"That I cannot answer," said the king. "And I'll not risk scouts or barracks men into those other lands to find out."

It was a sensible decision. Vharne wasn't so overflowing with men they could be thrown away on such a risky adventure. "This is what you wanted to tell me?"

The king thudded his goblet to the board. "No."

*Then what is it?* he wanted to demand. But he held his tongue, for his father was a deliberate man who frowned on being chivvied. Waiting, he retrieved his own goblet from the high board and drained it.

"Ewen, I want Padrig blooded."

He stared, feeling the pottage and egg curdle in his belly. *Blooded?* "Father—are you sure?"

"It's past time," said the king, his bleak gaze trained on the sky beyond the dining hall's one unshuttered window. "No stripling, he is. But he carries on like a youth, he does. It's a worry to me. If trouble's coming I need two sons I know can meet it. Blood him, Ewen. That's my wish."

Hand pressed to his heart, Ewen nodded. "If it's your wish, then I'll do it, of course I will. But why do you tell me? Why not tell Padrig yourself?"

"You'll ride nigh on five hours to reach the Eastern Vale and this poor, afflicted wretch," said the king. "In five hours he can wear his tongue out with questions, Ewen. You're blooded. Since you were fifteen it's six wanderers you've put down. He'll take it easier from you, he will."

Which was another way of saying the king and his younger son didn't always deal so easily together. Where Murdo was deliberate, Padrig could be careless. Where Padrig looked for laughter, Murdo preferred serious discussion. It was all to do with temperament, and little with the natural affection between a man and his son.

"Father," said Ewen. "What else must I know?"

The king pushed back his chair and stood. "You'll see your mother's cousin Nairn in the Eastern Vale. He's got the wanderer confined." He crossed to the nearest shuttered window, unbarred it and let in the light. Then he moved to unshutter the rest. "See this is dealt with out of the common eye, Ewen. I want tattling tongues silenced. When it's barracks scouts who find the brain-rotted, no news of them spreads. It's different, this is. I want Vharne and the Vale protected. I don't want it woken to unrest."

"What's happened won't be secret where this man was taken," he said, feeling fresh air stir through the dining hall. "He'll have family, most like. Friends. Unless he was taken in the dead of night, there'll be witnesses."

The king turned from the last unshuttered window, his face hard. "And you'll silence them. It's relying on you I am, Ewen. I must stay here, since it's needed I am for petitions in the Hall. But even if that wasn't so, I'd send you and Padrig."

Ewen swallowed, his belly still uneasy, and put down his emptied goblet. "Because it's blooded you want him?"

"Yes. And because you and Padrig riding out is not a matter for gossip. When I ride, it's noticed."

And that was true. He and his brother had grown to manhood racing about the Vale, first on ponies, then horses. Not a man or woman looked twice, save to greet them.

"I'll see no wild tales are spread, Father. I'll see Padrig blooded. But it could be we'll need to stay a day or two in the Eastern Vale, for this."

"Stay a week, if it's needful," said the king. "Ask Nairn for a bed, and food for your bellies. Your mother's cousin enjoys his high place where I put him. Bed and mutton is the least he can offer in return." Again, he rested his stern gaze on the pale blue morning. "That's all of talking now. The kitchen will give you bread and cheese—and before you ride from the barracks send Swordmaster Tavin and his scout to me in the Hall."

Ewen nodded. He thought it was a mistake for the king not to at least spare a kind word for Padrig, knowing his younger son would not be the man riding home that he was riding out. Some things were needful and cruel at the same time. Blooding was one of them. At fifteen and first blooded he'd had his mother for comfort, when the king's few plain words had failed to heal him.

*Take her place, I can't. But things are as they are. Padrig will have to make do with me, he will.*

Hand again pressed to his heart, he bowed low. "Father."

Padrig was mounted and restless in the barracks stable yard. "At last," he said, scowling. "And your jaw's not dropped off from talking? Waiting to see it dangled to your belly, I was."

Swallowing a sigh, Ewen kept on walking. One of the barracks brats had a hold of his own horse, which whickered to see him and tossed its dark grey head. An impatient beast. He should have named it Padrig, not Granite.

"Keep yourself," he told his brother, one hand raised in warning. "It's a word I need with Tavin, before we ride."

Ignoring Padrig's groan, still carrying the satchel filled with a clean shirt and food for the road, he ducked into the armoury where Tavin could almost always be found. And there was the swordmaster, running a long blade across a spinning whetstone. Scarlet sparks leapt and sizzled the air.

"You're off?" said Tavin, his voice pitched over the whining metal. He didn't look up from his careful honing of the blade. "Padrig says there's an errand, you've got."

*Padrig says.* Would his brother never learn discretion? "That's right."

Hearing his annoyance, Tavin eased his foot on the treadle then lifted the blade and his gaze. "That's all he said."

"I can't say more either. Not on that," he said, and slung the satchel across his chest. "The king wants you and Boyde in the Hall, he does. Best step lively."

Tav grimaced. "A mood's on him?"

"Not from what you told me," he said quickly. "It's this errand that riles him. He'll tell you, he should."

"Ah," said Tavin, his eyes narrowing, like as not seeing how one matter touched the other. He didn't need more than a few raindrops to know a storm was coming. "We'll talk when you ride back, we will."

He wished they could talk now, most of all on blooding Padrig. But that and the Vale man about to die had to stay secret 'til the nasty business was done with, and the king gave him leave to speak.

"Good," he said, backing to the armoury door. "Tav—if the king's more snappish than you'd like, he's got worries. Be easy."

Tavin grunted something, then swung himself off the whetstone. "You ride safe, boy. We'll cross swords when you're home."

"We will," he said, smiling, and ducked out into the day.

"Is that all your talking done, you old biddy?" Padrig demanded, grinning, watching him vault onto Granite. "Can we go now, can we?"

*Blood him, Ewen. That's my wish.* Remembering the king's command, he felt his smile freeze. "We can go," he said, and loosened Granite's reins. The horse bounded out of the barracks stable yard, and with a whoop Padrig kicked his horse after them.

"So, what did the king want?" he said, as they clattered abreast down the wide road leading out of the High Vale.

By now the sun was well clear of its circling sweep of woodland, which meant they weren't the only folk out and about. Ewen nodded at Brown Willem, passing them with his trio of brindled milch cows off to be milked at the dairy. Willem nodded back, cheerful enough.

"Ewen?"

He glanced at his brother. "Not here. We'll talk when only the sky's listening, I say."

Padrig gave him an odd look, but didn't argue. For the next small while they threaded their way past more well-behaved milch cows, a bevy of goats off to chew the edges of the common pastureland, and a few wives carrying trays loaded with proven bread dough to be set baking in the big oven down by Market Square. They knew everyone by face and name, and nodded or exchanged brief greetings. For all they were the king's sons, the High Vale was too small and its people too used to them for bowing and scraping. Besides, the king discouraged it. After countless generations of serving the sorcerer on their knees, he said the people of Vharne must never bow or scrape again.

At last they reached Humpy Bridge, arching its stone back over meandering Cottle Creek. It marked the boundary of the High Vale. No more cobbled road after this, just grassy tracks leading through open country and secretive woodland to the Vale's far corners. A good thing they'd spent their childhood and youth gallivanting. Knowing the Vale so well meant they could leave a guiding scout behind.

Feeling jaunty, the horses squealed and kicked as they cantered over the bridge. On the other side they reefed against their bits to go faster. Laughing, Padrig let his roan Larkspur have its head. Granite plunged after them and Ewen didn't argue, standing in his stirrups as the satchel of shirt, bread, cheese and apples banged and bounced against his back and the chilly autumn air whipped strands of hair across his eyes.

They drew rein at the old lightning-struck thrane tree, where the grass-and-dirt road forked. Walking now, the horses warm and blowing, they turned right for the Eastern Vale. The climbing sun was bright in their eyes.

"If that's food you've brought, I'll eat some," said Padrig, holding out his hand. "The king chased us off so fast my belly's still growling."

Ewen unlaced the satchel and pulled out an apple. "Make do with that, you can. The rest is for nuncheon."

"Worse than Tavin for orders, you are," said Padrig, taking it, and crunched through the small, tart fruit to spat-out pips in two bites.

"You'll thank me, you will, when your belly's rumbling at noon."

"I'll thank you for saying what the king wanted, I will," Padrig retorted. "The sky's listening, Ewen. Not a soul else."

Instead of answering, Ewen looped his reins into the crook of one arm, pulled the leather thong from his hair and re-tied it.

"*Ewen.*"

Spirit save him, he could almost hate the king for this. "It's quiet you were, when I spoke of the wanderers from Manemli."

"I was waiting for the king to start a brawl over Tavin," said Padrig. "But he didn't. Surprised me, that did."

He shrugged. "It's a fool who brawls with his brother when his house is caught on fire."

"Vharne's on fire, is it, Ewen? Is that what the king said?"

Padrig was young enough yet that he couldn't hide all his fear. "No. Not that. But if it's not on fire, Padrig, there's smoke in the wind. Smell it, I can. These blighted Manemlims. The others crossed to us from Iringa. Now this Eastern Vale man, brain-rotted. I've no proof, I say it plain, but I have a feeling where he's the first but he's not the last."

His brother was staring. "But that's not what the king said. That's not why you're skittish."

How to say it? How to tell him? Padrig was a feisty one, lusty and quick-tempered. As easily as he laughed, he clenched a fist or danced a jig.

*It's all his life I've known him, and never can I say what will tickle his fancy or strike him raw.*

Shifting in his saddle, Ewen looked his brother full in the face. "The king wants you blooded, Padrig. You're to put down this man in the Eastern Vale, you are."

The wind-whipped colour leached out of Padrig's lively face. "He told you that? You he told, and not me? What's his game there, Ewen? That's a nonsense, that is."

"Padrig." Nudging Granite closer to Larkspur, 'til his knee was touching his brother's, he breathed out hard to settle his own flighty emotions. "It pains the king, it does, to put this thing on you. He thought it might sound easier coming from me."

"It doesn't," said Padrig, his jaw tight. "It's sour news from you or anyone."

"I know," he said, aching. "But Padrig, there's dark trouble stirring beyond Vharne. The king needs you blooded to face it. He's got two sons and it's both of them he needs with more blighted madmen wandering over our borders."

Padrig's answer was to clap heels to Larkspur's flanks and bolt ahead down the road.

Curbing Granite's resentment, Ewen let his brother go. Chasing after him would only see both horses sweaty and tired. Let Padrig gallop himself to a standstill. After that they could talk like sensible men.

Underfoot, the open countryside began to rise and fall. A smudge of woodland appeared in the distance. That was Branin Forest, that was, and far on its other side lay the Eastern Vale. He could see Padrig ahead of him, dwindling. Was he going to gallop all the way to the trees?

For a moment he thought the answer to that was yes, but then his brother slowed, and slowed, and finally stopped. When it seemed Padrig had decided to stay put, he let fretting Granite bounce into a fast canter. The horse's long strides swallowed the gap Padrig had opened between them. but just as he reached his brother, Padrig urged Larkspur into a slow trot.

"Padrig, I'm sorry," he said, gentling Granite to keep pace with the roan. "I'd not have this for you ever, I wouldn't. But it's the king's command, it is. I can't disobey it."

Blue gaze resting on Branin Forest, every muscle in his face tight with temper and dismay, Padrig grunted.

"You know it's a kindness, putting them down," he added. "Brain-rot's a cruel way to die, it is. And putting them down keeps Vharne safe, Padrig. A man or woman with brain-rot will likely rot others. You know it happens."

Another grunt. Then a rabbit sprang from cover and dashed across the grassy track, almost under their horses' hooves. Granite and Lark-spur startled, and for the next few moments they were too busy to talk of blooding.

Once the horses were settled again, Padrig thumped one fist lightly against his saddle's brass-mounted pommel. "You like your swordplay with Tavin, you do. I never did."

"So it follows I've no qualms sliding my knife into a rotted man or a woman?" Offended, Ewen stared at him. "Harsh words, little brother."

"Life's harsh," said Padrig. "That's the king's song, isn't it?"

Angry, he kicked Granite forward then swung the horse athwart his brother, halting them both. "It's not willingly he sings it! Life is what it is, Padrig. Here's a task fallen to us, brother, and like good sons we'll see it done. There's a castle roof over our heads, there is, when others sleep beneath mouldy thatch and broken tiles. Keeping Vharne and the Vale safe is how we repay that, it is."

Padrig glared, rebellious. "Then I'll find myself a tumbled cottage with mouldy thatch, I will. Spirit knows how many there are scattered through this empty kingdom. Better an ague in my chest than blood on my hands, I say!"

Shifting Granite again, Ewen leaned over and took hold of his brother's wrist. "Padrig, it's not murder."

"*You* say!"

"The king says."

"He says what he says to see his commands obeyed," Padrig retorted. "If it's murder to me, I say it's murder, I do."

"Padrig." He tightened his grip. Beneath his fingers he could feel his brother's racing pulse. "I'd do it for you, I would. But this is your task, this is. Someday a life could depend on you being blooded. It'll be hard, I know, but you're not alone. I'll stand with you. Padrig—"

Padrig wrenched his wrist free. "You don't care it's not what I want?"

"I care," he said quietly. "But not more than what's good for Vharne, I don't."

"Oh," said Padrig. He sounded very young, and lost. "Ewen, it's a lover, I am. Not a barracks man. Not a swordsman."

He snorted. "Maise tell you that, did she?"

"This man in the Eastern Vale," said Padrig, ignoring that. "What wrong did he do, for me to slide a dagger in him?"

"That's boyish, that is," he said, thinking of Tavin's sharp reproof. "You know better, Padrig."

A long silence, then Padrig sighed. Piercing the cool morning, a lone eagle's cry. Larkspur stamped a hoof.

"Think, Padrig," Ewen said softly. "Where's the right in leaving a man to suffer, but not a broken-legged horse?"

"I know," said Padrig, and dragged a hand down his face. "It's right you are. The king, too. It's my task and I'll do it. But don't ask me to smile."

He'd won the argument. He should be pleased. But as he swung Granite out of the way, so he and Padrig could ride on for the Eastern Vale, he couldn't rid himself of the feeling that somehow he'd failed.

"It's in there, he is," said their dead mother's cousin Nairn, and pointed across the square to the Eastern Vale's squat stone council house. "Tied good and proper, five stout men with cudgels on guard. No chances taken."

Ewen nodded. If he'd not known Nairn shared blood with him and Padrig, there'd be no guessing it. There wasn't so much as a nose between them. Close to the king's age, but with less hair and all of it grey, the Eastern Vale's spokesman had greeted them on the last stretch of road into the village. Then he'd led them the rest of the way, riding a bony, spavined nag, his tongue running on and on about their capturing of the rotted man.

"And does he have a name?" he said, because not once in all his babbling had Nairn called the man he and Padrig had come to kill anything but "he".

Nairn opened his mouth to answer, but Padrig raised a hand. "His name's no matter."

Nearly five hours' steady riding, and they were the first words Padrig had spoken since the end of their short, desperate fight. As Nairn stared at him, uncertain, Ewen looked around at the gathering of Eastern Vale villagers. None of them had heard Padrig's harsh words, thank the spirit. Instead they clotted together in small groups, holding hands, holding breaths, sickened to silence by the tragedy.

"You know why the king's sent us?" said Padrig, his eyes so bleak they were unfamiliar. "You know what we've been tasked to do?"

"I thought—" Nairn cleared his throat. "We've goodwives in the Eastern Vale, know their way around healing herbs, they do, but up in the High Vale—you've got proper healing men there, you have—I thought—"

Ewen laid a hand on Nairn's shoulder. "It's sorry we are, but there's no cure for brain-rot. This man of yours is dead already, he is. But before he dies he could do some mischief."

"I know," Nairn said, his voice cracking. "Tried already, he did. We stopped him."

"Nairn, how did this happen? Do you know that?"

"For certain?" Nairn shook his head. "He was riding the rough, hunting wild goats. Need the meat and hides, we do. Could be he rode too close to Iringa."

Seven brain-rotted wanderers over the border in less than a month . . . 'What do you know of Iringa?"

"Nothing," said Nairn, flinching. "A scout rode through the Eastern Vale a while back. He tipped us a warning, he did. Told us we'd be wise to stay close to home. So we do, most of us."

A scout rattling his tongue? *Meaning well, but causing strife. Tav'll know who it was. Then there'll be sharp words spoken.* "But your blighted man paid no heed, you think?"

Nairn's brown eyes filled with tears. "His name's Jeyk. A friend to me, he is. There's a wife and four chil'en, he's leaving."

"It's the king's sorrow, they have. Nairn—" Ewen shook his mother's cousin gently. "Waiting makes this no easier. Take us to your friend. We all want this done with, we do."

A small, stifled sound of anguish, then Nairn nodded. "Come, then."

With the silent, staring villagers at their backs they crossed the square to the council house, Jeyk's prison. Four strides from its stone steps the door flew open and a woman staggered out, weeping, pursued by a ragged, shouting voice full of hate.

"—*bitch, you slut, you treacherous whore! I'll burn your lying eyes out, I'll plant a poison toad in your belly!*"

"Joan!" Nairn leapt for her. "Joan, are you mad? What sent you in there? Told to keep away, you were!"

"Five men with cudgels?" said Padrig, as the woman shivered and sobbed in Nairn's arms. "Deaf, blind and dumb, are they?"

The woman lifted her ravaged face. "Don't blame them, you can't," she said hoarsely. "Lied to them, I did. I said Nairn gave me leave to bid my man farewell."

"And they believed you?" Padrig shook his head. "So Nairn, it's none but fools live in the Eastern Vale, is it?"

Ewen touched his arm. "It's tossed about, everyone is, Padrig," he said. "Don't sharpen your tongue on him. Nairn, see her to a friend. Then come back and hold the door. Nobody else to come in, I say."

As Nairn led the distraught woman away, Padrig cursed under his breath. "I didn't want his name, I didn't want to know there was a wife and children. Ewen, they should've brought him to us in secret, in Branin Forest."

No matter what he said, or how gently, it would make Padrig angry. He sighed. "Let's go in."

They entered the shuttered, lamplit council house. Its round wooden conference table was shoved into a corner, leaving the centre of the small room bare. Seeing them, the five village men with their cudgels stepped forward. Ewen nodded at them, a curt greeting. For many reasons, they couldn't stay.

"The king's sons, we are. On the king's business. Wait outside. If you're needed, you'll know. Be sure the door's closed behind you."

The men glanced at each other and left, not one of them looking at their prisoner. Naked to the waist, the blighted man was roped to one of the table's chairs, bound by his wrists, by his ankles, with coils of rope tight about his middle. His lean face was stubbled, his dark hair lank with sweat. His brown eyes showed their whites, gliding round and round in their sockets. Small, blood-filled pustules disfigured his narrow, sun-browned chest and belly. Some of the pustules had burst, dribbling reddish-black blood and thin yellow muck.

Padrig slid his sharp dagger out of its sheath. "Are there words to say? Or do I stick him silent?"

Hearing the furious pain in his voice, Ewen took a deep breath. Easily, so easily, he could scream his resentment and rage. The king was right to ask this—and yet, and yet . . .

*I'm sorry, little brother.*

"Ewen—if I'm doing this, I want to *do* it," Padrig said, his fingers white about the dagger's slender hilt. "So if there's—"

"Wait," he said, and took hold of Padrig's arm. "I need to think, I do."

"*Think?*" said Padrig, shaking free—but he let the dagger drop to his side.

*How will we know what ghosts are stirring beyond Vharne's borders if we never wait long enough to ask a man who's maybe seen one?*

That's what he'd asked Tavin, and the swordmaster had given him short shrift in reply. But he'd been right. He *knew* he was right.

*This Jeyk's one of ours, not an Iringan, but still there's something he might know.*

Cautiously, he approached the man bound to the chair. "Jeyk. Jeyk. Can you hear me, Jeyk?"

"Ewen? What are you doing?" Padrig protested. "Don't talk to him. What if he understands you, and begs for his life? You want me to put him down while he's *begging*, do you?"

The man's lolling head jerked up. Such a terrible madness in his wild eyes. "Calling me. Calling me. Let me go, you. He's calling."

"Who's calling you, Jeyk?" he asked softly. "Jeyk? What's his name?"

The man's red-rimmed eyes narrowed to slits. "The power, the power!" he hissed, spittle flying. "Pathetic fool, on your knees!"

"Ewen, *enough*," said Padrig. "He's lost his wits, he has. Don't you see it?"

*Yes. I see it.* Choked with sorrow, he stepped back. "Remember your drills in the tiltyard, do you? One thrust, sure and swift, between the ribs and angled up. There's the heart, you'll pierce it for sure." Turning, he looked at his brother. "All your weight behind the thrust, Padrig. And when the hilt's home you twist the blade, you do. Cut the heart to ribbons and that's the end of him, it is."

Pale as milk, Padrig nodded. "I remember."

"And remember this too, you should. It's a kindness you're doing. His future's black blood and running pus and his mind shredding to tatters. See that, you can. Padrig, you're saving him."

Padrig stared. "Helps to think that, does it?"

He owed his little brother nothing but the truth. "Not now. But it will."

*When their faces come back to you, ghosts in the night.*

Breathing in harsh rasps, Padrig closed on the bound man. Halting before him, he took the blade in his left hand and wiped his right down the front of his dark green woollen coat.

Ewen swallowed. "Count down his ribs, Padrig," he said, staring at the bones beneath the madman's taut skin. "Slide your blade between fourth and fifth, you should."

"Ewen . . ."

"I'm right here, Padrig," he said, blinking. "Time to do this, I say. Waiting won't make it kinder."

*Not for him, and not for you.*

Turned to stone with tension, Padrig was. Muscles like rock, the air scouring his lungs like grit. He took the blade back in his right hand. The bound man stared up at him, a moaning gibberish clogging his throat.

"Hide his eyes," Padrig whispered. "Please, Ewen? I can't put him down with him looking at me. I can't."

*Don't touch a brain-rotted man past what's needful,* Tavin said. *Touch churns them, it does. Once they're bound the only touch they need is the blade's kiss, it is.*

But this was his little brother Padrig asking him. This was Padrig's blooding. He was scared.

*Told him I'd help, I did. What's my word worth? Nothing?*

He didn't want to ask Nairn for a cloth, and there was nothing in the council house to use for a blindfold, so he took out his dagger and sliced off the bottom of his linen shirt. Padrig watched him, speechless.

"Bind his eyes now, I will," he said. "And then, Padrig, you have to do it."

Padrig nodded. "I will."

Nairn's friend Jeyk spat and swore and cursed as the linen was tied tight around his face.

"Pity we can't bind his jaw shut as well," said Padrig.

"No. That would make this—"

"Butchery," Padrig muttered. "I know that."

Heartsick, Ewen kissed his brother's cheek. "Spirit guide your hand," he whispered. "Be merciful. Be quick."

But Padrig was nervous. He didn't thrust the blade home hard, he let it prick the bound man's skin first, drawing blood. Jeyk let out a piercing howl and thrashed in the chair, startling Padrig a pace backwards.

Ewen felt his fingers clench. "No, Padrig." *I should do this. I should. He's not ready—but the king gave his command.* "Padrig—"

"I know!" Padrig shouted, his face flushed, and raised his dagger. "Stand fast, Ewen. I'll do this, I will."

Fingers lightly touched to his own blade, Ewen watched his brother step close again to the bound man. Only this time Jeyk was ready, he knew his life was forfeit, and before Padrig's blade could slide home to its hilt he was screaming and thrashing, the chair was tipping, tipping, and before they could stop it Jeyk crashed to the floor.

The old timber chair split apart, and the blighted man, snarling, thrashed himself free.

Ewen leapt for him as Padrig turned to the door. "Help in here!" his brother shouted. "Nairn! *Nairn!*"

Howling, the blindfolded madman, still bound to bits of wood, flung around in a frenzy, wildly lashing out. A length of timber caught Ewen a crushing blow across his right forearm. He heard bone break. His legs buckled, dropping him poleaxed to his knees. As he struck the floor a bolt of pain seared through his body, making him cry out.

"*Ewen!*" said Padrig, whipping round.

Dizzy, his belly heaving, Ewen waved him back. "No, Padrig! See to Jeyk! Obey the king!"

Torn, Padrig hesitated. Then the council-house door banged open. Nairn tumbled through it, his five men with their cudgels at his heels. Half-blinded by suffocating, white-hot waves of pain, Ewen slumped to the floor, broken arm clutched across his chest, and watched as Padrig tried to blood himself by putting down the poor man Jeyk, who was lost to the blight.

Three shallow cuts he managed, not one a killing blow. The pain of them only maddened the brain-rotted man further, making him howl and stumble and throw himself around the room. Twice he caught Padrig with the timber still bound to his wrists, hard enough to hurt him. Stricken with horror, Nairn and the five Eastern Vale men held back. Padrig landed a fourth blow, opening a deep wound across Jeyk's spine. Screaming, the madman knocked the blade from Padrig's loosened grasp.

Ewen closed his eyes against a sting of tears. *I'm sorry, Padrig. I'm sorry, Father. I failed.* "Nairn!" he croaked. "You and your men — you have to take him!"

"No!" Nairn protested. "Ewen — he's my friend!"

*Useless, useless . . .* Nearly biting through his lip, Ewen lurched to his feet. "You men! Take him! Or you'll see the Eastern Vale under blight, you will!"

Jeyk's blindfold was sliding. He could see now, and he was lethal. Bloody tears streaked through his greyish stubble and all the pustules on his chest were burst. Slicked with blood and pus, stinking, he flailed and snarled, teeth bared and ready for biting, ready to spread his deadly, brain-rotting blight.

Padrig's dagger had slid beneath the council table. He was on his hands and knees under it, fighting to get the knife back.

"*Take him!*" Ewen shouted — and the five frightened men with cudgels obeyed.

Afterwards, with Jeyk's pulped and broken body decently covered and taken away, and dirt spread over the pools of blood soaking into the council house's wooden floor, Ewen sat silent while one of the Eastern Vale's goodwives looked at his arm.

"One bone broken, one cracked," she said, then bound his arm between two split boards and strapped it tight to his body so he could bear the long ride home. After that she went away, and that left him with Nairn.

"They'll not get over this, they won't!" his mother's cousin said, shaking. "Those men. They're *ruined*, Ewen, thanks to you and your brother. *I'm* ruined. It'll be with me 'til I die, that bloody slaughter!"

*And me.* "Nairn—" He hurt so much, he wanted to be sick. The goodwife had given him nothing for the pain. "I'm sorry. Send to the king. Complain of me and Padrig. We'll hold our tongues, we will. The fault here is ours."

"Send to the king?" Nairn snorted. "The man my cousin wed with, he never had time for me. You and your brother, go back to the High Vale, Ewen. Don't show your faces in the Eastern Vale again."

Dismissed, Ewen made his way through the village's angry silence, past men and women who hated him now, and found his brother at Nairn's stable with the horses. They were saddled and ready.

"It's a full moon tonight," Padrig said, his face bloodless still. The bruise on his cheek, from one of the blighted man's wild blows, stood out in stark green and purple relief. "We can ride after sunset."

"Padrig—"

His brother turned his back. "Swallow your tongue, Ewen. Unless there's a word you know to undo what's been done."

"Padrig," he said again, sighing. But that was all he said. It was too soon, and his brother was too raw.

Full of every kind of pain a man could suffer, he clambered awkward into his saddle, and with Padrig beside him rode away from the Eastern Vale.

# CHAPTER SEVEN

*Bright sunlight, warm and sparkling on a fountain. A pond. A mansion. It's smaller than King Gar's seagull-white palace, but almost as grand. Cautious, she looks around. The gardens are familiar. She's been here before.*

*A man stands on the mansion's balcony. Sunlight on his jewels. Gold on his fingers. Gold on his brow. His tunic is rich purple, his breeches midnight black. He turns and looks at her. His brown eyes warm in a smile.*

*Rafel. It's Rafel. He's safe. He's not screaming.*

*But then she realises, no. This isn't her brother, though this man wears his face. Those might be his eyes, and those his lips when he smile, still—it's not Rafel.*

*Without warning, a shadow crosses him. The smile dies, and his warm eyes turn cold.*

*"Who is it, watching me? Who dares to look?"*

*She feels the menace of him, sharp and piercing. She's frozen to her marrow and paralysed with fear.*

*Don't see me—don't see me—I'm not here. I'm a dream.*

*But as she wrenches herself free, before this terrible man can truly see her, she hears a faint voice crying for help.*

*"Deenie, it's me. Deenie, I'm here. Deenie, please, help me. You have to help me, before it's too late. Deenie . . . please . . ."*

"Deenie! *Deenie!* Deenie, for the love of Barl, *wake up!*"

Wrenched gasping from sleep, mizzily confused, Deenie opened her mouth to fratch at Charis for shouting — then gasped again as a new and different pain speared through her.

"Deenie!" Charis said again, clutching an oil lamp. In the glowing yellow light her face was blanched with terror. "Oh, praise Barl. Deenie, I—"

A bone-rattling crash of thunder overhead smashed Charis's words to silence, and the chamber lit up crimson as lightning stabbed the night.

"Deenie, is this it?" said Charis, into the ringing silence that followed. "Have we reached the end?"

Teeth chattering, Deenie shoved back her blankets and slid out of bed. "I don't know. I don't know." She felt as though she'd swallowed a bucket of burning coals, pain searing through her with every shaking breath. *Rafel.* "You mustn't go to pieces, Charis. I can't—"

Another crash of thunder. More flaring light. And then the rain came, full of spite and hail. She staggered to the uncurtained chamber window and looked out. Lumps of ice smashed into the glass panes, smashed against the Tower's stone walls and gouged holes in the unkempt lawn below. The raging night was lit in crimson fits and bursts, turning the pouring rain to blood.

"Oh, Deenie," Charis whispered, creeping to join her. "I think this is the end." She sobbed. "I'm not a brilliant mage like you or Rafel, but I can feel it. Our poor kingdom's trying to tear itself apart — and we're going to die!"

Deenie reached for her hand and held on tight. "Don't say that, Charis. It's not the end, it's just a bad storm, and—"

And then she screamed, a breathless cry, because the pain shooting through her was — was —

*Am I dying? Is this what dying feels like?*

Deep in the earth, a tremor was building.

"Charis—" She felt herself sink to the floor. "We have to get out. Go put some clothes on, as many layers as you can, then meet me in Da's room. Go on now. Hurry."

Charis let go of her hand. "Deenie, what are you—"

"*Hurry!*" she shouted, and slapped at Charis to make her run.

Alone again, she clutched at the windowsill and dragged herself, whimpering, onto her feet. Charis had taken the lamp with her, so she summoned glimfire. The pain of that made her eyes pop wide. When she could trust that she'd not fall down again, she shuffled to her wardrobe. Every step was a torment. The storm outside was nothing, *nothing*, to the storm in her flesh, and the storm outside was terrible. Rolling crashes of thunder like a rockslide in the sky. Whipcracks of lightning, torrents of rain. Rattle rattle smashing of hail on stone and glass.

The pain behind her eyes was stealing her sight. Blinking, unsteady, hands shaking and heart drubbing, she pulled off her nightshirt and battled into some smalls then leather trews and a wool longshirt and then two proper shirts over that. She pulled on her thickest wool skirt next, belted a leather coat around her, then dragged two pairs of socks on her feet and laced herself into her stoutest leather boots, wincing. Bulky and clumsy, she looked at the rest of her clothes in the wardrobe. Turned and looked through the window at the raging storm. Closed her eyes, and felt the earth clutching tighter and tighter, holding its breath.

So she took up her chamber footstool and smashed it through the glass, then snatched the hairbrush from her dresser and cleared the frame of splinters and shards. And then she pitched every stitch and shoe and boot she owned out of the Tower to the pummelled, hail-strewn grass below. Last of all she hauled out from hiding the stout wooden chest where she kept all her coin. How Rafe used to tease her for not keeping her trins and cuicks in the palace treasury. But she never liked other people knowing where to put hands on her small wealth, saved nice and regular ever since she was a tiddy sprat.

*And I was right, Rafe, wasn't I? It's a good thing this money ain't up at the palace.*

Emptying those hoarded trins and cuicks into her largest leather satchel, she felt a sob catch in her throat. *Rafe*. But there wasn't time to think of him or puzzle through her horrible dream. That would have to wait 'til later, 'til everyone in the Tower was safe.

She didn't dare throw the heavy satchel out of the window after all her clothes, so she dragged its wide strap over her shoulders, rested its clinking bulk against her right hip, and stood. Dizzy with the dream and the storm, groaning as she felt the earth's rising agitation, she staggered out of her chamber and took the spiral staircase to Da. Charis was there with Mama and Pother Ulys, who'd again come to sit with her father to give Mama some rest. Glimfire dimmed and shone and dimmed again as the crimson lightning flashed and died.

"Deenie!" said Mama, seeing her in the doorway. "What's this? Charis says—"

"Not now, Mama. We've got to go," she said, staring at Da. He lay still enough beneath his blankets, but even from a distance she could feel the blight in him, raging. As though the wild storm called to it. "There's a tremor coming. A bad one. We can't be in the Tower when it strikes."

"You're sure?" said Mama. "This isn't just another of your whirligig dreams?"

She looked up. Shadows smudged beneath her mother's eyes. In the fitful light she looked more frail than ever, and there was a bewildered softness in her face. It made her look like a stranger.

"No, Mama. It's real. Can't you feel it?"

Her mother pressed her thin hands to her head. "Yes. A little. I'm not—I'm feeling rather—Ulys gave me a posset." With an effort, she shook herself to a sluggish sharpness. "Deenie—"

"Mama," she said, and left the safety of the doorway. The roiling in her was so awful now that walking was like stabbing knives through her feet. But she couldn't mind it. She reached her mother, took both her wrists and tugged her gently away from Da's bed. "Fratch at me downstairs, as much as you like. But right now we have to leave the Tower. Please, Mama? Will you trust me?"

Mama stared at her. "You used to be so *timid*, Deenie. Where did our little mouse go?"

On a sob, she pulled her mother close in a swift hug. "Someone did a spell, Mama, and I turned into a cat." Letting go, she turned. "Pother Ulys—"

Pother Kerril's assistant jumped. "Deenie?"

She bit her lip. Ulys was a nice enough young woman, but she was hardly robust. *Except she's all I've got, so she'll have to do. Besides, Da's not heavy. Not any more.* "Ulys, I need your help."

Ulys's green eyes were bright with fear. "Of course."

A fresh battering of hail struck Da's chamber window. The storm was doing its best to break in. "Ulys, you and Charis get Da downstairs and outside. Wrap him in all his blankets and carry him, shoulders and ankles. Do it now, quickly. Mama and I will be right behind you."

"Deenie, your father's not well," Mama protested, as Charis and the novice pother leapt to the bed. "He can't be bustled about like this! Really, you mustn't upset him so. It's a storm, it will pass like all the rest—"

Whatever was in that wretched posset her mother had taken, clearly it had fuddled her good and proper. "No, Mama," she said. "It won't."

"All right," Mama said, uncertain. "If you're sure."

"We've got him, Deenie," said Charis, holding tight to Da's blanketed ankles. Anchored to his shoulders, Pother Ulys nodded her support.

"Then go!" she snapped. "Fast as you can. Don't wait for us—and make sure to get yourselves well away from the Tower, and anything else that might fall."

"But Deenie—" Crumpled with worry, Charis stared at her. "The hail, and the lightning—"

"Won't kill us half as dead as this Tower coming down on our heads!" Clapping her hands, she conjured scores of glimfire balls into the spiral staircase and the foyer so there'd be no chance of Charis and Ulys missing a step and tumbling with Da into a disaster of broken bones. "Now *go!*"

"We're going, we're going," said Charis. "Deenie—"

Far beneath her feet, she felt the earth groaning. "Don't worry, we're right behind you," she said, trying to smile. Trying not to show Charis the pain and the fear. "Hurry."

Charis pulled a face. "*You* hurry."

Another deep groaning in the earth. Forcing herself not to groan with it, turning away from Charis and Ulys hurrying Da from his room, Deenie took her mother's hands and tugged.

"Come on, Mama. We have to get downstairs."

"Wait," said Mama. "Deenie, you wait. I'm your mother, you're not to boss *me*." She pulled her hands free. "Now help me find dry clothes for your father. What use is there saving him from a tremor so he can die of an ague?"

There wasn't any, only—"Mama, *please*—"

But posset or no posset, Mama was still a slumskumbledy wench. "*No*, Deenie! This will take but a moment!"

It took more than a cat to drive her mother where she wouldn't go. "All right, all right," she muttered. "Only please, let's *hurry*!"

Mama flung open Da's garderobe doors and began hunting through his shirts and trews and weskits, clothes he'd not worn for months as he lay ailing in bed.

"Don't stand there dithering, Deenie!" she said. "Hold out your arms!"

Sick with nerves, Deenie did as she was told. Every instinct she possessed was screaming *run—run—run*—but she couldn't drag her mother out of the chamber, could she, and she wasn't about to leave her behind.

Mama pulled out two shirts and two pairs of woollen trews, muttering under her breath. She pulled Da's best winter coat off its hook and added it to the pile. She found woollen socks and his favourite boots.

"Mama, that's enough, isn't it?" she said, sagging under the weight of so much wool when she was already burdened with the satchel. "Mama, please, *we have to go*!"

Flapping a hand at her, Mama kept hunting through the garderobe. "Yes—yes—perhaps one more shirt—"

For the first time since childhood, Deenie stamped her foot. "*No*, Mama!" A fresh groaning in the earth, and a swiftly rising terror. "Mama, stop treating me like a spratling! Stop being *stupid*! I'm a mage and I'm telling you there's a tremor coming, a bad one!"

Shocked, her mother turned. "Deenie! Don't you—"

A lightning crack so sharp and loud it hurt the ears—a deafening crash of thunder and hard on their heels, a dreadful, rolling growl.

Dropping Da's clothes, Deenie grabbed her mother by the wrist. "Run, Mama, *run*!"

Protesting Da's abandoned clothes, Mama ran with her. She didn't have a choice—it was run or be dragged.

The Tower's blue stone bones were shuddering, the earth's agitation rising swiftly to its surface. Feeling the roil of releasing power, feeling the kingdom's long-buried, furious anguish, Deenie released her mother's wrist and shoved her through the main apartment door, out onto the landing beside the staircase. The balls of glimfire she'd conjured sputtered and sparked and winked.

"Hurry, Mama!" she said, sight blurring. The earth's pain was in her, so deep and hot she was nearly sick. "Don't fratch, I'm right behind you!"

And she was, for the first four steps. But then she had to stop, she had to snatch hold of the staircase railing, so nauseous and dizzy she nearly lost her footing.

*A moment, a moment, I only need a moment—*

"Deenie?" Mama shouted, out of sight now beyond the first spiral twist.

"I'm coming, Mama! Don't stop, I'm right behind you!"

But as she let go of the railing she heard a grinding run through the Tower's thick stone walls. Felt it grind through her own bones, so she had to cry out. Then, with a sparking sizzle, every conjured ball of glimfire died—and the groaning, grinding Tower was plunged into the dark.

And the dark was shattered by a terrible scream.

"*Mama!*" she shouted, and flung herself down the staircase, blinded anew by fresh terror and a choking wave of dread.

Another grinding groan shuddered upwards from the earth, shuddered through the Tower and through her bones and through her blood. She felt her home ripple around her. Heard things tip and fall and smash. Glass. Ceramic vases. Bookcases. Plates. Hands pressed to the unsteady wall, groping her way downwards to the foyer, her belly heaving, bile scalding her throat, Deenie tried to call out. Had to try twice. Tried to conjure fresh glimfire, but the magic wouldn't catch.

"Mama. Mama," she croaked, feeling her heels slide on each shaking stair tread. Feeling her heart painfully battering her chest. *"Mama!"*

She fell over her mother's motionless body at the foot of the staircase.

No time to cry out, or cry, or hold her. Time only to grab her wrists and haul her like a sack of flour across the foyer floor, which was shuddering and shivering and beginning to buckle. The foyer doors stood wide open, the sound of thunder bouncing off the circular wall, rain and hail blowing in, pooling and puddling. The lightning was still crimson, cracking in time with her heart.

Half-witless with the earth's pain she reached the doorway, dropped her mother's wrists and leaned into the storm. *"Charis!"* she screamed. *"Charis!"*

But Charis couldn't hear her.

*I can't do this. I can't. I'm not strong enough. I'm a mouse.*

Like a pond struck by a thrown rock, Lur's suffering earth rippled. The Tower swayed. Roof tiles slithered and smashed on the sandstone steps. A whip crack of lightning, high and hard and loud, very close, and the foyer lit up with eerie bright red light.

"Deenie! *Deenie!*"

She looked up from sheltering her mother, and there in the open doorway was Charis, soaked to the skin. She heard herself sob once, and then she strangled her grief-stricken panic.

"Help me, Charis! Quickly!"

Pummelled by rain and hail she and Charis half-carried, half-dragged Mama out of the foyer, down the Tower's juddering steps and across the forecourt's shivering gravel to the mouth of the carriageway, where Pother Ulys waited with Da.

"Help me, Ulys," she said, her teeth chattering, as she lowered her mother to the ground beside Da. "Mama fell down the stairs."

"Down the stairs?" Running with water, the pother pushed her aside and knelt beside Mama. "How many?"

"I don't know. It was dark, I couldn't see." Her voice broke. The hard rain drummed her skin, ran like tears down her cold face. "Is she all right?"

Pother Ulys hesitated. "It's so dark. I can't see."

"You don't have to see!" she retorted. "You're a pother. You heal people, so *heal* her!"

The muddy ground beneath them shuddered. Deenie doubled over, Lur's pain driving through her. She felt Charis's arm slip hard around her shoulders, holding. Another rippling rumble. More thunder. More crimson lightning, *crack crack crack crack*. The rain kept pouring, but mercifully there wasn't any hail.

"*Ulys!*" she said, shouting over the storm. "What's amiss with her?"

Another flash of lightning. It showed her Ulys's stricken face. "Deenie — I'm so sorry. She's — she's dead."

Dead? Mama was dead? *No, no, no. That can't be right.* Even as she heard Charis sob, felt Charis's arm close around her more tightly, she reached down and caught the pother's robe in fisting fingers. "You're wrong. You're just a novice. What do you know?"

"I'm sorry," Ulys said again. "Her neck's broken."

*Mama's dead. Mama's dead.*

The words bruised her like chunks of hail, tore through her like a tremor, pulling her apart. She could feel a howl building deep in her chest, pushing up, pushing up, trying to find a way out.

"— sorry, Deenie, I'm so sorry, Deenie, Deenie, it'll be all right. Deenie, I'm here."

And that was Charis, gabbling. The words rolled off her like the rain.

"Da?" she heard herself say. "What about Da?"

"He's still breathing," said Ulys. "He's soaked through, but he's alive."

*Da's alive and Mama's dead. Oh, what will he say when he wakes to that?*

Another shudder in the earth. Another. Another. The third one sent them sprawling, the solid ground turned malleable, rippling like a blanket shaken by angry hands. Somewhere close by the sound of large trees ripping free of the earth and falling. Breaking.

"Deenie!" shrieked Charis, terrified in the dark. "Deenie, what's happening?"

Tumbled across her mother's still, unbreathing body, Deenie gasped. The ground was shaking. No, the world was shaking. The rain and lightning stopped, abruptly, and there was only the tremor, building and building, like a giant gathering itself to roar its rage at the dark.

"Deenie?" said Charis, breaking the terrible silence. "Deenie?"

"Hold on," she whispered, the sickness surging through her in hot waves. "Hold on . . . hold on . . . it's coming . . ."

Pother Ulys was weeping, enormous hiccupping gulps she tried to strangle in her throat as the rain-soaked carriageway bumped and buckled beneath them.

Deenie groped through the darkness for the pother's cold hand. Groped for Charis's too, and held on tight to both. Somehow the lack of light made everything worse. If she was going to die, she wanted a last look at Mama's face. A last chance to kiss her father goodbye.

*I'm sorry, Rafe. I'm sorry. I did want to save you. I just didn't know how. I didn't—*

The tremor struck them like a blow from a mad blacksmith's hammer.

Out in the open, nowhere to run and hide, they rolled and bounced and bruised on the ground. Cracked heads. Bit lips and bit tongues. The small pains were welcome, because that meant they weren't dead.

Stone by stone by window by tile, the Tower broke apart and crashed to the ground.

Hearing it, Deenie felt herself break. Heard herself sob. Expected any moment to feel the earth tear wide and take her, swallow her, grind her to pulp. Another series of crashes. Terrified animal screams, cut short. The stables. The stables were smashing. Da's pride and joy, once, his second home. His great love. The horses. Dead or dying now, like Lur.

*Stay asleep, Da. Don't wake up. You don't want to see this.*

In the distance, still more crashing. What was that, then? The palace? Was the palace falling too? Was their whole world about to fall?

*Charis was right. This is the end.*

The earth's pain was her pain, ripping its way through her defence-less, vulnerable flesh. It showed no signs of easing, and neither did the earth's fury. Either she'd live through the brutal tremors or she'd die. Understanding that left her oddly calm, even as she whimpered at the flames teasing her bones.

*I wish you were here, Rafe. You'd know what to do.*

Poor Lur. Poor ruined kingdom. All because of Morg. Because of Barl. All because the Doranen had come here with their satchels full of trouble.

*You were right not to trust them, Da. This is all their fault.*

The pain in her eased so slowly for a moment she was sure she imagined it. But then Charis, huddled beside her, shivering, snuffled softly and raised her head.

"Is that it? Is it over?"

And she realised the earth had stopped shaking.

"I think so," whispered Pother Ulys. "Barl's tits, I hope so."

The unexpected crudity made her laugh. "Yes. It is."

They sat up. Holding her breath, Deenie summoned glimfire and this time the magic caught. The small, bobbing sphere showed her Charis, muddy and tear-stained. Showed her Ulys, white as milk. Showed her Da, most of him sheltered beneath his blankets, eyes randomly shifting beneath his eyelids.

Showed her Mama, deathly still.

Charis was trembling. "Oh, *Deenie*."

"I truly am sorry," said Pother Ulys, subdued. "If it helps, it would have been . . . quick."

Quick. Slow. What did it matter? Mama was dead. Deenie tugged off her coin satchel, letting it thud to the muddy ground, then struggled out of her soaking wet leather jacket and laid it over the waxen face of the woman who'd borne her, and loved her, and been her rock in the world. The earth's pain had scoured her hollow and numb. She'd feel this dreadful loss. She'd have to feel it. She just didn't know when, or how.

"I wonder what time it is," she said, folding her arms tightly. "I wonder what's happened down in the city."

Ulys glanced up from checking on Da. "I should maybe go and see. There are likely many people hurt. They'll need all the pothers they can get."

Deenie stared. "And leave Da? You can't."

"Deenie . . ." Ulys sighed. "There's nothing I can do for him. Not like this. Besides, as far as I can tell he's unchanged."

"He needs to be inside, in bed. He needs to be made warm and dry," she fretted. "But the Tower—" She had to wait a moment until she could trust her voice. *My mother is dead and my home lies in ruins.* "Perhaps the palace is still standing. Perhaps part of it is."

"Perhaps," said Charis, "but Deenie, we can't carry him that far."

"There is—there was—a handcart in the stables. For shifting bales of hay." She touched Charis's cold hand. "Wait here. I'll go and see."

The look on Charis's glimlit face said she wanted to argue—but instead, she nodded. "All right. But take care."

"And you stay here with them, Pother Ulys," she added. "Don't you go anywhere. Not 'til I get back."

Conjuring a second ball of glimfire, she went in search of the handcart. Found it, by some miracle, one of the few things left intact. Most of the stable yard was a series of gaping holes and piles of rubble. All but one of the stables was swallowed. The open-fronted hay-shed still stood, though. And the smithy. But not the horses. They were gone. *Oh, Da. Your dear old Cygnet.* Rafe's Firedragon. Her own mare, sweet Jade. And the lad gone, too. Tam.

*I want to weep for them. I do. I want to weep for all of us.*

But the earth's burning pain had boiled away her tears.

She skirted the edge of the wreckage, carefully retrieved the handcart and trundled it back to Da and Charis and Pother Ulys and Mama.

"We'll have to leave her behind," she said, her voice low, after they'd lifted and folded Da into the cart. "I'll come back in the morning. Once I know about . . ."

Charis squeezed her hand. "I'll come back with you, Deenie. Don't worry. We'll see her put right."

Put right? What was right about it? She'd be buried. Hidden in the ground. *Mama*. On a deep breath Deenie stowed her coin satchel beside Da. Conjured more glimfire to light the carriageway so they'd not tumble themselves into any holes, then took hold of one handle on the cart. Charis took hold of the other.

"Let's go."

Pother Ulys walked in front of them, as an extra precaution. The carriageway was rippled and bumpy but they didn't find any holes. What they did find was the palace, the new sections and the old, collapsed and sagging and not safe to go near.

Ulys gasped. "Barl's mercy."

"I can't believe it," said Charis, in a small, shocked voice. "It's the *palace*. It's *always* been here."

Deenie shrugged, too battered now to feel anything but tired. "Always ended tonight, Charis."

"Well—" Washed in glimlight, Charis turned to her. "That's it. We'll have to go home. To my house."

If her house was still standing. How much of the city remained after those terrible tremors? There was only one difficult way to find out.

*And if Charis's home is ruined, like the Tower? What do we do then?*

"Come on," said Charis, her chin trembling. "Your da needs a warm bed—and so do we, if we're not to catch an ague."

Pushing the handcart out of the palace grounds was exhausting, but at least it chased away the rain's chill. That cheered them . . . until they were far enough down the High Street to see and hear what had happened to Dorana City.

"I'm sorry," said Ulys, staring at the distant fires, the smashed shops and dwellings, the dazed and bloodied people milling on the rippled, glimlit cobblestones. A few city guards were trying to keep order, but they seemed as stunned and aimless as everyone else. "I have to help here. I'll come to see your father at the mayor's house, Deenie, as soon as I'm not needed. I promise."

"Go," Deenie said, resigned, because of course the pother was right. "We'll manage."

As Ulys ran to help the afflicted, Charis swallowed a sob. "Do you keep thinking you're going to wake up, Deenie?"

"Yes," she said simply. "Now come on. We shouldn't stay here."

It took a long time to reach Charis's home, on foot, pushing the laden handcart, having to weave their way around buckled streets and collapsed buildings and gaping holes in the ground. Nobody they came across offered to help them. There was too much grief and trouble, not enough unhurt hands to spare.

"Oh, no," Charis whispered, when at last they reached her street. The first two houses they saw were reduced to bricks and glass and broken roof tiles. "Deenie . . ."

"Keep going," Deenie said, making her voice hard to keep the grief at bay. "Don't look. Don't borrow trouble, Charis. We've enough of our own."

When Charis saw her home, unscathed save for two broken front windows and a handful of slipped roof tiles, she burst into tears. They pushed the handcart right up to the front door, which Charis unlocked with the key she kept on a chain round her neck. Then Deenie flooded the house with glimfire and they carried Da inside to the parlour. They were too exhausted to get him up the stairs.

Settling him on the old, sagging sofa, they stripped him out of his wet nightshirt and dressed him in one of Uncle Pellen's—eyes closed, because some things just weren't seemly—then made him as comfortable as they could with pillows and blankets and a pair of Uncle Pellen's thick wool socks on his feet. There was no wood for a fire. The blankets and socks would have to do. With Da settled, they pulled off their own wet clothes down to the deepest dry layer and laid them about the kitchen and parlour to air dry.

"Tea," said Charis, with all that done. "That's what we need. There's a scoop of coal left to heat some water. I'll make it, Deenie. You sit."

It wasn't in her to argue, so first Deenie fetched her satchel of coin in from the handcart and stuffed it under the sofa. Then she pulled up a footstool and held her father's hand between hers. It was cold, his hands were never warm these days, but there was life in him. She could feel it. There was the blight, too, but it had settled.

"Oh, Da," she said, helpless. "What do I do now?"

Da didn't tell her, and she had no idea.

She drank the hot, sweet tea Charis brought her, but couldn't eat the oaten biscuits and didn't stir from the stool. Charis ate and drank then curled up in an armchair and was swiftly asleep.

Da slept too. Even after such a terrible night, he showed no sign of waking.

Time passed. Behind the drawn parlour curtains the night slowly surrendered to dawn. When she judged the light strong enough, Deenie tucked her father's hand under his blankets then reached out to touch Charis on the knee.

"What? What?" said Charis, startled awake. "Is it another tremor? What?"

"No," she said. "Don't fret. I'm going out. I need to find Kerril. I need to know how bad things are. Will you stay and watch Da for me? I'll not be gone long, I promise."

"Well, all right," said Charis, sleepily frowning. "But you be careful, Deenie. And don't dally. Learn what you need to learn and come back quickly. And whatever else you do, don't fall down a hole."

Somehow, she managed a smile. "I'll try not to."

With a handful of coins from her satchel in one pocket, she left Charis to watch her father and ventured outside.

Water from the night's storm lay in sheets and pools and puddles. In the sullen dawn light fighting its way past the lowering clouds, the breadth and depth of the city's ruin was too easy to see. Not even the Wall's falling had left it wrecked like this, if she could believe dear ole Darran's stories.

And she could.

The early morning air was damp and chill, nastily tainted with the stink of death and destruction. Everywhere she looked she saw fallen houses, uprooted trees, ragged holes and buckled bumps in the streets and pavements. In too many front gardens she saw bodies, some under sheets or blankets, some left exposed. A few times she avoided the attention of a city guard doing his best to stop trouble brewing. She saw many weeping Olken. A few Doranen. Some of them were injured. None of them saw her, so lost in their own grief and horror were they. She didn't mind. She didn't want to face them, having no desire to say the obvious words.

*I understand how you're feeling. My home's wrecked too, and my mother is dead.*

She'd rather cut out her tongue with a rusty knife than say that.

Leaving the residential districts behind, she made her slow, careful way to the centre of the city. To find answers she needed to find someone in authority, someone from the General Council . . . though of late, the Councillors were sadly reduced. Or a Barlsman. Maybe even Barlsman Jaffee. Captain Mason of the City Guard. *Someone* whose business it was to keep Dorana on its feet and safe for its inhabitants.

But as she came upon Market Square, she slowed . . . and slowed . . . and stopped.

*Oh, Da.*

She had no words. The square was buckled and broken, Barl's statue reduced to scattered chunks of stone on the torn-up cobbles. And every last important building around Market Square was damaged — or destroyed. Justice Hall was half-collapsed. *Justice Hall*, where her father had helped make law in the kingdom. Where he and Prince Gar had first seen each other as real people, not strangers without one single thing in common. Stunned as she was, she felt the pain of that. Her family history, that was, lying in rubble. The Barlschapel was smashed to pieces, with not a Barlsman in sight. Uncle Pellen's Guardhouse too, and the grand General Council chambers. The tremors had spared nothing, spared no-one. Beautiful Dorana City was in *ruins*.

*Oh, Da.*

Save for one man stranded on the pavement before the Council building, the battered, silent square was ghostly empty. Approaching him, she saw it was Mayor Stott. She called his name four times before he realised he wasn't alone any more.

Eyes dull and red-rimmed, his bruised forehead scraped raw and his narrow shoulders surrendered in a slump, Stott looked down at her. He seemed too exhausted to be surprised. "Deenie."

"Meister Mayor—" She had to clear her throat. *Why can't Charis be right? Why can't I just—wake up?* "Mayor Stott—"

His expensive clothes were torn in half a dozen places. Beneath the rips she saw dried blood. There was dried blood on his hands. He touched his fingers to her shoulder.

"Deenie—you're Asher's daughter," he said, his voice harsh. "Can't you help us? Can't you fix this? Is there *nothing* of your father in you?"

Shocked, Deenie stepped back. "I don't—you've no right to—" She swallowed bile. "My mother's dead."

"Scores are dead," said Mayor Stott, his voice thick with grief. "Perhaps hundreds. Perhaps they're lucky. They died quick."

*Like Mama.* "Meister Mayor, where's the rest of the Council?"

"Dead or dying or broken or indifferent," he said, shrugging. "Barl knows, not I. I've not seen one of them yet." He dragged a hand down his stubbled face. His eyes were full of tears. "It was a mistake to let your brother cross the mountains. If he was here, he could fix this. He could put this all to rights."

She swallowed more bile. *Rafel.* "Mayor Stott—"

"What are you doing here, girl?" he said, frowning. "You shouldn't be wandering the streets. You'll get in the way. Go home, if you've not the wit to fix this. Care for your ailing father. That's a daughter's duty."

*As if I need you to tell me my duty.*

"I have no home," she said, snapping. Too tired and afraid to bother with courtesy. "The Tower fell down. Meister Mayor, would you know where I can find Pother Kerril?"

116

His frown deepening, Stott waved a vague hand. "She's out and about tending the injured. Deenie . . ." Briefly, he pressed trembling fingers to his lips. "Your father — he must be this kingdom's only hope. D'you think he'll wake? D'you think —"

She turned on her heel and walked away.

# CHAPTER EIGHT

D eenie wandered the almost deserted streets for nearly an hour, but she had no luck finding Kerril or any other pother. At last, feeling faint from hunger and knowing Charis would be fretting, she took bread and cured meat from a partly tumbled shop in Tag Lane, behind the Square, and left a silver trin in payment on the counter. Then she made her way back to Uncle Pellen's mostly unscathed house. Still nobody noticed her. She kept her head down and walked quickly. If another person asked her if she could fix this, or chased her about Da, likely she'd do something foolish.

Charis leapt up when she entered the parlour. "*Deenie*. You've been gone ages. I was sure you'd killed yourself down a hole!"

"I could have, easily," she said. "Barl knows there are dozens to choose from." She held out the bread and meat. "Are you hungry?"

Distracted, Charis took the provisions. "Is it terrible? The city?"

All of a sudden her legs wouldn't hold her. She dropped to the footstool beside the sofa. Da hadn't moved. She took hold of his hand and rested her gaze on his pale, quiet face. He was growing some stubble. He'd need a scraping soon.

"Yes. What's happened in Dorana—Charis, it's the worst thing I've ever seen."

"Worse than Westwailing?" said Charis, breathless.

She nodded. "Much worse. I think—I think—"

But she couldn't say it. Not yet.

"I'll make breakfast," said Charis. "And then we can talk about what to do."

She withdrew to the kitchen. Turning to her father, Deenie raised his hand to her cheek. "And that's the question, isn't it, Da?" she whispered. "What are we going to do?"

So still, so far away, he didn't answer. But for the first time since he'd fallen into his awful stupor, she wasn't sorry for it. Because so long as he was sleeping he'd never know Mama was dead.

*I'm not going to tell him, either. If I tell him he might go after her —and I'm not ready for him to die.*

After they'd eaten, Deenie told Charis everything she'd seen and learned in the city. Charis heard her out in silence, tucked back into the parlour armchair, and when the sad tale was done, sat silent for a time.

But, at last she stirred. *"Nobody's* in charge?"

"I s'pose Mayor Stott is, but all he did was bleat about Da saving us. I don't think he knows what to do, Charis. I don't think anyone does. Nothing like this has ever happened before. I don't even know how many of the Council's left to do the bossing he can't."

"Papa would never have carried on like that," Charis murmured. "He and your da between them saw Dorana put to rights after the Wall fell. They saw the whole kingdom put back together. And—and—" Her voice was small and hesitant. "And your mother, of course."

*Mama.* Without warning the parlour blurred, her eyes filling with hot tears.

"Deenie, about your mother . . ."

"I know, Charis," she said, blinking furiously. "I have to go back to the Tower, I have to—"

*Put her somewhere. Bury her. Give her to the ground.*

"Actually," said Charis, still hesitant, "I've been thinking. Perhaps you could lay her to rest in the royal crypt. If it's not been destroyed, I mean. So you don't have to—you know—dig a grave."

*The royal crypt.* "I think Da would want that for her," she said slowly. "*I* want it for her. Only—"

"I was thinking about that, too," said Charis. "Maybe she could share one of the other coffins. Just for a while. Until everything goes back to usual."

*If it ever does.* But she didn't say that out loud. "Not Princess Fane's coffin," she said. "Mama never said much, but I know Da couldn't abide her."

"Queen Dana's?" Charis suggested. "Everyone loved her, Papa said."

Yes. Queen Dana's coffin. That sounded right. Da always said Mama was the queen of his heart.

"You'll need help," said Charis. "You'll need me. It's not something you can do on your own, Deenie. Nor should you."

She certainly didn't want to. "Except I can't leave Da here on his lonesome, can I?" she pointed out. "Just 'cause he hasn't stirred doesn't mean he won't. And I can't take the chance he'll—"

Banging on the front door. She and Charis stared at each other, frighted. The city wasn't lawless yet, but that could come. With nobody in charge, giving orders, and everyone so fratched and desperate, that *would* come.

Charis went to see who it was and moments later brought Pother Ulys back to the parlour. The young novice was dirty and grey-faced with exhaustion. There were smears of blood and other things on her green smock.

"Kerril can't come to you," she said baldly. "She's sent me. I'm to look at your father and if there's any change, run and tell her."

Pother Ulys didn't look like she could run three steps, but Deenie didn't say so. "Thank you," she said, instead. "I'm grateful." She glanced at Charis and saw they'd had the same thought. "Pother Ulys, you look weary. Are you hungry, too?"

Ulys half-laughed, the kind of sound that said tears weren't far away. "It's been a long, bad night and a worse day, this far. So many hurt. So many dying."

"You should rest a while," said Charis. "You'll not help anyone if you're fainting left and right. And if you stayed here, and ate something, and drank some tea, and composed yourself, well, you'd be doing Deenie and me a kindness."

Mindful of Da, Deenie took Ulys's arm and gently nudged her aside. "It's Mama," she said, keeping her voice low. "I have to—take care of her. And I need Charis's help."

Ulys's expression changed. "Oh. Yes. Then of course I'll stay a while, Deenie. But—be wary. There's real fear brewing in the streets, now the first shock of what's happened is wearing thin."

Another glance at Charis. "I was out, earlier. It seemed to me there was a great deal of confusion."

"Barlsman Jaffee perished in his chapel," said Ulys, her eyes haunted. "Speaker Shifrin's dead, too. Guard Captain Mason's hurt. Half the city guard is hurt. And with the important Doranen long gone from here—"

"It's just Mayor Stott in charge," she said, her heart sinking. *Barlsman Jaffee? Oh, Da, there's a mischief.* "And Mayor Stott's wits are so rattled it's a wonder he can remember his own name."

"But I'm sure all will be well, in time," Ulys added. Plainly not sure at all, but needing to believe it. "Only don't linger up at the palace, Deenie. And come back before dark. For my sake, if not your own."

"I will," she promised. "But before I go, please, tell me Da's holding his own."

Charis retreated to the kitchen to cut up the last of the bread and meat and brew fresh tea. While she waited for her refreshments, Ulys took a quick look at Da, pressing a palm to his forehead, feeling his pulse, testing how strongly his breath fanned her cheek.

"He's taken no harm from last night that I can see," she said when she was done. "A miracle, to be sure."

Deenie smoothed her father's lustreless hair back from his face. "He's the Innocent Mage."

"Deenie." Ulys folded her hands before her. "I know what you say you can feel in him. Is it true? Do you feel it?"

"If I said yes, would you believe me? Kerril doesn't."

"Pother Kerril is a practical woman," said Ulys, with great care. "She believes what she can see."

Before last night she'd never really paid Ulys much attention, beyond the fact she was a Doranen and a pother-in-training and sometimes sat with Da. Now what she thought seemed terribly important.

"And you?"

Ulys looked round as Charis returned with a meal and a mug of tea on a tray. "I might not understand it, Deenie, and it might argue against everything I've been taught as a pother and a mage, but—I saw your face last night. I saw what you were feeling in the storm, and with the tremors. That was real. I couldn't feel it, but it was real. So . . ." With a polite nod she took the tray from Charis and retreated to the parlour's straight-backed wooden chair. "I'd be foolish to say you can't feel anything else, wouldn't I?"

"As foolish as Kerril," Deenie muttered. "And yes. It's true. There's some kind of blight in Da, trying to destroy him. It's taking all his strength to keep it at bay. I think that's why he won't—why he *can't* —wake up."

"And this *blight*," said Ulys. "Do you know what it is? Do you know what's caused it?"

"If I did don't you think I'd have said so long before now?" she snapped. *Silly woman.* "I've told you what I know, Ulys. I don't know anything more."

"You should pay heed to every word Deenie utters," said Charis, standing by the sofa with her arms crossed, belligerent. "She's the Innocent Mage's daughter, Pother Ulys. She's Rafel's sister. They're none of them regular Olken, you know."

"I know." Ulys took a mouthful of bread and meat, chewed, swallowed, then washed it down with tea. "I've another question. You might be angry with me for asking it, but—"

"But everyone else asks me, so why not you too?" Frustrated, Deenie pushed off the footstool and stalked to the parlour window. She felt like Da, doing that. She and Rafe used to laugh about it, sometimes, the way Da stomped about staring out of windows when he was fratched.

"Ulys, I'll tell you what I tell everyone else. If Da was awake, if he wasn't blighted, prob'ly he could do something to save Lur. He always has before. Mama—" She had to wait a moment, but even so she could feel the tears stubbornly threatening. "Mama said it was why he got born. To save our little kingdom. Only now he won't wake, so he can't save it, can he?"

"Can you?"

Two little words that felt like daggers shoved through her heart. She shook her head. "No."

"I thought Charis said—"

"Never mind what Charis said!" she shouted, and spun round. "Charis needs to learn when to hold her tongue. *Yes*, I'm Asher's daughter. *Yes*, I'm Rafel's sister. But that doesn't mean I'm like them. *I'm not*. I can't fix the weather. I can't save Lur. I wish I could. Barl knows it needs saving!"

Ulys shrank in her chair, meal and tea forgotten. "I'm sorry. I never meant to—I'm sorry."

"Deenie . . ."

Feeling cornered she looked at Charis, who hadn't deserved that scolding. "No, *I'm* sorry," she said unsteadily. "That was mean. It's just—people keep asking, and I have to keep on saying no, I can't help, and—" She had to stop again, her voice broken to pieces and cutting her throat.

"It's all right," said Ulys, full of sympathy. She wasn't really a silly woman. She was very, very kind. "We understand."

Except she didn't. How could she? Deenie bit her lip. "It's bad out there, isn't it, Ulys? I wasn't dreaming things."

"It's very bad," said Ulys, and wrapped her fingers round her mug. "I'm—I'm frightened."

"We're all frighted," Charis said. "But we can't let fear rule us. There's a way out of this. There must be. All we have to do is find it."

"Yes," said Ulys, nodding. Trying to be brave. "Yes, I'm sure you're right. Now, Deenie, I think you and Charis should go, if you're going. That way you'll be back all the sooner. I know I'm needed here, but with so much suffering in the city and not enough pothers I'm needed everywhere."

"We'll be as quick as we can, I promise."

"Good," said Ulys. Then she cleared her throat. "Ah—Deenie—your mother. Might she need preserving, do you think? Only I've done hospice work in my training and—and I have a spell, if you want one."

"Oh," she said faintly. She hadn't thought of that. She'd been trying her best not to think of Mama dead. "Yes."

So Charis fetched Ulys pen and paper and the pother scribbled down the words then handed them over. "It's not the easiest of incants, but you are Asher's daughter. I'm sure you'll have no trouble."

She wasn't sure at all, but she tucked the folded paper into her skirt pocket anyway. "Thank you, Pother Ulys. For everything."

So great was Dorana's upheaval that not even the pair of them trundling a handcart higgledy-piggledy through the streets roused much attention. A few people stared. A few people pointed. But most folk were too caught up in their own strife and misery to care what a couple of Olken lasses were about. Grimly determined, they pushed and pushed their way around the edge of Market Square until they reached the High Street. There they paused to catch their breath.

"It's awful," Charis whispered, daylight showing her the extent of the city's destruction. "Like a toy town that's been stamped on by a baby in a tantrum."

Fanciful, but true. Turning away from the collapsed shops and buildings and the dispirited Olken toiling in the debris, Deenie looked up the High Street and heard herself gasp. "*Oh.*"

The glorious seagull-white palace really was gone. All their lives it had sat above the city, shining bright in the sunshine, a familiar and comforting presence. Now there was just an ugly gap.

Charis's hand flew to her mouth. "Barl's mercy. Deenie, what are we going to do if the crypt's been destroyed too?"

She'd been trying hard not to think about that, either. "Don't let's borrow trouble, Charis. Come on. We need to hurry or we'll land poor Pother Ulys in strife."

Pushing the handcart up the High Street and into the palace grounds was a gasping, rasping, sweating affair. By the time they'd pushed it level with the fallen palace, dodging ripped earth and fallen trees, they were both cross and wishing they'd found a strong man to help. They stopped again, just to breathe and ease their aches.

Charis pointed. "Look."

There were Olken and Doranen poking gingerly through the rubble of the palace, where most of Lur's day-to-day governing had been done. All those important records, lost. Untold years of Lur's history. And buried somewhere in there, chests and chests of money. The treasury. Those city guards risking themselves in the ruins would have to stay behind, surely, to keep that money safe.

"They haven't noticed us," said Charis, keeping her voice low. "Should we say something, d'you think?"

Deenie shook her head. "No. I don't want to talk to anyone. I just want to do the right thing by Mama."

So they pushed on to the Tower, but there were city guards there, too, risking their lives and limbs in the mass of fallen blue stone that used to be a home. The first man to see them called out to his three companions, then hurried to meet them on the carriageway. Wyn, his name was. He and Rafe were friendly.

"Meistress Deenie! Meistress Orrick!" he said, shocked and pleased. "And there's us looking for you in all that tumbled rock."

"We were here, but we got out in time," said Deenie. "Most of us. Wyn—where's my mother?"

Wyn's pleasantly plain face sobered. "Meistress Dathne. I'm so sorry. We—we shifted her into the shade, there." He pointed. "Have you come for her, Deenie?"

If she kept on staring at Wyn's face, at his light brown eyes, at the deep, puffy cut along his left cheekbone, then she wouldn't have to look at the Tower. What was left of the Tower. She wouldn't have to remember what it had felt like, coming down. What the earth had felt like. How it had screamed in her blood as the pitch-black night flashed crimson with lightning.

"Wyn, I'm going to leave Mama at peace in the royal crypt," she said. "That's what my da would want. And it's what she's earned, with everything she did for Lur. I hope you're not thinking to cause me trouble on that."

"Trouble?" Wyn stared at her. "No. Why would I?"

"I don't suppose anyone's been to the crypt, have they?" said Charis. "To make sure it's still there?"

"I don't know, Meistress Orrick," Wyn said, alarmed. "I don't think so."

"Maybe you could look for us?"

"I can do that," he said. "You stay here, Deenie. I'll run there and run back."

"Thank you, Wyn," Deenie whispered.

Sometimes Rafe used to tease about Wyn, calling him a bit countrified, a bit simple. But right now, by her lights, he was the most wonderful man in the world. She watched him head for the palace gardens in a shuffling run, then turned and looked to where he and his fellow guards had kindly moved her mother. There she was — and not just moved, but respectfully wrapped in a sheet. Had they found it in the Tower's rubble? Or the palace's? Or had Wyn and his friends brought it with them, expecting the worst? It didn't matter. It was a blessing. The leather coat she'd left covering her mother last night had been folded and placed beside her on the uneven ground.

Charis took hold of her hand. "Come on. Let's wait with her."

Abandoning the handcart, they picked their way along the rest of the tremor-warped, tree-crowded carriageway. Now she had to look at the Tower. What was left of the Tower. A hole had opened up partway beneath it, so that half of its blue stones and windows and roof tiles and contents had fallen in.

Deenie heard herself sob, once.

"Be brave," Charis whispered, her fingers tightening.

She didn't want to be brave. She wanted to scream and howl. But what was the point? It wouldn't bring her mother back. It wouldn't rebuild her broken home, like magic.

The leather coat wasn't big enough for both of them to sit on comfortably, so they got a bit damp from the rain-soaked ground. Cross-legged beside her mother, Deenie couldn't bring herself to pull back the sheet. Not even the loosely wrapped linen could hide the doll-like stiffness in her mother's limbs. If she saw the same awful stiffness in Mama's face, she knew she'd lose control completely.

"Deenie?" Charis cleared her throat. "I hate to say this, but if you're going to use that spell Pother Ulys gave you . . ."

Yes. It would be best to use it now, while they were waiting. She pulled the folded paper from her pocket, flicked it open and read Ulys's swift scrawl. The pother was right, the Doranen preserving spell was tricky. Especially for her, with no reliable control over her magework.

But the hardest part about it was that she'd have to touch her dead mother.

*Oh, Da. Give me strength.*

"Can I help?" said Charis, diffident.

*No.* "You're here. That helps."

Tears filled Charis's eyes. "I wish I could do more. Deenie, I wish—"

"I know," she said quickly. "It's all right. Now hush, so I can do this."

Heart racing, feeling faint, she laid her palm gently on Mama's unmoving chest. Even through the sheet she could feel the unnatural chill. *Mama. Oh, Mama.* Clogged with grief, she recited the spell.

*Please work please work please work please.*

As she spoke the incant's last syllable, sick with fear of failure, she felt the power ignite and surge through her, felt it soak into her mother. She thought she could smell spring flowers, and feel a tingling swirl of warmth.

"Is that it?" said Charis, after a moment. "I thought there might be —I don't know. Sparks, or something?"

Sick with relief now, she drew back her hand. "No. That's it. All very simple." *And I did it. For once I worked a Doranen spell first time. Was that you, Da? Helping?* Her voice broke. "Mama, I'm sorry. I'm so sorry."

Now Charis was staring. "Deenie, don't. It was an *accident.*"

The other guards' voices rose and fell amongst the Tower's rubble. A crunching slide of stone against stone. A warning shout. A curse. A musical tinkle of broken glass, striking rock. Tickling her nostrils, the sharp scent of djelba sap from the uprooted trees. All the poor night-birds with their homes fallen down.

*And that's me. Just one more lost nightbird.*

"Deenie, I mean it!" Charis snapped. "Tell me you're not being so foolish as to lay this tragedy at your own feet."

Heavy-eyed and heavy-hearted, she looked at her friend. "I let her fuss about with Da's clothes, Charis. I made her go down the staircase first. Then the storm, the tremors—I turned so inside-out I had to stop. But I made her keep going. And then the glimfire died. If I'd kept her with me, or if I'd been with her on the stairs, if I'd been holding her, helping her—"

"She might easily have tumbled you down with her!" said Charis. "I could be sitting with her body *and* yours!"

"Don't fratch at me, Charis," she muttered. "I can't help how I feel."

Charis poked her knee. "No, well, nor can I. And I feel like slapping you, Deenie. *This wasn't your fault.*"

Maybe that was true. And maybe Da's not waking wasn't her fault either, even though she could feel the blight in him. Her not being mage enough to heal Lur, she wasn't to blame there. She couldn't help how she was born.

*But is Rafel my fault? Leaving him to rot on the other side of Barl's Mountains, wherever he is, when he needs me and he's screaming for me and I won't even try to get to him? Isn't that my fault?*

"Deenie?" said Charis, suspicious. "What are you thinking?"

*Something I really don't want to think.*

"Nothing," she said. And when Charis scowled at her, ferocious, added, "Nothing I want to talk about. Not 'til I'm ready."

Before Charis could argue, or wheedle, Wyn came back from the palace grounds. His torn and stained uniform wore smears of fresh mud and his sturdy boots were dirt-clotted inches past his ankles.

"The crypt's still standing," he said. The cut on his cheek had opened again, bright blood dribbling. He didn't seem to notice. "I'm sorry to say the Garden of Remembrance is mostly ruined, but—if you're bound to put Meistress Dathne to rest with the royal family, I suppose you can. Could be there might be a law about it, permission you might need from the Council, but—"

"I don't think there is a Council, Wyn," Deenie said. "Not much of one, any road. And like I said, my mother's earned this."

Wyn nodded. "That she has. Deenie—" He fidgeted a little. "With your father still poorly, I've not seen you for months. I want to tell you I'm heartbroke over Rafel. He was my good friend. And so was Goose."

Oh, Goose. She never let herself think of Goose Martin. All those girlish dreams she'd dreamed for nothing. She and Goose, they'd never kissed. Never cuddled. It was always *one day*. And now *one day* would never come.

"That's kind of you, Wyn," she said, not rudely, but in a way that would tell him he'd said quite enough. "Can you help us with my mother? And with what's to be done in the crypt?"

"Of course," he said. "I'll get Grif to help."

Watching Wyn and his friend Grif lift Mama like a bundle of sheeted cordwood into the back of the handcart nearly broke her, but she couldn't not watch. She couldn't turn away from any of this because that would be cowardly. It would disappoint her mother.

The young men took hold of the handcart's shafts and started pushing, and she fell into step behind them with Charis, who held her hand again. It was a strange and sorrowful funeral procession, one that made Uncle Pellen's funeral seem extravagant.

*Oh, Mama, you deserve so much more than this. Hymns in the Barlschapel, prayers from Barlsman Jaffee, and every soul in Dorana crowded to bid you farewell.*

Except now there was no Barlschapel, and Jaffee was dead. And every soul in Dorana had their own lost loved ones to mourn.

Charis leaned close. "Don't fret, Deenie," she whispered. "We'll do it properly one day. When this is over we'll make sure of it. I promise."

She nodded, not daring to speak. Opening her mouth would have let loose wails of grief.

They reached the crypt at last. She paid scant attention to the wrecked Garden, with eyes only for Wyn and Grif as they gently lifted Mama from the handcart and carried her into the crypt's cool darkness. Conjuring soft glimfire, she followed them inside with Charis her loving shadow.

Wyn and Grif said nothing, only nodded, when she pointed to Queen Dana's stone coffin. They settled Mama with care on the flagstoned floor, then without any sign of fear or hesitation slid the effigied lid from the queen's resting place. It was heavy, and made them grunt. Charis's fingers curled around hers, so cold. She was cold too, on the inside, where no-one could see. Without Charis beside her she didn't know what she'd do.

"You're sure, Deenie?" said Wyn, his voice hushed. He was being very careful to look at her, not the coffin. "In here?"

"I'm sure," she said. "And if you're fretted on doing this, don't fratch yourselves. I'll not tell."

She didn't know Wyn's friend Grif at all, a tall and rawboned young man with pimples on his chin. "I'm not fretted," he said gruffly. "It's your family. Your choice."

With an effort she found a smile for him. "Thank you."

As though she was their own beloved flesh and blood, they lowered Mama into the coffin. Then they replaced the effigied lid, grunting again with the weight of it, and stood back. Pressed their hands to their hearts and bowed their heads, paying silent respect.

"You need aught else?" said Wyn, after. "If not, me and Grif should —"

"No, no," she said. "You go, and take my thanks with you. Da's thanks too. I know he'd be so grateful." She turned. "Charis, you should go with them. Go back home. We don't want to keep Ulys from her pothering duties longer than we have to and—and I'd like some time to myself."

Tearful, Charis kissed her cheek. "Of course."

Alone at last, Deenie slumped to the flagstones and fell against Queen Dana's coffin. Maybe Charis was right, maybe Mama's death wasn't her fault, but she still felt responsible. Sliding all the way to the crypt's cold floor, suddenly and shatteringly exhausted, she pillowed her head on her arms and let the tears come, belated, in a hot and steady rain.

At last, emptied of tears if not grief, she felt herself slipping into darkness and sleep . . . where Rafel found her again. Just his voice this time, desperate and much fainter.

*Help me, Deenie. We're running out of time. You can find me. You have to find me. If you don't, the whole world will pay the price.*

And then he screamed, and she startled awake.

Heart pounding, fresh tears rising to her eyes, she pressed her hands to her cold face. "And how am I s'posed to find you, Rafe? Do you think I can sprout wings and fly across the mountains? Or snap my fingers and break the reef, make the whirlpools and the waterspouts disappear?"

He didn't answer.

Torn between despair and anger, she clambered to her feet and began pacing the coffin-crowded chamber. Agitated, distracted, she didn't pay close attention and shouted aloud when her hip caught one coffin's sharp corner. It belonged to King Gar. The effigied lid wasn't in place properly, a hazard for the unwary. Muttering, rubbing her bruise, she pulled a face at Da's best friend and kept on stamping.

*Oh, this is just like Rafe. Help me, he says, but he doesn't say how. If I can't fly or walk on water maybe he thinks I can harness a water-spout and ride it to where he is!*

As if she could. As if *anyone* could. Lur was fouled with dark magics and there was no escaping. How many boats had tried to defeat its blighted waters? Dozens—scores—and every one had sunk or been dashed to splinters against Dragonteeth Reef.

*What makes Rafe think I'll have any better luck?*

She wouldn't. She couldn't. She was Deenie the mouse, only pretending to be a cat.

Except . . . except . . .

*I feel things. It's the only magic I'm really good at. And when it comes to feeling, I'm better than most.*

Well. Better than anyone, according to Mama. According to Mama, nobody felt the twists and turns in earth and water the way her Deenie could. Until now the ability had been a curse, nothing more, but . . .

*What if it means I could feel my way across the harbour and past the reef?*

And that was a mad idea. Where had it come from? It must be her grief talking, or her fear for Rafe.

*Only—I am Asher's daughter. I have to be good for something. I can't let him down.*

Heart thudding, she turned and looked at Darran's effigy that Da had made so lifelike and beautiful.

"Hey there, you ole trout," she whispered, approaching him. That's what Da had liked to call him, when he was in a teasing mood. "It's Deenie. I know it's your fault I've got a stupid name, by the way. *Gardenia*. Did you think I'd not find out? Rafel told me."

The flickering glimlight shadows almost convinced her that he smiled.

"D'you remember what you used to tell me?" she said, still whispering. "How I was special, like Rafe, but in my own different way? Was that true, Darran? Did you mean it? Or were you only trying to comfort me after Rafe's teasing made me cry?"

He didn't answer. The crypt was silent.

"Darran, we're in so much trouble," she said, and brushed her fingers against his white stone hair. "And there's only me left to get us out of it. Mama's dead. Da's far away. Rafel's in strife somewhere over the mountains. I think if he and Da could work together, maybe they could save Lur. Only first Da has to get better and I can't help with that. I think maybe Rafe's the only mage to break his blight. So I have to save him first. Only . . ."

Bending over the old stone man, she clasped her shaking hands around his. Felt the cold marble under her cold fingers.

"Darran, please. You have to tell me. Am I addled, thinking maybe I can escape from Lur? Or am I special? The only mage who could?"

Oh, of course she was addled. She was noddycocked with grief. Like Charis, she was an orphan, as good as, and every sensible thought in her had washed out with her tears.

*I'm not a real mage. I'm Da's tiddy little mouse. Don't upset little Deenie, don't let her get riled up.*

That's what Da used to say. All her life he'd tried to protect her, especially after that awful time he'd called the warbeasts in his sleep and she'd felt them and woken screaming fit to pull the Tower down around their ears.

After that there'd been possets at bedtime, every night. Soothing herbs that Kerril said would dull her odd mage-senses. They'd tasted horrible and they hardly helped. But she'd never told anyone, in case they gave her possets that tasted worse.

"Oh, but Darran," she said, and rested her cold forehead to his. "Even if I could escape Lur, what then? Do I go traipsing alone through the wild world beyond the mountains? When I don't know what's out there? When I'm not a proper mage?"

Near to tears again, she struggled to stay calm. And then she thought she heard a voice. Darran's voice. Prim and proper, full of acerbic love.

*Your reprobate, ruffianly father was frightened, Deenie. He was so frightened he could hardly spit. And he was angry, you've no idea. He never asked to be the Innocent Mage. He hated everyone who told him that was his fate. But it was his fate and in the end he saved us. Deenie, you're his daughter. Can you do any less?*

Wrenching away from the coffin, she pointed a shaking finger at Darran's marble face. "Don't you say that! Don't you—I don't want to hear that, you—you—you silly ole *trout*!"

*Deenie, you're his daughter. Can you do any less?*

And of course she knew the answer to that . . . and was so frightened by it she could hardly spit.

"All right. *All right!*" she shouted at Darran, at Rafe, at the empty air and Barl and whoever else might be listening. "I'll do it. I'll try. If there's no other way, I'll try."

And there was no other way.

*There's only me. And I'm a mouse. But if I don't do this Lur will die.*

# PART TWO

# CHAPTER NINE

Pother Kerril was waiting at Charis's house.

"Ulys is sent about her duties," she said, looking wan and weary in the light from the parlour window. "And I must return to mine. But first, Deenie, though I know you'll likely shout, we must speak of—"

Deenie raised her hand. "A hospice for Da." It was all she'd been able to think of, walking back from the royal crypt. "Yes, Pother Kerril. I know."

Kerril and Charis stared at her, shocked.

Crossing to the sofa, she sat on the footstool and smoothed Da's untidy hair from his face. Fear and love and grief rose in her, tangled and strangling, so fierce she had to gulp for air.

*Forgive me, Da, but I can't see another way.*

"Deenie?" said Charis. "Are you—"

"I'm fine," she said, blinking away the sting. Of course it wasn't true, and Charis knew it, but what was the point in unpacking her woes? "A little weary, is all."

With a glance at Charis, Pother Kerril crossed to the sofa. "I'm truly sorry about your mother, Deenie. Her loss is a tragedy for all of Lur."

"For Deenie first," said Charis, snappish. "And most."

Kerril nodded. "Of course."

Biting her lip, Deenie looked up. If she didn't do this now her courage might fail. "Da's hospicing, Pother Kerril. How can it be arranged?"

"You're sure, Deenie?" said Kerril, faintly frowning. "Make no mistake, I still think it's for the best, but perhaps you should take a day to be certain. You're shocked, you're grieving, and—"

"I'm grieving, yes," she said, fighting to keep her voice steady, "but that's not why I've changed my mind. With Mama gone, with the Tower gone, where else can Da be safe and cared for? He can't stay here in Charis's house and I can't care for him alone. Not with Dorana in such turmoil." She swallowed. "Everything's changed, and I must change with it."

"You aren't alone, Deenie," Charis protested. "I'll help you. And of course you and Uncle Asher can stay here. Did you think I'd turn you out into the street?"

"No, Charis, of course not," she said quickly. "But it won't work. Da needs proper pothering, and with so many in the city hurt I can't ask Pother Kerril to spare me someone just for him—even if he is the Innocent Mage. Can't you hear him shouting at the notion?"

Charis pulled a face. "Yes. But Deenie . . ."

"Don't," she said, because she was already on the verge of weeping. "I know what I'm doing."

*I hope. Oh, I hope.*

"Deenie, I praise Barl you've made this wise decision," said Pother Kerril, her brisk self again now she had her way. "But I must tell you, there is a difficulty. As you say, we've many injured in the city and to make matters worse Dorana's hospice is damaged. Of course I could find a bed for him but in truth, I hope you'll let me guide you to another choice."

Eyes stinging again, Deenie looked at her unmoving, oblivious father. "You want me to send him out of the city?"

"At least for now," said Kerril. "Until our hospice is repaired and the worst of the injured are recovered."

*Or have died.* She pinned her hands between her knees, letting the small pain distract her. "Where?"

"Billington. I know, I know—" Kerril raised her hands, apologetic. "It's nearly two hours by carriage from Dorana. But it's a good hospice, Deenie, with excellent pothers. And I promise, once your father is settled, if you've a need to be with him then I'm sure something can be arranged."

*Except I won't be here. If I've not drowned myself I'll be lost in the wilderness, chasing after Rafe.*

"I'd like to take him there tomorrow," she said, hoping the pother was too tired to notice her dismay. "Can that be arranged?"

Kerril's eyes widened with surprise, then she nodded. "Yes. Of course. I'll come back in the morning with a letter for the hospice, and a strengthening posset to help your father with the journey. Deenie, you mustn't fret yourself. He will be the better for this, you'll see."

As the front door closed behind the pother, Charis fisted her hands on her hips. "All right, Deenie. What mischief are you brewing?"

Avoiding Charis's stern gaze, Deenie smoothed her father's blankets. He looked so peaceful, no sign of the silent battle he waged. She could almost pretend he was simply asleep.

*Almost.*

"Da needs nourishment, Charis. We should—"

"Kerril brought gruel," Charis said, impatient. "He swallowed some goodly mouthfuls. Now don't you think to fob me off. What's going on?"

She couldn't lie. Not to Charis. "You were right," she said softly. "I have to find Rafel and bring him home."

Charis collapsed into an armchair. "You mean that?"

"Of course I mean it."

"But how?" Charis demanded, and drummed her heels against the floor. "You were right too. There's no way out of this dratted prison of a kingdom."

Shifting round on the footstool, she gave Charis a wry look. "I've thought of a way, but I doubt you'll like it."

"I don't like *any* of this," said Charis, her expression severe. "So what is it, this plan of yours?"

Rising from the footstool, Deenie took a wander about the parlour, hugging her ribs. "I'm going to sail along Lur's coastline to the end of Dragonteeth Reef then slip between it and the cliffs into open waters and keep going past the blighted lands beyond the mountains until—"

"*Deenie!*" Charis was on her feet and staring. "Have you lost your wits entirely? Sail *how?* You said it yourself the other day—every harbour in Lur is ruined. And besides, it's years since you've set foot off dry land!"

Sighing, Deenie perched herself onto the parlour window's deep sill. "Sailing is like riding a horse, Charis. Once you've learned, you don't forget. And Da taught me well." A sweet childhood memory. A slow smile. "He said I was born to it, and it's true. I can feel the water and the wind like I'm a part of them. Like the boat's a part of me."

"That's nice," said Charis, caught between bewilderment and crossness. "But you don't have a boat. You'd have to—" And then she gasped. "*Deenie*. Stealing? You *can't*."

"Charis, I can't *not*," she said. Funny, really, how—now that she'd made up her mind to do this mad thing—all the objections Charis was making, the objections she'd made herself, seemed silly. "Rafe got himself in trouble—they all got in trouble, every expedition—by going over the mountains and trying to cross those poisoned lands beyond them. I won't be poisoned on the water. And sooner or later, if I sail far enough, I'll find a land that won't sicken me."

Charis didn't look convinced. "Maybe so, Deenie, but first you've got to survive Lur's blighted waters. What about the whirlpools and the waterspouts? What are you going to do about them, snap your fingers and make them disappear?"

A tickle of fear, deep in her belly. "No. I'm going to sail my way through them."

"You're cracked," Charis whispered. "Not even your da could do that, Deenie, and he's the greatest Olken mage who ever lived."

"Da's a great mage, it's true," she said, after a heart-thumping silence. "But not even he can feel magic the way I do. All my life I've called it my curse, but I think it might be my gift. I think this might be why I was born the way I am."

"Oh, *Deenie*." Charis shook her head, despairing. "That's wishful thinking."

"Is it? We're not a regular family, Charis," she said. "Mama was born to guard a prophecy and Da was born to fulfil it, the only Olken ever who could wield Doranen magic. And then came Rafe and me, and we ain't regular Olken either. There might not be a prophecy any more, but there's still *us*."

Charis's eyes were huge with trepidation. "No, Deenie. There's just you. You don't have an *us*. Not any more."

For one terrible moment she wanted to smack Charis for saying that. "You're wrong," she said, teeth gritted. "Only Mama's gone. I've still got Da and Rafel and they need me, Charis. They need me not to be a mouse."

Slowly Charis sank back to the armchair. "Rafe's lost beyond the mountains, Deenie! How do you think you're going to find him?"

"The way I always did, when we were spratlings," she said. "Wherever he was I used to find him. Made him ever so fratched, it did, but he'll be glad of it now."

"I don't understand," said Charis, baffled. "You were so sure this couldn't be done. What changed your mind?"

For a moment, just a moment, she did think about lying. But Charis didn't deserve that. "I dreamed him again. In the crypt."

Charis's fingers twisted her plain blue skirt like a dishcloth. "And it wasn't your grief conjuring fancies?"

"*No!*" she said fiercely. "It was Rafe."

"It was Rafe before," said Charis. "When you said he couldn't be helped?"

She couldn't bring herself to tell Charis about hearing ole Darran's voice in the crypt. She still wasn't sure if that part wasn't a grief-born fancy. And she didn't want to talk of saving Lur, either. Saving Rafe was difficult enough.

"Charis, you *wanted* me to do this. And now you've changed your mind? Do you *know* what you want?"

"Of course I do!" Charis leapt to her feet again. "I want Papa alive, I want Lur the way it was, I want Rafel here and asking to wed with me. I want the palace and your Tower standing proud and your parents holding hands. I want to walk out of this house and see Dorana laughing and whole. *I want to wake up.*"

"Well, Charis, that ain't going to happen," she retorted, and was shocked to hear the coldness in her voice. "So I'm going to find a horse and carriage to borrow and in the morning I'll take Da to Billington. And once I've got him settled in the hospice, I'll keep on going to Westwailing."

Charis smudged tears from her cheeks. "Not Restharven?"

"Too risky," she said, pulling a face. "Even though most of the fishing towns and villages have emptied now, there might still be family there. I mustn't be recognised. Anyway, Westwailing's the best harbour and I've a better chance of taking a boat there unnoticed."

"You mean *we'll* have a better chance."

"No, Charis. I'll not risk you. It's too dangerous."

"It can't be any more dangerous than staying here!" Charis snapped. "When any minute the ground could open up and swallow me!"

"Charis—"

"*No*, I said!" Charis insisted, pink with temper. "Deenie, I'm not a noddyhead. This isn't just about Rafe, it's about Lur, too. Well, the last time there was strife your da didn't save Lur on his lonesome. Papa was right there with him. So if you can fight on where your da left off, then so can I!"

Shifting on the windowsill, Deenie stared through the bobbled panes of glass. The afternoon was dying, a cold night coming on. In the back of her mind, a growing turmoil. There'd be another storm before sunrise. More misery for Dorana. Was it ever going to end?

*I'd be a sinking liar if I said I didn't want Charis to come. But if something should happen to her . . .*

142

"You're not the boss of me, Deenie," Charis said, quiet and steady. "And we both know you'll be safer with company."

"We could be gone a long time," she said, still looking out of the window at the tumbled houses across the street. "Likely we'll run into all kinds of trouble."

"I don't care," said Charis. "Deenie, you're the only family I have left. I can't stay behind."

*Oh, Charis, you're just like Mama—a slumskumbledy wench.*

She surrendered. "All right. But can you sit with Da a while? I need to go and find us a horse and—"

"I'll do that," said Charis. "There's folk I can ask, on account of being the mayor's daughter. You sit with your da, while you can."

Vision smeary, Deenie nodded. "Thank you, Charis. Now hurry along. It's going to storm again. You don't want to get caught."

With Charis gone, the house felt enormous and sad. So empty. Returning to the footstool, she took her father's hand and held it tight.

"I wish you'd wake up, Da, and tell me I'm doing the right thing. I wish I could hear you say you believe in me."

Da breathed in and breathed out, and didn't say a word. Deep in his bones, the blight raged on.

"I know I'm a mouse, Da. But I think I can be more. I *have* to be more, for you and Rafe and Lur."

Lost so far inside himself, Da stayed silent.

"I'll come back," she whispered. "I promise. I'll not leave you in that hospice, no matter how kind the pothers be. Da . . ." Gently laying his hand down, she folded herself in half until her cheek rested on him. "I love you. And oh, I miss Mama."

Listening to him breathe, feeling the slow rise and fall of his chest, she slid softly into that twilight place between waking and sleeping where memory danced and sometimes played tricks. Floating to the surface, a memory of recent, painful days. Mama, fuddled with possets and dreaming of secrets . . .

*That sinking diary. More trouble than it's worth. Horrible thing.*

*Full of old Doranen magic. He told me he'd burned it, but he lied.*

Barl's diary.

Drifting, Deenie thought: *I think I might need that. I think Barl's diary might be a good thing to have.*

Startled awake, she sat up and stared at her father. Certainty hummed and buzzed in her bones.

"Barl's diary, Da. Is that why you kept it? Did you know Lur would have need of it, one day?"

Da said nothing.

She leaned close. "I'll wager you did," she whispered. "And you were right. Da, where did you hide it?"

He loved her, but he didn't answer. He was too far away.

"Oh, Da." She rested her forehead on his slowly moving chest. *"Please."*

Where would he hide a thing like Barl's diary? Not in the Tower, surely. Too many people had wandered in and out of it over the years — and in the Tower, Mama might have discovered it. Or Rafe, being sneaky about his magic. He'd magicked his way into Da's locked trunk of spell books, hadn't he? As she tried to think where her father might've hidden something so dangerous, so precious, her fingers rubbed at the sore place on her hip where she'd banged it against the dislodged lid of King Gar's coffin.

The small pain prompted a wild, bursting thought.

*Why was that lid dislodged? Why would anyone need to open that coffin?*

With a gasp she sat up. "Really, Da? *Really?* You hid it *there*?"

But wouldn't that be just like him, to hide Barl's diary in his best friend's coffin? In the royal crypt that saw hardly a living soul? Wasn't that just like him to give the poor king one last important job to do, for Lur?

*Oh, Da. You clever man.*

When Charis finally returned, cock-a-hoop 'cause she'd found them a horse and carriage and arranged for it to be brought to the house first thing in the morning, Deenie used the excuse of needing to fetch the clothes she'd tossed from the Tower, and left her friend to sit with Da.

Reaching the palace grounds unchallenged, so preoccupied she'd hardly noticed the ruined city, she hurried past the deserted, collapsed palace and on to the crypt. First thing she did was brush her fingertips along the edge of Queen Dana's coffin.

"Don't be cross, Mama. You had to do difficult things when you were Jervale's Heir. Well, I'm *your* heir. And I have to do this."

With that said, she turned to King Gar's coffin and stared into his young, peaceful stone face.

"I'm sorry. I wouldn't disturb you if it wasn't important."

She'd never tried using a Doranen compulsion spell before, but she'd seen Rafe do one. The memory had stuck.

*Please, Barl, let it work. Don't let my Doranen magic fail me this time.*

Barl must've been listening. The heavy stone coffin lid jerked sideways, grinding. She only just managed to stop it crashing to the crypt floor. Beckoning her conjured glimfire closer, palms sweaty, she looked into the coffin, at the wrapped body it contained.

*Don't think about it being a person. Don't think of it as Da's dear friend.*

Straightaway she saw the diary, a small leather-bound volume, tucked between the dead king's arm and his side. Snatching it out of the coffin, she took a moment to swiftly leaf through it and felt a sting of dismay as she saw it was written in ancient Doranen. But then she found the scrawled notes tucked between some of the pages, the writing faded and unfamiliar but readable. Praise Barl for small mercies. Someone had managed to translate at least part of it.

Conscious of the time, she slid the journal into her coat pocket. Though it was awful, really, she couldn't help a surge of triumph. *I found it. I found it.* Because this was how well she knew her father. And if she knew him *this* well . . .

*Then I know I'm right about the rest, too. He is still inside himself, fighting. He hasn't given up—and neither will I.*

\*    \*    \*

She and Charis and Da left for Billington the next morning, after breakfast, with the tail-end of the night's storm still washing the rubbled streets with rain. The carriage was packed with her satchel of trins and cuicks, and her haversack full of clothes and a knife and some fishing line with hooks and the diary stitched tight in a double layer of oilskin, a secret for now, and Charis's haversack of clothes, and her own knife, and a little food for the journey. They'd buy more vittles as they travelled the rest of the way to the coast, not wanting to rouse questions in Dorana or take from the city. Food was dribbling in from the Home Districts but supplies still weren't plentiful.

"Barl's blessings be with you," said Pother Kerril, standing on the uneven pavement outside Charis's house. "Travel safely."

With the reins in her gloved hands, Charis beside her on the carriage's driving seat and Da tucked cosy inside, Deenie looked down at the pother, suddenly speechless.

*Will I see her again? I might not. Anything could happen.*

"Thank you, Pother Kerril," she said, managing a smile. "For all your help and guidance and your good care of Da."

Then, with a click of her tongue and a shake of the reins, she roused the sturdy carriage horse Charis had borrowed and guided it along the quiet residential street, heading for the main thoroughfare leading out of the city. A few folk were out and about, but nobody paid them any mind. They had too many troubles of their own to chew on.

"There's still time to change your mind, you know," she said to Charis, as the city's open gates loomed before them. "I'll not think any less of you."

Charis squirmed round on the driving seat to look at poor, broken Dorana City. "Of course it's too late," she said, almost under her breath. "It's always been too late, hasn't it? From the day Barl led the Doranen over the mountains, it's always been too late for Lur."

Deenie nodded, full of sorrow. "I know."

"Everything's falling apart so fast," said Charis. "D'you think there'll be anything left by the time we come back?"

"I wish I knew," she said, and took one hand off the reins to clasp Charis's arm, briefly. "Best we don't think on that."

"No," Charis whispered. "Best we don't."

And with nothing else to say, they settled into the long drive to Billington.

They passed a few fellow travellers on the main city road, some in carriages, some on horseback. Clip-clopping through the Home Districts they saw storm damage and signs of tremor, but both lessened as they took slantwise Fimble Way which would lead them, eventually, to their distant destination.

The horse Charis had found for them was dependable, not flashy, so it took them nearly three hours to reach the hospice that would be Da's home. Billington was a sleepy place, the town centre for a sheep district. The pothers and Barlspeakers at the hospice greeted them cautiously at first, but after learning who was in the carriage, and reading Pother Kerril's letter, they became quite excited and talked of "honour" and "welcome duty". Eager hands laid sleeping Da on a stretcher and rushed him into the long, low hospice building. Deenie offered to leave coin for his keeping but Brye, the senior pother, shook his head as though she'd said something dreadful.

He was a tall, stooped man whose blond Doranen hair was thinning. "You're a good daughter," he said. "But we've no need of your coin. And you've no need to worry, Deenie. We'll follow Pother Kerril's instructions exactly. And we'll not breathe a word that your father is here." His mouth turned down. "She has also written of your dear mother. I'm so sorry."

His sympathy stung her to tears. Mama's death was another thing it was best not to think on. She wept too easily now. She needed to be strong. "Thank you."

"Now, child," he added, "do you stay with us as we care for your father?"

"I'd like to, but I have some duties first," she said, hoping he couldn't read the prevarication in her eyes. "But I would like to come back and be with him, if I may."

Pother Brye smiled. "Of course you may. You're the Innocent Mage's daughter. Our doors are never closed to you."

Leaving Charis to mind the horse and carriage, she went inside the hospice to bid her father farewell. The pothers had dressed him in a clean nightshirt and settled him into a private chamber, sweet with fresh flowers and a window open to the country air. It was so peaceful. The misery and destruction of Dorana felt far, far away.

Bending over his narrow bed, Deenie kissed his forehead. "I have to go now, Da," she whispered. "But I'll be back, and I'll bring Rafe with me. I promise. So don't you go anywhere, you hear me? Da?"

He didn't answer. She kissed him again and walked away, before her courage failed her and she couldn't leave him, not even for Rafel or Lur.

Climbing back onto the carriage's driving seat, she took the reins and pulled a face. "Ready?"

Charis's cheeks were pale but her eyes were determined. "Ready."

Shaking the reins, urging the horse to get a move on, she bumped shoulders with Charis. "I'm glad you bullied your way into coming. I don't think I'd be brave enough to do this on my own."

"You're brave enough," said Charis. "You may be a mouse at heart, but you're a fierce mouse, Deenie."

For some strange reason, that made her laugh. Even as her heart broke, as she tried not to think of Da being cared for by strangers, of Mama alone and sharing a stranger's coffin, she turned the horse and carriage onto the road out of Billington, still laughing.

"What's so funny?" Charis demanded. "Are you laughing at me?"

Sobering, Deenie shook her head. "No, of course not. I don't know why I'm laughing. Maybe it's 'cause you're right, and I'm mad."

*Mad to think I can defeat the whirlpools and the waterspouts. Mad to think I can sail a boat so far. Mad to think I can find my lost brother.*

"Well, if you're mad, then so am I," said Charis. "And that's the last time we'll say it. Agreed?"

"Agreed," she said, and stirred the horse into a jog.

Three weeks and five days it took them to reach Westwailing. They didn't dare push harder or faster, because it wasn't their horse and the poor thing was doing the best it could, considering, and there wasn't enough coin in the satchel to stuff the animal full of oats. Not when they had to buy food for themselves, enough to last them to Westwailing and beyond.

That was the biggest worry—storing enough food to keep them alive as they made their way along Lur's coastline to the end of the reef and out into open water. Always assuming they managed to get even that far. They didn't talk about that, but Deenie knew Charis fretted. *She* fretted. She tried to seem confident but inside she was sick with doubt and fear.

But they'd come too far to turn back now.

The sun had slid almost to the horizon when they finally reached Lur's biggest fishing township. Slowing the carriage on the headland road that would in roundabout fashion take them down to the pier, they stared at turbulent Westwailing Harbour and the whirlpools and waterspouts that had swallowed it alive.

Deenie shivered. Even this far away she could feel the churning, vicious blight. It woke her mage-sense to shrieking, so that pain like fireworks burst behind her eyes.

"Oh, Deenie," Charis whispered. "You told me what it was like, but it's—it's—"

With an effort she kept the awful nausea at bay. "It's much worse seeing it for yourself," she said. "I know."

In chilled silence they watched the capricious magic-born waterspouts whip up, whip up, then collapse in foam and spray only to whip up again somewhere else, twice as large.

"What about the whirlpools?" said Charis, her voice croaky with fright. "Are they constant or do they shift about too? Because if they shift about, Deenie . . ."

This far from the water she could count seven—no, eight—whirlpools. There might be more, smaller ones. These eight were as large as the one that had swallowed Arlin Garrick's father and the other mages and helped to wreck that fishing smack on the reef, killing all those good Olken men.

"I don't know," she said, shrugging. "I think they stay where they start. But it makes no difference, Charis. Either way I have to dance with them and the waterspouts all along the coastline to the end of the reef."

"So far," said Charis, faltering. "Deenie . . ."

"I can do it," she said, as the reef's blight, Morg's twisted mage-work, curdled through her blood. "I have to."

Leaning sideways, Charis stared down at the township. "I can see a few people wandering about. The place isn't entirely deserted."

Maybe not, but it felt that way. Remembering how it had bustled the last time she and her family had come here, how busy and cheerful it was, when she'd been a child, she felt clogged with fresh sorrow.

*All ruined now, because Arlin Garrick's father and that horrible Fernel Pintte wouldn't pay attention to Da.*

"Look," she said, pointing. "Boats, moored at the pier. They haven't all been sunk or pulled to bits for firewood."

Charis looked at her. "You thought they would be?"

"I thought they might," she admitted.

"Now you tell me!" said Charis, crossly. Then she sighed. "Deenie, are you sure we have to steal one? Couldn't we find one you like and pay for it?"

They'd already discussed this, and more than once. "Charis . . ."

"And the horse and carriage," Charis said, nearly wailing. "However will I look Meister Barett in the face again after promising to return them? He must be frantic by now, and cursing me."

"You can always drive back to Dorana, Charis. I can go on my own."

"Oh, don't be a noddyhead," Charis muttered. "You know I won't leave you."

"Well, then."

Waking the tired horse with a shake of the reins, Deenie guided the carriage down the sloping cobbled street into Westwailing. Its emptiness was eerie, and so melancholy she could have wept. Two old men sat on upturned barrels in front of a boarded-up alehouse. They stared at her with surprised, rheumy eyes as she halted the carriage beside them and leaned down.

"Good meisters, my sister and I need a place to stay for the night. Can you tell me if there's an inn that could take us?"

The old men, fishermen it looked like, with their seamed faces and scarred, gnarled hands and the oiled wool coats and stout boots keeping them warm and dry, looked at each other, then back at her.

"The Mermaid's got beds," one of the men told her, his voice crackling with age. "It be the only inn we got left. Even the Dolphin shut its doors. Hiram walked away, like most everyone else." He sniffed. "Westwailing's a dead town these days, near as."

She wouldn't have stayed at the Dolphin anyway, on the chance she'd be recognised. But even so, she was sorry. Westwailing's slow dying made her sad. And the harbour . . . the blighted harbour . . .

*How will I stand it, when it makes me this sick and I ain't even got my feet wet?*

She didn't know. She'd just have to.

"The Mermaid?" she said, memory stirring. "That's further along this street, isn't it? Not far from the pier?"

"Been here afore have you, lass?" said the other fisherman. "Don't recall your pretty face, or your sister's."

"Not for many years," said Deenie. "Our thanks, good meisters."

The Mermaid's innkeeper greeted them with cautious curiosity. Deenie spun him the tale she and Charis had dreamed up on the road, how they were come down to the coast to find what was left of their family and tell them how their mother had perished further up north in a storm. Satisfied with that, he showed them to a room with two beds and called for a lad to stable the horse, house the carriage and bring in the young meistresses' belongings.

"Don't bother," Deenie said quickly, thinking of their sacks full of food. "We don't have much. We'll fetch them."

With the innkeeper paid and the day's light fast fading, they wandered down to the waterfront to see up close what boats they had to choose from for stealing. The few townsfolk they came across stared as though two strangers were the oddest thing they'd ever seen. And these dire days, doubtless they were.

Leaning against the stone harbour wall, feeling the blighted magic burn in her blood, watching the waterspouts rise and dance and die, Deenie breathed in the sharp salt air and sighed it out, gustily.

*If only I could breathe out this mage-pain as easily.*

"When I think of the stories ole Darran told me and Rafel, about the Sea Harvest Festival, it makes me so sad," she said. "Westwailing used to be such a grand place. Out there—" She pointed across the harbour. "That's where Da saved Prince Gar from drowning. The day of the terrible storm, when King Borne was so ill."

Charis sighed too. "It doesn't seem real, does it? Those days seem like something out of a book."

They did. A book with tattered pages now, thrown aside and forgotten.

And then she shook herself, because moping on the past wouldn't help them. Instead she shifted her gaze to the scattering of smacks and skiffs and runabouts tethered along the pier.

"Deenie?" Charis sounded nervous, of a sudden. "Are you sure you can sail one of those? They look awful big."

"The smacks are big," she said. "We can't take a smack. And the runabouts are too small for the open water past the reef. We'll have to take a skiff."

"A skiff? Which one's a skiff? They all look like boats to me."

Narrowing her eyes, Deenie looked at each rising and falling vessel, stirred at anchor by the endlessly restless water. For Charis's sake she was trying to sound confident, but her heart was beating hard and sweat dribbled down her spine.

*I can't do this. I can't sail a boat beyond the reef and up the unknown coastline for days and days. Look at those waterspouts. I'll never sail around them. I'll never be able to keep us out of those whirlpools.*

Not when the magic made her feel so poorly she could retch.

*But I have to.*

"Deenie?" said Charis. "What's amiss? Can't you tell which ones are skiffs?"

If Charis had forgotten how Westwailing had made her sick last time, she wasn't about to do any reminding. "Course I can," she muttered. "Now let's go back to the Mermaid. We need to pack everything good and tight and put our heads down early. It's not going to be restful, you know, sleeping on a boat. Especially if it starts raining or a storm blows in."

*And both are likely. Oh, Da. This ain't going to be much fun.*

But Charis didn't step away from the stone harbour wall. Instead she leaned over it, her bleak gaze reaching across the seething, surging, magic-poisoned water.

"He's out there, Deenie," she said, her voice fierce. "Rafel. And you and me, we're going to find him, and we're going to save him, and we're going to bring him back to Lur. Tell me you believe it. Tell me you know that in your bones."

*I want to believe it, Charis.*

But wanting didn't count. Not here and now. Not faced with this terrible thing they'd come so far to do.

*Not when Charis is risking her life on my say-so.*

"I believe it," she said solemnly. "Now come on inside. It's getting dark, and I'm cold.'

# CHAPTER TEN

✠

Charis woke before just before dawn. Months and months of caring for her dying father had honed that one small skill, being able to wake at the time she was needed. Lying in the darkness, she rolled her head on the inn's miserly thin pillow.

"Deenie?"

A faint rustling of bedclothes. "I'm awake."

Of course she was. Had she managed any proper sleep? Most likely not. The harbour and its horrible magics churned her so poorly.

*She thinks I don't see it. She thinks I don't remember what happened to her the last time she was down here, when Rafe—*

Her breath caught. Just thinking his name was hurtful. Ever since the day he rode off to cross the mountains with that horrible Arlin Garrick and those stupid councillors, every day since had been a day lived in pain. Loving him. Losing him. Fearing she'd never see him again.

*But I will. I'll not give up on him. I can't.*

"Charis . . ."

She knew what Deenie was going to say. She almost always knew what Deenie was going to say. Friends their whole lives, close as blood, she could read Rafel's sister like a recipe card—even when she had trouble understanding her, what it was like to *be* her.

And that was most of the time, really.

"No, Deenie," she said, but didn't bite, because her friend was feeling poorly, sick with worry on her account. "I'm not changing my mind."

"I know," said Deenie, her voice small in the darkness. "Only I thought I should ask. Just so I did."

They were all set to leave. Last night, after their stodgy hot meal of rabbit stew that Deenie hardly touched, they'd repacked their one haversack each, shoving their sharp knives and fishing lines and all the clothes they might need tightly inside. For wearing, Deenie had left out leather trews and a leather jerkin and a wool shirt and a leather coat, *not* the kind of clothes a good Olken lass would usually parade about in. She had nothing like that for herself, but she did have a pair of thick woollen hose and Papa's old Guard jacket. Deenie had told her to bring both, saying a boat on open water was no place for frills and skirts.

"But I *like* frills and skirts," she'd argued, because only boys wore *hose*. And Deenie had looked at her, lips tight, not a mouse at all, so she'd given in and packed them.

As for their food, it was safe in the carriage for collecting on the way to the harbour. Not that any regular person would call it *food*. More like teeth-breaking rotgut, it was. Hard-tack biscuits and strips of dried beef. Horrible. Only the nuts were truly edible. They had water, too. On the road to Westwailing they'd filled a score of waterskins bought here and there along the way, and packed them into a hessian sack. They'd have to be pinchy but their supplies should last.

*And if they don't we'll have to try our hand at fishing, and eat our catch raw. Or take our chances in the first bit of land we can find, mage-poisoned or not.*

It was thoughts like that that made her wince and wonder what Papa would say if he knew what she was planning.

Another rustling sound as Deenie threw back her blankets. "If we're going to go, we'd best go," she whispered. "At first light we want to be pushing away from the pier. We don't want to be seen loitering."

No, they surely didn't. She couldn't believe she was about to steal a boat, or that she'd *already* stolen a horse and carriage. As good as. And her father Captain of the City Guard *and* a mayor.

*Honestly, Papa, whoever would've thought the Innocent Mage's daughter would be such a bad influence?*

"What?" said Deenie. A clunking sound as she groped for the chamberpot under her bed. "What's so funny?"

She swallowed the rest of her breathy chuckles because really, none of this was funny. Especially not the horrible chamberpots.

"Nothing," she said, and quickly used her own pot.

That done, she waited for Deenie to conjure the teeniest, tiniest ball of glimfire, not much bigger than a glowbug, so they wouldn't crack heads as they dressed and found their haversacks. On with a linen shirt and the ugly woollen hose and thick woollen socks and a wool jerkin and Papa's Guard coat. Oh, she didn't mind wearing that. Wearing that was like having him with her on this mad, grand adventure. Then she laced on the stout boots Deenie had given her because she had no stout boots of her own. A blessing they could fit into each other's shoes. Last of all she pulled on her best leather gloves.

"Done?" said Deenie, dashing in her leathers. On her pillow she'd left the remaining trins and cuicks and the letter she wrote last night, asking the coins be used to send the horse and carriage back to Meister Barett in Dorana City. If the innkeeper didn't do it, well, the shame of that was on him, not them, said Deenie. Trying to convince herself as much as anyone.

She nodded. "Done."

So they hefted their haversacks onto their shoulders and by the tiny light of their glowbug glimfire tiptoed, hardly breathing, down the Mermaid's uneven staircase, through its side door—the front door had a bell on it—and round the back to where the carriage was housed.

Oh, Deenie had planned everything. For a mouse she had a surprising imagination. The sacks of food and water they'd tied with rope, leaving a loop free. The loops they threaded onto a thick wooden pole bought in a village called Trimtop, and they balanced one end of it each on their shoulders, walking single file. The weight was horrible, the pole digging in despite their clothes, but that didn't matter. What mattered was they'd not roused anyone, making their escape.

Westwailing slumbered as they made their way to the pier, so quiet they could hear the sibilant roar of the harbour's whirlpools and the higher-pitched thrumming hum of the 'spouts, the crashing splash as they fell apart and throaty roar as they were reborn. Unlike the township, they never slumbered. They were relentless and immortal like the magic that had spawned them.

"We'd best hurry," said Deenie softly, a note of strain in her voice. "The weather's going to change."

She felt a flutter of alarm. "A storm, you mean?"

"Could be."

*Oh.* Charis frowned at Deenie's back. She doubted she'd ever get used to it, the way her friend could feel the weather and Doranen magic and find Rafel on account of his power. Next to what Deenie could do, her own Olken magic was feeble.

*She's right about one thing. Her family's not regular. And I suppose I'm to be grateful for that. I suppose.*

The dregs of darkness were lifting, a greyish sheen glossing the sky. The pier was close now, the harbour's salt smell stronger, the sound of restless waves slapping against the ancient stone and the boats' wooden hulls louder and more urgent.

But even so she heard the sharp intake of Deenie's breath, and felt through the wooden pole connecting them the way her friend braced herself against the twisted magics in Dragonteeth Reef.

"Deenie," she said, keeping her voice down even though they were the only souls stirring. "Are you sure you're strong enough for this? If it's bad now, how bad will it be once we're out on the water?"

They'd almost reached the entrance to the pier. Deenie kept walking but turned her face, just a little bit. "I'll be fine."

She snorted. "You say that, but I'm not blind, Deenie. You talk of the lands beyond the mountains being poisoned, but you're poisoned too, aren't you? You feel sick and it's getting worse, not better."

"Charis, this is how it works," Deenie said, sighing. "This is how I'll get us safely through the waterspouts and the whirlpools, to the

157

end of the reef and past it. By feeling them. By them making me sick. It's how I know where they are and where they'll be."

"Yes, I *know* that's how," she retorted. "And I know you'll let them hurt you so we can escape Lur. But what will that cost you?"

"What's the matter, Charis? Are you frighted I can't pay the price? I promise I can."

Oh, *Deenie*. "Yes, but for how long? Days and days you said it would likely take us to sail up the coast and break our way past the reef. Can you be in pain like this for so long? Without any relief, having to think every moment about the next waterspout? The next whirlpool? *And* sail the boat while you're about it?"

Deenie managed an awkward, one-shouldered shrug. "I'll have to, won't I?"

She nearly let her own end of the burdened pole drop, she felt so cross of a sudden. "Deenie. Don't make light of this. We'll be no good to Rafel at the bottom of the harbour."

"And we'll be no good to him standing on the pier fratching, either," said Deenie. "Charis, if you don't want to come, then don't. I said all along you don't have to."

"You said you were glad I was coming!"

"I am. But you don't have to."

Charis pinched her lips shut. In his last few weeks Papa had relented of his stubborn tongue-holding and told her stories of Dorana's days gone by. Before that, just like Deenie and Rafel's da, he'd not liked to talk of the past. But then, as though he was of a sudden fretted that his time was running out, he'd sat her down beside his bed and held her hand and reminisced. Some of his memories had brought tears to his eyes, but a lot had made him laugh, even through the sadness.

Mostly those laughing tales were of Asher, the Innocent Mage. They'd made her laugh too. How the first time Papa and Asher met, the fisherman leapt onto the official Guardhouse table and scolded the Guildmeisters like they were a gaggle of naughty boys. How he'd talked back to the likes of Conroyd Jarralt, never once letting the hoity-toity Doranen lord browbeat him. How he'd won the King's Cup, the first

Olken ever to take that trophy. How he'd befriended Prince Gar. Saved his life. Stood for him when the king and queen died and made sure he wasn't bullied.

"He's the bravest man I ever knew," Papa had told her, his voice close to failing. So close to leaving her. "Morg tormented him. Dorana turned on him. I abandoned him when he needed me most. And he forgave me. He forgave Dorana. He was ready to die to save the rest of us from Morg. No better man ever drew breath in this kingdom, Charis. No better man. It's a blessing he was my friend."

Staring now at Deenie's stubborn back, as the sky overhead grew steadily paler, Charis felt her eyes sting. That was her friend's father Papa had loved so much. And Papa never could forgive himself for not believing in him until it was almost too late.

*Papa laughed at how stubborn he was. How he'd dig in his heels and say: This is me and I ain't changin'. And isn't that just like Deenie? Isn't she her father's daughter? And aren't I mine?*

Yes, she was.

"Deenie, I'm just asking," she said, as they staggered down the stone steps leading onto the pier. "I fret you might think you're stronger than you are."

"Well, I *don't*," snapped Deenie. "I know how strong I am, Charis Orrick. I'm strong enough to do this—with you *or* without you!"

And now she'd gone and made things worse.

*I never thought she minded that much, being called a mouse.*

"With me," she said meekly. "I'm not turning back."

"Fine, then," said Deenie. "Now hush up. I need to think."

There was enough light in the sky by now that they didn't need their little glowbug glimfire, so Deenie winked it out. Much more light and they'd likely be in trouble, get themselves spotted by someone wandering along the harbour road. She veered left across the pier so she could look at the first tethered skiff.

"No good," she said. "We want oars, just in case."

Oars? *Oars?* Did that mean they'd be *rowing*?

Deenie didn't like the second skiff, either. The third one had oars but she said its mast was spindly and three boards were waterlogged. That didn't bode well. There were only two skiffs left. The rest of Westwailing's boats were runabouts and smacks. Charis felt a little proud of herself that she could remember the difference.

"This one's got a spindly mast too," said Deenie, glowering at the last skiff. "But its oars are better and there's not a waterlogged board to be seen. And that's a spare sail, and a coil of rope, and a good solid bit of canvas, folded there. That'll come in handy for shelter. We'll take this one, Charis."

Just like that.

It was a horrible fiddly business, climbing down into the little boat. Though Deenie had sworn the waterspouts and whirlpools almost never sprang up this close to shore, Charis could feel the tightness of fear in her spray-slicked face, and sweat under her bulky clothes. It was a cold autumn morning but she was uncomfortably hot.

She knocked her knees and her ankles and her elbows on the side of the pier, and held her breath convinced she'd tumble straight into the water. There was meant to be a gangplank, Deenie said, but it was long gone. So she grunted and wriggled and trickled her way over the pier's rough stone edge, down, down, down to the skiff.

*I'd rather be in my kitchen, cooking.*

The moment her feet touched the skiff's floorboards the boat began to rock madly, and the horizon danced as though someone had it on a string. Swallowing a squeal of alarm she flailed her arms for balance. If she fell over the side now, well, that would be that.

Barl be praised, she stayed upright and out of the water.

With a small, encouraging smile Deenie handed down their haversacks and the hessian bags of food and water. Next she handed down the wooden pole, 'cause you never knew when that might come in useful, and last of all she unhooked the mooring chain and lowered herself into their chosen boat, landing lightly as thistledown.

*I mustn't be jealous.*

They took a moment to stow their supplies under the folded canvas at the end of the boat. *Aft*, Deenie called it. But it was also the *stern*.

And the front end was the *bow*. But if you went there, you were going *for'ard*. The steering bit was the *tiller*. There was a low wooden bench stretched side to side and that, said Deenie, was the rower's bench at *midships*.

Charis sat on it, grateful.

The spindly mast had a sail attached, but Deenie shook her head. "We need to row from the pier."

Oh. So there *was* rowing. Charis sighed. "I'm going to get blisters, aren't I? Even with gloves."

"Prob'ly," said Deenie, shrugging again. "Never mind. You'll live."

There were so *many* things she could say to that, but she bit her tongue. Deenie's salty-wet face was pale and her lips were thinned. Unpleasant shadows smeared beneath her dark brown eyes. Her father's eyes. Deenie looked a lot like him.

She watched as Deenie put the oars into their slots on each side of the skiff. *Rowlocks*, Deenie called them. As if knowing what they were called would make the oars any easier to use.

By now there was enough light to see waterspouts dancing in the distance. Light enough to see an ominous band of dark cloud swiftly building. A storm was coming in, just like Deenie had foretold.

"Right," said Deenie. "So we've got to row until we're a goodly distance off the pier, then I can get the sail up and we can fiddle ourselves away from Westwailing. But Charis—"

"It won't be easy," she said. "I can tell that, Deenie."

"It's not a big skiff, as skiffs go, but it was meant to be rowed by brawny fishermen," said Deenie, pulling a face. "We're going to crack our muscles and our backs afore we're done, I reckon."

Charis heaved another sigh. "I don't suppose you can fiddle the water, can you? Make a wave to help the boat along? You know, like Rafe did?"

"No, I can't do that water trick," said Deenie. She almost sounded cross. "I don't know how Rafe managed it. He always could. When he was a sprat he played magic in his bath. But when I tried, nothing happened." She pointed to the right-hand oar. "That one's yours. Wriggle over and brace your feet against the blocks there. The most important thing is that we pull together, as hard as each other. If we pull out of time all we'll do is row ourselves in a circle."

"I don't even know if I've *got* any strength," she said, under her breath.

Deenie pretended not to hear that.

When they were both settled on the rower's bench, the oars gripped tight in their hands, Deenie nodded. "On three, Charis. One—two—*three*—"

And oh, Barl's tits. With one pull she'd swear she'd snapped her spine in two.

"Again!" said Deenie. "Come on, Charis, pull again."

So she pulled again, and thought her eyes might pop right out of their sockets. Was the skiff even moving? She couldn't tell. She couldn't feel it. She heard the wet salt air rasping like sobs in her throat and chest. She felt a burning in the muscles of her arms and shoulders, her back, her legs. Her heart was pounding, sweat pouring down her spine.

"Good, good, keep on pulling!" said Deenie. "Only don't dig the oar in the water. Let it settle in and scoop and glide."

"Deenie, I hate you," she croaked, her popping eyes burned with sweat and tears. "I'll never forgive you this."

"Yes, you will," said Deenie, close to giggling. "Pull. Stay with me. Come on, Charis. *Pull.*"

So she pulled and she pulled and she scooped the oar, she didn't dig it. The skiff was moving, carving a slow passage through the water. Her tightly braided hair began to loosen and tug.

"At least there's a good breeze up," said Deenie, panting. "We'll have some speed behind us once I can raise the sail."

"How soon?" Her body was screaming at her. "Deenie, how soon?"

Sweat dripped off Deenie's chin. "Not yet. We've hardly moved at all."

From the corner of her eye she saw a twisting column of water, dark green and whipped white. "*Deenie!*"

"Don't fratch on it," said Deenie, impatient. "It won't come near us."

"How do you know?" she squealed, nearly letting go of her oar. "Deenie, it's heading this—"

"No, it ain't! Charis, either you trust me or you don't!"

"Sorry, sorry," she muttered, and hunched low over her oar. Closed her eyes so she wouldn't see the towering waterspout.

It collapsed in a distant gouting spume with an echoing whoosh. The breeze-driven spray splattered over her face.

"Charis," said Deenie, staring, "I mean it. You've got to trust me."

"I do. I swear I do."

"Then *trust* me — and *row!*"

Teeth gritted, chest heaving, the blood scalding through her veins, Charis rowed in time with Deenie and the skiff with great reluctance drew further and further away from the pier.

Whipped almost to shreds on the rising wind, a shout. Then another. Their theft had been seen.

"Don't look back," said Deenie, grimly. "They'll not come after us. They're all frighted of the harbour now."

"With good reason," she retorted. "Deenie, we're mad."

"Never mind about that," said Deenie. She was breathing hard too, even though she knew what she was doing. "Scoot over a bit and take my oar, Charis. Do your best to keep us steady while I set the sail."

Charis stared at her, aghast. "Deenie, I can't!"

"Take it!" Deenie snapped, nothing mouseish about her now. "We've got to use this wind while we can. There's no saying how long it'll last or if we'll end up becalmed."

More shouting, even fainter. She stifled a yelp. "Are you sure they'll not chase us down?"

Deenie glanced behind them. "It's one man and a boy and they're waving their arms at the end of the pier. They might as well be windmills. Or scarecrows. Charis, please —"

She scrunched herself to the middle of the bench and took Deenie's oar. The weight and drag of both lengths of timber caught her scalded blood on fire. Deenie scrambled about doing mysterious things with the mast and the sail, muttering under her breath. Not daring to look at the harbour, Charis kept her head down and struggled to keep hold of both oars, to keep their little boat steady. Sweaty inside her gloves, her hands ached and stung abominably, up her wrists, into her elbows and then to her shoulders.

"Nearly done—nearly done—" Deenie gasped. "Hold on, Charis. Nearly—*there!*"

With a snap and a flap the hoisted sail bellied with wind. Yelping, Deenie leapt aft, right over the rower's bench, and reached for the tiller as the skiff bounced and swung about like a fractious horse. Charis felt her belly heave, bile rushing up her throat.

"Hold the oars!" Deenie shouted. "Hold 'em tight, Charis!"

"I'm holding, I'm holding!" she shouted back. "But I can't hold 'em for long."

Cursing with words no nice young lady ought to know, Deenie wrestled with the dancing skiff.

"Right," she said, after a moment. Her breath was coming in short, harsh rasps. "I've lashed the tiller. It'll hold course on its own while we get sorted. Give me an oar."

Charis gave her one, gladly. "Now what?"

"Now we ship the oars," said Deenie, sounding more cheerful than she had any right to be. "And we let the wind do the work for a while. How does that sound?"

It sounded wonderful. With Deenie's help she *shipped her oar* then collapsed over her knees on the rower's bench while Deenie shipped her own. There wasn't a muscle or bone in her whole body that wasn't hurting.

"Poor Charis," said Deenie, returning aft to unlash the tiller. "I'm sorry I shouted."

Groaning, she sat up and cracked open her salt-stung eyes. "You should be. My arms feel like chewed string, Deenie."

"You could make yourself comfy on the floorboards, if you like," said Deenie, her eyes apologetic. She was sat on a box with the tiller's long handle in her hand, nudging it this way then that, a little bit each time. "I'll sail us for a while. You could even sleep a bit, maybe."

"*Sleep?*" She stared at her mad friend, Rafel's sister, then pointed over the side of the skiff at the three waterspouts writhing altogether too close to them. "How can I *sleep* with those horrible things right there?"

Deenie closed her eyes. Breathed in slowly, and out again. "No, we're safe from them," she murmured. "They'll not trouble us."

And a moment later two of the three waterspouts collapsed into spume, slapping the harbour's surface like big wet hands. The third one spun tighter and faster, growing thin, then thinner still, until it snapped like an overspun spindle of wool.

"See?" said Deenie, opening her eyes. She was trying to sound jaunty, but she couldn't quite mask her pain. "Charis, really, you should rest a bit. I need to think about what I'm doing."

In other words: *Charis, hold your tongue.*

So she did as she was told and made herself a little nest between the canvas and the rower's bench, using their haversacks as pillows to save her from the worst of the bumps. Westwailing's pier was a shadowy stroke on the water, the township dwindled to silence and roofs, falling fast behind them as Deenie swung their stolen skiff in a wide arc to the right, following along Lur's wriggly, southernmost coastline. Not so close to land that they'd be driven accidentally to ground, but making sure to keep them far away from the magic-poisoned reef.

The wind began to pick up strength. Uneasy, Charis realised there wasn't a real sunrise, just a murkish brightening. She glanced at the pewtery sky, where a bank of dark clouds was ominously growing. Deenie was right. There was going to be a storm. And they were so exposed out here. If it rained hard, or the storm threw down hail, there was nowhere to hide. Four new writhing waterspouts flailed across the harbour's choppy, foam-flecked surface. Filled with fresh fear she looked at Deenie, but her friend's milky-pale face was oddly serene. Even though, there was a pinch-line between her straight dark eyebrows and the corners of her mouth were turned down and tucked in tight. The pain of the harbour's blighted magic was growing stronger in her the longer they stayed on the water.

*And there's nothing I can do about that.*

Nothing except sit quietly, and not distract her, and let her be who she was, the Innocent Mage's strange daughter. Only . . .

"Deenie," she said. "I've seen waterspouts, but no whirlpools. Where—"

"Up ahead," said Deenie, her voice tight. "A clutch of 'em. We'll—"

"A *clutch*?" Lurching onto her knees, she grabbed at the skiff's side, waking her own aches and pains from all that rowing. "How many is a *clutch*?"

"Too many. Five. Six, maybe. They're running in a ragged line out to the reef."

"How long have you known?"

"Since we swung aside from the harbour."

"And you didn't *say*?"

"I was going to."

Of course she was. "Well—well—sail around them, Deenie! Get us closer to the coast!"

"Oh, yes, Captain Orrick? Like a turn at the tiller, would you?"

"No," she said, scowling. "But—"

"Charis, here's the thing," said Deenie, nudging their skiff a whisker rightwards. "There's a waterspout wanting to roar up 'tween us and the shoreline. If I shift us too far over then it might whip us to splinters. I've got to hold this course a while longer."

"Towards the *whirlpools*? Deenie—"

"Yes, towards the whirlpools," said Deenie. "And then I'll jink a dogleg and hopefully that waterspout won't rise. Charis, please. You're not helping."

"And neither are you," she snapped, leaning as far over the skiff's side as she dared, straining to see ahead. The boat bounced and splashed beneath her, spray flying. The salt was stinging and acrid on her lips. "Deenie, if we've got whirlpools ahead I've a right to know it! Don't you treat me like a noddyhead."

"I'm sorry," said Deenie, contrite. "I just didn't want you to worry."

If there were whirlpools she couldn't see them. She couldn't hear them, either, but sailing was a lot noisier than she'd expected: the canvas crack of the sail, the creaking mast, the rushing water and the wooden sounds of the skiff.

She flicked Deenie a look. "I'm going to worry regardless, so I might as well worry on what's *really* there instead of what I'm *imagining* is there."

"All right. Then what's there is—*there*. You see?"

She looked ahead where Deenie was pointing and felt her throat close. "I—I thought that was just more frothy waves."

Deenie snorted. "I s'pose that's one way of seeing it."

What she'd thought was harmless spume and spray was the edge of the first whirlpool. And now that she knew, and looked again, of course she could see there was something different in the way the harbour's water was surging. And if she listened more closely she could hear a throaty growl.

"*Deenie*—"

"Don't fratch yourself," said Deenie. "So long as we're not sideswoggled by waterspouts I can get us past them."

"And will we be sideswoggled?" Her voice was squeaking, but she couldn't help it. *Whirlpools. Those are whirlpools. They swallow people and boats alive.* "Deenie, what if a waterspout does whip up? What if there's *more* than one? What if—"

"Then I'll get us past them, too," said Deenie. "It just won't be as easy."

She could feel a whimper trying to escape.

*This wasn't supposed to be my life. I was supposed to find a good man and fall in love and wed him and bed him and have his babes. I did find a good man and I did fall in love and nothing after that has ever gone right. Oh, Papa—I'm frighted—*

The water around and beneath them was growing choppier. The distant growling of the whirlpools was getting louder. Coming close. And then a sudden freezing squall of wind shook them, slapping and snapping the sail against the skiff's spindly mast. Charis looked up and saw the pewter sky swiftly tarnishing black.

The storm.

"Stay down, Charis," said Deenie. "Get under the canvas if you can. Things are going to be tricky for a bit and you don't want to be playing pea on a hot frypan."

"Can't I help?" she said, as her skin goosebumped with cold and fright. "Deenie —"

"You can help by keeping out of the way! And not making me fratch!"

In the murky stormlight Deenie's face was whiter than milk. All boyish in her leathers, with her braided hair salt-soaked, she didn't look like Deenie at all. There was a fierceness about her that Lur had never seen. Staring at her, shocked, Charis felt oddly comforted. This was Asher's daughter.

*I'm not going to die.*

Then the first peals of thunder sounded, and as their echoes faded the wind shifted, sharply twisting their skiff to the left. Flung sideways, she hit the floorboards so hard she thought all her teeth were rattled loose in their sockets.

Head spinning, she sat up. Maybe she should crawl under the canvas, but she couldn't. That would be cowardly, with Deenie fighting to save them. Instead she pressed against the skiff's curved side, tugged as much canvas over her as she could manage — and remembered at the last moment to shove their haversacks under it too, to keep their clothes dry.

With another rolling crash of thunder it started to rain — fat, heavy drops that stung and soaked.

"Hold on!" Deenie shouted. "Charis, stay down and hold on!"

The harbour wasn't choppy now, there were truly proper waves, foam-tipped and rising, taking the skiff up with them, dropping it back to the water's surface with a stomach-lurching crash. And even though the rain was loud and thunder constantly rumbled, she could hear the whirlpools' deep, hungry roar. Looking to Deenie, because in this madness Deenie was her only source of solace, she saw pain shudder through her friend, the blighted magic's claws sinking deep. Then Deenie startled and looked over to the right. Not even the rain running down her face could mask the shock.

Charis turned, following her horrified stare.

And saw the beginnings of a waterspout rising out of the whipping waves.

# CHAPTER ELEVEN

*Don't be sick, Deenie. Don't be sick. You can't be sick. Charis needs you.*

"It's all right, Charis! That 'spout's not going to hold. It won't hold. We're all right!"

And how her mage-sense knew that, she could never explain. But it was true. The blight-spawned waterspout wasn't strong enough to last.

"Look!" Charis shouted, pointing. "You're right, Deenie. Look!"

With a splash and a splatter and an abrupt release of magic, the threatening waterspout collapsed. Dragging a wet leather-clad forearm over her rain-slicked face, holding tight to the tiller, Deenie nodded. "Stay down, Charis. This ain't over yet."

And it wasn't. She could feel the aching build-up in her blood and her bones, more waterspouts stirring beneath the harbour's rain-pocked surface. Her mage-sense surged and she swung around, seeking. Where? Where? Where?

*There.*

She was right. This time the 'spout whipped up beyond the ragged line of whirlpools. Small and feeble, it was, trapped between maelstroms. Trying to whip itself free, instead it whipped itself to pieces.

"Charis, please, you have to—"

Gasping, she couldn't finish. A doubled pain shot through her, a sour twist in the harbour's blight and a bolt of rotten magic in the air as thunder boomed directly overhead. The storm in her blood dimmed her vision and loosened her desperate hold on the tiller. She heard Charis scream as the embattled skiff lurched wildly sideways, succumbing to the suck and tug of the nearest whirlpool.

*No—no—no, please, no!*

She grabbed the tiller with both hands and hauled, putting all her meagre strength behind wrenching the skiff back onto the course she'd charted, the course her mage-sense demanded that would see them thread their way safely between the whirlpools and the struggling-to-be-born waterspouts.

Surly and sluggish, the skiff responded. The cold wind whipped hard, flogging rain into their faces, turning the waves to flying, stinging foam and cracking in the sail. Would it stay constant enough to power them? And if it did, would the canvas sail hold? And the spindly mast? Had she chosen the right skiff to steal? Had she chosen the right course? She was relying on her mage-sense as much as Da's lessons from her childhood. A born sailor, he'd called her, but what if he'd been wrong?

Most of the morning's light was storm-stolen now. The skiff battled through a dreary dusk, slapped and slopped by rain and spray. She felt so sick with the harbour's raging blight, by the reef, she could hardly remember what it felt like not to hurt. It wasn't only rain and salt spray on her cheeks. She was weeping, frighted almost beyond breathing.

*I'm a mouse. I'm a mouse. What was I thinking?*

Thunder rumbled again, and beneath it she heard the ravenous growling of the whirlpools. Felt the skiff skew sideways again, answering their hungry pull. Then came another spiralling surge in her mage-sense as the reef's blight spawned a new waterspout. This one was stronger, roaring loudly before it collapsed. Straightaway another formed, and one more beside it. But they smashed into each other, murderous siblings, and fell apart in more foam and spray.

The skiff lurched again, heeling over to kiss the waves. Huddled half-under the canvas sheeting, Charis screamed.

*What was I thinking? I should've made her stay at home.*

And then she didn't have time to even think that much, because three more waterspouts were whipping into life to starboard and the closest of the whirlpools, feeding off the storm, was picking up momentum. She'd never hold the skiff against them without help.

"*Charis!*" she shouted, above the battering noise of wind and water. "*Charis, I need you!*"

Tossed and bruised, Charis crawled her way to the stern. Uncle Pellen's uniform tunic and his ugly wool hose were soaked through, dragging heavy on Charis's limbs. Her hair, half unbraided, was plastered to her cheeks. She looked awful, chalky-white and terrified.

"Is this it, Deenie?" she said, her eyes wide. "Are we done for?"

"*No*," she said, pouring every skerrick of anger into her voice. "Grab the tiller with me, Charis, quick. It'll take both of us to hold our course."

With a choked cry Charis took hold of the tiller. Shoulder to shoulder, hip to hip and knee to knee, they hauled and they hauled against the drag of the whirlpools.

"Deenie—those waterspouts—"

"I know, Charis, I know," she panted. "Don't look at 'em. Just close your eyes and hold on."

'Cause *either they'll kill us or they won't. Either way there's nothing we can do.*

The wind still blew strongly, keeping the sail bellied fat and pushing the skiff through and over the storm-thrashed waves. Deafened, drowning in the noise and the pain, battered by rain and the magic in the whirlpools and the waterspouts, Deenie sank her teeth into her lip and held on.

*I might not be Rafel but I can do this. I can.*

Rafel, lost and needing her. Rafel, their only hope.

Beside her Charis was choking, terrible shudders racking her head to toe.

"Hold on, Charis," she said, almost pleading. "It's nearly over. Just hold on."

But she didn't know that for certain. Shocked, she felt the fury of the whirlpools and the wildness of the 'spouts. She felt her blood start to twist and whirl and spin. They were drawing level with the maelstroms now, the whirlpools calling to her with furious longing, and even as they called she heard more shrieking to their left. The triple 'spouts whipped and thrashed, struggling to spiral higher, to catch the skiff up and rip it apart. To destroy her and Charis and any hope of saving Rafe, and Lur after him. And Da.

Her strength was fading. Beside her, Charis was fading. She could feel everything but it wasn't enough. Feeling wasn't acting. It didn't change a thing.

*I'm Asher's daughter. I can do better than this.*

What was it Da always said, when it came to getting his own way? *If you can't beat 'em, join 'em, then lead 'em where they need to go.* Which meant she had to stop fighting.

With a sob, she surrendered. Straightaway the reef's blight rushed in, filling her, and instead of beating it back she opened herself even wider. Welcomed it, breathing it in right down to her toes. She tasted the taint of it, bitter on her tongue. Felt the icy scalding of it, curdling her blood. It felt so familiar. The same blight was in Da.

*And I'm his daughter. If he can survive it then sink me, I can too.*

So the blight was in her now, trapped within her shaking body. What could she do with it? How could she turn the evil against itself?

*Olken magic is all coaxing, a thing of subtlety and kindness. Doranen magic is brash and bossy. It wants its own way, no matter the cost.*

That much she knew, after a lifetime spent watching Ma, and Da, and Rafel.

*And I have both magics in me, don't I? Like Rafel and Da? So there must be a way to meld them. There must be a way I can use both magics to save us.*

With a moan of exhaustion Charis lost her grip on the tiller and slumped shaking to the skiff's water-soaked floorboards. "I'm sorry, Deenie," she croaked. "I can't—I can't—"

She was so full of ruined magic she couldn't speak, or even give her friend an encouraging smile. Never mind. She'd explain afterwards. If there was an afterwards. If her desperate hunch was right. Ignoring Charis's misery, because there just wasn't time, Deenie released her own grip on the tiller. The skiff slewed wildly, answering the whirlpools' greedy call. Charis screamed. She ignored that too, ignored the three howling waterspouts and the whirlpools that with each tight turn pulled the skiff ever closer.

Feeling strangely peaceful, she rose to her feet, riding the skiff's wild plunging as though she and the boat were one. Then she took a deep, salt-laden breath and held it, held it, until her lungs burned. Closed her eyes and imagined the blight an arrow with herself the bow. And then, just as she thought her lungs must surely burst, she let out the pent-up blight with her pent-up breath, aimed it straight and sure at the three whipping waterspouts . . . and let it fly.

The tainted magic burning through her made her shout aloud in pain. And then she shouted in triumph as the waterspouts collapsed.

Never in her life had she felt like a real mage. Not until this moment. And not until this moment had she realised how much she cared. Jubilant, she let the blight fill her again. Gathered it up, aimed it at the whirlpool closest to the skiff and again let it fly. Three more times she battered the whirlpool, and on the third assault she felt the maelstrom falter.

One final time she opened herself to the blight, pulling its poison inside until she thought her body would fissure and fall apart, so full of pain she couldn't remember when she wasn't.

This time, following instinct, she poured the blight's power into the water beneath the skiff. As she felt the waves lift them she dropped beside the tiller, grabbed hold and aimed the skiff's bow straight. Dizzy, she felt the boat skim through the air as the waves surged them past the line of whirlpools and the uneasy stretch of harbour where the waterspouts spawned. The sail rippled then bellied again, and she felt salt spray in her face.

Huddled on the skiff's floorboards, Charis stared up at her. "What did you do, Deenie? What did you *do*?"

There was so much lingering pain but still, she had to laugh. "Took a leaf from Rafe's book!" Her stomach churned. "Charis—Charis—take the tiller—keep us straight—"

Scrambling, Charis took it. Deenie folded over the skiff's side and was sick.

As she hung there, retching, she felt the rain stop and heard Charis give a little yelp. "Deenie, the storm's clearing! There's blue sky behind us and it's spreading this way!"

Blearily she straightened and looked round, still holding on to the skiff's side. Yes. There was blue sky. And just faintly she could feel an easing of tension. As the storm faded so did the roiling in her blood. Not by much—they were still too close to the ruined reef for that—but she'd gladly take what little she was offered. Her mouth tasted vile and her throat was scalded with acid.

And then her strength failed completely, and she slumped to the skiff's floorboards. "Keep hold of that tiller, Charis. There's wind enough to keep us going for a while."

"Me?" squeaked Charis. "But I can't! How can I? You're the sailor, not me! And what about the waterspouts? What about—"

Deenie pressed her palms against her salt-stung eyes, perilous close to tears. "Oh, Charis, stop *wittering*," she said, her voice like a tremor. "We've clear water up ahead. Just—I don't need long. I only need a few moments. *Please*."

Because she felt everything, she felt Charis's swift hurt and even swifter concern. "Deenie? What's amiss?"

"Nowt," she whispered, falling back on Da's funny word. "I'm a mite weary, is all."

"Then rest," said Charis. "I'll howl if something goes wrong."

*You won't need to. I'll feel it.*

But the offer warmed her, and she was so cold.

Curled on her side, with her leathers clammy and salt-stained and her soaked hair a burden, she listened to the harbour running swiftly past the hull. Smiled at the first light touch of fresh sunshine on her skin.

*I did it, Da. Sink me bloody sideways, I did it.*

Except they didn't sink. They'd faced whirlpools and waterspouts and a fierce storm on open water — and survived.

*This time.*

Sobered, groaning, she sat up. Caught her breath as every muscle and sinew starkly protested. Her leathers groaned too, shrunken and constricting.

"You all right, Charis?"

Her friend was clutching the tiller so tight it was a wonder the wood didn't split. She looked afraid to breathe too deeply, as though a twitch or a hiccup would send her skywards like a startled bird.

"*No*, Deenie," said Charis. "I'm *not* all right! How did you *do* that? Papa told me what happened when Rafe and your da fought the waterspouts and the whirlpool. But this was different, wasn't it? Rafe, he has all that power inside him and your da set it free. Is that what you did, all by yourself? *How?* Deenie — your face — it was *frightening.*" Her voice broke. "You frighted me."

She felt the dazzle of triumph fade. "Charis, I'm sorry. I was only trying to keep us safe."

"I know, and you did," said Charis. "But it's *how* you did. Please, Deenie, tell me. What did you do?"

Instead of answering, she stared across the calming harbour waters to the distant shore on their right. Where were they? How far had they come? With the storm's murkiness lifting she could just make out the rocky coastline. And there were the twin Gantling waterfalls, plunging over the cliffs and into the harbour.

*Not so very far, really. There's so much further to go.*

Would they have enough food? Enough water? How many more waterspouts and whirlpools would they have to escape? They'd sailed through one storm. How many more would blow in to plague them?

*Are we mad to attempt this? I think we must be.*

She felt like a weathercock, crazily swinging. One moment elated, the next drowned in despair.

*What if we're faced with calamity again and I have to open myself a second time to the blight? Then a third time? A fourth? How many times can I do that and not do myself harm?*

"Deenie!" said Charis, "if you don't talk to me I swear I will turn this horrible skiff about and sail us back to Westwailing!"

Still, she hesitated. Tipping her face skywards, she looked at the swiftly thinning storm clouds. Lots of reassuring blue to see now. And no sense of another storm riding in hard over Dragonteeth Reef. No sense of nearby waterspouts or whirlpools. This stretch of the harbour was clean. She could still feel the reef, though, broken glass in her blood. And if she squinted she would see waterspouts, dancing along its distant edge.

On a sigh she turned and looked at Charis. "We'll be sunny for a goodly while. You should shrug out of those wet clothes and change into dry. You mustn't go catching an ague."

Charis made a spitting sound, just like an angry cat. "I can tell for myself when I'm wet to the skin! Just you answer my question, Deenie —and take the tiller while you're about it. You're the sailor here, not me."

They swapped places, cagily shifting in the small boat as the bright breeze kept their sail filled and skimmed them along. Deenie watched Charis, on her knees, haul her haversack from under the sheltering sheet of canvas and pull out a dry blouse and skirt. Then, as she unbuttoned her wet, bulky guardsman's tunic, her friend glanced up and scowled.

"*Deenie.*"

"I don't know if I *can* explain," she protested. "And if I try I might end up frighting you again."

"Believe me," said Charis, shrugging out of the tunic. "I can't be frighted any worse."

That made her blink. "What do you mean?"

"There were shadows," Charis muttered. "Sliding under your skin."

She felt herself prickle up and down her spine. "Shadows?"

"I don't know," said Charis, shaking her head. "Maybe I was dreaming it. Maybe it was the storm playing tricks with my eyes. But that's what it looked like, Deenie. When you—when you were being a mage? There were shadows."

*Shadows, sliding under my skin.* "I used the blight against itself, Charis," she said, hushed. As though saying the words softly robbed them of strength and power. "I—I pulled it in and then I spat it out again, and when I spat it out it was changed. It was a weapon."

Charis tossed the wet tunic onto the rower's bench. "You pulled it in?" she echoed. "Into yourself, you mean? The blight? *Deenie!* What were you *thinking*?"

So now Charis was going to scold her?

*When I saved our lives, too. How's that for being grateful?*

Feeling waspish, she narrowed her eyes. "If you must know, Charis, I was thinking we had about half a dozen heartbeats between us before we both drowned!"

Mouth open, Charis stared. Then she pressed shaking hands to her face, shoulders slumping. When at last she lowered them, there were tears on her cheeks.

"Promise me you'll never do that again," she said, ragged. "*Promise* me you won't ever take another mad risk like that!"

"I can't," she said simply. "How can I? When it might make the difference between life and death for Rafe and Lur, how can I?"

"Of course you can!" Charis cried. "Deenie, it's the *blight*. It's what's left of Morg's poisonous magics. You can't muck about with that mank, you can't breathe it in like fresh air and think you'll not get sick. Didn't you hear me? *I saw shadows inside you!*"

Deenie shrugged. "It's no good, Charis. I can't—I won't—promise I'll not do it again. If we're going to find Rafel, if we're going to save him, then we can't be squeamish. *I* can't be."

New tears welled in Charis's eyes. "It's too dangerous. There has to be another way."

"And if I think of one, I'll use it. But if I can't? If there isn't? I'm trusting you to watch me, Charis. I'm trusting you to tell me if you notice anything else."

"Anything else like what? What d'you mean, Deenie?"

"I don't know!" Her headache was awake again, pounding pain behind her eyes. "I don't know what I'm doing. I'm making this up as I go, aren't I? And that's why I need you, Charis. You're an Olken mage. You feel things. You notice things. And you *know* me. So if you think I'm going wobbly, if you think you see me changing then—"

Charis sat with a thump, rocking the skiff. "Changing how? Into what?"

"I don't know, Charis," she said, and frowned. "Just . . . *changing.*"

"I'm starting to think this was a mistake," Charis said, hugging her knees. "Maybe we should turn back, Deenie. It's not too late. West-wailing isn't that far behind us."

"*Turn back?*"

Tearful again, Charis nodded. "I know I sound craven but Deenie, that was so *awful*. The storm and the 'spouts and the whirlpools. And now here you are telling me you're letting the blight in, and you might change, and I have to watch you because something could go wrong? Deenie, what if it does and I don't see it? Or what if I *do* see it but it's too late to save you?"

Poor Charis. How unfair it was, that her loyal friendship should be repaid with terror and pain. Aching for her, somehow Deenie managed a teasing smile.

"I thought I was the mouse here, Charis. Not you."

"Don't, Deenie," said Charis, looking down. "I'm shamed enough as it is. All those speeches I gave, all that fine, brave talk of rushing to save Rafel. About being Papa's daughter. Turns out talk's easy. Doing things? *That's* hard."

The last storm clouds were blown to tatters now, the sky warmly blue, the harbour lively but not lethal. This stretch of water remained clear, no grinding premonition of waterspouts spawning. The skiff fairly skipped along, its sail fat with the salt breeze. It was a perfect day for sailing.

Or it would be, if only the reef was free of blight. If only she could pretend she didn't feel its dark, looming menace.

"Aye, it's hard," she agreed, after a moment. "But here we are, Charis, and we're doing them. I know you're frighted. *I'm* frighted. But this isn't a mistake—and we're not turning back."

Charis sniffed. "We're not?"

Closing her eyes, Deenie lifted her salt-sticky face to the sun. "No."

"Oh." A damp shuffling sound, as Charis shifted on the skiff's boards. "Well." Another sniff. "How long do you think it'll take us to reach the far end of the reef?"

"I can't say for sure," she said, looking at Charis again. "A few days, it should be. But if we get more storms, or hit a few bad patches of waterspouts and whirlpools—most likely it'll take a week. Maybe longer. Don't worry. We've brought enough supplies."

"It's not the supplies I'm worried about," Charis retorted. "It's you getting enough rest so we don't sink, or worse. I think you'd best be giving me a few sailing lessons, Meistress Deenie. That way, when the sun's shining and there's no 'spouts or whirlpools, you can put your head down and rest."

And that made her stare. "Sailing? *You?*"

For the first time in what seemed like days, Charis grinned. "Aye, and why not me? Unless you don't rate yourself a teacher, that is."

"Saucy wench!" she said. "The question is, are you any kind of pupil?"

"I guess we'll see," said Charis. And then her smile faded. "Don't worry, Deenie. I'll keep a close watch over you. I'll not let anything dark touch you. I promise."

Warmed by much more than sunshine, she nodded. "And I promise I'll keep you safe from whirlpools and waterspouts and Morg's manky blight."

*And I will. If it's the last thing I do, I'll see Charis kept safe.*

Six days and five nights it took them to sail Lur's ragged coastline to the distant end of Dragonteeth Reef. Several times they caught sight of figures standing on the inhospitable cliffs that lined most of the water's edge. Word must have spread from Westwailing of the stolen skiff and the two mad girls braving Lur's unchancy waters. But with no harbours this far along the coast, no safe way at all down to the water, nobody came after them and that was all that mattered. Let all of the kingdom stare, provided they didn't interfere.

Charis wasn't a born sailor, but she soon learned enough rudiments of tiller and sail that she could confidently keep the skiff on course in daylight and clear water. Then Deenie crawled under the canvas tent they'd fashioned and snatched an hour or two of desperately needed sleep.

Not that the rest was restful. As soon as her eyes closed she dreamed of her mother, memories dredged from childhood that made her toss and weep. She dreamed of her father, too, alone in that Billington hospice. And she dreamed of Rafel, more little girl rememberings. Once she thought she heard his voice, as she'd heard it in the royal crypt, but it was faint. Too faint. Waking from that dream, all she could remember was fear.

*Don't give up, Rafe. We're coming.*

She wished she dared risk reading the scrawled notes in Barl's diary, but a funny feeling told her to keep the journal tucked out of sight. What Charis didn't know of couldn't get her in trouble — and besides, with the weather and harbour so unpredictable there was a chance she might lose it over the skiff's side.

And the same funny feeling told her that would be a disaster.

She and Charis grew miserably accustomed to being pickled in salt water, like brined herring, enduring sticky hair and sticky skin and grubby, salt-stiff clothing. They became used to the chafing and the blisters and the bruises as they battled their way towards the end of the reef. With no choice, they accepted the hunger pangs as they eked out their miserly hoard of nuts and hard-tack biscuits and dried beef, and drank sparingly of their stale water. Accepted too the crude necessity of a tin bowl for a shared chamberpot.

Three more times as they made their way along the coast they were battered by a storm blowing in across the reef from the uncharted, open ocean. To make things worse, as the bad weather crossed the reef it absorbed some of Morg's blight, so the thunder and the lightning cracked and crashed and flung them without mercy from wave to wave and stern to bow. At the height of the third storm their battered sail ripped in two. Deenie blessed the skiff's owner for that spare sail. It was patched and faded but it was *there* — which saved them.

And then of course there were the waterspouts and whirlpools. Every day they encountered them and every day she stretched her mage-sense to the fraying edge of its limits, pushed herself to nosebleeds and screaming headaches and half-fainting to keep the skiff from being sunk or pulled apart and herself and Charis drowned. That meant calling in the blight. It meant letting the darkness fill her so she could shoot it out again like an arrow, disrupting the ravenous tug of the whirlpools and collapsing the 'spouts in gouts of whipped-up water and foamed spray.

Even as controlling the dark power got easier with each use, the toll it took upon her grew. She could see that in Charis's eyes, in the way her friend's lips pinched and she said nothing more about shifting shadows, only held her hand tightly until the shuddering stopped.

Her only compensation was that in using the blight against itself, she became more keenly aware of its creeping rot, as though her mage-sense were a knife blade and she was whetting it, honing it to a lethal edge. It meant she could sense far more swiftly when a new 'spout was spawning, or where a whirlpool waited with its hungry mouth wide open, so she could jink the skiff to safety with plenty of time to spare. And that was a *good* thing. She couldn't begrudge that. But it meant she was changing.

She wished she knew into what.

Not enough sleep. Not enough food. She was living off the blight . . . and feeling it consume her.

Their fourth day on the open water was the hardest to endure. By her best guess they were somewhere close to level with Basingdown, Dorana City and home so close it was an actual pain. Just as the sun tipped over from noon and started its slow slipping towards the horizon, Deenie felt that prickling burst of uneasiness that heralded a spawning 'spout.

"Sit tight," she told Charis as her nerves sizzled, harder than ever. "This is going to be bad."

And it was. It was terrible. So many spawning waterspouts threatened them that she quickly lost count. No sooner did she collapse one than two or three more whipped up to take its place, twins and triplets dancing a wild, watery jig. The skiff spun like a leaf on a millrace and

**181**

they spun with it, teeth rattling, joints wrenching, every over-stretched sinew on fire and screaming.

In the end she couldn't sail the skiff and save their lives, so Charis took the tiller and she knelt in the bow, screaming "go left" or "go right" as she sought to thread them to safety somewhere up ahead. Choked with 'spouts, the waters churned to a frenzy of foam-capped waves, soaking them over and over until her eyes were so salt-burned she thought she'd go blind. After that her mage-sense guided her. Her mage-sense, and the blight. It filled her so completely she thought she was nothing but thin skin and darkness. Feared this would be the moment that changed her beyond help.

Afterwards, collapsed beside Charis on the skiff's soaked and sloshing floorboards, leaving the boat to fend for itself, she stared bleary at the blue sky. Feeling her heart thud. Feeling her blood pump and pool. Feeling every scrape and scream and bruise.

"Barl's tits," croaked Charis. "Let's not do that again."

"Spoilsport," she croaked back. And laughed. And laughed. And wept.

Then it was clear sailing until sunset and through the night. The next day saw a brief squall, two whirlpools and two bouts of waterspouts. It rained the night after, but not stormily, and they had to contend with five waterspouts—but were spared a whirlpool. As the sun rose on the sixth day, Deenie left Charis in charge of the tiller, crawled exhausted under their canvas awning and plunged into sleep.

Five hours later the blight woke her, dark and bubbling in her blood. And before she even opened her eyes she heard a familiar roaring, louder and hungrier than ever before.

Dry-mouthed, she crawled back out from under the canvas to find Charis sitting numb and silent in the stern, the tiller quiet in her hand.

"It's over, Deenie," she said, empty. "We went through all of this for nothing." She pointed. "Look."

After days and nights of struggle and fear, against every sensible hope of survival, they'd reached the end of the reef—and at its ragged end, between the ancient barrier and the rocky coast, roared a whirlpool seemingly big enough to swallow Dorana City whole.

Dismayed, Deenie stared at it.

*Oh, Da. Da, no. This just ain't fair.*

For a treacherous moment she trembled on the brink of overwhelming self-pity. Because it *wasn't* fair. Not after everything she and Charis had survived. Not after the hardship and the suffering and all that peeing in a tin bowl.

*There's no way around it and there's no way I can collapse it. I might as well try to collapse the sun.*

But even as she stared, ready to admit defeat, she felt a dreadful surge of fury, as vast and as powerful as the whirlpool now denying them the open ocean.

*Bloody sink that for a sackful of hammers. I ain't sailed all this way to turn tail on Rafe now.*

"Deenie?" said Charis, suspicious. "Deenie, what are you scheming?"

*If you can't beat 'em, join 'em.*

"Nothing you want me to tell you, Charis," she said, and gently shoved her friend away from the tiller.

*Am I mad, Da? I'm mad, aren't I? Prob'ly even you wouldn't think of doing this.*

"Deenie?" Now Charis sounded nervous. "Deenie—you're sailing us towards the reef."

She nodded. "I know."

"But—but *why*?"

"Because I'm not about to let that sorcerer Morg and his reef beat me."

"But *Deenie*—"

"Don't fratch at me, Charis," she said. "I need to think."

Muttering crossly, Charis gave up.

Deenie closed her eyes, willing her pounding heart to ease.

*I can do this. I can. I'm Asher's daughter. I'm Rafe's sister. And I'm stronger now than I was this time last week.*

Stronger . . . different . . . honed into a blade.

As though this was meant, they had nothing but clear water, all of Morg's blight poured greedily into the whirlpool. She nudged the tiller until the skiff was pointed as near to the end of the reef as she dared go. The morning breeze skipped them over the small waves, and the whirlpool's roaring seemed to cheer her on.

A long stone's throw from the ragged, jagged Dragon's teeth she swung the skiff sharply to empty the wind from its sail and bring the small boat to a rocking halt. Then she looked at Charis, who was cross-legged on the floorboards, her skirt torn, her shirt without three buttons, blistered hands fisted hard in her lap.

"Take the tiller, Charis," she said briskly. "And hold here until I'm done."

"Done?" Charis was glaring. "Done with *what*?"

She should be terrified—and a part of her was—but she was grinning, too. Because why not? Why shouldn't she? Why couldn't a mouse grin from time to time?

"You'll see," she said. "Now come on. Take the tiller."

Grumbling, Charis wriggled her way to the stern. And then she choked. "Deenie! What are you *doing*?"

"What does it look like?" she said, stripping herself of shirt and linen leggings, leaving only her manky smalls. She was barefoot already, they both were. "Now hold the skiff here, remember? I'll try not to be long."

And before Charis could stop her, she dived over the skiff's side and into the seething water's cold embrace.

So used had she grown to the blight beating through her blood, she hardly noticed how strong it was this close to the reef. Hardly felt the darkness bubbling as she swam to the Dragon's teeth. But she noticed it when she fetched up against the living rock and anchored herself to it with clawed fingers, opening herself to the source of the blight.

A maelstrom inside her, twisting power and might. This was nothing like collapsing waterspouts and dodging whirlpools. They were games for spratlings compared to this. As the reef's ruthless blight scoured her hollow she could hear herself screaming. It felt like Morg's tainted magic was ripping her apart. She was no rock reef; she couldn't sustain this. Her bones would break soon. She was going to die.

*I don't want to . . . I don't want to . . .*

And then in the midst of the madness she felt something new, something *gentle*, threading itself through her blood and bones. Heard a different voice, sweetly descant to Morg's brutal bass. Bewildered, she tried to make sense of it, but even as she drew another deep, shuddering breath she was deafened and battered anew by the sorcerer's lingering hate. By the sound of that monstrous whirlpool, roaring louder than a hundred storms.

*Help me, Da. Help me. We can't let Morg win.*

But Da was too far away, he couldn't hear her, and her mousey strength was ebbing, ebbing, like a tide. She felt the blight rise to swamp her, felt her fingers loosen on the reef. And that was all right, because if she let go the pain would stop.

*If I let go, Rafe will die.*

With a shout of fury she clamped her fingers hard on the reef again, heedless of the pain and the feel of warm, slippery blood. And then she stopped fighting. She had to use the blight, not battle with it, just as she'd used it to defeat all those waterspouts.

*But it hurts. Da, it hurts.*

With the tattered shreds of her endurance, closing her mind to the thought of shadows sliding under her skin, to the darkness thundering through her, she channelled the blight's power towards the enormous whirlpool. Danced her mage-sense around its spinning circumference, searching for a way in. Searching . . . searching . . .

*There.*

Holding her breath, she was dimly aware of that sweet, high voice at the very limit of hearing, teasing and tantalising. A warm note of hope. But it was a distraction, so she pushed it away.

Bit by bit she fed the blight into the whirlpool, like Charis in her kitchen adding sap-sugar to a sauce. At first the whirlpool resisted, tried to spit her and her mage-sense and the cloying blight into the sky. But she was stronger now, so much stronger. In her bones she'd been changed. Teeth gritted, bloodied fingers clinging, she pitted herself against the maelstrom.

*Let me past! You can't keep me here. I need to go. Let me go!*

She fought the whirlpool, and the whirlpool fought back. Bloated with Morg's malevolence, it tried to smash her to pieces, smear her to blood in the water. Weeping, she resisted. And when she heard that sweet, whispering note of hope again, she welcomed it.

*Help me. Please, help.*

A new strength poured into her . . . and she felt the whirlpool falter.

*Da . . . Da . . .*

She screamed as she felt the whirlpool die, killed by its birthing blight. Screamed a second time as she felt the last of the blight burn through her.

Everything went dark.

*Am I dead? Am I dead?*

But then she opened her eyes and saw blue sky. Heard her pounding heart in her chest. For the longest time she clung to the reef, too weak to move, almost too weak to breathe. Her clinging hands hurt horribly. Everything was hurting. She felt cold and shrivelled and so very, very small.

And then she heard Charis shouting. "Deenie! *Deenie!*"

Oh, yes. The skiff. She had to go back. But could she swim? Could she even move? Wouldn't she rather stay here and just breathe? Yes, but Charis needed her. That meant she couldn't stay.

Slowly, feebly, she paddled to the skiff. Charis had to help her back into it. Her bones had turned to string.

"Oh, *Deenie.*" Charis's teeth were chattering and her cheeks were wet with tears. "How did you *do* that? How are you not *dead*? Oh, Deenie, look at your poor hands!"

She didn't want to. She could feel them, and that was bad enough.

"Never mind my hands, Captain Orrick," she said, gently scowling. "You go man the tiller. It's time to fetch our missing Rafe."

# CHAPTER TWELVE

Alone in the barracks tiltyard, the sun just cresting the treetops, Ewen doggedly exercised his right arm. Though its broken bones had knitted well enough he wasn't yet returned to full strength, so he was training with the light sword he'd wielded as a youth. Running sweat despite the chilly air, he plunged the blade over and over again into the heart, lungs and belly of the sand-filled mannikin the barracks men had dubbed *Morg*.

And as he trained he heard his father's voice, just as he'd heard it day after dragging day since returning from the Eastern Vale, clipped and cold with a scarcely bridled fury.

*"Blood your brother, I told you. Not a hard task. One poor witless wanderer tied to a chair for a kind killing. And you failed! Ewen, how could you fail? No blooding, but a butchery. It's angry word from the Eastern Vale, I have. That witless Nairn, he rails to me of your blundering. What am I to say?"*

Weeks gone by since that confrontation and still the pain of it persisted. His ride home to the High Vale with a broken arm had been a retching agony, but gladly he'd have turned and ridden back to the Eastern Vale rather than endure one more pounding heartbeat of the king's bitter rage.

*"It's king after me you're chosen!"* his father had shouted. *"Wear a crown, can you? After this? I wonder."*

Next the king had rounded on Padrig, disgust and disappointment doled out with a heavy hand.

*"Is it a man, you are, or a milkish maid? What have I sired, a gelding? Have your balls dropped, boy? Do you shave? Can you rut? Should I send for a seamstress, should I, and have her sew you a dress?"*

The unexpected cruelty of the attack had left his brother speechless. But when he'd tried to take the blame, tried to see Padrig shielded, his brother had turned away. There was no forgiveness in him, either.

Remembering, stung anew by the unfairness of that, Ewen thrust his sword home to the hilt through the mannikin's heart, grunting as the impact jarred his mended bones.

"I'm sorry, Padrig," he told the empty tiltyard. "I let you down, I did."

He'd tried to say that to his brother's face, but humiliated Padrig hadn't wanted to hear it. Shamed by what had happened in the Eastern Vale, shamed again, deeper still, by the king's derision, he'd shut himself in his chamber with spare lamp oil and his books.

And then, four difficult days after their ignominious return, Tavin's three roaming scouts had ridden back into the barracks. The news they brought home with them had driven the Eastern Vale from their minds.

More blighted wanderers crossing into Vharne from Manemli. To swell their numbers, blighted wanderers from the long-silent lands of Ranoush. Worst of all, half a small village of men, women and children had been blighted because of it. The scouts had put them all down.

The king turned ash-pale hearing that, and stayed silent for a day.

Two days after that he'd ridden out of the High Vale with twelve heavily armed barracks men, two nephews and Padrig, still unforgiving, to hunt down the truth.

*"I'd rather you rode with me, Ewen,"* his father bluntly said, the night before. *"But the Eastern Vale took care of that, it did. So it's Padrig I'll take. I'll see him blooded in the north."*

Which had left him to sit his princely arse in the king's seat, in the

Hall, nursing his broken arm and pretending the crown belonged on his head.

"Spirit guide you, Padrig," he muttered to the cold tiltyard morning. "Find common ground with the king, you should."

Something else he'd tried to tell his little brother, that Padrig hadn't wanted to hear. Padrig held a grudge the way a miser clutched coin.

Grunting again, Ewen pulled his sword from the mannikin and watched the sand trickle out of its wound like pale yellow blood.

"Boy, what are you doing?"

*Tavin.* He turned, trying to mask the pain burning in his arm. "What does it look like?"

"Ewen—" His scarred face scrunched with displeasure, Tavin slapped the tiltyard's open gate with the flat of his hand. "Is this helping, is it?"

"You're the one said my arm won't find its lost strength with wishing."

"*And* I said," Tavin retorted, stepping into the tiltyard proper, "that it's more harm than good you'll do hating yourself, you will."

Easy for him to say, that was. He'd not disappointed a king and a brother at once.

"What do you want, Tav?" he said, the ache in his arm fierce, and in his heart even fiercer. "Is there word from the king?"

Joining him at the mannikin, Tavin shook his head. "No word."

He lowered the point of his childish sword to his boot. Painful or not, tomorrow he'd train with a proper weapon. Who would trust a prince wielding a blade made for a boy?

"Near a month since the last pigeon, Tav."

"Pigeons feed falcons," said Tavin, shrugging. "That's trouble for the pigeon, not for the king."

"The scouts spoke of wanderers from Ranoush, Tavin! *Ranoush!* That old enemy's been asleep since before I was born!"

"A handful of snowflakes don't make a blizzard," said Tavin, mildly enough. "A good king doesn't sweat himself before he needs to."

*But I'm not a good king. I'm a prince with a crown I never asked to wear.*

"Swordmaster, I say there *is* a blizzard," he snapped. "It's not whispers of blighted wanderers we're hearing. They've been seen. They've been taken and put down. Keeping count, are you? I am. Twelve since the king rode from the barracks, Tav. *Twelve*."

Tavin poked a finger into the mannikin's fresh sword-slits. "It's not a good number."

"No! It's not!" Breathing hard, he calmed himself. Shouting at Tavin wouldn't bring Padrig home safe. "That Eastern Vale man. Jeyk. Called, he said he was. Tav, we have to learn more. We have to find who called him. Then maybe we'll know why."

"You know who called him," said Tavin, brooding. "The north."

"The north is a place, Swordmaster. Say a valley called him and make as much sense, you would."

"Ewen . . ." Tavin sighed. "The king rode out to find answers. Scouts are riding the rough to find answers. You've been chewing this bone since the day you brought your broken arm home, boy. And if you want we can chew it again. We can chew it 'til our teeth break, we can. But there's no answer in this tiltyard or in the castle or in any corner of the Vale. So save our teeth, I say."

The swordmaster was right. With a shout of frustration, Ewen snatched up his blade and shoved it through the mannikin's throat. A flash of fire slammed up his arm, all the way to his shoulder. He shouted again, this time with pain, and pressed his right forearm hard to his chest.

Tavin listened to his cursing, one grey eyebrow raised. Then he pulled the sword free. "Boy, it's a stubborn fool, you are."

Scowling, he held out his left hand. "I'll have that back, I will."

"No, you won't," said the swordmaster, and snapped the blade across his thigh.

"*Tavin!*"

"A shoddy swordsmith made that, he did," said Tavin, eyeing the pieces of blade with disgust. "Child's sword or not, it needed better tempering."

"I'll temper you!" he retorted. "That blade was *mine*."

"And tempted, I was, to break it in half on your arse," said the swordmaster. "Treat that horse of yours if it was injured the way you're treating your arm, would you?"

The man deserved his own blading. "Decide for myself how hard to work, I can! It's not for you to tell me, Tavin."

Tavin's face gentled. "And the Eastern Vale's not yours for the blaming, Ewen. Padrig's his own man. You didn't trip him. He stumbled by himself."

"You're not a brother, Tavin," he said, teeth gritted. "You don't understand."

Tavin held out both pieces of the broken sword. "I understand, son. But loving can't mean saving. Some lessons get learned the hard way, they do."

*And some should never be taught at all*, Ewen thought.

But he couldn't say that out loud. Tavin was the king's man and so was he. Loyalty to the crown came first, even before family.

"Did you come here just to break my sword?" he said, taking back the pieces. "Or was there something useful you had for me?"

"I came to see how you're faring, I did," said Tavin. "I'm barracks busy and it's in the Hall you are, most days, polishing the king's seat and scrawling your name on the bits of parchment that secretary shoves under your nose."

He made a small, impatient sound. "Don't fault Clovis I'm not haunting the barracks. The king left a crown on my head, Tavin. It's heavy."

"I know, boy," said Tavin. Then he sighed again. "But I'm your swordmaster. Lean on me a bit, you could."

"I do," he said, trying to smile. "Every choice I make, that's your voice whispering in my ear."

"Not the king's?" said Tavin, quiet.

He felt his face heat. "And the king's."

"Then if my voice weighs as much as the crown, boy, *listen* when I tell you a king needs two good arms to rule," said Tavin, his face no longer gentle. "And it's ruining your right arm, you are, by mixing rest with stabbing sand men!"

The fire in his broken and cracked bones had burned out. Only a smoky discomfort remained. "It's not so bad, Tav. I've got potions I'm swallowing."

"Ask the goodwife for a potion to put addled wits to right!" Tav retorted. "That'll be a potion worth swallowing, that will."

Ewen dragged his left hand down his face, feeling the rasp of stubble he'd waited to scrape off. "I have to push myself, Tavin. You know it. Any moment of the day or night a scout could come riding, or a pigeon could return to its loft. One of your barracks men could stagger home with a tale. Any moment, the king could need me." He dropped his broken sword to the tiltyard's grass and held his mended arm out straight, willing it steady. "He'll need me ready to fight for Vharne and the Vale, Tav, with my left hand *and* my right. I failed him with Padrig. I can't fail him again."

This time it was Tavin who cursed. Then he punched the battered mannikin and turned away, heavy shoulders hunched to his ears. Cutting through the morning's chilly silence, familiar barracks sounds: horses whickering, men shouting, dogs barking and wooden cartwheels clattering over cobbles.

"The queen shouldn't have died, Ewen," he said at last, grief cracking his voice. "The king would know his sons better if his queen hadn't died."

Lowering his arm, he felt his throat tighten. "It wasn't that long ago, Tav. Padrig and I were years out of swaddle-cloths when we lost her."

"It was long enough," said Tavin, turning back. "You needed him, boy, and he wasn't to be found."

"Tavin—" He raised a warning hand. "It's thin ice, this is. Let's skate somewhere else."

The scar across Tavin's weathered face tightened with the clenching of his jaw. "I'll skate where I please. I'm old, and I've earned it. How can I do right by you and hold my tongue? If you're wrong, boy, I have to tell you. I have to slap your skinny arse."

"You do that, Swordmaster," he said, after a long, hard-breathing pause. "That's what you do."

Tavin closed on him, took hold of his right wrist and pushed back his long woollen sleeve to the elbow. Purposeful fingers probed along the muscles of his forearm, testing the mettle of the mended bones beneath the skin. He tried hard not to wince.

"When it was splinted and bound I only used my left arm," he said. "You were right. It needed strengthening. But Tav—"

Tavin pulled his sleeve down and let go. Beneath his pinched brows his eyes were searching and intent. "*Am* I your swordmaster, Ewen? Do you listen to me?"

"Do I—do *you* listen, Tavin? I just said—"

With a hiss, Tavin fisted a handful of his shirt and tugged him close. "A week, you'll rest it. A broken arm is more than knit bones, it is. It's not your friend Tav who tells you this, Ewen. This is the sword-master, this is, with the power to ban you from barracks if you disobey."

He blinked. "You'd ban me?"

"Son . . ." With a twisted smile, Tavin released his shirt and lightly slapped his stubbled cheek. "What do you think?"

*I think you're brother and father and best friend to me.*

Stooping, he picked up the two halves of his capriciously broken sword. "I think you owe me a new blade."

Tavin laughed, and led the way out of the tiltyard.

A full day in the Hall followed his barracks bath and breakfast. To start with it was reading the missives ridden to the castle by messengers from all over the Vale and the scattered villages beyond, handed to him by the king's secretary, Clovis. A meticulous man, he was, with his brain stuffed full of names and faces and the king's decisions made eleven years before. And once the reading was done with, Clovis wrote down his answers and he signed them and pressed the king's seal into a blob of soft blue wax.

That took five hours, and then he ate a swift, lonely lunch.

After lunch it was time to meet with the petitioners come to the castle to have their grievances and requests heard in person. Clovis sat with him for that too, whispering in his ear when whispering was warranted.

Spirit's grace, he'd have been lost without Clovis.

Every man and woman he saw thought he could and would give them what they wanted. Sometimes he did. Sometimes he didn't. He

was Prince Ewen, not King Murdo, and he went his own way. Whatever his decision, Clovis faithfully recorded it in the enormous
leather-and-brass-bound book kept for these matters. The secretary wrote
with a slow, careful hand, and each petitioner had to initial the entry
to show they understood what they had or hadn't received. It was altogether sobering, what happened in this Hall.

*When the king dies, I'll belong here for good.*

And that thought was more than sobering. Chilled him, it did.

*Spirit, let the king live a long time. I'd not swap the barracks and
hard riding for my arse in this chair while I'm still a young man.*

So many troubles in the Vale, and in Vharne. Some of them were
petty. Some broke his heart. A child drowned in a well left uncovered
by some careless villager. A stray dog turned goat-worrier and who
was going to pay? Hens ridden down by a heedless scout. The king
would pay for *that*. The village brewer who sampled too much of his
brew. Couldn't the king stop him from singing? His braying dried up
the cows' milk and set babbies to howls.

Problem after problem, all his to solve.

Though he was speaking for his father, it was his mother he most
thought of. Her commonsense wisdom that he remembered and passed
along. Beyond the Hall's unshuttered windows the afternoon slid through
his fingers, slippery as Shyvie's bath-house soap. The light was starting
to fade when Clovis checked his list of names put down for this day's
Hall.

"One last petitioner, Highness," he murmured discreetly. "A
bridleway dispute in the village of—"

And then the Hall's heavy doors burst open and Tavin blundered
in, his eyes wild with fear and grief. Two barracks men came close
behind him—it was Ren and Evon—and they were holding a third
man between them. Dressed in filthy, ragged clothes, hair darkened
with dirt, his head lolled to his chest, hidden. His hands were bound
before him and his bare and bloodied feet dragged across the Hall's
flagstoned floor.

Ignoring the secretary's shocked gasp, Ewen leapt down from the king's seat. "Tavin? What's this? Who is he? A wanderer? Is this a blighted man in the High Vale? *Tavin*, give me an answer!"

There were tears in the swordmaster's eyes. "Ewen. Boy. Best you sit down again, it is. Best you—"

And then he didn't need Tavin's answer, because the captive man looked up, revealing a dirty, bruised face and bloodshot eyes of pale blue.

*Padrig.*

But that wasn't possible. Padrig rode with the king, he was weeks and weeks away riding the rough country along the borders. He was hunting blighted men crossing into Vharne from Manemli and Ranoush.

*That's not Padrig. It can't be.*

"Ewen," said the swordmaster, his voice gravelly with distress. "It's your brother. Boy, I tell you, best you sit down."

He felt his eyes narrow, even as his heart threatened to break his ribs. "It's not 'boy' here, Swordmaster. In this Hall I'm the king. Ren—Evon—take your hands off the prince. And cut his bindings! He's not a criminal."

The barracks men looked to Tavin.

"Highness, they can't do that," said Tavin, his voice still rough. "He's not safe."

"Not safe?" he echoed. "Are you mad, Tavin? It's *Padrig*." Pulling his dagger from its sheath on his belt, he leapt the distance to the barracks men and his little brother. Not so little these days, almost a man full-grown he was, and robustly muscled. Or he had been. He'd been muscled when he rode from the Vale with the king. But now . . . 'Let him *go*, I said. Are you listening? *Give him to me!*"

Ren and Evon had to obey him. In this Hall he was the king. As they let go and stepped aside, he whipped his blade through the rope knotted around Padrig's chafed wrists.

"Padrig!" he said, sinking to the cold floor with this shrunken man, his little brother, held tight in his arms. "Padrig, look at me. Here I am. It's Ewen, Padrig. Look at me. Come on. Don't say you're still angry. Don't be angry, Padrig, *please*."

But Padrig wouldn't talk to him. He wouldn't look at him. He was like the mannikin in the tiltyard, a human shape filled with sand.

Ewen shook him. "*Padrig!*"

Now Tavin was kneeling beside him, one strong hand on his shoulder. He could scarcely feel it. "Highness, your brother's brain-rotted. For all our sakes, have a care."

He couldn't see anything. His eyes were full of tears. *Padrig*. "No, he's not, Tavin. Something else has happened, it has."

"Ewen—"

"*He's not rotted!*"

From the corner of his eye he saw Ren and Evon flinch, saw Clovis startle and Tavin bow his head. He ignored all of them. Fools. What did they know?

"Who found him, Tav? Ren and Evon?"

"That's right," said the swordmaster. "Halfway between our northern borders and the Vale."

"No sign of the king?"

"None."

And what did that mean? Was their father dead? "We must ride out to find him, Swordmaster."

"Highness, we will. Ewen—"

Ignoring Tavin, he dropped his dagger to the flagstones and chafed Padrig's cold, dry hands. "Come on, you little snot. I'm talking to you. It's not polite to ignore your big brother. What are you doing back here on your lonesome? Where's the king? Where are our cousins, and the barracks men who rode out with you? Padrig? Padrig, *look at me!*"

Pillowed on his chest, Padrig's head rolled. Then his crusted eyelids lifted. His eyes, their mother's eyes, were cloudy in their depths. His fleshless face was stubbled, his rasping breath foul.

"And in the last days there was a blood-red sun rising," he whispered. "The sundered parts all came together and oh there was a joining and the blighted world rejoiced."

"See?" said Tavin, his voice breaking. "Told you, I did. Brain-rotted. Not a word of sense out of him. Ewen—son—"

He knew what Tavin wanted to say. "Don't," he snapped. "You eat those words, Swordmaster. This is my *brother*."

Tavin loosened the grip on his shoulder and shifted until their eyes met. "This *was* your brother, Ewen, but it's a carcass now. It's wearing his face but Padrig is gone, he is. Boy, you know what happens next. You know what's to become of him. You know what's the right and merciful thing to do."

No. *No*. "Padrig," he said, and pressed his hand to his brother's cheek. "Padrig, it's me. It's Ewen. Please, Padrig. Talk sense to me. Prove our grizzled swordmaster wrong."

Padrig's eyes rolled like a bull's. When he was a little boy he used to make faces to frighten the servants. Here now was a face to frighten men. To frighten kings and older brothers. To break them down to tears.

"Bow down," said Padrig, his cracked and bloodied lips peeling back from his teeth. "Kneel. Bow down. Don't you know who is coming? Don't you know who calls? You weak fools. Bow down."

"No, no, no, don't say that!" he begged, and smoothed the strands of filthy hair out of Padrig's mad eyes. "Padrig, don't talk like that. You'll give folk the wrong idea, you will. Listen to me. Hear my voice. You're in the Vale. You're in the Hall. This is me holding you. Padrig, *please—*"

"*Ewen*," said Tavin, as Clovis and the barracks men retreated, their fear clotting the Hall's air and dimming its light. "He can't hear you. There's no understanding in him. Not any more."

"No!" he shouted, glaring. "I don't believe that. He needs rest, he needs a goodwife. Clovis, send for the—"

"It's too late for potions!" Tavin shouted back. Leaning forward he ripped open Padrig's tattered coat and shirt, baring his chest. "Look! He's half-gone already!"

The flesh of Padrig's torso was a mass of rotting pulp and pus. Seeing it, Ewen choked.

*Spirit, no. Please, no.*

But there was no point in praying. Tavin was right. It was too late. *Padrig.*

Easing his right arm free of his brother, he held out his hand. Tavin plucked the fallen dagger from the flagstones, then hesitated.

"Ewen . . . let me."

He shook his head. "No. He's my brother."

"And that's why I should—"

"*I said no.*"

Silenced, Tavin laid the slender dagger's hilt across his palm. The weight of it made his mended bones ache. It was a good blade. A sharp blade. His brother shouldn't feel a thing.

*I have to do this. I have to. Padrig's already dead.*

And it could be worse. It could be. There could be five men with cudgels.

Sick with rage and grief and guilt, he pricked the dagger's point between his brother's jutting ribs and pushed. The hilt thudded home. Padrig died without a sound.

*And so it's punished, I am, for that man Jeyk in the Eastern Vale.*

Clovis started weeping.

Heedless of danger, Ewen touched his fingertips to the thread of blood on Padrig's lips. "You know what to do now, Tavin. Do it. The king's lost, he is. We have to find him."

"Highness," said Tavin, his voice empty, and rose mountainous to his feet.

Mercifully they left him, Tavin and Clovis and the two barracks men. He sat on the Hall's cold flagstoned floor holding his brother, staring at Padrig's still face until the day died and the light with it, and everything was dark.

At sunrise he and Tavin burned Padrig in the pit, where every ruler of Vharne and his family had been burned since the first days of their ancient land. When it was done, the leaping flames died down to embers, all but a fistful of Padrig's ashes were scooped into the beautiful blue ceramic jar, made for him the day of his birth, and sealed inside it with scented white beeswax. That left-behind fistful of ash was mixed with the fistfuls of every other man, woman and child that had ever been given to the fire. Mixed with their mother, who had died too young. Those ashes stayed in the pit, for memory.

It was only the two of them. Him and Tavin. A burning was private, even for a king's son.

The pit was sited on top of the Vale's highest hill. It had a roof but no walls, and the cold breeze playing beneath it blew away the scented smoke of Padrig's fire. Holding the beautiful death jar, still feeling his brother's dead weight in his arms, Ewen stared at the new day's pale, flooding light. Watched as it gilded the scattered cottages, the grazing farm horses, and the bold stone castle with its barracks and tiltyard and bath house and stables and barns. Gilded the Vale folk stirred out of bed early, and toiling.

*The king's folk, they are. My folk 'til he's found. If he's found. And if he's not . . .*

Beside him, Tavin sighed. "You had a bad night, boy."

"I killed my brother, Swordmaster. What kind of a night should I have had, do you say?"

Tavin gave him a hard look, but held his tongue on that. "You're feeling well enough?"

"I'm not blighted, Tav, if that's where you're dangling."

Another hard look. "Sure of it, are you?"

"*Tav*—" Ewen schooled himself. "He was halfway rotted. His chance to blight me was long past."

"Ha," Tavin grunted. "Most like. But you'll not blame me for being cautious, you won't."

No, he wouldn't. But he was done talking of Padrig.

"So, now we ride to find the king," said Tavin, seeing it. "Who will you leave behind to sit in the king's seat? You've a handful to choose from, I say. Though best not your cousin."

"You've never warmed to Ivyn," he said. "When will you confide the reason?"

"Need to confide for not liking a man, do I?"

"When he's nephew to the king? I think you do."

Hunching one shoulder—a sure sign of his discomfort—Tavin blew out a sharp breath. "It's his eyes, boy. They sit too close together."

"His *eyes*?" If he'd not been holding Padrig he'd have struck his swordmaster a blow with one fist. "Condemn a man of my blood for where his eyes sit in his face, would you?"

"No," said Tavin, very quiet, after a moment.

"Then talk straight with me, Tav. Don't talk crooked like a thief."

Tavin's age-softened jaw tightened. "You think to push me?"

"Right into the pit if you don't speak plain."

Shocked, Tavin turned to him. "With that jar in your arms?"

"Yes, Tavin, with this jar! You think to push *me* on a morning like this, do you?"

*With the smoke of my burned brother in my throat? On my tongue? With my fingers remembering the dagger thrusting home?*

Scowling, Tavin dragged his callused fingers through his close-clipped badger hair. And then he sighed again, for he knew he could speak or he could walk away. And walking would be a thing of strife.

"Your cousin's eyes aren't the point of it, and neither's his blood," he muttered. "I'd condemn any man who shouts the king down in his own Hall. Ivyn spits too many bold, foolish words, Ewen. He doesn't think, he just spits them out. And when he knows he's wrong will he suck them back? He won't. No man like him can sit the king's seat in his Hall. Not without spitting enough words to cause trouble."

True enough, his youngest cousin blustered. But was that cause to condemn him outright? "It's you that's harsh here, Tav," he said, shaking his head. "There's no harm in Ivyn. He gets that bluster from his father, he does. My mother was the same. I was small when their father died, but I remember the old man well. Blustery as his children, he was, and not a jot of malice to it."

"Your mother," said Tavin, hot now, "never blustered a day in her sweet life, spirit see her. She spoke her mind straight to the king, as any good queen would. But she *never* blustered foolish at him nor overspoke him in his own Hall."

Ewen pulled a face. It was true Ivyn had done that, more than once. It was also true that, like Tavin, he didn't care for Ivyn's pushy ways.

But no man's wants could be placed above the wants of the man who wore Vharne's crown.

"You care for the king's dignity, you do, and that's a good thing. But Tav, if the king looks aside from Ivyn's bluster who are you not to follow his glance?"

"The king looks aside out of love for your mother," said Tavin, still hot. "The best of her pack, she always was. Ivyn's her blood, not his, like Nairn. Honours her, the king does, by excusing her family." A grimace. "He thinks."

"And what the king thinks I think," he retorted. "Ivyn's my blood too, Tav." He slapped a hand lightly to his swordmaster's arm. Could easily have slapped harder, only that wouldn't be clever. "If the king and I can bear Ivyn's bluster then so can you, I say. Besides, you cranky old fox, I never was about to sit my cousin's arse in the king's seat. A spring lamb, am I, to make a green mistake like that?"

"You're lambish enough, Ewen," said Tavin, unconvinced. "And this is a sunrise that sees you muddled with grief. That's your brother in your arms, boy, and it was your brother you put down like the poor rotted soul he was."

He came close to making good on his threat to push Tavin into the pit, then. The swordmaster saw it and took a clever step backwards.

"Now, now, Ewen—"

Pointed finger jabbing, he took back the space of that one clever step. "Be silent. *I'm* talking, I am. I treat you like a man of my blood and you think that gives you leave to *elbow* me, do you? There is *no* leave, Swordmaster Tavin. There is no—"

Tavin seized his shoulders between his callused swordsman's hands. His eyes were full of a painful pity. "There's leave, boy. What's my life for but honing you to be an honest king?"

"*Honest?*" he said, choking. "You say I need your help to be *honest*, do you? Tavin—"

"Have you wept for him yet, boy, our poor rotted Padrig? The mischievous little brother with the eyes your mother gave him? *Ewen, have you wept?*"

**201**

With a shrugging twist he forced Tavin's hands to drop. "So it's *weeping* makes me honest?"

"It's not hiding from the truth! No man can be a king if he can't look at what he's done!"

"Swordmaster, I spent all night looking," he spat. "I know what I did. Now tell me tears will bring Padrig back and I'll weep to fill the Spate River, I will. But if they won't, I'll keep dry."

Stony silent, Tavin stared at him.

"Tav, I grieve," he insisted. "Every breath I take is a dagger through my lungs. But I can't be womanish for him. Besides, if I weep myself empty now I might feel the lack of tears later."

It was the closest he could come to saying how much he feared for the king.

In his busy life Vharne's swordmaster had seen many sad and cruel things. He'd long since learned how to hide uncomfortable feelings — and he was hiding them now.

*Is that lying, Tav, is it? Or do you try to protect me? And on a morning like this is there any difference?*

"The king has my best barracks men with him, he does," Tavin said, after a moment. "You hold to that, son. He has your cousin Ivyn's two brothers and he has Ryne. I'd trust my Dirk in a skirmish as I trust myself. He'd not be my right hand else. Haven't I trained him hard for five years? Haven't I elbowed him over and over so he can take a harsh blow? I have. You've watched me."

But he wasn't reassured. "And you've watched the king with Padrig, Tavin. You know his heart, you do. He was angry over that butchery in the Eastern Vale but will you tell me he'd let the sprig out of his sight? Do you say he'd let Padrig wander the rough if he could stop him?"

The morning's light, brightening, showed him tears in Tavin's eyes. Showed him a bad night for the swordmaster. Showed him rivers full of grief.

"Ewen—" said Tavin, breaking, and roughly turned away.

Cradling Padrig's death jar, Ewen followed Tavin onto the grassy hillside beyond the pit. Down in the Vale milch cows gathered in their pastures, anxious to be milked, and dogs danced in the green grass as sheep and goats were unpenned. Mist curled off the duck ponds. Dew dappled the ground, sparkling.

A glorious autumn morning, it was . . . and here was the Vale without its king.

"Tavin," he said, and stood behind the swordmaster's broad back. "Padrig was yesterday. It's Vharne I have to think of today. It won't be Ivyn's arse in the king's seat when I ride out of the Vale."

Slowly Tavin turned to look at him, his grey stubble glinting silver. Understanding dawned. His eyes widened and then squinted and a scowl tightened his scarred face.

"Now that's a horse with a thrown shoe, Highness. Do what you will, you'll not get it to run, you won't."

Which was just what he'd expected Tavin to say.

"You'd defy your king?"

"I'd go hunting for my king!"

"And leave the Vale untended. Vharne ungoverned. That's how you'd keep your oath, is it?"

Tavin snarled. "My oath binds me to stand sword for the king. His danger's mine, it is. Whoever spills his blood spills mine and that's a crime to be paid for with death, it is." He spat on the grass. "You say I call you lambish, boy. You take offence. I grasp that, I do. So *you* grasp *my* offence at being held an old man who can't recall what oath he swore!"

Ewen held his glare unflinching. "Whoever sits in the king's seat stays true to his oath, I say."

"Then *you* sit in the king's seat, Ewen, since you're so keen to ruminate on oaths, and *I'll* ride out to find the man whose arse that seat should be warming!"

A good thing this was held a sacred place or they'd be brawling now. Tavin's face was mottled red with his temper, his bullish shoulders hunched.

"Swordmaster, I can't do that," he said, and with an effort set aside his own temper. "It's true you're the king's sword, but it's his son, I am. Break my blood bond, should I, for the sake of your oath?'

# CHAPTER THIRTEEN

Tavin let out a roar that woke the high hillside to echoes, then stamped towards the path leading down from the pit. But when his booted feet touched the beaten earth, he stopped.

"Tavin . . ." Sighing, Ewen joined him. "Who else can I trust with the king's seat? Who else can sit in the Hall and not shame it? Name me that man and I'll listen, I will."

"I say you should sit there," said Tavin, his shoulders slumping. "No other man in Vharne but you, I say."

"Tav, no other man but me can ride out," he replied. "What's the real flea in your shirt, old fox? I'm such a lamb, am I, I'll be devoured by the first wolf I find?"

Tavin turned. Resignation was in his face now, and bitterness in his eyes. "Leave me behind, and who will you take?"

"Ivyn," he said promptly. "Blustery or not, he knows how to hold a sword. And his brothers are out there, they are. It's his right to seek them. Bryn of the Croft, I'd take. It's a wily man, he is. A great tracker, and he knows the north-west. Noyce, with his dogs. A barracks man or three, if you can spare them."

"No more than that?"

"It's enough. Vharne's served best if we don't make a great fuss."

Tavin's nod was reluctant, as though agreeing gave him a pain. "Where will you ride?"

"In the king's footsteps to Neem," he said. "That's where he was when he flew us his last message, remember. Bryn will pick up his tracks from there."

"*If* the king's last message flew from Neem," Tavin muttered. "Falcons eat pigeons, remember?"

The swordmaster could be so contrary. "Well, Tav, unless I stumble across a pile of bloodied feathers and a ripped message to tell me otherwise, it's the best plan, I say."

Tavin grunted. "And if the Crofter and my barracks men find no tracks?"

He'd spent the long, hard night thinking of this. "Then I'll follow the northern borders west to the coast, head south 'til I strike the Spate's mouth then turn inland along the river 'til I reach the Vale. I'll find the king in there, I will."

*I hope.*

His leather coat creaking, Tavin folded his arms. "You should take more men, Ewen. That's a lot of riding over empty land, that is. Plenty of shadows for brain-rotted wanderers — or worse — to hide in."

"Worse?" Ewen stared. "*Beasts*, you mean? Tav, those days are long behind us, they are."

"You say." Tav hunched his shoulders again, stubborn. "But *I* say what I said before. *The north is stirring*. Vharne's infected with brain-rot, it is. There could be beasts in the rough country, I say."

The sun was climbing. He should return to the Hall. While he and Tavin burned Padrig, Clovis was sending a private summons to Ivyn, to Bryn of the Croft and the dog-handler Noyce. They'd be at the castle by noon.

*I don't have time for Tav to talk me in circles. Now I speak with the king's voice, I think.*

"Is there proof of beasts, Swordmaster?" he snapped. "Bring me a man who's seen one, or a horn, or a tail. A strip of bloodied hide. I'll fright at shadows after proof, I will." He stepped closer to Tavin then, Padrig's ashes tight in his arms. "There's folk like you in Vharne who remember the beast days, they do. I want the kingdom quiet, Tav, not frenzied with no proof."

Instead of blustering at that, Tavin only cocked his head. "What's your memory of them? Beasts?"

*His* memory? "Why?"

"Just answer me, boy."

Rude, that was. *Tavin, you try me.* But he was leaving his sword-master behind, so he let it go.

"Fear," he said. "Tusks and claws. Killing. And I remember they *died*, Tavin. Them and the sorcerer."

Tavin brooded across the Vale. "Know the haius blossom, do you? Falls fallow in autumn, it does. Sleeps all the cold winter. But when the earth warms it wakes, Ewen. Not all dead things stay dead."

His arms tightened round Padrig's death jar. *But most do.* "Tavin, I need your answer. Do you sit in the king's seat or do I choose again, against my will, and still ride from the Vale without you?"

"I'll sit in it," said Tavin, surly. "Deny the duty, can I, with the king's son demanding? And I'll handpick barracks men to ride with you into the rough. I'll do that for you, Ewen. And you do this for me, boy. Don't let my words of warning slip through your fingers like soap in the bath."

*Spirit be thanked.* "I won't. But I won't startle at whispers, either. It's cautious I'm being, Tav. Since when was that counted a fault?"

"Stand in front of a man running at you with a bared blade, you can, and tell yourself you're being cautious for not baring your own sword or leaping sideways," Tavin retorted, still surly. "They'll burn your cautious head and your cautious body in two fires, boy."

"That's an opinion, it is," he said, after a hard-breathing moment. "Tavin, you can keep it. I've got my own."

In reply, Tavin started down the steep beaten-earth path, his boots thudding hard. A sign of his distress, it was. As a rule he walked much lighter than that. Ewen stared at the swordmaster's broad, retreating back, what remained of Padrig so heavy in his arms.

*We're friends, we are. This will blow over.*

The swordmaster was halfway down the hill already. Resigned to being punished with silence, Ewen followed. When he caught Tavin up he slowed and kept pace at his side.

They returned to the castle without another word spoken.

His cousin Ivyn blustered into the Hall not long before noon, next to arrive after Bryn of the Croft. Richly dressed, his brown hair long enough to make a king frown, he walked the castle's stone floors as though he owned them.

"Why am I sent for, cousin?" he demanded. "I've cares of my own not to be dropped willy-nilly."

Ignoring Clovis's stiff-backed disapproval, and Bryn of the Croft's stifled surprise, Ewen kissed his cousin on both cheeks, a familial greeting. "There's news, Ivyn. Let's take a moment in private."

Leaving Bryn to kick his heels in the Hall and Clovis to wait for Tavin and Noyce to arrive, he led the way to the castle's spirit chamber. Ivyn knew the room. Straightaway he saw that Padrig's death jar was moved from the wall of waiting to a niche in the spirit wall, with its flickering flame. His sallow face drained sickly, all the bluster blown out of him and his pock scars standing stark.

"When?" he said hoarsely. "*How?*"

"Yesterday," said Ewen, pushing the chamber door closed. "A scouting party found him wandering, they did, and brought him home. Ivyn, he was brain-rotted."

Ivyn's fingers became fists. "Van? Lem?"

"There's no word from the king."

"They're *all* lost? Murdo and my brothers?"

He clasped his hands behind him. "I say there's no word."

A family's spirit chamber was a sacred place, for memory and mourning. Heedless of that, Ivyn paced the flagstones as though he longed for someone to kick. Two years older, he was, and liked to flaunt it. More years meant more freedom to disregard what he disliked. That was Ivyn.

"Padrig returned yesterday, you say?" he demanded. "Then yesterday is when you should have sent for me, Ewen. Concern for your own single brother and none for both of mine?" An angry glance, in passing. "I'm wounded."

*Ivyn, you don't know what wounded is.* "There's no proof the king or Van and Lem are dead."

Halting, Ivyn turned on him. "No proof but *Padrig's* dead!"

"More proof than that, I want," he said. "But I'm not sleeping on this, Ivyn. That's why you're summoned, it is."

Turning back to Padrig's beautiful blue jar, Ivyn looked at it in silence for some time. Then he sighed. "Was he dead when he got here? Or did he pay the price for brain-rot?"

*Oh, so now you think to ask me?*

"He died in my arms."

"I'm sorry," said Ivyn, meaning it well enough. "You loved him."

*And you didn't.* "Ivyn, there's trouble stirring in Vharne."

"No," said Ivyn, staring. "You've shocked me with that news, Ewen."

As much as he'd loved Padrig did he dislike this man, his youngest cousin. "Tomorrow you and I ride to find the king and your brothers. I've summoned useful men to maybe ride with us, Bryn of the Croft and a Vale man you might know—Iain Noyce. Swordmaster Tavin handpicks the barracks men who'll guard our backs. The castle will provision you. Your horse is fit for hard riding, is it? I'll find you another if it's not."

"Listen to him barking orders," said Ivyn, addressing Padrig's jar. "Like a king, he sounds."

"I could tell you the same in the Hall with my arse in the king's seat," he said, not rising to Ivyn's bait. "Would that chafe you less?"

"I'd be less chafed if you'd sent for me yesterday," snapped Ivyn, swinging round.

"Yesterday I was busy, Ivyn, stabbing my brain-rotted brother to the heart!"

"And that's sad, and I'm sorry for it!" Ivyn shouted. "But in a day or two or three I could be stabbing *both* of mine! Am I a barracks man, to be called here and told what I'll be doing, and when, and where, and who with? Piss on that, Ewen. I'll provision myself, no need for charity from the castle. And you should have sent for me when those scouts brought Padrig home."

Sick of him, Ewen headed for the chamber door. "Sing yourself to sleep with that song, Ivyn. Yesterday is done with. If I could unwind the clock, would I waste that time on you?" He wrenched the door open. "Light Padrig a candle, cousin. It's the family thing to do."

He returned to the Hall, where Bryn of the Croft still waited, contemplating his booted toes. "Highness," he said, with a respectful nod. He'd not yet been told the reason for his summons, but he seemed content not to know.

"Bryn. It's not too much longer we'll be, I hope."

Bryn shrugged. "I'm in no hurry, Highness."

A sensible man, Bryn was. Wived, and fathered twice over, he'd not lived in the Vale his whole life. Of his thirty-eight summers he'd spent the first eleven in Vharne's north-west, in the sleepy township of Croft. But then the sorcerer's beasts came for Croft's people — and inside a day Bryn was the only Crofter left in the kingdom. Found half-starved and wandering the empty township, he was made one of the king's foundlings until he came of age. These days he lived quiet, and never spoke of Croft.

*But he'll have to now*, Ewen thought, brooding at the man from beneath lowered lashes. *He's the only man I know who knows the north-west, he is. And he survived beasts, he did, meaning he's a man with an instinct for trouble.*

The Hall's doors swung open and in came Ivyn, his expression wary. Behind him came Clovis, and with Clovis walked Iain Noyce. Last of all was Tavin.

"Highness?" he said, one eyebrow raised, his look meaningful, and gestured him aside.

Ewen joined him near a window. "What?"

"Send Clovis to the king's chamber, son," Tavin murmured. "There's a map in his desk we'll be wanting."

A *map*? What was this? "Clovis. To me."

"Highness?" said the secretary, instantly attentive.

Still staring at Tavin, he said, "Fetch me the map you'll find in the king's private desk."

"Highness," said Clovis, discreetly baffled, and withdrew.

Tavin touched his elbow. "I'd have told you earlier, Ewen, I would, only—"

Only they'd been sharp at odds, then busy in different directions. "Tell me now."

"Best not," said Tavin, with a glance at boggle-eyed Ivyn. "A tangle, this is. But I'll steer you through it."

*Yes, you will, Tavin. Or we'll be more than at odds, we will.* He turned. "Choose a seat at the table, all of you. We can make great decisions on our arses, I say."

Noyce and Bryn found a chair each without fuss, but Tavin and Ivyn danced, hackles raised over who'd take the chair on the right of the king's seat. As swordmaster that place of power belonged to Tavin —but Ivyn, being Ivyn, saw the privilege as his.

Tavin won.

Hiding a grim smile, Ewen sat in his father's place. Clovis returned moments later, carrying a slender roll of parchment. He held it out. "Highness."

He took the king's mysterious map. "Sit, Clovis, and we'll begin."

Defeated, Ivyn had claimed the secretary's place to the left of the king's seat, so Clovis sat beside Noyce. With everyone attentive, even Ivyn, Ewen set the rolled map before him, folded his hands on the table and touched his gaze to each solemn face.

"You're summoned here on the king's business," he said. "First there's this for you to know: there's trouble in Vharne."

"More wanderers?" said Noyce, snorting. He was a man close to Tavin's age, fashioned of whipcord and as snappish as his dogs. "A kingdom of empty cottages we might be, but still *that's* no secret. Haven't

I been sending my hounds far and wide? No animal better scents brain-rot than my bloodlines. My bitches can't whelp pups fast enough."

Ewen eased himself on the king's seat. *I'm about to ruin lives. My bad night has given birth to a worse day.* "The trouble's more than wanderers. Prince Padrig is dead."

Noyce and Bryn gaped at him. "*Dead?*" said Bryn. His face crumpled. "Highness—"

"A tragedy it is, yes," he said, deliberately harsh. "But we'll hold our tongues on that, we will."

Noyce leaned forward. "And the king, Highness?"

"He can't say," said Ivyn, scowling. "No word there is of Murdo or my brothers. But my cousin died of brain-rot, so it's likely—"

"You snot!" Tavin bellowed, making Ivyn jump. "That's for you to decide, is it? Is that your arse in the king's seat? Was it you the king gave the Vale to, for safe keeping?"

"Swordmaster . . ." Ewen rested a hand on Tavin's arm. At odds they might be, but Tav would always have his back. "Stand easy. Ivyn's unwise in his fear."

"He's unwise in his puppery!" Tavin spat. "It's *your* arse in the king's seat, Ewen. That demands respect, that does."

He stared hard at his cousin. "Ivyn's nephew to King Murdo, Tavin. He knows about respect, he does."

Pocked face flushed dark red, Ivyn hissed a breath between his teeth. Then he nodded, stiffly. "I spoke out of turn, I did. My cousin's dead. I'm grieving."

"It's true?" said Noyce, breaking the taut silence. "Prince Padrig was rotted?"

*Stink and pus and festered flesh.* "Yes," said Ewen, blinking. "It's true."

"Spirit's mercy," Bryn whispered. "Then there's a chance the king's rotted too."

"A chance, but not certainty, Bryn. So I'm riding to find him, I am. And it's you I want, riding with me."

"Me, Highness?" said Bryn, uncertain. "How can I help?"

The trick was to sound confident, no matter what he felt. "The king was at Neem. Not far from the Croft, that is. Could be he struck trouble thereabouts. You know that part of Vharne, you do."

"Yes, but—" Bryn rubbed his face. "I was a boy when I knew it."

"Good enough, that is. You'll remember the land, I say. Bryn—" Ewen shook his head. "You've got family, I know. But I have to ask."

"It's the king," said Bryn. "I'll ride with you."

"You want me for my hounds?" said Noyce. "I've got a bitch and two dogs I can spare. They won't work for strangers, though. Strangers they look on for biting, they do."

"So you'll ride too?"

Noyce's smile was close to a snarl. "I'll ride."

*Spirit bless them.* Ewen let himself show a small smile. "So that's four of us, and three barracks men."

"And the swordmaster?" said Ivyn, glowering across the table at Tavin.

"Tavin holds the king's seat while I ride."

Ivyn choked. "A *swordmaster*?"

"Your choice is it, cousin?" he retorted. "Not where I sit, it isn't."

Pinching his lips shut, Ivyn dropped his gaze.

"Right then," he said, reaching for the rolled map. "There's this to consider now."

*Help me, Tav.*

He spread the parchment flat to the table, and every man save the swordmaster leaned close for a better look.

"What's this?" said Ivyn. "That's not a map I've seen before."

Tavin cleared his throat. "It's a spirit map, it is. Those red lines mark Vharne's spirit paths. The king used it to ride safe beyond the Vale, he did."

*What?* Ewen stared at him. *You know this, and I don't?*

"Spirit paths?" said Ivyn, disbelieving. "What are—"

"Places to walk in Vharne that hide a man from beasts and any sorcery-touched creature," said Bryn. "A spirit path saved me when those beasts ruined the Croft. Not that I knew what a spirit path was then." His plain face twisted. "If I had . . ."

Ivyn's disbelief hardened to suspicion. "How do you know now?"

"Bryn," said Ewen, when the man hesitated. "You've leave to speak. It's important, this is."

"The king told me," said Bryn. "A few years ago. When we spoke of the Croft, and how I survived. Still grieve that day, I do. Murdo wanted to ease the guilt in me, but said to keep quiet after. There were some who'd not understand, he said. Best it is spirit paths remain secret. So I held my tongue, I did."

Ewen stared at the map, his belly churning. So Tavin knew. Bryn knew. Who else did the king trust more than his eldest son?

"The spirit path that saved you, Bryn," he said, pushing the fresh hurt aside. "How did you find it?"

Bryn shifted in his chair. "Stumbled across it, I did."

"How?"

"Well . . ." Bryn rubbed his chin. "I felt it."

He glanced at Tavin, who twitched one shoulder in a doubting shrug. "What did it feel like?"

A slow, remembering smile warmed Bryn's face. "Like drinking sunlight, Highness."

"Drinking sunlight?" scoffed Ivyn. "And eating rainbows too, I suppose?"

Ewen flicked him a warning look. "*Cousin.*"

"Like I say, it's a boy, I was," said Bryn of the Croft, defensive. "But I swear, Highness, that's the truth."

"And I believe you," he said swiftly. "Bryn, would you know a spirit path again, crossing it?"

"I would," Bryn said, nodding. "It's not a feeling you forget."

So now Bryn *had* to ride with him, no changing his mind. With the king never once mentioning spirit paths, this survivor from the Croft might be his only chance.

*Why didn't you trust me, Father? Did failing in the Eastern Vale ruin me for you?*

"Spirit paths . . ." Clovis traced a fingertip along one faded scarlet line joining the Vale to the distant village of Arble, in the east. "I've read every book in this castle and found not a word about spirit paths."

Tavin stared at him. "*Secret*, man. Know the word, do you?"

"It's sorcery," Ivyn declared, leaning back in his chair. "Burn the map, Ewen. No sorcery in Vharne. That's the law."

Though he was hurt, and angry, he'd not hear the king accused. "Murdo trucks with no sorcery, cousin. *Spirit paths*. Given us by the spirit, they are."

"You say," said Ivyn, sneering.

"Yes!" he snapped, and slapped the table. "Here I sit in the king's seat, Ivyn. Until Murdo returns it's Vharne's king, I am. This map's no sorcery, I say."

"And this is you being king, is it?" said Ivyn, puffed up and set to bluster. "Banging your fist and laying down the law?"

Blustering back at Ivyn was a waste of good breath. "Are you chained here, Ivyn? You can walk. I won't stop you."

Ivyn folded his thin arms stubborn across his chest. "It's my brothers lost out there. Taken down these *spirit paths* by the king. Did Van and Lem even know what they travelled? Did the king confess his secret map?"

"Most like he did," said Tavin, rolling his eyes. "For that's the way you see a secret's kept secret, I say. By mouthing on it every chance you get."

Ivyn's face turned cold. "It's a rude man you are, Swordmaster Tavin."

"Rude or not, he's right," said Ewen. "Talk of the map stays between us, or there'll be trouble." He slid the parchment a little closer. "Now let's decide which paths the king most likely chose to ride."

"You don't *know?*" said Ivyn. "Cousin—"

"The king had no thought I'd need to follow," he said, struggling to hold his temper. "Ivyn, enough."

"Spirit paths," Ivyn muttered. "A sparkling notion, that is. And what's to save us from brain-rotted wanderers?"

"We'll have my dogs," said Noyce. "They'll scent a man with brain-rot long before he's dangerous close, my reputation on it."

"Really?" Ivyn sneered again. "Hide us like a spirit path, will it? Your reputation?"

"*Ivyn*—"

"Cousin, I'll have an opinion!" Ivyn snapped. "Best you accustom yourself to it. Best you don't mistake me for that cow-hocked horse you ride."

"Ivyn, you listen," he said, pitching his voice low. "Murdo is Murdo. What he swallows is his business. But you won't overspeak me in this Hall."

Ivyn scowled, his pocked face blotchy. "Padrig's *dead*, Ewen. My brothers' lives are risked. I'll speak on this matter, I will. Leave aside brain-rot, for now. Murdo rode these spirit paths to keep himself safe. And that means we've sorcery loose in Vharne, does it? With not a man beyond this castle warned of it? The truth's out tardy, Ewen."

Trust Ivyn to pick up that thread and tug on it. But before he could counter the claim, Tavin was slapping the arm of his chair.

"Sorcery in Vharne?" said the swordmaster, scornful. "Beetles in your brain, you've got, Ivyn. Every man in Vharne knows the rough's a dangerous place. Riding the spirit paths was Murdo being cautious, is all. Fault a king for caution, would you? That's clever, that is."

Ivyn ignored him. "Like you say, cousin, it's your arse in the king's seat. As the king, do you swear before witnesses Vharne's not fallen prey to sorcery?"

*Right now it's suspicion, with no certain proof.* "I swear," Ewen said, meeting Ivyn's hostile stare. Feeling the weight of Bryn and Iain Noyce, watching. "And I tell you this, *cousin*. The king followed these spirit paths and I'm following the king—to whatever end might come, be it sorcery or brain-rot or relief to find him whole. What you do, you can do. I'm done twisting your arm."

Chewing at his lip, Ivyn stared at the map. "It's my brothers out there," he whispered. There was pain in his voice now. For all his bluster, he did have a heart.

"Then ride with me to find them," said Ewen, and rested a hand on Ivyn's shoulder. "It's safe I'll keep you, I say."

Closing his eyes, Ivyn nodded.

He felt his mended arm ache, and his heart thud, and the sorrow for Padrig painfully simmering. Then he looked at Tavin.

"So it's settled, it is. Come the dawn we ride for the king."

Hours later, Ewen worked alone in the Hall. It was late, darkness outside the castle and beeswax candles within. Sworn to silence, Ivyn and the other two men were hurried home to ready themselves for leaving the Vale at sunrise. Tavin was back in the barracks, seeing to the horses and his barracks men's needs. Elsewhere in the castle Clovis organised provisions and prepared for his prince's absence. A good man, he was. Loyal. Not a soft-heart for flattery.

*Between him and Tavin I leave the Vale in good hands.*

"Here, boy," said Tavin, returning unannounced. "Best you take this, I say. Spirit knows what manner of strife you'll ride across beyond the Vale."

He carried his favourite longsword, Blood-drinker, in its elaborate leather scabbard. He'd killed that beast with it, and he loved it like a woman.

Slumped at the table, Ewen set down his inked quill and pushed aside his scrawl of notes. Then he held out his hands, and watched Tavin place the sword across them. The weight of it woke his right arm but he kept the pain from his face.

"Sure of this, are you?"

Tavin hitched a hip onto the sturdy table's corner. "What do you think?"

With the greatest care, he put down the sword. "I think it's an honour, I do."

"It is. And?"

He looked up. "And I think I should've known of that map before you."

"You were shitting in a nappy when Ewen the Elder told me of that map," said Tavin. "Every king tells his swordmaster, Ewen. He tells no-one else."

"He tells his heir."

Tavin nodded. "On his death bed."

"He told Bryn, he did."

"Take that up with him, you can. I swore Ewen the Elder *and* Murdo my silence, boy. I keep my oath."

He wanted to bang the table again. "You *broke* your oath. If you could break it today, Tav, why not break it last week?"

Eyes hooded, Tavin stared at him. "Because we didn't burn your brother 'til this morning."

A surge of pain. *Padrig.* He sighed. "All right."

There was a fireplace in the Hall and a fire in it, brightly burning. Tavin slid off the table and eased his way to the hearth. Fingers rasping his stubble, he stared at the flames. The fire's warm light stole years from his seamed face, painted it over with youth and vitality. But underneath that he looked old and weary.

Ewen stared down at the map his father had guarded his whole life. *Tav and me, we've been fighting all day, it feels like. And in the morning I ride out of the Vale into the rough and if this task goes ill with me I might never see him again.* "Tavin—"

"You need to hold your tongue a while, Ewen the Younger," said the swordmaster. "Some things to say, I've got. Not kind, all of them."

He propped his elbows on the table and rested his chin on his fists. "Words or swords, Tavin, you never spar kindly with me."

Tav flicked him a look. "Sure of that, are you?"

He dropped his fists to the table, feeling sick. "So you lied in the tiltyard? When you swore you never spared me, that was a lie to my face?"

"A lie of sorts," said Tavin, a touch of discomfort in his voice. "The whole truth is I never fought you to my full strength, Ewen."

Pushed to his feet, scalded, Ewen stared at Vharne's swordmaster. "*Why not?*"

Tavin's callused thumb jerked over his shoulder at Blood-drinker. "Why do you think, boy? My full strength killed a beast."

Three-quarters turned away from him, Tavin was, but enough of his

**217**

face was visible to reveal fear as well as weariness, harsh memories flickering like fire shadows.

"A battle-blooded swordsman can't unblood himself, son," he added, talking softly to the flames. "Sparring turns to warring in a blink, Ewen. I've seen it. The king's son, you are. Kill you, would I, not to prick your pride?"

"You say pride." Slowly Ewen lowered himself until the king's seat was polished and hard beneath him. "It might be. It might be I need to hear I'll ride from the Vale a ready man."

Tavin shifted round. With his spine to the flames his face was plunged into shadow. The tapered beeswax candles on the table picked out the whites of his eyes.

"I don't know if you are, boy. You're blooded, it's true, but our strife's bigger than that. Vharne's a land turned skeleton, Ewen. Sorcery near stripped its bones clean before you were born. We call your father king because even when beasts roamed amongst us we've always had a king. But Ewen, there are dogs in the Vale with more fleas than Vharne has subjects for your father to rule—or you, after him."

*I don't know if you are, boy.* Rankled, he folded his arms. "I know that."

Air hissed between the swordmaster's teeth. "Boy, could be I've got a useful thing or two for saying. So best make up your mind—am I Vharne's swordmaster or am I a sand-mannikin in the tiltyard?"

Ewen looked away. *Next he'll snatch up Blood-drinker and slap my arse with it, most likely.* "Tavin—" His turn to hiss air. "You talk. I'll listen."

Silence. Then Tavin nodded. "The Vale's a busy place, it is. Enough faces to look at so you won't be bored in a day. You ride out of the Vale and you ride into Vharne, into the rough country, where the trees outnumber faces. That's where sorcery lies in wait, I fear. In the valleys. In the silence. In the cold dark of night. That's why you'll take Blood-drinker. It drank sorcery once, it did. Could be time the sword drinks it again." He hesitated. "If it's strong enough, you are."

"*Strong enough?*" he echoed, and stared at his hands spread flat to the table. "Tavin, I killed Padrig. It's soaked, I am, in my little brother's blood. Strip my bones clean you'll see them stained bright red."

Heartsick, remembering, he watched Tavin cross to the table, hook close the nearest chair and sit. Watched the swordmaster's hands cover his own, fingers tightening on fingers. His gaze was steady. There was love in his eyes.

"Yesterday you released him. Last night you held him. At dawn you burned him. It was right, what you did. Ewen the Younger—it'll pass, your pain."

Was he a child, to take comfort from a comforting touch? Sitting in the king's seat, was he a child?

"What?" said Tavin, leaning back and dropping his hands to his lap. "There's a thought, there. What is it?"

He answered before he could stop himself. "It's happy I was, before the Eastern Vale. It's happy I want to be again, Tav. Is this what it felt like, when beasts roamed through Vharne? Remembering happiness? Being scared it's gone for good?"

"Yes," said Tavin, very quiet. "Just like this, it was."

*Oh*. Feeling lost, Ewen stared at Blood-drinker in its scabbard. "You truly want me to ride out with this sword, Tav?"

"I truly do," said Tavin. "I misspoke, before. You're swordsman enough not to disgrace it, you are."

"Thanks to you," he said, when he could trust himself.

"Goes without saying, that does," Tavin retorted. "But I'll smile that you said it."

*And I'll smile that I'm a swordsman, and not a disgrace. Soon as I remember how, Tav, I'll smile.*

Tavin tapped the parchment he'd been inking. "What's this, then?"

"It's safe with you the spirit path map stays," he said. "I'm making a rough copy."

"Rough enough so it won't make sense to eyes that might see it as shouldn't?"

"That rough, yes."

Tavin grunted, satisfied. "Other news for you. It's Duff, Refyn and young Hob I've picked from the barracks."

Duff and Refyn were seasoned men, tough as leather. Young Hob was two years behind Padrig, but what he lacked in age he made up for in ferocity. They'd often sparred in the tiltyard under Tavin's never-satisfied eye. Quick wits, Hob had, and a quickness on his feet to match them.

"Ready they are, and eager with it," Tavin added. "They want their king home in the Vale again, they do."

"And Ryne, and the barracks men who rode out with the king," Ewen said softly. "I've not forgotten them either, Tavin."

"No." Tavin cleared his throat. "So, boy, that's who I picked. You'll not lose sleep riding out with those lads."

"Or with Bryn of the Croft, or Noyce." He pulled a face. "Though it strikes me I should've left Ivyn in the dark so I could leave him well behind."

Tavin laughed, with little amusement. "No. It's right you were to tell him. He's a pustule, your cousin, but there's no rule of law says you can deny him the chance to save his brothers."

"I sit in the king's seat," he said, wistful. "Declare one before sunrise, I could."

That raised no bluster from Tavin. They both knew he wasn't serious.

"But he'll plague me," he muttered. "Tav, you know he will."

Tavin scowled. "I do. So it's best you know this. Strict orders, I've given my barracks men. The heartbeat your cousin climbs too high above himself? It's stepping in they'll be, to knock him back to the hard ground where he belongs."

Ewen drummed his fingers to the table. "And since you talk of *climbing too high . . .*"

"I don't climb a thumb higher than ever I should," Tavin snapped. "That Ivyn, he'll bluster you and overspeak you and call the sky green and the grass blue, boy, and you know it. He's widdershins like that, the king's nephew. And when he's blustering and you're shouting? Bryn and Noyce won't step between you. But my barracks men will."

"Tavin, I can take care of—"

"*No*," said Tavin, and slapped the table hard enough to splash the parchment ink in its pot. "Arse in that seat or out of it, boy, you're the king's voice until the king is found alive." Up came Tavin's finger, pointing. "Tell me the last time you heard your father bellow in this Hall—or out of it, come to think. Tell me, can you, Ewen? A tankard of cider says you can't."

It was a fair point. And true enough, the notion of wearying himself against Ivyn's bluster for all the days they'd be hunting through Vharne wearied him sitting here, no Ivyn in sight.

"It's a sweet care you have for me, Swordmaster Tavin," he said, gratefully. "You'll do fine in this king's seat while I'm away."

Tavin didn't relish the reminder. Eyes narrowed, he stood. "Finish inking that map, boy. You'll not find those spirit paths by spitting on your finger and waving it in the wind."

And that was their private, sentimental farewell.

# CHAPTER FOURTEEN

The early morning was thick with mist as Ewen led his hunting party from the castle's barracks, Blood-drinker in its scabbard laced tight to Granite's saddle. The weight of that famed longsword hung heavy, doubts gnawing despite Tavin's faith in him.

*I'm the swordsman to wield it, am I? If there's blood to be spilled, the courage and skill to spill it are in me, are they? Padrig was a merciful releasing, he was. The truth is a woman could've done that.*

Any farmer's wife in the Vale could have done it. Twice a week those women slaughtered goats. Even with his other bloodings, that was more blood than he'd ever shed.

Countless hours of his life spent in the tiltyard, thrusting and slicing and parrying with a blade, killing sand-filled mannikins, and now he carried Tavin's sword, a beast-slayer of a weapon. Only the tiltyard wasn't true battle and neither was putting down a brain-rotted wanderer. And while life in Vharne, in the Vale, could never be called easy, it wasn't hard the way life had been hard in the years and years the kingdom was overrun by beasts.

*If danger comes to us in the rough, I'm the man to face it, am I?*

His mended arm ached, doubting him. Angry, he pushed uncertainty aside.

*Tavin said I was, he did. I must trust to that.*

Ivyn on his lean black gelding rode at his right hand, smug he'd usurped Tavin from that prized place. Any fear he felt for his brothers was locked secret behind his face. Following them, Bryn of the Croft kept pace with Noyce and his three keen, panting dogs. Obedient creatures, they were, black and white and tan, long-tailed and short-coated, spike-collared and responsive to his snapping fingers and soft whistle. Bryn and Noyce straddled hardy brown Vale horses, good for leagues of trotting without breaking a sweat. Last of all rode Tavin's hand-picked barracks men, mounted on finely trained barracks horses. Fit and fierce in the eyes, Tav's men were, gazing left and right and left again as though a brain-rotted wanderer was like to spring out from behind a tree in the Vale.

*Spirit save us from that.*

Young Hob had been given the sour task of leading their packhorse. Its baskets carried food and waterskins and five pigeons for winging messages back to the castle.

*Spirit send me good news to send. Let me live to send Tav any news at all.*

Clatter clop clatter went the horses' hooves on the Vale road. The grey stone castle and its surrounding cottages were a distance behind them now. Around them spread the fields and farms of the High Vale. They rode so early there were few folk stirring. Even the milch cows were yet to gather at their pasture gates. The penned sheep and goats still slumbered and the farm dogs let them be. The handful of warmly dressed men and women who had risen with the misted sun stopped their labours to watch the hunting party ride by. He was well known so they waved at him, silently curious, and he waved back, leaving them none the wiser for his passing. There was no need for them to know of waking dangers in the north. Not yet. Time enough for that when such secrets couldn't be kept.

Closing his eyes, Ewen breathed deep of the damp green countryside. Whatever happened after his leaving, Tavin and Clovis between them would see the peace kept until his return. They'd keep order in the Vale, settle disagreements beyond it. Make sure the barracks scouts kept watch on Vharne's borders and along the grey, dismal divide between themselves and the blighted south.

But even so . . .

*It's Manemli waking to trouble now, and Ranoush. We're under siege in Vharne, we are, nowhere to run. Trapped, with the kingdom's coastal villages ruined years ago and our knowledge of sailing lost with them. If Tav's right and the north's waking—if Dorana's waking—*

Dorana.

That was a monstrous thought, that was. The sorcerer's home, the place they all thought was long dead. Sick with fear, he could make himself, thinking of that. He could tumble from Granite and cower mouse-like beneath a blade of grass. But what good would Tavin's Blood-drinker do him then?

He had no right to be cowering in fear.

*It's the king's son, I am. It's Vharne I'm carrying on my back.*

Folded tight and tucked inside his shirt, against his warm ribs, his copied map of the spirit paths rode with him. At a rough guess, following the king's direction, they'd take five dawn-to-dusk days to reach the Vale's northern edge. From there, with Bryn's help, they'd take the first of the spirit paths leading to the border with Ranoush, before swinging west into the empty places where Neem and the Croft and so many forgotten towns and villages had thrived before the coming of the sorcerer and his beasts.

*And we'll find the king there, we will, alive and well. We'll find Van and Lem and Tav's barracks men and his good right hand, Ryne. We must.*

Because he wasn't near ready to wear the king's crown for good.

"You're quiet," said Ivyn, with a narrow glance. "Thinking to keep your own counsel until this is over, are you?"

"What do you want me to say, cousin?" he replied, as beneath him Granite minced across a wide wooden bridge spanning one of the Vale's many swift-flowing creeks. "Spoke my piece yesterday, I did, in the Hall."

"And now you'll keep silent ever after, will you?" Ivyn's gelding baulked at the hollow hammering of hooves behind it. He dug his heels into its ribs and hissed a curse beneath his breath. "Witless slug. I should be riding my stallion."

Ewen sighed. "Your stallion can't be ridden within ten paces of anything else, Ivyn. If it wasn't such an ill-tempered creature—"

"Ill-tempered? He's honey-sweet, that horse," said Ivyn, his voice rising. "This is you on the king's seat again, Ewen. Only you can ride a horse with balls."

*And you're the only man I know, Ivyn, can split my head wide with words.*

"You want to keep *your* balls, cousin? Then keep a civil tongue, you should," he said, menacing. "This time yesterday I was soaking my brother in oil and torching him, I was. My temper's short. Don't tease it any shorter."

A snort from one of the following men. Ivyn whipped round in his saddle, offended and glaring.

"Ivyn . . ." Blowing out a breath, watching it thicken the chilly air, Ewen took his hand from the reins and touched gloved fingertips to his cousin's bony knee. They were all across the creek's bridge now, passing between brambled hedges draped in dewy cobwebs. A pretty morning. The feather-rustled pigeons in their wicker cage were cooing. "Ivyn, listen. It's blood that joins us, and a common cause. If I ride silent it's not a silent way of saying you don't deserve my speech. I ride silent for I've nothing to say."

"And why is that, Ewen?" said Ivyn. "Your brother died brain-rotted. Your father kept a secret map. You tell us we must ride these *spirit paths* and can only *claim* to know they're not sorcery. Every day more witless wanderers cross into Vharne, spreading death and ruin. Surely you have *something* to say."

"Clap tongue, Ivyn," he snapped, and kicked Granite into a trot.

Thanks to bad weather it took them nearly seven days to reach the edge of the Vale. When it started to rain, late the second day, they pulled on their oiled leather coats and wide-brimmed leather hats and endured the misery as cold water trickled down their necks.

Nearly three uncomfortable days, that went on for. Ivyn sulked through every one of them and only stopped when the rain stopped.

Trudging through greyish-brown mud smearing halfway to their horses' knees and hocks, basking in weak sunshine, at last they came across the weathered border stone warning them "Here ends the Vale'. It was barren countryside in these parts, stringy grass and stunted saplings and stones. If ever the soil had been tilled, the rough had reclaimed it years and years ago. Carried on the rising and falling breeze, an odd, stale taint. The horses, uneasy, swished mud-clotted tails and stamped hooves as they walked. Ravens huddled in the meagre trees, mocking them. Small bleached bones poking out of the water-logged ground were the only other hints of life.

Drawing rein, his right arm aching from the damp, Ewen tugged the copied spirit map from inside his shirt and unfolded it. The others eased to a halt around him, Tavin's barracks men hovering their fingers close to their sword-hilts. Always on the alert for trouble, they were. Noyce's three dogs flopped onto their bellies, pink tongues lolling, careless of the mud. But their ears were pricked and their amber eyes were watchful, and they never stopped scenting the breeze.

"Well, Highness," said Ivyn sourly. "Where do we ride from here?"

*Good question, cousin. Care to give me the answer?*

Though a red tracing on the map claimed the birth of a spirit path somewhere near to where they'd halted, he could see no marker or signpost for it. And with no first-hand experience of these hidden paths, finding one wouldn't be simple.

*Unless Bryn can stir his childhood memories. Drinking sunlight . . .*

If only the king hadn't kept his secret so close.

Ivyn sat a little straighter, suspicion dawning. "Ewen, you don't know where this spirit path is, do you? Not beyond a scrawl on that map."

Ignoring his cousin, Ewen turned to Bryn of the Croft. "Is any of what you feel here familiar? Sense a spirit path in these parts, can you?"

Bryn, who'd proved himself as quietly good-natured as Ivyn wasn't, cast a squinting look around them. "It's been a long time, it has," he murmured. "But—no. More rain's coming, it is. That's all I feel."

"So it's in the wrong place, we are? Already?" said Ivyn. He never tied back his long hair, not even for riding. It tangled over his face so he could pout behind it. "That's an achievement, that is." He hawked and spat. "Led us into ugly country for no good reason, you have."

Ewen felt his fingers tighten on the map. "If the scenery irks you, Ivyn, complain to the king, you can."

"Complain to my belly!" said Ivyn. "There's no game here, Ewen. What do we dine on tonight, cousin? Mud pie?"

He hated to admit it but that question was fair, too. With the help of Noyce's dogs they'd snared coney for supper a few times since leaving the castle, but still the cheese and smoked goat-meat they'd brought with them were running low.

"It's not here we're making camp tonight, Ivyn," he said, less biting. "We've got a good four hours' riding left before dark. Chances are we'll find fresh meat for supper."

"Chances," Ivyn muttered. "It's more than chances I want."

He was so gutsick of Ivyn's complaints he could have punched his cousin to the ground. "And it's less carping from you *I* want, Ivyn! Did you think we'd be sightseeing, did you? Did you think this journey would be anything but *grim*?"

Ivyn glared at him, and he glared back. Like always, his cousin surrendered.

"No. I didn't."

"Then bridle yourself, I say, or I'll send you home to the Vale, I swear." He breathed out hard. "This is Vharne. We're not going to starve, Ivyn. And the spirit path is here somewhere. Bryn will find it for us, he will. Won't you, Bryn?"

Bryn blinked. "Highness, I'll try, but—"

"But he can't promise it, Ewen," said Ivyn, scowling. The curse of him was he never stayed cowed for more than a handful of heartbeats. "You had to know that, you did, before you dragged us out here. So if Bryn's belly stays empty of sunlight, what then? You've kept tight-lipped since we left the castle, you have. And we've followed like meek lambs because you sit in the king's seat. Well, *cousin*, the king's seat is leagues behind us and here we are in the rough with no spirit path to follow."

He was sore tempted to slap Blood-drinker against Ivyn's arse. *It's a fool, I was, not to leave him behind.* "You're in my charge, you are, Ivyn. I'll protect you."

"That's so, is it?" said Ivyn, sneering. "Like you protected Padrig?"

Ewen had his dagger half unsheathed before he felt his fingers round its hilt.

Noyce's dogs lurched to their feet, softly growling. As Noyce snapped his fingers at them, Tavin's handpicked man Refyn nudged his horse closer to Ivyn.

"It's the prince's cousin you are, and Murdo's nephew," he said, his grey eyes cold and his voice biting. "So I won't put you on the ground this time. Next time, I will."

Finger by finger, Ewen let go of his blade. "He'll put you on the ground and I'll let him, Ivyn," he said, his throat tight. "Mention my brother again and I'll put you there myself and could be I won't think to let go of my dagger." Temper still simmering, he turned to Bryn. "You were on foot in the Croft, you were, when the beasts attacked. Could be you'll feel the spirit path if you slide off that horse and wander for a bit."

"Could be," Bryn admitted, his eyes anxious. "I'll try."

"And if you can't—" Ewen looked to Refyn and Duff, feeling Ivyn's burning glare on his skin. "You're three good trackers, you are. You'll find the king's trail."

"You hope," Ivyn muttered.

"Ivyn . . ." Ewen shook his head. "Clap tongue, else you'll have no words left for greeting your brothers, you won't."

His cousin offered a snarling smile. "It's plenty of words I've got, Ewen. For my brothers. For the king. And for you."

Suddenly weary, Ewen smoothed Granite's mane. Trouble was, he knew why Ivyn was so prickly. Behind the angry bluster his cousin was full of fear. He feared for his brothers and for himself. He feared that if they did ride into strife he'd fail to wield his sword like a king's nephew should. He was the youngest, in his brothers' shadows his whole life.

He understood that, he did. But even so . . .

*Ivyn, I should've left you behind.*

"Bryn," he said, turning again. "Do your best. We'll wait."

Sliding out of his saddle to the muddy ground, Bryn handed his horse's reins to Noyce.

"Highness," he said, and started to search.

Bryn found the spirit path roughly fifteen crow hops from the border stone marking the edge of the Vale.

Hearing his shout, Ewen cantered Granite to join him, the fingers of his right hand lightly clasped to Tavin's great sword. As he pulled up hard, the horse sitting on its haunches, a raven flapped complaining out of a nearby stunted tree.

Bryn of the Croft's plain face was lit up like morning. "It's here, Highness. Right here, the path begins."

"You're sure?" Ewen looked around, but he couldn't see anything unusual. Couldn't even see turned earth, or faded hoof prints—not a single sign to show that the king and his party had passed this way. Fallen leaves and scattered twigs, only. A hurrying of black ants. "Bryn . . ."

"It's here, my oath on it," Bryn insisted. "Climb down and feel it for yourself, you can. Or stay on your horse and ride where I point. It's strong enough you'll feel it mounted, I think."

The others were straggling over, Ivyn in the lead and ready to bluster some more. *Spirit, not another argument.* Clicking his tongue, Ewen nudged Granite forward—and let out a surprised cry.

"You see?" said Bryn of the Croft, his smile small and shy. "I said it right, didn't I? Just like drinking sunlight."

Granite's head was up, grey ears pricked, every muscle tensed with surprise. Ewen kept his fingers on the hilt of Tavin's sword. There *was* a lightness in him, that hadn't been in him a heartbeat before—and he could feel a gentle warmth rising from the earth. Then, as he kicked Granite forward another pace, he felt something in his path though his eyes showed him nothing.

"It's like trying to cross an unseen creek," he said to Bryn, astonished. "There's a drag against Granite's legs, there is. And I can feel a humming in my bones."

A humming that eased the ache in his broken, mended arm.

Pleased and relieved, Bryn nodded. "That's it."

"But you can still see me. I'm not vanished?"

"*Vanished?*" said Ivyn, halting his horse at a prudent distance. "Is your mind fogged, Ewen?"

"No," he said shortly, and swung Granite round. "There's a power here, right enough. Bryn, you say we stay with this—this *feeling*—and it keeps us safe, it does?"

"Yes, Highness," said Bryn, subdued again with Ivyn glaring. "It's how I survived the beasts."

"It's a boy, you were," he said. "How did you *know* the path would save you?"

Bryn looked away, his face a turmoil of sorrow. "I never did, Highness. Not at first. I had a friend with me when the beasts attacked. We both found the spirit path. But Alun got ahead of me, and he stumbled off it unwary. A beast saw him then. It didn't see me."

"This is madness, this is," said Ivyn, staring at the ground. "There's nothing *there*, Ewen." He turned to Noyce and the barracks men, halted off to his side. "You'll trust this, will you? With no proof? With nothing to see?"

Refyn glanced at his barracks companions, then rubbed his crooked nose and shrugged. "Our orders are plain. We follow where the prince leads."

Noyce's dogs weren't worried by the spirit path. They sniffed around the sparse undergrowth, seeking game.

Ewen nodded at them. "Mind the hounds, cousin? Bred to scent sorcery, they are. If there was trouble here they'd be hackled and howling by now. Ivyn, I can't prove this for you. Feel the spirit path yourself."

Ivyn glowered. "And if I can't?"

*If you say you don't feel it I'll call you a liar, I will.* "If you can't, and you can't trust me? Ride home, cousin. We'll ride on."

Still glowering, Ivyn kicked his horse forward. As the gelding crossed into the spirit path it snorted, head tossing. Ivyn gasped.

Ewen fought not to smile. *Gloating will lose him. Be smarter than that.* "A strange feeling, isn't it?"

"Strange," said Ivyn, sitting his saddle stiff as a tree. "I've never felt this in the Vale."

He hadn't, either. He looked again at Bryn. "Have you?"

"No," said the Crofter. "I don't know why."

"And never felt it in the Croft before the beasts came, did you?"

"No," said Bryn, shaking his head. "But where the beasts chased me and Alun, we didn't often play. It's all a mystery, it is."

And not one they had time for solving here. Ewen tightened his reins. "Mount up, Bryn. We need to ride on, we do. Hob—"

The barracks man tapped a fist lightly to his chest. "Highness?"

"Let loose a pigeon, so Tavin knows we're on the right track. Our swordmaster will be pleased to learn the king's son can read a map."

Grinning, Hob tugged their packhorse close, unlatched the pigeons' wicker cage, plucked out a bird and tossed it into the sky.

For a moment Ewen watched the bird's grey-and-white striped wings beat the air, escaping. Then he shrugged, and looked away. It would reach the Vale safely or it wouldn't. No use worrying about it, there wasn't.

"Ivyn," he said, "riding with us, are you?"

His cousin scowled at the ground as though a hard enough stare could make the spirit path reveal itself.

"I'm riding," he grunted, not looking up. "But I meant what I said, Ewen. There'll be words about this in the Vale, there will."

No use worrying about that, either. Ewen nodded at his companions. "So we're riding on. Noyce, give your dogs the signal. We're hunting now, we are. You barracks men, keep your swords to hand."

Refyn, Duff and Hob closed fingers round their blade hilts.

"Highness," they said, their eyes keen. Their horses danced a little, sensitive to the change in mood.

Ewen felt the spirit path hum through him, singing sunlight in his blood and bones. But where the sun shone, clouds gathered, they did. He pulled Tavin's Blood-drinker from its scabbard and rested the blade across his saddle's pommel.

"To the king," he said, and led his companions into the rough.

Vharne beyond the Vale was vast and silent. There were birds. There were conies. Wild sheep and other game. Ivyn's belly stayed full, and that stifled some of his complaining. They had creeks for water and sometimes a bubbling spring. But there were no fields of grain. No grazing flocks. The first spirit path they rode took them past two small villages, nameless and long deserted. Hardly a roof remained on the few upright walls. They saw bleached bones in the rubble. No sign of living folk. That path dwindled and died around noon on the third day, but after riding four nervous hours without their strange protection, with help from the king's map they found a second path that kept them riding north.

Sleeping rough was a hardship, aching backs and sore heads. Wherever they could, they made camp on the path. When they couldn't, when it led them down a ravine or into crowded woodland as the sun was setting, they camped as close to it as they could reach and Noyce stayed awake with his dogs.

Sunrise followed sunrise, and they never saw a brain-rotted wanderer. They didn't find a trace of the king. Falling asleep each night, with his saddle for a pillow, Ewen told himself: *Tomorrow. Tomorrow we'll find him.*

Not once did he voice the doubts gnawing his gut. But he could see their echoes in Ivyn's face, in Refyn's eyes. In the way Noyce and Bryn glanced at each other, and then looked away.

On the sixteenth day after leaving the Vale they saw dwellings in the distance, eastward off the spirit path.

*Neem.*

There the cautious villagers told them of the king, passing through with his people days and days before. Headed for the Croft, he was, heading west, along the northern border. Beyond that they knew nothing and cared less. What was the king to them in their lonely, miserable lives? Ewen tried not to hate them for it. It wasn't their fault the Vale had all the people it could feed. Instead he nodded and smiled and thanked them, working hard not to show anyone, especially Ivyn, the growing canker of his fear.

*The king is out here somewhere. I'll find him, I will.*

He sent a written message back to Tavin, letting him know they were pushing on from Neem, then consulted the copied spirit map. It showed a path out of Neem, most likely the same path Bryn had escaped on as a boy. Where it ended, there was the Croft. They found it after nearly an hour of searching and rode it for three days, seeing no-one. Finding nothing.

On the fourth day past Neem, still two days distant from the Croft, Noyce's dogs scented sorcery. Slavering and howling, the hounds led them across the treacherous countryside at a fast canter, until they reached a copse tangled with undergrowth . . .

. . . where they found a scattering of bodies, rotted to their broken bones.

Holding Granite hard between his hands and knees, Ewen counted them, bile rising into his throat, as Noyce struggled to leash his dogs and Tavin's barracks men beat the undergrowth with their swords, searching for more danger. Ivyn and Bryn sat their horses in shivering silence. The cool air was thick and wet with old death, the stench of it burning their eyes and coating their tongues.

Eleven men. Some of them were dismembered, limbs strewn about haphazard, the flesh torn off them in strips. At first glance he didn't think the king was among them, but to be sure he'd have to dismount and inspect each rotten corpse up close.

*And I will. I'll do it. Only first I'll catch my breath.*

There was no sign of the dead men's horses, just churned up ground and partly dried hoof prints leading away from the copse. Whoever—

whatever—had done this monstrous slaughter was gone. And while Noyce's eager dogs were still aquiver, tugging at their leashes, their frantic agitation had calmed. Not waiting for permission, Hob slid off his barracks mount, the packhorse abandoned, fell to his knees and started puking.

Grim-faced, Duff pointed. "That's Warin, that is," he said, and pressed the back of his four-fingered hand to his mouth. "Lost his left ear in the rough six years ago, he did."

"And that's Bailie," Refyn added, his face ashen, nodding to the half-devoured body beside Warin. "His face is eaten off, but I know the hilt of that blade. There's other barracks men there, only—"

Only they were rotted and ruined, and deciding who was who would be a gruesome task.

Ewen nodded. *It's glad I am, that Tavin's not here.* "I'm sorry. You knew them better than me, you did, but I know enough to say they were good men, they were."

"They were friends," Duff said heavily. "Every one."

Duff was a hard man, but he wasn't made of stone. His grief, and Refyn's, and Hob's, struck painfully close to home. *Padrig.* Hard riding and fear for the king had scabbed that wound over, but now it was torn loose and bleeding.

Then Duff nudged his horse a step forward. "Highness, look closer," he said, his voice low and grim. "Weren't no swordsmen here but our own—and some of those wounds, they're blade cuts, they are. And that means—"

*It means these good men turned their swords on each other, they did, as well as fighting whatever pulled some of them limb from limb.*

"I know, Duff," he said softly. "Sorcery." His belly churned. *The king. The king.* He turned to his cousin. "Ivyn, your brothers. Can you tell—"

Sickly pale, Ivyn shook his head. "I don't—I can't see—" His voice was high-pitched with distress. "I'm not sure."

And he never would be, if he stayed in his saddle. But it seemed Ivyn was nailed there. Ewen looked at Duff, beside him. "Hold Granite," he said, and as the barracks man took the horse's bridle he kicked his feet from his stirrups and slid to the ground.

*It can't matter that it's sorcery. I have to look for the king.*

He inspected every corpse, his heart hammering, his fingers tight around Blood-drinker's hilt. Tried not to see the maggots and the beetles and the gummy gleam of teeth. But the king wasn't one of the dead.

*Oh, spirit.*

Neither was Tavin's man, Ryne, one of the murdered. But he could name four other barracks men. The rest were too rotted. And he could name his cousins, Ivyn's brothers, Van and Lem. Van was in pieces, his skull split in two.

Ewen felt his eyes sting. They'd never been close, he and his cousins, not even as children, but still—they were blood. He looked up.

"Ivyn, I'm sorry."

Choking, his cousin leaned forward and spewed vomit down his gelding's shoulder and onto the trampled ground. Ewen stood and crossed to him, flicking a glance at Refyn. The barracks man, experienced, pulled everyone else back with a stern look and snapping fingers.

Ivyn swiped feebly at his vomit-flecked lips. "How can this be?" he mumbled, his eyes puddling with tears. "*Both* dead? There's only me left, is there? How is it just me?"

"Cousin." Ewen rested his hand on Ivyn's forearm. "I grieve with you, I do. I know—"

Nose running with snot, Ivyn snatched his arm free. "What do you know, Ewen? You only lost *one* brother. I've lost *two*, I have! I've lost—" His voice broke. "Spirit save me. How will I tell my mother?"

Weeping, suddenly boneless, he toppled sideways out of his saddle. Ewen dropped Blood-drinker and caught him, stifling a curse as his right arm protested. Ivyn slumped against his chest, hiccupping like a child.

And then he found a shred of self-control. "I'm sorry," he muttered. "That was unkind, that was. You're mourning Padrig." With a shuddering breath he pulled away and stood unsteady, but straight enough. "The king?"

Ewen shook his head. "Not here." Relief and fear shuddered through him. "Ivyn—" He had to clear his throat. "Will you ride with me to look for him, or ride back to the Vale? I'll understand if you ride back. And I'll give you Hob for an extra sword, I will."

Sickly pale still, but with a new hardness in his eyes, Ivyn looked at his dead, mutilated brothers, then dragged a sleeve across his wet face. "No, Ewen. I want to find the king, I do."

Ewen touched his cousin's cheek, lightly. "Good man. So do I." Then he looked at his companions, gathered sombre and close. "We can't linger to burn our dead," he said, brutally. "Let the spirit keep them. We'll come back if we can. Now we ride after the king—and the creatures who took our brothers from us so cruelly."

This time Ivyn did not bluster his choice.

Sooled on by Noyce, the dogs picked up a sorcerous scent again soon after, but this time Ewen ordered they be kept leashed. For three days they followed the trail steadily but with caution, travelling north-westwards towards the Ranoush border. They were nowhere near a protecting spirit path.

"It can't be helped," Ewen said shortly. "We keep going, we do, until we find our prey. There's not a soul in Vharne safe until the murderers are run to ground.

Again, not even Ivyn challenged him.

So they kept on hunting, but even though the wanderers' scent lingered and the dogs slavishly followed it they found no sign of the king or his surviving barracks men, or any other man or woman or child. Vharne's emptiness oppressed them. They felt like the only breathing humans in the land.

And then, as that third day waned cool and the long afternoon shadows summoned twilight, Noyce's dogs hackled and started to howl, threatening to strangle themselves as they fought against their leashes.

Ewen raised Blood-drinker, every instinct rousing, and looked at Refyn. "Close up. I fear we're—"

Out of the trees ahead of them lumbered two horned, scaly-hided beasts, taloned and tusked and stinking of evil. Ewen stared at them, sickened, Blood-drinker aching his arm.

*Beasts. In Vharne. You were right, Tavin. Curse you.*

Frenzied, Noyce's dogs wrenched free of his restraint and attacked. The beasts roared and grunted and killed them, ripping them to meat and blood.

Noyce slithered from his horse and fell howling to his knees.

"Bryn!" Ewen shouted, holding Granite against bolting. "Stay with Noyce and keep well back. If this goes ill, ride for the Vale and Sword-master Tavin! Ivyn and you barracks men—with me!"

No time for last words. Running sweat, they charged.

The vicious beasts were man-sized and nimble, the frothing horses mad with fear. Shouting defiance, Ewen wielded Blood-drinker in a fury, hacking and slashing, spurring Granite in for a strike, hauling the horse onto its haunches in feinting retreat. Dimly he knew Ivyn and the barracks men fought beside him but his vision was blurred scarlet, his blood a thundering flood through his veins.

Horses screamed. Men screamed. Duff went down, ripped in half, and his blood-soaked barracks mount fled. Hob went down next, his skull crushed with one blow. Refyn's horse died with its throat torn out and smashed the barracks man to the ground beneath it.

The two beasts were scarcely touched.

Half-unseated, mostly blinded with sweat, pain shrieking though his right arm, Ewen wheeled talon-raked Granite sideways and shook his head, trying to see. But the horse tripped over its own hooves and stumbled and it was enough to throw him clear out of the saddle. Granite panicked, shying away. He hit the bloodied ground hard—and dropped Tavin's sword.

A yowling roar. Beast hooves pounding. Winded and flailing, fumbling for Blood-drinker, Ewen looked up and saw curved horns, scarlet eyes, talons sharper than knives.

*I'm going to die.*

"Ewen!" Ivyn shouted. "Ewen, you fool, watch out!"

Snatching up Blood-drinker, he threw himself to the left and saw Ivyn ride his black gelding right over a beast.

The horse went down, forelegs breaking. The beast went down with it, talons sunk into Ivyn's thigh. Ivyn let out a choked cry of agony. Pinned beneath horse and beast he raised his sword-arm, the blade flashing, then plunged his weapon deep into dark blue scaly hide. The beast fought back, ripping at him, at his horse, yowling and screeching and fighting not to die.

Ewen staggered to his feet. *Ivyn*. But he couldn't help his cousin, and there was another beast. Turning, he saw it, splattered with blood, snuffling towards Bryn and Noyce.

*No. No. Not them too.*

He charged the beast, screaming. Felt the dreadful shock up his right arm as Blood-drinker sliced through heavy beast hide. Heard himself grunt as beast talons slashed his back. His body was on fire, and the pain spurred him into rage. He was his sword. He was Blood-drinker.

He hacked the beast down.

Heaving for air, running hot with sweat and blood, he stared at the butchered thing at his feet. And then, a feeble sound behind him. He turned.

*Ivyn.*

The beast pinned with his fractious cousin under the dying black gelding was still alive. He thrust Blood-drinker between its ribs, searching for its heart. The beast thrashed. The blade broke. Uncaring, he dropped to his knees and stared at Ivyn, speechless.

Ivyn stared back, breathed out, and died.

Silence in the woodland. A slowly sinking sun. Ewen looked around at his dead men, at the dead horses, at the dead beasts with their horns and hides and almost human eyes.

*Beasts? In my kingdom? Oh, spirit. The world is lost.*

# CHAPTER FIFTEEN

"Well," said Charis. "I think we might be in trouble.'

With a sigh, Deenie looked at what remained of their supplies. Six strips of dried beef, four paper packets of nuts and one and a half of dry biscuits, so stale now that even a miserly sprinkling of water couldn't turn them edible. And it had to be miserly, because only two full 'skins remained. They'd tried fishing, but that had proven unfortunate. Eating their catch raw made them so sick they thought they'd die.

"I'm right, aren't I?" said Charis, gloomy.

Deenie nodded. "Sadly, I think you might be."

The skiff sat becalmed on gently rolling water, days and days beyond Dragonteeth Reef. On one side of them the ocean stretched unchanging towards the horizon. On the other loomed the mysterious coastline, a brooding shadow. A constant menace. A blue sky sat above them, cloudless — for the moment. That tended to change swiftly, so they could never rest entirely easy.

And now they had yet another reason to fret.

"Deenie . . ." Charis shoved salt-sticky hair out of her red-rimmed eyes. "I know you don't want to, I know the thought makes you ill, but is there a *choice* now?"

*No, no. Please, no.* "We could wait one more day."

"Yes, we could," said Charis, close to snappish. "We could halve again what we're eating and drinking and wait *two* more days. Or three, even. But will three more days see us sailed past what's left of the blighted lands?"

She wanted to say yes so much her teeth ached. "Well, I'm not— maybe—" But she couldn't lie. Not to Charis. "No."

"Then we *don't* have a choice, do we?" Cross-legged on the skiff's floorboards, Charis slapped her knee. "We have to make landfall and take our chances."

Shivering, Deenie wriggled round on the rower's bench and stared across the slow, shallow up-and-down waves. Just the thought of travelling the lands beyond Barl's Mountains made her feel ill. Even with the skiff this far out—which was as far away as they could safely sail, any further and they'd lose all protection the coast afforded—the blight sickened her. It crept over the shifting ocean like a poisonous fog. Awake or asleep, she couldn't escape its foul taste. Since opening herself to the twisted magics in the reef it seemed she'd become utterly defenceless.

*I had to let the reef in, I had no choice. But I think I'll regret it for the rest of my life.*

"I'm sorry, Deenie, truly," said Charis. "It's just I'm not keen on the notion of starving to death."

"It won't be safe there, you know."

Charis snorted at that. "It's not safe here. Or haven't you noticed?"

*Yes, but I'd rather face a hundred storms or go back to sail the whirlpools than set one foot on blighted land.*

"Charis, we can make landfall, we'll find an inlet or a bay to pull into, but that doesn't mean we'll find anything to eat," she pointed out. "And even if we do, what we find could well be tainted. Or worse. I know you can't feel anything, but I can and—"

"And it doesn't matter! We still have to try!" From the look on Charis's face, she wanted to slap more than her knee. "Deenie, we talked about this before ever we left Lur. We knew from the start we'd have to forage wild food while we're hunting for Rafel."

She frowned at the brooding coast. The almost healed reef-cuts on her fingers were itching. "I don't want to forage in the blighted lands, Charis."

"And if we'd not taken so long to fight our way to Dragonteeth Reef and beyond it, and if we'd not lost nearly three days with no wind, and *another* day after that storm beyond the reef, we wouldn't need to," Charis retorted. "But all that happened, Deenie, so we do."

Never had she been so close to hating her best friend. She thought Charis was close to hating her back.

*We're exhausted. We're hungry. And worse than that, we're terrified.*

She looked at the flat and hanging sail, its belly as empty as her own. "We'll have to row."

"Then we'll row," said Charis. "I swear, Deenie, if I have to jump over the side and *push* this skiff to land, I will. I want firm ground beneath my feet. I want to drink fresh water and eat something that doesn't threaten to break every tooth in my mouth!"

"Jump over the side?" Somehow, she managed to smile. "Charis Orrick, you can't swim."

Charis threw up her hands. "The mood I'm in, Deenie, that trifling fact won't stop me!"

No, clearly it wouldn't. Charis had reached her over-stretched limit. "Then best you pack away what little food we've got left," she said. "For if the blighted lands disappoint us, and I think it's likely they will, then what we have will have to last us a while yet."

So Charis put the dried beef and the nuts and the stale biscuits and the waterskins back in their sack and stowed them safely under the skiff's sheet of canvas. Then they unshipped the oars and started pulling for land.

The closer they came to the coastline the worse she felt. By the time a quick glance over their shoulders showed them the shore close enough to make out details, her insides were knotted like old fishing nets and she could hardly see for the sick sweat in her eyes and the pain pounding behind them.

"Deenie?" said Charis, anxious. She was breathing hard too, but only because rowing on an empty stomach was miserable hard work. When they started this journey she'd been prettily plump. Now she was lean, like a Restharven fisherman. "Deenie, say something."

"Stop rowing a moment," she gasped. "So we can see what's what."

With a sob of relief Charis raised her oar and held it out of the water. Deenie, holding hers, tried to work out where they were and gave up.

"Take mine too. I want to have a proper look."

After all these days of learning, whether she wanted to or not, Charis was quite a tidy sailor. She shifted along the bench, took hold of the second oar then let both dip into the water so she could keep the skiff trim.

"Well? What do you see?" she said, after a few impatient moments. "Is there somewhere we can pull into shore?"

"Could be," Deenie muttered. On her knees in the bow, fingers bloodless on the skiff's sides, it was taking all her strength to beat back the roiling waves of blight. "There's a beach. It's small, and I think mostly stones."

"Who cares about stones? We've got boots."

"Yes, but—" Squinting, Deenie shaded her eyes with one hand. "Beyond the beach all I can see is lots of rocks and boulders."

"Rocks?" said Charis, alarmed. "What about grass or woodland? What about fresh water? What about *people*? Is there any sign of people?"

She shook her head. "None."

"Oh." Charis sounded crushed. "Then maybe we've picked the wrong place. Maybe there's somewhere better further along."

Deenie returned to the bench and took back her oar. "And if we do row further along and don't find anything? Charis, for all we know this is the only place to get onto dry land for days. It looks bad from here, but could be we'll find signs of life beyond the rocks."

"And could be we won't," said Charis. "Deenie—"

Sink it, she was the *most* contrary woman. "Charis, you're the one insisting we have to set foot on blighted land. You're the one says we can't afford to wait. So if we can't wait then we have to try our luck now, don't we? You can ride your horse or lead it. You can't do both."

"Fine." Charis sighed. "We'll set ashore on the rocky beach and cross our fingers for a miracle."

"Good." Deenie dropped her oar into the water. "Now let's keep rowing. It's past noon already and no matter what you say or how prettily you plead I'll *not* stay on blighted land after dark."

Huffing, Charis dropped her oar too. "I don't know why you're fratched at me. I'm not the one who turned the beach rocky."

"I know you're not," she said, contrite. "Don't mind me. It's my belly griping. I'm as hungry as you are."

Working smoothly together, not having to think about it any more, they rowed the skiff for the small, stony beach. The tide was on the turn, starting to run out.

"Is that good?" said Charis, as they eased the skiff towards the gently sloping shelf of water-tumbled stones.

Deenie shrugged. "I don't know that it's bad. At least we can get the skiff up high, away from the water's edge. Since there's nowhere to moor it that's the only way to stop it floating back out to sea."

"And when does the tide rise again?"

"To be sure, we shouldn't stay any later than dusk." *And hopefully we'll stay a far shorter time than that.* "Come on. We'll need to pull it the rest of the way."

They splashed into the shallows and wrestled the skiff as far up the stony beach as they could manage. The bright blue water was cold, goosebumping their skin. The air smelled briny and old. Stale. In her blood, in her bones, Deenie felt the blight seething.

*Don't think on it. Don't. Pretend you're somewhere nice.*

With the skiff as secure as they could make it, she pulled out the hessian sack full of emptied waterskins. Finding food was important, but replenishing their water supply was vital.

"Let's get on then," she said, the sack balanced over one shoulder, trying not to take her pain out on Charis. Trying to sound cheerful, and hopeful, and in no distress.

Not fooled, Charis brushed gentle fingers down her arm. "I'm sorry. I wish I could make it better for you."

*Dear Charis.* "So do I, but you can't. Don't fratch on it. None of this is your fault."

"Well, no," said Charis. "But—" And then she let out a startled squeak. "Deenie! My legs won't work!"

Without the skiff to drag, and with a moment to stand still and catch her breath after, the oddness of being on solid ground again after days and days on the ocean had caught the city girl unprepared.

"Yes, they will," Deenie said, amused even though the blight was seething. "Just keep walking. They'll remember what to do."

But it was more like a stagger, for both of them, as they picked their way to the ground beyond the beach.

"It's so *quiet*," said Charis, stopping to stare at the surrounding emptiness. Grey rock and brown rock, slicked wet in patches, dull dry in others. Cracks and little crevices, but no scuttling crabs or shy whelkies or rock pools sweet with anemones. "There aren't even any sea birds. And that's a pity, for where there are birds, there are eggs." She moaned. "I could eat a boiled egg."

Stopped beside her, Deenie grimaced. "Not a boiled seagull's egg, you couldn't. Rafel played that trick on me once, when we were spratlings. The first time Da and Mama took us down to the coast. I told you that story, remember? And you laughed and laughed 'cause I was sick the whole day after."

"I remember," Charis said, after a long pause. "And I scolded him for it, but he just laughed at me."

*Rafel.*

They rarely talked of him. There was nothing to say.

Deenie pushed her matted hair out of her eyes. "Mama did more than scold. She swatted him, good and proper."

And there was another pain, another bramble patch to stumble through. She had to bite her lip to hold back the tears.

"It'll get easier, Deenie," Charis whispered. "It will."

"So it's easy for you now, is it? With Uncle Pellen dead?"

Charis frowned at the ocean. "It'll never be easy. But the pain softens. With time."

*Or else you just get used to feeling it. Like the blight.* But Charis was trying to help, so she nodded. "Doubtless that's true." She looked ahead across the rocky ground. "Come on. Dusk'll be on us before we know it."

They started walking again. Soon after, Charis gave a little shiver. "I think you were right, Deenie. This place feels wrong. There's not so much as a hint that anyone's been here in years. It feels—it feels —*dead*."

*It feels worse than dead, Charis.* But she didn't say that aloud. "Prob'ly this was never a place many people came to visit. What's to see? Rocks and stones and a nasty little beach."

"More than that, I hope," said Charis, glumly. "We can't eat rocks and stones."

Which was true, and a worry. Lapsing into uneasy silence they pushed on across the harsh terrain, picking their way through boulders strewn careless like a spratling's marbles. The sky stayed cloudless, the air cool. Their wet boots and legs dried slowly and their salt-soaked clothing chafed. Oh, for a hot bath and soft soap. For a mattress and a pillow. For a belly not shrunk small and growling with hunger.

*And to walk through a land not blasted with blight.*

"Look!" said Charis, pointing. "Are those trees? I think they're trees!"

There was woodland ahead of them. Not lush, not exuberant, only green-brown grass and twisted saplings and older trees bent with age and lightning strike. A fringe of life on the edge of the barren landscape.

Charis laughed. "That's a good sign. Could be our luck's turning, Deenie."

Their luck hadn't been too bad so far. They weren't drowned or sunk or whipped up in a waterspout. They weren't dragged to the ocean's depths by a whirlpool. They hadn't smashed to pieces on the reef. Except—

*What if that was all our luck used up? What if things go from bad to worse from here?*

But that was another thing she couldn't say aloud. So much she couldn't say. So much she had to keep from Charis.

And in her blood the blight seethed and seethed.

There were birds in the woodland, plain brown things that clattered skywards in alarm at the sight of two weary, salt-stained girls.

"Maybe they've got eggs," said Charis, ever hopeful.

Deenie shook her head. "If they have they can keep them. I don't fancy climbing any of these trees."

"No," said Charis, and heaved a regretful sigh. "They are horribly spindly." Glancing at the twig-littered ground she gave a delighted squeal, then hunkered into a crouch. "Rabbit droppings. And they're fresh."

"Maybe they are," she said, uneasy, "but I don't see any rabbits. Do you?"

"They're around here somewhere," said Charis. "I can feel them. Their warrens must be close by. They must be practically underfoot."

And they were, as good as. Even through the blight, thinking on them, she could feel their tiny rabbit lives.

Charis noticed. "Ha! You do feel them, don't you? Good. Then that's supper solved. There's plenty of dry wood to be found, I'm sure, so we can get a fire going. Oh, Deenie!" She pressed a hand to her middle. "A hot meal at last. I *so* want a hot meal. I never want to eat dried beef or nuts or hard-tack biscuits again, *ever*."

And neither did she, only . . . 'Charis, to cook rabbits first we have to *catch* rabbits. And to catch them we have to see them. Feeling them isn't seeing them."

Pouting, Charis stared at the droppings. And then, slowly, she looked up. "Deenie . . ."

She knew that look. She'd come to mistrust that look. Despite her aching bones, she straightened out of her slump. "What?"

With a little grunt of effort, because she was very tired, they both were, Charis stood. "You told me once how Rafel called fish in Dragon's Eye Pond. When he was a boy. And your mother used to call wild rabbits sometimes, Rafel told me that."

"Yes," she said, wary. "So?"

"So *we* can call some rabbits, can't we?"

"Call them and kill them, you mean?"

Charis gave her another look. "Well, we can't eat them alive."

She'd never seen Mama call rabbits for the oven. She'd never done it herself. Just the notion had made her cry. Poor helpless little things. Rafel poked fun at her for it and said she was a noddyhead for caring. If she could eat rabbit pie then she should know how it was she came to be eating it. He'd been right on that, but it made no difference. She never could go with Mama to catch wild rabbits.

*But that doesn't mean I don't know how it's done.*

"So we'll do it?" said Charis. "Deenie, I think we have to." ·

So many horrible things they had to do, these days.

She sighed. "Have you ever called a rabbit before?"

All this time on the open water had turned Charis's pink face a deep brown but still, the blush was there. "No. But you could tell me how. You know I'm counted a fair Olken mage and this is Olken magic we're talking on. Or — or you could call them and I could kill them."

"*You* kill them?" Deenie stared. "What do *you* know of killing rabbits?"

Charis looked around. Pointed. "There's a good stout branch. One whack on the head and the job's done."

"And if you missed? If you only half-killed the poor thing? What then?"

"Then — then I'd whack it again."

"With the rabbit bleeding and shrieking in pain?" Deenie pressed a hand to her face. "I don't think so, Charis."

"Then I won't miss!" said Charis hotly. "I'll make sure I kill it first blow. Deenie, I am *not* leaving here without cooked rabbit in my belly!"

She let her hand drop. "It's not just killing them, Charis. It's skinning and gutting them, too."

"So? We've got knives, haven't we?"

"Yes, but—"

"Deenie, I will skin and gut them with my bare teeth if I have to!" Charis shouted, and snatched up the stout, fallen branch she'd pointed to. "Now call the sinking rabbits! I'm *hungry*. I want to *eat*."

Without Charis she never would have been able to break free of Lur's blighted waters. Without Charis she'd stand no chance of finding Rafel.

"Put down that horrible branch, Charis," she said, so tired. "And stand away. Stand still. I've never done this before. I don't want to spill over on you."

Charis dropped the branch and backed to the shelter of the nearest spindly tree. Her eyes were wide and suddenly uncertain. "Deenie? What are you going to do?"

"What needs to be done."

"Oh, Deenie." Charis chewed her lip. "Are you sure?"

And how *Charis* that was, to suddenly wonder if what she'd said, what she wanted, was the right thing after all.

She couldn't help a little smile, even though she felt so sad. "Yes, Charis. I'm sure." Her stained leather leggings creaking, she dropped to the cold ground. "Now hush."

Drifting her eyes closed, she took a deep breath and slowly, deliberately, loosened some of the tight grip she held upon her mage-sense. Straightaway the blight surged, eagerly seeking her weakened places. Seeking out the parts of her the reef's blight had touched and changed, that she couldn't change back again no matter how hard she tried. Scars on the inside, where no-one else could see.

She touched her mage-sense to the rabbits in their warren. Five in all. She let it stir them. Beguile them. Lull them to thinking they could come to no harm.

*I'm sorry. I'm sorry. But we can't afford to starve.*

She heard Charis gasp as the rabbits appeared out of the woodland's undergrowth. Heard her friend gasp again, almost a cry, as one by one she snapped their necks with a thought.

"Deenie! How did you—*that's* not Olken magic. Olken magic doesn't *kill*."

Shuddering, ashamed, even though she knew it had to be done, Deenie stared at the kindly killed rabbits. "I know."

"Then how did you kill them?"

She looked up. *It's only fair that I tell her. She deserves to know the truth.* "Charis, that last whirlpool—it was so strong. It was too strong. To break it, I had to—I had to let the reef in." A deep breath. A slow sigh. "And some of its magic stayed in me."

Charis's eyes opened wide. "Dark magic, you mean? *Morg's* magic?"

"Part of it is, yes," she said, struggling to meet Charis's shocked stare. "But Barl magicked the reef first, remember? There's some of her in me, too. I think. It's hard to hear it. The blight shouts so loud. But I'm sure I can feel her. At least, I can feel something that isn't dark."

"*Deenie.*" Charis blinked back tears. "Why didn't you tell me?"

"I didn't want to fright you. And I'm still trying to make sense of it myself. But it's hard. I'm so tired."

Frowning, Charis tugged at her salty hair. "If you're right about Barl, well, that's a good thing. Seems to me we can use all the help we can get. Only—it's not Barl's magic that showed you how to kill those rabbits. Is it?"

"No," she said, very quietly. "It's not."

"Well, that does fright me," Charis said at last. "I'm sorry to be hurtful, but it's the truth."

"Don't worry, it frights me too," she said, hugging her ribs, feeling her heart thumping them, hard. "But what's done is done, Charis. I can't get rid of it. So I'll have to find a way to live with it. And use it for the right reasons. Like now."

After a moment, Charis nodded. "I suppose." And then she was frowning again. "But I do wish you'd told me sooner."

*Told you what, Charis? That there's a darkness inside me I don't know what to do with?*

"I wanted to," she said, staring at the dead rabbits. "Only I was afraid you'd look at me like I was—"

"A monster? Like Morg?" Charis stamped a foot. "*Shame* on you. As if I ever would!"

"You just said you were frighted!"

"And so I am!" retorted Charis. "But that doesn't mean I think you've turned into a *monster*."

"Maybe you don't, Charis," she retorted. "But maybe *I* do. I'm turned upside down and inside out, ain't I? The things I've done since we stole that bloody skiff? I'm Deenie the mouse! No-one ever said I had *that* kind of magic! Nobody ever told me I could kill a rabbit with a *thought!*"

"Don't shout, Deenie," said Charis, her voice small. "I'm as turned about as you are, one way and another. Last time I looked I wasn't s'posed to be a sailor. I'm Mayor Orrick's pretty daughter. I keep house and I dance and flirt with young men. I'm not s'posed to be galli-vanting about blighted lands wearing men's woollen leggings with a knife strapped to my hip."

Breathing fast, they glared at each other. And then Charis laughed, wildly.

"No, no, it's not funny," she said. "But I don't want to cry. I've had enough salt water on me to last two lifetimes." She pressed her hands to her face for a moment, then let them drop. "You should go and find us some water. I'll stay here and roast these rabbits. We can eat our fill then take what's left back to the skiff. Cooked and covered, the meat will last a day before it spoils."

It was a sensible suggestion, only—"You can do that?"

"Of course I can," said Charis, scornful. "I'm three times a better cook than you, Meistress Deenie. And my magic's dab at fire starting. Off you go. I'll be right as rain."

*And now it's my turn to be uncertain.* "You're sure?"

"I'm sure. Just—use that fancy mage-sense of yours to check again we're alone in these parts."

She'd been about to do that. Closing her eyes, Deenie unfurled her feelings and pushed them through the cloying blight. "There's no-one. We're lonesome."

"Then off you dawdle," said Charis briskly. "And if you get yourself lost, just follow the smell of roasting rabbit."

She'd never tell Charis, but it was an aching relief to find herself alone for a while. Close quarters in that small skiff, peeing with company, trying to wash in salt water with company, grieving with company — and she'd spent her life 'til now quiet and a lot of it on her own. Not lonely. Never lonely. Content in her own company. It made no difference she loved Charis like a sister. She needed her solitude.

Especially now.

The countryside beyond that narrow belt of woodland was, in its own way, as barren as the rocky shore. A tussocked stretch of open land, it reminded her of Crasthead Moor's vast stillness. Only the moor smelled sweet with wildflowers and its crisp, untainted air carried the skirling of eagles.

Here was dour sourness and the ever-present taint of poisoned magics.

Mindful of the sun in its slow slide to the horizon, Deenie strode the stinging grass with the hessian sack of empty waterskins slung over her shoulder, resolutely in search of a spring or creek or pond. The blessed freedom of walking, of striking boot heels to the ground, was so exhilarating it almost managed to banish the oppression of the blight.

Almost.

*It's bad here because these are the blighted lands. Once we've sailed past them, I'll feel better. And when I'm past them I'll be able to feel Rafel again.*

She'd not felt him for days. Not since she gave herself to the reef and broke the last whirlpool. She hadn't even dreamed him. Not childhood dreams, not anything. That sense of him that linked them, that let her know she was travelling in the right direction, travelling towards him . . . it was gone.

*Not broken. It can't be broken. For it to be broken he'd have to be dead and he's not dead. He can't be. That, I would feel.*

It was as though they'd spent their lives tethered and now, careless, she'd let go.

As to what the rest of it meant? The mage-sense and the magic seared into her by the reef? That was a mystery whose unravelling would have to wait. If it meant she could call and kill rabbits, kindly — if it meant she and Charis wouldn't starve on their way to rescuing Rafel — then that was enough.

In truth, it was all she wanted to know.

She was breathing harder now, the countryside tilting upwards in a long, slow rise. Inside her leathers she began to sweat. If only she weren't so hungry, so parched. If only the ancient dark magics soaked into the soil weren't so brutal.

By the time she reached the top of the rise she was giddy with the effort, sucking in air like a broken-winded nag. Every beat of her labouring heart was like the banging of a fist on a wide, wooden door.

But when her clouded vision cleared, the sweat and pain and banging were worth it, because she could see in the distance a spreading patch of bright green and hear on the fitful breeze the breathy chuckle of running water. Relieved beyond tears or laughter, she broke into a wavering, tottering run.

*Barl be praised. If you're there. If any power's watching over me.*

It was a spring, bubbling up between a cradle of rocks from deep underground. Cold and sweet, the only sweet thing in this forsaken land, she was sure, the water had worn a thin bed for itself and ran down the hill in a swift, narrow stream.

Having tasted it once, quickly, Deenie cast aside the hessian sack full of waterskins and flung herself face down on the grass. She drank in great gulps, panting, desperate to drink all the swallowed and breathed-in sea salt out of her body. No sooner was she so full she thought she'd burst than she felt the urgent need to pee.

There was nobody to see her. She kicked off her boots and her socks, stripped off her leather jerkin and her shirt and her leather leggings, and squatted on the grass like a country sprat of three. After that she drank some more. Peed again. Drank deep for a third time. And then, not caring that the water was so cold, regretting only that she'd not thought to bring her puny sliver of soap, she sluiced herself as clean as she could. Oh, if only she could wash her hair too. It felt so horribly filthy it made her want to cry.

To dry herself off Deenie lay on the grass and rolled like a horse. Poor Charis, cooking rabbits. If there was time she should come here and drink her fill and wash then warm her naked body in fresh, salt-less sunlight. That would only be fair.

Relaxed beneath the open sky, it seemed that even the weight of the blight was lifted. For the first time in a long time it felt like she could breathe. What a shame she had to pull her manky clothes back on. But the sun was still sliding and she had waterskins to fill.

Carrying them back to the woodland, and Charis, was a wearisome task. But the pain of that heavy burden vanished as she watched her friend gratefully guzzle a whole waterskin dry.

"There's water enough to bathe in," she said, as Charis washed her hands and knife blade free of gutted rabbit. "I did."

"Oh," said Charis, longingly. Then she looked at the fire with its flame-heated rocks and jointed, roasting rabbits. "Maybe after we've eaten. I can't believe I'm saying this, but I want food more."

They burned their fingers and their tongues and the insides of their mouths on that rabbit, and they didn't care. After nothing but nuts and dried beef and dry biscuits for so long, the feast of flavour nearly brought them to tears. Between them they ate three and a half of the rabbits then sprawled on the ground afterwards, replete.

"I'm like to pop," said Charis. "And I truthfully don't mind."

Deenie smiled at the paling blue sky. Sorrow lingered for the rabbits, but she couldn't entirely regret their deaths. Not with her belly full for the first time in so many days.

"I know these lands are blighted," Charis added. "But I can't help thinking they're peaceful, too. I wonder what this place was named?"

She felt her smile die. Felt the sinking sunlight cast colder. "I'd rather not know. I think they must all be dead, Charis, the people who once called these lands home. It grieves me to think on them."

"Then don't," said Charis simply. "You didn't kill them, Deenie, and you can't bring a single one back to life. The dead stay dead and the living go on without them." She sighed. "Is it still bad? What you're feeling?"

Her respite by the spring hadn't lasted long. The blight's darkness was back, humming through her blood and bones, trying to spoil the pleasure of their meal.

"Yes."

"Deenie?" Charis sat up, bits of dead grass and dead leaves stuck in her hair. "I don't mean to nag, but I have to ask. What's doing with Rafel?"

She closed her eyes, feeling her stomach churn. "What do you mean?"

"You know what I mean," said Charis. She sounded afraid. "Where is he? And how much further must we sail to find him?"

"I'm sorry, Charis. I don't know."

"But you must," Charis insisted. "You must know *something*. We can't be travelling blind, Deenie. Can we?"

*Charis, Charis . . . why did you have to ask?*

"And if I said we *are* travelling blind? What would you do? Demand that we sail all the way back to Lur?"

"Well?" Charis's breathing quickened. "*Is* that what you're saying?"

Reluctant to answer, Deenie let her forearm fall across her face.

"Deenie!" Charis's voice was sharp now. "I've been patient. I haven't asked you to share everything you're feeling or complained when you sit hour after hour in silence, pretending I'm not there, so the least you can do is be honest with me. I think I deserve that much. Don't you?"

"That much and more," she said, sitting up. "But all I know for certain is Rafe's not dead. For the rest? I don't know. We just have to keep sailing north and see what we find."

Charis's eyes filled with tears. "I thought we were going to find Rafel."

"We are. We will." *I hope. Oh, please.* "But right now I can't tell you when or where or how. I'm sorry, Charis. I'm doing my best."

"I know you are," said Charis, sniffing. "And I know you're suffering and I know you hate being here and I know you probably wish I'd stayed behind in Dorana."

Leaning over, Deenie grabbed Charis's hand. "*No.*"

Another sniff. "Good. Now we'd best get back to the skiff. The sooner we sail away from this place the better you'll start to feel and then maybe—" Charis's eyebrows went up. "—Barl willing, you'll dream of Rafel again."

*Oh.* "I never said I'd stopped dreaming him."

"You didn't have to," said Charis, clambering to her feet. "I'm not blind, Deenie. I can see it in your eyes."

She didn't want to talk about that. "You're sure you don't want to bathe? You're a bit manky, you know."

Charis wrinkled her nose. "Sorry to say this, but you bathed and you're *still* manky. The only hope for us is hot water and soap."

"True," Deenie sighed, and held out her hand. Charis hauled her upright and together they kicked over the fire and stamped its embers to death, put the remaining cooked rabbit in the sack with the water-skins, then began the long trudge back to the beach, and the skiff.

# CHAPTER SIXTEEN

⌖

Two days later, just after dawn, racing along with a strong wind at their backs, they sailed past the last of the blighted lands. Feeling the darkness lift, like a cloud clearing the sun, Deenie burst into tears.

Charis sat up, smeary with sleep. "What is it? Deenie, what's wrong?"

Folded over the skiff's tiller, she could only shake her head and sob.

Charis moaned. "Oh, Barl save us, it's Rafel, isn't it? He's— he's—"

"No," she said, sitting up. "No, it's not him. It's me. I can think again. I can *feel* again. *Properly.*" She let out a shuddering breath. "Charis, look at the coast. That's unblighted land."

"*Un*blighted?" Turning to look, Charis laughed. "Oh, Deenie . . ."

After so long weighed down, she thought the lively salt wind might blow her away. "Can you take the tiller, Charis? I feel so strange. I need to sleep, just for a little while. I need to find my balance again."

Charis shooed her. "Go. Go. I'll be fine. I'm as good a sailor as you now."

Barely past the horizon, the sun lacked any heat but still she took refuge in the gloom of their rough-made canvas shelter. Though they'd eked out the remains of the cooked rabbit and the rest, their food had come to an end last night. It meant she was hungry but they had plenty of water. They'd manage. All that mattered was that they were past the filthy, blighted lands. Once she was rested they'd sail close to the coast and make landfall again the first chance they got. The thought of walking on clean, blight-free grass, of breathing blight-free air, almost had her weeping again.

*We're coming, Rafe. I'm coming. Hold on. Don't give up.*

As easily as a swimmer sliding beneath the surface of a lake, she slipped into the cradling darkness of sleep. And for the first time in a lifetime, or so it felt, she dreamed of her brother.

*Alone, deep in darkness, he wanders lost and afraid. He's not big brash Rafe now, he's a sprat again, tizzed like he was tizzed the day he called those fish in Dragon's Eye Pond. She can feel him. She can't see him. His pain shines brightly but still, he's in the dark. She calls his name, but he can't hear her. He can't speak. She can feel that, too, how his voice has been stolen. A fist has closed around his throat. A fist has closed around his heart. He's slipping away from her. She's losing him, she's losing—*

"Deenie. Deenie!"

"*Rafel*," she said, and opened her eyes.

But it wasn't her brother calling, it was Charis.

"Deenie, wake up! Come and see what I've found! Deenie! Are you awake?"

"Yes," she called back. But she had to wait until her breathing steadied and the storm of grief inside her had eased.

*Rafel, what's happening? Why are you so frighted? Hold on. Please. I'll never find you if you don't hold on.*

The odd link between them had weakened so badly. So *quickly*. And was that her doing? Had she damaged it somehow, perhaps by opening herself to the dark powers in the reef? But if she'd not done that she'd still be trapped in Lur and he would still be lost—and in danger.

"*Deenie!*"

Oh, Charis. What could be so important? Feeling fratched, she crawled out from under the canvas to see what had the wretched girl so het up.

"Is it a whale?" she said, squinting. The sun was tipped at least two hours past noon. She'd been asleep for *ages*. "Tell me it's a whale. If it's not a whale then I'm crawling back to—"

The words died on her tongue, salted and shrivelled with astounded disbelief.

"Charis?" she croaked. "Barl's *tits*, what—"

Uncle Pellen's crazy daughter was beaming like a bride at her wedding. "No, it's not a whale. It's better than any silly big fish. Look!"

The skiff was sailing down a *river*.

Stunned, Deenie gaped at her. "Charis Orrick, what have you *done*?"

"What does it look like?" said Charis. Any ticktock now she was going to burst with pride. "I've found us somewhere to stop and catch our breaths. Somewhere that isn't going to make you feel ill. Look at the countryside. Wonderful, isn't it? I'll bet there are rabbits galore. And wild cherries and blackberries and eggs we *can* eat."

She was so sinking *pleased* with herself. She had no *idea* . . .

Deenie clamped her teeth shut. It was all she could do not to stamp about the skiff shouting and waving her arms. A good thing Rafe wasn't here. *He'd* toss her over the side, head-first.

"Charis, this was—this was *foolish*," she said at last, when she could trust herself not to shriek. "You don't know *anything* about this river. You don't know how deep or wide it runs or how sharp the currents are. You don't know where it goes. What if it turns back and runs into the blighted lands? What if we run aground and we get stuck here—or if we sail far enough that we *do* end up back in the blighted lands and get stuck *there*? Charis—" If she wasn't careful she really would shriek. And then most likely she'd throw herself to the skiff's floorboards and drum her heels until the boat sprang a leak. "What if choosing this path takes us *away* from Rafel instead of *towards* him? You should've woken me sooner. You should've woken me when you found the river's mouth so we—so *I*—could decide if this was the best choice to make."

Finger by finger, Charis let go of the tiller. "And since when do you decide for me, Meistress Deenie?"

"Since I'm the one with a fisherman for a da who spent most of his whole life on the water and taught me a clever trick or three about sailing," she retorted. "Since I'm the one with the mage-sense that feels strife up ahead of us. Since I'm the one with the missing brother. *That's* since when, Charis."

"But Deenie, what's the use of sailing straight to Rafel if we're like to starve or die of thirst before ever we get close?"

"There's no use, I do know that, only—"

"So what would you have done if you were me?" Charis demanded. "Sailed us right past the river's mouth? Crossed your fingers we'd find landfall somewhere further along this unchancy coast when you don't know what's ahead any more than I do?"

Suddenly weary, her dream of Rafel lingering, prickling, Deenie bumped herself onto the rower's bench, propped her elbows on her linen-legginged thighs and rested her aching head in her hands.

"No, Charis. Prob'ly I'd have sailed into the river's mouth and down its throat with my fingers crossed I'd find no trouble. Just like you did."

"Then who are you to scold and wag your finger at me, Deenie? It's not enough to say you're Asher's daughter and Rafe's sister. I might be neither but my life's risked here as hard as yours."

As suddenly shamed as she was weary, Deenie looked up. "I'm sorry. It's just—I was such a mouse, Charis. And then everything went wrong and I had to *stop* being a mouse and now I'm frighted, you see, I'm frighted . . ."

"That if you stop bossing you'll be a mouse again?" said Charis, no more temper in her voice. "Deenie, it doesn't have to be one or the other."

"Maybe," she muttered. "But Charis, I can't take the chance that if I stop wagging my finger I'll turn mouse again and *stay* mouse. Rafe's so lost and he needs me strong. He needs me bossy. So I need you to *let* me be bossy. For him."

Charis was staring. "And if that's not the *sneakiest* thing!"

The smallest smile. "I know. I learned it from Rafel."

Sharply sighing, Charis pulled on the tiller and swung the skiff round to drop the breeze out of its sail and leave them rocking. Very smartly she did it, looking like a sea-born sailor. Looking nothing like the mayor's daughter with her salty braided hair and her baked-brown face and her shirt and her woollen hose, barefoot and chin up. The young Olken men of Dorana, her flirts, and maybe even Uncle Pellen, they'd be hard put to recognise her.

*This new Charis is grand.*

"So, we're not too far down the river's throat," Charis said briskly. "Best we make sure we've not been swallowed by trouble." She waved a hand. "And seeing you're the powerful mage on this skiff, you can look ahead to what's waiting. If it is trouble, well, the river's wide enough that we can turn round and row our way out of danger."

*Look ahead and see what's waiting.* Just like that, eh? Like a mage in a children's story? When she felt so altered and out of sorts? When even though she'd tried and tried, she couldn't work out exactly how much was changed in her, or what other frighting things she could do besides kill rabbits with a thought?

She frowned. "I'll try."

Charis was right about one thing, at least. The river was wide here, with room and spare to turn. Now that the first shock of disbelief and anger was subsided, she was able to look properly at where they'd fetched up.

With the river's mouth and basin behind them they were into the waterway proper. The river's banks along this stretch were sheer and rocky. No hope of landfall. A lacy fringe of trees, branches weeping downwards to the greenish-brown water's lazy surface. Deep silence. The rich, green smell of plant life, growing. Muted birdcalls. A distant hum of autumn insects.

Tranquillity.

*But how long will it last?*

As the afternoon sunlight soaked into her bones, Deenie dropped her eyelids and reached for her mage-sense. Was shocked, again, to feel its changes. How long before she'd be used to the new Deenie who looked on the world with such altered eyes?

*Or maybe I'll never get used to her. Maybe I shouldn't even try. Maybe—*

But she couldn't let herself think like that. No matter where the power came from, if it was helping her, helping Rafe, she had to accept it.

"Well?" said Charis. "Do we sit here until we grow barnacles or do we sail on?"

"Hush," she murmured, and let loose her mage-sense to roam the unknown countryside around them.

Emptiness. Stillness. A whispered memory of blight. Not soaked into the land's bones as it was soaked into the reef, just a faded smear on its surface. But even a whisper was enough to make her shiver. Scattered throughout the still emptiness she felt small, animal lives, but no people. It seemed they were alone. Alone and not in danger— at least for the moment.

She nodded to Charis. "We're safe."

"And Rafel? Does he grow closer if we keep going or will we have to turn back after we've found food and more water?"

She only had that one recent dream to guide her. But surely she'd not have dreamed him if they travelled the wrong way. "I think we can keep going. I think we're heading towards him, like this."

Charis beamed like a bride again and tugged on the tiller, swinging the skiff round to catch the lively breeze. As the sail flapped and filled, the skiff scooted forward. Deenie slid off the rower's bench, braced her back against it and stretched her feet towards the bow. Tipping her face to the cloudless sky, she let herself settle then, on a sighing breath, sent her mage-sense seeking.

Nothing. Nothing. And then, so faint it was like the faded memory of a dream, she felt her brother's presence. Felt a tug on their strange link. Blinking and blinking, she thrust away the stinging tears.

*It's me, Rafe. I'm coming. Don't be frighted. You're not alone.*

\*    \*    \*

It took nearly three hours to sail the length of the rocky cliffs lining the sleepily winding river. For long stretches the breeze played hide and seek, capricious, and they were forced to unship the oars and row. But then it sprang up once more and stayed and Deenie, taking a turn at the tiller while Charis snatched an hour of sleep, watched the cliffs shrink and shrink and give way to grass-and-moss covered banks. They were high, still no chance of landfall, but her flagging hopes began to revive. And as the cliffs dwindled so the river started to narrow, gradually at first and then more and more sharply until if she'd had a stone to throw, she easily could have tossed it from bank to flowered bank.

From up ahead, around a gentle bend, came the urgent sound of racing, splashing water. Deenie felt her skin prickle and her mage-sense stir to life. Swinging the tiller she dropped the breeze from the sail.

"Charis. Charis, wake up! We might be in a spot of bother."

An upheaval within their makeshift canvas tent, then Charis squirmed into the light. "Bother? What kind of bother?"

"I'm not sure. Hush."

In silence they listened. Then Charis pulled a face. "That doesn't sound good."

Still there was nowhere they could leave the skiff and clamber ashore. The river was hardly being helpful. Deenie winced as her mage-sense stirred again, sharply.

"I think it's best to row until we know what that is."

She and Charis took their places on the rower's bench, took hold of the oars with hands that had long since worn through their gloves and were now callused, like fishermen's hands.

"Slowly, mind," she cautioned. "I don't fancy a swim or any kind of watery tumble."

Charis rolled her eyes, and they started to row.

As they neared the river's sweeping bend the water began to flow more swiftly, fighting against their drag on the oars. Glancing over the skiff's side, Deenie felt her heart skip.

"We've lost a goodly bit of depth. It's a blessing we're flat-bottomed."

Sweating, breathing deeply, Charis flicked her a grin. "Speak for yourself. My bottom's got a nice womanly curve to it, thank you."

Her mage-sense was humming, but she managed to grin back. "Mind your oar there, Meistress Orrick. You'll have us in circles any tick-tock."

Charis snorted, derisive, but she minded her oar.

The sound of swift splashing was growing steadily louder. And it roared louder still as they swept round the river's bend—to see a stretch of white-capped water frothing and racing over a wide scatter of sharp, slick rocks, some small and tricky and some frighteningly large.

Charis nearly dropped her oar. "Barl's tits! How are we s'posed to row through *that?*"

"I don't know," said Deenie, feeling her jaw clench. "But we have to. Look—"

Not too far beyond the treacherous white water the river smoothed again, inviting. And on either side, past its low and kindly sloping banks, stretched open fields lightly thatched with woodland. On the left, in the middle distance, a hint of long, low roofs. A village, maybe even a township. She couldn't sense any people in it but then, she was awfully tired. Maybe there *were* people and she was just too weary to feel them.

"Sink me," said Charis and turned, her eyes wide. "Deenie—"

*Don't let her panic. We'll be swoggled for certain if she panics.* "Well, for a start, I don't think *sink me* is exactly the thing you should say just now," she replied. "Here. Take my oar."

"Why?" said Charis, startled. "What are you—"

"I've got an idea. Charis, my oar!"

Charis shifted and took the oar, her expression mutinous. "Deenie, you're not going over the side again, are you? Why do you have to keep going over the side? You can't—"

"Yes, I can," she said. "I have to. Now hold the skiff *right here*. I need to put my boots on."

A good thing she wasn't in her leathers today, or that would be more wasted time in changing out of them. Boots laced on tight, with an effort she hoisted herself over the side, making Charis curse as she tried to keep the skiff from tip-tilting too hard. The water reached just past her waist and was cold enough to start her teeth chattering almost at once.

"And what does that prove?" said Charis, battling to keep both oars under control. "Deenie, please, get back in the skiff."

Walking slowly, bobbing a little, feeling the river try to knock her off her feet, Deenie shuffled through the water until she was well clear of the oar.

"No," she said, shaking her head. "I'm all right. It'll only get shallower from here. You'll have to get out too eventually, but for now you do your best with the oars and I'll do my best holding on close to the bow. Between us we should be able to keep the skiff from running away or capsizing."

"*Capsizing?*" Charis's jaw dropped. "Deenie—"

"Oh, do stop wittering," she snapped. "We can't possibly turn back, Charis. We have to keep going forward—and that means some fancy footwork past this horrible stretch of water. Now let's get a move on, shall we? Unless you want to let Rafe down."

It was a cruel thing to say, but it was all she could think of that would stiffen Charis's resolve.

Slipping and stumbling, the riverbed stony underfoot, she walked beside the skiff as Charis wrestled to control it with the oars. *She* tried to control it with her oddly altered magic, but she'd never learned the kind of spells that could help in a task like this and whatever magic the reef had left in her, she couldn't seem to make it work in their favour.

All that left was muscle and luck.

Splash by splash the river's water level dropped, first to her hips and then down to mid-thigh. If it dropped to her knees there was going to be trouble, with the first scattering of boulders getting closer—and closer—

"It's no good, Charis," she said, panting. "You'll have to get out. We can't afford the skiff hitting the riverbed. If we do we'll spring a board, and that'll be that."

So Charis shipped the oars, pulled her boots on and slipped over the skiff's side into the cold and shallow racing water. They each took a side, grabbed a rowlock, and struggled to partly drag, partly lift the skiff against the flow of the river.

Even if they'd been tall, brawny men it would have been a monstrous task.

Over and over they lost their footing and plunged their knees onto the riverbed's smooth rocks. Banged their shins and their elbows and even their chins on the skiff. Caught splinters. Burst blisters. Scraped their skin to blood. Twice they nearly lost hold of the skiff and once it banged so hard into a boulder Deenie was certain it would fly apart into spars.

They staggered past the first tumbling of rocks. Past the second. There was only one more. The water barely reached midway up their calves, now, and that made their job harder. They had to bend to keep hold of the skiff, making their backs ache and their arms and shoulders burn. The river was so shallow and flowed so fast it was hard to take a step without it nearly swept them along with it. And the skiff —the skiff—

"Whatever you do, Charis," Deenie panted, groaning, "don't let it go!"

But that was easier said than done.

The river snatched it away from them as they reached the third race of rocks. Leaping and spinning the skiff tore from their desperately grasping hands and sent Charis flying, crashing sideways and shoulder-first into a humped boulder.

"*Charis!*" Deenie shouted. And then she couldn't care about her friend any more, because the skiff was bouncing and racketing its way back down the race.

Their clothes. Their waterskins. Their knives. And Barl's diary . . .

"Deenie! Deenie, what are you *doing?*"

Ignoring Charis's pained cry, Deenie flung herself after the skiff. *Come back—come back—you have to come back!*

Even though the reef had changed her, she still wasn't strong enough to summon the skiff with a thought.

Staggering like a drunken sailor, she chased after their small, errant boat. Rock after rock after boulder it banged into, tipping and spinning but still staying afloat. The further she pursued it the deeper the river grew, slowing her, dragging her, until she could hardly see and hardly breathe and all her body felt on fire.

*But it's our clothes and our waterskins and our knives and Barl's diary.*

The skiff surged ahead of her, carried along by the river. It surged past the race's first scattering of rocks and swept towards the bend. As soon as the water was deep enough, Deenie started swimming. His little fish, Da had called her, when he wasn't calling her his mouse.

At last she caught up with the skiff—but only because half its boards were sprung loose and it was starting to wallow and sink.

Lost in a haze of exhaustion, Deenie dragged herself over the sagging skiff's side. One haversack she could rescue, only one. She had no hope of carrying two. Sloshing across the flooding floorboards, she reached the sheet of canvas, hauled it aside and dragged out her haversack, not Charis's, because Barl's diary was in it. Double stitched into oilskin, oh, praise Barl indeed. She found Charis's knife, though, and shoved it into the haversack with her own. Pulled out half of her own clothes, making sure to keep her leathers, and shoved some of Charis's on top of them instead. The empty waterskins were floating in the skiff now. She grabbed four and stuffed them on top of the clothes. And that was that. She'd run out of time.

And then she remembered: *Charis can't swim.* Half-shrugging on the haversack, she flailed and staggered and splashed her way to the rowlocks. One oar had slid free, the other was in pieces, floating, banging into the bench. She snatched up the biggest piece—it was the blade end, that was lucky—then managed to get herself back over the side and into the river just as the skiff began to go down for good.

The weight of the haversack dragged her under with it.

An odd moment, then. A kind of tired and wondering surrender. The river closed over her head and she remembered Darran's story about Da and the king. Well, the prince, as he was then, down in West-wailing. The terrible storm. Prince Gar being knocked overboard and Da diving in after. Finding him. Saving him.

*He was a hero that day.*

Now here she was, all these long and terrible years later, and she was in the water. She was going to drown. And there was nobody to save her. She wasn't a Prince Gar and she didn't have a champion.

*Which means I'll have to save myself, won't I?*

A hot surge of fury flashed through her.

*I'm not drowning. Not today. I'm too busy.*

Kicking and thrashing, she flailed her way to the surface — still holding the haversack and the broken piece of oar. She mustn't let go of either, because Rafel needed Barl's diary and Charis couldn't swim.

*You swim, Deenie. You're a fish, not a mouse.*

She swam as far as she could and then she walked — staggered — through the shallows to the top of the race, where Charis was waiting. Sitting in the water, her back pressed against the boulder, looking terrified and furious and shivering cold all at once.

"Deenie —" she said, gulping. "Deenie — where's the skiff?"

With a groan, she let the haversack slide off her aching shoulder. "Sunk to the riverbed, by now."

Horrified, Charis stared. "*Deenie!*"

"Don't look at me," she said, her own teeth chattering. "This is all your fault. You're the one who said *sink me*. Didn't I tell you that was a bad idea?"

No sound but rushing water. And then they both started to laugh.

"It's not funny, it's not *funny*," Charis wailed, rubbing her bruised shoulder. "Deenie, what are we going to do?"

Deenie looked further up the river, at the low banks and the open fields and the thatching of woodland. "We're going to get out of this horrible water. And once we've dried ourselves, and had a hot meal and a good night's sleep, we'll keep going on foot."

"On foot," Charis said faintly. Then she frowned at the wet

haversack dropped onto another, smaller rock. "Deenie, I don't mean to sound ungrateful, but is that really all you managed to save?"

"Sorry," she said, shrugging. "Trust me, we're lucky I saved this much."

Charis sighed. "I know." And then she frowned at the stretch of river between them and the distant meadow. "How am I supposed to get to dry land?"

"With this," said Deenie, holding up the length of oar. "You'll hold on to it and dog paddle. I'll be right beside you, Charis. I won't let you drown."

"You make it sound simple," said Charis, trying to smile.

Deenie shrugged again. There was no point sweetening the truth. "Well, it's not. But you'll manage. You're a mayor's daughter, remember? A *hero's* daughter. You don't have a choice."

And manage Charis did. Barely. It was a cruel trial for both of them. It wasn't such a great stretch from the end of the shallow, treacherous race to the first section of river bank that was low enough for them to climb up, but they were both shatteringly tired, bruised and cold and dazed with shock. And the waterlogged haversack didn't make things any easier.

On hands and knees, heads hanging, streaming water, they crawled over the bank and into the river's bordering field. There, in the pale warmth of the slowly sinking sun, they sprawled face-down in the grass and laughed and wept in turns.

At last Deenie sat up, and poked Charis in the ribs. "Come on, Meistress Orrick. Stir your stumps. We can't stay here all night."

Whimpering, Charis rolled over. "I think I have to. I don't have any bones left. They dissolved in the river."

Ignoring that, Deenie squinted across the field towards the nearest huddle of trees. "There'll be dead branches there. We can start a fire. I swear, I could sleep on a bed of hot coals."

"I tell you I can't move a finger," said Charis, groaning again. "I'm one big bruise from my head to my toes."

"So am I. So what?" Grunting, Deenie bit by bit pushed to her feet. "Charis, come on. If we don't warm ourselves soon we're going to catch our death of ague."

Stiff and cold they trudged to the straggle of trees, with the haversack hung on the piece of broken oar and carried between them. There was dead wood aplenty. They made a fire and laughed at the heat of it. There were rabbits, too. Stifling the regret, because it couldn't be helped, Deenie called them, and killed them, and while Charis skinned, gutted and jointed the poor things she upended the haversack and spread its contents out to dry.

"What's that?" said Charis, pointing. "I've not seen it before."

Sink it. The diary. Wrapped and stitched in the double layer of oilskin, it had survived its river-dunking intact.

"Charis . . ." Deenie chewed at her lip. "If I ask you to forget you saw it, could you? Would you?"

Flickered with flames and shadows, Charis looked at her steadily, in silence. Of a sudden she seemed older, and burdened with cares. Then she nodded. "Yes."

"It's nothing bad," she added. "Only—it might be safest if I keep it secret a while longer."

Another silence. Then Charis smiled, dimpled and swift. "Was I dreaming or did I see a hint of roofs, from the river?"

Bless her. "I saw them too. With luck we'll find a village with people in it who can tell us where we are."

"Yes," said Charis, suddenly doubtful. "Only they won't speak Olken."

Yet another problem. *I'm sinking tired of problems.* "We'll manage somehow. Is that rabbit cooked yet?"

"Not yet," said Charis. "Hold your horses."

The stars came out as, at last, they ate their fill. When they couldn't swallow another bite, they piled the fire high with all the dead branches they could find and, too tired to care that they slept on nothing but hard ground, curled up in the billowing warmth and plunged straight-away into sleep.

Hours later, in the deep chill of night, Deenie roused with her mage-sense roiling. Opened her scratchy eyes and saw that she and Charis were no longer alone.

She could hardly breathe past the stench of blight.

"Charis." She sat up slowly, staring at the four shadowy figures at the very edge of the slumbering fire. They weren't moving. They just stood there. Mumbling. A sound to stand the hair on the back of her neck. "Charis, *please*. Wake up."

Charis muttered. Whimpered, then groaned. "What? Oh, oh, everything hurts. Everything—"

"Charis, hush," she said, her voice low and urgent. "And stay still. We don't want to startle them."

"Startle who?" said Charis. "What are you—" And then she sucked in a sharp breath. "Barl save us. Who are they? And what's *wrong* with them?"

"I don't know," she murmured. "All I'm sure of is they're blighted. And I think . . . not in their right wits."

Inch by inch, Charis crept out her hand. "Deenie, what do they want?"

"I don't know that either, Charis," she said, and tried not to snap. "Why would you think I'd know?"

Charis swallowed another whimper. "Have they been watching us since we got here?"

She stared, her heart madly thudding, as the four shadows melted closer. Then she crept out her own hand and took hold of Charis's, hard. "No. I swear, I never felt them. But look where the moon is. We've been asleep for hours. They could've come from miles away. From that village, maybe."

"Why?"

"Maybe they smelled the smoke. Or the cooking rabbits."

Charis nodded. "Maybe. But what do they *want*?"

The shadowy figures melted closer again, so close this time that the firelight lit their faces. Their bodies. With the blight roiling in her, curdling and foul, Deenie made herself look at what it had done to them.

Open sores. Running pus. Pulpy gangrenous flesh hanging off them in strips. Four of them, all women. Mostly naked, wholly putrid. The stench of their corruption made Charis turn her head and retch.

Frozen, feeling just as sick, Deenie couldn't ease her own belly. Looking at them, *feeling* them, she could hardly breathe.

*This is what Da's fighting. If he wasn't Da . . . if he wasn't Asher of Restharven, the Innocent Mage . . . this is what he would have become. This is how he would have died.*

She didn't know how she knew it. She only knew it was true. And the truth was a dagger, plunged between her ribs.

The tallest blighted woman gargled horribly, deep in her throat. Coughed. Spat. Teeth landed at her feet. "And he will come in splendour," she said, her voice grating. "He is mighty. The world will weep blood for him."

"Weep blood," the other three women mumbled, red pus dripping from their wounds. "Blood. Blood."

Eyes rolling, the tall woman tried to raise her rotting, stinking arms. "And in the morning of the last days there was a blood-red sun," she crowed. "The sundered parts all came together and oh there was a joining and the world rejoiced."

"Deenie—" Charis's voice shook. "Have you any idea what they're saying? I can't make head or tail of it."

Stunned, Deenie listened to her thundering heart. "Can't you? That's funny. I can understand every word."

Except it wasn't funny. It was terrible.

*The reef magic again. It must be. Oh, Da. What am I now?*

The horribly rotted woman let out a keening cry. "He's calling us! He's calling! *We must be whole!*"

And as though that were some kind of command, or a signal, she and her companions again began to shuffle forward.

"Deenie!" said Charis, and scrambled backwards as fast as she could. "Barl's mercy, we mustn't let them touch us. Deenie—"

It was a nightmare come to life, those four disgusting creatures shambling predatory towards them, their eyes no longer human, blight hanging round them like a shroud.

"Deenie, we can't try to outrun them," said Charis, close to tears. "It's pitch black past the fire. We'll fall and break our necks."

"I know."

"Can you—Deenie, I think you have to—"

But Charis couldn't say it, and neither could she. Not out loud.

*Kill them? With magic? As though they were rabbits?*

She felt her belly heave. *No.* How could she? That would change her worse than anything Dragonteeth Reef had done. Morg had killed with magic.

*I can't turn into him.*

"Deenie!" Charis cried. "Deenie, *do* something! *Please!*"

The rotted creatures were spreading out, trying to circle them like a pack of hunting dogs trapping prey. Her eyes flooded with tears, blurring. Sobs crowded her throat.

*Da . . . Da . . . what do I do? Mama? Help me!*

But she was on her own.

So she reached for her changed mage-sense and killed the rotting people like rabbits. And afterwards sat with Charis in the firelight, silently weeping and waiting for dawn.

# CHAPTER SEVENTEEN

"*You wish to serve me, little Doranen? Little Lord Garrick? Very well. You can serve me. But first we must see to your sadly inadequate education.*"

So Morg had told Arlin, grandly, upon his servant's return with more gathered pieces of himself. After he had consumed and then carelessly discarded them.

He was growing very strong.

Taken into the mansion's locked library, a place forbidden him 'til then upon pain of gruesome death, Arlin had watched in silence as Morg first extinguished a powerful general warding, then perused the chamber's serried ranks of shelves. Continued to watch as he trailed his fingers along the books' old and mottled spines. Tapping one. Tapping another one. Leaving the next untouched. Leaving half a shelf. A whole shelf. There seemed to be no pattern or reason behind his choices. The spine of every book he touched glowed with a crimson sigil. When he was finished perhaps three-quarters of the books were marked.

"And those books you may not touch, Arlin," Morg told him. "The rest are made safe."

He didn't ask what would happen if he touched a protected book. The answer was in the gleam lurking deep in Morg's eyes.

Without asking permission, assuming permission was granted by the fact that he stood in the library, he plucked a safe book from the nearest shelf and let it fall open in his hands. Could Morg see them trembling? Most likely. But that didn't matter. Let the sorcerer mock him. Let him laugh. Let him sneer. These were books of magic the likes of which his father had dreamed his whole life.

*And me. I dreamed them. I wanted this too.*

"It's not the complete sum of our knowledge," said Morg. "Barl and her cowardly dupes managed to steal some volumes away with them when they ran."

He looked up. "Durm's secret library?"

"Yes," said Morg, smiling thinly. "Are the books still there?"

"No," he said, and felt the touch of bitter rage. "The collection was ordered destroyed, after—"

"After Asher killed me. And Lur's Doranen destroyed it?"

"Yes."

"So." Morg sneered. "The cowardly blood breeds true."

"I'm sorry," he said, and he meant it. Not a single Doranen voice had been raised against that infamous act. Not even his father had dared to protest it, at least not in public. Of course in private he'd condemned it every day of his life.

"And would you have spoken up, Arlin?" Morg asked, idly curious. "Had you not been a puling infant in your cradle? Would you have decried such wanton destruction?"

The trick, he'd learned, was not in lying to the sorcerer. That was fruitless. The trick was in telling him a truth that would serve as a lie. Or else the plain truth, if no harm could come of it.

"I don't know," he said, feeling the weight of the precious book of magic in his hands, his wrists, his forearms. "I like to think I would have. I like to think I'm not a coward. But those days were confused. Feelings ran dangerously high. There were Olken who thought all Doranen should be put to death."

Morg smiled again. "Because of me?"

"Yes, Master. Because of you."

"And yet they weren't. Why was that?"

"Asher wouldn't allow it."

"*Asher.*" Morg's face twisted to ugliness. It always did when anyone spoke the fisherman's name. "His misguided compassion will be his undoing. I look forward to rousing him from his stupor so I might gift him with the death he deserves."

Arlin looked down at the book again, so Morg might not see his eyes. Years of childhood study meant he could read the text's original Doranen easily enough. Its ink was faded, the thick paper mottled with age. Apparently this book was a treatise on the question of low-level transformations. Nothing like beast-making, though. Nothing at all that could be used to do the sorcerer harm. Not that he could anyway, so carefully warded as he was.

Morg waved his hand, indicating every permissible book in the library. There were dozens. "Unless I send for you, Arlin, remain here at all times. Complete your education. An ignorant man is of no use to me. But I warn you. No experimenting. Theory only. I'll tell you when the time is ripe for you to spread your little wings."

"Yes, Master," he'd said, bowing, and had happily obeyed.

Outside the mansion, days and days of time passed. Within its walls, however, passing time held no meaning. Human servants changed the linens on his bed, saw him with clean clothes and hot baths. They cooked him meals which the idiot Goose brought to him on trays in the library, shaking with terror because he'd watched the necessary killing of Fernel Pintte. He wished they wouldn't send Goose, but he knew better than to complain.

Every time the idiot looked at him, he felt Fernel Pintte die.

He neither saw nor heard Morg. The sorcerer remained secluded in his eyrie, incomprehensible. Unknowable. Waiting for a summons, Arlin steeped himself in ancient magics. The texts he'd been given to study covered an astonishing range of subjects. Translocations. Transmutations. The harnessing and coercion of natural powers: wind, lightning, water, fire, even the powers locked deep in the earth. He learned methods of working that would let a mage melt rock and flow it into any shape of his desire. Shift mountains. Freeze rivers. Think sand into glass and that glass into lofty towers.

Remembering the paltry magics he'd been permitted in Lur, remembering the way his father had raged, and Ain Freidin had raged, he felt his own buried temper stir. Father had been right about this much, at least. These Doranen magics should never have been denied them, should never have been kept secret. Barl had no right to leave them behind in Dorana to die.

*This was our birthright. This was our heritage. And out of fear we let ourselves be gelded into Olken. We lost ourselves. No. We threw ourselves away.*

Like a starving man he feasted on book after book. Glutted himself and cursed the need to pause, to eat, to sleep, to piss. The outside world stopped mattering. All he cared for was the magic.

Once, standing at the library window as he let the weight of his newfound knowledge settle into his bones, he saw a horde of beasts march down the carriageway towards the road leading to Elvado. Even as his skin crawled he had to admire their brutish perfection. Another time he saw beasts herding a motley collection of humans along the carriageway up to the mansion. He counted some fifty captives. From the look of them they weren't hosts to any more of Morg's sundered pieces, which meant they would soon walk back down the carriageway with hides and horns and tails.

Besides, if Morg had sensed the coming of any more hosts he'd have sent for his tame, compliant Doranen to go and collect them.

The temptation to use what he was learning burned him with every breath he took. But he knew better. Disobedience would lose him what little of Morg's trust he'd so far earned, and to defeat such a sorcerer he must be in his trust completely.

*And I will defeat him. I must. Until Morg is dead I can't return Dorana to the Doranen.*

Sometimes, before he could stop himself, he did think of Rafel. He did wonder if the Olken was still alive inside his stolen body—and wondered if there was yet any way to reach him.

But every time he let himself think it might, just *might*, be possible, he straightaway abandoned the hope. That brief glimpse of Asher's son had shown him a man being slowly extinguished. And surely, even if there was any part of Rafel remaining when Morg was defeated . . . if he was defeated . . . that part of him could not possibly remain sound. Sarle Baden and the idiot Goose and every witless, gibbering host brought to Morg from the wilderness, were all proof that no mere mortal's mind survived holding a piece of Morg, no matter how briefly.

And Rafel held more pieces than anyone ever had—and for longer.

*If only I knew how many more were still to come. If only I knew how much more powerful Morg will be.*

But short of asking the sorcerer outright, he'd never know. Not until he was witness to some great feat of magic. And by then . . . by then . . . it might be too late.

*If it's not too late already. If Dorana and my people aren't already lost.*

Eighteen days after his studies began, Morg sauntered into the library.

"Well, Arlin? Are you finished? Are you *educated*?"

Arlin looked at the pile of books he was yet to tackle, neatly stacked on the floor beside his chair at the large reading table. How many were left? Thirty or so? Not a bad effort, considering he'd started with nearly sixty. He was so full of new magic he thought he might fly apart at the seams.

He bowed, because Morg expected it. "Master, I'm certainly more educated now than I was the last time we spoke."

The sorcerer laughed. "I'm pleased to hear it."

There was something different about him. He seemed brittle. On edge. Watching him pace from wall to wall, from shelf to shelf, Arlin cleared his throat.

"Master, is there something you need? Something I can do for you?"

"Yes," said Morg, without pausing. "You can stop prattling, Lord Garrick. And I advise you to do so—if you want to keep your tongue."

Ah. He pulled back to him the book he'd pushed aside on Morg's entrance, lowered his gaze and busied himself with reading.

Three pages later, Morg stopped pacing. "Rafel truly believed you would oppose me, Arlin. He did not believe you would kill Fernel Pintte. He thought that despite your differences you and he could find common ground against me."

Arlin shrugged. "He thought wrong."

"Did he?" In the light from the window Morg's jewelled rings sparkled as he smoothed back his hair. A familiar gesture, made less familiar now by an undercurrent of tension. "And I'm to believe that self-serving declaration, am I?"

For a second time he pushed his precious book of magic aside. "Master, have I done something to displease you?"

"I don't know," said Morg, his eyes narrowed. "Have you?"

*Breathe, Arlin. Sweetly. Show him your best face.*

"Not to my knowledge, Master. Everything I've done, I've done because you asked it of me. Is that displeasing?"

Morg walked from the window to the table and looked down at him. "That was insolent."

"I'm sorry, I didn't—"

The blow came hard and fast and knocked him from his chair to the floor. Morg stared down at him, dispassionate.

"Why do you think I'll brook insolence from you?"

One of Morg's rings had opened the flesh over his right cheekbone. He could feel the blood trickling, carving a thin line through the pain.

"You have no answer?" said Morg. "Why, Lord Garrick, what has happened to that glib tongue of yours?"

He nearly said, *You told me to hold it.* But that would be tantamount to cutting his own throat. Braced on his elbows, he lifted his head. "Master, I don't know what to say. You're angry. I don't know why. I'm afraid that however I answer, I will be found wanting—and you'll punish me."

Hissing, Morg flung about and returned to the window. Arlin let his eyes close, just for a moment. It was life with his father, all over again.

The violent rages. The casual beatings. His dutiful obedience that was always, *always*, called into question.

*I survived that. I will survive this.*

Warily he sat up, but didn't stand. That too would be a deadly mistake. He could feel his bruised, bleeding flesh swelling. Throbbing. He'd memorised some healing incants found in one of the sorcerer's books, but it was too dangerous to summon his power. Best he play Olken and sit dumb on the floor.

Long minutes of silence. And then, still standing with his back to the chamber, Morg stiffened his spine. "You know already I am sundered, Arlin. That is no secret. What is secret, what I tell you now, is that I cannot bring all the pieces of myself home." His voice was tight, as though speaking was almost beyond him. "Some are dead. Some are dying as we speak. And when they die, I can feel it. As though Asher had a knife in his hand and cut from me pieces of my living flesh. I am *bleeding*. I am . . . diminished."

Arlin felt his heart leap. *If I was a hypocrite I'd praise Barl for that.* He made sure to speak softly. "Master, I find that hard to believe."

Morg laughed, without amusement. "Believe it. Lord Garrick, I am not the sorcerer I was."

*And if that's true, why are you telling me?*

"Master," he said, with all the earnest sympathy he could summon, "you will be that sorcerer again."

Turning, his eyes sullen, Morg nodded. "Yes. But it will take time."

"Do you not have time? Do you not have all the time in the world?"

Another hiss of rage. Morg's face twisted with contempt. "If you knew what I have lost, little man, you would not ask such an ignorant question."

"Forgive me, Master," he said quickly. "I am trying to understand."

"Are you?" Morg folded his arms and tapped his fingers to his forearm. "Perhaps you are." He roamed his gaze about the shelves and shelves of books. "Have you not asked yourself why this mansion remains when the rest of Elvado—of Dorana—lies in sad ruins?"

Of course he had, but he'd resigned himself to not knowing. "Yes, Master."

A hint of smile. "And yet you did not ask me."

"If I had needed to know, you would have told me."

This time Morg's laughter was definitely amused. "Arlin . . . Arlin. Your father trained you *well*."

*My father trained me better than you could ever imagine.*

A touch of eagerness, now. A hint of fawning hope. "I confess I would like to know, Master. If you feel inclined to tell me."

"Yes, I do feel inclined," said Morg. "But only to suit *my* purpose. Do not mistake these confidences for an admission that we are *equal*."

Arlin looked down. "No, Master. Never."

"After the mage war — after I defeated every one of my enemies," Morg continued, breaking his own silence, "I needed somewhere to live while I perfected myself. I returned here, to my family's ancestral home. I had servants. My needs were tended. And I worked. Arlin, I worked as no mage before or since has ever worked. I cannot tell you the number of times I nearly perished, or share with you my sufferings as I pursued the greatest mage secrets."

That was a pity. He'd have liked to know more of Morg's pain. "And you succeeded, Master," he said, nothing but admiring. "You broke out of your cage of flesh and bone and became . . ."

"The air," Morg whispered. "I was free. Arlin, *I was magic*."

There was so much pain and longing in Morg's voice he could almost imagine feeling sorry for the sorcerer. He could certainly feel envy.

"It must have been glorious."

Morg's eyes were glowing with the fervour of cherished memory. "It was."

"How long did it take you?"

The fervent glow died. Morg's eyes turned bitter cold. "Centuries."

Arlin felt that cold knife through him, as though any moment snow would fall from the ceiling and frost crackle over the window and the floor.

*I don't have centuries. And I can't let him have them, either. But I must make him think I want them, for him.*

The truth. The truth. He had to tell lies with the truth.

"Yes, that first time it took centuries," he said, warmly encouraging. "But must it take you so long again? You know what to do now, Master. You know—"

"Yes, I know!" Morg shouted. "But I am not *strong* enough! I told you, Arlin, I am *diminished*. And it will take *years* for me to rebuild that lost strength. Those dead and dying sundered parts of me are years and years of toil and pain. I will not become my true self again with a mere snap of my fingers!"

So much raw anguish. So little self-control. Heart thudding, Arlin risked climbing back to his feet. "How much is lost, Master? How far are you diminished?"

Morg raised a finger. "Not so far or by so much that I cannot kill you where you stand."

*Oh, careful. Be careful.* "Yes, Master. Of course. But I wonder—" He had to know. He had to risk asking. Sickened, he made himself meet Morg's terrible eyes. "Why are you telling me this?"

"Because until I am myself again I must live in this world," said Morg, as though the words stabbed him. "I must live in this prison named Rafel, a mortal man, and when I rule again I must *rule* as a mortal man. That means I need Elvado restored. It means I need men of power to command."

His pulse was racing. "Men like me, Master?"

"*Is* there another man like you, Arlin?" Lazily contemptuous now, Morg smiled. "Rafel doesn't think so. Rafel thinks that if you weren't so corrupted, you could have been the greatest Doranen mage in Lur. You think so too, don't you? It's all right. You can admit it. I'll not call you vain."

*Rafel* thought? And what would he know? He was ignorant of what it meant to be a Doranen mage. "What the Olken calls corruption, Master, I call ambition. I have power. I'm not ashamed of it. But in Lur I had no hope of becoming my true self."

Lightly, kindly, Morg stepped close enough to brush fingertips across his wounded face. "You have that hope here, Arlin. In Dorana. With me."

"I know," he said. "Why do you think I killed Fernel Pintte?"

Another smile, cruel this time. "I think you killed Fernel Pintte because you didn't want to die."

His cut cheek still throbbing, Arlin knelt on the floor. Lowered his head until his chin touched his chest. "Master, command me. I am your man."

"Yes, Arlin. I think you are," Morg murmured. "Rafel thinks you are too. He's weeping again. I tell you, Lord Garrick, I could grow fat on his tears."

"Would that I could grow fat on them with you, Master." Smiling, he looked up. "He can hear me?"

"When I permit it, he can. Yes."

So here was his chance. Choose the right words, the right tone, and Morg would never doubt him again.

*Do I care if I hurt Rafel? What is his pain, compared to what I must achieve? It's not like he can help me, trapped inside his own skull.*

"Then let him hear this," he said, unleashing himself. "Fernel Pintte was only the start, Rafel. When we are done here in Dorana, when Elvado is restored to her beauty and the might of Morg again shudders through every land, then will the Olken be set into their rightful place. Every man, woman and child in Lur will wear the face of a beast because that's all your peasant people ever were. Dumb, mindless animals, bred and born to serve."

Morg laughed, delighted. "He heard you. He's howling. Now, Lord Garrick. On your feet. We have much work to do, you and I."

They rode from the mansion to Elvado with an escort of *dravas*. Deep into autumn now, the air was thin and cold, the sky sharp blue, the sun distant. Arlin had pulled on a leather coat but Morg rode in his silk sleeves, relishing the fresh wind's bite. Daring it to discomfort him.

At length they reached the ruined city of mages, Dorana's cradle of learning. So silent, so haunted. All its beauty become decay. They rode along cracked and rutted streets to its heart, where Morg drew rein. Halting his own horse, hearing the *dravas* clatter to a stop behind them, Arlin looked around in grief and wonder. How many nights had his father dreamed of this place? Of this moment? How often had he and his friends, Sarle Baden especially, sat by the fire in the study drinking their brandy and imagining what they would find when they set foot in the Doranen's long lost home?

*Would you have wept to see this, Father? To find Elvado so broken down and forgotten?*

Before them was an enormous ornamental pool full of dirt and dead leaves and dead, desiccated birds. It was tiled in a series of intricate mosaics but the pictures they formed were obscured by centuries of grime.

He couldn't bear it.

With a word, with a whisper, all his newfound magic aching inside him, he dragged his fingers through the air and made beauty beautiful again.

Morg stared at him.

"I'm sorry, I'm sorry," he said, flinching, his gaze fixed on his horse's tangled black mane. "I didn't use what I learned in the library. That magic was mine. It's tame. It's *harmless*. But—Master, I had to."

He sat there, waiting for another blow across the face.

"Of course you had to," said Morg. "Why else are we here?"

Surprised, he risked looking up. "Master?"

"Can I rule in rags, Arlin?" said Morg, his eyebrows raised. "Can I set my throne upon a dirty dais? Elvado must be made glittering again. It must again be the brightest jewel in my crown. Little lord, you and I have come here today for a working. Together we will restore Elvado to its highest splendour. Then—and only then—can I summon my disobedient subjects so they might kneel and renew their fealty to me."

Magework the whole city? By themselves? But—"Master, that will take days. Weeks, even."

Morg shrugged. "So? You're the one who said I've all the time in the world."

"The whole city," he murmured, imagining it. "Made new again. Made beautiful."

"Ha," said Morg, pleased. "The idea appeals to you. It speaks to your romantic streak—a sadly Doranen weakness. But I'll overlook it, this once, since it can be made to serve me."

*Mageworking an entire city.* An astonishing notion. And yes, one that appealed. Staring at the ornamental pool, letting his eyes caress the blue and crimson and emerald and black and gold and purple tiles, caress the mermaids and the unicorns and the dolphins and the eagles, Arlin remembered that time in his father's study when he transmuted a crystal glass into a falcon. Remembered his pride in that beautiful thing—and the grief soon after when he was told to destroy it.

"This pool has a fountain, you know," said Morg. "Or it's meant to. Make it dance again, Lord Garrick. Show me your worth."

And that didn't mean a tame spell he'd brought with him from Lur. That meant using the magic he'd learned in Morg's library. For a moment he sat still, his gaze blurring on the mosaics.

*If I do this, I'll be changed. If I do this, I'll have taken a step closer to him. I killed for him, and that was dreadful. So why do I fear that doing magic for him will be worse?*

"Arlin?"

Such a gentle voice, when it wanted to be. Kind. Cajoling. Not unreasonable at all.

*I have to do it. I must. Or I'll have killed that peasant Fernel Pintte for nothing.*

And besides . . . he really wanted to.

It seemed the magic was waiting. He didn't even have to think. He opened his mouth and the old Doranen words were there, ready on his eager tongue, and the triggering sigils burned like fire in his fingers.

"*Hync a'teah,*" he whispered. "*Tavek. Rot'u. M'hal.*" With each word he traced a sigil on the air, laughing to see the green flames flare then swiftly die.

Nothing. And then he felt a shiver in his blood. A distant rumbling in the earth beneath his horse's hooves. For a moment he thought *tremor* and felt the breathless urge to run.

Morg laughed at him. "Sapskull."

It was such a Rafel word he was shocked out of his fright. "Master?"

"Look," said Morg, and pointed. "Nicely done, Lord Garrick. Indeed, a good beginning. But we've a long way to go."

Water leapt and bubbled at the centre of the ornamental pool, splashing the festive mosaics and painting the autumn air with rainbows. The horses pricked their ears and tossed their heads, nostrils flaring. Behind them the *dravas* snuffled and stamped.

Ridiculously pleased with himself, Arlin watched the gushing fountain. Then he glanced at Morg. "What's next?"

"You see that?" said the sorcerer, pointing to a cracked and faded tower, with gaping holes in its walls, smashed windows, buckled roof. "That was the most important, the most revered place in all of Dorana. The Hall of Knowledge, where the finest, brightest, greatest mages of the time gathered to share their understanding of magework. So much fierce brilliance there, Arlin. You would have wept to see it. *I* wept. In that Hall of Knowledge we *knew* magic was all."

Morg's face was alight with memory and passion. Six centuries behind him, and he hadn't forgotten. It might have been yesterday that he last walked through the tower.

"The first time ever I saw Barl, it was in the Hall of Knowledge," he said softly. And then his face convulsed with hatred. "The bitch. The slut. The treacherous whore."

His attentive *dravas* shifted on their hooves and feet, made uneasy by the venom in his voice. Their scaly tails whipped side to side as claws and talons clicked the cobbles.

"Be still!" Morg commanded, and the *dravas* turned statue.

Arlin shifted in his saddle to take in the rest of the battered buildings surrounding the ornamental pool. None was as tall as the Hall of Knowledge, but each one hinted at past glory, showing the world now only a dilapidated grandeur.

"The Hall is mine," said Morg. "You shall not touch it. You, Arlin, will take half the *dravas* and make your way to Elvado's outskirts. They'll keep you safe while you begin your working there."

Keep him under guard, more like. "Master."

Morg was smiling again. "Have no fear of disappointing me, Arlin. The magic you need for this is in you. Why else did I task you to all that learning in the library? Trust yourself, my little mage. We'll meet here by your beautiful pool at the end of the day."

They'd brought no food with them. No water. And heavy mage-working placed great demands on a mage.

"Arlin," said Morg, sighing, "don't make me regret giving you this chance to serve me. Did you or did you not learn the spells of translocation?"

He felt his face heat, waking the pain in his split cheekbone. It was frightening, made him ill, the way Morg could read him with no more effort than it would take to read a child's storybook.

He bowed. "Master. Of course." Because his father had beaten him if ever he forgot a spell, once read.

"Of course," said Morg, sneering. "But be sure to leave enough food in the mansion's larder for our dinner." Turning to the *dravas*, he snapped his fingers and barked a sharp command. Five of them stepped forward. "Go with Lord Garrick. Guard him with your lives."

"Master," said Arlin, bowing again, and rode away from the pool and the sorcerer, the *dravas* in his wake.

The street he chose to follow to Elvado's edge was, like so many of its streets, pitted and decaying with age and weather. Smiling, he repaired it and then, liking the newly smooth thoroughfare so much, allowed himself to be sidetracked from the task Morg had given him and repaired every crumbled street he could find.

Straightaway Elvado took on a different feel.

But soon enough the city's emptiness began to disturb him. Thousands of people had lived here once, yet he couldn't see so much as a finger bone remaining. No sign at all that any Doranen had lived here. Birds' nests he saw, yes. Small bones of birds and rats and other feral creatures that had made their homes in the city's abandoned buildings. And yes, he felt the lingering remnants of Doranen magic soaked deep in the earth, the rasp and tang of angry, violent incantations.

But no people.

Although, if he could feel their magic, six centuries after the city's destruction, the thought of what it had been like in Elvado at the height of the mage war . . .

*Enough playing with streets, fool. There's a city to remake.*

His long-dead ancestors had favoured tall, airy buildings. A lightness in their construction spoke of their lightness of thought. The bright colours Barl and her refugees had taken with them into Lur were here, faded but discernible. Greens and yellows and pinks and blues — for one blinding, unexpected moment he was homesick for Lur.

*You really are a fool, aren't you? It's probably broken to pieces by now, ripped apart and flooded and drowned. Don't think of it. You'll never set foot there again.*

The *dravas* were watching him with their once-human eyes, incuriously waiting. If he tried to run, they'd run him down.

A shiver in the back of his mind turned his head towards the city's centre. Morg was mageworking. He'd best follow the sorcerer's lead. After all, he was Lord Arlin Garrick, Morg's eager right hand.

*Or so Morg believes. Because he believes me — and Rafel, of course.*

Rafel. *He's howling.* Surely, though, the Olken's pain and despair had been an act.

*Surely he knows I was only pretending. Because if he believed me . . .*

Then he might just — give up. But Rafel couldn't. He *couldn't*. Not when the life of every Olken born depended on him.

*He couldn't give up. Could he?*

He didn't know. Not for certain. He just had to hope that deep in his prison, in his cage of familiar flesh and bone, Rafel was working to defeat the sorcerer.

*Just as I am, caged out here in the world.*

\*     \*     \*

Three weeks and four days it took them to make Elvado beautiful again.

By the end of the city's working Arlin was so exhausted he could barely sit upright on his horse, or even stay in the saddle. Racked with pains throughout his body, skewered by headaches and struggling to keep food in his belly, he stood at Elvado's heart, by the ornamental pool with its bubbling fountain, and tried not to collapse in a heap at Morg's feet.

If the long days of mageworking had overtaxed the sorcerer, it didn't show in his face. If anything he seemed invigorated. Inspired by what they'd wrought. The Hall of Knowledge was magnificent now, a soaring dedication to everything right and true in magic.

All it needed now was mages to bring it alive.

"Oh, I don't think so, Arlin," said Morg, lazily. Reading him again. Beneath the casual carelessness, a newly honed edge. "For now, I think two mages are sufficient. But do you know what we *are* lacking?"

He was far too weary for playing games. "No. What?"

"Subjects. Supplicants. Servants." Morg smiled. "*Slaves*. The time has come, Lord Garrick, to remind the world of who I am."

He clapped his hands once. Echoes bounded and rebounded around the beautiful, mageworked buildings. Heartbeats later the air shivered, and shimmered, and out of it stepped a pack of *dravas* herding seven naked, captured men.

Arlin swallowed his shock. That was the same kind of mageworking Rafel had used to send those three useless Olken Councillors back home from the blighted lands beyond the mountains. But where Asher's son had needed sigils and words, Morg needed only to think his desire and it came to pass.

*So much for hoping his lack of completion might cripple him.*

The *dravas* shoved and bullied the captives into a straight line on the polished granite of Elvado's central court. Numb with shock and terror the men didn't resist or utter a sound. All seven were young. Tall. Healthy and well-made. Like a buyer at a livestock market, Morg inspected them one by one, poking their muscles, flattening his hands to their faces. Grasping their wrists and testing the mettle of their bones.

When he was finished he nodded. "They'll do."

Arlin frowned. These past weeks of mageworking had seen a kind of rapport build between himself and the sorcerer. He'd pleased Morg, he knew that much, with the quality of his work. With his instant compliance. With his deference and constant submission to every passing whim. It meant he now had a certain, narrow freedom.

"Do for what, Master?"

"My purpose, Lord Garrick," said Morg, not looking at him. "Don't ask stupid questions."

"Master," he said, and took a step back.

They were now well into the tail-end of autumn. The cold afternoon air thickened, almost to a fog. Curls of mist rose off the ornamental pool. Power stirred, and the mist stirred with it. Morg stood in front of the first captive and touched a fingertip between the man's terrified eyes.

"*Iringa.*"

The man's eyes rolled back in his head.

Morg snapped his fingers, and the frightened man changed. Became a beast with a human face and an almost human body. His skin darkened and thickened 'til it looked like soft saddle leather. His arms lengthened, lost their fingers, turned to talons instead, and great flaps of skin like bat-wings joined his upper arms to his ribs. His mouth widened, his teeth jutting and sharpening themselves into tusks.

Again, Morg nodded. "And that will do."

Silent, his belly churning—though he should be used to it by now—Arlin watched the other six men transform. Listened as Morg gave each new-made winged beast a different word. Trindek. Feen. Manemli. Ranoush. Vharne. Brantone.

*Brantone.* A name he recognised. So these were messengers, were they? Harbingers of doom.

The transmutation complete, Morg laughed. "Delightful. You know your purpose?"

The beasts nodded, as one man. "Master," they replied, a sibilant chorus.

"Then see my wishes carried out. Return to me when you are done."

"Master," they said again, their voices slushy around the curving tusks.

Morg snapped his fingers a second time and the creatures took to the air in a leathery flapping of wings. Hideous. Arlin watched them out of sight, and when at last they were disappeared lowered his gaze to find Morg watching him.

"The beasting distresses you," the sorcerer said, curious.

There was no point in lying. "Yes."

"And yet you've promised Rafel nothing but beasting for his kind."

He made himself smile. "For the Olken, Master, I'm prepared to stifle my dismay."

And that made Morg laugh, as he was almost certain it would. "Come, my little lord," said the sorcerer. "The wheel is set in motion, but there is yet much work to do.'

# PART THREE

# CHAPTER EIGHTEEN

B ecause he'd been given charge of the king's seat, Tavin couldn't ride out to meet the king's son and his companions as they crossed into the Vale from wider Vharne. But with word sent ahead, being told they were coming, he sent ten barracks men to meet them for an escort. Such a clatter they made, riding back to the castle.

Tavin was on his feet and waiting for them in the Hall, where lamps and beeswax tapers were lit and fat logs burned in the fireplace. Shadows danced up the walls, hinting at darkness.

Seeing him after his long weeks in the rough, after all that he'd seen and done there, Ewen was hard-pressed not to weep. Especially when the swordmaster's broad, relieved smile faded as he counted only three men walking into the Hall, stubbled, filthy and stinking.

Clovis closed the doors behind them.

"Highness," said the swordmaster, strangely formal, a terrible fear dawning in his eyes. "The king?"

Ewen halted, Tavin's broken, blood-sated longsword hanging heavy at his side and burdened saddle-bags dragging down his left shoulder.

"I didn't find him, Swordmaster," he said, his voice a hoarse rasp. "And Lenyd and Refyn and Duff and Hob died searching, they did. Lenyd's brothers are dead too, they are, and nine more barracks men."

Tavin swallowed. "My barracks Dirk? Ryne?"

**293**

He made himself meet Tavin's stare. "Vanished, like the king. Three barracks men gone with them."

"No sign of Murdo?" Tavin's fingers opened and closed at his sides. "You're sure?"

*No, Tav. I'm guessing.*

"Searched for five days we did, Swordmaster," said Bryn, stepping forward. "Right to the border. Tracked the rough on our hands and knees. Not a hair of the king or your men to be found, there wasn't."

Tavin was frowning. "The dogs caught no scent?"

"The dogs died," said Ewen. And Noyce had burned their ruined bodies, weeping. "Tavin—"

He wasn't listening. "You say all three of my barracks men I picked for you perished, Ewen? *And* your cousin?"

Ewen flinched. *Disappointed, old man? Not like I am, you're not.* "Tavin . . . there were beasts."

And he heard that, Tavin did.

"*Beasts?*" the swordmaster echoed. He sat sudden in the king's seat. "So it's right, I was. Spirit save us."

"Two beasts, there were. The prince slew them both," said Noyce, his voice cracking. He wasn't a young man any more, and it showed. "Ewen did the king and Vharne proud."

"I slew one, Iain," he said sharply. "The other beast Ivyn killed mostly." Leaving Tavin aside for the moment, he looked at the two men who'd survived with him. "I've words to share with the swordmaster. Get to the barracks bath house, if you like. Shyvie and his brats will take good care of you, they will. After you're clean you're welcome to a meal in the castle. Only one caution—you won't speak of what happened beyond the Vale. Not 'til I give you leave."

Bryn and Noyce exchanged glances. Friends, they'd made of each other, over these long weeks. Then Bryn shuffled his feet. "Highness, it's home for me without the bath house or the meal. My wife'll skin me if I don't."

"Your choice," he said, dredging up a smile. "I'll not argue it. Iain?"

"I'll take both gladly," said Noyce. "It's only my kennel boy at home." His lined face twisted. "And my dogs."

"Then go," he said. "And take my love with you."

They nodded, not quite a bow, and left the Hall together. Silence after the doors closed. Tears in Tavin's eyes.

"Boy—" he said harshly. "Ewen—"

Bones and muscles aching, the half-healed, rubbed-raw beast marks in his flesh smarting, Ewen slid the saddle-bags off his shoulder and let them thud to the floor. Then he unbelted Blood-drinker in its scabbard and held it out.

"The blade snapped, Tavin. I broke your sword."

"Fuck the sword," said Tavin, and leapt up, and held him.

Endless days of desperate riding. Not a night's sleep that he didn't dream of those beasts. Of Lenyd. Of Padrig, and Vharne's lost king. Ruined Blood-drinker slipped from his fingers.

*Fuck the sword. Fuck all of it.*

"I knew you'd ride back to the Vale, boy," Tavin said, a fierce whisper. "I knew you wouldn't leave me stranded in this Hall, I did." His grip convulsed tighter, then he let go and stepped back, glowering. "Ewen, I could blade your arse, I could! *Two* pigeons you send me? Boy, you took five!"

"Lost the packhorse," he said, biting his lip. "The pigeons were still on it."

Tavin pulled a chair out from the table and sat. "Tell me all of it."

Slowly pacing, Ewen unfolded the past weeks for him. By the time he'd reached the part where the beasts attacked, and Lenyd died, and the three barracks men, he was shivering in the warm chamber and Tavin was ashen-faced. And after that . . .

"We couldn't bring any of the dead home for burning," he said, still hurting for it. "So we burned them where they fell." He looked at the saddle-bags. "And I carried back enough of their ashes for their death jars, and their pits. Brought their blades, too. Taken into the barracks, they are. I'll sort my cousins' swords from the barracks men's later. My aunt will want them with the ashes, she will."

"That's a proper thing you did, son," said Tavin, his own gaze heavy on the saddle-bags.

He rubbed his stinging eyes. "Tav, I wish I'd liked him better. Luyn. I wish I'd liked his brothers better too, but I didn't. It's more honest grief I've got for Refyn and Duff and Hob. But they were *blood*, my cousins. How is *that* proper?"

"It's not," said Tav, shrugging. "But you feel what you feel. Let it go. Bigger troubles, we've got."

*And that's true, that is. Much bigger.*

Crouching, he unlaced the saddle-bags from each other, hefted one to the Hall's table and upended it in front of Tavin. Severed horns and talons and smashed tusks tumbled out.

"Tried to burn the beasts too, we did," he said, revolted. "But the flames wouldn't take them. So we buried them shallow and covered them with rocks. It's desolate country out there, but I didn't want the chance of a scout or a hunter stumbling on them. Even in the rough that's word to spread fast, it is."

Tavin kept his hands to himself, but his eyes feasted on the beast remains and his face darkened with dreadful memories.

Crouching again, Ewen picked up discarded Blood-drinker in its scabbard. Held it for a moment, feeling an ache in his arm, reliving the desperation and the terror. Then he set the sword gently on the table beside the horns, tusks and talons.

"I'm sorry, Tav. I wanted to bring both pieces back to you, I did, but—" He shook his head. "There wasn't a sword could cut open the beast that stole half your blade."

Tavin's fingertips lightly touched Blood-drinker's hilt. "Swordsmith who made this, he's long years dead. Not another man in Vharne ever matched Nilym in forging a blade. Belonged to my grandfather's father, this sword. Handed down, son to son." He glanced up. "Always meant it for you, I did. Knew my whole life there'd be no son from my loins."

"Spirit save me," Ewen muttered. "Making it worse, you are. Tav, I *broke* it."

Tavin's fist thumped the table. "Boy, you and Blood-drinker, you

296

slew two beasts! If a blade's got to die, what better death is there?"

And then both his fists thumped the table and he was on his feet, raging.

"We were fools, we were, Ewen! Me and Murdo, and Ewen the Elder, we were *fools*. Believing an evil that could spawn beasts would melt like ice in summertime? Babby-brained, that was. I told you at the pit, I did. *Haius blossom*. And I should've remembered it years ago. The north never died, it only slept, and now it's woken."

Ewen watched the swordmaster roam about the Hall, kicking chairs in passing, thudding his fists to the stone walls. He looked like a bear in his anger, rumpled clothing and spiked hair and eyes alight with the desire to kill.

"Tav, how's this your fault? Name me one man who ever *dreamed*—"

"It's my fault 'cause I'm the *swordmaster*!" Tavin shouted. "Sworn to guard the king's back. To guard Vharne. Youngest swordmaster ever chosen, and *why*? For my instincts, Ewen. For slaying a beast and knowing evil when it slunk across my path. I was trusted for that, and what did I do? I *slept*, I did, with evil crawling to my door. If any man deserves a flogging, *I'm* that man, I am."

Stepping in front of him, Ewen took the swordmaster by both shoulders. "Clap tongue, Tavin. Murdo's king in Vharne. Serve him, you do. Told him to 'ware the wanderers when they first stirred, you did. 'Wait,' the king said. Then we had more wanderers and the king still said 'Wait.' Then one touched the Vale. Murdo said, 'I'll ride to see this.' Tavin, you said, 'Don't.' You said, 'Send me. Send more scouts. Vharne can't risk its king.' Murdo wouldn't listen."

Tavin scowled. "Felt guilty, he did. He knew he should've listened sooner. Then he wanted to prove himself, after. But Ewen—" His eyes were haunted. "Things happen. If Padrig had blooded himself in the Eastern Vale—if you'd ridden with Murdo—if you'd ridden *instead* of Murdo—"

*Then it's dead now, I'd be. It'd be my ashes in that saddle-bag. My bones burned in the rough.*

He turned away. "I know."

"Things *happen*," Tavin insisted, tugging him back. "Don't you flog yourself, son. I'd face what's coming with you before *any* man, I would."

It should've been a comfort, to hear it. But there was no comfort in the Vale. Not any more.

"And what's coming, Tav?"

"What d'you think?" the swordmaster whispered. "It's the sorcerer."

"*Morg?*" He felt a roil of sickness. "How can that be? Morg's dead."

"With beasts in Vharne?" Tavin cuffed him. "*Think*, Ewen. They're his creations, they are. If beasts are walking so is he! The sorcerer's *alive*."

Ewen tried to step back as the swordmaster, barrel-chest heaving, snatched up a fistful of his stained leather coat. "But Tav—"

"*No!*" Holding hard, Tavin shook him. "Boy, don't you be Murdo's son now. Don't you be a fool and close your eyes and ears to me. There's no *time*. If we've got two beasts in Vharne, we've got more than two, I promise. You and me, we've got to make our people ready."

"Make them *ready*?" He prised Tavin's fingers from his coat. "How? When beasts ruled in Vharne nothing Ewen the Elder did saved us. Nothing my father did saved us. Beasts ruled here for generations before that, they did, Swordmaster, and *no king* could stop them."

"Ewen, you slew two of them!" said Tavin, his eyes furious. "More than any king's done, any *man's* done, since the first beast set foot across our borders."

"I slew two of them and broke the greatest sword ever forged," he retorted, desperate. "What do you want from me, Tav? You want me to forge the people of Vharne into a sword so I can break *them* next, do you?"

"Boy, they're going to break be they forged or no!" roared Tavin. "Morg's beasts hunger for slaughter, they do. There's not a pile of broken bodies they see that they've no wish to pile it higher."

"Then what is there to make ready? Save for pits and more pits to burn our dead."

"*Ewen*—" On a groaning sigh, Tavin put himself into one of the empty chairs at the table. "With you Vharne's king now, there's need for—"

"I am *not* the king, Tavin," he said hotly. "Not until Murdo's death jar is brimful with his ashes. I'll protect the kingdom as I can, I'll sit in the king's seat and hear disputes and sign my name, I'll do what Clovis tells me a king of Vharne must do—but claim the crown before I *know* my father's dead? I can't."

Tavin shook his head. "Ewen, don't do this. You know the truth of things. You know what's happened to Murdo, you do. He's Padrig in a ditch with no kind dagger shoved in his heart, he is."

"*No!* Tav, he's not dead in a ditch unless I *find* him dead in a ditch." Shaking, Ewen set his fists on the table and leaned low and close. "The king's out there somewhere, I say. And I say there's a chance he's out there alive. Once I'm bathed, once my belly's full, I'm taking the best men in the barracks and I'm finding him, I am."

"You can't do that," said Tavin, brutal. "Ewen, let him go."

"Let him go?" he echoed, straightening. "And if you had a son, Tavin, you'd want those words on his lips, would you? 'Let him go.' What's the king to me, then? A lost dog?"

"Dog or man, it makes no difference," said Tavin. "He's lost."

"*You don't know that!*"

"I do! And, son, so do you." His breathing harsh, Tavin doused his temper. "Face facts; you have to. If Murdo was alive you'd have found him, you would. If he was alive he'd have heard you calling, even on a spirit path. And if he'd heard you he'd have come running. Only reason he wouldn't is if he'd run away. Is *that* what you're saying, is it? Murdo ran away, with his nephews and his barracks men brainrotted and beast-hunted and needing him? Son, is that the king?"

*Clap tongue, Tavin. Clap tongue, you old man.*

He pressed one hand to his eyes. "No."

"Then it's you I'll call king, I will."

"*No!*" He dropped his hand. "Call me king custodian if you must, Tav. But not king."

Folding his arms, Tavin sat back in his chair. "You bandy words, Ewen. You make words a pig's bladder and you pat it about this Hall as though we play a game. King or king custodian, find the difference and show me, if you can." His eyebrows lifted. "But you can't, can you?" He pointed to the empty king's seat. "So there's where you need to cradle your arse."

Beyond the Hall's one unshuttered window, the sky was fast fading from dusk to dark. Those fat logs still burned in the fireplace but even so, he shivered. He was cold on the inside, where no flames could reach. He felt his eyes sting again. Felt the tears rise and tip onto his cold cheeks.

He was too tired to stop them.

"*Fuck*," said Tavin. He'd never sworn so much before. Not outside the heat and scuffle of mock-battle in the tiltyard. "Ewen—"

Shamed, he turned away. "I'm fine."

"I'm not," said Tavin. Shoving his chair back he stood, then came round the table. "Let me see."

He let Tavin drag him closer to a smoky lamp and examine him head-to-toe in its yellow, flickering light. "Well, there's no more of your bones broken and your face is in one piece. But you're more than tired, you are." He scowled, suddenly suspicious. "Beast-clawed?"

"Not badly."

"*Ewen!*" Tavin slapped him, a swordmaster's reproof.

He rubbed his cheek. "But that doesn't help."

"Get to the bath house," Tavin growled. "Scrape that scraggle of beard off, get your stink out of my nostrils, and make sure to spread Shyvie's salve where it's needed. Then you'll eat and put your head on a pillow and come morning we'll talk of what to do, we will."

Bemused, Ewen stared at him. *And I'm the king, am I?* "Tav, my cousins' ashes. I—"

"I'll see to them," said Tavin. "And telling the barracks who we've lost, and how."

He shook his head. "No. It's me should tell them that, Tav."

Another scowl. "I'm swordmaster, I am."

"Named you that, have I?" he said, pushing a little, because he was tired of being pushed himself.

*Because I'm tired.*

Tavin pointed a finger. "Boy, I'm warning you—"

"Clap tongue, Swordmaster," he said, almost sighing. "You're right. I need a bath."

They left the Hall, silent, and walked to the barracks together.

Ewen found the bath house empty, save for Shyvie and his brats. Noyce had come and gone, and the rest of the barracks men were seeing to barracks business. Let Tavin bark his orders, he could have called for a tub in his own castle chamber—but it seemed pointless to send servants scurrying with buckets when Shyvie's huge cauldrons were never empty and the barracks' tubs stood idle with their jars of ready soap.

The water was so hot it nearly scalded him raw, but he didn't cool it from the cauldron of cold. He needed it hot, to thaw him. Breath by breath the heat unravelled the knots in his muscles and sinews and lulled the grinding ache in his broken, mended arm. The beast's claw-marks burned, making him hiss, but of all his pains it was the one that pained him least. A lost father, three dead cousins, and a brother burned to ash. Luyn's mother and Nairn in the Eastern Vale were the only family he had left.

*As good as orphaned, that makes me. Spirit be thanked for Tavin.*

Because he was alone he could at last let himself feel exhausted. Let himself admit the cost of riding to find the king and remember clearly, not dreaming, his battle with the beasts. Let himself think about what those beasts meant.

*Morg.*

A small and childish part of himself wanted to pretend none of this was happening, that Padrig wasn't ashes, or his cousins, that the king wasn't lost and good barracks men with him, that Morg the ageless sorcerer hadn't risen from the dead.

But it was all true, and he had to face it.

For the first time in a long time he was sorry he lacked a woman. No bastards in the castle, that was the rule, so though he did tumble a willing wench now and then, to keep the king happy he kept himself mostly wenchless. And that was a pity, that was. At least it was a pity tonight. If ever he needed a woman to hold him, to lose himself in, it was now. For there were beasts loose in the kingdom . . .

*. . . and my father's likely dead.*

But sitting naked and dirty in a tub wouldn't bring Murdo back, or kill his grief—or any beast. Taking up the soap jar, he lathered his hair and body frothy and scrubbed away the dried sweat and grime. Scrubbed away the scabs of his beast-clawing, too, on his back and his shoulders and across his right thigh. That drew blood and hissed air between his teeth. But he had to. Shyvie's famous ointment liked raw flesh to work on.

On the wall beside the hanging towels and the box of ointments and liniments, Shyvie kept another box full of freshly stropped razors. Ewen fetched one, climbed back in his bath and scraped his face down to bare skin. Used it to pare his nails, too, fingers and toes, even though Shyvie disapproved of that. Then, with all his cleaning and scraping done, he climbed out of his bath for good, towelled himself dry, and spent five minutes cursing as Shyvie's wound salve set him on fire.

When he looked to his clothes, he shuddered. Stinking, torn, filthy and bloodstained—what a fool he was, not to think of sending for a clean shirt and trews. He needed Tavin like a nursemaid. After tossing everything but his boots into the bath-house fire, he shoved his bare feet into the boots, smothered himself in towels and clopped his way back up to the castle to find a meal first, then his bed.

The barracks men who saw him stopped and stared, but didn't laugh. And that was clever, for he was in no laughing mood.

Early the next morning, after breakfast, he met in the Hall with Tavin and Clovis to talk with them about saving Vharne.

The beast horns and tusks and talons he'd brought home from the rough had remained overnight on the table. Waiting for Clovis to finish setting out his ink and paper, he brooded at the filthy things, refusing to be intimidated.

*If I killed two of you I can kill two more, I can. If I have to, I'll kill two hundred. Hurt my people of Vharne and I'll kill you all, I will.*

But that was bluster, and he knew it.

Clovis inked his quill, then tapped it almost dry. The secretary's nerve was holding well enough, even with the beast parts sitting so near. Any grief he felt for the king was buttoned neat inside his shirt.

He glanced up. "If there's something you need to keep between us only, Highness, say the word and I won't record it."

"Good. So—" Ewen looked from the secretary to Tavin, seated at his right hand. "First we need more scouts, I say. Those beasts came from somewhere, they did. Ranoush, or Manemli. I favour Ranoush. It was closest." Despite that hot bath and a night in his own bed, his neck was aching. He rubbed at it hard, digging his fingers into the knotted muscles. "Those borders need regular scouting, they do. And the border with Iringa. As much rough country as we can cover, I say. How fast can you train new scouts, Tavin?"

"How fast can you find them?" Tavin countered. "If a man or woman can sit a horse without blistering arse or falling off at a sneeze—if they know a bit of knives and they're not so squeamish they can't kill what needs killing—then I can train them to scouting a whisker inside a week, I can."

That was fast, even for Tavin. *It's glad I am my training's done with.* "Clovis, it's in law for me to command and not recruit, isn't it?"

"It is," said the secretary, after a moment. "In times of dire need. A proclamation from the seat, it's called."

*And if these times aren't dire they never have been, I say.*

"Then here's me, proclaiming," he said. "How many to start with, Swordmaster?"

Tavin grunted. "Twenty-five. We'll need more, but I say let's not fright folk too much. Not yet."

*No. Not yet.* "We'll word the order last thing, Clovis. Swordmaster, what of the barracks?"

"I've men to see the Vale protected," Tavin said, his gaze narrowing. "I could use more."

Of course he could, with so many recently lost. "And you'll get them. But it's beyond the Vale I'm thinking about, Tav. Those villages in the rough. The folk I met out there . . ." He shook his head. "There's no barracks for them. And there's no stand a swordless man can take against a beast."

Tavin pulled a face. "Even with a sword, that stand's not likely, boy. If it was I'd not be called Mighty Tavin Blood-drinker from one end of Vharne to the other, I wouldn't."

"I know," he said, impatiently. "But how can I leave those folk in the rough defenceless? If there are beasts in Ranoush or Manemli and they cross into Vharne or chase the folk there across the borders to hide in our rough country—"

"So you want to proclaim scouts *and* barracks men, do you? And you want me to train them, then send them back to the rough?" Tavin slumped in his chair. "Train them with me, you can."

He tried to smile. "I will."

"And barrack them where? There's no time or spare hands to build our barracks bigger. Not when the men need to be training for beasts."

He knew that, too. He'd done some thinking since his bath. "They can take beds in the Vale."

Clovis choked a little. "Turn Vale folk out of their homes, Highness?"

"Turn them out? No," he said, mildly enough. "But there's no harm sharing a roof can do."

Clovis's raised eyebrows said he didn't agree.

Ignoring that, Ewen turned again to Tavin. "A week to train new scouts, you say. How long for new barracks men?"

"Ewen—" Tavin sighed. He'd reached for a beast tusk, and was running his finger over and over its sharp, wicked curve. "Depends what you mean by train, it does. To hold a sword right way up, that's one thing. How not to cut their own legs off at the knees or the next man's head when they're skirmishing? That's another, it is."

Oh. "You're saying it can't be done? The beasts can't be fought?"

"No. They can be fought."

"But not beaten."

Tavin's eyes were bleak. "Not by some poor fool dragged out of the rough and given a week or three to learn swordplay."

He was right. That would never work. *But I can't abandon them.* The desperate faces of the folk in Neem haunted his dreams, too.

"Only we can't tell them that," Tavin added, and tossed the beast tusk onto the table. Clovis winced. "They have to think there's a chance, they do. You take hope from a man, son, best you slide a dagger 'cross his throat while you're about it."

*Not* tell them how poor their chances would be?

"Tav, I can't *lie* to Vharne's people."

The swordmaster shrugged. "Ewen, sometimes a lie is the kindest thing you can tell a man. Sometimes if you tell him the lie often enough it'll turn into truth. You want to ride from one side of Vharne to the other telling folk to turn up their toes, it's all over, they're going to die?"

"Of course not!"

Another shrug. "Then you tell them it's time to pick up a sword, or a pitchfork, or a toasting fork if that's all they've got. You tell them Vharne is their home, you do, and the time's on them to fight for it."

"Against beasts," he said, and felt the ache stir in his arm. In his heart, for the bloodshed he knew was coming.

"If it's beasts come to kill them?" Tavin's bleak eyes flickered full of shadows. "Yes, son. Against beasts."

He looked at Clovis, who'd put his quill down and was staring at his partly inked paper. Now his grief was showing. Now his hidden pain was revealed.

His own grief spiked him. *I had Blood-drinker and years of training and I nearly died.* "Tav, it's going to be a slaughter."

That made the swordmaster laugh, grimly. "Ewen, it'll be a slaughter whether they're holding swords or twigs."

"Then it's best they're holding swords," he said, feeling sick. "But if we're asking folk in the Vale to share their beds and their floors, we'll have men from the rough in the castle, too. If I can't live with what I'm asking the Vale to do then I've got no right to ask it, I say."

Tavin's pinched lips softened into a smile. "Spoken like a king, that was."

*But I'm not a king. Vharne has a king.*

He turned to Clovis. "Here's a task for you. Survey every dwelling in the Vale. How many heads in each home. Who's friendly and who's feuding. I want to know how many rooms are under each roof and how many strong men there are in each family. Who can be spared for scouting or the barracks, and who can't. Some of that I know, but not all. If you're asked a reason, it's the king's business. Once I've got those answers, I'll make that proclamation, I will."

Clovis, taking notes again, nodded. "Highness."

"Sensible, you're being, son," said Tavin. "But before you proclaim anything there's a wrinkle to think on."

*Of course there is.* "What?"

"Word's out wide on your brother, it is. And while you were in the rough, scouts put down a fistful of brain-rotted souls in the Southern Vale. There's no hiding this, Ewen. Too many wanderers are crossing the borders."

*The Southern Vale, now? Spirit, we'll soon be over-run.*

Ewen scowled at his swordmaster. "You couldn't tell me this last night?"

Tav lifted an eyebrow. "Could you change it last night?"

*I can't change it now.* "No."

"And you can't proclaim scouts and barracks men without you break silence and tell Vharne about the north. Clap tongue on that, son, and it's a lie you won't be forgiven."

*Break silence and break hearts. Turn day into night and feed Vharne's people nightmares instead of porridge.*

"I'll tell you another lie Vharne won't forgive me," he said, meeting Tavin's grim gaze. "Declaring Murdo dead when I don't have a body."

Tavin's fingers tightened. "Ewen—"

"Tav, if word of Padrig's spread, and him a younger son, word of a missing king will spread through Vharne like fire. And here's me in the king's seat, claiming his crown? Vharne will call me a usurper, and that *won't* be a lie."

Clovis jumped as Tavin slapped the table, hard. "Ewen, this got put to bed last night, it did. When will you *listen*, boy?"

"I listen, Tavin. If I hadn't heard you I wouldn't have killed two beasts. But that doesn't make you right every time."

"I'm right about this!"

"So I should listen to you tell me I can't be a good son?"

Tavin grabbed his right forearm, unthinking. "It matters more you're a good king."

He clenched his jaw against the pain. "How can I be a good king when I *abandon* a good king?"

"When you keep his kingdom safe, boy," said Tavin. "Besides, the dead can't be abandoned, I say."

"Tavin—" He couldn't bear it. He pulled his arm free. "I don't—"

"Highness, your swordmaster's right, he is," said Clovis, unexpectedly. "When Murdo left the Vale, he left Vharne in your keeping. It's yours to keep safe whether he's dead or alive. Best you don't leave the people uncertain. Best you claim the crown, and have done."

Shocked silent, Ewen stared at the secretary.

"And another thing," said Clovis. "Though could be you've thought of it already. The spirit paths, Highness. Can't they help keep Vharne's people safe?"

The spirit paths? *Ewen, you fool.* "Yes," he said, forgetting the woken pain in his arm, his frustration with Tavin. "Clovis—I could *kiss* you, I could."

Blinking, Clovis sat back.

"We need copies of the spirit map," he said. "Scores and scores of copies. And scouts to ride them into the rough. Bryn and Noyce, they can show the scouts how to find the paths, how to feel—"

Beyond the Hall's closed doors, a woman screamed in terror.

Screamed again. Then more screams. As Ewen leapt to his feet, the doors flew open.

"Best you come," said Typher, one of Tavin's barracks men. He was sickly faced, his voice hoarse with shock. "It's—it's a beast."

A *beast*? Leaving Clovis to gape, Ewen bolted with Tavin close behind. And then Tavin shoved by him and he was racing to catch up.

The beast stood unafraid in the castle's forecourt, ringed by barracks men with swords. It was tall and thin and leathery brown. Naked. Hairless. Sexless. Its eyes were green and horribly human. It had tusks instead of teeth, talons for fingers and toes. It had wings —of a kind.

Heart thudding, regretting Blood-drinker, Ewen stared at the filthy thing as Tavin dragged his barracks man back over the castle's threshold.

"What's this, Typher?" the swordmaster demanded. "What are you men doing? Think a sword's a prick, do you, needs a woman for—"

"It spoke, Swordmaster," said Typher, shaking. "It said to fetch the king."

Tavin thumped him. "It said—and you do its *bidding*? Man, are you *brain-rotted*?"

"Leave him be, Tav," Ewen snapped. *It spoke? A beast spoke?* "And let me pass."

"No." Tavin's face was taut with dismay. "Ewen, no, you can't—"

*Clap tongue, Tav. I have to.* Pushing swordmaster and barracks man aside, he stepped through the main doorway and onto the forecourt.

"*Ewen—*"

He paused, his gaze intent on the beast. "I've never heard that they speak, Swordmaster. Have you?"

"Only with swords and clubs and talons," said Tavin. "Not words. Ewen, you can't—"

"Hold there, Swordmaster."

Tavin groaned under his breath, but for a wonder didn't argue.

The silent barracks men surrounding Morg's beast were frightened, but holding their ground. Passing between them, Ewen took the sword from the man on his right, Fergil. Kept walking, his fingers sweaty on the hilt, until he was within spitting distance of the creature. Then he stopped.

The thing's green, human eyes blinked. Bile-yellow spittle dripped from its tusks. "You are king of Vharne?"

*I am today. Spirit save me.*

"I am Ewen, the beast-slayer," he said, freezing his voice. "Go back where you came from, beast. You're not wanted here."

The beast was indifferent. "I bring a message from my master. The lord Morg will see king of Vharne. The lord Morg will see him kneel. The lord Morg will have Vharne."

*Morg.* Curse Tavin for being right. *If I show fear, it might kill me.* "Morg's not wanted here either, he's not."

The beast blinked again. "You are king, Ewen beast-slayer?"

Ewen tightened his hold on Fergil's sword. How he wished it was Blood-drinker. *I'm sorry, Father.* "Beast, I am king."

In a blur of brown motion the beast took to the air. Startled, Ewen raised the sword but there was nothing there to kill. He spun on his heel, looking for the thing — and instead saw another blur of brown motion.

And then a barracks man ripped to pieces in front of him.

Before he could defend the rest of his men another died, then another and another, so swift, so brutal, they didn't even have time to scream. He felt blood spray across his chest, over his face, into his mouth.

Twelve men in the forecourt, slaughtered in heartbeats, and he never had a chance to strike.

*Spirit. Spirit.*

Morg's beast dropped lightly to the blood-soaked ground. "Ewen beast-slayer kneel to my lord Morg in Dorana, give Vharne to him. Or—" It raised an arm, one talon pointing at the severed heads and scattered pieces of flesh and bone that had been men "—this is Vharne. My lord Morg waits in beautiful city Elvado. My lord Morg does not wait forever."

In a brown blur the creature took to the air again, and was gone in a cracking, flapping of wings.

Bending over, Ewen heaved up his egg-and-bacon breakfast.

"You can't go," said Tavin, reaching him, grabbing him by the arm. More cries of alarm and horror were sounding as the castle's people looked out of windows or came onto the forecourt and saw the butchered barracks men. "Ewen, you *can't.*"

"Tav . . ." He rested a hand on Tavin's shoulder. His fingers were splashed with somebody else's blood. He could still taste the iron of it, burning his tongue. "I must."

Anguish in the swordmaster's scarred face. "Ewen—"

"*Tavin, I must.*" He wanted to be sick again. In all his life he'd never felt such fear. "To save Vharne's people—and give you time."

"Time for *what?*" Tavin demanded. "Boy—"

He cupped his hand to Tavin's cheek. Slapped it lightly. "To spread word of the spirit paths, for one thing. And to prepare Vharne for battle. *Think*, Tavin. When did the sorcerer *ever* send a messenger? Something's different. Something's *wrong*. And we can use it against him."

Tavin shook his head. "No. No, this is a trick, it has to be, you can't—"

"I *can*," Ewen insisted. "And while I'm kneeling before *my lord Morg* I'll study him for weakness. Because there is weakness, Tav. I can *smell* it. And when I'm done kneeling then it's home to the Vale I'll come, I will . . . and together we'll work out how to beat him.'

# CHAPTER NINETEEN

"Are we lost?" said Charis. "We are, aren't we? We're lost."

Deenie let her clammy forehead thud against the rough bark of the tree that was the only thing keeping her upright. "Charis, we've been lost since we left Dragonteeth Reef behind."

"Yes, I s'pose, only, what I mean is—"

It was no good. She had to sit before she fell. Letting her legs fold, she slid down the tree trunk until she bumped onto the damp grass.

"Yes, Charis. I know what you mean."

*You mean I've led us far, far astray. You mean there's a good chance we're only wandering in circles. You mean you think it was a mistake ever to trust me.*

Prob'ly it had been. Prob'ly blind faith in her odd mage-sense had blinded her to the harsh truth of the matter: that it always was madness to think she could find Rafel over such a distance.

She'd stopped feeling so much as a hint of him days ago. Now she could scarcely recall what that humming link between them had felt like. There were even moments she doubted she'd ever felt it at all.

Poor bedraggled Charis was looking down at her, face smeared with dirt and trickled with sweat from all their steady tramping. Where had bright and flirty Charis gone? Where was the girl who'd danced down Dorana's streets?

"Deenie, you look awful," she said, so subdued. "Are you sure you're all right?"

"I'm fine," she said, even though she felt as awful as Charis's expression told her she looked. "I just need to rest for a few moments."

Charis pushed a straggle of damp hair back from her face. "That's a good idea. You rest. I'll have a little look around and see if I can find anything worth eating."

Oh, and didn't that make the guilt stab? "No, you should rest too. I know there's not a terrible lot of daylight left but there's time enough for a sit down, before we push on."

"Don't be silly," said Charis, rallying. "I've got plenty of bounce. There's no need to fratch about me, Deenie."

Except there was. She didn't look bouncy. She looked pale and thin and worn ragged by their adventures. She was trying so hard not to show how frighted she felt.

*She hasn't even fussed about how I could understand those poor rotting people. But I know that it frights her. It must. It frights me.*

"Charis . . ."

Charis dropped to a crouch. "Hush. Close your eyes and don't think about anything. Not even Rafel. I won't go far, I promise. I won't lose you."

If she lost Charis she would truly be lost. "You'd better not."

Charis wriggled her fingers. "See you soon."

Eyes obediently closed, Deenie listened to Charis's feet sliding on the grass, breaking twigs, as she faded into the distance. It was nice, this little patch of sunshine filtering through the heavy woodland canopy. Though there wasn't much heat, still it felt like a friendly whisper against her skin.

Somewhere close by a bird called, three quick high cheeps, then a longer, lower whistle. So pretty. She'd never heard a birdcall like it before. Dragging her heavy eyelids open she looked for it. A rustle of feathers, and there it was. A small bird, perhaps the size of her fist. Dusky brown and bright yellow plumage, with a startling white cap on its sleek, narrow head. A needle-sharp beak. Bright, curious eyes.

Calling again, the bird fluttered its wings. They were banded with black. *Such* a pretty thing.

Without warning her eyes flooded with tears.

*Oh, Mama. I'm so tired. And I'm frighted. I don't know where we are . . . and I think we're going to die.*

She'd lost all notion of time. Couldn't make sense of how many days and nights had passed since the skiff sank on the river. Since she and Charis had woken on the cold ground to see—to see—

*Stop it. Stop thinking about it. You had no choice. They were going to kill you and Charis, or worse.*

And that was true. She'd saved their lives. But knowing that didn't help. Killing rabbits was horrible enough. But killing *people*? Even people like *that*, mad and rotting and falling to bits?

*Now I know how you felt, Da. When you did what you did to stop Morg, and King Gar died. You had to do it, you didn't have a choice either, but now I know exactly how you felt.*

And because she'd grown up with him, watching him, feeling him, she understood that no matter how many years went by she'd never feel any better about the terrible thing she'd had to do.

Those waiting tears trickled down her face, and the sun wasn't warm enough to dry them. She was too tired to dry them. Her arms were so heavy it was like someone had turned them to stone.

*Oh, Da.*

They'd seen no signs of life since that terrible night. But there'd been people living in this land, once. After wandering through the village near the river and finding it empty, she and Charis had come across more tumbledown cottages. Their stone walls were broken apart, the scattered pieces wrapped up in ivy and pretty, pink-flowered climbers. Nothing left of their roofs, either timber or thatch. The second time they'd found fruit trees, gone wild and late blooming. Funny little red fruits on them, almost like apples. She'd taken a tiny nibble first, 'cause Charis had been afraid to try eating one. Perhaps it hadn't been very clever, but her peculiar mage-sense didn't warn her not to and she was so sinking *tired* of rabbit. The fruit had tasted dry, almost dusty. Not much juice in it, but the flavour was good. They ate a few handfuls each and then stuffed as many as they could carry into their haversack.

After dinner, though—more rabbit—they'd both been taken with a terrible gripe. They only ate one fruit a day after that, until they were all gone. It was a lesson well learned.

The weather was holding, Barl be praised. No rain. But it was cold once the sun went down. Without so much dead wood to burn they might have perished of it by now, or come down with a fearful ague. Even so they wore all the clothes they could to help them stay warm. Oh, how she missed her leathers. That ducking in the river, after days of salt at sea, had done them no good at all. They were too stiff to put on any more. They might even be ruined.

Another thing to fret about. It was so easy to fret these days—or weep. The smallest things fratched her. A bramble caught in her hair, a scrape on her finger. The drag of the haversack over her shoulder, and the way Charis flutter-snored through half the night.

*It's because I've lost Rafel. It's because I don't know where he is, or where we are, or where we're going, or how we're s'posed to save him when we get there. If we get there. It's because of the dreams.*

The dreams she had now weren't about her brother. They were about the creatures who'd attacked them and awful beasts with horns and tusks. Trapped in sleep she heard screaming, she smelled burning. She knew she stood on the brink of something dreadful and nothing she could do would stop it.

Just one pleasant dream she'd had. Well, a sort of dream. A snatching glimpse of a man's face. Dark red hair. Green-gold eyes. She'd dreamed him once before, long ago, the night Da called the warbeasts, but why she'd dreamed him she still couldn't say. At least this time he wasn't weeping tears of blood.

A soft breeze soughed through the branches above her, rattling leaves. This was a strange place, whatever country it was they'd found. She could still sense the memory of blight here, but underneath that, she could feel something else. Something warm.

Something sleeping. But she couldn't wake it or hear its whisper in her dreams.

Very strange.

A rustling in the woodland undergrowth snapped her head around. Charis? No, Charis would've called out. Was it more of those maddened people? She didn't think so. Her mage-sense barely stirred. Heart hammering, sweat prickling beneath her disreputable clothes, she held her breath.

A plump, rust-brown chicken stepped into the clearing, amber eyes curious, head tipped to one side, clucking and crooning deep in its feathered throat. Close behind it stepped two more plump chickens, both hens, one brown-and-white and one black.

*Chickens?*

Astonished, Deenie stared at them. The chickens stared back.

*Those are chickens.*

Without thinking, without hesitation, using her magic, she killed them.

Some little time later she heard more rustling in the undergrowth. Footsteps, this time. A familiar presence. Charis.

"Deenie! Deenie? You'll never guess what I—"

Weeping over the dead chickens, cradling them in her arms, Deenie looked up. "Never guess what you what?"

Her own arms full of glossy brown pears, Charis gaped. "Chickens?"

She shrugged. "At least they'll make a nice change from rabbit."

"*Chickens!*" Charis said again, delighted. "Where did they come from? I didn't see them in the village."

"Village?" Deenie's fingertip kept stroking the plumpest hen's glossy black feathers. "What village?"

"Out beyond this stretch of woodland," said Charis, carefully kneeling to put down her pears. "Deserted, like the others. I don't think anyone's been there in years. But there's a proper orchard, Deenie. Gone wild, but still. And not just pears, we've got apples too. And cherries, only this is the wrong time of year. And there's a well, with water in it! I dropped a stone in and there was a splash. The bucket's tin and it's on a chain, but the handle's rusted." She pulled a face. "I tried to magic it unstuck but that didn't work. You'll be able to, though. Best of all?" Now she was beaming, echoes of the Charis who'd danced through life without a care. "Some of the cottages aren't tumbledown. They're a bit manky inside, but we can magic them clean. Oh, *Deenie*." She laughed. "How long since we've slept under a proper roof?"

She wanted to feel as excited as Charis, but she couldn't. *Poor little chickens. This was their woodland, their home.* And in she'd blundered and because she was hungry, because she was so sick of *rabbit*, she'd taken her unwanted mishmash of Olken and Doranen magics and killed them.

Charis sighed. "Honestly, Deenie. You do know, don't you, that those chickens were always going to die some day? Either they'd drop dead from old age or a fox was going to get them. Does it really matter they died so we can eat them?"

"I'm not a fox," she said, with a sharp upwards look. "If I am going to kill things then I think I should *care*. Because if I don't care, Charis, if I just romp willy-nilly through the countryside killing things and *not* caring, well—"

"Deenie, we've talked about this," said Charis, and slumped onto her heels. "You don't have to kill them with magic. You don't have to kill them at all. Why won't you let me wring their necks? Or hit them with something?"

"You know why, Charis," she muttered. "My way's kinder. They don't have time to be frighted and they don't feel a thing."

"But you do," said Charis, frowning. "And then you gloom about it afterwards."

Yes, she did. She tried not to, but she did.

Charis flicked her a glance. "I wish you'd talk to me. I know I'll never properly understand your magic or how the reef's changed you, but I'd like to try. I'd like to help."

"I know, Charis," she said. "The trouble is, you can't."

*No-one can. I'm different, and I hate it, and there's nothing to be done.*

She poked a finger at the pears. "If we're going to spend the night in that village, why did you bother to bring these back?"

Startled, distracted—just as she'd intended—Charis blinked. "I don't know. I s'pose I wanted to surprise you. Are you hungry?"

"Silly question."

They were always hungry. Walking from dawn to dusk, day after day, a bit of rabbit here, a mouthful of berries there, once or twice some hazelnuts, half-ruined by maggots. After a lifetime of well-stocked kitchens and bakeries and sweetmeat stalls, never a second thought about where a meal would come from, scrounging in the wilderness was a frightening thing. Not even the hardships of Lur and its failing weather had prepared them for only ever being one twist of bad luck away from an empty belly.

"Deenie, I've been thinking," Charis said slowly. "I reckon we should stay hereabouts a day or so. The thing is, you see, I'm *tired*. I don't know what I thought this would be like, but I *never* thought . . ."

Reaching across the chickens and pears, Deenie took her friend's grimy hand. "No, *we* never thought. We were so worried for Rafe—*I* was so worried for Lur, for Da—and then Mama died and—Charis, I'm sorry. You came because you believed me when I said I could find Rafel. Save everyone." She looked at the quiet woodland surrounding them. "And now, well, you said it. We're lost."

"Yes," said Charis, sniffing. "We're lost. But Deenie, we're lost with chickens. Things could always be worse."

Taken aback, Deenie stared at her madcap friend. And then she laughed. "You're right. They could. So let's eat a pear, then you can show me this village."

Probably it was foolish of them not to press on. But they really were tired. What harm could it do to snatch a day or two of respite? To sleep out of the damp night air, on dry ground? Surely there was no harm in that. And perhaps, if she got just a little more rest, she might be able to find Rafel again.

*If I can sit quietly for a time, if I'm not so weary, so hungry . . .*

They ate all the pears. Then, sticky with juice, they picked up their bits and pieces and the dead chickens and trudged through the rest of the woodland until the trees thinned. And there it was, the abandoned village, as overgrown and mournful as the rest of this odd land. Charis set about plucking and cleaning their dinner, a messy task. She was welcome to it.

"Deenie, you choose us a cottage," she said, then blew chicken-down off the end of her nose. "Use your fancy magic to make sure it's clean. No spiders. And then—" Her face lit up with a thought. "Deenie, the *well*. We can have a hot bath!"

Deenie looked at her. "Out of a tiddy tin bucket, Charis? Really? With no soap?"

"Oh, stop being a killjoy," Charis retorted. "We'll make do. We can soak a shirt and scrub ourselves with it. It's better than nothing." Her nose wrinkled. "It's better than stinking. We haven't had a wash since we fell in the river! *And* we'll be able to get the last of the salt out of our hair!"

Because not even their river-dunking had washed it clean entirely. "That's true."

"Then *smile*!" said Charis. "Things are looking up!"

The afternoon dwindled as they saw to their many tasks. At last, once there was a clean cottage to call home and all three chickens were roasting, jointed and threaded onto water-soaked green branches balanced over a banked fire, they took turns with their ridiculous tin-bucket bath. Hoping to find a second bucket they'd scoured the tiny village's abandoned twelve cottages, but not a stick of furniture or one more bucket remained. *Nothing* to tell them who had lived here or why they'd left.

Still. The inconvenience and painful slowness of the process couldn't dim their pleasure at feeling warm water on their skin and sluicing through their sticky hair. With a sopping, squashed up shirt they scrubbed themselves free of dried sweat and days of grime. And once they were as clean as a bath without soap could make them, and dressed in their least manky shirts and leggings, they cleaned the rest of their clothes as best they could and draped them over low-hanging pear tree branches to dry.

By this time the sun was fast sliding towards dusk and the chicken was cooked. After sharing the pieces between them they added more wood to the fire, stirring its flames to greater leaping. Light and warmth billowed as they devoured their meal.

"I've been thinking again," said Charis, frowning at her greasy fingers. "We should go on a chicken hunt tomorrow. There must be more hiding somewhere close. We could—what? Deenie? What's wrong?"

She couldn't answer. Could scarcely breathe, the stab of blight shafting through her was so cruelly sharp. Her belly heaved and a half-eaten piece of chicken slipped from her loosened grasp.

"*Deenie!*" Charis reached out, her face in the firelight stark with alarm. "For Barl's sake, what is it? What can you sense? Deenie—"

And then thrumming through the gathering twilight, the distant sound of hoof beats and shouting. A crashing through the woodland. Another dreadful wave of blight.

Grabbing Charis by the wrist, Deenie staggered to her feet. "We have to hide. Hurry, Charis. *Run!*"

They stumbled the short distance from their fire to the cottage. Tumbled through the open space where its front door had been, gasping.

"Charis, get *down*," Deenie hissed, dragging her to the dirt floor. "And don't move. Don't make a sound. No matter *what* you see or hear."

"But—"

She slapped a hand across Charis's open mouth. Held it there even as Charis tried to prise her fingers free. More shouting, louder now, almost on top of them. Hooves thudding hard and fast on damp ground. Charis tried to bite her fingers, so she snatched her hand away.

And then a terrible shriek, a high-pitched animal squeal of agony. A man's deep voice, shouting and desperate.

"*Ride on! Ride on! Ride, spirit take you!*"

Mounted horses burst out of the woodland, galloping and frenzied.

Deenie peered round the door frame and saw terrified faces and blood and terror as their riders swerved and zigzagged, fleeing—fleeing—

Charis screamed.

Her mage-sense was screaming too, howling inside her. Dizzy with it, sickened, Deenie fell against the cottage's doorway and watched four beasts burst out of the woods. Crimson hide, blue hide, black and sludgy grey. Horns and tails and tusks and talons. The beasts she'd been dreaming, the beasts Darran once told her of in his tales, people who'd been wickedly changed. The blight in them wasn't ancient, like the blight in Dragonteeth Reef. It was minted new and bright, fresh as a flower.

Another horrible horse scream. She whipped her head round and saw another beast attacking from the other direction. The horses and their riders were pinned between them, nowhere to run. The horse that screamed went down, plunging, half of its light brown neck torn away. Soaked in the hot blood, its rider was tossed from the saddle and the beast that attacked them pounced. Not even the man's drawn sword could save him.

She couldn't count how many men and horses were tangled in this chaos. All she could see was blood and slaughter. Moaning, she clawed at the doorway and pulled herself to her feet. Felt Charis's fingers plucking at her leg.

"Deenie—Deenie, no, Deenie, what are you—"

The beasts weren't rabbits. They weren't chickens. They weren't anything born of nature. But they lived, so they could die.

Another horse went down screaming, its rider screaming with it as he was crushed beneath its bulk. Almost blinded with tears, Deenie stepped out of the cottage. Opened her mage-sense to the ravening beasts. The blight in them burned her, set her racing blood on fire. She didn't care. She couldn't care. It was only pain; she wasn't dying. Those poor men were dying and she had the power to save them.

Softly exhaling, she closed her eyes.

Images in crimson and black danced behind her eyelids. Outlines of tails and tusks and horns. Pulsing deep within each beast a dark heart of blighted magic, the poison that had twisted people into mind-less, murderous *things*.

*I'm sorry. I'm sorry. You can be at peace now. I hope.*

An incredulous shout. Not Charis. A man. "Girl! Girl! What are you doing, girl? *Run!*"

Opening her eyes she saw a beast charging towards her, firelit and savage. No mercy in it. Nothing human left at all. Was she frighted? Maybe. Mostly she felt oddly calm.

Her hand came up, fingers spread. "Die now," she told it. "Beast, drop dead."

She felt a surge in her mage-sense. Felt the magic light her blood. The beast dropped in its running. It dropped dead at her feet.

The remaining beasts rampaged about the abandoned village. She killed every one of them and then she folded to the ground.

"*Deenie!*"

That was Charis. Huddled on the cold grass, no strength in her to talk or stand, she looked up as Charis crouched beside her.

"Deenie, are you all right? How did you *do* that?"

"How d'you think?" she said weakly. "Really, they're not much bigger than chickens."

Charis almost laughed, and then she gasped again.

"Girl," said the man who'd shouted. He was off his horse and striding towards them, a sword in one hand. He had long, dark red hair tied back from his face and green-gold eyes and she *knew* him. This impatient stranger was the man from her dreams. The sound of his voice was like a clear bell, tolling.

*Oh. It's you.*

Behind him, his surviving companions on their horses gathered close in the near-dark of late twilight, swords raised and ready. Nine of them, all silent. All staring. What was the matter? Had they never seen a girl?

The dead beast that had run at her was a lump on the grass, fire-light flickering warmly in its dead, open eyes. She felt a pain in her, somewhere. It had been human before it was blighted. Someone should grieve.

"Girl," the man with dark red hair said again, and halted directly before her. His lean face was stubbled a dark reddish gold, and the same flickering firelight danced up and down the length of his blade. "Who are you? Where have you come from?" He jerked his head at the dead beast. "And how did you do *that*?"

Charis stared up at him, perplexed. "*More* gibberish? Please, Deenie, tell me you understand him."

The man's companions stirred, uneasy, hearing Charis speak. The man glanced at them, his hand raised, then turned back. "It's strange, your tongue is. You're not from Vharne, you aren't."

*Vharne.* Was that the name of this land? Vharne. She'd never heard of it. "Yes, Charis," she said softly. "He wants to know who we are and where we're from."

Charis shivered. "That reef magic. Deenie . . ." Then she scowled at the man. "We mustn't tell him anything. Who's to say he's a friend?"

But he was a friend. She felt it in her bones, even if she couldn't explain how or why. "It's all right, Charis. He's not going to hurt us."

"You don't know that! He could run you through in the blink of an eye. Deenie, I *swear*—"

"Charis, *hush*." With a cross look at her, Deenie stood. The man with the dark red hair, who was so familiar though they'd never once met, took a wary step back. She pressed a hand to her chest. "*Deenie.* My name is *Deenie*."

He frowned. "Deenie."

"That's right." She touched her fingers to his chest. "You?"

Knocking her hand aside, he took a second wary backwards step and raised his sword. He wasn't handsome, not precisely, but there was something astonishing in his face. A strength. A steadfastness. Beneath that, a deep sorrow. It tugged at her soul and pounded the blood hard and fast in her veins.

*Goose Martin, Gardenia. Remember Goose?*

And she did. Of course she did. She was very fond of Goose. But she'd *dreamed* this man. That had to mean something. Something out of the ordinary.

*And when I look at him, I feel . . . I feel . . .*

Staring into his green-gold eyes, she felt her pulse leap. "I'm Deenie," she whispered. "Please, won't you tell me your name?"

Quizzical, he touched his chest. "My name, you want?"

She nodded. *Trust me. Please, trust me.* "Yes."

"My name." He looked to his men, then at the dead beast, then back at her. His jaw tightened. "Ewen."

"Ewen." She turned to Charis. "His name's Ewen."

"So?" said Charis, still suspicious. "Should I turn a cartwheel?" Cautiously she got to her feet, one eye on the men with the swords. "Deenie, what's going on? Why are you so willing to trust him?"

"It's hard to explain."

"*Try.*"

Deenie bit her lip. *She's really not going to like this.* "I dreamed him. Once before we left Lur, and again a few nights ago."

"Oh. Really?" said Charis, unimpressed. "And when were you going to mention that?"

"I wasn't. I thought it was nonsense. I had no idea we'd stumble across him in the wilderness." She shook her head. "It's very peculiar."

"Peculiar?" Charis snorted. "That's a word for it. Deenie, who *are* these men? What are they doing here? And why are you dreaming about them?"

"Not them. *Him.* And honestly, Charis, I don't know. But—"

She broke off, then, because the man Ewen was retreating, returning to his companions. They gathered close around him, talking in low voices, and she couldn't hear them.

"Deenie, those—those *things*," said Charis. She was staring at the dead beast slumped on the grass. "Am I going mad or do they—"

"You're not going mad, no," she said grimly. "They're what Da and Mama and your papa fought, the day Morg died. It was a beast like this that took his leg."

"You're saying that was a *person?*" Charis whispered, horrified. "All those creatures were people? Oh, how *awful.* And you—Deenie—"

Such a dear friend, she was. "I'm all right, Charis," she said, suddenly

**323**

tired. "I had to stop them. They'd have killed every last one of us, else-wise."

"I know. But still."

Yes. But still. Here was another memory that would haunt her to the grave.

Shivering, Charis hugged herself. "I don't understand, though. *Morg* made the beasts Papa fought in Dorana. So if they're of his making, and he's dead, then who made these ones? Has someone else learned his magic?"

Deenie stared at the dead beast. She could still feel the blight in it, that foul, corrosive touch. It stirred the reef's darkness inside her. Made her feel sick and faint.

*It's the same, Da. In you, in me, in the reef—and in this beast. It's the same.*

"No, Charis. I don't think so."

"But that has to be what happened," said Charis. "Because other-wise it means—" Her eyes widened. "Oh, Deenie. Deenie, *no*."

She thought of her dreams. Rafel on that unknown balcony, feeling somehow not like Rafel. The way he'd felt smothered. Silenced. Wrapped in darkness. The way he'd . . . disappeared.

It broke her heart to say it. "I think it's yes, Charis. I think it's Morg. He's not dead."

"But he has to be," Charis whispered. "Your da killed him. King Gar *died* so he'd die. Deenie, *he has to be dead!*"

Staring at the beast, she shook her head. "No. We want him to be dead. It's not the same thing."

"But—but—if he's alive—and I don't see how he can be, but if he *is*, then who's going to stop him, Deenie? *Us?*"

She felt her chin tilt. "And Rafe. 'Cause we are going to find him, Charis, and when we find him he'll join the fight. You'll see."

Charis's face was vivid with anguish. Tears like little snail tracks trailed down her cheeks. Deenie opened her mouth to say something brave, but sharply raised voices distracted her. Whatever Ewen and his companions were talking of, things were getting heated.

"*No*, Ibbie," said Ewen, glaring. "And that's a fool thing to say, that is."

"Deenie?" Charis inched closer as the men continued to brangle. "We should sneak away while they're not looking. 'Cause there's only two of us and we're girls. What if they—"

"They won't," she said. "I told you. We can trust him. Ewen."

Now Charis was glaring. "And you're sure of that, are you, after knowing him such a long time?"

"You, there! Girl!"

She turned. Ewen was going to have to stop calling her that. "Deenie," she said, and put a snap in her voice.

Leaving his men, he came back. His sword was in its scabbard now, but one hand was on its hilt. "Deenie. You understand me?"

She nodded. "Yes."

"Hold up three fingers, so I'm sure."

Sighing, she held up three fingers. "See? I can count, too."

His lips twitched. "It's strange, your tongue—but you're being sassy, I say."

"*Sassy?* That's a new word. Where I come from I think you'd say *slumskumbledy*." She shrugged. "Either way, I won't apologise. I used to be a mouse once, but that Deenie got herself drowned on the way here."

"Stop your nattering," he said. "No point to it, is there, when I can't understand you?"

"No," she said. "I s'pose not."

He looked at the dead beast, his eyes grim. "Sorcery was it, that killed them?"

Ah. Now here was a sticky bit. "You could call it that, I s'pose."

He glared. "Yes or no?"

She nodded. "Yes."

They could understand that much of her, then. His men muttered, dangerous, and every sword came up.

"*Sorcery*," said Ewen. There was murder in his eyes.

Not shifting her gaze from his face, she knelt before him then tugged aside her damp tangle of hair, baring her throat. "I won't hurt you, Ewen."

"Deenie, what are you doing?" Charis demanded. "Do you *want* him to cut off your head?"

"He won't," she said, her heart pounding. "I frighted him. That's all."

"And now you're frighting me!"

"I'm sorry. Don't fratch. We'll be all right."

"*Deenie*—"

Still, she looked at him. "Mama was prophecy's keeper, remember? And I'm her daughter. I dreamed him. He won't hurt me."

"And what about me? I don't want my life in his hands!"

"It's not, Charis," she said steadily. "It's in mine."

Charis groaned. "Deenie, I could smack you! *Fine*. But if it looks like manky business then you drop him like you dropped those beasts. I mean it. You *have* to."

Fingers still on his sword-hilt, Ewen was frowning. "Charis, she is? She's afraid?"

"Yes."

"Are you afraid, Deenie?"

She shook her head. "No."

"*Sorcery*," he said, close to growling. "I should put you down, girl." Then his gaze flicked to the dead beast. "But it's our lives we owe you."

She sank onto her heels. "You're welcome."

Doubt was churning in him. "Who are you, girl? Where are you *from*? Iringa? Trindek? Feen?"

"We're Olken, from Lur."

"Lur? That's your country? I don't know it." He dragged a hand down his face then, surprising her, dropped to one knee. Took her chin between his thumb and finger and stared hard into her eyes. "Trust you, girl, can I? Or will you murder us in our sleep?"

He might not understand her words, but with luck he'd sense that she wasn't a threat. "No, Ewen. I won't."

He let go of her. "Spirit," he muttered. "It's glad I am Tav's not here." In a single, smooth motion he stood. "Get up. You and Charis are safe, you are."

"What? What did he say?" Charis demanded.

"That we're safe," Deenie said, standing. Ewen watched her, and didn't offer a helping hand.

Charis snorted. "And I suppose no man ever said *that* and broke his word?"

"We'll bide here 'til sunrise, we will," said Ewen, glancing at his men. "Come dawn, you ride with us."

"Don't tell me, let me guess," said Charis. "We're his prisoners?"

"He thinks we are," Deenie murmured.

Ewen pointed at the cottage. "Going to sleep in there, were you?" She nodded. "Yes."

"This stretch of rough country's rotten with beasts, it is," he said. "I'll watch you, I will." He turned to his men. "Make yourselves some torches, then get the horses settled and—"

"No need for torches," said Deenie, and with a snap of her fingers called glimfire. To a man they cried out—even Ewen was startled— and suddenly every sword was pointed at her throat.

Ewen spat on the grass. "*Sorcery.*"

"No," she said. "It's just light. But if you don't like it?" She snapped her fingers again, and the glimfire went out.

In the dying firelight he blinked at her. Scowled at the darkness. Glanced at his men. Scowled at her.

"Bring it back."

She raised an eyebrow. "*Please.*"

"What?" he said, baffled. "Girl—Deenie—bring it back. We can't watch for beasts in the dark."

Sighing, she summoned several balls of glimfire, spread them about so everyone could see properly, then took Charis's arm and turned for the cottage.

"He's going to nursemaid us. We'll have to talk later."

Their own bobbing ball of glimfire showed them the cottage's doorway and the bare, clean floor within. With Ewen a few paces behind them they ducked inside and sat themselves with their almost empty haversack, then watched as he sat by the empty doorway opposite, his drawn sword across his bent knees and his back to the wall. His gaze roamed the cottage's small, single room. Sadness again, swiftly suppressed. And then it settled.

"It's a strange girl you are . . . Deenie."

Deenie shrugged. "No stranger than you, Ewen."

"What's he saying?" said Charis.

"Nothing important." She patted Charis's hand. "Get your head down. You can have the haversack for a pillow. Just—wait a moment—"

But as she tugged her stiff, folded leathers out of the haversack, to use for her own pillow, her fingers brushed against Barl's oilskin-stitched diary. An odd shivery sensation went through her, waking the other, kinder magic she'd absorbed from the reef. On impulse, or instinct, she shoved the diary between her leathers' folds and pulled both out together.

With a last, baleful glance at Ewen, Charis slithered onto the floor. "I'll not sleep, you know," she grumbled. "Not with him glooming there."

Smiling, she bumped Charis's shoulder. "Yes, you will. If you stop wittering."

Charis huffed. "I really did like you better when you were a mouse!"

But she settled down and in a little while, because she was weary, she slept, soft flutter-snores filling the hushed cottage. And that left her and Ewen, her dream man of the dark red hair and green-gold eyes, in the glimlight, in the silence.

*Well, Da. What now?*

# CHAPTER TWENTY

⚜

The girl was dozing, knees pulled to her flat chest, arms folded on them, face buried. Shoulders pressed to the cottage's rough wall, fingers lightly curled about the hilt of his sword, Ewen watched her through half-closed eyes.

*Deenie.*

What kind of name was that for a girl? But then, what kind of girl could kill beasts with a word?

*A sorcerer, that's what kind. Tav would tell me to kill her, he would.*

But she was a sorcerer, so how could he? If he tried to hurt her she'd drop him, like she'd dropped those beasts. Besides. He had to do what he thought was right, no matter what he knew Tavin would bluster.

*The tiltyard's behind us now. I rode into the rough a son in search of his father, I did. And when I rode back I was a man with a crown.*

Still, he missed Tavin's counsel. Hip-deep in their desperate plans to save Vharne's people from Morg, the swordmaster had only fought a little against being left in the king's seat a second time, and so soon. He knew there was no other choice. With Murdo's nephews dead, no more of his blood in the Vale, there wasn't another man to be trusted. Well, save Clovis. And Clovis was busy.

*You'll blade my arse when you hear of this, Swordmaster. I can hear you now, I can. No sorcery in Vharne, boy. Kill this girl. Find a way.*

Only he didn't want to.

Maybe because she'd saved their lives. Maybe because he might need her to save them again. According to the king's secret map there were no spirit paths to hide them from beasts and wanderers in this part of the rough. And there wasn't time to run about testing that. Morg was expecting him, and it was Vharne's people who'd pay the price if he was late.

*Or maybe it's because she knelt at my feet, she did, and bared her slender throat to my blade.*

She could have killed him, but she made herself vulnerable. When she looked at him he'd seen something compelling in her eyes. And her voice, it was kindly. He couldn't hear any cruelty in it.

*It's a scrawny thing, she is. And she's plain as a mouse. But when she looks at me . . .*

He didn't want to think about that.

The strange light she'd created hovered high in the corner. She'd snapped her fingers and dimmed it so her friend Charis could sleep. And the girl was sleeping. She was snoring. Even a beast might not start her awake. Deenie easily could've left the light bright.

Light with a finger-snap? How was that possible?

*How is it possible to kill with a word?*

The girl—Deenie—breathed in deeply, and lifted her dark-haired head. Her blurry gaze sharpened, then softened. She smiled. "Ewen."

Wary, he nodded. "Deenie."

She said something else. Not a single word of it made sense. She was from *Lur?* Where was that? Not in the blighted south. Nothing lived there. She had to be lying. She was Feenish. Or maybe from Brantone.

She was staring at him, her straight brown eyebrows pulled low in a scowl and her bottom lip caught between her small, white teeth. As she stared, thinking, her hand strayed almost stealthily to the stiff, mishandled leathers she'd tried to use as a pillow but quickly abandoned. Her fingers crept between the folds then crept out again, holding an oilskin-wrapped packet.

Startled, she looked at it. As though she hadn't realised it was there — or hadn't realised she wanted it. The expression on her thin, angular face was strange as she traced her fingertips over the packet. *She* was strange. Small and slight and fearless.

*And every word I say, she understands, she does.*

Sorcery.

"Girl," he said. "Deenie. What's that you hold?"

She made an impatient sound, her eyes narrow. Said something scornful. And of course she was right. Hadn't he scolded her for nattering when they both knew he'd never understand? Shaking her head, she reached for the blade belted at her hip. He'd not taken it from her, or the blade from her snoring companion, thinking it might ease their distrust of him.

Tavin would say that was a mistake.

He raised his sword. "Girl—"

She said something else, her voice soothing this time. Using his name. He felt himself relax, which was foolish. He had no business trusting her.

*So I must be brain-rotted, because I do.*

For a moment she did nothing with the knife, just held it loosely while she stared at the packet. That dimmed, sorcerous light showed him a hint of tears in her eyes. Showed him fear and confusion in her shadowed face. Revealed to him a sad, grim resolve. He felt his own sleeping pain wake, seeing it.

She said something else. She was talking to someone. Not him. Her voice was wistful. Yearning. Then her face tightened, hardened, and she pushed her pain inside.

*I do that, I do.*

Ignoring him, she used the tip of her blade to cut the oilskin wrapping's stitches—and then she put the knife on the hard dirt floor, its point turned away from him. A message, was it? *I mean you no harm.*

He watched her pull the oilskin off the thing it protected, which proved to be a thin, leather-bound book. Her eyes said it was important and frightening. And if it frightened her, a sorcerer . . .

"Should I fear it?" he said. "That book. Maybe I should burn it."

Shocked, she shook her head then rattled words at him. They sounded threatening.

His fingers tightened on his sword. "Girl—"

"*Deenie!*" she snapped.

Her outlandish name. How he hated it being the only word of hers he for certain understood. "Deenie, will that book hurt me? Will it hurt my men?"

She wanted to say no, he could see the struggle in her, but instead she lifted her skinny shoulders in a shrug. *Maybe.* So did that mean she was an honest sorcerer, that she wouldn't tell a lie?

*I want to believe her, I do. Is that a spell? Has she beasted me, on the inside, where no-one can see?*

"Give it to me," he said, and held out his hand.

She stared at him, her eyes wide and faintly hostile. Shook her head again as her slender fingers clutched the book. So it frightened her— but it was important.

*If I try to take it she might kill me.*

"Deenie, do you mean to hurt me with that book, do you?"

Another headshake. She said something, sounding earnest, one hand pressed to her heart.

"I'm to trust you on that, am I?"

She nodded. "Ewen," she said, and pressed her heart a second time.

"But you won't trust me."

Dropping her gaze to the book, biting her lip again, she touched her fingertips to its mottled cover. Not a word spoken, but her answer was clear enough.

*Not with this, I won't.*

If he had his way they'd soon be riding the rough together. But he couldn't keep her under his nose every step. And if she didn't trust him she might get them all killed, not with sorcery but argument. Maybe if he did a kind thing for her . . .

The leathers she'd discarded were clearly unwearable, and she should be wearing them. Travel in the rough needed leathers, not wool and linen.

"Bide here," he said, and put down his sword. "I'll be back, I will."

Her eyebrows lifted but she didn't reply.

The sorcerous balls of light she'd created still glowed outside the cottage, brightly enough that he could see to walk without turning his ankle. He made his way to the horse-line, his own leathers soft and supple. The horses were unsaddled and drooping, their tack neatly stacked to one side. He found his saddle-bags, rummaged for what he sought, pulled out a measure of dried beef after it then went to be certain all was well with his barracks men. His surviving barracks men. Two dead, to be burned come the sunrise: Grame, his Dirk on this journey, and young, feisty Drooe. His heart ached to think of them, lost. And now he'd have to choose himself a new right hand.

*I'll think on that come sunrise, I will.*

His barracks men looked to him, solemn, as he joined them at the fire they'd kept alive with fresh wood.

"All good out here, is it?"

"All good, Highness," said Robb, most likely the man he'd choose for his new Dirk. Him or Hain. "We'll—"

"Captain, not Highness," he said sharply. "Our business is ours. Hold your tongues around those girls, you should."

"Not girls," Neel mumbled. Cross-grained as bad timber, he was, but one of the best swords Tavin ever trained. "Trouble, they are."

He frowned. "Maybe. But I'll mind them, I will. Keep beast watch and rest. We're riding on at sunrise, we are."

Leaving the men to mutter, he returned to the cottage. The girl Deenie looked up as he ducked back inside. She was still holding the book. Her friend Charis kept on sleeping. A poor barracks man, she'd make.

Eased to the floor again, he held out his hand. "Give me your leathers."

Her straight eyebrows lifted.

"I'll give them back," he said. "Steal them, would I? When they won't fit?"

She hesitated, then tossed them. This would be a task—they felt like old tree bark. He shoved dried beef in his mouth to silence his belly's rumbling, then opened his grease bag and got to work. Likely he'd use up every dab of it. He'd have to beg more from his barracks men to keep his own leathers soft.

Her eyes were on him as he suppled her trews enough so she could wear them. Glancing once at her, he caught a kindness in her eyes. That made her look down. Light colour touched her cheeks.

After a time, she opened the book. Her shocked gasp had him dropping his grease bag and reaching for his sword.

"What's wrong, girl? Sorcery?"

Her breathing came in short sharp pants, but she shook her head.

"What then?"

She said something, trying to explain, then pulled a face.

A pain in the arse, this was. If it was sorcery let her understand him, why couldn't she fix it so he could understand her?

"Deenie. Not sorcery? It's sure, you are?"

This time she nodded.

Shake for no, nod for yes. He could understand her that much, at least.

"Not beasts?"

She shook her head again.

"Harm to any of us?"

Another headshake. And when he kept staring, patted a hand to her heart, her eyes pleading.

*Trust me.*

He lowered his sword, slowly. "You say," he muttered and then, uneasy, kept on greasing her leathers.

She returned to the book, working through it page by page. From her quick breathing, and the look on her face, he thought it amazed her. Strange, that was. Didn't she know her own book?

At last, with a sigh, she let it fall to her lap.

"Ewen."

"What?" he said, still wary. There was a gleam in her eyes that made his blood stir, not pleasantly.

She thought for a moment. Then she pressed a hand to her heart again and lifted those straight, purposeful eyebrows. A question.

"Do I trust you?"

She nodded, pleased.

He wasn't pleased, not at all. "To do what, girl?"

With a snap of her fingers she summoned a tiny ball of light, then blew on it so it danced across the space between them. He made himself sit still. Just as it touched his cheek, warm and soft, she vanished it.

"Sorcery?" he said, feeling his mouth go dry.

Another nod.

"On *me*?"

Her eyes were warm, now. Understanding.

"Why?"

She used her hands and fingers to mimic two ducks, quacking face to face.

He stared at her, guessing. "You mean — so we can talk?"

She smiled.

*She's reading my mind now, is she? That's sorcery, that is!*

He put aside his grease bag and her slowly suppling leathers. Then, with his sword on the floor beside him and sweat springing to his skin, he rested his hands on his knees and made his fingers stay unclenched.

"Will it hurt?"

She twitched her shoulders. *Maybe. I don't know.*

"If you make me a beast," he said, heart thudding, "I'll gut you, I will."

She rolled her eyes. "Ewen." She might as well have said *fool*.

"And it is a fool I am, to let sorcery touch me," he retorted. "So do it quick, girl. Before I change my mind."

It riled her when he called her that, but it made him feel better. Gaze narrowed with annoyance she eased herself away from the opposite wall and her sleeping friend Charis, shifting across the floor towards him 'til they were close enough to touch.

And then she touched him.

Her slender, callused fingers were cool on his face, and not quite confident. He could feel the tremor in them. She closed her eyes, hiding from him, then whispered under her breath in a tongue different from her own. A shiver ran through her. Ran through him a heartbeat later. He felt a flooding warmth. Oddly, it reminded him of a spirit path. And then he was startled by an *unfolding* in his mind. Her fingers fell from his stubbled cheek. The loss of her touch hurt him. He wanted to snatch her hand back.

"Ewen," she whispered. "Can you understand me now?"

His mouth fell open. Spirit, spirit, what had she *done*? "Girl—"

"I *swear*," she said, her thin face scrunched to a scowl, "if you call me *girl* one more time I shall find a spell to make your tongue fall out and then I'll sinkin' *use* it."

"Sorcery," he said, hearing his voice hoarse with shock.

"Not sorcery, Ewen. Magework. And where I come from it's nothing to fear. *I'm* nothing to fear."

*You say.* "The beasts you killed. Born of magework, are they?"

"No," she said, so certain. "*That's* sorcery. The wicked use of power."

He could see she believed it, but he wasn't so easily convinced. "Magework killed those beasts, did it?"

Shadows shifted in her eyes. "Yes," she said, after a long silence. She was struggling, he could see it. "But I promise I won't you hurt you or your men."

*And I'm to believe that, am I? On your say-so, no more?*

He had to fight not to pick up his sword. "We know sorcery in Vharne, we do. It comes from the north." His guts tightened. "From Dorana."

And she *knew* that name. He saw it stab right through her. But before he could chase that, the girl Charis stirred and sat up, yawning.

"Deenie? What's going on?"

Deenie turned. "I've found a spell that lets him understand Olken."

"Really?" said Charis, prickly as a hedgehog. "Plucked it from thin air, did you?"

Oh, she was a frisky one. He watched Deenie's gaze drop. "No."

The leather-bound book was on the floor. Charis glanced at it, her eyes sharp. Suspicious. Interesting, that was.

"And will this spell work the other way?" she demanded. "If it will, you can use it on me. I'm tired of not knowing what he's saying to my face."

So Deenie used her magework on her frisky friend, who showed no fear. Should he be reassured by that? When it was done, the girl Charis looked at him. Even so thin and weary she was beautiful. But oddly, she didn't stir him. It was Deenie who made his heart thud. Spirit save him. Was *that* a spell?

"Well?" said Charis, snappish. "Don't just sit there staring like a lummox. Say something!"

Say something. "I want to know where Lur is, I do."

Charis's eyes widened. "It worked!" Then she jutted her chin at him. "But don't imagine that means we're going to tell you about Lur."

Deenie sighed. "Charis."

"*No*, Deenie. We don't say a word about anything important until we know who he is, and where he's from, and what is *happening* in this land. It's full of beasts and mad people. For all we know *he's* mad."

"Charis, he's not mad," said Deenie, with another sigh.

Charis sniffed. "Why? Because you dreamed him?"

That made him blink, and forget *mad people*. "You dreamed me?"

"Don't listen to her," said Deenie, blushing. "She's addled. She hasn't had enough sleep, poor thing."

"*Deenie!*" Charis poked a finger in her friend's ribs, then turned on him. "You haven't answered my questions."

He shrugged. "Answer mine first, you can."

"Certainly not," the girl Charis retorted. "We've far more to fear than you. All you strong men with swords. You could spit us like chickens for roasting and there's not a thing we could do to stop you."

He smiled, not kindly. "Deenie could kill us, she could."

"But she won't," said Charis. "Not even if you deserve it."

He looked to Deenie. "Why not?"

"Because I ain't a murderer, Ewen."

He pressed his back and shoulders against the wall behind him. "You say."

Gaze lowered to her lap, Deenie bit her lip. "Lur's a long way from here, Ewen. It's—"

"*Deenie!*" said Charis, imploring. "*Don't.*"

"I have to, Charis. This is his home, not ours. Why should he trust us if we keep secrets?" She looked up. "Lur lies beyond the blighted lands to your south. Over the mountains."

He stared, disbelieving. "You travelled the blighted lands?"

"No. They're poison. We sailed past them, along the coast."

*Sailed?* She knew boats? "Why? To escape your own land? This Lur, it's blighted too, is it?"

Deenie and the girl Charis exchanged wary looks. "It wasn't," said Deenie. "It is now. Ewen, our kingdom is dying."

And that was no lie. Though why her pain should pain him . . . 'Your king thought Vharne could help you? Why?"

Again the girls looked at each other. "Lur's king is dead," said Charis.

Was that the truth? He thought so. But it wasn't the whole truth. And it didn't explain how Deenie knew of Dorana.

*I'll have that answer from her, I will.*

"Then why—"

"We're not here on purpose, Ewen," said Deenie, so earnest. "We sailed up the river to find food and water, and then lost our skiff to rocks."

*That* was a lie, surely. "You sailed the Spate. Two girls."

Charis's eyes glittered. "Two *mages*. And yes, we sailed the river. So?"

"*Two* mages?" He raised his eyebrows. "It's a beast-killer you are, like Deenie?"

"No," she said, not pleased to admit it. "Deenie's the only mage like Deenie."

And that was interesting too, but he wasn't about to let them see he cared. "If it wasn't your king sent you sailing, why did you leave Lur?" A thought struck him, and he straightened. "Did a beast come to you? Are you summoned to Dorana?"

Again, the name touched Deenie hard. It touched both of them. Then Deenie shook her head.

"I never saw a beast before tonight, Ewen. Charis and I sailed from Lur to find my brother, Rafel. Months ago he crossed the mountains into the blighted lands, trying to find a way to help our kingdom. But—" Her voice was wobbling. She breathed hard, to steady it. "But something must have happened, something terrible, 'cause he never came back. So Charis and I, we've come to find him."

Her pain was real. As real as his own. He recognised her suffering like he recognised his own face in a mirror. The king. *Padrig*. And yet . . .

"Aren't there barracks men in Lur?" he said roughly. "What of your father? Why did he send you after your brother with only another girl for company?"

Her breath caught. "Da lies gravely ill. He doesn't know about Rafe, or me. Besides, Rafe's given up for dead. Charis and I are the only ones who believe he still lives." A second time, her voice broke. "Ewen, we have to find him. He has the power to save Lur and its people. To save Da."

Ah. "He's a mage, your brother?"

"As great as any Lur has ever seen."

He looked at her, brooding. Every word she'd spoken was the truth, he'd swear his sword on that. But still, there was no denying she'd told him a tale full of holes.

"If he's not lost in Vharne, where is he, d'you think?"

"I don't know, exactly," she murmured at last. "All I can say for certain is we need to keep going north."

North? Chilled, he closed his fingers so they'd not reach for his blade. "How do you know that?"

"If I try and explain, you'll call me a liar."

"Explain and *I'll* decide if it's a liar you are."

Her jaw clenched tight, stubborn. "Fine. But don't say I didn't warn you. I feel him, Ewen. I've felt him my whole life. That's how my mage-sense works. I feel things. And since he went missing I've dreamed him. I've heard him calling me for help. He's alone and afraid and hurting, and since I'm the only one who can save him, here I am."

*Dreamed her brother, dreamed me . . .* 'I want to know about these dreams, I do."

She looked down again, hiding. "My dreams are mine, Ewen. I don't share them."

"But *you* could share something," said prickly Charis. "Turn and turn about, it's only fair. What's the matter with this land of yours? We've been tramping for days and days and there's *nothing* out here but abandoned villages. Where are Vharne's people? The ones who aren't mad and rotting, I mean."

He felt his skin crawl. "You've found wanderers?"

"If wanderers are mad people falling to bits, then yes." Charis shuddered. "We found some. Four women."

Women? *Not Murdo, then.* But even so—"Where?" he said, urgently. "Near here?"

"No," said Deenie. Her eyes were dark with the memory. "Near the river."

Too far behind them for him to turn back and search there for the king. "What happened?"

"They died," said Charis, and shuddered again.

"*Died?* Every one?"

Deenie nodded, watching him closely. "They were desperately ill, Ewen. Do you know what afflicted them?"

"Brain-rot, we call it," he said, and wondered if she could feel his pain. *Padrig.* "It's a mystery, the cause of it."

"Not to me," she said. "They're blighted, like the lands south of Vharne. Like Lur is now. It's a kind of sorcerous infection."

Sorcery? Then somehow Morg was to blame. Spirit save him, he wanted not to be wrong about her, but—"How do you know?"

She met his stare without guile, yet he'd swear she still kept secrets.

"I told you. I'm a mage who feels things. I feel the blight, wherever it is. Whatever it's touched."

He shook his head, unsettled. "Girl, it's strange you are."

"That's not for you to say," Charis snapped. "And don't think I don't see you pushing the talk back to us, either. *I'm* not a noddyhead. Now, why are you and your men rampaging about in the middle of nowhere?"

What a pity he couldn't make her clap tongue. "I can give you an answer," he said, shrugging. "Freeze your blood it will, but I can give it."

"You'd best believe our blood's difficult to freeze," said Charis. "We've lived through things you'd not dream of."

Deenie gave her a chiding look. "*Charis.*"

The girl Charis sniffed, but said nothing else.

Easing his shoulders against the hard wall, Ewen half-lowered his eyelids. Their whole truth they'd not give him? Well, he had secrets too and he'd keep them, for now. But some truth they should know, and in hearing it they might reveal more of themselves.

"Your kingdom. Lur. I've never heard a word of it."

"You wouldn't have," said Deenie. "For hundreds of years Lur was lost to the wider world. Now it's found again. Does that matter?"

It might, but he'd chew the question over later, by himself. "Lost or found, did Lur ever know Morg?"

In the deep silence that followed he heard the horses on the horseline, shifting and stamping. He heard a hunting bird call and a fox bark, distant. He heard Charis's quick breath. In Deenie's eyes he saw a dreadful shifting of memories.

"There are stories," she said, at last. "Very old ones. He was a sorcerer, I think."

Ewen watched his fingers clench. "He was. Ruled over many lands, he did. Vharne was one of them."

"I'm sorry to hear that."

He thought she truly was. "He never ruled Lur?"

"No," she said. "Never."

The truth again, no question. "What saved you?"

She shrugged. "No-one knows."

And *there* was a lie, he'd swear his life on that, he would. But to challenge her now would be to lose her, he knew it. Besides, she was a beast-killing mage. Dancing on thin ice, he was.

"Lur was fortune-kissed," he said, his voice low. "Ruled Vharne for centuries, he did. His sorcery helped him live more years than was natural. But in the end, he died." He felt a stab of pain. "We thought he died. But it's back, he is, with his beasts and his dark magic. And it's summoned north I am to his new court in the city of Elvado. In Dorana. He wants Vharne, he does, and he's determined to have it."

"*You're* summoned?" said Charis, her eyebrows lifting. "Who are you to be summoned for Vharne?"

That was something else he'd keep secret, for now. "The king's man, I am. A captain of his barracks. He can't travel so it's me he's sent."

Cross-legged on the cottage's dirt floor, Deenie leaned forward. Her eyes were full of disbelief—and disgust. At *him*. "To give Morg your kingdom? Willingly?"

"*Willingly?*"

He couldn't sit still for that. Braced against the wall, he pushed to his feet. Bile was rising thick and fast into his throat.

"I've never been less willing, girl. But Morg sent a beast to the Vale, he did, to the king's house. It butchered the king's barracks men. Butchery for every soul in Vharne, it promised, unless we give Morg what he wants."

"You can't fight him?"

"*How*, girl? Vharne has no mages. There's no power here to stand against sorcery."

Now her eyes were full of sympathy, as if she knew how it felt to be helpless like that. "Even so, there must be *some* way you can fight back."

Their only weapon was Vharne's spirit paths, a frail straw for clutching. But he wasn't about to trust her with them. "Easy for you to say, that is. You can kill beasts with a word."

His sneering hurt her. He was glad—and he was sorry.

"Rafel will help you," she said. "If I can find him."

He laughed. "One man can destroy a sorcerer, you think? *One man?* Girl—girl—you are—"

"Stop calling her *girl*," said Charis. "You ignorant, arrogant *captain*. What do you know of magework? Or Rafel! Rafe can—"

"Don't, Charis," said Deenie, chiding again. Warning? It seemed so. "He doesn't understand. He doesn't trust magic. And why would he?" A little shiver ran through her. "After Morg?"

"He'd understand if he listened instead of talking!" Charis retorted. "But he's so busy doubting us he can't be bothered to find out if we can help!"

"Charis, that's unfair," said Deenie. "We're sprung on him without warning. Give him some time to get used to mages wandering around his kingdom without an invitation."

Charis folded her arms. "I swear, if I find a spell that'll turn you back into a mouse . . ."

Ignoring her, Deenie turned to him. "Ewen, please, I know this is hard. But I'm not lying, I promise. Rafel can help. And so can I."

He stared down at the girl, wanting to believe that promise. Knowing it was foolish. It was a foolish hope, to think anyone could stand against Morg.

*And it's a fool I am to think one girl and her brother can make a difference.*

He looked past her, to the floor. "That book of yours, there. It's for magework, is it?"

She hesitated, then nodded. "Yes."

"Use it against Morg, can you?"

"No. Rafe can wield those magics. I can't."

*No?* Suspicion stirred. "But you spelled me out of it, so we can talk."

"That spell's different," she said, her gaze steady. "I can't use the rest."

He held out his hand. "Let me see it."

"Don't," said Charis, glaring. "It's nothing to do with him."

Deenie unfolded herself from the floor and faced him, no more flinching. "I'm sorry, Ewen. If I let you have it, I'll be breaking my word."

He wasn't sure he believed her. "To your ailing father?"

"And to my mother. She's dead."

It was a new pain, he could see that. He wished he couldn't feel it. Lost her mother, lost her brother, her father far away and dying. A bad way, she was in.

*But what is her pain to me? It's the caretaker king of Vharne, I am. Vharne's pain matters, not this girl's.*

"What do you want, Deenie?" he said roughly.

She tipped her head. "What do *you* want?"

"No sorcery in Vharne! This kingdom's *choking* on sorcery!"

Stepping close, she touched her fingertips to his arm. "Then we want the same thing. I want sorcery gone from Vharne, from Lur, from every land it's touched. I want Morg properly dead, *never* to rise again."

So small, she was, so slight and so plain—and so full of venom he had to take a step back. Her hatred was blazing. If he held out his hands he could warm them against it.

*What haven't you told me, mage girl? What do you know of Morg that I don't?*

If he asked her, she'd lie to him. He could see that in her too. But if he was patient . . . if he gave her time . . .

*I'm a wheedler, Tavin says. I'm a man who sits in the king's seat and waits and listens and coaxes secrets like mice from their little hidey holes.*

And if he did coax her secrets? What difference would it make? A mage girl and her brother—if he lived, if she could find him—they'd never stand against a sorcerer like Morg.

*It's spinning dreams, I am. Tav would clout me so hard.*

But even so . . . 'We're both travelling north. Travel together, we can."

The blaze in her died down to hot embers. "Except Charis and I don't have horses."

"You're not heavy," he said, carelessly. "Ride with me, you can. One of my barracks men will take Charis. You're right about Vharne. Full of wanderers and beasts, it is. Not safe even for mages. And this is my land, it is. I won't get us lost here, or see us starve or die of thirst."

"And beyond Vharne?"

"It's a long time we've stayed inside our borders," he admitted. "But we still know more of the lands beyond them than you do."

Lips pinched, Deenie looked at her friend. Charis grimaced. "He's right about that much."

"I know," said Deenie. "All right. Ewen, we'll travel with you, at least as far as it helps me find Rafe. But even though you're the king's man and Vharne is your kingdom, it doesn't mean we're bound to you. If we need to, if Rafe needs us to, we'll leave you behind and make our own way."

He had to laugh. "And that means what, you say? You say I'm the king's man and I've no authority to bind you?"

"Ewen." She met his eyes without fear. "I'm a mage. *Can* you bind me? Truly?"

He went cold. Small and slight she was, and there was pain in her that he could feel, that pushed him to her . . .

*But it's a sorcerer she is, even when she calls herself a mage.*

"So now I see you," he said, and spat on the dirt floor. "Take a mislike to me and in a blink I'm a beast, is it? I'm your slave, wearing chains forged from your magic? It's a fool, I am, to think of trusting you. What a blessing there's a man who knows me who's not here to see it. For I'd be breaking his brave heart giving comfort to you."

As tears brimmed in Deenie's eyes, the other girl Charis leapt up. "And isn't that just like a man," she said, scornful, "to have his bubble pride pricked because he can't trample roughshod over a woman. *Noddyhead*. She only means she'll follow her conscience and do the right thing. That's all Deenie ever does. Even when it's *killing* her, she does the right thing!"

He glared at the girl, his gaze slitted. "It's a sorcerer, you are. Sorcerers lie."

"*No*, noddyhead, I'm a *mage*!" said Charis, a spitfire now. "And believe me, not a scary one. I call glimfire and grow flowers and lure rabbits into the pot. That's what *I* do." She pointed. "But Deenie kills beasts! *And* she feels them coming. She feels your awful wanderers,

345

too. You prattle about us being safer with you? Trust me, Captain, it's *you* who's safer with *us!*"

Scowling, resentful, he turned to silent Deenie. "It's true I can't bind you. But you can bind yourself, girl, when it makes sense to be guided. I'll be your captain then, I will. For riding safely. For knowing Vharne where you don't. For knowing how to reach the borders and where to cross them without a man being lost or hurt. These things are *my* conscience, I say. Respect that, can you?"

Deenie nodded, quiet and small, that blazing hatred died down. "Yes, Ewen, I can. I will. I promise."

He rubbed a hand across his face.

*Tav would knock me turtle for trusting her. But Tav says it's a clever man who trusts the voice in his heart. And the voice in my heart says trust her, it does.*

"You *dreamed* me, girl?" He shook his head. "Happier, I'll be, if you don't do it again."

Her lips twitched. "I'll do my best."

She looked so *weary*. So did Charis, though Charis doubtless wearied herself with scolding more than anything.

"Get some sleep, you should," he said. "We ride early. You should put out your little light."

"The glimfire?" Deenie looked up at it. "You don't need it?"

"Not for greasing leathers, I don't."

"Oh. Yes. My leathers." Her cheeks pinked. "That's a kind thing for you to do, Ewen."

"Girl," he said, looking to ruffle her, "it's a kind man I am."

And that made both mages huff and flounce and lie down with their backs to him.

In the darkness, with Charis snoring, he greased Deenie's leathers by sure touch. Thought of his questions, and their answers, and all the things they hadn't said. Those thoughts made him grimace. But he'd made his choice, hadn't he? It was too late to turn back.

*And spirit alone knows where that choice will lead us.*

# CHAPTER TWENTY-ONE

Caged behind his own eyes, Rafel watched Morg remake the world. And though he tried so hard that he thought he'd tear his soul to strips and tatters, he couldn't break free and he couldn't crush the sorcerer who'd stolen his body.

*I thought Arlin would help me. I'm a sinkin' fool.*

It was hard to remember now why he'd trusted Arlin Garrick. Why he'd believed what he saw and heard in that brief, desperate moment when he'd managed to speak as himself. Lord Garrick was a Doranen, and the last good Doranen had died fighting Morg. One taste of power and the man who'd sworn to help him had shown his true face.

*How could I trust him, when I've known him my whole life?*

Sometimes it was hard to know who he hated most: Morg, Arlin . . . or himself.

Life in his prison of bones was strange. Sometimes he heard and saw everything. Sometimes Morg smothered him, putting him to sleep. There was always a panic after he woke. Until he worked out how much time had passed, and what Morg had done while he'd been kept unaware.

And then, once he knew, came the grief—and the rage.

*Da, if only you'd trusted me. If only you hadn't kept my power a bloody secret! If you hadn't, I could've stopped this. I could've kept Morg out.*

But he tried not to think on that. Morg liked to eavesdrop. He fed on pain. He was fat with other people's suffering.

*Every time I fratch at Da, he laughs.*

And there were other things he didn't dare think on, not even while Morg was preoccupied, like he was now. It wasn't safe. Not for him. Not for anyone.

He'd been so hopeful about Arlin, about them joining hands to defeat Morg. But all that hope was gone now. Shame. Grief. Despair. They'd devoured it.

Caged behind his own eyes, he felt the confines of his prison. Every time Morg swallowed another piece of himself, it meant less room for him. He was being crowded out of his own body, pressed and pushed into a corner, growing smaller and smaller.

*He says he's lost some power, but he don't feel weak to me. Sink me bloody sideways, if he's weak now then what'll it be like when he's found what's left of himself and swallowed it?*

Morg liked to torment him with that, too. Everyone in Lur thought Da had killed the sorcerer, but all he'd done was throw glimlight on a shadow. Da and his friend the king, they'd got it all wrong.

*I wish I knew how Da was. I wish I knew if—*

But that was something else he shouldn't think on. Not only because Morg liked it, but because the fear he felt for Da threatened to break him to pieces, when he was too close to breaking already. When he was scrabbling and scrabbling like a crab in a bucket.

Him and Deenie, when they were spratlings, having a looksee down on the coast. Splashing in the rock pools with Da and Mama wading nearby, hand in hand and laughing. Watching the sails on the fishing smacks full-bellied in the wind. Stirring the little waves with his magic when his parents' backs were turned. And Deenie with her eyes wide, feeling what he did.

*No, you sinkin' fool! Don't think about Deenie.*

Morg was up in his eyrie, locked inside the mansion's attic with his stolen eyes closed and his sharp, cruel mind drifting. He spent time here every day, calling for his scattered bits and pieces . . . honing his growing power . . . making his plans . . .

*And there's not a sinkin' thing I can do but watch him. I can't fight him. I can't hurt him. I can't—*

"That's right," said Morg, smiling. "You can't escape."

Shattering pain blasted through him. Morg could do that, hurt his prisoner without hurting himself. He'd done it all the time to Sarle Baden. The Doranen mage had fought Morg as hard as he could, but he'd lost.

Morg sighed. "Of course he lost, Rafel. *Everyone* loses. But Sarle was an idiot, so of course he paid the price."

Sometimes, at odd moments, he thought he could hear Baden screaming.

"But you still don't believe that, do you, Rafel?" said Morg, musing. "Even now, after so long, part of you refuses to accept your defeat. What a sad thing you are. How pitifully defiant."

He didn't answer.

"*Rafel!*" Morg snapped, and hurt him again.

Pitifully defiant, a scrabbling crab in a bucket, he froze and tucked himself as small as he could.

*Hurt me all you like, you sinkin' blowfish. I don't have to answer to you.*

Piqued, Morg took them outside, in the mood to soothe himself by savouring his last night in the mansion. Come the morning he and his ragtag court would take up residence in his new palace.

The sun was sinking, glowing dark gold in an eggshell-blue sky. It glittered on the distant spires of reborn Elvado. Knowing what its rebirth meant, Rafel tried to look away.

Morg wouldn't let him.

"Deny me my due, would you?" the sorcerer said, mage-claws sinking into his mind. "What a pustuled little toad you are, Rafel. What an insect. What a *grub*. You *stink* of jealousy, did you know that? Even Arlin can smell it. Did you think you could *hide*?"

*I ain't jealous, Morg. Sink me bloody sideways if I want what you've got.*

"Sink you? *Sink* you? Olken, I'll —"

And then Goose shambled out of the cobwebbed stables and into the slowly dusking light.

"Goose!" said Morg, brilliant with a vicious delight. "You idiot. You useless lump of wood. Come here."

Rafel felt a different kind of pain blast through his captured mind.

*Run, Goose. For pity's sake, wake up to yourself and run.*

But Goose wasn't Goose any more. Carrying a piece of Morg had fuddled him. If it had stayed in him longer than a day it would've killed him, for sure, but that small, sundered piece of sorcerer had swiftly jumped to Sarle Baden. For a while he'd thought his friend was getting better. But then Goose saw Arlin murder Fernel Pintte, and his half-mended mind broke again.

*Come on, Goose-egg, you can do it. Run!*

Uncertainly obedient, Goose shambled to Morg and stopped. Rapped knuckles to his forehead and stared at him, anxious.

"Dolt," said Morg, took a handful of Goose's hair and twisted, buckling his knees and putting him on the grass.

Goose's eyes stretched wide with shock. "Rafe?"

There was nothing he could do. Morg sailed him like a boat.

*Sink it, Goose. Sink it. I wish you'd bloody died.*

"Ha," said Morg, smiling. "He'll wish he'd died too — won't you, my plump little Goose?"

The pain and terror in Goose's face as Morg hurt him made Rafel kick and scream and batter the bars of his cage. Morg hardly felt him. He just laughed and pushed him away.

But not so far away he couldn't see Goose pay the price for his pride.

At last — and it took too long — Morg grew bored. Watching Goose crawl back to the stables, weeping, he wiped his hands down the front of his blue velvet tunic.

"When will you learn, Rafel?" he said softly, his voice icily intimate. "I won't be defied. I won't be denied. That treacherous whore I loved more than life *killed* herself rather than face my displeasure. How can it be you learned *nothing* from that?"

Shivering in the darkness somewhere deep behind his eyes, hearing again Goose's pitiful gasping, Rafel felt his rage burn.

*I learned, you sinkin' bastard. And you know what Barl taught me? She taught me you can be stopped. Not by me, maybe. It's too late for me, I reckon. But there's someone who can do it. You ain't invincible yet.*

"Well, little toad," said Morg, staring at distant, glittering Elvado. "You're right about one thing." Sighing, he set his inner world on fire. "It really is too late for you."

Standing with Morg on the Hall of Knowledge's highest balcony, Arlin stared across the remade city of Elvado. The city of beauty, of wonders, that he'd helped raise out of its ashes and into a glorious, wondrous rebirth.

*I should have seen it burn a second time. I should've lit the flames myself.*

Beside him, the smiling sorcerer stroked blunt, ringed fingers down the front of his crimson tunic. Were he a cat he'd be purring, so sleekly self-satisfied he was.

"And so the past becomes the present. What was now is, and will be forever." He laughed. "Come, Arlin. Confess the truth. You never thought it could be done."

"Master, I never doubted you could do it," he said, bowing. "To doubt you is to doubt the sun. But myself? Myself I doubt always."

"Little mage," said Morg. "Little lord. Don't judge yourself so harshly."

He sounded almost affectionate. But that was deceptive. There was an odd edge to the sorcerer this morning, a treacherous volatility. Something had irked him. Three *dravas* lay dead in the road behind them, smoked to stinking embers because they'd displeased their creator.

*I wonder . . . is it Rafel? Is he still alive? Still struggling?*

He hoped so. Like it or not, he still needed the Olken's help.

"Arlin? Your mind is wandering."

"Forgive me, Master," he said quickly. "I'm overcome by the view."

Morg's hand came to rest on his shoulder, a companionable gesture that could easily turn to pain.

"As well you should be, Arlin," he replied. "And by your good fortune, too. Confess *this*, since we are in the mood for confessions. Every last small dream you ever dreamed in Lur, that rotten kingdom of rotten fools, they are come true here in Elvado. They are come true in service to me."

Not only would it be foolish to deny Morg's claim, it would make of him a liar. Morg's unique library had glutted him with magic. And in Elvado, set free of all restraint, he had far surpassed his father, and Ain Freidin, and every Doranen mage he'd ever known.

*I have surpassed Asher and Rafel. In this place my father dreamed of, I have done more than ever I dreamed.*

Morg's fingers tightened. "Arlin—you think because I am who and what I am, it is not in me to understand your struggle. You're mistaken."

"My—struggle, Master?" It was an effort to keep his voice light, puzzled. "Master—"

"*Arlin.*" Morg laughed again, but still he glittered with that dangerous edge. "I was a *man*, once. I loved. I lost. I lusted. I wept. I yearned for greatness. And when it seemed that greatness would be denied me, I despaired. Talent is a *burden*, Lord Garrick. And the man who bears its burden is heavy-hearted indeed—for it makes him a man apart. He does not see the world as others see it. He cannot walk in it as other, lesser men must walk. Arlin, little mage, it takes *courage* to be great. To step off the path lesser men demand that you follow and forge your own way in the world. But if you are to be true to yourself then you *must* forge it. Greatness cannot be served else."

"Master . . ." He cleared his throat, discomfited. *How can he be so evil and so right?* "You sound like my father."

"You forget, Arlin," Morg said, his lips curving in dry amusement, "though I wear the face of a young man I am indeed old enough to be your father. And your grandfather, and your great-grandfather, and so on and so on. Tell me—" Letting his hand drop, he shifted a little on the balcony. "Are you accustomed yet to seeing this face? To seeing Morg look at you with Rafel's eyes?"

What was this now? A trick question? A genuine enquiry? Was the sorcerer merely amusing himself, or did he have a deeper meaning? Trying to read him was exhausting. And terrifying. And hard.

"Master—" Arlin moistened his lips, buying a moment's time. "I don't give the question much thought. To me, that face stopped being Rafel's when you—when you—"

"Stole it?" said Morg, delicate. "Or—usurped it, perhaps?"

"Won it."

"*Won it?*" Intrigued, Morg rolled the words over his tongue. "Won it. Yes. I *like* that, Arlin. You're right, I *won* it. There was a battle, I was triumphant, and Rafel is my prize."

"Exactly, Master," he said. "Asher's son died in the blighted lands. His face is yours, now. Rafel? Who is he?"

Winter was closing fast on Dorana, but there was still a little heat in the sun. Standing on this balcony, so high above the city, a chill breeze rustled their clothes and whipped their hair.

Morg's eyes chilled with it. "And tell me, Lord Garrick. Do you miss the son of that fisherman?"

*No need to lie now.* "As one would miss an ague, Master."

"Or grieve?"

"Master, I grieve his death as keenly as I grieve the fall of Barl's Wall," he said promptly. "Which is to say, not at all."

And that too was the twisted, bitter truth. For the destruction of the Wall in its roundabout way had led him here to Elvado—and here in Elvado he'd become the mage he was born to be. The glory of that was so great, sometimes he was tempted to disregard the cost, to abandon his secret resistance and let the glory take him.

Sometimes.

Smiling again, looking nothing like Rafel, Morg stepped to the balcony's balustrade and stared down at Elvado's streets far below.

Mindful always of the sorcerer's mood, Arlin stepped to his side and followed his avid gaze. What he saw stirred a tangle of feelings. Scant weeks ago those wide, mageworked thoroughfares had been empty. Desolate. Now they were cluttered with throngs of bewildered men, women and children culled from the lands Morg had once ruled and was determined to rule again.

The sorcerer had everything meticulously planned. First, his winged beasts. A setback there, for two of the seven originally created had failed to return. He'd created two more and sent them back to the wilderness beyond Dorana's borders. Next he'd created another ten winged *dravas*. His trusted emissaries, they were, his sharp eyes above the world. Within days of their departure a trickle of human tribute began arriving in Elvado from those nations lying closest to the border. Now the trickle was thickened to a flood. The city was coming alive again, slowly but surely, as more and more voices filled the ancient silence.

A cheerful thing, provided no attention was paid to what the voices were saying.

These flesh-and-blood tributes were like sheep now, all the same, herded and chivvied from place to place by their unforgiving *dravas* guards. But soon enough they'd be sorted into ranks. The most amenable would join the *dravas* in imposing law upon the rest. Of those remaining subordinate, the men and the children were destined for work and the women for breeding. And death awaited anyone who was foolish enough to resist.

"After all," Morg had said, so reasonable. "We must remember: I am a ruler. Therefore there must be those who are ruled."

"Of course, Master," he'd replied, because what else could he say?"

And Morg had smiled. "I'm glad you agree, Lord Garrick. For it's you I'll rely upon to see this task carried out. Not just here, in Elvado, but throughout all Dorana—and beyond."

Remembering that, Arlin shivered.

"Yes, it is a magnificent sight, isn't it?" said Morg, stirring beside him. "We spoke of grief before. I tell you truly, Arlin, it is a strange thing to realise that *I* was grieving. I gave up my body willingly. I embraced the power that came with its loss. But there can be no denying that there is *pleasure* in flesh." He lifted his face to the cool sun, eyelids drifting closed, almost dreamy. "I remember when I took that fat fool Durm. My first mouthful of his breakfast? I thought I might die from the pleasure. I had *forgotten*, you see. And so I was reminded, the sensual life is not to be wholly despised. It cannot last. I must outgrow it in the end. But until I do . . ."

He sounded so greedy. Arlin shivered again.

*Until you do, you are vulnerable. That's the only hope I have left.*

"Master, since you have touched upon the matter—might I ask if any more pieces of your sundered self approach?"

"Why?" said Morg, staring. "What is that to you?"

An edge had returned to his voice. He was so quick to take offence. Again, a truth might best disarm him. So far it had proven the most reliable weapon.

Arlin clasped his hands before him and lowered his head. "Master, forgive me. There is no greater honour than to be entrusted with their safety but—I confess, I would not be parted from the library. If you must know, I am drunk on the knowledge your books contain. And I have so much more to learn, that I might more perfectly serve you."

"Ah." Relaxing, Morg smiled. "Then to answer you, Arlin, even as we speak the last surviving parts of my scattered self creep towards Dorana. And I am strong enough now to guide them without need of you as their shepherd."

He made no attempt to hide his relief, knowing Morg would misread it.

*So I still have time to learn how to unlock the warded books and find the spell that will destroy him.*

"Also creeping," Morg added, "are the rulers of those subject nations who forgot, and will be reminded, that they are themselves ruled. And when the last paltry princeling has come crawling to my feet I will teach them all what they must learn in order to serve me."

He lifted his bowed head. "Of that, Master, I have no doubt."

355

"Therefore enjoy your solitude in the library, Lord Garrick, but be aware of this: soon I will ask you to curtail your pleasures there. For when my court is a true court again, when my kingdom is reconvened, remember there are other duties awaiting you."

He'd grown adept at disguising how he felt when Morg touched him. Smiling as the sorcerer laid a palm to his cheek, he looked and looked—but still could see nothing of Rafel in those dark, Olken eyes.

"Master."

Morg turned aside, abruptly cold again. "Go, little man. Your ambition wearies me."

Always, *always*, it was the same: a smile followed by a blow. He bowed. "Master," he murmured, and retreated.

If he should discover some ancient text in the library proving to him that Morg and his father shared a common seed, nothing would have left him feeling less surprised.

Morg had chosen the Hall of Knowledge as his new palace.

Walking its lofty halls and staircases and corridors to his refuge, the library, Arlin admired yet again the majesty and perfection of the sorcerer's solitary mageworking. Stained glass and alabaster and marble and gold captured, reflected and enhanced the mid-afternoon sunlight. The air was soft with music, faint and lilting. A woman's high, sweet lament.

He wondered if it was some magical capturing of Barl from the ancient past. He didn't dare ask.

Some ten days had passed since taking residence here, and like the city, the palace was no longer deserted. Servants bowed as he swept past them, cowed by his golden hair and his gifted authority from the sorcerer. Morg's *dravas* stood sentinel at every staircase, every door. By now so many of the beasts had been created, they teemed through Elvado like overgrown rats.

The second day of his solitary mageworking in the city, with only his *dravas* escort for company, he'd tried to insinuate his own magic into one of the creatures. A dangerous act, but too tempting to ignore. The backlash had left him stunned and bleeding in the street.

Terrified that Morg would know, would discover his insincere loyalty, he'd abandoned his mageworking and sought out the sorcerer.

"Master, forgive me," he'd said, abased on his knees. "The *dravas* would not heed my call for help. I thought only to bend it in service to me, that I might be a better servant."

Morg had accepted his apology, then made good on his promise of punishment.

It was a full day before he could stand again, and another before he could return to his mageworking. If he'd not grown up under Rodyn Garrick's roof, he had no doubt he'd have broken then and there.

*Thank you, Father.*

Bent now on finding a different way to thwart the sorcerer, upon entering the palace library he found the idiot Goose studiously polishing the round reading table that had graced Morg's mansion. The idiot looked up as the door closed, dropped his cloth and beeswax and lurched a few steps towards him.

"Arlin."

Yes, Rafel's ruined friend was speaking again. Well. Mumbling. A word here. A word there. Never more than that. No actual conversation. Still no better than a dog, but useful. His cruel and casual tormenting of the half-wit kept Morg passingly amused—and lulled.

But that was for show. In truth, with Pintte dead, he saw the idiot clothed and housed and fed and kept him away from the *dravas*, hoping that Rafel could see what he was doing. He needed Asher's son to understand that Arlin Garrick merely played a part. That he was *not* Morg's willing, compliant puppet. Because if Rafel gave up fighting, if he surrendered to his captivity . . .

*He's supposed to be helping me. He swore himself Morg's enemy. But all I see is Morg getting stronger by the day. What a fool I was to trust in an Olken's strength.*

"Arlin," the idiot Goose said again. His eyes were damp and anxious to please. The worst grief of Pintte's death had passed. Adrift in a world he lacked the wit to comprehend, the man clung to any kindness he could find. Forgave those casual, deliberate cruelties because he knew enough to know that otherwise, he'd be alone.

It was pathetic.

"Thank you, Goose, yes, I do know my name," he said, and slammed the library door behind him. "Be about your polishing, dolt. Your garbled blathering is more than I can bear. But leave that table. I want that table. Find yourself something else to polish."

Flinching, Goose took his cloth and beeswax to the library's other reading table and resumed his servant's duties.

*Idiot.* Ignoring him, Arlin selected one of the few unwarded books he'd not yet studied, slid into a beeswax-scented chair and opened it at random.

*Section Twenty-three: being a treatise regarding the efficacy of moon phases upon river tides: viz. the relative growth and retreat of lungbottom.*

Lungbottom?

He flipped the book closed and read the faded, handwritten inscription on its papery leather cover. *Herbal Decoctions.* Oh. This was a pothering manual.

He wasn't studying to be a pother.

Although — but no. It was unlikely in the extreme that Morg would have left him free to read a pothering manual that contained a recipe for a potion capable of harming him.

"But there's harm, and then there's harm," he murmured, fingers lightly tapping the book. After all, pothers weren't perfect. They'd been known to give a man possets that failed to sit well side by side in the stomach. "I wonder . . ."

"Arlin?" said the idiot Goose, startled, and fumbled the tin of beeswax.

He didn't bother to glance up. "Be quiet. I'm not talking to you."

Pothering. Yes. As Morg said, he was flesh now — and he'd remain flesh for some time yet. Sorcerer or not, flesh was vulnerable to more than magic and knives.

*If I can learn herb lore — if I can discover a combination of potions to render him weak —*

Such an attack would be a drawn-out affair. First he'd have to learn which herbs he needed, then find them without his plan being discovered and then, last of all, manage to poison Morg with them. That was the greatest challenge of all. He was still warded against turning any magic against the sorcerer. But was herb lore magic? Would a potion trigger the ward? And was he warded against intent, as well as deed?

He didn't know. To find out he'd have to act, and in acting he might betray himself. So best he read the book first, and any others like it in the library. The ones that wouldn't harm him. A tedious task, to be sure.

*I'm grasping at straws, of course. But if straws are all I have to grasp . . .*

He opened the book to its first page and began reading. *Being a remedy for flatulence brought about by mutton fat.* What? Surely the remedy was obvious—avoid the consumption of mutton.

*This, I'm afraid, will prove more than tedious.*

Time shuffled by. Beyond the library's window, the day seeped towards sunset. The idiot Goose moved on from polishing the other table to polishing bookshelves. And then he started a grating, tuneless humming under his breath.

Arlin slapped his palm to the table. "*Idiot!* How am I expected to concentrate when—"

Startled again, clumsy Goose spun round. His hand struck a row of still-warded spell books and with a punch of power he was thrown screaming to the floor.

"Goose!"

Leaping for him, his chair overturned, Arlin felt a flash of pain as power from the discharged ward skimmed his exposed skin. The wash of sorcerous magic knocked him off his feet so that he landed on hip and elbow beside the stricken Olken. The idiot was whimpering, staring at his blistered fingers in shock.

"Stop blathering," he said roughly. "It could be worse. You could be dead. You would be, if Morg didn't have such a care for me." And the sorcerer must have a great care, or he'd have set the protective wards to killing strength. "So I saved your life, dolt. Have you wits enough left to be grateful for it, I wonder?"

Idiot Goose, snivelling, held his fingers out like a child.

"Yes, you fool, you're hurt. I can see that, I'm not blind!" he snapped. "What do you expect me to do about it?"

A fat tear trickled down the idiot's cheek.

"I'm not a pother, Goose! I've read six pages of herbal remedies. If you were farting like a sheep I could help you. Perhaps next time you won't beeswax the shelves!"

Another tear. Then another. Mired in the half-wit's baffled woe, a terrible hint of comprehension. Seeing it, Arlin felt a wave of sickness flood through him.

"*Enough*, you useless, ignorant Olken! I'm not a nursemaid any more than I'm a pother! You're a trifle singed, that's all. It's not the end of the world. You're not *dying*. Now get back to your work and leave me to tend mine!"

The dolt's blisters were blood-tinged, angry scarlet welting down to his palm. Eyes anguished, he reached out his unhurt hand.

*Help me. Please help.*

Arlin shook Goose free of his sleeve and scrambled up. "Leave me be! Did I say for you to touch me? Did I say you could *look* at me? *Pintte, Pintte, Pintte*. Is that what you want?"

When all else failed, that cursed fool's name always cowed Rafel's friend.

The idiot Goose curled his arms over his head and wept.

*Curse it, curse it, curse all mages and magic.*

Heedless of the pothering book's age and fragile paper, he blundered his way through the pages looking for something, anything, to shut the Olken up.

*Being a charm to soothe a minor wounding.*

He ripped the spell from the book, returned to the Olken and snatched at his hurt hand. The idiot cried out as though it were murder.

"Fool!" Arlin hissed at him. "Do you want me to help you or not?"

Eyes wide and tearful, Goose stopped struggling.

"Good," he said, fiercely. "Now hold still, you beast-witted dolt. And be quiet. Interrupt me and I could well burn you to cinders."

Goose hunched into himself, his trembling lips pressed tight.

The charm was four phrases and a sigil, repeated three times. Resentfully Arlin chanted them and painted magic on the air. The power caught. The charm ignited. Goose's angry, welted blisters vanished.

*Well. Look at that. Perhaps I missed my calling, Father. Perhaps you should've made me into a pother.*

"Idiot," he said to the astonished Olken. "Anyone would think you'd not seen magic before."

Leaving the fool to his servile polishing, he tossed the ripped page of pothering charms onto the table then turned to brood at the rows of books Morg had warded. Their sigiled spines glowed, silently taunting.

It irked him beyond measure, knowing that a pompous fool like Durm had once managed to break a ward near as powerful as these. His father had never called King Borne's Master Magician anything but a toad. And to be found wanting against a *toad* was nigh impossible to stomach.

*There is a way to unravel these wardings. There must be. I am steeped in Morg's magics from dawn 'til dusk. I have spent weeks mageworking beside him. Together we remade Elvado. I know him. I stink of him. These bindings will not stand against me. They can't.*

The difficulty was that no two of Morg's warded books shared a single binding. So were he to break even one ward, a hundred more must be broken after, each one of them different. If the answer to Morg's destruction lay somewhere in this library, then every book the sorcerer wanted kept secret had to be laid bare.

*And I can't even open one.*

He winced, memory waking. The sharp pain of his father's chastising hand whenever he dared admit a weakness or doubt. He was Doranen, and a Garrick. There was no weakness. There was no doubt.

Rafel had brought incants with him, over the mountains. Ancient Doranen magic he'd had no business possessing, remnants of Barl that hadn't been destroyed. Morg had those parchments now. Might they hold a solution to his current dilemma? It was possible. But even if they did, Morg would never let him see them. Perhaps in time, as he continued to prove himself trustworthy, he'd be granted the privilege.

But how much time? And by then would it be too late? With every new sunrise the sorcerer drew closer to invulnerability.

Ruthlessly he crushed the first faint stirrings of desperation. He was Arlin Garrick, a Doranen mage. One of the greatest ever born. All that prattle of prophecy, of Olken born to save the world? Idiot lies. The Olken had failed, hadn't they? First Asher and then his arrogant son. Touted Lur's champions . . . and in their wake nothing but death and destruction. Waterspouts and whirlpools and a father dragged to his death.

*The burden weighs on me now. Arlin Garrick called to greatness.*

And he would answer. He had to.

*I cannot fail.*

In silence, in solitude, Morg drifted through his palace. And for the first time since his exile in the blighted lands ended, he was quietly alone. No other voice disturbing him, screaming in his mind.

First it had been Sarle Baden, that shrill, disbelieving Doranen. After so long as little more than a memory on the wind, he'd needed to hear a mage's voice again. He'd spent so long sundered, fragmented. A shattered mosaic of himself. He had dim memories of the magickless bodies he'd taken before Sarle. But one by one each frail, worthless vessel had failed him. And everywhere he was, every scattered piece of himself had felt every small death whenever a temporary host died. When a sundered part of himself died. Terrible. Annihilating. The grief had burned him worse than acid, over and over and over again, year after year after desperate, endless year.

Not until Sarle Baden had he found a true home.

But in the end even Sarle had disappointed. It seemed Doranen blood flowed like water these days. Well. Except for Arlin's. Little Lord Garrick had a touch of the old days' fire in him. A whisper of true power.

*And yet, compared to Rafel, Arlin's power is like mist.*

Asher's son, in the wilderness. Asher's son, defying the blight. Asher's son, with a power to eclipse even his own, when he'd been a man.

*Asher's son.*

Without Rafel to ride he'd have ridden to his death months ago.

He remembered Asher, of course. How could he forget that blunt, arrogant Olken and his little blond friend? The eunuch prince. The neuter king. It pleased him enormously to know that Asher had killed Gar to kill him. To know that Asher had suffered for that murder every day since. To know that while he had risen, triumphant, Asher's friend mouldered in his grave.

*Because I won. I always win.*

His other great pleasure was in tormenting Rafel with his father's pain. Asher, being a coward, had never told his son their whole story. So he did. In great detail. He let Rafel relive it as though the memory were his own. The son's screams, echoing his father's, soothed the troubled places in his soul.

But not tonight. Tonight he had Rafel locked away, rendered mute. Ordinarily he was content to let the Olken mage batter and rail and smash his mind against his own skull, but his mood had shifted.

*Tonight is for memories.*

His *dravas*, standing sentinel, would not move without his command. His warded human servants were locked away underground. Arlin was sleeping, his broken pet Olken on the floor by his bed.

And he drifted through his palace with the ghosts of his past.

There. That corridor. That was where he first saw Barl. She'd been waiting for an appointment with Lord Hahren, so frightened, so hopeful of being noticed, of being approved. Newly arrived in Elvado, not a soul to call her friend. He'd had mage business with Hahren himself that day, and with his wishes made clear he'd left the ignorant fool's chamber. One stride through the doorway and he saw her: small and slender, wrapped in blue linen, her golden hair like a crown. The scented air had shimmered round her, rippled by her raw power.

He'd felt his heart stop. Felt his blood seize. Forgot how to draw breath.

It was love. And it was *painful*. He never knew love could hurt.

She didn't see him. Not properly. Not then. But when she did? Oh, when she did . . .

*The bitch, the slut, the treacherous whore.*

With the lift of his finger he sounded her voice through the halls. Listened to her singing. Let Rafel's eyes weep.

*It was perfect, Barl. We were perfect. What led you astray? Who convinced you to betray me? I gave you my soul, woman. Why wasn't it enough?*

She didn't answer. She never did. Six hundred years of asking and still he didn't know. He stopped the tears. He stopped the music. He walked in silence. Alone.

# CHAPTER TWENTY-TWO

It was Charis who found the spirit path, four days after they fell in with the barracks captain and his men.

Deenie hadn't noticed a thing. Wrapped up in her fears for Rafel, distracted by the truth of Morg's survival, by the growing sense of blight curdling through her the closer they rode to Vharne's crossroads border with the lands of Manemli and Ranoush, she was as startled as Ewen when her friend hurtled back into their makeshift camp.

"Deenie! Come quick! You have to feel this!"

Scorning any suggestion of danger—"*Deenie would know if there are beasts hereabouts, Captain*"—she'd gone off to look for wild mushrooms and berries. Ewen had tried to stop her, but short of tying her to a tree Charis was unstoppable. So irritated it was almost funny, Ewen had let her go. "*And if you fall face-first into trouble, girl, don't bother calling to me for help, you needn't.*"

Now he was on his feet, sword half-pulled from its scabbard, his barracks men following their captain's lead. "Feel what?" he demanded. "Girl—what are you—"

Charis flapped a hand at him. "Hush. You're not Deenie."

"Charis, don't be tiresome," Deenie sighed. "What have you found?"

Charis was jiggling with impatience. "I don't know. Not exactly. You have to come and *feel* it, I tell you."

365

With another sigh she put aside the torn shirt she was mending, thanks to Ewen's needle and thread. "Charis doesn't imagine things, Captain."

There was an odd glint in his eye. "We'll all three of us go, we will." He turned to his new Dirk. "Robb. Stand sharp."

The look on the barracks man's face said he didn't approve, but his captain was his captain. He nodded.

Following Charis, they plunged into the surrounding thick woodland, heading away from the mostly overgrown path they followed north and the mean trickle of stream and kerchief-sized clearing they'd found to sleep in that night. The treetops blotted out the sinking sun and the ground was choked with brambles and rotted fallen branches and travelling vines and clumps of dubious mushrooms. It was cold in the shadows, winter's promise being kept.

Deenie felt Ewen glance at her as they clambered over an uprooted sapling. "No, Captain. I still don't feel any beasts nearby. Or wanderers."

"Know what I'm thinking to ask before I ask it, do you?" he said, glaring. "More sorcery, girl?"

*Girl*. She gritted her teeth. "Of course not. It's just you hardly ever ask me anything else." 'Cause she made him uneasy, though he'd never admit it. "So I thought it was a fair guess."

"More to think on than blathering, I've got." Then he looked at Charis, forging ahead. "What's she found, d'you think?"

Her foot slid on a fallen branch hidden by rotting leaf mulch. Ewen caught her elbow, keeping her from a stumble. His unexpected touch jolted her anew. There was safety and warmth in it. She pulled free.

"I don't know, Captain. Why don't you tell me?"

"Who says I know?"

"You do," she retorted. "Four days I've been riding behind your saddle, remember? You're not so much of a stranger now as you were when we first met."

And he didn't like that overmuch. "Sorcery," he muttered, and pushed on after Charis.

She let him go. It was easier to feel for beasts and wanderers and other trouble when he wasn't close by her, fogging her mind.

*I'm tired of him clouding me. I wish he'd leave me alone.*

Deeper into the woodland Charis led them, hardly glancing behind her to make sure they kept on her heels.

"How much further, girl?" Ewen called after her. "We're a ways from camp, we are. I don't like it."

Charis laughed. "Frighted of tree-boggles, Captain? Don't fratch, we're almost there."

"Fratch," said Ewen, unhappy. "Fratch you, girl, I will. Rampaging me through the woods."

But Charis didn't hear that, or else she didn't care. She was slowing of a sudden, one hand lifting.

Then, just as sudden, Deenie could feel it too. An odd tingling of power. A tickling reminder of that sleeping presence she sometimes felt in this land.

"Deenie?" said Charis, turning. "You can feel it now, can't you?"

Astonished, chagrined — *I should have felt it first* — she nodded. "I can."

"There!" Charis pointed. "I marked the spot. See?"

A scrap of Charis's green linen shirt fluttered on the branch of a low bush laden with dark blue berries.

"Stand right there," said Charis, her eyes shining. "Where I marked. Go on. It won't hurt you."

But instead of proving Charis right, Deenie looked at Ewen. "If I stand there, Captain, what will I find?"

"Oh, never mind asking him," said Charis, scornful. "Just because you saved his life, why is that any reason to trust us?"

Ewen's eyes narrowed, but still he didn't answer.

*Barl's tits, but he's fratchsome.*

She turned her back on him and went to stand beside the berry bush waving Charis's little flag — and felt her mage-sense shudder as her feet touched a blaze of power sunk deep in the earth's bones. Mind whirling, she dropped to her hands and knees. Dug her fingers through the leaf litter, into the damp soil, feeling that unexpected power thrum through her. Then she stared at Ewen.

"What is it? *Tell me!*"

Charis smirked. "Perhaps he doesn't know."

"He knows. He—" And then she had to stop talking, and simply breathe, because the waves of light and warmth washing through her were making it hard to remember what she wanted to say.

"Deenie!"

"I'm—I'm all right. I think," she murmured, as Charis knelt beside her. "Only—Charis, it's so strange. The blight's gone. At least, I can't feel it. And the mankiness inside me, because of the reef? I can't feel that either. I feel—I feel—*safe.*"

As safe as when she rode behind Ewen with her arms clasped tight about his narrow waist. Then she felt the way she had as a spratling, with Da. Like nothing awful in the world could touch her.

But she wasn't going to think about *that.*

"Well," said Charis, frowning, "I can't feel the blight so I'll have to take your word on it. But there is *something* here. D'you know— it almost feels *familiar.* A bit like I feel when I'm working in the garden."

Charis was right. "You think it's Olken magic? But how can that be?"

"No, not Olken magic. Its kissing cousin, maybe? But if that's true, then—"

But before they could explore the notion, Ewen kicked through the leaf litter to stand a stone's throw away, in line with the berry bush.

"It's a spirit path," he said, his voice tight, as though he was fighting to get the words out.

Deenie took another deep breath, pushing against the strange power's flooding heat. "And what does that mean?"

"I don't know," he said. "Told about it not long ago, I was. Vharne's greatest secret, they are."

"And what's their use?"

Ewen hesitated, then sighed. "Hide a man from beasts, they do. I've a map—" He slipped his hand inside his shirt, pulled out a grubby piece of parchment and unfolded it. "Only—"

"This path isn't on it?"

He lifted his gaze, frowning. "No."

"Is that a surprise?" said Charis, standing to consider their surroundings. "We are awfully off the beaten track. Perhaps this path's been forgotten."

Knowing he'd not hand the map over, Deenie got up, dusted her hands and knees free of dirt and dead leaves and approached him. "Can I see?"

Ewen angled the map towards her, tapping it with a fingertip. "It's here, we are. Roughly."

"And all these squiggly lines—" She traced one. "Those are Vharne's spirit paths? Then you're right. This one's not here. But that one—" Her turn to tap. "Is that what you're trying to get to? Is that why we've been following such a higgledy-piggledy line north?"

Nodding, he refolded the map and shoved it back inside his shirt. "Yes. Spirit paths defeat sorcerers and sorcery."

"Really?" Charis raised an eyebrow. "Then perhaps you'll stop expecting us to turn you into a frog any ticktock, Captain. Because here's me and Deenie standing on your spirit path and neither of us has burst into flames. Which I s'pose means we ain't sorcerers after all."

Deenie swallowed a smile. Ewen's fratched scowl reminded her of Da and Rafel—and for once the reminder didn't cause her pain.

"If you're right about these spirit paths' power," she said, "then I agree we should travel them when we can."

She felt the tight knot of tension inside him ease. "That's the plan, it is," he said. "But we won't travel this one. Not when I don't know where it'll take us." He looked at the fading sky. "Dusk's coming, it is. Robb'll be worrying. Back to camp, girls. Starting early in the morning, we are."

Sure of his way, he pushed ahead of them. Deenie lingered, reluctant to leave the cradling warmth of the spirit path. As soon as she stepped off it she'd be steeped in blight again. And it felt so *good* to be free of its roiling, curdling taint.

Charis was glaring after Ewen. "*Girls,*" she spat. "Tell me, Deenie, is it in you to turn him froggy? If it is, I wish you would. Just for a night, to teach him a lesson."

*Is it in me? I don't know. I don't want to find out.*

"He means well, Charis," she said, and took her friend's arm. "Besides, he only says it to fratch you. Smile when he does it. That's your best revenge."

"I s'pose," said Charis, sighing.

"*Girls!*" Ewen shouted, almost out of sight. "Want to walk north, do you?"

Charis spluttered. "Please, Deenie. *Please.* Just a little frog? For five minutes?"

"*No,*" she said, laughing. "Charis Orrick, clap tongue!"

It was one of Ewen's expressions, and the look on Charis's face for her using it made her laugh again. But the laughter stopped as she set foot off the unseen spirit path and the blight rushed back through her, more ravenous than ever.

Gritting her teeth, she kept on walking.

Two of Ewen's barracks men came back from their hunting with a scrawny wild goat, already skinned and butchered and ready to cook. They let Charis do that, wary as ever but prepared to be coddled a bit. Ewen, being sarcastic, asked if she was leaned on against her will.

"I don't mind cooking it," Charis retorted. "At least this way I know I'll eat more meat than charcoal tonight."

And he couldn't say anything to her about *that*, because last night his men had burned their rabbit dinner to cinders.

Eavesdropping, Deenie had to smother a laugh.

Later, having eaten her fill and so relieved she hadn't had to kill her dinner, she lost herself in the leaping flames of the fire she and Charis shared, trying to lull the blight in her to sleep.

Charis sat beside her on the small sheet of oil-cloth Ewen had given them for the damp. In her baggy, borrowed leather jerkin—it was one of the barracks men's spares—and her woollen hose and her boots, she'd never looked less like Charis Orrick in her life. She sighed. She sighed again. And then she cleared her throat.

"Deenie."

Stirred from reverie, Deenie bit her lip. "What?"

"I think I've been good," said Charis. "I think I've been patient. But you've not said a word and I think I deserve to know."

"About?"

"About *everything*!"

But though she *said* everything, what she meant was the diary.

"Charis, keep your voice down," she muttered, glancing at Ewen and his men. They weren't so far away that they'd not overhear two girls fratching. Not that Ewen's men would understand the words. They hadn't been spelled to understanding—his decision. But *he'd* understand, and his men would be roused suspicious of them all over again. "And any road, there's nothing to know."

"Nothing to *know*?" Charis said, her voice nearly a squeak. "When you put a spell on me I've never heard of and suddenly I can understand every word that—that Captain *Noddyhead* says? When you tell him bold-faced lies about the things you can do? Really, Deenie? *Nothing?*"

Charis sounded more than cross. She sounded hurt. And who could blame her? She was right. She'd been patient, and trusting. Four days of hard, fast riding across rough country, bouncing and banging piggyback on a horse, and she'd not complained. She'd not demanded. She'd endured all of it and never once badgered for the truth about the mysterious little leather-bound journal.

*Be honest, Deenie. You knew you couldn't keep your secrets forever.*

"It's safer he doesn't know everything I can do, Charis. I can't believe you'd fratch me on *that*."

"I don't," said Charis, after a moment. "That's sensible. But the book?"

"It's Barl's diary," she said, still brooding at the flames. "Da lied. He never destroyed it, like he said."

"Oh," said Charis, hushed. "*Barl's diary.*" She hugged her ribs. "Now there's a thing. And you can read it, even though it's in Old Doranen. Is that because of the reef?"

"Yes. I think it must be."

So many things different in her now, because of that sinkin' reef.

"So the understanding spell's in it," said Charis, trying so hard to be practical and matter-of-fact. "What else?"

*Barl's regrets. Warbeasts. The way to keep a tiny kingdom safe. Other spells, small and helpful. And the Words of UnMaking, the worst Doranen magic of all.*

"Nothing to help us find Rafel," she said at last. "And that's the only magic I care about, Charis."

Charis shivered. "You still can't feel him?"

"No," she whispered. "I've tried and tried but he's not *there.*"

Flames crackling in the silence. The barracks horses shifting hooves. Deep voices murmuring, as Ewen's barracks men passed the time dicing with bones. Ewen played too. He didn't hold himself apart. She liked that about him, that he wasn't lofty. That reminded her of Da, too.

Charis reached for a stray piece of kindling and dug it, vicious, into the dirt. "Does that mean he's dead, Deenie?" No tears. No wobbly voice. This adventure was tempering her, like steel in a forge. "Is Rafe dead?"

Turning her head, Deenie met her friend's furious stare. "*No.*"

"Is that true, or are you just saying it?"

"I'd feel if he was dead, Charis. I *would*. And I'd tell you."

"Deenie . . ." Again, Charis dug at the dirt with her piece of kindling. "If he's not dead, I'm wondering—d'you think he might be held prisoner in Dorana?"

Deenie felt her heart thud. "Morg's prisoner, you mean?"

"Mmm," said Charis. "He could be. That could explain why you can't feel him any more."

*Morg.*

"I don't *understand,*" Charis whispered, with a cautious glance across the camp to the dicing barracks men. "My papa *saw* your da kill Morg, and he wouldn't *lie*. Neither would your mother, Barl rest her. They *all* said Morg was dead. But with these beasts about, and Captain Noddyhead summoned by him, then—"

"Who said anything about lying, Charis?" she retorted, just as whispery. "Could be Da made a mistake."

"A *mistake?*" Charis nearly laughed. "And that's likely, is it? Asher of Restharven, the Innocent Mage, making a mistake about something like *that?*"

Deenie closed her fingers around her friend's wrist. Four days they'd gone not talking about this, and she'd happily go four hundred more.

"Charis, *clap tongue*."

"Let go," said Charis, her eyes wide. Almost frightened. "You're hurting me."

*Sink it*. She snatched her hand back. "I'm sorry. Charis, I'm *sorry*, I just—" She rubbed her stinging eyes. "I don't see how I'm s'posed to fight Morg. If *Da* couldn't beat him . . ."

"You'll find a way," said Charis. Now her voice was wobbly. Now she sounded close to tears. "Only do you think Rafe's his prisoner?"

*Oh, Charis, why d'you have to ask a question like that?*

"I don't know."

But Charis could be slumskumbledy too. She wasn't about to leave this alone.

"When you dreamed him," she persisted, "he was dressed all fine in velvets and jewels, you said. If he is Morg's prisoner, he'd not be treated like that, would he? When Morg kept your papa prisoner—"

*Yes, Charis. He did dreadful things.*

Not that she was meant to know about it. A city guard, trying to impress her once, had spun her a few tales he'd heard of those days. She gone straight to Darran and asked. The ole trout said it was nonsense —but he'd not been able to keep the truth from his eyes.

"Deenie?"

"No," she said, and had to clear her throat. "When I dreamed Rafe he didn't look like a prisoner."

*But when I dreamed him the second time I knew something was wrong. And when next I dreamed him, I couldn't see him at all.*

Charis still didn't know that, and she wasn't going to tell her. Not when hope was hanging by a thread.

"Well," said Charis. "That's something." She knocked the piece of kindling against her knee, dislodging the dirt, then tossed it into the fire. "But he still might be in Dorana, Deenie. Don't you think he might?"

"You know Rafe," she said, cautious. "If he found out Morg's not dead he'd go after him."

"And what about Arlin Garrick?"

*Oh, Charis. One calamity at a time.* "I don't know."

"But you're certain sure if we keep riding north with Captain Noddy-head and his barracks men, we'll ride across Rafe?"

*Certain sure? How can I say? Sometimes it feels like I'm not certain sure of my own name.* But Charis didn't need to hear that either.

This time she clasped Charis's wrist gently. Felt her friend's thudding, scudding pulse beneath her fingers. "We'll find him. I promise."

"How?" Charis whispered. "When you can't feel him any more?"

Good question. *Time for a hopeful lie.* "It's the blight, Charis. That's why I've lost him. When we reach a spirit path we can ride, chances are I'll be free of it again. And then I'll go looking for him."

Charis made a little scoffing sound, her lips pinched. "Best you ask Captain Noddyhead first. If he thinks you're doing sorcery on his precious spirit path he'll have a tantrum."

*Captain Noddyhead.*

Charis refused to call Ewen anything else. She'd taken against the red-haired, green-eyed king's man, and never lost a chance to be prickly and rude. He stomached it well enough, but . . .

*I expect that's the main reason he won't let me spell his barracks men to understanding. He doesn't want Charis to make him look bad.*

"You're not being fair," she chided, keeping her voice low. "He's trying. But he's not easy with magework—and you nagging him on it doesn't much help."

"Not easy," said Charis, scornful, and pulled her knees to her chest. "I notice he's easy enough with it when it saves his life or fills his belly. He's easy then, Deenie. Don't deny it."

She couldn't, because it was true. He made use of her mage-sense and her magic when he had to because it helped keep them safe. Didn't mean he could be comfortable with it, though, after growing up in a land that hadn't been lucky, like Lur, able to hide from Morg behind a wall of magic.

"You're so strict on him, Charis," she said, watching Ewen grin at something his barracks man Robb said. "Honestly, I think he's a bit like us. The Olken, I mean. The way we must've been before Barl. We'd never seen pushy magic until the Doranen came. Those Olken must've been frighted out of their wits. Ewen's no different. He just needs a little time."

Charis rolled her eyes. "Hear yourself. *Ewen*. You dreamed him and you ride behind him and now you're mooning over him. Deenie—"

"Mooning?" Offended, Deenie tossed a clod of dirt. "Charis Orrick, I do not *moon*."

"It's Goose Martin you like, I thought," said Charis, darkly. "Fickle, are you?"

And that was a *hurtful* thing to say. With Goose gone across the mountains and most likely dead in the blighted lands. "*Charis!*"

The firelight played fitfully over Charis's discomfited face. "I'm sorry. That came out wrong. I didn't mean—" She hunched her shoulders, cross with herself. "It's just there's a lot Captain Noddyhead's not telling us, Deenie."

Her cheeks were still hot over that crack about Goose. "Like what?" she said, showing a little scorn of her own.

"Like why is he so fratched about finding wanderers?" said Charis, leaning close. "*I'd* think we'd want to keep as far away from them as we can. They're horrible. They're *dangerous*. But how many times a day does he ask if you can sense one?"

"A few," she muttered.

"More than a few, and I'd like to know *why*. You should ask him, Deenie."

"I did."

"And?"

*He wouldn't tell me. But you already don't like him, so I'm not about to make things worse.*

"He's worried for Vharne, Charis. Like you say, those wanderers are dangerous. He's worried for the people they can hurt."

Charis knew her too well. Eyes narrow, she didn't even try to hide her doubt. "Hmm. I still think there's more to it than that. Perhaps if we stumble across a wanderer between here and the northern borders we'll find out why Captain Noddyhead's *really* so worried."

"Perhaps," Deenie sighed. "But I hope we don't. I'd rather I never saw one of those creatures again."

"And *I'd* rather your Ewen told us the truth," Charis replied. "I know I'm not Asher's daughter and my mother wasn't Jervale's Heir, but my papa was City Captain and mayor and a canny, canny man and Deenie, I take after him. So could be for once you'll listen to me."

"Charis, that's not fair," she protested. "I always listen to you."

"And then you go your own way!"

Ewen and his barracks men had finished dicing and were settling to sleep. Their campfire was banked, their saddle-bags plumped up for pillows. The night's first lookout had taken his post at the edge of the clearing, sword drawn. High overhead, the moon shone like a new-minted trin, small and silver amongst the stars.

Deenie pulled a log from their pile of firewood and fed it to their own campfire. "It's late, Charis. Best we put our heads down."

Grumbling, Charis took the hint. Moments after she closed her eyes, she was snoring—but Deenie couldn't rest. Not because she was cold or uncomfortable. Ewen had given them the sleep-sacks belonging to his two barracks men killed by the beasts in that village, so they were as protected as they could be.

No. She couldn't rest because her mind churned without respite, dully thudding with her fears. *Rafel. Da. Morg.* And Lur. What kind of new strife was the kingdom in now? Had there been more storms?

More tremors? Was anything left of Dorana City? In all her life she'd never felt so helpless or alone.

*I've come such a long way and nothing's any better. If anything, things are worse. Oh, where are you, Rafel? I'm here. Find me. Please.*

Sighing, shifting, she curled herself tight and tried to will herself to sleep. It didn't work. And then, sink her sideways, she needed to pee.

Passing the horse-line on her stealthy way back from the sheltering woodland, in the light of her tiny ball of glimfire she saw two of the barracks horses had tangled their head-collar buckles. Ears flattened, heads tossing, they were about to make a fuss.

"Here now, here now," she said, reaching for them. "Don't you do that. You'll have the whole camp in a kerfuffle."

Caught up with freeing the silly things, she nearly shrieked when she felt a touch to her shoulder from behind. Spinning round, she lost her balance and had to clutch at Ewen's arm.

"Suck on a blowfish, why don't you!" she gasped. "Weren't you never taught not to sneak up on people?"

His green-gold eyes gleamed in the pinprick of hovering glimlight. "I wasn't sneaking."

"No? Well, it *felt* like sneaking!"

Embarrassed, she turned back to the horses and busied her fingers with their head-collars. Barely up to his shoulder, she reached. He was Doranen tall and he liked to use that. She could feel her heart thudding, and not just from startlement. And she could feel him smiling, teasingly amused.

"What woke you?"

She tucked a leather strap-end into its buckle. "Not beasts or wanderers. Any road, I wasn't asleep."

"Only a day or two from the border, we are," he said. "If we ride hard and strike no trouble."

"And when we reach it?"

"Depends on what we find, that does."

There was nothing more she could fiddle with on the horses' head-collars. She had to face him or risk looking like a ninny.

"What do you think we'll find?" she said, turning.

Ewen shrugged, painted with shadows. "Don't know. Beasts, most like, I say."

"Beasts." She shivered, feeling bleak. "Will you want me to kill them?"

"They're beasts, girl," he said, as though the question was foolish.

The barracks horse beside her snorted, shaking its head. She stroked its brown cheek. "They used to be people."

"*Used* to be," he said. "They're monsters now, they are."

"I know. But still . . ."

"Deenie—" He took her arm and pulled her round. "*They're monsters.*"

"I know!" she said, smacking him loose. "And if we run foul of any more and they threaten us then *yes*—Captain, I'll kill them. But I don't have to like it, do I? Besides, I don't think you've thought this through."

He didn't much care for contradiction. "You say?"

"Yes, I say!" she retorted, and poked his chest with her finger. "They're more than monsters, Ewen. They're *Morg's* monsters. He made them and he's a sorcerer. So, what if he can feel when they die? What if he can find us out here because I'm romping through the rough killing his beasts with magework?"

Arms folded, he brooded down at her. The glimlight showed her his dark red hair tied back in a tail, and his gleaming, suspicious eyes. "And is that a true thing?" he asked at last. "Or is it a thing you say because you don't like to kill?"

So, he was twisty when he wanted to be. "Could be both."

He snorted. "Could be—but is it?"

She didn't want to talk about herself. She wanted to make him see that she was right. "You're a brave man, Ewen," she said, trying to coax. "But are you foolish, too? Do you risk your barracks men on a whim?"

"No." He sounded insulted. "That's a girlish question for a mage who's ridden leagues behind me."

"Oh, do stop using 'girlish' to pay back a slight," she snapped. "Or you'll prove Charis true with her Captain Noddyhead nonsense."

And though he was fratched, that made him laugh. "She doesn't like me, your friend."

"She doesn't trust you. Our home is so far behind us, Ewen."

"It is," he agreed. Then his lips curved, very faintly. "But you trust me, you do."

After four days of snatched conversation with this man she'd almost forgotten that it was Doranen magic, Barl's magic, that let them understand each other. But every so often her ear caught an odd inflection and it reminded her that his tongue was a long way from hers.

Even with his faint smile, his eyes were grave. "You trust me because you dreamed me?"

And wouldn't she like to make him forget *that*.

"'Cause once or twice I went to bed on a full stomach," she said, glowering. "If I think hard on it, I'll prob'ly recall it was a bogwight I dreamed of and I just mixed you up."

"*Bogwight*," he said, and his faint smile blossomed into a grin. Her heart thudded again. "Girl, you should do better than that, you should." But then he turned grave again. "You're troubled because the killing's done with magic, I say."

He hardly knew her. How could he know her so well?

"I told you before, Ewen. Rafe's the mage in my family. Him and Da. The power in them's special." She felt her lips tremble. "The killing? That's not meant to be in me. But something happened, and I'm changed."

She waited for him to ask how, but he didn't. Instead he hesitated, then smoothed a strand of unruly hair from her cheek. "Want me to say I'm sorry for that, do you? When I'm standing here breathing instead of being burned to ashes, like my men?"

*Burned to ashes*. Those funeral fires in the abandoned village had been horrible. Riding through the rough, in the fresh air, sometimes she thought she smelled them again. Smelled the thick, hot stink of dead, burning men.

"No."

"Want me to be sorry that you found a way to eat so you're not starved to a pile of bones, you and Charis?"

"No."

"Girl," he said, softly, "why can't you sleep?"

She blinked back the stinging tears. "Why can't you?"

"I was sleeping. You woke me, you did. Deenie . . ."

There was still so much she didn't dare tell him. But he'd sniff out a lie. "I'm frighted for my brother."

Nodding, he shifted his gaze across the campsite, where his barracks men were changing lookouts. "Deenie, what'll you do if he's not in Elvado?"

She pinched her lips. "Keep on looking."

"And if he is there, but he can't help you bring down the sorcerer?"

"Who says I'm after Morg?"

"You said it, in that village. Changed your mind, have you?"

If only she could. "No."

"So—if your brother can't help you?"

"You think I'm lying about his magework?"

Ewen's leathers creaked in the midnight silence as his knuckles came up to brush her cheek. "I think things go wrong, I do. If there's no brother waiting, take the sorcerer on your own, can you?"

The question made her flash ice-cold.

*Take Morg alone? Not even Da could do that. He needed King Gar's help.*

Except—no, he didn't. He'd had the spell to kill Morg. He'd had Barl's Words of UnMaking. He could have used them by himself and died, killing Morg, only King Gar wouldn't let him.

*And was that why Morg didn't die? 'Cause when the king jiggered the spell, it turns out he jiggered it wrong?*

She'd never asked herself that before. Then again, she'd never had to. But some horrible deep instinct told her she'd found the truth, by accident.

*And now I've got the diary. I've got the proper Words of UnMaking.*

"What is it?" said Ewen. "Deenie, what's wrong?"

She stood before him, shivering, feeling hot tears crowd her eyes. *Rafel.* If she found him and told him she had Barl's diary, with that spell in it, he'd take it from her and UnMake himself to destroy Morg. 'Cause he was Asher's son and he'd not been able to save Da when the Weather Magic went wrong.

*He blames himself for that. So he'll kill himself saying sorry.*

"Deenie!" said Ewen, and took her by the shoulders. "Say something! Girl, it's spooking me, you are!"

She couldn't speak. Her knees wanted to buckle, and drop her to the ground.

*Oh, Da. What do I do? Keep the diary a secret from him and let Morg go his merry way? Give it to him, and watch him die? Or not try to find him at all—and confront Morg alone and speak the Words of UnMaking myself?*

She didn't know. Overcome, she rested her head against Ewen's chest and sobbed.

Arms closing tight, he pulled her hard against him. He smelled of greased leather and horse and sweat. It was familiar. Reassuring. She liked it. She liked him.

*And ain't that a madness? When he's from Vharne, and I'm not?*

"Don't be crying, Deenie," he said, pleading. "We'll find your brother, we will."

"I know!"

"Then, girl, why are you crying?"

She shoved away and punched a fist to his leather-clad ribs. "I'm not. And *don't* call me girl!"

Smiling again, he touched a fingertip to her spilled tears. "Deenie . . ."

Another truth. A pain to drown her. "I miss my mother."

He pulled her close again. "Ah. Girl, that's a thing to weep for, it is. There's no shame in shedding tears for dead family."

She could feel his heartbeat, muffled beneath her cheek. Feel the blood pounding through her own veins, hot and swift. He was making her feel a lot more than *safe*.

*I was wrong. This ain't madness. I'm meant to be here, with him.*

She closed her eyes. "Who did you lose, Ewen?"

A long silence. Somewhere in the surrounding woodland an owl screeched. The night's chill was deepening and if he hadn't been holding her, prob'ly she'd feel cold. The horses in the horse-line shifted and stamped.

"Padrig," he said, his voice low, full of memory and hurt. "My brother."

"Oh." She wriggled her arms round him. "I'm sorry. What happened?"

"Sorcery, it was," he said, after another long silence. "Nothing to be done."

Sorcery? Then no wonder he was wary. No wonder he was anxious about beasts and wanderers and keeping his men safe.

*The wonder is he trusts me at all when he knows I'm a mage and my da and brother mages too. When I could kill him with a thought.*

"Ewen, you mustn't worry," she said, and tipped her head back to meet his eyes. "I'll keep us all safe 'til we find the spirit path you're looking for. Any beasts we ride across, I'll kill them. I won't blink. Wanderers, too, I promise. I already—"

Too late, she remembered he was the king's man.

"Ewen, I'm sorry," she said, almost stammering. "I didn't want to kill those poor women, I swear, but—"

His finger pressed against her lips. "Hush."

Heart pounding, she stared at him. Was he angry? Was she a murderer? His face was shadowed again. She couldn't tell.

"They truly were all women, those wanderers?" His voice was cold enough to freeze fresh milk. "Not telling me you killed them, was that the only lie you told?"

She jerked her head aside. "I never lied. I just didn't tell you how they perished." Bewildered, she stared at him. "Ewen, what's wrong? Why does it matter if they were—"

He turned from her, one hand pressed across his eyes. "Get some sleep, girl," he muttered. "Deenie. Rotten you'll be, tomorrow, if you don't sleep tonight."

She watched him retreat to his campfire, aching for him. Knowing that something was terribly wrong, but with no idea how to ease his grief.

"And what was *that* about?" said Charis, poking her nose out of her sleep-sack.

Deenie extinguished her little glimlight and slid back into her own sack. "Nothing. Go back to sleep."

"Sink it," said Charis. Even in the near-darkness it was easy to tell she was scowling. "I was right. You've gone giddycakes over him."

She felt herself blush. "No, I haven't."

"*Giddycakes*," Charis repeated, slumskumbledy. "Over a man with red hair and cat's eyes who calls us *girls* to make us stroppy — and that's all we know of him."

"That's not true. We know he's brave. We know his men love him, and he loves them. We know his king trusts him to speak for his people. And Charis—"

"You dreamed him," Charis groaned. "I know. I just wish . . ."

Deenie curled into a ball. "That I'd dream Rafel. Believe me, Charis. So do I."

*Rafel floats in darkness, chained like a dog. Morg is no fool. He remembers Conroyd Jarralt. He remembers how the trapped Doranen helped bring about his temporary demise. And so this captive is kept close-confined. Confident in his mastery, in the punishment he's meted, Morg chains Rafel deep and walks away, content.*

*Abandoned, discarded, Rafel nurtures the gossamer thread connecting his wounded soul to his sister.*

*And there she is.*

*"Deenie," he whispers. "Deenie. It's me."*

*She can't hear him. He's too far away. Even so, he can feel her. And what he feels is a fright to him. Deenie's been changed. And in those changes he can sense a new danger, to her . . . and to Morg.*

*If the sorcerer senses it he'll hunt her. His sister will die.*

*He's chained like a dog, but a chained dog can still bark. And if the murderer walks too close, a chained dog can bite.*

*Deep in the darkness, Rafel hears himself laugh. But softly, so his tormentor won't know. Then he bends his mind to the thought of revenge and a way to keep his sister hidden from Morg.*

*He's a mage. He's Asher's son. He can do this. He must.*

# CHAPTER TWENTY-THREE

A day and a half later, Ewen and his barracks men found the spirit path that would guide them safely through what remained of Vharne's northern rough. And that Charis girl, again, piggybacked with Robb, was the first to feel it, even before Deenie.

"Stop!" she said loudly, her voice joggled by the trotting. "Captain Noddyhead! *Stop!*"

Ewen gritted his teeth. *Captain Noddyhead.* He *ached* that she wasn't one of his barracks men, that he couldn't break a sword-blade across her arse. *Captain Noddyhead.* Beautiful or not, Charis Orrick was a scold.

*Call me Noddyhead, would she, if she knew I wear Vharne's crown?*

Most like. Most like she'd shrug and call him *King* Noddyhead because she was just that kind of woman, she was.

Robb rode a stone's throw from his left hand, so he only had to turn his head. "Told you to pee before we rode on from the last stop, I did, girl," he advised Deenie's scolding, disrespectful friend. "Can't be stopping to pee every half a league."

"Ewen," said Deenie over his shoulder, as Robb snickered appreciatively into his fuzzy, new-grown beard. "I don't think she needs to—"

"Peeing?" shouted Charis. "Who said anything about *peeing*? Your precious spirit path's hereabouts, in case you're still interested."

385

"Deenie?" he said, because he trusted her mage-sense more than her friend's. Charis wasn't the one who killed beasts with a word.

He felt her arms tense around his waist. Heard her breathe out, a lot like a sigh. "You'd best stop," she said. "So I can concentrate."

Raising a clenched fist, he looked left and right at his barracks men. "Hold!"

The barracks horses knew that command, and they dropped from jog to halt in a stride. Charis squeaked and bounced; she was no horseman. And then she slid backwards off Robb's horse, catching hold of its tail for balance as her feet hit the uneven ground.

Robb gave him a barracks look. *Why me?*

His answer was a swift, wry smile. Then he looked behind him at Deenie. "Getting down, are you?"

"Yes," she said, letting go of him. "Best you keep your men and horses here."

He watched, biting his lip, as the two girls walked off a few paces, whispering. Deenie wasn't right. Her cheeks were chalky, there were shadows beneath her eyes, and she was more quiet than ever. Was it because he'd been a fool and frightened her about those wanderers? Most like. And most like he could trust her with the truth about his father. But he wasn't ready to take the chance. Not yet. Not when his blood burned to tumble the girl, and her a mage. Suspect, that made his judgement.

*It's a cobble I'm in, Tav. Wish you were in it with me, I do.*

A cool breeze sprang up, sighing through the tall grass and fluttering his hair and the horses' manes. The country they travelled was wide open and pocked with rabbit holes. Slow riding it meant, to keep the horses' legs from breaking. Smudgy in the distance, a suggestion of more woodland. He didn't know this part of Vharne, but Hain remembered it. Used to scout up here as a youngster, he did. Catching the man's eye, he beckoned him closer with a jerk of his chin.

Hain nudged his horse over. "Captain?" he said, with a straight face. All the barracks men were used to calling him that now.

"Hain—" Ewen tugged out his spirit-path map and shared it between them. "That Charis says she feels the spirit path close. You know where we are, you do." He pointed. "That's the path we're aiming for. Is she right? Are we stopped in that bit of the map?"

He was a foxy-faced man, Hain. Sharp nose, sharp eyes, a thatch of thinning, gingery hair, and threads of grey in his scraggled beard. That foxy face went still and blank, his gaze shifting to his horse's blunt brown ears.

"Hain?" Ewen frowned at him. "Empty your basket, you should. Think I'll smile at you for holding something back?"

"No, Captain," Hain mumbled, then dragged a forearm across his mouth. "See, it's not a thing you talk on. If you come across it. Some things you don't talk on, see? Scouts, some scouts, we know. We don't talk on it. Sorcery, see? Say nothing, lose nothing. That's the way of it."

He stared at his barracks man, forgetting Deenie and Charis for the moment. "Hain, is this you saying you *knew* about spirit paths?"

Hain licked his dry lips, nervous. "Didn't know what they were called, did I? Not 'til you told us the day we clattered out of the Vale."

"But you've rode them?"

"A time or two, yes," said Hain. "Here and there. In the rough. I stumbled on this one we're looking for, but it was years ago, it was. Couldn't point to it now." His gaze flicked to distant Deenie and Charis, trying to sniff out the path. "Most like they'll find it." He shuddered. "Those sorcerers."

"Mages," he snapped. "There's a difference, there is. Hain, how many others have stumbled on Vharne's spirit paths?"

"Couldn't say, Captain. There's scattered folk in the rough know. But they don't say." Hain shrugged. "No point. Never do a thing, these paths, only run a tingle up your legs."

Ewen swallowed a curse. *What else don't I know?* "And in case it's sorcery, folk who've felt them clap tongue."

"That's the way of it," Hain agreed. "Safest to do, all round. And—"

A shout. It was Deenie. As Charis leapt for her, Ewen dropped his reins and slid out of his saddle.

"Deenie!" he shouted, running. "Deenie!"

Charis reached her first, where she was sprawled on her back on the grass. "Deenie? Sink it, *say* something!"

Deenie blinked at the pale blue sky, with its scattering of clouds. "I'm all right," she said, dreamily. "It's just such a relief."

As soon as he set foot on it, Ewen felt the spirit path's warm hum. "Relieved, you are?" he said, glaring down at her. *Making me run, showing me startled in front of my men.* "Why?"

Tutting, Charis took his arm and tugged him off the path for scolding. "You're blind, aren't you?" she accused. "I call you Noddyhead for teasing, but it seems I was right." She pulled him round and pointed. "*Look* at her, Captain. Wearing down to the nub. She *told* you, she feels sorcery. And the further north we ride, the worse it gets. It churns her up and makes her sick."

He wasn't blind. He'd seen it. But there was nothing he could do and he knew she wanted no talking about it.

"Feels better on the spirit path, she does?"

"Yes," said Charis. "And praise Barl for it. She'll get some respite now, at least until we reach the border."

"No, I won't," said Deenie, sitting up. Blades of dry grass and bits of faded flowers clung to her hair. "If I stay on the path I'll not feel any beasts or wanderers."

"If we stay on the path it won't matter!" Charis retorted. "Because they won't see us either and we can trit-trot past them like little spring lambs!"

"Except," said Deenie, her dark, pained eyes watching him, "that might not suit Captain Ewen."

And it wouldn't. Not when he still held out hope that one of Vharne's lost wanderers might be the king.

Charis's hands were on her hips. "Is that so? Well, sink me whether I care whether it suits him or not!"

Sighing, Deenie got to her feet before he could help her. "Ewen, I'm right, aren't I? You'll keep clear of beasts if you can, but you need the wanderers?"

"Could be they can tell us useful things," he said, nimbling round the truth. "The ones not so far gone."

A little colour had blushed back into her cheeks. "Then I'll do my best to find some for you."

Charis gasped. "*Deenie*—"

"And it's grateful I am, Deenie," he said swiftly. "But you're poorly, Charis says, for not riding a spirit path. Take turns, we could, riding on it and off it."

"No," said Charis. "That's not good enough. She needs a proper rest, she needs—"

Deenie raised a hand. "It'll do."

Turning, he started to whistle—then remembered he rode a wiry, rough-bred barracks horse, not his own Granite. But Hain saw him and rode to join them, leading his horse. Taking his reins back he vaulted into his saddle, as behind him Charis fussed at her friend.

"I wish you wouldn't do this, Deenie. You'll be no good to anyone if you fall in a heap."

"Then I'd better not fall, had I?" said Deenie. "Don't fratch at me, Charis. I'll be fine. Captain?"

She was a feisty one, and no mistake. His mother would've liked her. He thought even Tavin would like her, once the swordmaster forgot she was a mage. Leaning down, he took her outstretched hand and leaped her up behind his saddle. As she settled herself, arms holding him, and Robb rode up with the rest of the men, Hain cleared his throat.

"It's coming to me a bit, where we are, Captain," he said. "A village there was, beyond that stretch of woodland up ahead."

Ewen nodded. "Then ride on, we will, to see if it thrives. Charis, why are you standing there with your mouth open? It's flies you want for supper, is it? Get on Robb's horse, I say."

Charis glowered, but did as she was told.

Kicking his horse onto the spirit path, feeling that odd drag against its legs, he threw a glance behind him. "I'll stay on the path a while, Deenie. But after that . . ."

"I know."

He hated to hurt her, even if it was for Vharne. "It's my thanks you've got."

"You're welcome, Ewen," she said, tightening her arms in a warning. "But don't think I won't have a proper explanation from you, when we're done."

Like Charis, she sounded. He snorted. "I'll explain if I can, girl. If I can't, I won't."

She didn't answer, and so they rode in silence as the sun slid steadily across the sky.

With no hint of beasts or wanderers, they reached the nearest edge of the woodland and made camp for the night. Pinch-faced, Deenie brought down a score of autumn-plump pigeons for supper. After a swift meal they slept 'til sunrise without trouble, filled their bellies with cold pigeon and rode the spirit path into the woodland's shadows not long after. The track between the close trees was narrow but sound so they cantered and trotted and cantered, to make up for all the times they'd had no choice but to walk.

"You slept?" Ewen asked, keeping quiet so the thudding hooves would muffle him.

Deenie's head nudged his back as she nodded. "A little."

"It's sorry I am, but I can't keep on the spirit path as much today," he said, feeling cruel. "Not with the trees crowding so close. Easy for beasts and wanderers to hide, it'll be."

"That's all right. I understand."

She sounded weary. "Deenie? What's it like, feeling sorcery?"

"I can't explain it," she said curtly. "Just be glad you don't."

And he was, but it didn't feel right to say so.

They rode for hours through the green hush, through dappling pools of shadow and sunlight, chilled and warmed in turns. The air was cool and damp, rich with rotting mulch and tree sap and a thin, sweet note of flowering creeper. Pigeons rattled through the branches overhead. Whenever he guided his horse off the spirit path he felt Deenie's arms tighten, heard her breathing quicken. And in the short respites he could give her, then he felt what Vharne was costing her in the way she slumped against his back, almost gasping, and the shiver running through her flesh and bones. It nearly broke him.

*But I can't care more about her than this kingdom. That's not the king Tavin trained me to be.*

Around noon, as best he could judge by the fingers of sunlight pointing straight to the woodland floor, he once again, with regret, rode his horse off the spirit path. And when the gap between the path and the encroaching woodland widened, he pushed on into a canter. A dozen strides later, Deenie sucked in a sharp breath.

"Ewen! *Stop!*"

Up went his fist. "Hold, I say! Hold!"

Snorting and stamping and cursing as his barracks men, still riding the spirit path, hauled their horses to a halt.

"What is it, girl? Beasts or wanderers?"

She was gulping for air, her arms so tight around him that he could scarcely breathe either.

"I'm not sure," she said, her voice strangled. "I think it's beasts. Up ahead. Not very far. Oh, Ewen, so *many.*" She was nearly sobbing. "And people—I can feel people—and they're *terrified*—"

People? That meant the village Hain remembered must still be there. Scooping his reins into his left hand, he covered her icy fingers with his right. "Deenie, listen. Can you take them all, can you? If we ride hard to that village and there's a horde of beasts like you say, can you put them down? I don't want to risk my men."

A shudder ran through her. "Yes. But Ewen—"

"If Morg feels it, then he feels it, he does," he said harshly. "But it's k—" *Fool, think before you speak!* "It's a captain of Vharne, I am, girl. I can't give our people to beasts." He looked at Robb and Hain and the rest of his barracks men. "Swords out, but you'll not risk yourselves, you won't. Keep your distance. You, Robb—hold at the back, you will. Charis can't kill beasts but she's a mage. Could be we'll need her."

Charis's face, chalky white, peered over Robb's shoulder. "Deenie? Are you all right?"

"Save your womanish sympathies for after, girl," he snapped. "And hang on to Robb. A fall could kill you, it could."

"I'm all right, Charis," Deenie said, choking. "Do what Ewen says. And don't you *dare* fall off!"

Heart thudding, Ewen unsheathed his sword then rested his spurs lightly against his barracks horse's flanks.

"Deenie?"

"Go," she said. "*Go*. And stay on the spirit path as long as you can. I need to gather my strength."

In a thunder of hooves he led his men out of the woodland, following the path around blind corners, up and down steep slopes. They leapt a streamlet in one dry bound, crashed through undergrowth and hurdled fallen trees. Sick with fear and fury for what they'd soon face, he could scarcely feel the spirit path beneath him.

Up ahead the trees were thinning, the woodland gloom giving way to full light.

"Deenie?" he said, over the drumming of hoof beats. "Are you ready?"

She didn't speak, only slapped his belly. He took that as a *yes*.

The spirit path swept into a long, slow bend, and as they rounded it, clinging to their horses, Ewen saw the small village, its dwellings huddled beyond the last fringe of woodland.

It was a fair distance off the path—and being plundered by beasts.

Fresh rage scalded through him, blinding him, making him sweat. He reefed at his horse's mouth, hauling the animal to a plunging halt, and counted seven—ten—no, *eleven* beasts. The unclouded sunlight gleamed on their hides and horns and tusks as they chivvied a wailing, weeping crowd of Vharne's people—*his* people—into the open ground between their plain homes and the woodland. There were children among them. Babbies clutched to breasts. Hidden from beast-sight by the spirit path, he could hear their terrified crying, floating on the breeze. And he could see torn, blood-soaked bodies, scattered on the grass. But the beasts weren't killing anyone else. Squinting, he thought he made out grey hair on the murdered villagers.

So this was *theft*, this was. The beasts were stealing people from Vharne. But only the people strong enough to survive. Strong enough to be useful when they were put to work.

A moan of horror from Deenie. Her clasping arms tightened, threatening his ribs. Behind him, the muttered cursing of his barracks men and a stifled sob from that Charis girl. He heard his own stricken breathing and his heartbeat pounding in his ears.

Every story the king had told him—every tale Tavin shared in the bath house—they were brought to life before his eyes in that village.

*This is Morg's world, this is. If he lives, this is his world.*

"Girl," he said, belly churning, "kill so many beasts from here, can you?"

"Maybe," Deenie said, full of doubt. "But I'd rather be closer."

*Closer* meant leaving the protection of the spirit path.

"Deenie, no," Charis protested, tearful. "It's too dangerous. You can't—"

"Charis, I must."

For once he wanted to argue on Charis's side. But then Deenie's crushing hold vanished as she slid to the ground. He heard Charis gasp and raised his sword in warning. *Clap tongue.* But he didn't look at her, or any of his barracks men. His gaze was pinned to Deenie. Slight. Fragile. Hardly more than a girl. Dark hair untidily braided, dressed head to toe in the leathers he'd worked so hard to supple for her, she stood on the shrouding spirit path, staring at the terror and slaughter before them.

"Whatever happens, Ewen, don't you interfere," she said. She sounded like Tavin. "You might mean well but I promise, you'll only be a ruction."

And then before he could answer, before he could change his mind, she stepped off the path.

"*You there!*" she shouted, her voice clear and carrying. "*You there! You beasts!*"

The villagers stopped their wailing. Confused, the beasts swung their heads, snuffling, talons clicking. Tails lashed.

"*You beasts!*" Deenie shouted again, and swaggered towards them, a sorcerer, as though *she* owned the world.

"Deenie—Deenie—what are you *doing*?"

That was Charis's frantic whisper, but he didn't rake her for it. She was only putting his own dismay into words.

"*Beasts!*" called Deenie, still swaggering. "Come and face me. Come and *die*."

One beast saw her. Its cloven hoof stamped the ground. The other beasts followed where it pointed and they all saw her. Snarls and clashing tusks. Horrible, animal growls. Then they abandoned their captives and walked towards Deenie. Slow. Hesitant. Snuffling the air.

"No, you're not dreaming," Deenie taunted them. "I'm real. I wonder, is Morg listening? Is he watching? Well, sink me bloody sideways. He can watch. *I don't care*."

Halting, she snapped her right hand high above her head, fingers spread wide. Every line of her girlish body proclaimed her rage. Then she clenched her spread fingers into a shaking fist—and a beast with dull blue hide and pronged horns and talons like small scythes dropped dead without a sound.

The ten beasts surviving looked at their slain companion. Then they threw their inhuman heads back and howled. Hearing them, the villagers wailed in fresh terror.

Deenie snapped up her left hand. Even though he couldn't see her face, Ewen knew she was smiling. Knew that the mage in her was given free, furious rein.

"You beasts," she said again, her voice full of contempt. "This kingdom of Vharne has no need of *you*."

As she uttered her last word the beasts flung themselves at her in a howling, snarling rush.

Holding her ground, Deenie clenched both her fists. Another beast fell. Another. Another. But that still left seven, it did, and they were closing on her . . . they were closing . . .

"Captain, what are you doing, you—you *noddyhead?*" Charis demanded, still tearful. "Don't sit there, *help her!*"

"No," Ewen said, not taking his eyes from Deenie. He was slicked with sweat down his ribs, down his spine. His horse was skittering, fretting beneath him. It remembered too well what happened the last time there were beasts. "She told me to stay put, she did. And I told *you* to clap tongue!"

The girl's angry protest cut short as Robb's fretting horse whipped round on its haunches. His other barracks men were wrangling their animals too, but he couldn't worry about that. He only had room in him for worry about Deenie.

She still held her ground. Another two beasts collapsed, but the other five kept coming—and she was starting to shake.

*Help her, spirit. Help her.*

If he stepped off the path, if the beasts caught scent and sight of him, she'd be fighting to protect him and kill them at the same time.

*She'd die faster if I put my sword in her now, she would.*

So he stayed put. It nearly killed him.

The last five hideous beasts were almost on top of her. Heartsick, he watched Deenie shudder then sink to her knees. On an anguished cry her slender body convulsed, small fists battering the air.

And then her fisted fingers flew apart.

The beasts dropped dead in their tracks, rolling and sliding across the tussocky grass. Feebly Deenie tumbled herself out of the way. After that it was a race between him and Charis, to see who reached her first.

"Oh, look," Deenie murmured at last, cradled against him. "It's Captain Noddyhead."

Charis, who'd run slower, was chafing Deenie's hand. "You—you *noggin,*" she scolded, weeping. "You slumskumbledy wench! If your da was here—if he could see you—"

Deenie's face was death-white. Blood trickled from her half-closed eyes like tears. "Clap tongue, Charis," she said, trying to smile. "You're worse than ole Darran."

"I don't care," Charis retorted. "Deenie, all those *beasts*!" She spared a look at their gruesome, scattered corpses. "I can scarce believe it. *You*. Deenie the mouse. Deenie the beast-slayer, we'll have to call you now. All the people you saved! Captain Noddyhead will have to tell his king to give you a procession." She turned. "You can do that, can't you?"

Ewen smothered a smile. "I can ask him, I can. Fair to say he'd say yes, I think."

"There!" said Charis. And then she sobbed. "Deenie, I swear, if *ever* you fright me like that again . . ."

Deenie gave her friend's hand a little pat. "Sorry. I didn't mean to."

Ridden off the spirit path, Robb and the other barracks men kept a respectful distance but Ewen could feel their awestruck stares. Sorcery under a blue sky. And he thought they were unsettled by the king's son with a sorcerer in his arms.

*And I'm not? I am. How is this my life?*

"Robb," he said, quietly, with a glance behind him. "Ride on. See to the villagers. I'll be there, I will."

"Captain," Robb said, and led the barracks men to their duty. Their horses squealed and shied as they trotted past the dead beasts.

"Ewen . . ."

He looked down into Deenie's horribly pale face. "Lie still, girl. It's proper coggled, you are." Then he frowned, relief frosting with fear. "Eleven beasts, Deenie. D'you think the sorcerer felt that?"

With an effort she touched her fingers to his unshaven chin. "I don't know. Let's hope not."

He captured her fingers in his. "It's a debt, I owe you. Saved my people, you did."

"Well—" She coughed, wincing. "In that case, could be you'll forget me and Charis are trespassing."

He laughed at her, so thankful. She laughed with him. Then she wept. And then pulled out of his arms and heaved her breakfast onto the grass.

\*     \*     \*

They stayed to help the villagers burn their dead, and bury the beasts in the woodland. Charis left Deenie to sit quiet on the grass, warmed by a patch of sunshine, while she busied herself tending the hurt and frightened as best she could. Deenie wanted to help her, but Charis would have none of it.

For once, Ewen found himself agreeing with the girl.

By the time the burying was done and the burnings started, and Charis had used up all the village's salves and ointments on the wounded, the afternoon was almost slipped away. The villagers begged them to camp the night, because they were grateful—and in case more beasts came.

"One night," Ewen said, talking private with Robb, near where they'd helped bury the beasts. Smoke was curling from the new funeral pits dug beyond the village, and the clean woodland air was miserably tainted with death. "But we ride on come sunrise."

"Agreed," said Robb, his lean face and balding head coated with ash and sweat and dirt. "Think they'll spare us a bath, do you?"

His Dirk sounded wistful. He didn't chide. He was feeling desperate to be clean himself. "A good thought, it is, but I don't want these folk run out of water."

"I'll ask," Robb said, pleased. Then he sobered. "Highness— Captain—"

"I know," he said. "If more beasts come, they'll be taken. Robb, what can I do? They turned down my offer of a place in the Vale, they did. I can't stay to protect them and I can't command them to leave. Not when I'm a plain barracks man."

"No," said Robb sadly. "They'll take their chances." Then he looked to where Charis kept Deenie company. "That was a sight, that was. All those beasts the girl dropped dead."

"Settled with it, are you?"

Robb grimaced. "Highness, it's sorcery."

"And she saved a village with it, she did. She saved us."

"This time," Robb muttered. "I'll see about those baths, I will."

Ewen frowned after him a moment, then crossed the open ground to Deenie.

"Don't fratch her, you," Charis said, under her breath, leaving. "She's still feeling it. In fact if you want to be useful, Captain Noddyhead, make her shift onto the spirit path. She won't listen to me."

"You mustn't mind Charis, truly," Deenie said, with a wan smile. "She's practically my sister."

He sat beside her, pleased to ease his aching bones. "She's right, she is. You still look coggled."

"*Coggled*. What a funny word."

"No funnier than *fratched*, I say," he said, wanting to tease her into feeling better.

But she wasn't listening. Instead she'd turned to stare past the village, towards the north. "We're almost at the border now, aren't we?"

"Almost. Late the day after tomorrow, I say. How do you know?"

"Oh . . ." She shivered. "I can feel it. Blight and sorcery, growing so thick, so fast, they hurt my heart."

"You should listen to that Charis, you should, and sit on the spirit path," he said, half-rising, alarmed.

Her cold fingers closed around his wrist. "No. I need to feel this. For a little while, any road. I need to know what I'll be fighting." She let go of him and pointed towards the north-east. "That way, we need to ride. That way's Dorana . . . and Elvado."

He stared, of a sudden feeling churned, like Robb. "Certain of that, you are?"

"Yes," she said, her voice small and tight. "I'm a drum, Ewen, and the blight beats me so hard my bones are shaking."

*Girl . . . girl . . .* 'Deenie, *sit on the path*. It's coggled, you are."

She gave him a barracks look. "And it's coggled I'll be once the spirit paths run out. So I might as well get used to it, Captain. There's nothing to be done, you know. Morg's workings, they sicken me. They always have."

But Morg never ruled her land, she said, so how could that be? What hadn't she told him? So much trust he'd given her but really, what did he know?

*I know she makes my heart race, she does. I know she's the fiercest beast-slayer Vharne's ever seen. Her father's sick, her mother died and she loves her brother. But it's risking Vharne, I am, trusting her. I need to know more than that.*

Eleven beasts buried, killed with a word.

"Girl, who *are* you?"

"I don't—" She blinked at him. "Ewen, I told you."

He wasn't going to let her coggle him, with her sweet eyes and her lilting voice. "Your name, you told me. Where you come from. Tells me nothing, that does. How many Olken can kill beasts with a word?"

She shrank into herself like a blossom touched with frost. "Ewen—"

His turn to grab her wrist, but not to link fingers or to kiss her sweet, callused palm. *"How many?"*

"I don't know," she said, sitting still. "But I think—just me."

"Why not Charis? She's a mage, she is, you say."

"Ewen, we've talked on this," she said, bewildered. Or pretending. "Olken magic, it's—it's like the spirit path. It's warm and gentle and it can't be used to hurt."

"But girl, *you're* Olken! If that's true, how can you *kill?*"

"I can't tell you how, Ewen," she said softly. "Because I don't know."

He'd stake his life she wasn't lying. Only—"Then tell me this, you can. Why didn't Morg ruin Lur like he ruined Vharne and Iringa and the rest?"

Her eyes turned cold, like a sorcerer. "You'll have to ask him. I wasn't there at the time. Ewen, let go of me. You're hurting my wrist."

And now she was lying, even as she told him the truth. Her refusal to trust him jabbed, like a knife-point. Not even eleven dead beasts made it easier.

He let go. "And Rafel? Found him yet, have you?"

"No," she said, hugging herself. "But I will. And when I do, he'll help us."

Now she sounded sick and weary. A long way she and Charis had come to find this brother of hers, but if he wasn't to be found . . .

*Or if he's found, and found wanting, we'll not defeat the sorcerer.*

*Killing beasts is one thing. But killing Morg? She can't do it. Not alone. So it's kneeling at his feet, I'll be. And then I'll be giving him Vharne and its people. The ones he hasn't already stolen, that is.*

"Ewen . . ."

He looked down at her fingertips, touching his knee. Looked up to see her eyes warm again.

"If I frighted you killing those beasts," she said softly, "if that's why you're so fratched of a sudden, I'm sorry. If it makes you feel better, I frighted myself."

She'd frightened him spitless, but he'd never admit it. He scowled. "You'd best be right about your brother, I say."

"I am."

"Then, girl, you can swear to me, on your life, he's the mage to kill Morg."

Her eyes filled with tears. "I don't understand, Ewen. I thought you trusted me."

He wanted to, so hard it hurt him, but in truth he didn't know. Not with all her secrets crowding the air between them. He wished he'd not left Tavin behind in the Vale.

"It's a barracks man, I am, girl," he said heavily. "I trust my sword-master's training and my sword."

"Then Ewen, think of *me* as your sword," she whispered, and pressed her hands to his. "Think of me as the blade in your fist."

Eleven beasts buried, killed with a word.

*And if she's my sword that means Vharne's saved, does it?*

"Fine," he said, sharply nodding. "You're my sword. But Deenie —if you cut me? I'll break you in two, I will."

It broke her heart to leave the villagers behind. She couldn't understand why Ewen didn't bully them back to his Vale, to safety. Explaining how the spirit path could help them wasn't enough. They couldn't live on it, could they? And sooner or later it was likely more beasts would find them.

"And when they do," Ewen said curtly, "those villagers'll run to the path and hide 'til the beasts leave, won't they? This is Vharne, girl. We do things our way, not yours."

Oh, he was so *fratched*. Partly because he knew that path or no path the villagers wouldn't survive even one beast for long—but mostly because he knew she'd not told him the whole truth.

"Tell him to suck on a blowfish," said Charis, niggling that horrible conversation out of her as Ewen and his men saddled their horses. "Who's Captain Noddyhead to complain, I ask you, when there's eleven beasts buried in those woods thanks to you!"

And although that made her laugh, she knew it wasn't so simple.

In sour silence Ewen led his barracks men away from the village, and in resigned silence she rode piggyback behind him. At least she had the spirit path to blunt the growing pain roiled up by the blight. And at least, according to his funny little map, that respite would last all the way to Vharne's border.

Except it didn't.

Some two hours before sunset after a relentless day of riding, the path came to a shattering end, just as if they'd ridden over a cliff. The malevolent, creeping power of the blight struck her so hard that she let go of surly Ewen and tumbled like a rag doll from his horse to the bare, stony ground.

"Stop!" Charis shouted, smacking Robb on his shoulder. But then she didn't wait for him to listen, she just slithered backwards over his horse's rump, the way she always got off, and rushed over. "Deenie! What's happening? Why has it gone so *wrong*?"

Her travel-worn leathers had mostly saved her from cuts and bruises, but her left hand was scraped a bit. Shaking the sting out of it, she let Charis pull her back to her feet.

"It's Morg's blight," she said, and pressed a fist to her churning belly. "It's creeping, Charis. I think it's eaten away the spirit path."

"What are you saying, girl?" Ewen demanded, kicking his horse close. They'd all had a welcome bath in the village and he'd scraped off most of his beard. It was odd seeing his face again. Thinner now, with his eyes seeming greener than ever. "The path's eaten away? But I'm standing on it, aren't I?"

Loyal Charis glowered at him. "And if we explain, Captain Noddy-head, will you believe us? Or accuse us of playing some nefarious trick?"

"Don't, Charis," Deenie murmured, then looked at Ewen. "Yes, you're standing on the path now, but you won't be for much longer." She pointed ahead. "It ends there. Morg's sorcery's ruined it. I'm sorry. We can't hide from beasts and wanderers any more."

His hand was already on his sword-hilt. Now he half-pulled the blade from its scabbard. So did his barracks men, every one of them ready to fight.

"Morg's done this?"

"His sorcery has, yes. That's what it does, Ewen. It poisons things."

The look in his eyes told her he wanted to say, "*And how do you know?*" But he didn't. He slid his sword back into its scabbard and looked at Robb.

"We'll ride on. Stay wary."

"Deenie." Worried, Charis bit her lip. "You're looking awful again."

She was feeling awful again. "It's not so bad. Any road, what can't be cured must be endured. That's what ole Darran liked to say, and he was right."

"And if we ride across more beasts? If you're fighting the blight . . ."

*Will I be strong enough to kill them?* She didn't know. But how could she say that? "Don't fratch. I'll keep us safe."

Ewen kicked free of a stirrup and leaned down, hand outstretched. Clasping him wrist to wrist, her foot in his stirrup, she leapt and he pulled. It was a familiar dance now, but there was no smile from him this time. She settled behind the saddle, feeling sad. Feeling ill.

As they rode on, barracks men on either side, he surprised her with a question. "The spirit path's poisoned, you say. How long before the poison spreads back to that village?"

Another question she didn't want to answer, but at least this time she could tell the truth. "I don't know."

He grunted. "Poison them too, will it? Morg's blight? Or just the path?"

"I'm sorry, I don't know." She could feel him, tense and angry, within her loose embrace. "Ewen, why does your king not protect those villagers, instead of leaving them to fend for themselves all the way out here?"

"Clap tongue, girl," he snapped. "The king does what he can. Vharne's history's a sorry tangle, it is."

Clearly. And then she was struck by another horrible thought. "Ewen, do you even know how many villages like that one are lost in the rough?"

"No," he said, after a long, uncomfortable silence. "It's the rough, it is. And it's not enough scouts we've got to look under every rock and blade of grass."

*So when he said Morg ruined his country, he wasn't stretching the truth.*

His voice was full of pain and shame. But it wasn't his fault. He was a barracks captain, he couldn't order the king to find all the people he'd lost in Vharne's wilderness.

"I'm sorry," she said again. "I didn't mean to—" She sighed. "I'm sorry."

"I know," he said, weary.

And there was nothing else to say.

# CHAPTER TWENTY-FOUR

With dusk swiftly approaching they were picking their careful, glimlit way through another stretch of shadowed woodland when the blight roiling in Deenie surged a sharper pain through her.

She gasped. "Ewen. *Wanderers.*"

"You're sure, girl?" he said, over his shoulder. "It's wanderers, not beasts?"

"I'm sure," she said, as sickness churned her. "They feel different."

"How many?"

"I don't know. A few." She pressed the back of her hand against her mouth. "Please, Ewen, can't we ride on? Can't we leave them be?"

*Because I feel so sick and I'm not sure I can kill them.*

He made a curt, impatient sound. "No. Where are they?"

*No.* Just like that. She felt a sizzle of anger. So her feelings didn't matter? *She* didn't matter?

*And if I refuse to tell him, what then? He'll abandon me and Charis here, like his king abandoned those poor, helpless villagers?*

She thought that in this mood, most likely he would.

Robb, riding beside them, had one hand on his sword-hilt. Beneath the beard he'd not scraped off, his weathered face was taut with alarm at the notion of wanderers nearby. Slumped behind his saddle, her arms loosely clasped, Charis dozed with her cheek squashed against his broad back. He jabbed his elbow, not gently, and she jerked awake.

"What? What?" She stared around, fuzzled. "Deenie?"

"Wanderers, Charis," she said. "Shake off the cobwebs."

Charis squeaked. "Wanderers? Barl save us. Where?"

"Tell her, Deenie," said Ewen. "Then we'll both know, we will."

"It doesn't matter where they are," said Charis, clutching Robb's lean middle. "They're not here, that's what matters. Well? What are we waiting for? Are we galloping away or aren't we?"

Ewen ignored her. "*Deenie.*"

Had she been pleased to find him? Had her heart missed a beat at the sound of his voice? Had she felt safe in his sheltering arms?

*I'm the noddyhead, I am.*

But she had to tell him. She'd promised she would. Pounded with pain and sickness, stabbed through with misery, she pointed. "That way."

Spurring his horse to jittering, Ewen wrenched hard to the left. "Barracks men!" he shouted. "Barracks men, to me!" And then he spurred his horse again and leaned forward, slackening the reins.

The horse leapt wildly, narrowly missing a tall, thin tree. These woods were different, the ground thickly cushioned with fallen needles, not leaves. The air smelled different too, cleanly sharp instead of rich and peaty. With no undergrowth to tangle them they could ride fast, and Ewen did. His barracks men kept pace behind him, Charis's breathless protests almost lost in the muffled drubbing of hooves.

Deenie hid her face and held on, not caring if she cracked all of Ewen's ribs.

*Don't fall off, Charis, whatever you do. He won't stop to help you and you'll likely be trampled.*

Oh, this was madness. The day's light was almost faded, glooming shadows blotting out the way ahead, and the glimfire she'd conjured for them couldn't make a difference at this pace. They were cantering, *cantering*, weaving like a gaggle of drunken loomsters between the woodland's slender, haphazard trees. One misstep, one mistake, and there'd be a calamity.

"Ewen!" she bawled into his ear, mercilessly bounced and jostled as the horse's hindquarters bunched and thudded beneath her. "Sink me, you fool of a man, slow down! Someone's going to get *killed.*"

"Clap tongue, girl!" he shouted back at her. "Steer me to the wanderers!"

He'd lost his reason. He must have. She risked a glance to the right, where Robb was cantering apace with them, Charis still piggyback, clutching and desperate. *Oh, Charis.* What was Robb thinking? He was Ewen's Dirk, his trusted right hand. Why did he let Ewen ride roughshod, and so dangerous? And for what? For wanderers? He'd called them *brain-rotted*, and he wasn't far wrong. What could he possibly hope to learn from those poor lost souls?

She caught a glimpse of Charis's face, drained bloodless with fear, and for a moment sheer anger blotted out the blight.

"Ewen! *Stop!*"

And still he wouldn't listen. She was tempted, so tempted, to wrap her fingers round his tail of red hair and yank it 'til he howled or fell off the horse.

*I can mage him. I can use a spell from the diary, the one that keeps a man harmless without having to lay a finger on him. I think I can. I can try. Only—*

Only he'd never forgive her if she did that, and she needed him for reaching Rafel. The chances of her and Charis making it safely to Dorana, to Elvado, without him and his barracks men were slim.

"Deenie!" he shouted over the sounds of pounding hooves and jangling harness. "Where are they? How far?"

*Him and his sinkin' wanderers.*

"I can't tell! I can't think straight!" she shouted back. "Slow down and I'll maybe feel them!"

She heard him growl in frustration, and then he raised a clenched fist. "Hold! Hold!"

Plumed with hot breath, sweat steaming from their coats, the barracks horses slowed, canter to trot, trot to walk, walk to a huffing, puffing halt.

Before Deenie could even open her mouth, Ewen turned to glare at Charis. "Clap tongue, girl, I say. *One* word and I leave you here."

Shocked, Charis gaped at him, breathing hard. But she believed Ewen's threat. Only a noddyhead wouldn't.

"Deenie," he snapped. He was hardly panting. "The wanderers."

Close to tears of a sudden, she rested her forehead against his back. Undistracted, the rotten taste of them slapped her viciously, like a waterspout. Threatened to drown her like a whirlpool. To find them exactly she'd have to stop fighting the blight.

*And I don't want to. I don't.*

Pestilent. Filthy. Rancid as fly-blown meat. The wanderers' decay savaged her until she groaned.

"Up ahead. Keep your eyes peeled. Ewen—"

"Ride on," he told his barracks men. "Behind me. *Any* man rides past me, it's him I'll leave behind, I will. Deenie, it's more light, we need."

She conjured fresh glimfire. That small act of gentle magic stirred the blight into revolt. *Barl's tits. I can't bear this.* But Rafe was counting on her, and so were Da and Lur.

*No wonder Da never wanted to be the Innocent Mage, if this is how it feels.*

Ewen spurred their horse into a steady, prancing trot. The barracks men pranced behind him. Then he eased into a slow canter, and the following hoof beats started dancing. The glimfire bobbed above them, tethered by magic, spilling light on the ground. Then the woodland floor dipped, a shallow scoop in the earth. It dipped again, more deeply. The snorting horses shortened their strides, bouncing. Deenie felt a swamping surge.

"*Ewen.*"

He nodded, but that was it. Save for the hard, steady hammering of his heart he might've been made of stone, like King Gar on his coffin.

The sloping ground eased, the trees thinned, and there was a clearing ahead of them. And in the clearing, rag-dressed and stinking, a muttering, maundering huddle of brain-rotted wanderers.

Ewen leaned back, banging his shoulder blades into Deenie's face, hauling the horse onto its haunches. The poor beast came near to sitting down and that sent her flying. Again. She hit the needle-soft ground hard and rolled over fallen branches and a sharp, half-buried rock that bruised her side. Dizzily she sat up, spitting dirt and twigs, to see Ewen in the glimlight slide from his saddle. Sword drawn and lifted, he strode towards the wanderers with an ominous purpose.

The creatures' stink churned her. Her mage-sense rebelled. Belly heaving, she staggered to standing and took a step after him.

"*Hold!*" said Robb, knowing she'd understand him. "Don't you move, girl, or the captain'll put you down, he will."

Turning, she saw that he and the other barracks men were slid from their horses with their swords out, but not a one of them looked like they'd follow to guard Ewen's back. What were they doing? Were they Ewen's men, or not?

Robb saw her confusion. "We stand ground 'til he calls us, girl. Understand?"

"Listen to him, Deenie," said Charis, down off her horse and propped against the nearest tree. She looked seasick. "And don't you lift a finger. Let those horrible things tear Captain Noddyhead's face off. It would just serve him right."

Blight-struck, she still managed to shake her head. *Oh, Charis. Can't you see? There's something terribly wrong.* "Robb," she said, and held out a cautioning hand. "I need to know what's happening. A little closer. A few steps. Please?"

Wary, understanding her pleading tone if not her words, he didn't protest her shifting a few paces nearer to Ewen. Because he was loyal, she thought Robb was frighted for his captain. Watching him carefully, she thought she saw him nod. So she shuffled closer again, inching round so she could see Ewen's face. Then Robb's eyes narrowed, his fingers tightening on his sword-hilt, so she stopped.

Ewen had almost reached the wanderers. Lost in their madness they hadn't seen him, or didn't care. He'd taken the glimfire with him, and now she'd shifted close enough that it showed her three men and a woman and a sorry, blighted youth.

"I want to see you properly, I do," Ewen said to them, his blade gleaming liquid fire. "Let me see you!"

As though his voice was a spell-breaker, the wanderers cried aloud and broke out of their huddle. Bloody, rotting and pustuled, their clothing torn to rags, the stink of them was rank in the swiftly cooling dusk air.

"I need more light!" he shouted. "Deenie—"

Smothered with blight, hurting, she conjured him more glimfire. And then, baffled, watched him ignore the woman and youth and drag the nearest rotted man into the brighter light. Watched him search those ghastly features with an alarming intensity. She glanced back at Robb. His bearded face was stiff with self-control, but his blue eyes were full of pity and fear.

"Deenie?" said Charis, pushing away from the tree. "Deenie, what's he doing?"

She shook her head. "I don't know. Hush."

The first rotted man abandoned, now Ewen stared at his companions, just as intently. But who was he looking for? What was this *about?*

Disappointed, Ewen stepped back. "You're people of Vharne, you are," he said, his voice close to cracking. "My people. I can see that much left in you, I can. Speak to me. How are you rotted?"

Deenie bit her lip again. He was close to begging. The pain in his voice hurt her almost as much as the blight.

"Tell me your names!" he demanded. "And your villages. I'll find your families, I will. I'll give them your ashes for the spirit wall. Don't leave them not knowing. Don't be cruel, I say."

Days and days of riding, fleeing rain and cold and beasts, and *never* had she heard him like this. Desperate. Almost frantic.

Instead of answering him, the wanderers started swaying. And then they started crooning, their hoarse voices eerie in the glimlit gloom.

"*And in the morning of the last days there was a blood-red sun. The sundered parts all came together and oh there was a joining and the world rejoiced.*"

Ewen fell back a pace and his sword came up, as though he had to defend himself from the nonsensical words. Hearing a sound behind her, Deenie turned to see Robb and the barracks men crowding close. Their faces chilled her, full of rage and pain and fear.

"You're from Vharne!" Ewen shouted over the wanderers' madness. "It's your *king* I'm seeking! Help me find him, I say!"

Shocked, Deenie turned again to Robb. The barracks man met her eyes once, then looked away.

"Did he say *king*?" said Charis, her eyes wide. "He's looking for Vharne's *king*? But he said—"

"It's missing, Murdo is," said Robb gruffly. "Thought maybe to find him in the rough, the captain did, on the way to Dorana."

*Vharne's king.*

No wonder Ewen had been so determined to chase after wanderers. Deenie stared at him.

*Why didn't he tell me? He could've told me.*

The wanderers they'd found and caught were still crooning—but there was a rising note of danger in their voices, the same warning she'd heard in those other wanderers near the river. Could Ewen hear it? Or was he deafened by grief?

Robb heard it. "Captain!" he called. "Captain—it's done here, you are!"

If Ewen heard his barracks Dirk, he gave no sign of it.

"*Captain!*" Robb bellowed. "Do you need me?"

There was something odd in the way Robb asked the question. Deenie exchanged glances with Charis, then took another step closer to Ewen.

Robb flung up his hand. "*Hold*, girl. Leave the captain to himself, you will."

"Do as he says, Deenie," said Charis. "That's a bloody big sword."

"Captain," Robb called again, as the other barracks men shifted and shuffled, their uneasiness stirring the air like the blight. "Do you need me?"

"No," said Ewen, his voice tight. "Stand ground, Robb. This is mine."

And without warning, with five swift strokes of his glimfired blade, he killed every one of the blighted wanderers. And when they were all dead, mercifully silent, let his sword fall and dropped weeping to his knees.

Stricken, Deenie pressed her fingers to her lips.

"Girl," said Robb, his hand touching her shoulder. "The captain's brother. Padrig. He died like that, he did."

What? "No! But that's *awful*. Who—"

Guessing her meaning, Robb flinched. "The captain."

*Oh, Ewen.*

She ran to him, heedless of his sword, of any danger. But as she reached him, her blighted heart breaking, he used his blood-stained blade to help him stand, then turned. His face was worse than stony. It looked like ice carved into a man.

"We ride on, we do," he said. "I'll not camp in these woods."

And then he pushed past her, unseeing, as though never once had he held her weeping or danced his fingers over her hair.

It was a bad night after, cold and damp with only two small rabbits between them. Dismayed, churned with blight, Deenie stayed awake in case of more wanderers. Ewen stayed awake too, but never uttered a word. Once she tried to talk to him of Padrig. Of his missing king. If he'd been a sorcerer his furious glare would've dropped her cold dead. At dawn they saddled the horses and kept going, and just after noon they reached Vharne's crossroads border.

"So we decide now, we do," said Ewen, brooding at the weathered border stone jutting out of the dirt. "Ride Ranoush, ride Manemli, they'll both get us to Dorana, they will."

Charis leaned past Robb to gaze at the brown grass plain and the stunted saplings dotting it.

"Which way's most direct?"

Ewen pointed east. "Manemli. Head west and it's Ranoush then Brantone then an eastwards turn for Dorana."

"Well, I've no idea," said Charis, resigned. "Deenie? Does your mage-sense have a suggestion?"

Letting go of Ewen, Deenie slid down their horse's rump to the ground. As she walked towards the border stone she closed her eyes, let down her flimsy guard and tasted the blight.

Worse here. Much worse. As though Morg's pernicious magics were soaked right to the earth's heart. There was a flat, coppery tang in the back of her throat. Her blood had turned corrosive, burning her veins.

She opened her eyes. "Not Manemli."

"Why not?" said Ewen, belligerent. "It's weeks longer we'll take if we ride Ranoush then Brantone."

"Manemli's blighted the worst. I won't ride that way."

When he didn't reply, she swung round. He was staring at her, his warm self hidden behind that icy stone mask. He hadn't taken it off since killing those wanderers in the woodland. His barracks men were staring too, waiting for their captain to react.

"And once we're over Vharne's border," she said, ignoring them, keeping her voice cool and aloof, "I won't help you hunt down any more wanderers, either, or chase after beasts. I'll keep us well clear of them and kill meat for our supper if I need to, and that's all. Agree to that, Captain, and we'll ride with you, me and Charis. Refuse and we'll part company here and now."

Ewen needed her talent for sensing trouble, and they both knew it. His lips tightened a moment, then he nodded, grudging.

"Agreed. Only — what if beasts or wanderers come hunting us?"

"Don't worry," she said curtly. "I'm no keener to perish than you are. If it comes to a choice between dying or killing . . ."

*Then I'll kill, won't I? I'm not a noddyhead.*

"Captain, I'm sorry about your missing king," she added, risking an outburst of his temper. "I am. But he's not why I've come and I won't be distracted."

Ewen raked his gaze over the beckoning plain. "We've no map past Vharne. Lead us to Dorana, can you?"

She tilted her chin at him. "I said so, didn't I?"

And she would. Even without Rafe to guide her, she could. Morg would coax her there, an ugly spider sitting in a cobweb made of blight.

Ewen pulled his foot from the stirrup and held out his hand. "Then let's ride," he said. "Elvado's a long way from here, it is."

And a miserable journey it proved to be.

The weather closed in over them, three days of pelting rain. There was nowhere to shelter and any road, Ewen wouldn't stop. If there were spirit paths in Ranoush, she and Charis couldn't find them. So they picked their way across muddy plains, through stony ravines and treacherous rivers and forests dangerous with wolves and bear, and to keep them all safe she kept herself open to the blight.

Charis gave up asking after her. She grew tired of having her nose snapped off for her pains. Deenie felt bad for it, but couldn't spare the strength to make amends. The blight drummed her without mercy. She had nothing left for niceness. She'd not survive by turning back into a mouse.

Ranoush wasn't as empty as Vharne, but it was empty enough. Of people, at least. She sensed a great many beasts—but no wanderers —and bullied Ewen into crisscrossing the countryside to avoid them, even when it slowed them down or took them over risky terrain. A few times they spied hints of townships, or villages, once-travelled roads and roofs in the distance. But she always sensed beast presence most strongly there, and so they never rode any closer.

Twice, beasts came upon them because she was too sick and weary to feel them. Once they were caught because the blight was so thick it hid them. Each time she killed them, and then the others had to wait and wait afterwards 'til she was strong enough to ride.

Only then did Ewen come close to kindness. She'd given up hoping they'd get back what they'd had, whatever that was, however brief it had been. He was lost in a wilderness of his own personal blight, and it seemed she wasn't strong enough to rescue him. Even if he'd wanted rescuing—and he'd made it clear he didn't.

She carried Barl's diary snugged against her ribs. Took it out every night after the others fell asleep and re-read it by glimlight, no longer bothered by the fact that she could, taking comfort from the bits and pieces the Doranen mage wrote about the land she'd loved and fled. About the hardships she and her fellow mages endured as they battled their way to safe harbour in Lur. Reading those entries in the diary, she thought she could feel an odd kinship with Barl, a stirring in that part of herself the reef had changed that didn't belong to Morg.

She made sure to learn the diary's spells too, even the awful Words of UnMaking. It was hard to think on but she couldn't hide from the truth, that maybe those words would be her only way to stop Morg. Every time she closed her eyes and recited the spell, being careful not to twitch her fingers in its sigils, she felt a cold shiver. Remembered the reef, and his touch, and knew that because she was changed this was a Doranen spell she could surely wield.

And she couldn't even resent it, for without that lingering memory of Morg and his blight she doubted she could ever find Dorana.

Though each long day's riding took them closer to Elvado, no matter how hard she tried she still couldn't feel Rafe. The failure would destroy her if she let it, so she refused to think on that, too. She didn't talk of it with Charis. She kept the wound to herself.

Poor Charis. She was the loser here, and no mistake.

At last, with the weather turning colder every day, they reached the end of Ranoush and crossed the border into Brantone, heading east.

"Charis," said Deenie, pulling her aside as Ewen and his barracks men settled the horses and gutted the river fish she'd called and killed for their supper. "Charis? Can we talk?"

Charis pulled a face. "I don't know, Deenie. Can we?"

It was a slap at her for countless days of withdrawn silence. "Please? It's important."

Grudgingly, Charis clambered to her feet. "You can help me fill the waterskins."

They took as many 'skins as they could each carry down to the nameless river, which they'd have to cross tomorrow. Lean now, in a way she'd never been before, Charis hunkered down at its stony edge and dipped the first 'skin under the water's slow-flowing surface.

The sliding sun's light threw her face into sharp relief, revealing all the new hollows and planes. Two days after crossing into Ranoush she'd taken her knife and hacked all her hair off, boyish short. Its raggedy ends framed her cheeks and jaw, making her eyes look twice as big.

Crouching beside her, never mind waterskins for now, Deenie cleared her throat. "Charis, about Dorana. I think we'll be reaching it inside a week, if we're not bothered too much by any more beasts."

Charis plugged the stopper into her waterskin, laid it aside and reached for the next one. "And there's still no hint or sense of Rafe?"

"I'm sorry," she whispered. "I'm trying to find him, truly I am."

Carefully, Charis dipped the waterskin into the river. "I know. I'm not blaming you, Deenie. I'm just asking."

She sounded so weary . . . and *hurt*. Flooded with sudden, scalding contrition, Deenie stared at her. "Oh, Charis, I never should've let you come. It was stupid and selfish and *wicked* of me." Her voice broke, and she was weeping. "Charis, Charis, can you ever forgive me?"

"Forgive you?" Charis pulled her waterskin from the river and dropped it. "This was *my* choice. Since when are you the captain of me? If I'm fratched at you, Deenie, it's 'cause you've gone so quiet and far away!"

"I never meant to," she said, stricken. "I didn't want to be a burden."

"A *burden?*" Charis gave her a little shove. "You—you *noddy-head*!"

They clung to each other, both tearful. The river swished and chuckled its way through the shadowing silence, and further along the bank Ewen's barracks men laughed. Hardy men, they were, to find lightness when so much around them was dark. They'd started a fire. The smell of cooking fish was enticing.

Deenie let go, and wiped her sleeve across her face. "Any road. About Elvado. I've been thinking, and I don't reckon it's a good idea for us to stay with these barracks men once we reach the city. They're going there to pledge Vharne's loyalty to Morg but we're going to find Rafel, and when we've found him, *kill* Morg. Now Ewen might say he wants the sorcerer dead, and prob'ly he does, but I reckon if there's a chance harm could come to Vharne because of us? Well . . ."

"Hmm," said Charis, after a moment. "And there's me thinking you were still giddycakes for the man."

Scowling, she busied herself with a waterskin. "When we've hardly swapped two polite words since those wanderers? Don't be silly, Charis."

"All right," said Charis, taking up another 'skin to fill. "No need to fratch." And then she grinned. "Here's a notion. We can steal a horse each and gallop to Elvado on our lonesome, so maybe Captain Noddy-head and that sour lemon Robb can ride piggyback the rest of the way. Serve them right."

Though she was scoured with blight and racked with misgivings, she had to laugh. "*No.* I'll not risk any of them with such a daft scheme."

"Pity," said Charis, sniffing, and swapped the filled waterskin for another empty one. "What's *your* notion, then?"

She'd been giving it considerable thought. "Once we reach the city, we'll have to give Ewen the slip. But we'll not pass as any kind of barracks men. Well—I might, at a pinch, since I've got my leathers. But all you've got are your woollen hose, and Charis—"

"I know," said Charis, her nose wrinkling with distaste. "I've stitched 'em and stitched 'em, but they're falling apart. So what—"

They both turned at the sound of someone approaching.

"Girls," said Ewen, politely enough. "Best you leave filling those 'skins, you should. Rivers in these parts aren't safe at night, they're not. There's more than fish swim these waters."

"Really?" said Charis, glaring. "And you couldn't warn us *before* we started filling the waterskins?"

He shrugged. "Didn't see you leave, did I?"

"Noddyhead," Charis muttered under her breath, collecting her share of 'skins. Then she looked up. "Me and Deenie, we've been talking. You'll need to find us a place to stop before we enter Elvado, so we can change into our girlish clothes. We'll get looked at in leathers and hose. We need to be strumpets."

Startled, Deenie stared. Really? When did they decide that?

Ewen's eyebrows were lifted. "Strumpets?"

"Yes," said Charis, impatient. "Light-skirts. Don't ask me to believe you don't—"

"Tumble-wenches," said Ewen. "I know." His gaze shifted. "Deenie? You can't magic your way in?"

She hesitated, then shrugged. "I could summon warbeasts. I've got the spells in Barl's diary, but I'm thinking that might prove too fratchsome. Besides, Elvado is Morg's city. He'll feel my magework there, for sure."

"He hasn't felt it yet, I say."

"And I say we've been lucky. I'll not risk my magic right under his nose!"

Something softened in his cold green-gold eyes, and a shadow of pain, or regret, shifted over his heavily stubbled face. Instead of arguing, he nodded.

"It's right, you are. I'm sorry."

She felt herself thaw. "You've a lot on your mind."

"Come up from the river," he said, closer to smiling than she'd seen him in days. "Dinner's cooked, it is."

"You go on," she said. "We're right behind you."

As Ewen retreated, Charis sighed and shook her head. "What did I say? *Giddycakes*. Now come on, before they eat all the fish."

Five more days of riding followed, through green, silent Brantone, past deserted villages and empty townships. Just before noon on the sixth day after crossing the river they came to a narrow, baked mud-brick road. It was worn with old wheel-ruts and stretched in almost a straight line towards a distant hint of buildings.

It was the first proper road they'd come across, and the horses' hooves made a cheerful clatter. Deenie pressed her face to Ewen's back. Couldn't quite stifle a moan. She felt anything but cheerful. The blight was in her like a whirlpool, trying to drag her down.

Ewen's head turned a little. "Deenie?"

"I'm all right," she muttered. "Don't mind me."

His answer was to break into a song.

*"Eryn was a likely lass, with cherry lips and eyes sky blue. When Eryn danced the sun rose twice, and when she danced the sun danced too and when she danced she danced my heart, she broke my heart, what's a likely lad to do?"*

It was a lively, lilting ditty and despite her pain it made her smile. He had a rich, deep voice that soothed the roiling blight within her. As he started the ditty over, Robb and the other barracks men joined in and of a sudden, hearing the chorus of male voices was like being home again, in Westwailing, standing by the harbour singing the Festival songs to bring the fish.

Eyes pricked with tears, Deenie let their lovely voices close over her aching head. Let them deafen the blight and every yammering fear inside her and lull her to a gentle drowsing.

The stab of blight came so hard she nearly tumbled off the horse. She clutched at Ewen so desperately he was half-wrenched from his saddle.

"What?" he demanded as his barracks men raggedly let their singing die.

Heart pounding, she saw the road was taking them through a small township. But unlike the other villages and townships they'd seen so far in Brantone, this one wasn't dead.

"Beasts," she hissed. "Ewen—"

A shout from one of the barracks men. "Captain. There!"

And the beasts showed themselves, six of them, stepping onto the main road from a shadowed side street. They had captured people with them, bloodied and weeping and afraid.

One beast was different. Tusks and talons, yes, but it was tall and bony, with leathery skin that hung in flaps like great wings. It turned its naked head and saw them.

Ewen sucked in a sharp breath.

"You know it?" she whispered. "You've seen it before?"

"Or one like it," he said. "Deenie, not a word. They slaughter in a blink these beasts, they do." He raised a fisted hand to his men. "Hold here."

This wasn't like him. She could feel his shuddering fear. "Ewen, I can kill it."

"*No*," he said fiercely. "This beast's not brutish. It speaks for Morg, it does. You kill it, you risk Vharne. Girl, you'd best get down."

The sweet man who'd sung her to drowsing was gone. Deenie slid off their horse and watched Barracks Captain Ewen ride towards the staring beast. Its wings flapped once, idly, and then it walked to meet him, talons clicking on the dusty road.

"Man of Vharne," it said, its voice oddly dry. Its eyes made her feel ill, storm grey and wrongly human. "Come to kneel."

Ewen's head lifted. "You know me, then."

"Morg knows you."

The other beasts, horned and tusked and hooved, with thick hides and claws like farm scythes, closed tightly around the captive humans, who stared at Ewen and his barracks men with dull, hopeless eyes. Not one of them a wanderer. Just poor taken people. She didn't want to know for what.

*If I don't stop Morg this will happen to Lur. All the Olken, even the Doranen, his beasts will take them too.*

The winged beast licked its lips with a thin, pointed tongue. "Man of Vharne, you carry a sword. That is a mistake. There are no swords in Elvado."

Ewen's head lifted. "Then I'll take it off." His voice shook. "I'll throw it away, I will. So will my men. Only don't—"

Hissing, the beast raised one winged arm. In the sunlight its curved talons glittered. Ewen whipped his head round, the look on his face so awful Deenie lost her breath.

"Robb!" he shouted. "Drop swords!"

And then came the sound of a shrill, childish scream. Ewen whipped back to stare at the winged beast, and then a heartbeat later Charis screamed too, because the horned beast that had snatched a little boy from his father's sheltering grasp snarled and ripped the child's slight body in two.

Deenie felt herself collapse. The captives' screaming, the beasts' roaring, Charis's cries, and the clatter of swords dropped to the mud-brick road, they sounded odd and far away. She watched the winged beast knock Ewen off his feet with a single blow. Watched it bend over him and take up his sword. Break it with contemptuous ease and throw the pieces on top of him.

She wanted to kill it, she wanted to kill every last beast here, only Ewen had said "don't". But it was so hard to follow that order when the winged beast took him by the hair and dragged him back to his feet, then struck him twice more across the face so that he went down hard on his knees.

"Man of Vharne," it said. "Defiance is death." It laughed, a bubbling hiss. "You forget the dead men at your pretty castle?"

"No," said Ewen. His voice was thick with pain. "Never."

"Good," said the beast, and released him. "Come with us to Elvado. Morg is waiting. Leave horses. Leave swords and knives. Walk on your feet."

Ewen groped his way to standing and turned. Still slumped on the ground, Deenie swallowed a cry at the blood slicking his cheeks and forehead, torn by the creature's wicked talons.

He limped back to them.

"It's done." His eyes were wild, as they'd been wild that night in the woods, after the wanderers. His breathing was unsteady as he fought the pain of his wounds. "Strip saddles and bridles. Take care of themselves, the horses can. Leave your weapons behind with them."

Charis slid off Robb's horse. "*Deenie.*"

The father of the slaughtered boy was howling, held close by some of the other captives. Blood from his ruined son ran and pooled between the road's mud bricks. The discarded bits of the child's body were attracting flies.

With Charis's help Deenie got back to her feet.

"Ewen," she said, urgent, as he began to unsaddle their horse. "I can still kill them."

"No," he said tightly. "Don't ask again."

"He's right," Charis whispered. "We can't risk another child. Deenie, *please*, don't look like that. This isn't your fault and there's nothing you can do."

No. There wasn't. So much for her hope of them finding Rafel on their own and killing Morg. She wanted to lie down and weep her disappointment.

Ewen dropped the saddle and saddle-bags and her haversack onto the road. Bending, she rummaged in the saddle-bags until she found the small clay pot of salve he used on the nicks and cuts and scrapes travelling had earned him. She took that, and a half-full waterskin and one of her shirts from the haversack and while his barracks men saw to their own unsaddling she wiped his bloodied face with the damp-ened shirt then packed his wounds with the salve. Every gentle touch hurt him, but he didn't make a sound.

"There," she said, when she was done. Dropped the spoiled shirt and the emptied waterskin and tucked the salve-pot into her pocket. Barl's diary was safely snug against her ribs. "Perhaps there'll be a pother in Elvado who can pull those together with a stitch or two. Or maybe Morg will heal you. I believe he's capricious."

"Man of Vharne!" the beast called. "Time to walk."

Ewen looked at her, his eyes gone from wild to desperate sad. "You and Charis, drop your knives and walk in the middle of us. The beasts don't see you now. Keep it that way, I say."

Deenie nodded, feeling Charis's fingers wrap cold around hers. No sniping at *girls* this time. There was death. There was brutality. In her blood the blight raged.

*It's real. The journey's over. We're being taken to Morg.*

# CHAPTER TWENTY-FIVE

A fter seemingly endless hours, the dreadful day came to an end. The sun, reluctantly sinking, dragged twilight in its wake and the air cooled, slowly at first and then faster and faster until not even walking could keep the cold at bay. Darkness followed the brief twilight, stars like scattered chips of crystal. Sickle-thin and tilted, the moon hid Brantone in shadows.

Captive, Deenie trudged with Charis, Ewen and his barracks men well behind the beasts and their Brant prisoners. It was a small, defiant gesture but the winged beast seemed indifferent. So long as they attempted no escape it was satisfied. Ewen trudged in silence, a few paces in front. What was there to say? Obeying his lost king, he was bringing Vharne to Morg. Despite the pain in his torn face he kept his head high and his shoulders back, he had that much pride in him — but inside, Deenie knew he was weeping. She could feel it.

Inside, she was nothing but Morg's burning blight.

Every step was a battle to keep the darkness from swallowing her. The raw heat of Morg's power tried to beat her to her knees. Had the reef been overwhelming? The reef had been nothing to this, mere candlelight to the sun.

The night deepened and dragged on. They walked and they walked and the herding beasts showed no mercy, clashing tusks and flashing talons at the first hint of lagging. Terrified for their remaining children's lives, the Brant prisoners passed their little ones from arm to arm to arm, not daring to let them fall behind. No-one dared to fall behind. When they stumbled, exhaustion crushing them, somehow they managed to find their feet and keep going.

Courage or terror? Perhaps they were the same.

Without glimfire Deenie couldn't see Charis's face, but she could feel her friend staunchly walking beside her. Sometimes their hands bumped, their fingers linked. Poor Charis. Sad as she'd been, she should have stayed in that graveyard, mourning her father.

*And should I have stayed in Billington, watching Da slowly die? Being the dutiful daughter and nursing him like a pother?*

She didn't have an answer for that. All she knew for certain was Da needed her to be brave, and that she had to save him. She knew she grieved for her mother and she knew she feared awfully for Rafe. All those feelings were a tangled complication, not one to be separated from the others. She was here now, walking, because of Da. Because of Mama and Rafel. Because she'd not been able to save one and needed the second to save the third.

And then there was Morg.

So full of blight, so battered and aching, she wasn't sure she could feel *him*. She thought maybe all she was feeling was his terrible power, that he might be like a stone thrown in a pond—and all she could see of him was the ripples. But the stone was there, and waiting for her in the city of Elvado.

"Deenie," Charis whispered. "Are you all right?"

She realised then she'd been whimpering. Letting the pain and fear and doubt escape her throat.

"I'm fine," she whispered back. "Don't fratch on me, Charis. And don't fret. No matter what happens, we'll find our way home. You'll see."

Charis's breathing hitched. "You promise?"

"Yes, Charis." She linked their fingers again. "I promise."

"And so do I promise," Ewen whispered over his shoulder—though he had to know as well as she did that the words were empty bravado. "Now clap tongue, girls. We don't want trouble."

"Captain Noddyhead," Charis grumbled. But this time there was a surprising affection in her voice.

Ewen. Dark red hair and green-gold eyes. Tall and splendid and dreamed for a reason. Holding on to that, Deenie kept walking, desperately searching for Rafel . . .

. . . as the blight roared louder and louder in her blood, turning every step into a torment. Trying to beat her into pulp.

Marching through empty, open countryside, under a distant, indifferent night sky, they reached another deserted township just after dawn. There the winged beast let them rest for a while, hunkered by the road-side in a scarlet hum of exhaustion. Then its beast underlings watered them from a central well, a few prisoners at a time. After that, their raging thirsts slaked, they were bullied onto the road again.

"And what use is giving us water?" Charis muttered. "When we're about to drop dead for want of food?"

"We'll die parched before we die starved, we will," said Ewen. "Clap tongue, girl. Don't give them reason to look at us now."

As Charis opened her mouth to scold him, beasts or no beasts, Deenie clasped her wrist. "He's right," she said, so tired. "And any road, Dorana's not far away. They'll feed us there. They must do. We won't be any use to them dead."

They were walking three abreast now, with Robb and the other barracks men on their heels. As Charis doubted under her breath, Ewen took hold of her elbow.

"Dorana's close? It's sure of that, you are?"

Glancing up at him, she felt her heart thud harder. Churned beneath his courage there was so much grief and fear—and she could no more ease him free of its pain than he could save her from suffering with the blight.

"I'm sure," she said, blinking the sting from her eyes.

"And your brother?"

If she let him see her face, answering, he'd read the lie. She knew it, because he'd come to know her. On her other side, Charis tensed. She looked ahead, to the huddle of Brant prisoners.

*Oh, Da. This might get tricky.* "I think—"

"You need to stop being such a noddyhead," Charis snapped. "She'll know where to find him once we reach Elvado. Prodding her on him now doesn't do any good. Besides, she's too tired to feel much of anything but blight. Isn't that so, Deenie?"

*Bless you, Charis.* "It is bad," she admitted. Ashamed of herself, but having to, she let the blight's brutal pain tremble her voice. "That's how I know Dorana's close."

To her surprise, Ewen slid his fingers around hers. They felt cold. Or maybe it was her. "Could be a shame you ever helped me, Deenie. Could be when you dreamed me, it was a nightmare you dreamed."

"*No,*" she said, as the blight beat fiercely in her blood. "Don't ever say that. This isn't over, Ewen. We've not reached the end of our road. You have to stay strong. How can I do this if you don't stay strong?"

"*Giddycakes,*" said Charis, pretending to clear her throat.

So much for blessing Charis. She flicked her friend a dark look. *Clap tongue, you.* "I mean it, Ewen. Charis and I need you. So do Robb and your barracks men. You can't lose hope now. You don't have the right."

He let go of her hand. "A tongue like a dagger you've got, girl."

"She has," agreed Charis. "And if you don't talk nonsense she won't sharpen it on you. All right?"

And with that smartly settled they trudged on, their thoughts their own.

The sun was sinking towards their second night as Morg's captives when Deenie felt something new stir beneath the beating blight. Still walking beside her, limping a little now, without complaint, Charis caught her breath.

"Deenie! What *is* that? Am I imagining things, or is it Doranen?"

Shocked, she looked at her friend. "You can feel it too?"

"Feel what?" said Ewen, his hand reaching for the sword he'd been forced to leave behind. "Deenie—"

"I'm not sure," she said, her eyes half-closed, her pain-dulled mage-sense reaching. "Some kind of magical barrier, I think."

"No, it's more like a bell on a shop door," said Charis. "The kind your mother's bookshop had, Deenie. Somebody wants to know when there's a mage come a-calling."

"I think you're right, Charis," she murmured. "It's pure Doranen magic. Not blighted. And I think it's been in place for a very long time."

"Then—"

"Yes," she said, and opened her eyes wide. "We've reached Lost Dorana."

Even as she spoke, the winged beast flapped into the dusk-darkened air, hissing commands. The herding beasts roared and lashed their tails and clashed their tusks, cowering the Brant captives to a ragged stop. As they stopped too, keeping their careful distance from the others, Ewen spared a warning glance at his barracks men—*keep your heads down, no trouble*—then looked at her.

"How far is Elvado, Deenie? Can you tell?"

For the last hour or so she'd felt a colder, sharper shadow in the blight, as though at last the shape of that thrown stone was being revealed. The shadow was Morg, she had no doubt. And that could only mean one thing.

"It's not far now, Ewen," she murmured. "This will be over soon."

In more ways than one. Because the conviction had been growing in her, as they walked and walked and walked, that with Rafe's fate a mystery and all their plans sunk by this captivity, the only sure way of defeating the sorcerer was if she used Barl's terrible words of UnMaking herself. She didn't want to. Every time she thought on it, the notion brought her close to retching. But for the life of her, she couldn't think of any other way.

*Charis will be so fratched with me when she finds out.*

"Deenie?" said Charis, suddenly sharp with suspicion. "What's wrong?"

Only everything. "My head hurts. And I'm hungry."

Charis snorted. "That makes two of us. I wonder—"

"Clap tongue," said Ewen, urgently. "Girls—"

The winged beast was approaching, talons scraping the mud-brick road. Deenie exchanged a look with Charis, then grabbed her wrist and ducked them behind Robb and the other barracks men. The barracks men closed up tight, doing their best to keep them unnoticed.

"Pretend this is Lur in the old days, Charis," she muttered. "Pretend you had no idea there was magic in you. Push it deep. Close enough, this creature might be able to sniff us out. And I don't think that'll do us much good."

Then she took her own advice, sluggishly scrambling to bury her mage-sense before Morg's dreadful beast reached them.

With a leathery rustle of wings and a leering, sneering smile the creature halted before Ewen. "Man of Vharne," it said, hissing, "here is Dorana. Here is where you will kneel to Morg. I fly for my Master. The *dravas* stay. The *dravas* kill disobedience. You understand?"

"I understand," said Ewen. He sounded grim and resigned. His torn face was hurting him again, the pain humming in his voice. "And how is that, I say? How can a beast know the speech of my people?"

The winged beast laughed. "Morg speaks all tongues. I speak with Morg's tongue."

Ewen came dangerously close to spitting. "Sorcery?"

"You say," said the winged beast, and laughed again. "I go."

With a flapping of its wings, the beast leapt into the air. Dregs of daylight showed its oddly graceful retreat, a dark spiralling shape flying north, higher and higher and finally gone.

Warily, Deenie stepped out from behind Robb. "Now what?"

"Asking me, are you?" Ewen stared at the beasts—the *dravas*—left behind to guard the captives. The creatures showed no sign of goading everyone back to walking, which was odd. "A waste of breath, that is."

She flinched. He sounded so beaten. "Ewen—" She risked her hand on his arm. "This isn't your fault."

"No?" A sudden fierce light glittered in his eyes. "What do you know, girl? Of me? Of Vharne? How do you—"

"Hold," said Robb, his head tipped to one side. "Captain? Hear something, I can."

And then they all heard it: wooden wheels creaking and a rhythmic clopping of horse hooves, coming closer.

Ewen stepped to the very edge of the road, risking punishment from the guarding beasts. The nearest one gave him a hard stare, barbed tail lashing, but no more than that when it saw he was simply looking ahead.

"Carts," he said, self-contained again. "Three of them. It seems we're driving to Elvado, we are."

"Praise Barl," said Charis, close to moaning with relief. "Because my feet are falling off."

Stepping back again, mindful of the staring beast, Ewen frowned. "You praise this Barl a lot, you do."

Deenie shrugged, pretending indifference. *Sink it, Charis.* "It's a figure of speech, is all. Just like you say 'spirit', I think."

"That's right," said Charis, sniffing. "Any road, why do you care who I praise? Or curse, for that matter."

Ewen gave her a barracks look. "And why do you bite me, girl, every chance you get?"

"Don't ask silly questions and I'll not have reason to bite, will I?" Charis retorted, no hint of affection in her voice now. "I swear, you're as bad as Deenie with all your bossing."

For once Deenie didn't care that they squabbled, if it meant no more awkward questions about the woman Morg had loved. Only that staring beast was staring harder, hearing them, and the lashing of its barbed tail signalled a rising danger.

*If it attacks I can't kill it. Even if I could reveal myself I'm too tired. I hurt too much.*

"Ewen—Charis—*hush.*"

And if that was her being bossy, so be it.

They fell silent, glowering at each other. And then the squabble was forgotten, just like mention of Barl, because the carts were almost on them and the beasts were beating and roaring their captives into groups, heedless of families desperate to keep together.

"Deenie!" Turning, her wide eyes desperate, Charis reached out. "If we're separated, if they—"

It didn't bear thinking of. "I'll find you," she promised. "Charis, I won't see you abandoned. I *swear*."

And she wouldn't, not even if she had to die killing Morg. Somehow she'd make sure Ewen cared for Charis, whether Charis wanted his caring or not.

But it turned out they'd feared for nothing, because the beasts did no worse than herd them into the last cart, along with a handful of weeping Brant captives. It seemed the man of Vharne and his people were to be afforded a rough kind of respect. The silent human slaves driving the carts turned them around, one after the other, and headed back the way they'd come. Urged into a steady trot, the horses' hooves sounded loud in the chilly, gathering dusk. Loud too was the clicking and scraping of the beasts' hooves and taloned feet on the road as they escorted their captives at an easy jog.

There were baskets of bread and cheese, and a barrel of water, in the cart that carried them towards Elvado.

"Well," said Charis, cheering a little. "At least we won't starve."

Deenie tried hard to smile. "Yes. At least there's that."

Briskly taking charge, Charis began sharing out the food to the Brant captives and Ewen's barracks men. Though her own belly was growling empty, Deenie eyed the dry bread and stinking cheese with misgiving. The blight's constant churning made the notion of food seem unwise.

Ewen leaned close, his lips almost touching her cheek. "You're hiding something, you are. What haven't you told Charis? What haven't you told me?"

She shook her head, feeling so unwell. So sad. "Nothing that can make the slightest bit of difference."

He tensed and pulled away from her, full of hurt and doubt. "You say."

"Ewen, please don't fratch at me," she whispered. "Please . . . just hold my hand."

For one horrible moment she thought he'd refuse her. But then he sighed, and took her hand in his, and didn't fratch at her again.

And the carts full of captives drove through the darkness, to Elvado.

*If I live to be one thousand . . . if Morg lets me live that long . . . I know I shall never accustom myself to this.*

Naked and hairless, with elongated limbs and leathery wings and gleaming eyes — *oh, their eyes* — the sorcerer's most trusted, most intelligent *dravas* stood before Arlin in the Hall of Knowledge chamber Morg had granted him as his own.

"Lord Garrick," said the beast, most recently returned from Brantone. "It is done. The last summoned leader sits below in the Master's dungeons."

Ah. Morg would be pleased. *He* was pleased. Of late the sorcerer had been growing dangerously impatient. "And the slaves? They are brought to Elvado in the numbers I commanded?"

The *dravas* dipped its head. "Lord Garrick, they are brought. They are held in the slave pens. See them for yourself."

Yes, he'd have to, though the stench sickened him and the misery kept him awake afterwards. "And what of the Master's final, precious vessels?"

Hissing with pride, the *dravas* flapped its wings. "They are found, Lord Garrick. They await the Master."

*Found?* Yet again, his father's harsh training stood him in good stead. Not even Morg would see a hint of his crushing disappointment. "You have pleased him." He breathed in and out, softly, then shifted his gaze to the other *dravas*. "This is claimed by all of you?"

Ranged on either side of the grey-eyed *dravas*, the other quasi-human beasts solemnly nodded. Their wings shifted, thick skin rubbing thick skin, a sibilant, unnerving sound. Twenty there were now, their ranks increased again by Morg so that the ruling of Dorana and the subjugation of the lands surrounding it might proceed even more swiftly and smoothly. Arlin never showed the creatures his loathing. It was a weakness they might be clever enough to exploit. Instead he flicked bored fingers.

"If all is done as it should be done, then you are done here. Go."

With a dull clicking of talons upon marble tiles the winged *dravas* withdrew from the chamber. As two human slaves swung the doors closed behind them, he let himself breathe out hard. Beneath his sumptuous blue velvet and gold brocade robe—more finery courtesy of Morg's abandoned mansion—his skin slicked with cold sweat. They made him sick, those hideous things. They sucked his mouth dry and set his heart beating too hard. He'd seen them kill. When he closed his eyes he could feel them kill him, feel their cruel talons tearing vulnerable flesh and snapping bones. He could see his blood spreading in pools on the marble. A nod from Morg and they'd do it. If he misspoke himself but once, if he smiled at the wrong time or didn't smile when he should, if he trod too swiftly or too slowly, if he should ever betray so much as a *hint* of the truth—

*How long can I dance this dance? How long before I grow weary and dance myself to bloody death?*

"Stop it, Arlin," he said, and listened to the lilting echoes of his voice in the still air. "Stop it."

*They are found, Lord Garrick. They await the Master.*

The *dravas'* words were enough to make him weep, for their success meant that he had failed. For all his days and days of trying he'd not unbound one warded book of magic that could help him stop Morg before the sorcerer grew too powerful to ever be defeated. And now, very soon, Morg would consume the last rescued remnants of his sundered self and in doing so complete his unlikely resurrection.

*In large part thanks to me. Father, Father, would you be proud?*

Cool afternoon light spilled through the chamber's windows and onto the blood-red marble floor. Another day was slowly dying and with its death came the death of Lur and the last of his own people, the Doranen, those innocent descendants of the cowards and traitors who'd sided with Barl and fled the mage war.

Of course, they might be dead already. Lur's misery could only have deepened in the time since he and Rafel crossed the mountains. In a way he hoped they were. Cheating Morg of his final, longed-for revenge might be *his* only revenge.

*I wonder how long I'll have to savour it?*

Leaving his small, personal audience chamber, he made his way up and up and up through the lofty Hall of Knowledge, up to Morg's spacious, private domain, his eyrie. Outside its closed doors he stood and waited. Waited. Felt the tiniest stir of hope when it seemed Morg might not know he was there. Which in turn might mean—

*Is it possible? Could it be—*

Soundless, the wide, brass-bound doors swung open.

Heartbroken, and hiding it, Arlin entered the chamber and halted before the sorcerer's throne.

"Master," he said, his voice perfectly controlled, "it is done."

Eyes closed, his face smooth and still, Morg nodded. And it was Morg. Even in repose there was a difference between him and Rafel. After so long within his stolen body the sorcerer had remoulded it in his image. New lines around the eyes. A different way of holding his mouth. This Rafel looked older. Colder. More cruel.

Never in his life did he expect to grieve the loss.

"So the last of the puppet rulers is come," said the sorcerer, dressing his satisfaction in Rafel's deep voice. "Four kings to kneel before me." He frowned. "I would have preferred seven."

But of the seven lands surrounding Dorana, three had never recovered from Morg's earlier predations. Iringa, Manemli and Feen had collapsed in his wake, descending into chaos. Or so the *dravas* sent to them had said, and the *dravas* did not lie.

"Are these kings assembled, Lord Garrick? Do they await my pleasure?"

"Master, they do," he said. "They are held in readiness to pay you homage."

"And the last of my sundered pieces?"

He couldn't control the shudder. "Master, the *dravas* have delivered them. They are housed with the others, and await your loving reunion."

Morg smiled. "They distress you."

Distress? It was too mild a word. The rotting flesh, the putrefied minds, the ceaseless raving and chanting. He'd never seen a filthier thing.

"Master, their time grows short, I fear," he said. "Few humans are strong enough to hold even so small a part of you for any time."

"That is true," said Morg, and opened his eyes. "In all the wide world, there is only one Rafel."

"Yes, Master."

"If I had chosen you, Arlin, it is what you'd have become, quite quickly," Morg added, so gentle. So kind. "A raving, bleeding, rotting monstrosity. But I looked within you and I saw you deserved more than that. One day you will be the last Doranen. Tell me that pleases you."

"Master, I—" And then he shook his head. "Forgive me. I cannot."

The fading light through the windows picked out Morg's steady breathing in flashes of ruby and opal and emerald. "You think I should spare them?"

"I think they're your people. I think they should be given the chance to serve you, as I serve you. Those who would serve you should not be put to death."

Morg's eyes glittered. "Ah, but little mage, the question is: would they serve me? They are Barl-rotted, these cherished Doranen of yours."

"Not all. I have told you, Master. Some of us kept our wits."

"Yes, Arlin," Morg agreed. Ringed fingers glided thoughtfully through his long black hair. "You did tell me that."

Standing, waiting, as Morg stared at nothing, lost in thought, he looked into those dark Olken eyes, Rafel's eyes, his enemy's eyes, and searched there for any sign that Asher's son still lived.

*Blink, Rafel. Twitch your cheek. Weep one tear. Something. Anything. I know you hate me, but still. You can't leave me here alone with him. Please.*

Nothing.

And then—did he imagine it? No. *No*, there *was* a change. A shifting in the dark, open Olken eyes. Beneath the surface of Morg's face, a realignment of muscle. New lines smoothing here . . . lost lines reappearing there . . . and a subtle readjustment of the stubborn mouth. Yes. That was *Rafel*.

But before he could say a word, before he could take one step toward the Olken, Rafel opened his mouth and screamed. Screamed again as he clutched the arms of Morg's throne, screamed for a third time as his spine bowed him almost in two. Screamed and screamed again as his heels drummed the marble floor. Anguish and agony and a mind lost to reason. Madness in his face and his wide, staring eyes.

And then it stopped and there was stillness. A sweet, blessed silence. Muscle by muscle, Morg returned. And then he smiled.

"You wanted to know of Rafel, Lord Garrick? And now you know. And you may leave me. One hour, little Doranen. In one hour I will rejoin myself." The smile vanished and within a heartbeat he was angry again. "So much of me lost in the wilderness, Arlin. There are parts of me *murdered*. Did you know? Did I tell you? Parts of me murdered, parts of me starved and rotted and trapped to die with the vessel not strong enough to bear me. Parts of me set free from their flesh prison that could find no other vessel and so perished in the wind. Oh, Arlin, I am *diminished*. There are pleasures in flesh but oh, I am so *small*."

It had become a tediously familiar, self-pitying refrain. "You won't remain small, Master," he said, because it was expected. Because it was one of the reasons Morg kept him alive. To reassure him, flatter him, act as an echo of his dominion dreams and so keep the dark, looming fears at bay.

Morg closed his fingers on the arm of his throne, shuddering. And then he had himself under control. "You're right, Arlin. I was infinite once and shall be infinite once more. *Go*, I told you. You have only an hour. See that everything is prepared—or be prepared for my wrath."

Arlin escaped the chamber. Fell shaking against the wall outside as its doors banged shut. And when he could stand again, withdrew to do his master's bidding.

"Deenie!"

Mind reeling, stomach heaving, Deenie rolled over and spat bile on the dungeon's cold stone floor. If there'd been food in her belly she'd have heaved that up instead, but there'd been no food offered to them since they'd reached Elvado.

"Deenie," Charis said again, pleading. "What's wrong? Is it the blight? Do you need a pother?"

She almost laughed. Ewen needed a pother for his torn face. She'd used up the salve on him in the cart, to no good use. The wounds needed something stronger than salve. But it was clear there'd be no pother. Not for him. Not for any of them. Weakly, she patted Charis's anxious hand.

"No."

"Then what's the matter?"

*I can't tell her. How can I tell her? I don't want to break her heart.*

"Nothing," she said, turning away to rub her face's sickly sweat on her sleeve. Hiding. Lying. "A bad dream. An upset stomach."

But Charis knew her too well. "What kind of bad dream? Deenie —is it Rafel?"

Barl's tits, yes. It was Rafe. A rush of tears filled her eyes, so she had to keep her face hidden. For weeks and weeks *nothing* . . . and then *this*.

"*Deenie*—"

"Leave her be, girl," said Ewen. His voice was slow and stiff, the talon-wounds in his face paining him anew. "You raise a ruckus, you'll have beasts in here, you will."

"And did I ask you, Captain Noddyhead?" snapped Charis. "Think I care about beasts when my best friend's sick to weeping?"

"I care about beasts when it's my men they'll kill!" he snapped. "Girl, you need to think clever, you do."

Deenie bit her lip until she thought her voice could be trusted. "Don't fratch, you two. Ain't we got enough strife as it is?"

"Sorry," said Charis, and took hold of her hand, chasing away some of the shivering cold. *Rafel*. Oh, she was hard put not to weep. The *pain* in him. The *anguish*. No words, not even a cry for help. Just a loud and terrible screaming, worse than any blight she'd ever felt. And then he'd vanished, as though he'd never been. Had he died? Is that what she'd just felt? Her brother's sudden dying?

*I think it was. I think I've lost him. Come all this stupid long way for nowt.*

"Please, Deenie," said Charis, anxious. "Don't cry. We'll be all right."

And that was a stupid thing to say, but it wasn't in her to bite at Charis. Sitting up, she smeared her face dry then slumped against the nearby dungeon wall. "Don't mind me. I'm just weary."

Their fellow captives stopped staring and returned to private, murmured conversations. It was a small chamber she and Charis and Ewen and his barracks men had been pushed into by Morg's beasts, made smaller still by the number of people already crowded within its four windowless walls.

Like them, the other prisoners were road-stained and odorous. On being shoved through the door, Deenie had counted eleven unfamiliar faces. Three of them belonged to important men, if their dirty, dusty garments were any guide. Faded silks and moth-eaten velvets and tarnished jewels, they wore. Riches from a kinder time. It was odd to see such finery after so long with Ewen's plain, practical leathers. The other captives were attendants, or so she guessed.

With the worst of her grief and shock receding, she touched Ewen's knee. "So," she said softly. "Our fellow prisoners. The important ones. Do you know who they are?"

He looked at her, his face self-contained beneath the pain of his wounds. "They'd be kings, I say, from the lands Morg means to swallow again. Their names I can't tell you. Vharne keeps to itself."

"Only three?"

"We'd come to think Iringa was lost," he said, one shoulder shrugging. "Could be more than Iringa never rose again after Morg. Still. Three or thirty, girl. What does it matter, I say."

And now he sounded so defeated. Reminded, could be, of his own lost king. But there was nothing she could do about that, and talking of it fratched him. As for any of it mattering, she s'posed it didn't. But it was something better to think about than killing spells or the burning blight in her blood and the new, aching loss of her brother.

*Oh, Rafe.*

Shifting a little, she felt Barl's diary unstick from her ribs.

*So much for not thinking on it.*

And so she should think on it. She couldn't be a mouse. Not about this. The sorcerer had to be put down, no matter the cost. Besides, being truthful—with Rafe gone, somehow the notion of dying to kill Morg didn't seem so bad. Mama gone . . . Rafe gone . . . her gone too, soon. And Da would never know. Perhaps his blighted sleep was for the best.

*He never forgave himself for killing King Gar. Could be, in a twisted way, I can set that right.*

Feeling Charis's fingers tug her dirty sleeve, she turned. Leaned close. Charis's eyes were so frighted.

"Deenie, there has to be a way you can magic us out of here," she said, her voice little more than a sigh. "How will we find Rafe if we're cooped up in this dungeon?"

Her heart thudded, painfully hard. "Charis, I'm sorry," she breathed back. "I can't."

"But you *must*," Charis insisted. "Rafe's here. I can feel it. And I came with you, I risked everything, I sailed the whirlpools and the waterspouts, tramped all those leagues so I could find him. You *have* to get us out of here. You have to—"

*I'm sorry, Charis. I can't hear this.*

"Girl, what did you do?" said Ewen, as she eased Charis's limp body to the floor.

She scowled. "I swear, if you're not careful *I'll* start calling you Captain sinking Noddyhead."

He leaned over her, his green-gold eyes full of a startling suspicion. *"What did you do?"*

Nothing so great Morg would notice, she hoped. Smoothing a stray wisp of Charis's hair back from her used-to-be-so-pretty face, she risked a glance at him. "I nudged her. All right? She's worn to the bone and frighted spitless for Rafe, so I nudged her. She'll sleep a tiddy few moments and when she wakes, she'll feel better."

"And she'll wake, will she?"

The question thumped her like a clenched fist. "Of *course* she will. What do you take me for?"

He crowded her so close his torn forehead almost touched hers. "*A liar.*"

"Ewen . . ."

But she couldn't hold his fierce gaze. Robb and his barracks men were staring, sudden tension singing through them. Ready to leap if she used her magic on their captain. The strangers crowded in the chamber with them, they were staring too.

"Ewen, *please*," she murmured. "Please don't stir trouble. We're in enough strife, ain't we?"

Fingers closing around her upper arm, he tugged her against him. She felt his heat. Smelled the familiar horse and sweat of him. His heavy heartbeat thudded through her.

"It's the truth I'll have of you, girl," he said, his voice so low, so dangerous. "Or the strife here will be yours, I say. Is your brother in Elvado or isn't he?"

He was hurting her. Roped and corded with muscle, he had strong swordsman's fingers. He was important. She'd dreamed him.

*I have to trust.*

"He was. I'm sure he was. But Ewen, he's dead. It was Rafel dying I woke from." She was weeping again, and didn't care. "I came too late. *I couldn't save him.*" Saying it aloud broke her. And as he felt her break he released his cruelly tight fingers and instead sheltered her within his arms, as though he'd never once looked at her with cold mistrust.

"You could be wrong," he said, his voice unsteady. There was grief in him too, for the loss of a brother. "It's as weary as Charis, you are. That could've been a fright dream, Deenie, it could've been—"

"No, no, it wasn't." Struggling to kill the tears, she pulled away from him. "I'm a mage. *I know*. Only you mustn't tell Charis. It's for me to say." Her breath caught. "It'll nigh on kill her, I think. She loved him so much. And Rafel was a fool, he danced around her this whole last year. He flirted with every pretty girl he crossed paths with but he *loved* Charis. He just wouldn't say. And now it's too late."

His eyes bleak, he touched the drying tears on her cheeks. "You lied to her, Deenie."

"I *had* to," she said fiercely. "And I'll keep on lying 'til it's safe to tell the truth. I can't have her fall to pieces on me now. Look around you, Captain Noddyhead. This is Morg's domain and we're his prisoners. And with Rafe . . . gone—" she clenched her fists, willing herself to stay strong. "I'm the only mage here to stand against him. Unless a king of these other lands is mageborn?"

"Not a one of them," said Ewen, sighing. "The Doranen were mages, in this city of theirs. No other race of men I know has the power of magic." Then he frowned. "Except your people, that is. Doranen and Olken. No more."

Deenie covered her face.

*And between us just see the trouble we've caused. Da was right all along. Magic's nowt but a curse. And look at me now. Cursed to try and save the world.*

# CHAPTER TWENTY-SIX

A while later, Ewen stirred. "Deenie." He was frowning again. "It's one girl, you are. Can one girl stand against a sorcerer like Morg?"

She wasn't sure how to answer.

Should she tell him now about the Words of UnMaking and what she had planned, or should she wait? No. Best that she wait. He'd kick up such a fuss. Most like he'd do his best to stop her. And to stop him she'd need to use strong magic. Morg would feel it, and that would be that.

"I can try," she said, and fussed a bit over drowsy Charis so he'd not see her eyes. "I have to."

Huddled on the floor beside them, Charis moaned softly and stirred. Her eyelids fluttered open and she blinked in the dungeon's smoky lamplight.

"Deenie?" she said muzzily. "What happened? Did I *faint*?"

"You did," said Ewen. "You're the noddyhead, I say."

With a scornful hiss, Charis struggled to sit up. He helped her, and she let him. "Noddyhead yourself." Then she gasped a little, remembering. "Deenie—"

She couldn't look at Ewen. "Don't fratch, Charis. We'll find Rafe, I promise. I didn't drag you with me all the way from Lur to give up. But—"

The ever-present boiling of blight in her leapt high, stealing her breath, and a moment later the dungeon's door opened revealing two of Morg's winged beasts. The crowded chamber thickened with sudden fear as every man, king or commoner, shuffled and kicked and pushed himself as far from the creatures as he could get.

Every man but Ewen and Robb and Vharne's other barracks men. They sat stone still, frighted sick but refusing to show it. They were so brave. Bursting with love for them, Deenie reached for Charis's hand. Chances were she'd soon be dead, with no time to explain.

*Forgive me, Charis. You have to. It really is the only way.*

"Men of the lands," said the winged beast with brown eyes. "Your kneeling time is come to you. We go."

"Men of the lands," said the other beast. Its eyes were bright blue, vivid as lightning in its flat leathery face. "Disobedience is death."

Rustling and shuffling, they got to their feet. The four kings whose lands hadn't fallen to chaos in the years after Morg's sundering, they did their best to look royal, set an example for their men. Filthy and terrified, they weren't very convincing. Ewen looked more a king than all of them put together. Deenie couldn't take his hand, but she glanced at him from beneath her lashes.

*I'm sorry, Ewen. I wish things could've been different.*

The winged beasts stepped back from the dungeon's open doorway. Behind them, lining the long stone corridor beyond, more beasts. The brutish kind, made for strength and slaughter and little else. She'd seen so many beasts now but she still wasn't used to them. Every time she saw one she felt fresh sickness curdle through her. Men, they'd been. And women. Sometimes they'd been sprats. Even transformed she could feel their lingering human echoes. Could feel that somewhere inside them lived a spark of what they'd lost. Because Morg couldn't kill it completely . . .

*. . . or because it pleases him to know they suffer. I don't under-stand it, Da. He was a man once, an ordinary Doranen. He lived. He loved. How did the man Morgan become the monster Morg?*

The first captive king and his servants were shuffling from the chamber, eyes down, flinching as they crept past the winged beasts to be herded by the brutes along the corridor.

"Oh, Deenie," Charis whispered, watching the next king and his men creep out. "I'm frighted."

"You are not, Charis Orrick," she said, desperate. "And neither am I."

She and Charis and Ewen and his barracks men were last to leave the dungeon. The winged beasts looked at them, dispassionate, uncaring that two girls were among them. All they cared for, it seemed, was the kings kneeling for Morg. The kings and Ewen, who was his king's man.

The chamber they'd been penned inside was deep beneath a soaringly beautiful building at the heart of Elvado. Almost unconscious with exhaustion after the relentless journey from that Brant township to this city centre with its mosaic pool and its splashing fountain and all its colourful, beautiful buildings, still Deenie had been struck by the majesty of the tower—even as its wreathing darkness ribboned cruelly through her blood.

Now the winged beasts and their brutish underlings herded their panting captives along the maze of dungeon corridors and up ranks and ranks of stairs until they reached the spacious, glimlit ground floor. Then they were herded further, hustled, given no time to catch their breath or ease their aching legs, hungry and thirsty and dazed with pain and fear, into yet another windowless chamber. Brightly lit with more glimfire, its glassy walls and floor were deep black marble. At the far end of the chamber rose a long crimson marble dais. The sound of hesitant human feet on cold stone was loud as they entered. The clack clack of talons and hooves, strong with purpose, was louder. The silence beneath those sounds was crushing.

More beasts entered behind them, ten with wings, a score without, crowding their captives forward towards the empty crimson dais. The wingless beasts made up for that lack with their horns and their razor-tusks and the claws like curved daggers. Heart thudding hard again, Deenie closed her eyes. The urge to slaughter all of them made her feel sick.

*But I can't. I need to wait. I'll kill them when Morg gets here.*

Because that would alarm him. Seeing his precious beasts drop dead without warning would startle him enough that he'd be thrown off course. Jinking him, tossing him sideways, that would give her the chance she needed to UnMake him, *properly*, the way Da thought he'd done.

*And that's why I'm here, looks like. It's why I was born and why I dreamed Ewen. So he could get me to this place, at this time, for me to die killing Morg and make Jervale's Prophecy come true.*

And it would come true, in a roundabout way. The Innocent Mage was her father. Morg's death would be his doing as much as it ever was hers, for without him she wouldn't exist.

*So you see, Da? You and me and Mama and Rafe, we'll win after all.*

As one, as though she'd spoken aloud, Charis and Ewen looked at her, the same expression on their faces.

"Girl," said Ewen, leaning close. "What are you thinking?"

Even if there was time to tell them, she wouldn't. They'd try to stop her. And this wasn't about her, about her life and how she'd hardly lived it. It was about being Asher's daughter . . . and doing the right thing. Feeling strangely serene she smiled at Charis, then at Ewen. How terribly odd. She wasn't frighted. These were her final moments, most like, and all she could think on was how much she loved these two fine people.

"Ain't nowt for you to fratch on," she said softly, being her father's daughter. "We'll sink Morg between us, you'll see. Only I can't have you both fratching. I want you friends, I do. No matter what."

And because Charis knew her too well, she knew something wasn't right. She opened her mouth to say so—and then said nothing at all, because a section of black wall behind the crimson marble dais slid open and a man stepped into the glimlit chamber. Tall and blonde and slender, he was, resplendent in rich gold and blue brocade.

Charis nearly swallowed her tongue. Hand clutching, breath rasping, despite the vigilant beasts and the press of bodies around them she took a shocked step forward.

"Deenie! *Deenie!* That's—"

*Lord Arlin Garrick.*

The beasts were hooting and snarling and grunting and flapping their leathery wings, greeting Arlin as though they loved him. The captive kings and their servants huddled together, brothers in dismay. Ewen's barracks men were muttering. Ewen said nothing, just stood unmoving with his green-gold gaze fixed to the dais.

"That's a Doranen," he said, his voice grinding, almost lost in the louder noise of the beasts. "They're meant to be died out. Girl, is that *Morg?*"

Deenie looked back at Arlin. For a moment, just a moment, she thought—she hoped—it was. But no. Though he was brimful of mage power, all of it was his. Pure Doranen, no blight. Just arrogant, hateful Arlin Garrick.

*Arlin, you toadstool. Did you kill my brother? I swear, if you killed him I will get revenge. Arlin, I'll kill you. My word as a mage.*

Her fingers ached to fist, the killing blight blinding in her, but she didn't dare drop him. So instead she stepped mostly behind Ewen. The black-walled chamber was crowded with humans and beasts but it wasn't so large she could be easily lost in it and Arlin knew her, sink him. As thin and as dirty and dressed as she was, still he might recognise her. And if he did . . .

Charis was jiggling like a pea in a frypan. "Deenie—Deenie—"

"*Clap tongue*," she muttered, burning Charis with a look. The beasts were still dinning the air but they could fall silent any ticktock. "And for pity's sake stand still."

"Girl, is that Morg?" Ewen said again, insistent, as Charis crossly did as she was told. His fingers were round her wrist, crushing the bones.

"No," she said. "Ewen, you're hurting me. Let go. And don't you *dare* do a thing to get me noticed."

"You know him." He released her, sounding shocked. Disappointed. With all his grief riding him, it could quickly turn to anger.

She pressed her palm to his back. Every muscle was rigid. "I promise you, Ewen. That man is *not* my friend."

"But he's Doranen? And you *know* him? Deenie —"

*Oh, Ewen. Not now!* "I can't explain. There's no time. Ewen, be *quiet*."

Robb and the other barracks men were muttering and jostling. They loved their captain so much they were going to get him killed.

"And quiet your sinkin' men," she added. "Our lives hold by a thread, Ewen. Do you want to see it cut?"

After a moment that lasted a lifetime, Ewen raised a clenched fist. His barracks men fell silent. On the imposing marble dais, arrogant Arlin Garrick clapped his hands for beast silence. Instantly obeyed, he then wrote in crimson sigils on the air and uttered the words of a complicated spell. Deenie felt the air ripple with something vaguely familiar.

"There," Arlin said, once the sigils were faded. "And now you'll understand me. This is to the good. You are brought to this place to lay your lives at the Master's feet. Forget the past. It is over. Your firefly freedom is dead and gone. There is no purpose under the sun but to serve the Master of Dorana. If you please him he will reward you. If you don't, you will die. His name is Morg. You know him. He will know you. Think not to hide any truth in your heart, in your liver, in your bones or in your blood. The Master sees everything. The Master knows all."

As he paused to let the words sink in, to let the captive kings and their servants mutter and moan and shake with their fear, too terrified to wonder that they could understand Arlin's threats, Deenie glanced at Charis. She was silently weeping. To see Arlin like this, to hear those words from his lips, she had to know he'd done something to Rafel.

Her pain was like the sharpest knife.

Ewen said nothing, his breathing swift and shallow. Deenie took hold of his leather coat with a clutch of her fingers. She wished she could kiss him. She wished she could hug Charis. Morg would be here soon. It was time to prepare.

Squeezing her eyes shut she reached slowly for her mage-sense, for the odd, reluctant power she'd never fully understood. And there it was, simmering in Elvado's shadowing blight, full of twists and kinks from her undoing of the reef. How she had hated that, loathed the changes inside her, that had given her the power to wield strong Deranen magic. And now she was grateful. In a strange way Morg would be killing himself. Realising that, she nearly let her mage-sense escape.

*Careful, now. Careful. Mustn't startle Lord Garrick.*

Summoning her mage-sense like this was like calling fish with a magickless song. But it was working. And Barl's terrible Words of UnMaking were sitting ready in her tongue.

"*Kneel!*" Arlin shouted, startling her. "*You paltry kings of vermin lands, you king's servants, kneel to the Master. Kneel before Morg!*"

Grunting and squealing, punching, slapping, kicking, the chamber's beasts surged forward and forced them all to the marble floor. Cursing, with no choice but to kneel with Ewen and Charis and Vharne's barracks men and the rest, Deenie snatched at her mage-sense — but her concentration was shattered. She'd have to start again.

Then that panel in the chamber's black glass wall slid open a second time . . . and another man stepped out of the darkness, into the glimfire light.

*Rafel.*


As the chamber's beasts burst into fresh howls and shrieks, Ewen felt a shock run through Deenie and Charis as though both girls had been struck by the same bolt of lightning.

Charis gasped something and lurched forward, intent on pushing through the captives in front of her, but Deenie grabbed her arm. "*No,* Charis," she said fiercely, her voice almost lost in the noise. "He mustn't see us. *He mustn't!*" She turned. "Ewen, *help!*"

The beasts still clamoured for their Master, heedless of the captives cringing on the floor. Ewen looked to Robb and his barracks men, his grand men, Tavin-trained, and nodded. They knew without a word spoken to move in around him and the girls. As he shoved his way to

Charis, bruising his knees on the cold marble, getting an arm tight about her from behind and a hand to her mouth so she couldn't cry out, he threw another look at the dark-haired sorcerer on the crimson marble dais.

*Dark hair? But Morg was—is—Doranen. What's happening here, Tav? He's got the look of Deenie and Charis, I say.*

And why that was he couldn't begin to understand. But his guts were churning, warning trouble—and his guts were rarely wrong.

The sorcerer's weathered face was a mask of ecstasy, as though he pumped a tumble-wench with his seed pouring out. The other man, the Doranen—*the man Deenie knows, and how can she? What else don't I know?*—stood aside from the sorcerer, hands clasped behind his back. He stared at the dais beneath his feet, and what he felt for his Master, for the cowering captives, for the beasts or the dreadful noise they made, none of those feelings were on show.

But he'd think about that later, because Charis was struggling against him. She tried to bite his hand, tried to wriggle free and kick him. He could hold her harder, he could choke her until she dropped. If she didn't stop trying to bite him, he would. Deenie crushed close, her voice urgent.

"*Please*, Charis. We'll sort this out, I promise. But we can't if you get us killed. Charis, stop *fratching*!"

With a muffled sob the girl Charis gave up. Ewen could feel her warm tears splashing onto his hand.

"Good," he said, releasing her. "But girl, I'll put you down if you danger us with your thrashings. Understood?"

She nodded, barely listening. "Deenie—"

"I know," said Deenie, and she was weeping like her friend, a river of tears pouring down her pale, thin face. "I think this must be like Conroyd Jarralt. Remember?"

Conroyd Jarralt? Who was he? Churned with a terrible rising suspicion, under cover of the beasts' still-deafening clamour, Ewen turned on her. "You *know* him, Deenie? You know *Morg*?"

On a shuddering breath, the girl shook her head. "No. I don't."

He could have slapped her. He wanted to. "You're lying. *Don't lie.* Girl, that sorcerer. *Is he your brother?*"

And she flinched as though he had slapped her, as though he'd stuck a knife between her ribs. She might as well have shouted *yes.* "Ewen—"

"Silence!" said the dark-haired sorcerer on the dais, over the squeals and grunts and groans of his beasts. "Hold your tongues, slaves, lest I be forced to tear them out."

His raised fist rolled thunder round and round the chamber. The air beneath its high ceiling curdled into thick black clouds and forks of lightning flickered blue-white and crimson. A painful crackling followed, and hair stirred and stood on heads. The sorcerer laughed as his captives cried out their fear and dropped to their hands on the marble floor before him. His beasts cried out and bowed their heads in swift obeisance.

Dizzied by Deenie's betrayal, Ewen pulled his barracks men flat to the floor with a look. Pulled the girls down with him so the sorcerer would have no reason to see them. He wasn't about to die because of her.

*It's her brother, he is. The sorcerer's her brother. How can that be, Tav? And how did I let her mage me like this?*

"I am Morg," said the sorcerer. "You will call me Master. You and your offspring have forgotten me, but I have not forgotten you. There was a man, once, who thought he'd killed me. He was wrong. He is dying. When it suits my purpose, I'll see this mistaken man dead." His ravenous gaze slashed around the chamber. "Any creature who denies me will join him. Any creature who denies me will lead the way for him. You are called here to remember me. Who are the summoned kings among you? Stand now. I would know your faces."

Utter stillness. And then one bold, foolish man found his feet. He was fat, olive-skinned, and his bald head was covered with ink. His thin nose was pierced with many small blue gemstones. He wore a dirty blue silk tunic that reached to the floor.

"I am Ranoush," he said, his voice nasal. "The Tarkalin of Ranoush."

The sorcerer smiled at him. "I am Ranoush, *Master.*"

His fist clenched again and the Tarkalin of Ranoush fell to the floor, howling, even as new thunder rumbled and forks of crimson lightning threatened to tear the thickened air to shreds.

"On your knees, Ranoush," said the sorcerer. "And bow your head to me like a proper slave."

Piteously groaning, blood dripping from his pierced nose, Ranoush's ruler fumbled back to his knees. The blue silk tunic rippled with his shudders.

"Master," he said. He was choking on his own blood.

Ignoring him, Morg again savaged the chamber with his eyes. "That is one. There is more than one before me. Kings, I can gift you with such pain you will never know yourselves after. On your feet. On your feet. While you can still stand."

There was no hiding. There was no escape. Feeling his barracks men's fear for him, Ewen breathed out a sigh and stood, and the other captive kings stood, and the beasts with wings prodded them between the other cowering captives until they joined kneeling Ranoush at the foot of the dais, before the sorcerer Morg—Deenic's brother—and the Doranen who served him. A man Deenie knew. One by one they were forced to kneel again. High above their heads, the sorcerer's conjured clouds writhed.

Morg bared his teeth. "*Speak.*"

"I am Brantone, Master." A young man, barely bearded.

"I am Trindek, Master." An old bent man, mostly dressed in livid scars.

No Feen or Manemli here, then. Like Iringa, it must be ruined.

These kings, these ruling men, all were punished by Morg to blood and twitching, to shrieks and moaning as they bowed their heads and offered him their souls and the souls of their people.

Sickened, Ewen waited his turn.

*I must do this. I must. Vharne lives or dies on Morg's whim.*

But the pride in him was howling that a man of the Vale should be so thrown down. Would Murdo kneel like this? Would he shame the king, with his kneeling?

**449**

*Murdo's dead. I'm the king now. Tav would say to do my best for Vharne, he would.*

Today, his best was kneeling.

And then Morg looked at him.

He stared up into the sorcerer's dark, pitiless eyes. Familiar eyes, with a look of Deenie in them. He cleared his throat. Forced the craven words to his tongue.

"Master, I am Vharne."

They came close to cutting his throat to ribbons, those words. It came close to killing him, knowing he'd given his people to Morg.

"You are Vharne," said the sorcerer, and for the fifth time smiled and clenched his fist.

The pain that ripped through him then woke the lightly sleeping pain in his beast-torn, salved face. Robb and his barracks men were watching, Deenie was watching, the girl Charis who called him Noddy-head, she was watching too, but he couldn't stop a shout of anguish bursting from his lips. Like the four kings before him he collapsed and writhed on the cold black marble floor. Spat blood. Vomited moans. Thunder and lightning cracked the cold, cloudy air.

"I am Morg," said the sorcerer, releasing him, "and you kings belong to me. Your lands belong to me. Whatever is left of your runting people, they too belong to me. Every blade of grass, every pebble, every cow pat under the sun is mine. *Everything* in this world is mine . . . or shortly will be. It was a lesson learned once that your grandparents forgot to teach you. Now *I* will teach you, and I do not spare the rod. *Get up.*"

Along with his fellow kings Ewen slowly stood, shaking. Five of Morg's winged beasts stepped forward at his glance and next they were roughly pulled to one side of the crimson dais. Cruel pressure on their shoulders put them once more on their bruised knees. The winged beasts stood behind them, talons resting on their heads. The warning was plain.

*Protest and you die.*

"You are granted a privilege known to very few," Morg told them, as though they should be grateful. "At this time, in this place, do I take back the last found tattered pieces of my lost and sundered self. Only by my unmatched skill have I kept them intact for so long. No other mage in history was strong enough for that. You slaves are called here to witness this. To witness my majesty. In your fallow time as I was sleeping you came to think of yourselves as free. You are not free. Here, in Elvado, freedom's illusion dies."

Ewen watched the blond man, the Doranen, who was meant to have died out with the rest of his cursed kind, who was not looking at Morg, who Deenie *knew*, and saw something unexpected flit across his milk-pale, handsome face. Contempt? Revulsion? Grief?

*No. That can't be, it can't. A monstrous man, he is. Like Morg.*

At a glance from the sorcerer, Deenie's Doranen snapped his fingers. The beasts nearest the chamber's doors lumbered to open them. More beasts came in soon after. Was there no end to their number? Those beasts in the lead kicked and shoved their way through Deenie and Charis and his barracks men and the four kings' servants, clearing a path to the crimson marble dais.

And shuffling behind them, crowded together by more beasts, came a putrid, eye-watering gaggle of naked, brain-rotted wanderers.

Within heartbeats the chamber's cloud-thickened air was thickened further with their stench and rang with the harsh sound of their mindless mumblings and chantings. Ewen felt his throat close, bile rising, as the unhealed wound of his brother's death stabbed him. *Padrig.* The men who'd come to Elvado with their kings, his own barracks men, treacherous Deenie and Charis, they choked and shivered as the wanderers shuffled between them, leaving blood and pus and shreds of rotting flesh in their wake.

Ewen caught Deenie's eye. Pale and sickened, holding frightened hands with Charis, she saw him staring and tried to smile. Her eyes were bright with tears, and anxious. In return, he showed her his bitter, blinding rage.

*Girl, it's a pity you dreamed me, it is.*

The Doranen had retreated, breath by breath, to the furthest edge of the crimson marble dais. Morg hadn't noticed. Too busy, he was, devouring the wanderers with his greedy dark eyes. Like a starving man he stared at them, a man presented with a feast.

Reaching the dais, the wanderers stopped their mindless shuffling. A beast seized the nearest mumbling, brain-rotted wanderer and tossed her at Morg's feet. That look came to his face again, the look of a man pumping his loins empty. He knelt beside the babbling wanderer and took her rotting face in his hands. The moment he touched her the ruined flesh began to slip from her bones. A terrible keening howl broke from her bloody mouth. The other brain-rotted wanderers howled with her, as though they felt her pain, and the captives on the black marble floor cried out in fear and wrenching disgust.

Morg heard none of it. The rotted woman's rotting flesh coated his fingers and slicked his rich clothes. With a soft popping sound the woman's eyes burst in their sockets but still he stared into them, as though he would see her soul. Blood and jelly poured down her ravaged cheeks.

And then the sorcerer threw back his head and let out a great cry. Something loathsome shivered the air, brushing sickly against all their skins. Something foul and evil streamed from the wanderer into Morg's wide, straining mouth. He shuddered and convulsed with it. He squealed like a tumble-wench pierced to pleasure.

The brain-rotted wanderer fell to pieces on the dais.

Though his belly was empty Ewen heaved and heaved, and his fellow kings heaved, and their fellow captives heaved. Even Robb and his hardened barracks men heaved. The brutish beasts roared and grunted. The winged beasts behind Morg's slave kings pressed with their talons. One move more than heaving guts and heads would be torn off.

After that, Ewen couldn't look. There were some score of wanderers brought here like sheep to a shambles and though he was a swordsman trained, though Tavin's honour was at stake, he could not bring himself to look. He stared at the black marble floor and listened to the wet flesh flappings and the cries of pain and the cries of pleasure and the soft collapsing of rotted flesh and bone on more rotted flesh and bone as the pile of the discarded grew higher and higher.

*A sorcerer, this is. It's magework. It's the world.*

If there'd been tears to weep he would have wept them, but his heaving belly had dried him out. He couldn't even look at Deenie. She was caught in this, she was somehow to blame. Called herself a *mage*, she did, and lulled him into lowering his guard. Showed him a sweet face, a brave face, made him think that she cared. She didn't care. She'd used him. Deenie was a lie.

*And it's a fool I was, to trust her.*

A good thing Tavin would likely never know of it. Such foolishness in Murdo's son would break the swordmaster like a blade.

*It's sorry I am for this, Tav. So sorry.*

One by one the rotted wanderers were consumed, until only a single babbling voice remained, chanting the same mindless gobblings he'd heard from Padrig and every brain-rotted wanderer he'd crossed paths with since.

*"The sundered parts all came together and oh there was a joining and the world rejoiced."*

Except it wasn't a mindless gobbling any more. This moment was what the wanderers had meant, Morg sucking them dry of the madness infecting them. Sucking them dry of *himself*. Remaking himself. Becoming what he'd been before, the most soulless, powerful sorcerer beneath the sun.

*Padrig. Padrig.*

And then he felt his guts twist, as something familiar in that last babbling voice made him look up. The face before him was rotting, burst pustules and running pus and wet gaping holes in the cheeks. But despite the foul, distorting ruin, he knew it.

*Those are my eyes, they are. Those cheekbones? They're Padrig's. But see that? There's my jaw. And there's the way the hair springs sideways on my forehead. There's the man whose seat I gave to Tavin, so I could come here and give Vharne to Morg.*

A beast seized Murdo by one stinking, rotten arm. Cast him like he was a dying dog into a small, clear space on the blood-smeared marble dais. Morg failed to notice. He seemed drunk now, glutted, his muckish face oddly blurred. His dark eyes were closed as he swayed on his feet.

*"The sundered parts all came together and oh there was a joining and the world rejoiced."*

Hearing his words dressed in another man's voice, the voice of utter madness, Morg opened his eyes. Smiling, he took a step towards Vharne's rotted king. With the winged beast behind him, its talons light upon his head, Ewen felt the tilting world stand still.

*"Get away from him, sorcerer! It's a stinking abomination, you are!"*

Morg hesitated, his greedy eyes widened in shock. As the brutish beasts howled and roared their fury, as the winged beast at his back hissed and flapped, before it could strike Ewen dropped and twisted as Tavin had taught him hour after hour after hour in the tiltyard. Scant heartbeats free of the creature he threw himself at the marble dais, at Morg. He heard a girl scream his name. *Deenie*. His fingertips reached the dais—touched Morg's shod foot—*touched Morg*—and then the winged beast he'd evaded sank its talons into his shoulder and his hip and raised him so high he thought he might touch the black and roiling clouds beneath the chamber's ceiling.

Drenched in scarlet agony he heard the captives shouting, the brute beasts growling. The winged beast with its talons in his flesh was pulling him apart. He felt sinew stretch and threaten to tear, felt blood pour from his breached, battered body. He was going to die. He didn't care.

*Sorry, Tavin.*

Then he heard the winged beast scream, and moments later felt himself falling, falling, then strike the marble floor. The winged beast fell beside him, its blue eyes open in abrupt, astonished death. Its fellow beasts were yowling, flapping wings, clashing tusks and horns. The floor shuddered beneath him as they came to tear him apart.

"Stand back! *Stand back!* Touch him, touch any captive, and you die!"

It was the Doranen. Morg's right hand. His Dirk. The beasts obeyed him, howling their dismay.

Stunned, Ewen blinked up at the dais, at the Doranen, whose milk-white face was a mask of rage and disbelief and—and hope. *Hope?* But how could *that* be?

"Ewen—Ewen—what are you *doing*?"

It was Deenie, dropping to her knees beside him, hauling him against her leather-covered chest, as the winged beasts and the brute beasts yammered all around them. He hated her, but it didn't matter. Nothing mattered but Morg.

"Kill him, girl!" he croaked, struggling to free himself, to see Murdo, as the pumping blood slicked his cold skin hot. "Kill the sorcerer! Kill Morg!"

"I can't, I can't!" she said, holding him. "Ewen—"

He sank his fingers into her arm, still struggling, ignoring the pain. "You have to, Deenie. That wanderer is Vharne's king, he is. *My father.*"

Her eyes blanked with shock, she shook her head. "No."

Sick with hating her, he wrenched himself free. Rolled half-over, tried to get to his feet—*Father! Father!*—but he was too late. Morg was feeding on Vharne's king.

Deenie behind him, her hands clutching his arm. The Doranen on the crimson dais, watching them, his clever mask still awry. Murdo in the sorcerer's grip, the flesh sliding from his bones. Morg with his mouth wide open, drinking himself in. He cried out, slumping, the king tumbling through his hands. Deenie's Doranen leapt forward to catch the sorcerer—*her brother*—in steady, eager arms. So much for revulsion. So much for contempt and hope.

Cradling Morg so gently, the Doranen looked up. Looked at him, and at Deenie. The girl gasped, shivering. He heard Charis whisper her name. He heard a man, softly sobbing. It was Robb, his Dirk. But the grief of his barracks men was too shallow to touch him.

"*Dravas!*" said the Doranen, his voice a carrying command. "Take the captives whence they came, not a mark to be put upon them. The King of Vharne and his people lock in a cell on their own. All but one *dravas* to stand guard over them. One winged *dravas* with me, for the Master's chamber!"

Crude, clawed hands claimed him, dragged him up from the floor. Dragged him with the other captives, kings and servants, barracks men and lying mages, out of the stinking charnel house chamber. He felt nothing in his bleeding, punctured hip and shoulder, nothing in the talon-wounds scraped into his face. Somewhere on that marble dais, in that towering pile of rotted flesh, was the king. The king. Murdo.

*My father.*

# CHAPTER TWENTY-SEVEN

⚏

Arlin sat on the floor, in the corner of Morg's eyrie, back flat to the wall, knees pulled to his chest, arms wrapped around his knees. Aside from the sorcerer, he was alone. The winged *dravas* he'd commanded to carry Morg into his private chamber was long since dismissed. Vaguely he was aware of pain behind his eyes and in his haunches, raging thirst, and a stomach both queasy and hungrily hollow. He'd been sitting here for some time now, and despite his various discomforts intended to sit a good while longer. Until he had an answer, one way or another.

Morg slumped on his eyrie throne, profoundly unaware.

Floors and floors and floors below them, Rafel's sister and her silly friend and some kind of parochial royalty they'd managed to trip over on the way to Elvado were locked in a dungeon dug deep into the earth.

Arlin cleared his dry throat. "Rafel? Deenie's here. Shall I tell her you're at home?"

No answer.

"*Rafel*," he said, sharply this time. "I shall have to speak with her. What should I say?"

Still no answer.

He held his breath, waiting for Morg to reappear, to chide him or beat him or burn him for trying to rouse the Olken. But Morg, it seemed, was as distant as Rafel. Indeed, he looked like a corpse sitting on his throne. Only a sporadic flicker of eyelid suggested he was still alive.

*A corpse.*

Shuddering, Arlin pressed fingers to his saliva-soured mouth. Would the day ever come when he could forget the sight of those grossly repugnant vessels? When he could breathe and not breathe in their cloying, putrid stench? The sorcerer was clean now, he'd seen to that first, but how long before the sight of his clean face would not provoke the memory of smeared blood and pus and gobbets of rot?

*I think I'm wasting my time. If Rafel is alive in there, surely he must be driven out of his wits.*

To the best of his understanding, before today Morg had taken back to himself no more than four sundered pieces of his soul at a time. And how many ruined vessels had the beasts pushed into that chamber? Nineteen? Twenty? Which meant Morg might well be in this trance for days.

*And here I sit on my arse, the great Arlin Garrick, stuffed to bursting with magic and powerless to end him.*

"Rafel, for pity's *sake!*" he said, moved to sudden violence. "Make an effort, you useless Olken peasant. This could be our only chance. Well. *My* only chance. Chances are you're too far gone. But I know you want to stop him. So stop hiding, you feckless coward. Come out. Come out and *help me!*"

Again he held his breath, heart sickly pounding, so afraid of Morg's resurgence he was sore tempted to say a prayer.

*Blessed Barl, this is your fault. Care to lend a hand?*

But Morg said nothing, did nothing. The sorcerer remained oblivious, too deeply lost in the arduous task of reclaiming himself. And Rafel said nothing, because he was Rafel.

To his unspeaking shame, Arlin felt his eyes burn with tears. Breathing harshly, he hid his face behind his hands. Weeping now? *Weeping?* When he'd not wept since childhood?

*You fool, Garrick. You fool.*

But berating himself did not dry up his grief. He was tired, so tired.

Every night when he closed his eyes he saw Fernel Pintte. Every night when he closed his eyes he felt the killing dagger thud home. Saw the shock in the old fool's eyes. Felt the life shudder out of him and heard the idiot Goose's wailing, heartstruck cries. Every day, serving Morg, he felt another small part of himself shrivel and die. And no longer could the glory of the magic sustain him.

*This wasn't supposed to be my life. I was not born to be a sorcerer's lackey.*

But now he could see no escaping that fate. He was shackled to Morg, bound with chains of darkest sorcery, and though he was Lord Arlin Garrick he wasn't strong enough to break free. Which meant he was no less a prisoner than the fisherman's son. What a good thing his father was dead. Though his son was a man now, Rodyn Garrick would still beat him for this.

The thought wrung fresh tears from him, a drowning wave of despair. *"Arlin . . . Arlin . . ."*

He lowered his hands. They were shaking. "Rafel?"

For one heart-stopping moment he thought it was a trick. There was no change in Morg's face this time, no suggestion that the Olken was once again behind his own eyes. His eyes were barely open. His mouth remained slack. That sporadic *tic tic* in one eyelid was unchanging, blunt hands lax in his lap.

*"Arlin."*

He didn't move, in case the moment shattered. The Olken's voice was so faint and thready, a slurred mumble.

"Rafel?"

A blink for a nod. *"Yes."*

"Imagine that. I thought you were dead."

Another blink, this time for a shrug. *"Is that why you're crying? Arlin, I'm touched."*

Bastard. "Your sister's here, Rafel. When Morg wakes, he'll kill her."

The tears this time belonged to the Olken. *"No."*

"Yes," he said, brutal, because there was no time for mercy. "Unless you help me stop him."

Ghosting across Rafel's face, disbelief. "*You?*"

"Yes, Rafel. Me. But I won't defeat him without you."

A long silence. Then Rafel managed to twitch a finger. "*Can't.*"

He wanted to leap up from the floor and shake the Olken 'til his teeth fell out. "You *have* to. I can't do it by myself!"

"*Deenie.*"

He sneered. "She's no mage."

"*She is,*" said Rafel. "*Trust her.*"

*Trust* her? Trust Rafel's drab little wallflower of a sister? *With his life?* "And why should I?"

Another long silence. Rafel's breathing turned to groans, as though the effort of surfacing, of speaking, was a physical torment.

"*Changed.*"

"*She's* changed?" he demanded. "And how would you know?"

"*Arlin . . .*" Another shallow, groaning breath. "*Trust me.*"

He banged his head against the wall, choked with frustration. *Trust me*, said Rafel. And he'd have to, wouldn't he? His nonsensical idea of poisoning Morg with herb lore had gone nowhere. This appalling Olken was his only weapon.

*But now he asks me to believe his sister's a weapon too. Idiot.*

Except—except—she was Asher's daughter and somehow, *somehow*, she had escaped Lur—and survived. Surely that argued some kind of mage ability, even though he vaguely recalled her as incompetent. And Morg had sunk no binding wards in her.

*So I suppose, if worse comes to worst she could always run a sword through him.*

He gave Rafel a sour look. "And how exactly can your paragon of a sister help me?"

"*Books. Arlin, books.*"

Books? What was that supposed to mean?

And then he realised. "In the library? Morg's warded books?"

Almost Rafel's groaning breath sounded like a laugh. "*Yes.*"

"Rafel, you're deluded. They're warded. Changed or not she'll *never*—"

"*She will.*"

So faint and sickly, and yet he sounded so sure. *I must be mad, to trust him.* "Which books?"

Deenie's brother didn't answer.

"*Rafel! Which books!*"

Nothing. Nothing. Then another groaning breath. "*Everry. Novil. Baden.*"

Baden? Then—"Those are the authors?"

"*Yes.*"

"And those books contain what I need?"

"*Yes.*"

For the first time in such a long time, he felt a surge of hope. "You'd best be right about your sister, Rafel."

He waited for Rafel to say, *I am.* Then he waited some more, for him to say anything at all. The fisherman's son said nothing. His groaning died away.

Tentative, disbelieving, Arlin leaned forward. "Rafel?"

Morg's eyrie stayed silent.

When she could bear the hostile silence no longer, Deenie risked a touch to Ewen's ankle. "I'm sorry. I'm so sorry."

Staring at the ceiling, Ewen didn't reply.

She tried again. "I swear, I had no idea anything like this would happen. If I'd known, I would've—I mean, I'd have *tried*—but I'm not sure if I could've stopped it even if I *had* known. But I am sorry. You have to believe that."

Still he said nothing, and his stony refusal defeated her. Folding her hands in her lap, feeling the cold seeping into her from the dungeon's stone floor, she looked down.

*Why are you surprised, girl? He's just seen his father die the most horrible death, and 'cause you didn't tell him everything he's convinced you're to blame.*

And she couldn't blame him for that, even though he'd been keeping secrets too.

*He's not a barracks captain. He's the King of Vharne.*

Well, it certainly explained some of the odd looks she'd seen Robb giving him from time to time.

She heard nearby Charis stifle a small sigh, but didn't look at her. Ranged against the dungeon's opposite wall, Ewen's Dirk Robb and the other barracks men sat with their eyes shut and pretended they weren't listening. Separated from the other kings and their men, hustled into this smaller prison chamber, they were waiting to see what would happen to them next. But simply waiting wasn't good enough. They needed to talk about what had happened. They had to make a plan.

"*Ewen*," she said again. "Please. This is important."

His grieving eyes flickered, one hand clenching to a fist. Beside himself because of his king's beast-made hurts, Robb had insisted Ewen lie flat on the floor, insisted everyone take off their coats and jerkins to cushion him on the cold flagstones. And now everyone's coats and jerkins were mucky with blood, even though Robb had stripped his shirt off as well and used it to staunch the wounds in Ewen's shoulder and hip.

"Leave him be, Deenie," said Charis, sitting with arms crossly folded and her back to their wall. "Can't you see Captain Noddyhead's sulking?" And then she rolled her eyes. "Oh. I'm sorry. *King* Noddy-head."

"Clap tongue, girl," Robb growled, glaring, as the other barracks men muttered. "Show some respect, you can."

Charis sighed. "I do wish you'd take that understanding spell off them, Deenie. I miss our private conversations, I do."

Charis's tongue always sharpened when she was most afraid. And Ewen's loss of his father cut too close for her to be kind.

"It's all right. I can't complain. Da used to fratch at anyone who was rude to King Gar."

"From what Papa used to say, Deenie, your da fratched at everyone with no reason at all!"

And because that was true, if ole Darran's claims could be trusted, despite everything she grinned at Charis, and Charis grinned back. But not for long.

"Deenie." She let out a shaky breath. "Deenie, that was *Rafe*."

Deenie had to swallow hard before she could answer. "No, it wasn't, Charis. That was Morg. Rafe's not done a thing wrong. *Not one thing*."

"Then I'll tell you what this is," said Charis, her thin, pale face twisting. "This is Arlin Garrick's doing."

And she really wanted to believe that herself, only— "I'm not so sure." Troubled, she picked at a nick in her leathers. "He could've told those beasts to kill us. Instead he had them bring us back here. Why would he do that? And did you see his face, when—when—"

But she didn't want to say it, not with Ewen listening. Not after what had happened to his da. *The killing of his brother was kinder. And if that isn't an awful thing to think . . .*

Charis sat a little straighter. "Deenie, what are you getting at?"

"Well, if you ask me, I'd say Arlin doesn't want any part of what's going on here. I'd say he's desperate to find a way out."

"Desperate?" Charis hissed. "Arlin Garrick? Now who's the noddy-head? He's a *Doranen*. Isn't this his dream? Finding Lost Dorana? Making his people great again?"

"Yes." She bit her lip, fretting. "Only I don't think his dream included Morg. Honestly, Charis, weren't you watching him? I mean, I don't like him either, I sinkin' well hate the poxy shit, but—I don't think he's fooling. I think he's afraid."

"If you're asking me to feel sorry for him, don't waste your breath," Charis retorted. "He hates Rafe, remember? He blames Rafe for his father's death. I don't give a fat rat's arse about Arlin Garrick. All I care about is saving your brother."

"And so do I care about Rafe! Only—"

"Only what?" Charis stared at her. "Deenie? *Only what?*"

She didn't want to say it. If she said it, out loud, then that might mean it was true. Goaded, close to tears, she scrambled to her feet.

"*Deenie!*"

Reluctantly she turned back. "Only I'm not sure how much of Rafe is left to save."

Charis slapped her hand to the flagstones so hard she woke echoes.

"Don't you *dare* say that! Papa told me something of Conroyd Jarralt survived when Morg took him. And Rafe's twice the mage that nasty Doranen ever was, I'll wager!"

"Darran told me and Rafe the same story," she said. "But the thing is, I think that was different. I think there's more of Morg in Rafel than was ever inside Conroyd Jarralt. Charis, I think Morg's taken him over. I think—I think Rafe's gone."

"You *think*? That means you don't *know*, not for sure!" Charis scrambled to face her. "So how can you stand there and say you're giving up? You've got Barl's diary, haven't you? There *has* to be a spell in there that can save Rafe and kill Morg!"

"Oh, *Charis*, don't you think I want there to be?" she said, shivering. "And don't you think that if there *was* I'd have used it already? But there *isn't*! I don't know a single spell that will kill Morg and save Rafel. All I've got are the Words of UnMaking."

"Then use them!" said Charis. "If what we're after is getting rid of Morg, use them! They got rid of him last time, didn't they? All right, the spell was meant to properly kill him but I say getting rid of him for a few years is better than nothing. And while he's all scattered bits and pieces again you and Rafe can work out how to kill him for good when he comes back."

Bumping her shoulder against a nearby stretch of wall, Deenie shook her head. "Charis, it won't work. Morg didn't die, but Conroyd Jarralt did. And so will Rafe."

"Oh, well, you've got an answer for everything, haven't you?" Charis demanded, scathing. "Anyone would think you didn't *want* to—" And then she choked back the rest of her hurtful accusation. "Fine. Then how about this? If you're so sure Arlin Garrick is on our side against Morg, get him to help you fuddle with the spell. Isn't he s'posed to be a great Doranen mage? Get him to fix it so Rafel stays safe!"

*Oh, Charis.* "That won't work either," said Deenie. "I think fuddling with the UnMaking spell ruins it. I think that's why Da couldn't kill Morg when he tried. King Gar fuddled the spell so he'd die instead of

Da, remember? But it only half worked. He died, Da lived—and so did Morg."

Charis blinked at her. "What are you talking about? I don't remember any such thing."

"You don't—you mean Uncle Pellen never told you? I thought he told you everything."

"No," said Charis, and stepped back. "He never would talk about the magic that killed Morg. Not even at the very end. All he'd ever say was King Gar died helping the Innocent Mage destroy Lur's greatest enemy. That's all anyone ever said. I never heard anything different. *You* never told me."

"It was a solemn sworn family secret," she muttered. "I couldn't. *I* wasn't meant to know, only Rafe found out and he told me and there was such a commotion."

But Charis wasn't interested in old family ructions. "So what you're saying is the proper UnMaking spell will kill whoever says it? You're saying that the only way to defeat Morg is for you to die with Rafe?"

And there it was, in the open. The one thing she'd never wanted Charis to know.

"Deenie, you *can't*," said Charis, her voice breaking. "I won't let you. I won't—"

"*Clap tongue!*"

Startled, they whipped round to see Ewen shoving himself upright, his deeply lined face twisted with pain and rage. Realised a moment later that Robb and the other barracks men were gaping at them with their mouths wide. So upset, so lost in angry despair, they'd tipped out all their dirty linen . . . forgetting they weren't alone.

*Barl's tits*. Deenie blinked at Charis, and Charis blinked back. Then she turned. "Ewen—"

"Clap tongue, I say," he snapped at her, struggling to prop himself against the wall. Robb moved to help him and was glared at for his kindness, so he raised one hand in apology and made no further attempt to help his king.

When at last he was sitting up, more or less, his hurt shoulder hunched, one hand pressed to his hurt hip, the scabby talon-wounds in his cheek and forehead split a little, and weeping blood, Ewen let his head fall back against the stone wall and narrowed his eyes in a cold glare.

"I knew you were hiding secrets, I did, girl. I knew in my gut they had to do with Morg. But you saved my men, you did. You saved the people of that village. You saved me. So every time I shivered, every time I had a doubt, I wouldn't let myself hear it." He swept that cold glare round the dungeon. "Now look where we are."

Deenie felt her face heat. "You're not fair, Ewen. This isn't my fault."

"You've the power to kill Morg, you say," he spat. "You let him live. I should *trust* you?"

"Don't you understand? He holds my brother captive!"

"And he held *my* brother captive, he did. He did worse, girl. He *rotted* him. Girl, I put my knife in Padrig. I held him as he died." Ewen thrust his hand at her. "My fingers sifted his burned ashes, they did. Don't you rattle to me about dead brothers. Not when yours is still alive."

"Except he might not be," she retorted. "Or else what he's living through is worse than death. Worse even than brain-rot."

Ewen's green-gold eyes were pitiless. "Then put him down, you should. That's if you love him."

She heard Charis's angry gasp and gave her a sharp look. *Don't.* Then as Charis bit her tongue, she made herself again face Ewen's ice-cold anger.

"I was afraid to tell you everything. I didn't think you'd understand. I thought you might think we were somehow in league with Morg. I thought you might not believe our story. I know it's outlandish. And knowing what Vharne has suffered, I know you've reason to fear."

Ewen eased himself against the dungeon wall, wincing. "Your father killed Morg?"

She grimaced. "Apparently not."

"He killed a *king?*"

"He didn't want to," she said, hearing herself defensive. "That king was his dearest friend."

Ewen's lips pressed tight. There was no softness in him anywhere. He'd turned into a sword. "Morg never ruled your land, you said."

"No, he didn't."

"Then girl, how do you know him?"

So she told him Lur's story, all of it, no more secrets. He didn't look away from her once. When she was finished, she dropped to one knee and tentatively took his hand. He let her. Even curled his fingers lightly around hers. And then he smiled, his eyes thawed to a gentle warmth.

"That's a tale, that is."

Her heart was beating so fast it was hard to breathe. "But do you believe it?"

"Yes, girl. I do."

The relief nearly drowned her.

"So these few years we've had without the sorcerer," Ewen murmured. "They'd be owed to your father, they would."

"To Da," she said, struggling to hold back a flood of tears. "And Mama, and Uncle Pellen, and King Gar."

Ewen frowned. "A Doranen."

"They're not all bad, Ewen. I don't like them very much, the ones I know at home, most of them, but that's not the same as saying they're bad."

"This Arlin Garrick's not bad, you say?"

*Arlin.* Oh, her head was spinning over Arlin. "I don't know. I don't think so, not any more, maybe, but—I don't know what happened in the blighted lands. I don't know how Rafe ended up Morg's prisoner."

Cross-legged on the floor again, Charis snorted. "I do. Arlin betrayed him."

"Could be he did," said Ewen, looking at her. "But it's trained, I am, to read a man's face. Deenie's right, I say. Your Arlin's tormented."

"He's not *my* Arlin!" said Charis, offended. "And I'll thank you to remember it!"

The merest hint of a smile tugged the corner of Ewen's mouth. "Yes, Meistress Orrick."

"Ewen." Deenie lifted his hand and kissed his bruised fingers. "I am so sorry. For everything. I clapped tongue because I thought it was for the best. But if I was wrong, if by keeping my secrets I made things worse for you, for Vharne, for—"

He slid his other hand behind her neck, leaned forward, and pulled her lips to his. She was startled, just for a moment, and then she relaxed. Didn't care about their barracks men audience. Didn't think of Charis, teasing *giddycakes* under her breath. Amidst the pain and the terror and the grief here was one moment of pleasure. Of love.

And then the still-simmering blight burst into hot, dark life. A familiar, horrible presence. A sudden, crushing certainty.

*It's coming for me.*

She wrenched free of Ewen's lips and gentle hands. "Winged beast!" she gasped. "On its way." She pulled Barl's diary from its safe home against her ribs and thrust it at him. "Keep this hidden. If things go wrong try and get it to Arlin. If I fail he could be our last chance to defeat Morg."

Ewen didn't even glance at the diary as he shoved it inside his bloodied shirt. Beyond the dungeon, faint sounds of beast doings. "The sorcerer wants you?"

She tried to smile at him. "Someone does. And if it's Morg, he'll soon regret it."

"Deenie, *no*," said Charis, her voice cracking. "There has to be another way, you can't—"

"Charis, I have to," she said gently, pushing to her feet. "How can I be Asher's daughter and say the world can die for me?"

"And if you do this, girl?" said Ewen, his voice close to breaking, "Say these Words of UnMaking? How will we know?"

She wanted to smile, but she couldn't. "Don't worry. You'll know."

Grim-faced, Robb and the other barracks men got to their feet. Charis stood too, tears streaking her cheeks. When Ewen tried to stand, Robb moved to help him and this time wasn't rebuffed. Turning from him, Deenie flung her arms around Charis in a convulsive embrace.

"I don't know if it's possible, Charis," she whispered. "But if it is I'll save Rafe for you."

Sobbing, Charis nodded. "I know you will, you slumskumbledy wench!"

As she eased free of Charis, they heard the bars on the dungeon door being lifted. Ignoring that, Deenie looked at Ewen, standing uneven from his hurt, grief and rage stark in his face. Dark red hair. Green-gold eyes. The man of her dreams. She kissed him again, desperate. Hello and goodbye. A last taste of what might have been, if things were different. If she'd not been born who and what she was.

Then the dungeon door swung open.

"Come," said the winged beast, pointing. "Woman of Lur. You will come."

Without protest, without another word, she walked from the dungeon. And because she was still a mouse at heart, she never once looked back.

In silence she followed the winged beast through lofty corridors and across open halls with stained-glass windows, their patterns hidden by the night. Followed it past more beasts and terrified human servants and up many elegant stairways. The extravagant beauty failed to touch her. Since stealing that skiff in Westwailing she'd lost count of the times she thought she was about to die. So now, even though death seemed more likely than ever, she couldn't feel anything. Instead, she made her plan.

*It's quite a short spell, but Morg will know it. So I have to start saying it before I see him, so I can trigger the final sigil and kill him before he kills me. But I can't say it too soon, either, or the magic won't catch.*

Decisions, decisions. How odd, to feel so numb, so dispassionate. So completely indifferent to the prospect of her death. Was there something wrong with her? Had Da felt like this?

*Rafel.*

She stumbled.

*Noddyhead. Don't think on him. You told Charis you'd try to save him to save her feelings, not because there's any hope.*

Now the winged beast was leading her along a dead-end corridor.

She saw the enormous, ornate double doors up ahead and felt her mage-sense stir. Felt a sudden prickle of sweat and slowed her pace, just a little. The lethal Words of UnMaking burned behind her eyes.

"*Senusatarum*," she said, her voice the merest whisper. "*Belaridovarik*." And then with the tip of her finger, she sketched the first sigil. Deep in her blood and bones her magic stirred, questing. "*Kavartis*." The second sigil. "*Toronakis*." The third. One more word. One more sigil. Morg would die—and so would she.

*Ewen.*

The winged beast halted before the closed double doors. She halted behind it, dizzy with the painful pressure of the incompleted spell. *Da. Da, I'm sorry*. Without knocking the beast pushed open the doors, snatched her by the arm, shoved her into the chamber and slammed the doors behind her.

It was a library. There were books, shelves and shelves of them. Most were sunk deep with warding incants, cruelly effective. Tall, narrow windows drawn with blue velvet curtains. Lamps. Chairs. Two glossy reading tables. A low sofa. There was a man hunching in the lamplight shadows. As she saw him he moved, and the light fell on his face.

"*Goose!*"

Shocked, she extinguished the deadly spell shuddering in her blood.

"Goose, it's me! Deenie!"

Shambling, uncertain, his dear, familiar face so changed, he covered his head with his arms as though he expected her to run at him, shouting, or beat him about the face with her fists.

"No, no, Goose—no," she said, creeping forward. "Goose—it's Deenie. Rafe's sister. Oh, Goose, don't you know me?"

Goose Martin, Rafe's friend from boyhood, as dear to him as Charis was to her. Brave and bold riding over Barl's Mountains. A master brewer in the making. A kind man to make her smile. Not to make her heart beat the way Ewen did, she knew that now. But still. *Goose*. He'd been so sweet to her the night of Uncle Pellen's farewell ball, when things had gone so badly wrong. When their world began to fall apart in earnest. But what had happened to him? How in Barl's name had he become *this*?

Goose lowered his sheltering arms and peered at her. Such a struggle in his face, his gentle eyes, as though he was trying to remember, to know her. His lips, gone slack and trembling, worked as though he wanted to speak. It broke her heart.

"Deenie?" His hand hovered, on the brink of reaching out to her. "Deenie?"

"Yes, Goose," she whispered. "It's me."

Their fingertips met. Gasping, he snatched his hand back. She kept hers outstretched.

"It's all right, Goose. I won't hurt you."

"*Deenie*," he said, smiling, *knowing* her, and took hold of her hand.

"Well, well," said a cold voice out of the room's shadows. "Isn't that touching? I might shed a tear."

She turned, ignoring her thudding heart, and lifted her chin. "Sink me bloody sideways. If it ain't Arlin Garrick."

Arlin stepped into a soft pool of lamplight. It shone on his golden hair, on his pristine velvets and his jewels. Showed her his smooth, handsome face. But beneath the arrogant mask she could feel his disquiet . . . and something terrible writhed in his eyes.

"Deenie." His lip curled. "The ruffian Rafel's forgettable sister."

"Not so forgettable, Arlin," she pointed out. "You remember my name."

"Actually, I had forgotten," he said, careless. "Only you were bleating it at this idiot and as it happens, I'm not deaf."

Hating him, she clenched her fingers. *Did I defend him to Charis? That was foolish of me, wasn't it?* "Don't you call Goose an idiot!"

Arlin shrugged. "Why not? It's what he is."

"What he is," she said, teeth gritted, "is my friend and a dear, good man." She swallowed, fighting tears. "What happened to him, Arlin? How did he come to this sorry state?"

"He was a vessel. He held a sundered piece of Morg."

*Oh, Barl's mercy.* Only — "Are you sure? He's not dying. He's not . . ."

"Putrid? No," said Arlin. "It wasn't for very long, and it wasn't a big piece." His turmoiled eyes went dark. "Fortunately for him. You've seen what hosting a big piece for more than a day or two will do."

He was standing so still. She could hardly see him breathing. And Goose stared at him so strangely, a little afraid, a little anxious. Muddled between the two an odd kind of trust. But she didn't have time to think about that.

"Are there any others here?" she said. "From the first expedition? Or is Goose the only one?"

"Pintte's dead," said Arlin, curtly brutal. Goose whimpered at the sound of his name. "The others annoyed the Master, so he turned them into beasts. Which is a kind of living, I suppose. Oh—and Sarle Baden's dead too. He was Morg's host for a while, until your brother and I found him."

He wasn't going to make her cry. *Nothing* he said was going to make her cry. "And I s'pose you arranged for the sorcerer to exchange Baden for Rafe, and not you?"

"I had nothing to do with that. It was Morg's decision." Shadows danced across Arlin's face. "Believe me or don't believe me. I don't care. But it's the truth."

Oddly, she did believe him. He was hateful; he'd always be hateful, but she knew she'd not been wrong about him in that terrible chamber. Arlin Garrick was a deeply troubled man.

"Arlin—what am I doing here?"

The question made him laugh. It was an awful sound, full of sick despair and fury. Flinching, Goose hunched his shoulders and whimpered. Arlin paid no attention.

"I thought perhaps you could tell me, Deenie," he said. "And tell me this, while you're about it." He took a step towards her, his pallid face and dreadful eyes intent. "How did you escape Lur? You can't have crossed the mountains. Not *you*. And there's no way past the reef. Was it that Doranen incant Rafel used to send those idiot Councillors back to the city? Is that how you did it? *Tell me!*"

She didn't even try to hide her mean triumph. "Actually, Arlin, I *did* get past the reef."

His eyes widened, and his throat convulsed in a swallow. "*Liar.*"

"Suit yourself," she said shrugging. "But you asked."

"You broke the reef?" he whispered. "*You?* An Olken?"

"I don't know if I broke it, Arlin." *It's more likely the reef broke me.* "But I tamed the 'spouts and the whirlpools and sailed past it into open water. You keep forgetting I'm not just any Olken. I'm Asher's daughter, remember?"

"And Asher couldn't break it," Arlin spat, livid with resentment. "Rafel's his son and *he* couldn't break it. My father couldn't break it with the best Doranen mages in Lur! And you stand there with the gall to claim that you — that *you* —"

Goose was whimpering again. Ignoring Arlin's near-incoherent outrage, Deenie took Goose's hand in hers and stroked it until he calmed.

"How?" said Arlin, once he'd mastered himself. "How did you do it?"

Turning away, she smiled at Goose. He tried to smile back — and that did make her weep.

"Why should I tell you, Arlin?" she said, letting her tears for Goose fall. "Telling you is like telling Morg, isn't it?" She turned back to him. "Why don't you tell me something? Do I still *have* a brother? Or did Morg kill Rafe, too?"

She thought Arlin would lie. She thought he'd say something taunting, something cruel. Instead he stared at her, silent. And as he stared his arrogantly handsome face emptied of all expression until it was pale and blank, like a fresh fall of snow.

"I wonder, Deenie," he said at last, softly. "Is it possible to hate someone, yet not wish them ill?"

She smiled at him, fiercely. "Well, Arlin, I hate you — but I don't particularly want you to die. On the other hand I do want Morg dead. So I might not be the best person to ask."

Arlin nodded, his gaze drifting around the room. "I hate your brother, you know," he said, after another long pause.

What was he playing at? What did he *want?* "Yes, Arlin, I know."

"I still can't decide *why,*" he continued, as though she'd not spoken.

"I can't decide if it's because I was raised to hate him, as an Olken, as Asher's son, or whether I would have hated him anyway because he's an arrogant shit. And even you have to admit, Deenie, he is an arrogant shit."

She scowled. "It takes one to know one, Arlin. And even if he is, I don't care. Rafe's my brother. I love him."

Nodding again, Arlin tapped a thoughtful finger to his lips. In the lamplight its heavy ruby ring winked and flashed. "Rafel's not dead."

Her eyes pricked with tears. There was no reason to think he would *ever* tell her the truth. "I don't believe you."

"Why would I lie?"

"So you could hurt me with the truth later, of course!"

Her raised voice upset Goose. Whimpering again, he raised a protective arm to his head. Arlin gave him an impatient look. "Idiot. Fool. No-one's going to hurt you."

"Don't *call* him those things!" she said hotly. "Sink me bloody sideways, Arlin! You can say mean things like that and wonder why I won't believe you?"

Incredibly, he almost smiled. "You sounded like Asher, then. Is *he* dead?"

"No, he's not," she said, waspish. "Sorry to disappoint you."

Arlin raised an eyebrow. "You mean, he wasn't dead when you left Lur. But anything could have happened since then. For all you know Lur's ripped itself to pieces with tremors and fallen piecemeal into the sea by now."

Rage came on her so hard, and so fast, she couldn't breathe. Shaking, she took a clenched-fist step towards him. Killing magic rose choking inside her. And because Arlin was a great mage he felt her seething, murderous power. He stepped back, his arrogant face stilled to a knife-edged wariness.

"Careful, Deenie. Kill me and you kill Rafel—and I don't think Asher would be happy about that.'

# CHAPTER TWENTY-EIGHT

**D**eenie stared at him, scornful. "I'm not a noddyhead, Arlin. You'd say or do anything to save your life."

His wary expression didn't change, but a muscle ticced in his cheek, and in his watchful eyes the shadows shifted. She'd scored a point. She didn't think she wanted to know how or why. It was enough that she could keep the poxy shit off-balance. She needed the advantage — and he deserved to squirm.

"Rafel was right," he murmured. "You *have* changed, Deenie."

"Really?" Ruthlessly she smothered a surge of hope. "So now you expect me to believe he's alive *and* you've spoken to him?"

Arlin nodded. "Twice. Twice he's been able to break free of Morg's control and talk to me. The second time not long ago."

"Oh, *Arlin*! How much of a noddyhead do you think I am?"

"Your brother's in grave danger, Deenie," said Arlin. "If you want to save him I suggest you stop fratching at me and listen to what I have to say, before it's too late."

*I don't have to kill him. I could just hurt him, a little bit.*

The dreadful urge was almost overwhelming. Fingers clenched, she beat it back. At the very least she'd have to wait until he'd outlived his usefulness.

*But after that, Arlin? I make no promises, I don't.*

"And why should I believe you care what happens to Rafel?"

Arlin smiled. It was ghastly. "Because as much as I hate your brother, Deenie, I hate Morg much, much more."

"And why should I believe *that*?"

Silence, as Arlin's ghastly smile faded. "You think because I'm Doranen I worship him? I *despise* him. He's the reason my people lost their birthright, have been deprived of the power and glory that's rightfully ours. He's why we were cast out of this city, out of Dorana, and banished to exile in your pathetic little Lur. He *ruined* us, Deenie. He ruined you, too. Not that I care, but you should know I know it."

She almost laughed in his face. "And that's why you hate him? Not because he's evil. Not because he's cruel. Not because he's a perverted monster who turns people into—into *things*. Into *beasts*. You hate him because he took away your magical toys. Oh, *Arlin*."

With an impatient curse, Arlin turned away to pace the library. Goose, closely watching him, ducked behind the nearest reading table. Deenie shifted and shifted, not letting Rodyn Garrick's horrible son out of her sight.

"And where is Morg now? What is he doing while you're skulking in here?"

Arlin glanced up, as though looking through the library's ceiling. "He's in his eyrie, recovering. Every time he takes back more pieces of his mind—his *soul*—he retreats into a trance to reacquaint himself with himself."

And did that explain why the sorcerer felt somehow *muffled*? In the heart of his domain, was that why she could hardly feel him?

"This trance—how long will it last?"

"Hours. We've time."

Falling silent, Deenie watched Arlin pace and pace. Waited for her mage-sense to warn her of treachery. When it didn't, she breathed a little easier.

"What do you want, Arlin?"

"What you want," he snapped. "Morg dead."

"Why? So you can take his place?"

Shocked, he blundered into the other reading table. *"No."*

And oddly enough, she believed that. Arlin really had suffered. The twist of mage-sense that had gifted her—cursed her—with the ability to feel things that others couldn't meant that even standing on opposite sides of this library, she could feel the raw, weeping places inside him. Lord Arlin Garrick was on the brink of breaking.

*So here's my choice, Da. I can push him and smile as he smashes to bits . . . or I can pull him back from the edge.*

"Rafe said I'm changed, Arlin? What else did he say?"

For a little while he simply stared at her, as though he couldn't believe she believed him. And then he sighed, the high, discordant note of tension in him easing, and gestured to the ranks of books around them.

"He said there are three books in this library that will help us defeat Morg."

She tipped her head to one side. *"Us.* You can't defeat him without me?"

A touch of colour in Arlin's pale face. "I'm warded. My power is limited."

Holding his gaze, she crossed the floor to stand before him. Lightly pressed her palm above his heart and opened her senses. Morg's binding blight whispered sibilant in her unsettled blood.

"And so you are," she said, letting her hand fall. "I could unbind you, but I'm not sure you'd survive." And then she smiled. "Besides. I think I prefer you on a leash."

Arlin's lips twisted. "Changed? Your precious brother doesn't know the half of it."

Had he felt Morg in her? Perhaps. It didn't matter.

"The books are warded too," he added. "I can't break them."

"But I can?"

Brimful of doubt, he pulled a face. "Rafel thinks so."

He wasn't lying about Rafe . . . but he wasn't telling the whole truth, either. Grief and fear churned her, 'cause this was Arlin Garrick, who'd stood before the General Council and accused Da and Rafe of murder. Now he expected her to *trust* him? When scant hours ago she'd watched him stand beside Morg and not lift a finger as the sorcerer destroyed a score of innocent men and women with as much compunction as she'd swat a mosquito?

*It's not enough that he's tormented for it. It's not enough that he's bound. He should have done something. He should at least have tried.*

Something of her thoughts must have shown in her face, because Arlin frowned. "Deenie, what you saw in that chamber—it was terrible, I know. But you must understand, if I'd ever tried to save one of those rotting vessels, if I'd tried to dissuade Morg from seeking to restore himself to himself? I'd be dead. And you'd have no chance of defeating him."

It galled her to admit it, but Arlin was right.

*And I didn't do anything to save them, did I?*

Somewhere above her, Rafel was trapped in a prison of his own flesh and bone. Below her Charis and Ewen and his barracks men were trapped in a different kind of prison. Far away in Lur, in Billington, Da was trapped too. The whole known world was trapped . . . and it needed her to free it. All she had to do was trust Arlin Garrick.

*Barl's tits.*

She pressed a hand to her eyes, willing the pain and dismay to retreat. Then she looked at Arlin, showing him nothing but a grim resolve.

"You said we could save Rafe before it's too late. Is he dying?"

Arlin's hesitation answered her.

*Sink it, Rafe. Hold on.*

"Which books?" she demanded. "Show me. *Hurry.*"

Goose watched anxiously, mumbling in the background, as Arlin pointed out the three warded books.

"You'll have to break their bindings where they are," he said stiffly. "I can't even touch them."

Mostly ignoring him and his grudging resentment, she hovered a fingertip above the first guarded book. An interesting binding sigil. Touch it once, receive a warning. Touch it twice and die. Morg's distinctive magic stirred her, waking memories of smashing waterspouts, unravelling whirlpools and dropping beasts in their tracks.

She closed her eyes.

*It's a knot. It's a tangle. All I have to do is tease it apart.*

Gently. Gently. This wasn't a brute waterspout or a ravenous whirlpool. She had to kill this binding kindly, not bludgeon it to death.

"Deenie . . ."

"Clap tongue, Arlin," she said, her voice dreamlike. "Stop buzzing in my ear."

Fooled by the reef changes in her, seeing her as harmless, Morg's ward made no protest as she touched it. No protest as it died. Opening her eyes again, she watched the glowing sigil on its narrow spine fade . . . and fade . . . and disappear.

*"How did you do that?"* Arlin demanded, almost ugly in his shock.

She had no intention of explaining. "Does it matter? I did it."

The second book surrendered as easily as the first but the third and final book Rafel wanted her to see, it fought back. Pain burned through her body. She felt blood trickle from her tight-closed eyes, from her nose and down the back of her throat.

Goose cried out, terrified, as at last the ward broke with a flash and a loud crack. The force of its breaking flung her into Arlin's arms. She struggled free of him, staggering backwards until she struck a chair and sat down.

Arlin handed her a kerchief. "For the blood."

She dabbed her face clean, the blight roiling through her so thickly she was afraid she'd be sick. But the nausea passed, sparing her. Looking up, she found Arlin watching her intently.

"Deenie, how did you do that?"

Not demanding, this time, but plaintive. Confused. As unlike Arlin Garrick as ever she'd heard.

"It's a long story, Arlin," she muttered. Quivered with nerves, she took a few deep, settling breaths. "For now, we need to look at those books, and see why Rafel wanted us to have them."

"They're written in Old Doranen," said Arlin, scornful. Of course he'd not remain plaintive for long.

"I reckoned they might be," she said. "Will you need my help reading them?"

Offended, he snatched up one of the unwarded books from the reading table and stalked to the nearest curtained window.

The third unwarded book was splayed on the carpet, tossed there by the force of its unbinding. Bending to retrieve it, Deenie felt a wave of faintness wash over her.

"I've been kept starved, Arlin," she said, straightening. "I need food and drink."

Still scornful, Arlin sighed and stared past her at Goose. "Idiot. Kitchen."

And oh, how she hated him for speaking to Goose like that. But Goose didn't seem to mind. He nodded, pleased to be noticed, she thought, and made his shambling way out of the library.

"He has some wits left," said Arlin, mistaking her look. "Enough to follow a simple command. If you're lucky he'll make it back here with half the food on the plate."

"Arlin, your compassion moves me to tears."

He raised an arrogant eyebrow. "It should. Morg wanted me to kill him."

And what was she s'posed to say to that?

While she waited for Goose to return with her supper, trying not to think of Ewen and Charis hungry and thirsty in the dungeon, frighted for her, waiting to learn if she was dead or alive, she sat at the reading table and opened the third book. A thick volume bound in heavy crimson leather, dryly titled *Incants for Judicial Application*, the author's name on the age-mottled frontispiece read *Sarle Baden*. Startled, she drew in a sharp breath.

"What?" said Arlin, looking up from his own book. Stubbornly he refused to sit down. "Can't read it after all? I *am* surprised."

*Poxy, arrogant shit.*

Ignoring the jab, she touched her fingertips to the parchment page. "Sarle Baden's ancestor wrote this." She looked up. "I wonder, if we kept looking would we find a book here written by some other Arlin Garrick?"

Arlin's face tightened. "What's your point?"

"It must be difficult," she said, almost sorry for him. "Being here. Seeing everything your people lost."

"Deenie," he said, thinly smiling. "Your compassion moves me to tears."

Scowling, she returned to the book, which proved to be an extensive and stomach-churning collection of incants designed to punish miscreant mages for the misuse of their power. Reaching the surprisingly terse section on death penalties, she again caught her breath.

*Oh, Da. This magic's in me already. This is how I can kill with a thought.*

"Deenie?"

Not scornful this time. Arlin actually sounded concerned.

"I'm all right," she said, because she didn't want him to know. "I'm hungry, is all. What's keeping Goose?"

Arlin snorted. "Goose."

Shoving the Baden book aside, her hands not quite steady, she opened the other one instead. Slender and hand-written, the ink spidery faint like Barl's diary, it was a succinct compilation of powerful binding hexes. Just reading them made her mage-sense shiver.

And then the library doors opened, and in shambled Goose with plates of food, a jug and two elegant glasses on a tray. He smiled shyly, seeing her, and clumped his broken way across the library to join her.

Reading the judicial incants had mostly robbed her of appetite but she'd hurt his feelings if she didn't eat. Besides, she needed the nourishment. Pouring herself a glass of strong cider, she watched him pull a second chair to the table then look anxiously at Arlin.

"Supper, Arlin. Supper."

"Idiot," said Arlin, still reading. "I'm not hungry."

Goose's hurtfully changed face crumpled. "Arlin. Supper."

Arlin looked up, glaring. "Are you *deaf* now, dolt? Are your ears full of wax? I said *no.*"

Shivering like a scolded child, Goose pressed his fingers against his mouth.

"For pity's sake, Arlin!" Deenie snapped. "Must you be so cruel?"

A motley of emotions shifted over his face. And then he stalked to the table, flung himself into the chair Goose had fetched for him and with ill grace helped himself to bread and cold sliced duck.

Goose nodded his approval, wounded tears forgotten.

Staring into her glass, Deenie struggled to hide her grief. If Arlin mocked her now she wasn't sure what would happen. But when she risked an upwards glance, she saw the grief in him, too.

*Oh, Da, he's a strange one. I can't begin to figure him out.*

Goose was still hovering beside the table.

"You should eat too," she told him, and gestured to the plate of duck. "Goose? Please, eat."

He looked at her, uncertain.

"Here." She added duck to a piece of bread and held it out. "This is yours."

"Deenie," he said softly, and shattered her with a smile. "Deenie."

She ate the food and drank the cider, quickly, barely tasting them. Piled her crockery and Arlin's back onto the tray, stowed the tray on the other reading table, spared a glance for Goose, slowly eating in the corner, then dusted her hands and turned back to Arlin.

"The other book. What is it?"

He had it open before him on the table. "It's more a journal than a book," he said, frowning. "A series of essays on magework by an eccentric called Novil. I think—"

"What?" she prompted, as he drummed his fingers on the page. "Arlin, what?"

"Some of Novil's ideas. They're uncomfortably familiar. I think Morg might've stolen his work at some point. He writes of *expanding a mage and his mage-sense beyond the confines of the corporeal*."

Uncomfortably familiar? That was one way of putting it. *Morg's immortality.* "Well, that's disturbing, Arlin, but I'm not sure how it helps us."

Instead of answering, Arlin pulled to himself the two books she'd been reading and swiftly perused them. Then he sat back in his chair, fingers drumming his knee.

"No?" he murmured. "How terribly dim of you, Deenie. What a good thing I'm here."

She felt her face heat. "You can be snide or you can explain, Arlin. I doubt we've time for both."

"*Think*, Deenie!" he said, impatiently. "Three books of magic. Binding hexes, judicial murder—and a way to pull a mage from his body."

She took a few moments to think it through, just to be sure she'd understood him aright. "So," she said at last. "You want to trap Morg in his eyrie, pull him out of Rafe and execute him?"

Smiling, Arlin clapped his hands. "Exactly. Well done."

It was an audacious notion, and no mistake.

"And you think Rafe will survive it?"

"I have no idea," he said. "I'm not even certain it'll work. But I *am* sure he won't survive decapitation with a sword. And while that might kill Morg with him, I'm not prepared to take the chance, even if I could convince you to cut off your brother's head."

*Cut off Rafe's head? No, Arlin. I don't think so. But if I have to I'll kill him with the Words of UnMaking.*

She hesitated. Should she tell Arlin she had that spell at her fingertips? No. Not yet. He might prefer that she use it—the perfect revenge. He might hold Ewen and Charis forfeit until she did. With Morg in a trance, he was the Lord of Elvado. And even with his bindings Arlin was a formidable mage.

But not formidable enough.

"I think you're right," she said. "I think this could work. Only I can't do it by myself. What you're suggesting will require two mages."

He sneered. "Not being dim, Deenie, I had worked that out. So you'll unbind me. Now. There's no telling how soon Morg will wake."

Unbind him? Deenie looked down so he'd not see her eyes.

*Unbound, he'll be even more powerful. And Barl alone knows what magics he's been learning from Morg. If I unbind him, how do I know I won't be creating another monster?*

"Deenie," said Arlin sharply, leaning forward, "I thought we understood each other. I want to end this madness. I want to end *him*. This land belongs to my people and I want it back. The Doranen need to start afresh, away from the Olken. And the Olken?" He shrugged. "Your people have a right to a life without us."

She stared and stared at him, but still she couldn't sense any deception. But there was fear. The notion of her unbinding him? He knew he gambled with his life.

Arlin's face was tight with impatience, and trepidation. "Well?"

"All right," she said at last. "But if you're lying, Arlin, I'll kill you." Then she smiled, not sweetly. "I might kill you anyway. Breaking the reef was one thing—but you're flesh and blood."

He smiled back at her, so arrogant. "Perhaps I'll break you."

*Sink me sideways, Da. What Arlin Garrick needs is a clip round the ear.*

Shoving her chair back and standing, she looked around the library then pointed to a clear space on the rich carpet. "Lie down."

When he was stretched out on his back, eyes fixed on the ceiling, she sat on her heels beside him. Rested her right hand lightly on his chest and folded her left hand in her lap.

"Before we start," she said, "do you know an incant to muffle the room? There might well be screaming and I'm not sure I could explain this to one of Morg's winged beasts."

Arlin gave her a scorching look, but did as she said.

On a slow exhalation, Deenie sank her mage-sense deep into him. Immediately felt the intricate twists and turns of Morg's bindings, even more complex than the ward on that first Sarle Baden's book.

*Oh, Da. This is tricky. This'll hurt him, no mistake.*

"Hold fast, Arlin," she murmured. "I'll be as quick as I can."

But she couldn't be quick, she had to be painfully slow—or risk killing him. And though she did hate him, she wasn't eager for his death. The thought of Rafe as Morg's prisoner, the fear of Morg waking, too powerful for defeat, pressed her and pressed her to go faster than she should. She resisted the temptation. And when Arlin screamed, she wept.

And then it was over and he was broken, like the reef.

It took some time for both of them to stop shaking. Goose hovered, fretting, making small sounds of distress.

At last Deenie looked down at Arlin's sickly pale face. "I'm sorry," she said, meaning it. "I did try to be kind."

Still lying flat, he managed to shrug. There was a strange resignation in his red-rimmed eyes. "No. I deserved it."

She didn't want to know why. "Can you stand? Are you strong enough? Arlin, we need to go."

"A moment," he whispered. "Just give me a moment."

Leaving him, she returned to the table and again looked through the three books Rafel had found for them. Pushed aside the collection of binding hexes, then opened the Baden to the incants of execution and, wincing, ripped out the page. *Sorry, Mama.* Then she ripped out the page in Novil's journal with the incant that would coax a soul into the air. Arlin still looked wretched, unable to move, so she slid onto the chair and studied the spell. Like the Words of UnMaking it was deceptively simple. The words seemed to slide comfortably under her skin. As though she already knew them, and had simply forgotten. She shivered.

*This is wrong, this magic. It shouldn't be.*

Only Rafe had said to use it, so that was that.

Nervously, she glanced at the ceiling. They had hours, Arlin had said. But even so, to be safe, surely they should be on their way?

"Arlin? Which of these binding hexes will we best need?"

Stifling a groan, he sat up. "All of them."

So she handed him the book, tucked the folded torn-out pages inside her shirt, kissed Goose on the cheek, and left the library at Arlin's side.

No beast challenged them as they made their carefully unhurried way to Morg's eyrie. Instead the horrible things bowed their heads, grunting obeisance, as Arlin passed by. The Lord of Elvado, indeed. Mouse-like, Deenie trailed in his wake, head down, gaze down, no sinkin' threat at all, with every humble step a desperate prayer.

*Let this work. Let Rafe be there. Don't make me UnMake him. We don't want to die.*

Cautiously she stretched out her mage-sense, but she still couldn't feel Morg. Despite all the beasts, even his blight was easing. There was a lot of Arlin's magic in Elvado. Maybe that made the difference.

Or maybe there was only a respite because the sorcerer slept.

There were no beasts at the top of this prison called, Arlin told her under his breath, the Hall of Knowledge. And then he told her, climbing still more stairs, that Morg had recreated it himself. She found the notion unnerving. How could such a monster make something so beautiful?

By the time they reached the sorcerer's eyrie she was trickled with sweat from all the climbing and Arlin's face was fish-belly white.

"Can you do this?" she said, her voice low. "Are you strong enough?"

Eyeing her with contempt, his prone frailty vanished, he thrust the book of binding hexes at her. "Yes. Wait here."

He pushed open the eyrie's doors and entered, leaving her to pull the sweaty folded papers from inside her shirt and flap them dry.

*Oh, Da, now we're down to it. Now we find out if I'm truly your daughter.*

Floors and floors and floors below her, Ewen and Charis fretted in a cage. If she let herself, she'd feel his burning wounds and her fear. If she let herself she'd crumple in a heap on black marble.

*Please, Barl, let me be good enough. Please, Barl, let us live.*

Arlin reappeared in the chamber doorway. "He's still in trance. Hurry."

Heart thudding, she tucked the pages into her leather trews waistband and entered the softly glimlit chamber. Arlin swung the doors closed behind her then held out his hand.

"Give me the binding book. We'll need to share warding this chamber. This many bindings, this kind of magic, it will take a toll—and it's only the beginning."

"You start," she said, giving the book to him, her gaze fixed to the back of the single tall throne. From behind it looked empty. "I'll join you in a moment."

He wanted to argue, she could see it, but instead he opened the book of binding hexes, turned another page, and ripped it in two.

"Here."

Holding her half of the book, she edged around the chamber until she could see who was sitting in that tall, imposing chair.

*Rafel.*

Motionless, lightly breathing, he didn't stir at her approach. The glimlight showed her his closed eyes, his thin face, his crooked nose, his long hair. Oh, how he must hate that. First thing, once she freed him? He'd be shouting for scissors, he would.

"Rafel," she whispered, as the tears rolled down her face.

Arlin hissed at her. "Be quiet."

She blotted her cheeks on her sleeve. "If Morg's still tranced, can't we wake Rafel?"

"No."

And Arlin was right, of course. It was too risky. Only there he was, her fratchsome big brother. She'd stolen a skiff and dared waterspouts and whirlpools and a poisoned reef to find him. She'd been broken, remade, become something entirely new. She had death at her fingertips. She could kill with a word.

And all she wanted to do was hold him.

*"Deenie!"*

Arlin was glaring at her, furious, his half of the torn binding book clutched in his hand.

"Get away from him!" he said. "Are you truly dim? We must bind this chamber *now*."

*Poxy, arrogant shit.*

But as he raised his right hand to draw the first hex's sigil on the air, she leapt towards him. *"Wait!"*

He stared at her, incredulous. "Why?"

"'Cause I just realised something," she retorted. "Arlin, only a noddy-head locks himself in a room then swallows the key. If this goes topsy-turvy we'll need a way out."

"Yes," he said, grudgingly, after furious thought. Then he closed his eyes, spoke swiftly under his breath, and sketched five sigils onto the air. They burned briefly crimson and then burned out.

She blinked, feeling the surge die down in her mage-sense. "What was that?"

"Think of it as a quick-release knot," said Arlin. Even taut with nerves, he managed to be smug. "Now the whole binding won't trigger until I say the word. And when I say it again, the binding will snap back open. As good a key as any, yes?"

Really? Just like that, he thought of it? And then made it happen? She took a moment to reach out with her mage-sense. Caught the shape of his incant and had to smile. It was a typically elegant Doranen creation. She might not like Arlin—she *didn't* like him—but she couldn't deny he was a magnificent mage.

They began the task of spinning a binding web round Morg's eyrie. Following Arlin, as she finished her first spell Deenie felt it thread onto his *quick-release knot* and smiled again. So clever. And then she felt his eyes on her and swallowed the smile.

"What? Did I say it wrong? Was my sigil lopsided?"

"No."

"Well, then?"

Baffled, he shook his head. "Who are you, Deenie? *What* are you? An Olken who can wield Doranen magic? An Olken who can unbind Morg's wardings? You and your brother, you shouldn't be possible. You shouldn't *exist*."

She would *never* show him that his words hurt her. Instead, she bobbed a curtsy. "Why, Lord Garrick. You say the sweetest things."

He scowled, ugly again, and began the next binding hex. Once he was done it was her turn. Then his. Then hers. The weight of the untriggered hexes pressed heavy against her skin. She felt her mage-sense shudder under it, felt the changed places inside her chafe. Taking a deep breath, she prepared to recite her next—oh, her last—hex. Turned . . . and saw that Rafel was watching her from beneath half-lidded eyes.

She held her breath.

"*Deenie.*"

And yes, it *was* Rafel. She'd know the feel of him anywhere. She knew the feel of him when he was a thousand leagues away. Morg was still sleeping. This was Rafel. It was Rafe.

"*Deenie*," he said again. His lips twitched, as though he wanted to smile. "*You're here.*"

But oh, he sounded terrible. More distant even than when he was a dream. She could hardly understand him. She leapt close, full of tears.

"Don't touch him!" said Arlin, and roughly pulled her back. "You could wake Morg."

He was right, but it hurt not to hold onto her brother.

Arlin stepped in front of her, his eyes savage. "Deenie, we can't stop now. You can snivel over him later."

Snivel? *Snivel?* This from the man who'd turned the General Council upside down howling for blood over the accidental death of his father?

"I'm not *stopping*!" she hissed. "I just want to make sure he's all right." She shoved her pages of the ripped hex book at him. "You do the last one, Arlin, so we can finish this."

And he didn't like that, but he didn't argue further.

She stepped back to the chair. Had to lock her fingers together, not to touch her poorly brother. "Rafe," she said, bending low, "hold on. It's nearly over, I promise."

He was so still and pale, he could have sat atop a coffin.

"*Beat Morg*," he said, the threadiest whisper. "*Hid you.*"

For a moment she didn't grasp what he meant, but then understanding flooded through her. So *that* was why Morg never felt the deaths of his beasts? Rafe had hidden her? A prisoner inside his own body and he'd managed to keep her safe? More tears, hotly rising.

"Oh, Rafe. I do love you."

Behind her Arlin made a scathing, impatient sound.

"*Deenie?*"

"Hold on, Rafe," she said, smearing the wet from her cheeks. "It's nearly over. Now, I'm sorry, this next bit might hurt. But then you'll be free of him, and we'll go home. I promise." She turned to Arlin. "Once the binding hex is triggered I'm going to pull Morg out. And when he's out, you can kill him. Since he's a Doranen, I think that's only right."

Arlin hesitated, then nodded. If he felt any qualms he kept them well hidden. "Agreed."

She pulled the folded page of execution incants from her waistband. *Death in her fingertips. Death in a word.* But there could be no grief or remorse this time. Morg wasn't a poor, crazed, brain-rotted wanderer. He wasn't any kind of innocent. What did it matter if he made beautiful buildings? He was the man who swallowed men's souls alive.

With iron in her own soul, she gave the page to Arlin.

As he read through the judicial incants, she shifted her gaze back to Rafe. Was it awful of her to be so relieved he wasn't fuddled, like Goose? That by some miracle he'd escaped his friend's heartbreaking fate?

*Maybe it is, but I don't care. And we'll see Goose right, somehow. If there's a cure for him, we'll find it. And if there's not we'll make sure he's never hurt like that again.*

"Ready?" said Arlin. "We've wasted enough time."

*Wasted.* Well, she'd take that up with the poxy shit later. She was still holding the page from Novil's journal, but she didn't need it. Shoving it back inside her shirt, she nodded.

"I'm ready."

On a deep breath, Arlin triggered the incant tying all those binding hexes together. Sigil after flaming sigil burned in the air. Deenie felt the power crackling against her skin, calling to the Doranen magic sunk deep in the bones of this ancient land. Calling to the power that had remade this ancient building. It called to her mage-sense, which was also remade, dark and light tangled. Her blood surged, her senses spun.

And then she felt a shudder of terror, and in its seething wake a wild whipping of blight.

"*Arlin!*"

Igniting his quick-release knot incant had hurt him. Bent double, struggling with the pain of so many binding hexes, he twisted sideways to look at her.

"Arlin, something's *wrong!*"

Another brutal slap of blight, stunning her. And then she felt an ominous stirring. Heard a rustling of silk. Felt cold crawling on her skin. She turned.

Rafel had straightened out of his slump. Eyes closed, his face was changing. Remoulding. Becoming *not Rafe*.

Morg opened his eyes.

For one odd, caught-out-of-time forever heartbeat, the sorcerer stared at her . . . and she stared back. She watched the incredulous recognition dawn in his eyes—saw the blank shock of her presence strike him a hammer blow and felt his rage rise as swift as a waterspout, whipping and thrashing and seeking to destroy. She felt *him*, in all his terrible power.

She couldn't feel Rafel. Her brother was gone.

Someone grabbed hold of her arm, pulled her back from the chair. Arlin. It was Arlin. He was shouting something but the words made no sense.

*Rafe.*

Was he dead? Had Morg killed him? Or was he caged again like before? She didn't know. She couldn't tell.

*Da, Da, what do I do?*

Morg's UnMaking was in her, the words on her tongue and the sigils at her fingertips. She could end this right now, she could kill the world's great evil. The sorcerer was still struggling, not yet himself. She had this moment, this fleeting moment, when she could set the world to rights.

*And maybe kill Rafel. He might not be dead.*

Arlin was still shouting. Something about getting out, leaving Morg trapped in here, working together to destroy him another way. Her arm hurt where he held her. Distracted, she flicked him aside.

"Rafel!" she said, almost sobbing. "*Please*, Rafe, you've got to *fight*. I can defeat him, but not on my own!"

She waited to see him change back. She waited to see Rafe.

Nothing.

Morg clutched at the arms of the chair, dazed and unfocused, trying to stand. Something had stirred him from his trance too soon, perhaps Arlin's incant, perhaps Rafe. For these few brief heartbeats, he was vulnerable.

*I can end this. I should end this. He can't leave here. He can't.*

But she couldn't bring herself to UnMake him and kill Rafel. Not without trying another way first.

On a sobbing cry of despair she seized Morg's face between her shaking hands and abandoned herself to his evil. Opening herself to him, abandoning all her defences, she heard the screams of every murdered innocent, tasted the putrescence of each maddened, rotted soul, felt the grief of every trust betrayed and the fury of all his principles denied.

Century after century of depraved cruelty burned through her. Power unimaginable crushed her bones to chalk. The reef—the reef was nothing—a pale, watercolour imitation—and her power, her little power, her pathetic Olken mage-sense, how could it help her? Ripping to pieces, she threw her head back and screamed.

In the midst of the maelstrom she heard a gloating, triumphant laugh. Heard Rafel scream and felt him writhing in pain. Heard a hateful voice, a lover's whisper, tender in her ear.

*Defeat me? As if you could. You bitch, you slut, you treacherous whore.*

And she saw between breaths the world Morg would make. Saw Charis and Goose turned into beasts, and the rest of the Olken, saw Ewen and the people of Vharne beasted too, saw Arlin and Lur's Doranen flayed alive and left to die, saw Da—saw Da—

*No.*

She opened her eyes. Clawed her fingers into Morg's face. Pulled him close, pulled him closer, until their sweating foreheads touched. She bared her teeth at him and showed him her soul.

*"I broke the reef, Morg. And I'll break you, I will!"*

# CHAPTER TWENTY-NINE

✵

She could feel the eyrie's myriad wardings, shivering and trembling as Morg's blighting power thrashed against them. She could hear Rafel screaming as the sorcerer flogged him to punish her. And she could feel — she could feel —

*Da! Da, he's afraid!*

It must mean she was winning. He was *afraid*. It meant *something*. But sheer will and desperation wouldn't be enough. She needed Novil's incant to beat him, even though she knew to her marrow that kind of magic was wrong. The dangerous spell was in her, eager to be spoken, its sigils searing her fingertips and tugging at her arm.

*Hold on, Rafe. Hold on.*

Lost in her mage-sense, in this thing she'd never asked for, never wanted, she let prophecy have its way. She was the child of Jervale's Heir and the Innocent Mage, born to finish what they had begun.

She pulled Morg out of Rafel one atrocity at a time.

Blood streamed down her face, from her eyes, from her nose. Blood dripped from her open mouth. She didn't care. Screaming, clawing, clutching, Morg fought and fought but the broken reef was inside her . . . his scars were inside her . . . Barl's mysterious strength was inside her . . .

*Sink it, Morg. You won't win.*

The whipcrack of power as she ripped him out of Rafe's body sent her flying across the warded chamber. She struck a wall hard, felt something break, heard someone laugh.

*Oh. That's me.*

And then someone was shouting at her, tugging her, slapping her face.

"Deenie! Deenie!"

For a moment she thought it was Rafe. Then she opened her eyes and saw Arlin Garrick's arrogant, handsome, terrified face.

"*Deenie!*"

The warded eyrie was so bursting full of blight she wanted to scream with the pain of it. Belly heaving, bones burning, she struggled to her feet. Arlin helped her, not gently. The pain that woke in her left shoulder made her shout.

"Deenie, we have to go!"

Ignoring Arlin, she spun round and nearly fell again. Rafe sagged boneless in Morg's high-backed chair, his face beeswax pale. A thread of bloodied spittle dangled from his slackened, open mouth. He looked dead. *Oh, Rafe, no!* Sobbing for air she staggered to his side.

"Rafe—Rafe—"

His skin was ice-cold. But when she touched him with her battered mage-sense she felt an answering spark flicker. Fingers under his chin, she tipped his head up and stared into his vacant, half-lidded eyes.

"Rafe? Can you hear me? Rafe? It's me, Deenie."

He didn't answer.

"Deenie, it's no good," said Arlin. "We failed. We have to get—"

Spitting blood on the floor, she turned on him. "I'm not going anywhere. Not 'til Morg's finished!"

"*What?*" Incredulous, Arlin looked at the ceiling. "Deenie, are you sheepwitted? Not even you can finish *that!*"

And *that* was a seething, roiling cloud of power, stinking the air and springing sweat through her skin. It was pure blight and unleashed fury, Morg without face or form, thrashing round and round the chamber against the eyrie's iron wards. There was madness in it, and murder, and if they stayed here they'd not survive.

Deenie felt grief and guilt stab through her. *Oh, Da. I got it wrong.* "Arlin," she whispered, "take Rafe and get out. And once you're outside seal this chamber behind you."

"*Seal*—" Arlin gaped at her. "You stupid, *stupid*—you're as mad as the sorcerer. Deenie, if you stay in here with him you'll *die*."

"Prob'ly," she snapped. "But what do you care, Arlin, so long as you're safe?"

He flinched as though she'd struck him, then stared again at the formless, furious sorcerer she'd unleashed into the air. "I don't know how long those binding incants can hold."

"Well, I reckon we're about to find out," she said. "Any road, he won't go anywhere while there's me to reckon with. So I'll entertain him while you find a way to keep this chamber sealed for good."

"*How?*"

Oh, she could slap him. "How d'you *think*, you sinkin' noddyhead? The books Rafe gave us. That Novil, he was chockful of ideas. Look for something in his journal."

"And if I can't find anything?"

"Arlin, for pity's *sake*! How long d'you think we've got to stand here bickering? That sinkin' bastard's going to find himself any tick-tock!"

Already she could feel the incoherent blight changing, feel Morg's crazed, scattered mind trying to collect itself. And once it did . . .

The banging pain in her collarbone was ferocious, close to drowning the pain of Morg's blight. She wanted to drum her heels on the floor and weep. But there was no time for weeping. There was no time for fear. Pressing her left arm hard against her body she staggered back to Arlin, snatched him by the sleeve and dragged him protesting to Morg's throne.

Arlin's face twisted as he stared down at Rafe. "Deenie, he's dead."

"No, he *ain't*!" she shouted, and did slap him. The pain of it cleared

**495**

her dizzy head. "Now you get him to safety, Arlin. You go, you go, or I *swear*—"

He must have seen his murder in her face, 'cause he hauled poor lolling Rafe out of the chair, draped one slack arm around his shoulders and clamped his own arm round Rafe's ribs. Then he stared at the lashing, seething cloud of blight that was Morg. His face twisted again, this time in despair.

"You'll not defeat him."

She shoved him. "We'll see." Another shove. "Now *go*."

Resisting, Arlin shook his head. His eyes were tormented again, full of terrible memories. "It should be me. I should stay."

Almost, she shoved him a third time. But then, prompted by some odd instinct, instead she laid her palm gently against his cold cheek.

"If you want to make amends, Lord Garrick, you see Rafe and Goose looked after. You see Ewen and Charis safe. You undo the damage you helped Morg do. *That's* how you can make amends. Now *go*."

Arlin's eyes were glittering. "I still don't like you. Or your brother."

"Well, that's my heart broken," she snapped. "*Arlin, would you go?*"

But as he started for the warded doors she snatched his sleeve a second time.

"No, wait." She kissed Rafe's waxen cheek. Stroked his hair. "*I love you.*"

And then Arlin was taking her brother away.

Rafel could barely shift his own feet. Arlin had to drag him to the doors. Deenie watched them, blinking away tears. Then, on a shuddering breath, she backed to the far side of the chamber and looked up at the raging thing that used to be a man.

*Oh, Da. I think Arlin's right. I'm cracked.*

From the corner of her eye she saw Arlin reach the chamber doors, Rafe a sagging dead weight, and look back at her. With her left arm useless, she shifted a little and raised her right hand. *Not yet—not yet.* And then she let down her guard and beckoned Morg close.

*Here I am. Here I am. Want to try again?*

A moment of silence. A moment of calm. Then Morg's blight came roaring at her, and knocked her to her knees.

Through the burning pain she felt Arlin's binding ward collapse. Terrified of Morg feeling it, she summoned her wavering strength and fought to distract him. Remembered the reef and that final whirlpool and poured everything she had left into collapsing him too.

But Morg wasn't a whirlpool.

She screamed as she was picked up and hurled across the chamber. Screamed again as Morg smashed her from ceiling to floor. As the smothering cloud of blight descended she saw Arlin hauling the chamber doors open, hauling Rafe into the corridor. Nearly there. Nearly there. And then he was outside the chamber, Rafe was outside the chamber, and its imposing doors were banging shut. A pounding heartbeat later she felt the binding wards reignite.

Sprawled on the cold eyrie floor, she laughed. And then she screamed as Morg took her and shook her like a dog with a rat. She thought any ticktock her bones would fly apart.

*But it doesn't matter. It doesn't. Da, our Rafel's safe.*

Abruptly, Morg let go. Exhausted, hurting so terribly she could scarcely breathe, Deenie stared at the blight-shrouded ceiling. Waited. Waited. But the sorcerer held back. Warm trickles of blood crept from her eyes, her nose. Trickled between her parted lips.

*Oh, Da. I'm so tired.*

She felt scoured raw inside, smashed to quivering pieces. Felt herself drifting, like a cloud.

*Is this it, then? Am I dying?*

She thought she must be, and was sorry, in an odd, far-off way. Very slowly, she blinked. Prob'ly Da would want her to keep on fighting, but she couldn't. *I'm sorry, Da. I'm all fought out.* Just like her mother. *I'm sorry I was fratched, Mama. I had no idea.* So it was up to Arlin now. He could be the Doranen hero. He'd like that. He really was a poxy shit.

As she lay there, idly drifting, she felt her mage-sense stir. *Go away. Leave me alone.* But it wouldn't. She felt it stir again, that horrible prickling that warned of beasts and wanderers and whirlpools and 'spouts.

Hovered beneath the chamber's ceiling, the cloud of blight shivered. Shivered. Trembled into life. But there was no crazed writhing now, no furious thrashing from wall to wall to wall. No. It moved steadily, with purpose, sinking towards the marble floor, gathering in upon itself. Cunning and sly.

Heart thudding, Deenie stared at it. Then, with a groaning effort, one-handed, her injured shoulder on fire, she sat up. Dragged her sleeve across her face to clear her smeary, bloodied vision. Blinked. Blinked again.

*Oh, no.*

The cloud of blight was changing colour. Changing *shape*. She could see through it now as its menace bubbled in her blood. Her mage-sense was shrieking, chattering her teeth. The blight shivered again. Became a figure. Became a man. Blond hair. Piercing eyes. A thin, cruel mouth.

*Morg.*

Churned almost to vomiting, Deenie scrambled to her feet.

A familiar voice whispered: *No running this time. This time you're mine, you bitch, you slut, you treacherous whore.*

The places within her that he'd scarred with his touch leapt to burning, blighting life. And then she felt a terrible pressure, felt the weight of his remade self bear down on her, felt Morg seeking his brutal way in, determined to take her and break her and make her his new puppet.

Inch by inch she was driven to her knees.

*I can't . . . I can't . . .*

Not even the reef had prepared her for this. And being Asher's daughter wasn't enough. Not this time. Though she fought with all her strength her soul was splintering and Morg, laughing and triumphant, poured himself through the cracks. She was drowning. She was drowning. And there was nothing she could do.

Then she heard a hiss of fury. Felt the sorcerer's onslaught falter, felt him draw back in dismay and disgust as he encountered some deep, hidden part of her mind.

*Barl.*

As Morg thrashed inside her, furious, Deenie reached out and touched this other, kinder scar left behind by Dragonteeth Reef. And there was an echo of the magic she'd read in Barl's diary. Incredibly, there was an echo of *her*. So she hadn't imagined it. What remained of Barl in the reef *had* changed her.

Morg was still raging. *Bitch. Slut. Whore. Traitor.* But it was more than anger, it was grief and pain and despair. Feeling it, Deenie realised Barl's ghostly presence had overpowered him—just as he was over-powering her. So she had this moment, this tiny ticktock, to turn his brief overturning into his defeat.

A sliver of her mage-sense remained unconsumed. Weeping, she clung to it with the tattered remnants of her strength and struggled to find a way to use it while she still could.

*Beautiful Elvado, the city of mages. Centuries of magic seeped into its bones.*

So Barl wrote in her diary, lamenting all she'd lost.

*Centuries of magic.*

Doranen magic, the most powerful ever known. In its pure form not blighted. Not tainted by Morg. And what was Deenie the mouse, the Innocent Mage's daughter, if not a conduit for power? So that meant she could use it, surely—if she could find it beneath Morg's ravaging blight. But to find it she'd have to abandon what remained of her pitiful defenses and pray she succeeded before Morg won.

*Oh, Da.*

Sick with terror, she stopped fighting. And of course Morg felt it, he felt her resistance collapse. Fury flashed to fresh triumph. His gleeful laughter thrummed her bones.

*Don't listen to him, Deenie. Listen to Barl instead.*

With that stubborn surviving sliver of mage-sense, with the slum-skumbledy part of herself that belonged to her mother, she embraced the scar Barl had left behind and reached for the memory of ancient Doranen power.

*Beautiful Elvado, the city of mages. Centuries of magic seeped into its bones.*

With a sharp pang she felt Morg's surprise, and then his explosion of anger for this one, small trick. She pushed his rage aside so it wouldn't distract.

*Help me, Barl. Help me. It'll be your victory too.*

She could feel Morg's searing blight and his passion for her destruction. She could hear herself screaming as he punished her with pain. It didn't matter. It couldn't matter. *This* mattered. Nothing else.

*Help me, Barl. Help me.*

And there it was. *There it was.* Doranen magic. Doranen power. Faint but unmistakable, faint but familiar, filling her with a strange sense of home. Shouting her relief, Deenie invited it in. And the magic poured through her, more powerful than blight.

Morg was howling. She opened her eyes. Towering above her, the sorcerer raged and flailed.

*You bitch, you slut, you treacherous whore!*

Instinct. Desperation. On a cry she lunged upwards and plunged her right hand through the shimmering evil before her.

*And the power . . . the power . . . the power coursing through her veins . . .*

Morg caught fire. He was a man turned to paper and she was the flame. He burned — he burned — he burned —

He died.

Biting his lip, Ewen shifted himself carefully so he wouldn't wake Charis. The wounds in his shoulder and hip burned with a constant, dull resentment, the pain not helped by the girl using his unhurt shoulder for a pillow — but he couldn't rid himself of her. The tears had dried on her hollow cheeks, but even asleep he could see she still grieved. The man she loved dead, her best friend taken away by beasts . . .

Her best friend. *Deenie.* He felt his own grief stir, waking his dull pain to a sharper suffering. The diary she gave him was pressed against his ribs.

Robb looked at him. "Captain?" he said softly, out of habit. "You all right?"

It was a fool question, and Robb knew it, but—"It's fine, I am."

"And it's sorry about the king, I am," said Robb, his mouth turned down. Hain, listening and not drowsing like his fellow barracks men, nodded agreement.

Letting his head rest against the dungeon wall, Ewen closed his eyes. "Murdo deserved a better death, he did." Like Padrig, and every brain-rotted soul fallen victim to the sorcerer. "But it's done, it is, Robb. Best let it go, I say."

As Robb nodded, accepting the gentle scold, Charis shifted against him, disturbed by their voices. Then she lifted her head. "Is she back? Is she all right?"

She chafed him like ungreased leathers, this girl did, but still he felt a surge of pity. "No. Charis—"

A terrible howl of agony burst out beyond their barred dungeon door. On and on and on it sounded, skincrawling and horribly inhuman. Robb leapt to his feet, the other barracks men right after. Charis scrambled up, then offered him her hand. Ewen hesitated, then wrapped his fingers round her wrist and let her help him to standing.

"It's the beasts," said Robb, his voice raised, and took a step towards the door. "Something's happened to the beasts, it has. D'you think—"

The terrible howling stopped. Fighting treacherous hope, they stared at each other.

"When Deenie's da killed Morg—well, scattered him," said Charis, the faintest thread of excitement in her voice, "his beasts dropped dead and vanished. Every last one."

Robb turned, fighting to keep his barracks man face. "So he's dead, you say? The sorcerer?"

"He might be," said Charis, suddenly cautious.

*Deenie.* Heart thudding, Ewen kept himself in hand. *Her lips on his. The sweetness of her smile.* "If his beasts are dead he must be, I say. And if he's dead—"

Charis shook her head. "No. Don't you say it. Don't you *dare.*" She clapped her hands to her ears. "I'm not listening to you, Ewen. I'm *not.*"

But she'd have to face the truth, sooner or later. If Morg was dead then Deenie had killed him with her filthy Words of UnMaking. And that meant . . .

In dreadful silence, they waited. And waited. And waited. Charis began weeping again, soundless tears sliding down her face. In the end Ewen returned to the floor, defeated by his wounds. And still they waited.

When at last the dungeon door opened, they thought at first it might be some kind of trick—especially when they saw who it was in the doorway.

"Arlin Garrick!" Charis spat. "What do *you* want?"

The Doranen mage looked exhausted. "It's over. Morg is dead." And when they gaped at him, unmoving, twisted his lips in a bitter smile. "And Deenie lives."

"Is that true?" Charis demanded. "Or do you think to sport with us, Arlin?"

Ewen glanced at her, approving. She'd stolen the words from his tongue.

The Doranen sighed. "It's true."

This time it was Robb who helped him onto his feet. Unevenly standing, shaken, he fixed the man with his coldest stare. "Take us to her."

"By all means, your Majesty," said the Doranen, with another twisted smile. "Follow me."

Garrick led them up empty stairways, along empty corridors and through empty halls until they reached a chamber at the end of another empty corridor. Its door stood open.

"After you," he said, pretending generosity.

Charis bolted inside, crying, "Deenie! Deenie!"

Ablaze with pain, needing Robb to lean on, Ewen followed her. His heart was pounding.

The lamplit chamber was a library, crowded with books. Morg— *no, remember, that's just Rafel now, it is*—lay on a low sofa. Deenie, kneeling beside him, turned at the sound of Charis's voice. Her left arm was bent and bound close to her chest, the pain of the injury plain to see. Another man hovered behind the sofa, an Olken from the look of him, with a foolishness in his face that spoke of a mind gone awry.

The girls embraced awkwardly, laughing and weeping. Then Deenie retreated so Charis could weep over the man she loved.

Robb stepped aside, leaving him to stand alone.

"Ewen," said Deenie, her smile a trembling, beautiful thing. Was she different? She looked different. But he couldn't say exactly how. "Did I worry you? It's sorry, I am."

He didn't care that he was hurting, bad enough to make him retch. He opened his arms and whispered her name and, when she ran to him, held her close through the tears and the pain.

Later, some four hours past dawn, after empty bellies were filled and wounds were treated and the aftermath of their captivity was dealt with, they gathered again in the comfortable library.

Thanks to Robb and Vharne's barracks men the dungeons of Elvado were emptied of the other kings and their servants and every living man, woman and child stolen into slavery. They'd fled soon after being freed, no matter their hurts, on foot and in horse-drawn carts. The once-empty city of Elvado was empty again, but for them.

Now Robb and his barracks brothers stood sentinel around the bookshelves. Looking at them, Tavin's trained and handpicked men, so self-contained and competent, Ewen thought he could burst with pride.

The Doranen, Arlin Garrick, who'd explained to Robb where to find the rest of Elvado's dungeons then disappeared about his own business, sat at one of the reading tables, a pile of parchments before him. Like Deenie, he was changed. His eyes were still shadowed but his torment had eased, and when he looked at her there was awe and a grudging respect.

Charis perched on the low sofa's edge, holding Rafel's hand. He still slept. Deenie's brother looked like a breathing corpse, he did, sunken eyes and sunken cheeks and not a word spoken, even in a dream. The foolish man, his friend Goose, sat on the floor by Rafel's feet, mumbling softly under his breath now and then. A tragedy, he was, and the luckiest man alive.

*Padrig.*

"I know I sound like a noddyhead," said Charis, shamefaced, "but —you're *sure* Morg's dead this time? He won't come back?"

Deenie exchanged looks with the Doranen. "I'm certain sure, Charis," she said quietly. "I felt him die."

There was a chasm of darkness beneath her simple words. Ewen felt his guts twist, hearing it. She sat beside him on a second sofa brought to the chamber, her broken collarbone set and bound by Hain, Tavin's best barracks healer, her hand warm in his, their knees lightly touching . . . but even so, she was leagues away.

*"I'll tell you one day what happened, Ewen. Just not today."*

He hadn't argued when she said it. How could he? But her silence left him cold with dread.

"So the sorcerer's properly defeated," he said. "What of his beasts? They're truly dead with him?"

"All dead," said Garrick, with a vicious satisfaction. "Never to come again."

*Unless you hanker after them, you do.*

As if he'd heard the thought, the mage stared at him. So haughty. Deenie was right, Arlin Garrick was an arrogant man. "Sorcery died with Morg. The world is scoured clean of blight."

Deenie pressed her lips to his cheek, careful not to touch his freshly salved wounds. "Don't fratch yourself, Ewen. Arlin won't betray us."

He had to believe she'd know.

"I want to go home," said Charis. "Can't we please go home?"

Deenie nodded, sombre. "Yes. Tomorrow."

Home. *Lur.* He looked down. Of course Deenie had to go. Her father was ailing. She had a people to save, just as he did. All those villagers lost in the rough. And Tavin waiting in the Vale, uneasy in the king's seat, not knowing if Murdo's son was alive or dead.

Only the thought of losing Deenie tore fresh wounds in his heart.

"Though I wonder how much of home is still standing," Charis added, her voice unsteady.

He felt Deenie shiver. "You mustn't think like that, Charis."

She was trying to keep faith, but he had his doubts. From what she'd told him of her small kingdom's sufferings, they'd be going home to heartbreak. Indeed, what she'd told him gave him pause for thought. But before he acted he'd have to consult Tavin, he would.

"Whatever we find, Ewen," said the arrogant Doranen, making free with his name, "you should know this. I intend to bring Lur's Doranen here, to Elvado. Dorana is our ancestral home and we have been away too long."

He straightened, disbelieving. "You'd make this a land of mages again? After *Morg*?"

"Ewen." Deenie's fingers tightened. "They have a right to a home, just as the Olken and the Vharne do. I'm sure once the dust has settled you and Arlin and your fellow kings can sit peaceably together and find common ground."

Unconvinced, he shook his head. "You say."

"And *I* say," Garrick said, his eyes sharp. "*Sorcery is dead.*"

Which was a simple thing to say, but who could know what mages yet unborn might dream of?

*But that's a worry for tomorrow, it is.*

Garrick tapped the parchments on the table before him. "I've retrieved from Morg's apartments some ancient spells Rafel brought with him over the mountains. Among them is the incant to send a man many leagues in a heartbeat, but I don't care to test it on so many at once, or this far from Lur." His gaze shifted to Deenie's brother, so silent, so still. "Nor do I care to risk anyone in frail health."

"Well, that's easy fixed, that is," said Deenie, less cheerful than she sounded. "Robb and his men kept back horses and carts, didn't they, Ewen? So we'll ride back to Vharne, all of us, and decide what's next when we get there."

\*     \*     \*

The last thing Deenie did before leaving Elvado was secure Morg's library with every binding incant she could find, finishing with a personal ward that only she could break. A reef legacy that she was pleased to claim, she said.

"And that's that," she told Arlin.

The arrogant Doranen was too clever to complain.

With Morg's beasts dead and no more wanderers to fear and the weather kind enough, if cold, they travelled straight through Dorana into Manemli, then into Vharne and on to the Vale. Fifty-one days, it took them, and in fifty-one days they saw no other living souls. Broken bones and torn flesh healed, Arlin Garrick minded his Doranen manners and they struck no trouble. Only Deenie's brother never spoke, though at long last he opened his eyes and could walk with some help. Charis and the foolish Goose between them saw to his care. Deenie seemed content to let them. Seemed content to drive one of the two carts and walk and ride a little, sometimes, and hunt for their supper when Robb and the barracks men came up empty handed. But when she thought no-one was looking, her face crumpled with grief and some dreadful memory. Heartsick, Ewen kept her secret and prayed that she'd find ease, that her father still lived and her addled brother would recover his wits.

In fifty-one days she said nothing of Morg.

This time, warned of his pupil's coming, Vharne's Swordmaster rode break-neck through the Vale's late morning sunshine to meet him.

Hurtled off his barracks mount, stood straddle-legged and weeping in the middle of the road where it crossed into the High Vale, Tavin bellowed a greeting.

"Boy! Boy! Is this your idea of timely, is it? Get off that horse so I can blade your skinny arse!"

As Robb and his barracks men chuckled into their fists, and Arlin Garrick looked down his Doranen nose, Deenie, riding beside him, raised one dark, purposeful eyebrow.

"That's an interesting way to talk to a king."

Ewen grinned. "That's Tavin, that is." Then he kicked his feet free of his stirrups. "Hold everyone here, girl—and take care of this nag."

As Tavin's arms closed around him he was sure his ribs would break, and when at last they stepped back from each other he was weeping too, unashamed.

"Boy," said Tavin, his breathing harsh, "it's lost I thought you were, I did."

He managed a shaky smile. "It's lost I thought I was, Tav, more times than I can count." Then his smile faded. "Murdo's dead, Swordmaster. I watched the sorcerer kill him."

"Spirit," Tavin murmured. "That's not an ending worthy of him. Son, it's sorry, I am."

He'd held the grief at bay for so long, feeling it now somehow made it harder to bear. He let himself take comfort from Tavin's comforting embrace. "You never did tell me what the rub was between you."

"And I won't," said Tavin, letting him go. "It's no matter now."

No. It wasn't. "Vharne held its own, did it, while I was gone?"

"Well enough," said Tavin. "Son, what's that you've done to your face?"

He touched fingertips to the puckered talon-scars. "Sliced myself shaving, I did."

"Careless," said Tav, going along with the joke. But his eyes weren't laughing. "Seems you've brought a crowd home with you."

"I have," he agreed. "See that girl on the horse?"

Purse-lipped, Tavin looked. "I do."

"That's Deenie. She killed Morg, she did."

"The sorcerer's dead?" Tavin whispered. "Ewen—"

"He is, Tav. I swear it."

"And *she* killed him?" Tavin's mouth dropped open. "That *girl*?"

He laughed. "A word to the wise, Tav. She's a mage, she is, and she doesn't take kindly to being called *girl*."

"A mage," Tavin said blankly. "Boy, are you run mad?"

Well, he'd never thought Tavin would take kindly to this at first glance. "It's a long story, Swordmaster. Cutting it quick, I'll tell you now — she's a mage, and her friend Charis in the cart is a mage, and so's her poorly brother, Rafel, he's in the cart with her friend, and *his* friend, Goose, well, he used to be a mage, and that snitty blond man driving the other cart? That's Arlin Garrick, that is, and he's a mage too. Only Tav? He's Doranen."

Tavin took a step back, hand shifting to his sword-hilt. "Is it Ewen, King of Vharne, you are? Or has the sorcerer sent me a changeling in his place?"

Slowly, deliberately, with one fist raised in a warning to Robb and the others, Ewen dropped to his knees in the road.

"I'm no changeling, Tavin. It's Murdo's son, I am, and Padrig's brother. I'm the King of Vharne and you're my beloved right hand. Look in my eyes, Tav. You'll find the truth there, you will. Or if you can't? Take my head. I won't stop you."

Tavin stared down at him in anguished silence, fingers clutching and loosening on his sword's hilt. "A *Doranen*?" he said at last, looking ready to spit. "Where are your wits, boy? A Doranen in Vharne?"

With his beast-clawed hip hardly paining him at all now, Ewen stood easily enough. "I'd still be kneeling before the sorcerer if it wasn't for him. Ride easy, old man. There's a lot more to tell, there is."

"That's as may be," said Tavin, glaring past him at Arlin Garrick. "But do I want to hear it?"

He kissed Tavin's stubbled cheek. "No. But you will, Tav. For me."

They rode for the castle side by side, leaving the others to follow in their wake. And as they rode he told Tavin most of what had happened since the day he left the Vale, and after that he explained what he had planned for the kingdom, and was patient as his swordmaster protested and swore and cursed him and argued. But in the end Tavin gave in, because he wasn't a foolish man and he knew, like it or not, what Vharne needed most.

"Only is it sure, you are, Ewen, I'm to have that girl *mage* me?"

Ewen shrugged. "Tav, I told you, the spell's on me and it's on Robb and Hain and the others, it is. It doesn't hurt. And you'd best believe it makes life less tricky. Besides, if it's leaving Charis and Rafel and that poor Goose behind with you, I am, what's the good of you never understanding a single word they say?"

Casting a glance over his shoulder, Tavin grimaced. "And it's bound to leave them behind you are, is it?"

"You won't ask me that once you clap eyes on Deenie's brother. He's not fit for more travelling. Tav —" He couldn't hide the shiver. "I thought what Padrig and the king suffered was bad, I did. And it was. It was bad. But *Rafel?*" Another shiver. "I'd rather burn alive than live through that, I would. He never stopped fighting Morg, Deenie says. No matter how the sorcerer hurt him, he stood firm. The Doranen says it too, he does, and there's no love lost there."

"Another long story?" said Tavin, sounding sour.

"Most like. It's heartsick for her brother Deenie is, and I can't see a thing to be done for him."

Riding through the afternoon's shadows, between the High Vale's green fields, *home*, Tavin thought about that. Then he raised his straggled eyebrows.

"So. It's tumbled into love with this Olken mage girl, have you?"

He'd not said a word about love. "*Charis?*" He showed Tavin his horror. "That scold? Bite my head off soon as look at me, Swordmaster, *she* would."

And that bit of play-acting earned him a stern look. "*Ewen.*"

He should've remembered who he was talking to. "And if I am in love with Deenie?" he said quietly. "That's tricky for you, is it?"

Tavin grunted. "Expect me to answer when I've not swapped three words with the girl, do you?" He rubbed his chin. "Son, if you love her she's a girl worth loving, she is. But that doesn't make her any less of a mage. And what the Vale will say to it? To any of it? That's a puzzle, that is."

"The Vale will smile about it, Tav," he said, not in the mood to hear otherwise. "And so will the rough. Her people feel our spirit paths. There's a meaning in that, I say."

Tavin nodded, and didn't say any more.

They rode in silence for a time, with the sun in their faces and the carts creaking behind them. Foolish Goose sang some ale songs in a cracked, deep voice.

"Charis thinks he'll get Rafel talking, she does," said Ewen. "Best friends they were, Deenie says. Good as brothers."

"Sad it is, that," Tavin agreed. "Son . . . what haven't you told me?"

So many lonely weeks he'd lived through without Tavin's rough guidance. He had to wait a moment, and just breathe.

"Deenie," he said, making sure to keep his voice down. "She won't tell me what happened when she killed Morg."

Tavin let out a long, slow sigh. "And these secrets, boy. Mage secrets or woman secrets are they, do you know?"

"You're asking if I trust her? Clap tongue, Tavin. That's a stupid question, I say."

Another sigh, impatient this time. "And if you trust her, boy, does it matter how long it takes her to tell you?"

"No," he muttered, scowling.

"Then you clap tongue," said Tavin. He pointed. "Look. You're home."

And there it was, bright in the distance, the king's castle in the Vale, set on gently rising ground, its slate roof shiny in the sun. He lost sight of it through a blur of tears, lost the sound of horses and cartwheels in the pounding of his heart.

Spinning his nag on its haunches, he kicked it back to Deenie. She was driving her brother's cart now.

"What is it?" she said, startled. "Is something wrong?"

He shook his head, close to laughter. "Give the cart to Charis to drive and climb on behind me."

Nimble, she handed over the reins, slid to the horse and closed her arms around his waist. As he urged their nag back into a canter, clattering down the road past Tavin without a pause, she leaned a little sideways.

"We had a castle," she said, over the horse's drumming hooves. "It fell to pieces. So did my home."

She'd not told him that before. For all the things she'd told him, there was still so much he didn't know. Reins in one hand, he covered her fingers with his.

"Then we'll find you a new home, girl," he said. "One that can't fall down."

He heard her shaking, indrawn breath. "You promise?"

"I promise."

She kicked their horse into a gallop.

# CHAPTER THIRTY

※

Ewen saw Rafel settled in the room that used to be his brother's. And once he was settled, with a gentle *"Find me if you need me, Deenie'*, withdrew so she could sit and have some private time with him before she had to leave for Lur in the morning.

"I'll give Da your best love, Rafe," she said, holding his cool, disinterested hand between her own. "He'll be so pleased to know you're on the mend."

*If he's still alive. If I haven't lost him too, along with everything else.*

Rafe was sleeping again. Barl save him, he did so very little except sleep. And even when he was awake, he wasn't really *awake*. He wasn't *Rafe*. He was a wax doll who looked like Rafe.

*And this is Morg's revenge, I think. This is me and Da and Rafe punished 'cause we wouldn't give in. Oh, Rafe.*

His hair was clipped short again. Charis had done it, Arlin's scissors held in trembling fingers as she hacked and hacked and hacked. Hoping that with his hair Rafe-length again he'd look more like himself and less like Morg. And he did, there was no doubt.

Only it would be a long time before she'd forget Morg's crimson marble dais in that black chamber, and the brain-rotted wanderers, and Ewen's father as he died.

512

"It wasn't you, Rafe. I know it wasn't you," she whispered. "But you were in there. You couldn't stop him. And I know that's why you won't come back."

Or it was part of why he'd not come back.

"I know you're hurt, too. I know he hurt you worse than ever, at the end, 'cause of me. 'Cause I fought him. But I had to fight him, Rafe. You *wanted* me to fight him. And now I want *you* to fight. You *have* to fight, or else it's just me. I know there's Ewen, but that's a leaky boat. Or it could be. I don't know yet. Rafe, you can't leave me alone. If you do, I'll be so *fratched . . .*"

His eyes were closed. Was he listening, or sleeping? And if he was listening could he even understand?

Goose understood. Goose was getting a little better, she thought. Charis thought he was. And Arlin. So that was cause for hope. Though he'd never be *Goose* again, not the way he was. But she couldn't complain. Not after Ewen's father and brother. Ewen was pleased about Goose, for her sake, but she could feel the splintered pain in him whenever he looked at Rafe's friend.

*Every time he looks at Goose he feels his dagger thudding home in Padrig's heart. He sees his father, dying.*

And there was nothing she could do about that.

She lifted Rafe's hand to her cheek and pressed it there, frighted. Would this be her life, now? Was she about to become her mother, trapped in a silent chamber with a man who'd never speak? Or would that fate fall to Charis, her best friend, so steadfast in her love?

Swallowing fresh grief, Deenie hid her face against her brother's slowly rising and falling chest.

*Please, Rafe. Please. You have to come back.*

She heard the chamber door creak open. Thinking it was Charis, so there was no need to hide, she kept herself pillowed on Rafe.

"Deenie. I'm sorry to disturb you but I wanted a word."

*Arlin.* She snapped up straight. Took a moment before showing him her face. "Yes?"

He closed the door. "It's about returning to Lur."

Arlin looked so *peculiar* dressed in borrowed Vharne leathers. The few clothes they'd travelled with from Elvado were rags, or nearly. They'd all been given castle or barracks clothes to wear. Discreetly inspecting him, dressed in her own barracks man trews and shirt, she hid a dry smile.

*Leathers or velvet, he'll always be Arlin.*

"Yes? What about it?"

Standing just over the threshold, he was careful to keep his gaze away from Rafel. "Did you know Ewen — the king — intends on coming with us?"

Was there any use pretending in front of this man? She thought prob'ly not. He knew her, and she knew him, in ways that would never leave them comfortable.

"No."

"Ah. Then if you don't like it, I'll refuse to take him."

*Why* wouldn't he look at Rafe? 'Cause he still saw Morg, even with the long hair gone? 'Cause he still blamed Rafe for so much, and couldn't let it go? Or was it 'cause he blamed himself for Rafe's suffering?

*It's all of that, I reckon. And there ain't a thing I can do to help him, either.*

She tipped her head a little. "You think I can't use that fancy travelling spell, Arlin?"

"I have no doubt you could," he replied. "But I thought it might be more comfortable if the refusal came from me. If you wanted to refuse."

*Dear Ewen.* "I don't."

All those weeks on the road and not once had she and Arlin talked of what happened in Morg's eyrie. Of what had happened before that, in the time he'd been Morg's faithful servant.

Still holding Rafe's hand, she sat back in her chair. "Is there anything you wanted to ask me, Arlin?"

Pale and silent, wearing rough leathers like silk, Arlin stared at her. Then he shook his head. "No."

"Is there anything you want to *tell* me?"

Another headshake. "No." His lips twisted in that small, bitter *Arlin* smile. "Anything you feel like telling me, Deenie?"

She looked at Rafel. "No."

"Then I suggest you find your bed early," he said. "It's likely tomorrow will prove itself . . . grim."

Charis did come in, soon after Arlin departed. Goose was with her, faithful shadow at her heels. "He's still sleeping?"

Letting go of Rafe's hand, Deenie slid from the chair. "Yes. Still."

"You're not to worry about him while you're gone," Charis said, taking her place at the bedside. Goose stood behind her, one protective hand on her shoulder. "King Noddyhead's promised us all the soup and soft blankets we need. Goose and me, we'll keep him safe. You see about your da, and about Lur. Deenie—" Her voice was shaking. "What are we going to do if it's all ruined?"

She couldn't bring herself to think on that. "I don't know. Let's hope it isn't, eh?"

Leaving Charis and Goose to their vigil, she went in search of Ewen. A castle maid said His Majesty was in the Hall, but when she found her way there she only found his swordmaster, Tavin.

"Girl," he said, not standing out of his chair at the rough-hewn table. Once returned to the castle he'd let himself be spelled to understanding. Hadn't liked it overmuch. She thought he didn't like her.

*But Ewen loves him, so . . .*

"Swordmaster," she said politely. "I'm looking for Ewen."

A grizzled bear of a man, he was, with scars and memories she didn't want to share. "He's not here."

"Can I wait?"

"It's a mage you are, girl," he said. "Seems to me you can do what you want, I say."

"Thank you."

She crossed the Hall's flagstones to the flame-leapt fireplace and stood with her back to the welcome heat. Tavin pretended to busy himself again with his quill and parchment, but really he was watching her. The game lasted only a few minutes. Dropping the quill, not caring for splattered ink, he planted his elbows on the table and stared at her, unblinking.

"Just one thing I want from you, girl. One thing. If you give it me, we'll untangle the rest as we go, I say. But if you don't? If you can't? Then we'll be in the tiltyard, you and me."

If she smiled, she'd offend him. He'd never accept she wasn't mocking, only seeing an odd reflection in him of a fussy ole man who complained and stamped about and loved without reservation.

"Swordmaster," she said, softly, "I'll never hurt him. Not on purpose, any road. He's in my heart, he is."

Ewen entered the Hall while Tavin was still staring.

She turned to him. "Arlin says you want to come with us to Lur."

"I do," he said, cautious. "I was looking for you to talk on it."

"There's nothing to talk on. Come."

Relaxing, he smiled at her—but beneath his smile she could feel pain. He wanted her to confide in him. He wanted her to tell him about killing Morg and the ways that had changed her. 'Cause it had, and he knew it. *She* knew it.

*I just don't want to say.*

Instead she borrowed from Arlin. "I'm to bed, now. You shouldn't stay up late either. The magic to get us home—to Lur, I mean—it's powerful. Best you're rested for it. And when we get there, well . . . I don't know what we'll find."

He stopped her in passing, and lightly kissed her lips. Despite the salve, those talon-wounds in his face had scarred. Every time she saw them, she wanted to magic them away.

"Whatever we find, Deenie?" he whispered. "You'll not bear it alone."

And what they found was utter destruction.

"*Arlin,*" said Deenie, one hand pressed to her mouth, eyes flooding with shocked tears.

Though he'd never made a secret of his disdain for Lur, even Rodyn

Garrick's arrogant son looked shaken at the sight greeting them as they stepped out of magic and into Dorana City's desolate Market Square.

Gaping holes. Ripped up, buckled cobbles. Piles and piles and piles of rubble. Bricks and tiles and glass and timber. The few buildings that had survived that last enormous tremor hadn't survived the tremors that came after. Nothing was left standing. The air smelled rank and old and rotten. Storm clouds clotted the sky and beneath their feet, the soaked earth shivered. Not a soul stirred. Not a sound but their own breathing. Dorana City was abandoned.

"I don't see any mageworking that can fix this," Arlin said at last. "Not even Morg could have fixed this."

Chilled to her marrow, Deenie banished grief. "No."

*Not Morg, or Rafel, even if he was himself. I doubt the three of us, Rafe and me and Da, could fix this.*

"Deenie . . ." Ewen slid his arm around her shoulders. "It's sorry, I am."

She shrugged free of him. She couldn't risk his sympathy. Not now. She had to stay strong.

*Da, please. Don't be dead.*

"Arlin, do you know Billington?"

Wary, he shifted his gaze from the ruins. "I know of it. Why?"

"Da's there. Will you take me? Is it safe to use the incant again so soon?"

"Safe?" He raised an eyebrow. "For me or for you?"

She bit her lip. *Poxy shit.* "For us all, Lord Garrick."

"I don't know," he said, his eyes glittering. "Shall we find out?"

And it was safe enough, though the journey left them twice as dizzy.

They found ruin in Billington, too. Uprooted trees, a handful of toppled buildings. Maybe half the township's streets turned into humps and holes. Not as bad as Dorana City, but even so . . .

Seeing it, Deenie felt a welling of despair. Was all of Lur ruined? If she took the ancient Doranen incant and magicked herself the length and breadth of the kingdom, would she find nothing but heartbreak and destruction?

*I think I would. I think Lur's truly dying.*

And yet again, she was fighting back tears.

Standing in the middle of the township's main street, pointed and stared at by cowering, startled Olken, Ewen ran a hand down his scarred face.

"Morg did this, you say?"

"Not directly," said Arlin. "But when he broke Barl's Weather Magic he started the rot."

"I thought Vharne was troubled, I did. But this?"

"Yes," Deenie said shortly. "It's far worse than I dreamed."

This time Ewen knew better than to touch her. "It's a fool I feel like, saying it, but — Deenie, I'm sorry."

"I know you are."

"It's still blighted is it, your kingdom?"

And it wasn't until Ewen asked the question that she realised. "No. No, it's not. At least, not like before. I can still feel it, taste it, but . . ." She wrinkled her nose. "It's not growing."

Arlin looked at her. "You think you killed the blight when you killed Morg?"

*Burning and burning, his screams echoing in her mind.*

"I don't know. Maybe." Leaving him and Ewen, she crossed the street to accost the nearest startled Olken. "You. I'm sorry, I don't know your name. The hospice here. Is it still standing?"

The woman nodded, torn between fear and fascination as she gaped at Ewen. "Who's he, then? Where's he from? He's got *red hair.*"

Deenie nodded. "Yes. He has." And while that might be the first time she heard someone say so, already she suspected it wouldn't be the last. "He's a friend. Please. The hospice?"

"That way," said the woman, still gaping, and flapped a vague hand. "Ask for Pother Brye. Meistress—"

Deenie turned back. "Yes?"

"Who are *you?*"

There seemed little point in keeping it secret. "I'm Deenie. I'm Asher's daughter."

Many of the townsfolk heard her say it. They stopped staring at Ewen and stared at her instead.

"Asher?" said the woman. "The Innocent Mage? Ain't he dead? Him and his son and his wife, the word was, all three." Her careworn face softened. "You poor child, you. Orphaned." And then she hugged herself. "There's a mortload of orphans in Lur these days."

"I have to go," she said, hearing her voice faint and disbelieving. "I'm sorry. I'll help you all as soon as I can."

One look at her face and Ewen snatched hold of her arm. "Deenie?"

"The hospice is this way," she muttered. "We have to hurry."

She broke into a run, heedless of maybe twisting an ankle or worse. Arlin swore, then he and Ewen ran after her.

Though countless weeks had passed since she'd been here, and then only the once, instinct guided her back to the hospice. And terror sent her barging through its front doors and into the entrance hall, shouting for Pother Brye. Startled pothers who weren't Brye hurried to hush her and find out what she wanted.

"I want Brye!" she snapped. "Are you deaf?"

"Steady, girl," murmured Ewen, as Arlin stepped well out of the way. "Setting the place in an uproar, you are."

"I don't care! I want to see Pother Brye and—"

"And here I am," said a calm voice. "Barl be praised, child. Barl be praised. We long ago gave you up for dead. Lur has mourned Asher's daughter. And now we can rejoice!"

In the weeks she'd be gone he'd lost more of his blond hair, and the lines on his face were carved even deeper. Staring at him, suddenly speechless, Deenie felt herself trembling so hard she thought she'd break her healed collarbone. She tried to speak, but her teeth were chattering with fright. She could hardly feel Ewen's hand holding hers. The words were crowded in her throat.

*Is he here? Does he live?*

"Fear not, child," Brye told her, smiling. "We have your father. And he's awake."

If Ewen hadn't pulled her against him, she'd have fallen to the floor.

*Awake. Awake.* "What does he know?" she said faintly. "What have you told him?"

"That your brother vanished, child, and you vanished after him."

And if Ewen hadn't still been holding her, she might have slapped the old Doranen. "*Why?* Why would you tell him that, why would you—"

Movement behind the pother, in one of the hospice's shadowed doorways. She felt her breath catch, her heart thump.

Slowly, painfully, a man stepped into the light, dressed in baggy woollen trews and a linen shirt. Medium height. A fratchsome tilt to his chin. Broad shoulders and blunt, capable fisherman's hands.

"*Da*," she said, and ran to him.

They held each other, weeping. He was thin, he was so *thin*. But then so was she. They'd snap each other to pieces if they held on too tight.

At last she let go of him, and stepped back, and stared into his— oh, his thin face. And his hair, he'd gone almost all grey, and there was a cloudiness in his dark, sunken eyes.

"Da . . ." She shook her head, disbelieving. "How did this happen? How are you healed?"

"It's a miracle," said Pother Brye, stepping a little closer. "He was sinking, fast. Not a posset or a potion we gave him made a difference. We'd abandoned hope. And then out of nowhere, Deenie, some seven weeks ago, your father burst into a terrible high fever. In all my years of pothering, I've never seen anything like it. Then the fever broke, as swiftly as it came on him . . . and he revived. His return to health has been slow and steady ever since."

A fever? Was it Morg's burning, then? The timing fit. And that meant she'd been right all along, she had. It was the sorcerer's blight in him that kept him so ill . . . and when Morg died, like all his workings it had died with him and set Da free.

*Praise Barl. Praise Barl.*

"Mouse?" Da's thin fingers came up to touch her cheek. He was smiling. She never thought to see him smile again. "Was it you?"

She nodded, then turned to Pother Brye. "I need a few moments with Da alone. Somewhere we can sit."

"There's my chamber," said Da. "We can sit there, mouse." Then his clouded gaze shifted past her. "Sink me. *Arlin Garrick?*"

She kissed his cheek. "I'll explain everything, I promise."

"And who's that makin' sheep's eyes at you?" he said, frowning. "He's got *red hair.*"

*Oh, Da.* "Yes, but it's very nice red hair. Come on. You should sit down."

With a flicking glance at Ewen and Arlin — *stay right there* — she retreated with her father to his small, airy chamber. Da sat on the bed and she took the room's small chair. Where to start, where to start . . .

"I found Rafe," she said, leaning forward and taking his hands. "He's poorly, but he's mending." *Please, please, let him be mending.* "Charis is nursing him. Her and Goose. Poor Goose, he's—"

But Da wasn't listening. His eyes had lost focus, tears sliding down his cheeks. "You found him," he whispered. "You found my boy. *Mouse.*"

She could never get tired of hearing that silly pet name.

"Da?" She tightened her fingers. "Da—I killed Morg."

He stared at her in silence so long that his tears of joy for Rafel dried on his cheeks. "He weren't dead?"

"No." She had to tell him all of it. She couldn't lie, not to Da. Even the softer, kinder lie of holding back the full truth. "Da, he took Rafe. The way he took Durm, then Conroyd Jarralt."

And of a sudden, right in front of her, there was Asher, the Innocent Mage, his unleashed mage-sense roaring through him. Shocked, she let go of his hands as he trembled with fury, with the power he'd kept hidden from her all her life.

*I never knew. I never realised. Rafe never said.*

"And *that's* why Rafe's poorly?" Da demanded. "'Cause that filth, that monster, he—he—"

"Da, Da, don't fratch yourself! Da, I told you, he'll be all right!"

Abruptly exhausted, Da slid off the bed to the floor. Frantic, Deenie dropped out of the chair beside him and grabbed his hands again, chafing them warm.

"Deenie . . ." Now his voice was cracked and hoarse. He sounded old. "You tell me the truth, mouse. Morg don't ride a man and leave him right as rain after. That don't happen. You tell me the truth."

So she told him. And then she wept with him.

At last, Da sighed and looked at her. "Mouse? Why weren't Morg dead?"

*Sink it*. She'd hoped he'd not think to ask. She'd hoped that was one truth she'd never have to share. But she had to, so she told him, and held his hand while he grieved anew.

"Bloody Gar," he muttered. "Bloody Doranen. Always think they know best. And he died for *nowt*."

"Well—not *nowt*, Da," she said, carefully. "'Cause if he hadn't, there wouldn't be me. And there wouldn't be Rafe."

Da snorted. "Aye. That's true."

"So could be prophecy had its reasons for things working out the way they did."

"*Prophecy?* Mouse, if you love me, don't you say that sinkin' word again."

She lifted his hand and kissed it. "Sorry. I won't, I promise."

"*Good.*"

And now there was just one last terrible thing to tell him. She felt her heart thud. "Da—"

He patted her knee. "It's all right, mouse. I know."

"You *know?* About Mama? How could you know? Did Pother Brye—"

Da's smile was so gentle. Now he kissed *her* hand. "Your mother told me, Deenie. She came to me in a dream."

Stunned, she stared at him. "Oh." She didn't know what else to say.

Side by side on the hospice chamber floor, holding hands, they mourned their dreadful loss.

After some time, Da shifted a little. "Arlin Garrick."

Deenie felt her lips curve, just a little. "A poxy shit. That much ain't changed."

"But?"

"But in his own way, Da, he got himself hurt as bad as Rafe did." Then she sighed. "It's a tangled tale, what happened. And there're parts I don't want to tell twice." Didn't want to tell once, but there was no sailing around it. "So I'm wondering . . ."

"Who is he, then?" said Da, sounding resigned.

And now she was shy. Now she felt like the old Deenie, who'd not say boo to a cat. "His name's Ewen. He's the king of Vharne. It's a kingdom over the mountains, past the blighted lands. Me and Charis fetched up there, looking for supplies."

"And instead you found him?"

"He's a good man, Da. I'd have sunk without him. It's his castle Rafe's in now, mending."

Da grunted. "And he's got red hair. *Long* red hair."

"And a swordmaster named Tavin. You'd like him, I reckon. I reckon you'll like Ewen."

Another grunt. "Do you? Well, *I* reckon prob'ly we've sat in here on our lonesome long enough."

He was prob'ly right, only . . . 'Da? There is one last thing." And since it was easier to do than to explain, she touched his forehead and spelled him to understanding.

"Sink me!" He blinked at her. "What was that?"

She shrugged. "Nowt much. A little trick I picked up." And reminded, she pulled Barl's diary out of its hiding place inside her shirt. "From this."

Eyes slitted, Da stared at it. Then he stared at her. "And what's your little trick do, ezackly?"

"It lets folk from different places understand each other. It's the spell Barl used when the Doranen first crossed the mountains."

"Deenie—" Da swallowed. "Gar never translated any spell like that."

"I know," she said softly. "Like I said, Da. It's a tangled tale. I'd have kept you from it, if I could."

A terrible sadness washed over him. "Ah, Deenie. My tiddy mouse."

She kissed his cheek. "Don't fratch on it, Da. It was for the best, in the end."

Ewen and Arlin, at opposite ends of a bench in the now potherless entrance hall, stood as she and Da came out of his small chamber. Walking slowly, but with all his familiar purpose, Da ignored Ewen and crossed to Arlin instead.

Deenie held her breath.

Silence, as Da looked at him, and Arlin looked back. But if she listened carefully, the roar of a whirlpool . . .

"Arlin," said Da, nodding.

Arlin nodded back. "Asher."

And that was that.

Scowling, Da turned to Ewen. "So. Meister King of Vharne. Makin' sheep's eyes at my daughter, are you?"

"*Da*," she said, anguished, but Ewen just laughed.

"I am, I say. If she'll have me."

Da blinked, once, feeling the new magic in him work. Then he shrugged, and jutted his chin. "Oh, aye. And will she?"

Ewen shrugged, his eyes glinting. "Ask her, you should."

"Reckon I don't need to, Ewen," said Da. "Reckon I know my tiddy mouse well enough." And then he scowled again. "And I reckon she'll be livin' in this kingdom of yours. In your castle, where you're givin' care to my son, I'm told."

"Your son's earned every care I can give him, I say," said Ewen, gently. "He's a man to be proud of, Rafe is."

Deenie, watching, couldn't remember the last time she saw her father pushed so close to tears like this.

"But it's not just Deenie I'd have come live with me in Vharne," Ewen added. "I'd offer a place in my kingdom to any Olken who wanted one, I would."

"*What?*" Deenie stepped forward, astonished. "Ewen, when did you—"

"In Morg's dungeon," he said, his smile warm and intimate. "What you said of Lur, it got me to thinking, it did. I wondered what you'd find here after so long away. Asher—" He looked at Da. "I'm a king of empty cottages, I am. Morg killed most of us, in his time. We've folk in the Vale, but out in the rough? The rough's empty, it is. Deenie'll tell you, she will. Plenty of space for the Olken to start over."

"But Ewen—" Reeling, Deenie stepped closer. "Your people. They don't trust mages."

He shrugged. "They can learn, girl. I did, didn't I?"

"Well, yes, but—" She was too shocked to pay attention to his teasing. "Leave Lur? Start again, in a strange land? Ewen, I'm not sure you understand what you're asking. Your people and mine, we have so little in common."

"It's everything in common, we've got," Ewen retorted. "Everything that matters, I say. Your kingdom and mine, smashed to pieces by a sorcerer. Your people and mine, trying to rebuild. And Deenie—don't forget the spirit paths."

*The spirit paths?* "What about them?"

His green-gold eyes saw only her. They might've been alone in the wilderness, for all he cared they were stared at. Closing the distance between them, he cupped his palm to her cheek. "We feel them. You feel them. That means something, I say."

And was this prophecy again, sticking an oar in their lives? "I s'pose."

He smiled, making her heart pound. "My people, they'll listen to me and Tavin, they will. Yours—they'll listen to you and your da. Won't they?"

"They'll listen to Da," she said. "Da's the closest thing to a king Lur's got."

Da growled at her. "Don't you go bloody callin' me a king, mouse! Ain't I said that for the last twenty years and gone? Sink me, you be a slumskumbledly wench."

"Yes, Da," she said, unrepentant. "Mama's doing, that is."

He smiled at that, but it didn't last long. "It all sounds promisin'," he said to Ewen, scowling again. "But here's the thing. The Olken ain't the only folk as live in Lur." He jerked a thumb at Arlin. "What about his lot?"

The warmth died out of Ewen's face. "The Doranen. I know."

"My people aren't interested in living anywhere but Dorana," said Arlin.

"Oh, aye?" said Da, his spine snapping straight. "So you can set yourselves up as lords of the world again, eh? Ain't that what your da always dreamed of, Arlin? Ain't that what—"

"My father's dreams and mine are . . . different," said Arlin, very quiet. Remarkably subdued. "I give you my word, Asher. As a Garrick. There will be no more Morgs. There will be no more . . . *lording.*"

"Da." Deenie rested her hand on his arm. "He said the same thing in Dorana. I believed him then, and I believe him now."

"You do, mouse?" Da considered her, unconvinced. "And why's that?"

She looked at Arlin, who was a great deal more than just a poxy shit. "'Cause he knows now that some dreams cost too much."

Arlin said nothing to that, but his watchful eyes softened. For a moment, no more.

"Well," said Da, shoving his hands in his pockets, "here's what I reckon. You can make your folk the offer, Meister Garrick, but that don't mean they have to leave. Whoever wants to stay in Lur, Doranen or Olken, let 'em stay. It's their choice. A fool's choice, it might turn out, 'cause this poor land's done for. But I'll have no arm-twistin' either road. Agreed?"

Arlin nodded. "Agreed."

"And you," said Da, turning on Ewen. "Meister King Sheep's Eyes. There's a boatload of this 'n' that for you and me to talk on. Slumguzzled me sideways with this offer of Vharne, you have. But so long as it's understood that any Olken as comes is just as free to go if it turns out your tiddy kingdom ain't his boatload of mackerel, then we can start talkin', I reckon."

Ewen looked at Da, then turned. "That understanding spell of yours, Deenie. Wears off after a while, does it?"

And oh, it felt so *sinkin'* good to laugh. "No."

"No?" Ewen raised an eyebrow. "So that was a yes, it was?"

Standing tiptoe, she kissed him. "Aye, Ewen. I reckon it was."

But it was one thing to decide the fate of Lur's Olken and Doranen in a hospice — and quite another to decide it in Lur.

Firstly, even using in part the Doranen travel incant, it took nearly two weeks for word to spread to every township and village that a momentous decision had to be made. Then came more weeks of debate and argument and compromise and fisticuffs, at least for the Olken.

Deenie travelled to each meeting place with Asher and Ewen, patiently answering questions, talking through what their people's choice was, what they'd be gaining in starting a new life in Vharne, what they'd be losing if they left Lur behind. She began to think she could cast Barl's spell of understanding in her sleep.

She fretted over her father, who wasn't strong yet, and might never be. Not the way he'd been strong before he was struck down by the blight. But there she was helped by Ewen, who kept a watchful eye on him and with a grin overruled Da when he was determined to do too much. And though Da blustered, claiming great offence, she knew it was for show.

The weather helped make the Olken's decision less complicated. Though Morg's blighting magic was dead, its echoes stubbornly lingered. There were more storms, more heavy rain, more flooding, more deaths. Much of Lur was poisoned and might never be clean again. Food supplies grew ever scarcer. Sheer hunger prompted many to take the chance.

Nigh on four weeks after the first meeting was called, every Olken in the kingdom had cast a ballot, yea or nay. And in the end less than a thousand decided to stay behind the mountains and inside the reef. The rest of Lur's Olken fell to with their preparations, having agreed to travel by boat, in relays, along the coast until they reached their new home. With Lur's waters at last free of whirlpools and waterspouts it was the best way for the great adventure to begin.

For the Doranen, as Arlin had always claimed, there was nothing to discuss. They were chastened by the news of Morg's resurgence and death but once told of their rediscovered lost homeland, they were eager to quit Lur.

And quit it they did, using magic.

Arlin was the last to leave. With Deenie, Asher and Ewen making ready for their sea voyage to Vharne, ahead of everyone else so the groundwork could be laid, he travelled down to newly bustling Westwailing to make his brief, circumspect farewell.

Greeting him out front of the Dancing Dolphin, Deenie looked his sunlit silks and velvets up and down. "D'you know, Meister Garrick, I think I prefer you in leathers."

He looked down his nose. "And I think, Meistress Deenie, it's a good thing for both of us that I no longer need to care what you think."

"Sink me bloody sideways, Arlin," she said, sighing. "You really *are* a poxy shit."

Da was waiting for them in the Dolphin's shabby parlour.

"So, Meister Garrick," he said, at ease in a comfortable chair, "this is the back of you, we're seeing?"

"For now," said Arlin, just as comfortable on his feet. "There will be conversations at a later date. Treaties and so forth between Dorana and its many neighbours."

"Aye," said Da, nodding. "So Ewen says. And Deenie here—" Reaching out, he patted her arm. "She reminds me that she trusts you, Meister Garrick, and I've got no cause to fratch on you or any Doranen or them nasty books of magic Morg left behind."

"And she's right, Asher," said Arlin, frowning. "The past is the past. You have nothing to fear from me or mine."

"Oh, aye? Well, that's good to hear," said Da, and then he leaned forward. "Now you hear this, Arlin. My hair's gone grey but I'm still a mage. Rafel? Poorly or not, he's a mage too. And Deenie? Well, we all know *she's* a mage, don't we? And we'll be watching you and yours, Meister Garrick. 'Cause one mage like Morg is one mage too many. And it ain't likely we'll be lettin' him happen again any time soon."

"Da," Deenie said, when a tight-lipped Arlin had banged the parlour door shut behind him. "Did you really have to say that?"

Tugging her into his lap, he pressed a swift kiss to the top of her head. "Aye, mouse. I did. Now, what say we head on down to the harbour? 'Cause that red-haired king of yours might be a dab hand at swordplay and suchlike, but when it comes to sailin'? He's got a few tiddy things to learn. And if he ain't managed to tangle hisself upside down in some rigging by now, then my name ain't Asher of Restharven. And I be tolerably sure it is!"

"Oh, *Da*!" she said, and slid from his lap. "Is that any way to talk of the man I love, is it?"

He scowled. "Mouse, it's the *only* bloody way to talk of him, I reckon."

Hand in hand, laughing, they went to find Ewen.

# EPILOGUE

Two days later they sailed a small, refurbished smack out of West-wailing harbour, looking to follow Lur's calm and kindly coastline past the quiet reef and all the way up to Vharne.

Proper sailing with Da for the first time in her life, in waters empty of 'spouts and whirlpools and blight, Deenie felt the hurt of the past weeks ease a bit. And watching her father come alive, sailing, seeing the fresh colour in his cheeks and the rekindled spark in his eyes, she wept a little. Despite everything, he was happy. *Properly* happy. He'd found his true self.

*Look, Mama. Ain't that grand?*

Da praised her sailing skills, and his pride in her helped keep sorrow at bay. So did laughing at Ewen, who was no sailor born and bred and most likely never would be. But he tried, and she loved him for it. Loved Da for teaching him, and helping him overcome the terrible loss of his father and brother.

"He's a proper man, he is, Asher of Restharven," said Ewen, as they shared the stars on the third night of sailing, with Da tactfully snoring in his tiddy captain's cabin. The breeze was lively, keeping the sail fat-bellied and tickling them with salt.

She rested her head on his shoulder. "Aye."

"There's a lot of him in you."

"And Mama," she said softly. "What's best in me I get from them."

His arm tightened around her. "Sell yourself short there, you do."

"Maybe," she said. "But not by much. I wish you could've known her, Ewen. I wish I could've known your father, and Padrig." She sighed. "We've so much to be grateful for, I know that, but . . ."

"There's no sunshine without shadow," said Ewen. "Not a one of us gets everything we want."

He sounded sad, yet somehow at peace. As though he'd found a way to make sense of all that had happened. Found a way to grieve without losing hold of their blessings.

*And if he has, so can I.*

Reaching Vharne at last, with daylight dwindling to dusk, they anchored in a small, deepwater inlet that Tavin had seen prepared for them. Then she used the Doranen part of herself to whisk them to Ewen's castle in the High Vale.

As they stepped out of magic and into the torchlit forecourt, Rafel emerged from the castle to greet them. Dressed in barracks man leathers, he was still thin, still pale—but he was himself again.

He smiled. "Da?"

Deenie heard her father sob something under his breath. She thought it was *Dathne* but she couldn't be sure. Then he crossed the forecourt with the stride and speed of a much younger man, arms wide. Rafe rushed to meet him halfway. A heartbeat later they were holding each other, and she could scarcely see anything because she was weeping too hard.

*See, Mama? We're a family. We're a family again.*

Charis and Goose came out of the castle next, both of them proud and tearful. There was even a hint of strength now in Goose's soft, foolish face. Tavin followed, and the castle secretary, Clovis. They waited, and she waited, Ewen holding her hand tight, while Rafe and Da convinced each other that this was real, and they both lived.

Then Da let go, and it was her turn to greet her miraculous brother. At first she couldn't say anything useful. All she could do was pound her fist against his leather chest and call him a noddyhead. Tiring of that, he pulled her close and rested his cheek on her hair.

"Deenie. Gardenia."

She'd called him noddyhead, a lot of times, so she couldn't complain. Easing back, she looked up into his altered face, his shadowed eyes. Showed him only what he needed to see, his feisty little sister.

"I'm so proud of you, Rafe. There ain't a brother in the wide world I'd rather have than you."

His trembling smile came close to breaking her heart.

"Goose looks brighter," she said, thinking to cheer him. Instead he bit his lip, stricken.

"It's my fault, Deenie," he said, his voice low so the others wouldn't hear. "What's happened to him. I'm to blame. I swear, I'll go to Arlin Garrick if I have to but I'll find a way to undo what Morg did."

She kissed him. *"We'll* find a way, Rafe. I promise."

"Charis and the swordmaster told me what's going on," he said, wide-eyed. "Are you sure about this, Deenie? D'you really think it can work, the Olken coming to Vharne?"

"I think if it doesn't work, it won't be for want of trying," she said, staunchly, 'cause it was happening either way and there was no point sinking the boat before it even set sail.

"I s'pose," said Rafe, sounding doubtful.

"Rafe . . ." She brushed her fingertips down his arm. "We have to. It breaks my heart to say it, but the cold truth is there ain't nothing left for us in Lur."

His lips tightened. "What about Mama? You're saying to leave her behind, in the crypt?"

So. Charis had broken the news. Did it make her a coward, that she was glad the duty had been taken from her?

*Prob'ly. But I am.*

Still, he raised a thorny question, one folk were wrestling back in Lur. The dead were dead and buried, but even so . . .

"I know," she whispered, feeling the familiar ache of loss. She thought she'd live the rest of her life feeling it. "We need to think on that. We need to talk on it with Da and Ewen. We need to talk about Mama. But not now."

He nodded across the forecourt. "That's Ewen? Charis told me about him, too. Giddycakes."

Bloody Charis. "Aye, Rafe, that's Ewen," she said, warning him. "And if you value your life you'll say nowt of red hair!"

He grinned and oh, he was Rafel again. He was Rafel, her brother.

After that it was hugs and kisses with Charis, so brightly in love, and with Goose, who kissed her cheek, shyly smiling, then introductions all around and finding their way into the castle for hot food and mulled wine and more talk.

Tugging her aside, dimpled with happiness, Charis said, "There's so much to tell you, Deenie. Find me at bedtime and we can have a good gossip."

"I will," she promised, and couldn't say any more, 'cause love for Charis welled up in her, stealing her voice.

*It's thanks to her that me and Da have Rafe again. We owe Charis his life.*

She didn't begin to know how they could repay that. But somehow, they would.

Watching Goose and Rafe together as they ate in the castle's dining hall, watching her brother's pride and sorrow and Goose's simple kindness, the true heart of him laid bare, Deenie had to bite her lip and hide her face in her wine goblet until she could trust not to make a fool of herself. But then she watched Da and Swordmaster Tavin size each other up across their plates and become thick as thieves an instant later, and that made her laugh.

With supper finished, they gathered in the main Hall. Robb and his barracks brothers joined them there for ale and cakes and making music with fiddles and pipes. Charis danced with Goose and after him, Ewen. Then she excused herself to take some cool ale with Da, and Ewen hunkered down with Tavin, and the barracks men started up their singing as they piped and fiddled another spry tune.

Finishing a little dance with Goose, Deenie saw Rafe on his lonesome, tucked into a corner. He looked up as she joined him, and tugged a stool close so she could sit.

"Mouse."

"Rafe." She touched his knee. Glanced around. This might not be the best time or place, but she had to ask. She had to know. "Rafe, how much do you remember?"

Instead of answering, he looked at Charis as she giggled and danced a jig in Da's sturdy embrace. Love of her was in his face, no silly pretending any more. Then he sighed.

"I remember all of it, mouse."

She blinked back tears. "Oh."

"I tried to stop him. I did. Only—"

"Don't," she said, and took his hand. "It ain't your fault, Rafe. He was Morg."

"Feels like my fault," he muttered. "Couldn't stop him, could I? Couldn't kill him. You killed him."

"No, *we* killed him." She gave his hand a little shake. "Think I could've done it without you? Think if you hadn't hidden me from him I'd still be alive? I wouldn't. You saved me. And don't you ever forget that."

The barracks music was jaunty, echoing to the Hall's rafters. Da handed Charis back to Goose so he could hunker with Ewen and Tavin. The smallest smile tugged at Rafe's lips, watching the girl he loved laugh. Watching his best friend Goose laugh.

Then his smile faded. "Reckon I won't forget a heartbeat of it, Deenie. But I want to. I can still feel all those poor souls, dying. I can still taste—"

"Don't," she said again. "Rafe, it's done with. Don't you torment yourself on it. Don't you spoil this. If you let Morg spoil this he might as well not be dead!"

He stared at the floor. "Can't hardly say a word to that Ewen of yours. Can't hardly look him in the eye."

"You think he blames you for Murdo?" She tightened her fingers. "He doesn't. Rafe—"

"Rafe! Rafe, come dance with me!"

And that was Charis, flushed prettily pink and standing with her hand outstretched. Flirting and cheeky in barracks leathers, the mayor's carefree daughter again. Well, mostly. She was still whipcord slender, though. Some things had changed. They were all four of them changed, one way and another. Changed and scarred and different people.

*But we'll always be friends.*

"Dance with her," said Deenie, softly. "There's always sunshine after rain."

"Deenie—"

She gave her brother a little shove. "Dance with her, noddyhead. We can talk again later. We've all the time in the world to talk, you and me."

So Rafe danced with Charis, Goose clapping his hands to the pipes and fiddles, and she watched them through her tears a while. Then she caught Ewen's eye and they slipped out of the Hall under cover of Da and Tavin swapping tall tales and being raucous, making everyone laugh.

The castle grounds were silvered with moonlight. Spring was upon them but a late frost glittered the grass. Sweet beneath the chilly air, a hint of fresh blossoms. It was the first time since leaving the smack at anchor that they'd had a proper moment alone.

"So, girl," said Ewen, his fingers laced with hers. "It's home, we are."

*Home.* The thought would take some getting used to, but he was right. This was home.

"And there's your brother on the mend," he added. "And his friend with him, and bossy Charis bossing both of them, and your da and my Tavin like peas in a pod."

"Aye," she said, sighing happily. "And don't call me *girl*."

He snorted. "Girl, will you wed me?"

She made him wait, and wait, and wait. And then she smiled. "Aye, King Noddyhead. I will."

Laughing, he kissed her. Kissed her again. And again. After that he cupped her face between his warm hands and gave her his best barracks look.

"If you love me, I'm telling you, *don't call me that!*"

The scars on his face were fading. She had to believe all scars faded, in time.

"All right. I won't."

"Deenie. Deenie." He was half laughing, full of wonder. "You'll be my Mage Queen, you will. Sink me, that's a thing, that is."

"And you'll be my Sword King." She grinned. "Sink me. Fancy that."

Lightly, lovingly, his fingertips touched her lips. "I do, girl. I fancy it. It'll be a new world, it will."

On the night's breeze they heard music, drifting jaunty from the Hall. She pressed her hand to his chest and felt his heart, beating there.

"It's already a new world, Captain."

And then she danced glimfire like fireflies, just for him, beneath the moon.